Bücher bewegten die Welt /
Books and the Western World

A translation of the 1968 second edition of
Bücher bewegten die Welt: Eine Kulturgeschichte des Buches
by Karl Schottenloher, published in two volumes
by Anton Hiersemann Verlag, of Stuttgart (first edition, 1951–1952).

KARL SCHOTTENLOHER

Books and
the Western World

A Cultural History

TRANSLATED BY
WILLIAM D. BOYD AND
IRMGARD H. WOLFE

McFarland & Company, Inc., Publishers
Jefferson, North Carolina, and London

British Library Cataloguing-in-Publication data available

Library of Congress Cataloguing-in-Publication Data

Schottenloher, Karl, 1878–
  Books and the Western world.

  Translation of: Bücher bewegten die Welt.
  Bibliography: p. 423.
  Includes index.
  1. Books–History.   2. Libraries–History.
3. Book collecting–History.   4. Book industries
and trade–History.   5. Civilization, Occidental.
I. Title.
Z4.S3813 1989   002   88-42501

ISBN 0-89950-344-6 (lib. bdg.; 50# acid-free natural paper)

Printed in the United States of

McFarland Box 611 Jefferson

Translators' Preface

Karl Schottenloher, the author of these volumes, has been dead now for over thirty years, but his name is well remembered and highly respected in the German-speaking scholarly world. His reputation and works are less well known in the English-speaking community. A few remarks concerning him are therefore in order.

Karl Schottenloher's name is associated with outstanding achievement in both the sphere of practical librarianship and the rather more theoretical world of serious learning and scholarship. His life and work represent the scholar-librarian at his best. If Karl Schottenloher was indeed but one among a number of Germans who through the centuries have embodied so well the ideals of the scholar-librarian, he nevertheless was and is outstanding among them.

Born January 11, 1878, at Rodau near Regensburg, his family background as well as the immediate environment of his early years served to give him a good foundation for the solid humanistic education he later pursued in the New Gymnasium and subsequently in the universities of Munich and Berlin. In the latter institutions, Schottenloher initially devoted himself to studying classical languages, but he was soon focusing his interest on history, in which he was to maintain a steady as well as avid interest for as long as he lived.

Schottenloher's work as a librarian began in October 1903 with volunteer duties he undertook at what was then the Royal Court and State Library in Munich. In less than a year, however, Schottenloher was called as assistant to the Royal Library in Bamberg. There, in the midst of a collection especially rich in Franconian history and culture, he followed (in addition to the special cataloging responsibilities assigned him) his own research interests, publishing in this period a number of articles concerned with the history of Franconian printing as well as with the depiction of Nuremberg as a significant center of the early printed book.

The pattern Schottenloher set for himself during his four years in Bamberg, namely the combining of the duties of librarian with the industrious scholarly utilization of the collection itself, was not only furthered but fulfilled in the thirty-year period of Schottenloher's tenure in various positions (including that of library director) at the State Library in Munich, to which he returned in 1908. In that very rich (bibliotecally speaking) environment, not only did Schottenloher carry out his librarian's responsibilities in an exemplary way, but he also produced most of the items that were later to be listed by Otto Schottenloher in a quite extensive bibliography of his father's works.[1] The elder Schottenloher gave special attention in his activities to the many incunabula that were in the great collection of the State Library, and he even inventoried the incunabula held in the smaller libraries throughout Bavaria. It is therefore little wonder that he was invited to become an active partner in the great German bibliographical project begun in 1925, the *Gesamtkatalog der Wiegendrucke* ("Whole Catalog of Incunabula").

But scholarly recognition had come to Schottenloher long before that. When the Prussian Culture Ministry in 1917 created a special commission for the thorough and impartial examination of the two great sixteenth-century cultural movements that we commonly call the Reformation and the Counter-Reformation, it was to Karl Schottenloher that they turned for the preparation of the *Bibliographie zur deutschen Geschichte im Zeitalter der Glaubenspaltung 1517–1585* ("Bibliography of German History in the Period of the Confessional Split, 1517–1585"). This great undertaking, which was to occupy him for over twenty years, was published between 1932 and 1940. (A final volume in the set, which Schottenloher had planned but not completed, was wholly frustrated due to the destruction suffered by the Munich State Library from Allied bombardment in the Second World War.)

Schottenloher retired from his official duties in the State Library on November 1, 1938; his scholarly pursuits, however, he continued. Among several other works, the cultural history of the book in two volumes that we here present in English translation was published in 1951–52. (A second and mostly unaltered second edition was brought out by the publisher, Anton Hiersemann Verlag, in 1968.) Schottenloher, we are told, deliberately gave this work the title *Bücher bewegten die Welt* ("Books Moved the World") on account of his deeply-felt conviction that the book is "das wesentliche geistige Agens der Weltgeschichte" ("The essential spiritual force that moves world history").[2]

When this work was first published, few knowledgeable persons would likely have gainsaid the central cultural role that Schottenloher thus assigned the printed book. But developments in the electronic means of communication have now been the cause for a fresh questioning about the place of the printed book in our culture. Some would-be futurists say that we are seeing the last of the book as we know it, and that, however important it may have been for us before, the printed book is passing away, after the fashion of all things temporal. Meanwhile, more and more books are being issued by thousands upon thousands of publishers—a partial phenomenon itself of the so-called information explosion.

Had Karl Schottenloher been aware of the technological changes that have occurred, would he perhaps have altered his somewhat presumptuous title for this cultural history of the book? We cannot know, of course, but we are strongly inclined to doubt it. One can hardly help wondering how this consummate scholar and librarian might weigh the events of the last decades since his work was published. Not having been the beneficiary of our more recent cultural experience, Schottenloher naturally does not here consider questions that some inevitably have now concerning the printed book. But we believe his work in these two volumes is not thereby essentially devalued. The work, furthermore, possesses an integrity of its own, something that any supplementation either by us or others in order to reflect more recent cultural realities, would seem seriously to compromise. Excepting our work of translation, then, these volumes stand as the author left them.

Bücher bewegten die Welt was acclaimed by knowledgeable critics in the fifties as well as in the early seventies as an extremely important history of the book. Works have appeared since then which, for students of the history of the book, of the history of libraries, and of Western culture generally as well as German literature and culture in particular, would nicely accompany or supplement Schottenloher's work; none, however, has replaced it. It therefore seemed to us especially unfortunate that this signal work on the cultural history of the book should continue to be inaccessible to those persons interested in the subject treated in these volumes but who lack a reading knowledge of the German language. The making accessible of important and relevant sources of information that, without mediation, might remain quite inaccessible to many potential users—this sort of effort is the librarian's stock-in-trade, as it were; and it is with a deeply bibliotecarial sense that we offer this translation, which is made possible not least by means of an agreement with the Anton Hiersemann Verlag of Stuttgart. Mr. Gerd Hiersemann has, incidentally, personally inspected our work in the first volume, and we would here express our appreciation to him for his cooperation in this entire project.

Our effort in these pages has been to render the German text into a reasonably readable style for American and other readers in the English language. It will be evident that we have accomplished our aim more successfully in some instances than in others, German style (particularly of the type often employed by Schottenloher) being notoriously challenging in the difficulties it can present to translators. We have regularly used standard reference works in handling the numerous proper names that are encountered in these two volumes.

An attractive characteristic of this work is the international scope of the author's consideration and treatment. At the same time, however, Schottenloher evidences a particular interest in German contributions to the history of the book, and now and then within the text there are expressions of the very special pride that Schottenloher seems to have taken in his own national heritage. Those who personally remember him assure us that Schottenloher's patriotic fervor derives from his formative years, which were lived within the context of a nation still euphoric over the significant reunification achieved in 1871. That is to say that Karl Schottenloher, whose basic outlook was quite humanistic, was not and is not representative of the spiritual extremities to which Germany fell prey in the third and fourth decades of the present century. In any case, these expressions of a nationalistic consciousness did not, for us, detract from the value we found the work as a whole possessing in unusual measure. We trust that others will agree with these sentiments, and discover in these pages, as we did, a rich mine of knowledge and information concerning the book and its development within the cultures of our Western world.

William Douglas Boyd
Irmgard H. Wolfe
Hattiesburg, Mississippi
December 1988

Table of Contents

Dedicated
to
The Bavarian State Library

Original Foreword

The book published here has been written just before the Second World War; through the events that then ensued, the process of bringing it to completion has twice been frustrated due to bombardments. Now, following the terrible downfall of the German nation, does it still have some meaning, so that, improved, it tries yet a third time to find its way to the reader? Can it bring something uplifting and encouraging to him? We hope so. Certainly the book is among the good spirits in our national life; it is indeed the best foundation for rebuilding the nation. So, in spite of the bad times, may the biography of the book offered in these pages still find a pleasant acceptance, and serve also to communicate here and there a measure of hope and comfort.

Everything the world of books has given me in the course of a grand experience I owe to the extraordinary wealth of material in the Bavarian State Library in Munich. The hundreds and thousands of manuscripts and printed works that I myself have handled there have compelled me to understand the book as the incomparable thoughts of the creative human spirit and, at the same time, they have impressed upon me, in an overwhelming fullness, the development and influence of the world of books.

I had the good fortune (I was perhaps the last person to do so) to be able to draw on the full extent of the then yet unharmed treasures of the Munich collection before the bombs of hostile aircraft fell on them on March 9, 1943, and destroyed entire ranges of them. It is with a profound sadness that I remember that proud collection when it was intact.

Reviewing my work, I especially have to thank the publishing house of Hiersemann in Leipzig, and now of Stuttgart; despite all the difficulties that the war generated, Hiersemann remained faithful to its work and, indeed, it has in a gratifying manner taught me an important presupposition necessary for living in the book world, viz., the harmonious cooperation between author and publisher. Over and beyond this, I am indebted to Herman D. Wilhelm Olbrich, the head of the publishing division of the house, for so many valuable suggestions and practical hints that, in many parts, my obligation to him is much like that owed to a formal collaborator. The head librarian of the State Library, Dr. Wilhelm John, through his untiring assistance, has made it possible for me to carry out the initial printing, despite all the events of the war that stood in the way. At that time my son, Otto, had just come from the Russian Front, and now he has also supported me again, by reading the proofs with me. To Dr. Walter Kunze I am especially indebted for the kind help he gave.

K. Schottenloher
Munich
November 1951

Introduction

Outline of a Cultural History of the Book

In the pages that follow, we wish to tell the story of the book: of its nature, its mission, its efficacy, and its fortunes. Much has already been written (among which are some excellent treatises) covering manuscripts, printing, type-casting, binding, book formatting, the book trade, the care of books, book collections, or on other matters, all of which belong to the book, but which embrace neither the book solely for itself, nor the entire book in its most essential nature. When the history of literature or the history of thought come to address the matter of the book, it is accomplished with only a few words, while a history of writing, which would above all have to include the book, still does not exist, generally speaking.

Adolf von Harnack once said: "All of us deal with books everyday, just as we deal with human beings, but we know less about the modern book than we do about human beings. Its multifaceted genealogical tree is as unkown to us as is its physiology."[1] Karl Julius Weber has been thinking in a similar vein: "We have a book that has received a big but undeserved reputation: Baron von Knigge's *Über den Umgang mit Menschen* ("On Getting Along with People"); who will give us a classic book concerned with an equally important matter, viz our handling of, or dealing with, books?" Even our presentation here will still be capable of bringing no formal solution to the appointed task; but at least it may provide a beginning toward this goal and be a guidepost to the most important questions for an extensive consideration of the book, and of its significance within the history of culture.

If we would here address ourselves to the book, it is not the individual book that we have in mind, nor even its external get-up, nor its content, but rather its total nature, the entire book domain, the world of books, which has a life of its own, a force, just like the forest which in itself is something other than the individual plants or the total number of trees contained within it.

What is the book? It is one of the most remarkable and incredible miracles of human culture. Not the body itself, nor the spirit by itself, but both of these together — almost like the human beings whose image it is. The essential nature of the book is mental activity with life in all its richness, the address of the I to the you, of the individual to the community. Intellectual power, however, no matter how significant it may be, is without its proper effect, and in the long run there is no guarantee it will endure, so long as it merely reposes in the brain, or at the writing table. It is only by making the transfer into the material world, only through its transformation into the book, that the boundaries of space and time which have been established for mankind are overcome; it is only this that reproduces the secret of the intellectual connection with the world of external things; only so is the work loosed from its creator and only so does it become something new: it becomes the community's property with its own independent powers, which are no more those of the author alone; it is deprived of the accidents of individual existence, and it enters into the realm of the spirit.

That which is applicable for each and every book is properly true in the highest sense of the word first of all those great intellects which are only given to mankind from time to time. While human beings and chronlogical periods disappear, the eternal books, detached from time and place, go through the worlds of the centuries — the entire work of a Homer, of a Vergil, Dante, Cervantes, Shakespeare, Molière, and Goethe. If one once imagines in how many editions, translations, and printings the *Odyssey*, the *Iliad*, the *Aeneid*, the *Divine Comedy, Don Quixote, Macbeth, Le Tartuffe*, and *Faust* have been disseminated throughout the entire world, and if one additionally takes into account all the treatments that are concerned with these peak performances, one will then be able to get an approximate idea of the meaning of books for the world of culture. "Jene Großen haben denen, die ihnen lauschten, die ahnende Sehnsucht nach der Sonne gegeben: und das ist alles." ("Those great intellects have given to those who listen to them the presageful yearning for the sun; and that is everything.") (Gustav Roethe.) There are about 4500 editions of Goethe's works; and added to that are 70,000 publications about him.

The state of affairs is similar with the works of an Aristotle, of Plato, Marcus Aurelius, Augustine, Thomas à Kempis, Erasmus of Rotterdam, Luther, Voltaire, Rousseau, or Kant. If mankind in all its transitoriness seeks and yearns for that which remains, for that which is essential, for the complete, for the infinite, for the eternal, it is in books that it has the most effective and faithful aid. To preserve cultural values in the face of transitoriness and annihilation — that is the ultimate and the highest significance of the book. Everywhere the cultural heights arise, there the book also has its shining hour.

Thus it is that in an historical survey concerning the world of books in the period of Antiquity, in the Middle Ages, in the Renaissance, in the Enlightenment, in the Romantic period and in the modern period, there is always to be kept in mind also the most important mission of the book, viz. its impact as an expression and communication of the active mind, as a fountain of youth for fresh renewal, and as the bearer of, and the witness to, the dominant culture. If we consider the book's impact, occupying a preferred position will therefore have to be the book's cultural history. The mighty ascent of the book from the restraint of the earlier period up until today's wealth of communication, and the splitting off into newspaper and journal — these must likewise be so emphatically inquired into, as the intellectual, technical and economic sources and their effects, as well as the development of the national literary language in the book, or the gradual penetration of the world of books into ever broader classes of readers and vocational groups through the most diverse forms of literature, such as the popular book, youth literature, the school book, the picture book, the text-book, subject literature, the scientific work, the conversational lexicon, and the voice of daily life, or finally, the development of the public communications of certain fields of literature, such as biography, literary reports of one's own work and thought, diaries, and collections of letters. In the libraries, the book that is reflective of its period becomes the mediator of the limited time that is part of human destiny, as well as of that eternal realm in which the spiritual life reposes. Arthur Schopenhauer, who had so many nice things to say about the significance of the book, has called the world of books the "papered memorial of mankind," in which alone the largest part of all of human knowledge continues, while only a small portion of it lives in human heads. No less deserving of attention therefore (as something additionally to be followed through the various periods) will be the increasing will toward preservation, and the generally available public libraries, and their work in the interest of art and science, of popular education and of the social education of particular peoples.

What, further, is the nature of the relationship at any one time of the society, the nation and the political leadership to the world of books? As a rule, the leading classes in the individual centuries which read and love, and care for and collect books are: in the ancient period, the priests, the scholars and the philosophers; in the Middle Ages, the clerics, especially the monks and canons, and also the emperors and princes, in their devotion to the luxury book on account of its lifting the level of courtly splendor, or the aristocracy, which took pleasure in the knightage registry with its heraldry. Since the Renaissance period, fully since the discovery of printing, the city, burgherdom, officialdom, and the scholary world, have come into the foreground, until gradually, following the victory of the national languages over Latin, the entire nation has participated in the book, and is ever creating out of it the world that is in accord with, and of the same quality as, its own nature. In a penetrating history of the book, the book's influence as well as the influence of the world of readers will have to be given special attention.

What does the world of books signify for one's own nation? It is one of the highest goods of the culture; it is the issue and the mirror of the soul, of the vitality and character of the people, a living witness to, and symbol of, its history, of its destiny, of its bright days and of its dim ones, of its power and of its need, of its devotion to all that moves the soul, piety, mysticism, chivalrousness, the longing for beauty, melancholy, the will to live, the impulse to inquire, and the eternal question concerning life's meaning. It is like the towering cathedrals, citadels and castles; it is like the immortal works of the fine arts, and like the incomparable creations of muscial art; it is our proud legacy with endless rows of ancestors, the great chronicle of our national existence. Hugo von Hofmannsthal calls literature a nation's cultural space, which is something other than its political space.

So far as the relationship of specific political leadership to the book is concerned, the world of books has experienced the most diverse evaluations. Belonging here are such things as the occasional promotion of books by the emperor and by princes, the procedures that have been taken by authorities against immoral books, or against ones considered politically dangerous, the granting of imperial or princely privileges for certain publications, the instituting of imperial book commissions for supervising the book trade in Frankfurt am Main and in Leipzig, the requirement of depository copies, the legal measures taken to protect intellectual property through copyright, the building of public book collections for the advancement of scholarship, for the preservation of the national literature, and for lending support to the book trade by purchasing the most important work that were being published. A purposive national politics of culture will always give special attention to this valuable national possession and visible standard of culture.

As a corporal creation, the book is the subject to all the changes brought about in its production by industrial and technical forces. To be portrayed here will be its development in the papyrus roll of the ancient world, in the parchment codex, and the paper manuscript of the Middle Ages, and in the printed work of the modern period. Further to be observed are the script, the type, the decorations, the figurative embellishments and the increasing of the book's effectiveness by means of book illumination, woodcuts, engravings, lithography, and the more modern modes of production, and further, the deeply engaging cooperation of technology, through the discovery of papyrus, parchment and paper, of xylographica and printing, the setting and printing machines, and the transformation in bookbinding. The book is here again very closely allied with cultural history, in a relationship that, for the book, is more acquiescent than active, while forces that are essentially alien influence its development.

With the cultivation of a comprehensive industry, the book in increasing measure has become a significant economic commodity. At the heart of the questions that arise here is the discovery of printing with its enormous economic consequences. Entire professions came into being which devoted themselves to producing the disseminating books: the printer, the typefounder, the bookkeeper, the publisher, the bookseller, the binder, and the antiquarian. What has the book given to these professions, and what again have these given to the book? The book becomes an object of the political economy; the venture, the capital, the economic striving—all of these factors enter into its service; supply and demand determine the book's turnover, and the book trade grows mightily. Economic power, the popular standard of living and of cultural life—all of these enter into connection. Cultural property becomes an economic commodity and its economic possibilities increase toward infinity.

What does the book give to the individual person, i.e. to each of us? It enables us to participate in all that is and in all that happens in the world. We thus broaden our life and give it depth, and we achieve greater clarity about ourselves. Whoever reads deeply in Goethe's works will feel himself somehow transformed thereby. And how many persons have not already experienced Goethe's poems! Precisely in the limitless number and in the diffusion of the book (which cannot indeed be said often enough, so far as the ultimate fulfillment of the idea of the book is concerned) lies the infinite efficacy of the world of books. What we ourselves have once experienced, say, the beauty of nature in a flower, a landscape, a satisfied summer day, works at its most profound depth in us if a book of poetry paints a similar experience for us. And the images that are shaped for us by poetry become our own, even without our having had such experiences previously ourselves. The reed songs of Lenau, the North Sea songs of Heine, the heathen songs of Droste-Hülshoff charm us, never having seen them, as clearly as if they had been seen before. Heller's famous epic has revealed the beauty of the Alps for the world, Goethe's *Erlkönig* has grippingly made known the mysterious harmony of man with nature. What the thinker and the poet have fathomed and observed concerning life's order and meaning, about guilt and fate, about fortune and misfortune – all these go unhindered throughout the world. In the biographies of great men we happily see before us the proficient activities of blessed talents. In religious books, we find the way to the Transcendent. There are thus infinite enrichments everywhere.

What meaning has the world of books to all mankind, to humanity, to its spiritual progress, and to the education of the nations? It is in the book that the most effective exchange of ideas among the various peoples takes place. No nation comprehends the essence of the world and of life in its entire infinity, and each people shapes the world differently, in accord with its natural disposition and its gifts. Exchanging these various experiences, which is something that is nurtured by the book, belongs among the most effective forces for educating the human race. The books of the world, which are related to the great and eternal things of life, make their way like the sunlight, which knows no national boundaries, and they belong to a kingdom which is indeed invisible, but which is everlasting. That is the greatness of the book's efficacy – that the Bible, Homer, Vergil, Dante, Shakespeare and Goethe belong to the entire world and to all centuries – yes, they have today something to say to infinitely more people than their first readers.

To the intellectual creator of a pattern of ideas, the reproduction and the diffusion of his wares offers an inner satisfaction. It is indeed significant if an author has something to say which delights, which elevates and enriches hundreds and thousands of people. This reactive effect is simply the most essential power circuit that keeps the entire book industry moving. The increased assessment of cultural work as an accomplishment to be highly valued, and its issue in the book, have gradually brought to the creator also an economic share in his production. This history of the professional writer and poet takes its beginnings from the effectiveness of the book.

With respect to publishing, it consciously or unconsciously exercises the greatest influence on both the inward and outward formation of a written work. During the process of its transformation into a book, a world of ideas scarcely remains entirely untouched by the consequences of this – something that is, as it were, automatic. Each cultural product is formed according to certain viewpoints, during which it becomes a book, so as to address the reader, or its public. One may almost say: The expectant reader, and indeed the whole contemporary world, are there as co-creators. The history of literature is inextricably bound up with the history of the book.

A survey of the development of the book has also to show us, finally, the principal fortunes of the book and of book collections, the various degrees of the care of books and of bibliophily, the ups and downs of preserving books with the encroachment of wars and the concluding of eras, the shifts in the priorities of particular peoples, and the change in the centers of books, as this is shown in the names of the great book cities such as Athens, Alexandria, Pergamon, Rome, Constantinople, Florence, Mainz, Venice, Paris, Frankfurt am Main, Leipzig, London and Berlin.

One can speak of a cultural history, a social history, a national history, an art history, an economic history, and of a technical history of the book; but one can also speak of a cultural history of the book, which comprises all these — and which attempts to present the nature of the phenomenon in its totality, its dependence on the culture in an everlasting proclamation and transmission of the human spirit. What the task is for an emphatically cultural history of the book could be most effectively illustrated in a great exhibition that would present the most significant books of all times. If our gaze were to rest on one of the venerable Nibelung manuscripts, then again on the Gutenberg Bible, and yet again on one of the complete Goethe editions, it would then become fully clear to us, what the transformation and the influence of the world of books has to say within the great history of culture.

Set within such perspectives, this guide through the ages, based in the history of the book, should now begin.[2] I believe that it makes no difference if everything that has gone through the world in books that was superficial, defective, foolish, irresponsible, and even inimical to life, remains unnoticed. There is no good on earth that has not been slighted, corrupted and misused. Even nature loves the overflow, and it suffers failures, in order to enhance the survival of life according to the law of selection. So may the following presentation quietly become a great anthem to the book, and perhaps thereby strengthen our sense of responsibility for a precious commodity of our national life, and no less confirm our reverence for, and love of, it. It is not the mere knowledge about becoming and being that is the essence of all knowing, but the profound faith in the power of perceived good, and the inspiration that flows from it. In the following survey, reference will purposely be made to as many significant books as possible, so that we may thereby become memorably aware again and again of that which the world of books has to give to us.

1
The World of Books in Antiquity

Knowledge about the development of man's cultural life, as this presses back in time, gets lost only too soon in the gray twilight. The beginnings of culture, with man's earliest ascent out of the purely natural life of instinct, into the development of his initial mental and moral powers, are scarcely known to us. What we do know of mankind's most ancient period, shows that it had already attained a significant peak, which must itself have been preceded by immeasurable times of advancement and reversal, periods of remote antiquity which can be surmised only by making comparative references to the life of the more undeveloped primitive races.

One of mankind's most significant steps toward knowing, feeling, willing, and shaping, and toward his essential nature as a forward-thinking, religious, artistic, and economic creature was the adapting of gesticulatory signs and the natural sounds to the mystical art of words and of language; these were the means whereby man, through shaping and ordering with phonetic symobls, recreated the world that surrounded him, brought these symbols into meaningful relationship with one another, and thus initiated a second world that belonged only to him—his most original creation full of original power. "A people has no idea that has no word for it," says Herder. With language there was achieved the most important means toward mutual understanding, and for the lasting transmission from one generation to another of ideas and of human experiences.

It was from this—mankind's highest good—that script gradually grew; little by little, one wrote with ingenious tools in mysterious signs on inventively fashioned material, the fleeting ideas, the fading speech, the dying song, as symbols of sounds, concepts, and objects, and then these were transmitted as signals to the eyes. But this made it possible for the signs of script to be changed back again into words, into language: here sound and the ear, and there sign and the eye, entered into a wonderful relationship. In writing, the words were mysteriously illuminated; they became visible and re-transformed. Thus there was created, in addition to the oral tradition, the infinitely extended diffusion of ideas beyond their own time and place. If cultural development, as a totality of accomplishments, depends primarily on the exchanging and transmitting of ideas and skills, so it was in the more and more developed languages and scripts (which, according to Jakob Grimm, enabled man in the situation "to make the most cultural use of his hand"), that the most important representatives of culture, and thus of progress, were produced. Pliny was already saying that human culture depends on the use of papyrus, on the historical

memory and on man's immortality, and Vitruvius, in the foreword of the ninth section of his ten books on architecture, marvelled that ancient Greece awarded such
great honors to the victors in the Olympic games, and that no one had remembered
the storyteller, who had performed such valuable services for all peoples and all
times. They should, of course, have been accorded the usual recognitions, with
palms and branches, but they should not only have been awarded these; they
should also have been granted triumphs, indeed, those with special accomplishments should have been given a position among the gods. It was already
fully known to the world of antiquity that it is in literature that humanity's eternal
sources flow. It is odd that, for the word, temporal and spatial limits are set, while
the fixed art of symbols which we have in writing, the shadow image of language,[1]
is almost limitless in its possibilities. Through writing, the individual's memory was
transformed into a corporate memory of the tribe, of the nation and of humanity.

Even if we knew nothing of the nature of the book in the flourishing periods
of antiquity,[2] books could be inferred on basis of the highly developed literature
of the ancient world, which has been transmitted to us: the literature of the Egyptians, Assyrians, Greeks and Romans in the flourishing periods of the ancient book.
But there is also a series of historical witnesses that allow us to look directly into
the world of books in antiquity. A priceless residue of buildings leads us toward
Nineveh, the buried capital city of the Assyrian kingdom on the Tigris, where in
1849–1853, numerous baked clay tablets with cuneiform characters have been
found among the excavated ruins of a palace, valuable testimony to the administration of the Assyrian king Asshurbanipal (668–626 B.C.), who shortly before the
breakup of the Assyrian kingdom, had assembled collections of writings from
public life and in the fields of religion, history, astronomy, mathematics and
medicine.[3]

Hermann V. Hilprecht has similarly found, since 1895, the extensive temple
library of a buried and forgotten city, with many thousands of cuneiform tablets
which partially pertain to daily life and are partially of religious-scientific content;
they date from the period 2500 B.C.[4] This discovery was made in the alluvial plain
south of Baghdad in the area where Nippur (one of the four major cities of Nimrod's
empire) once stood, and thus an important cultural site of old Babylonia. With this
find, there emerged from the ruins and rubble the great, wide world of Assyria and
Babylonia, which until then was almost unknown to us, and which has unlocked
for us on the soil of the lands of the Euphrates the flourishing human history of three
thousand years before Christ. In these monuments we have at the same time the
oldest public provision for the care and preservation of transmitted texts that we
know about; there cannot be any doubt, however, that these high cultures have proceeded from developments that are far older.

Just as the totality of our Western European culture cannot be traced back to
the time ages and ages ago in the Eastern world, but comes to us primarily through
the mediating Greek and Roman antiquity, so is it also with our designations for
the book: Library, Liber and book; these go back not to the ancient clay fragments
of the Assyrian and Babylonian writing, but to the later widely used writing material
that came from the bark of plants: from βίβλος (the bark of the papyrus shrub),

as with the ancient Greeks, from *Liber*, as with the Romans, and then to the German *Buch*, from the wood of which the small runic sticks have been shaped. It was primarily the fibers of the papyrus shrubs (which today has been almost eradicted but which was one of the reed plants much cultivated at one time in Egypt) that for some time supplied the material for writing for the entire Greek world. Pliny has given us a detailed description of the way it was produced. One cut strong stalks of the high plants into thin wide strips, then laid two strips crosswise on top of each other and glued them together into a fabric-like polished mass, on which one could write.

Generally speaking, the writing material thus attained was rolled up, especially if several strips were attached to one another (there were frequently over twenty of them) in order to be able to accommodate lengthy pieces of writing. Nowadays, the roll is familiar to us only through the storing of maps; but in antiquity, the roll (Greek, Κύλίνάρος ; Latin, volumen) was part of the characteristic Greek and Latin book, and it was also readily employed figuratively. Thus Xenophon once spoke of the reader who "unrolls" the books, and holy scripture refers to heaven, which rolls itself together like a book (Isa. 34:4); pagan and Christian pictures present the poet or the scholar, Christ or the apostles, with a roll in the hand, and Theodore Birt has in a fortunate combining of ideas recognized the sculpture of the Trajan column as an unrolled illuminated roll. If we would imagine how the writings of Homer, Aristophanes, Sophocles, Euripides, Vergil, and Cicero have at one time appeared, then we have to conceive of roll upon roll, each one being about six meters long, each one of them inscribed uniformly letter after letter, and line after line, without any subdivision.

The art of preparing the papyrus plants so that they became useful writing material (something of which today we are indeed no more properly conscious) is among the most significant accomplishments of human culture; in some manner it has also prepared the way for the use of parchment and paper for writing. Language and script are thus inseparably bound up from the very beginning with the craftsman's work.

Of the oldest Greek book we do not know much.[5] In the earliest literary period, Homer and Hesiod stand out like lighthouses beaming forth from the darkness. The great heroic poems, the *Iliad* and the *Odyssey*, march in their triumphal procession through the storms of the centuries and they become the first of humanity's enduring "world books." Concerning Artistotle, (384–322), who was Alexander the Great's teacher, and who was the grand philosopher and the master of the whole of knowledge in his time, and who with his widely disseminated works belongs to world literature,[6] it has been transmitted that a portion of his books have come in a roundabout way to Appelicon of Teos and later have been carried away by Sulla to Rome. The grammarian, Tyrannos (the teacher of Strabo and Andronicus of Rhodes) used them there; he was the first one to compile Aristotle's complete works.

Athens, the cultural center of the Grecian world, with its famous philosophical school, was the place where the magnificent statue of the Apollo of Belvedere was created. One simply cannot conceive of the city without rolls of books and public

rooms, where a teacher and his pupils wandered to and fro, inquiring and disput-
ing; but time has forever spread its veiled cloak over all that. Under Pericles
(499–429 B.C.), Greek literature attained a brilliant pinnacle; Aeschylus (d. 456),
Sophocles (d. 428), Euripides (d. 406), Aristophanes (d. 387), Anaxagoras (d.
428), Herodotus (d. 428), and Thucydides (d. 396) wrote their immortal works.
The chief knowledge that we have of antiquity's world of books rests on the
Hellenistic period, the "first unity of the world" (Droysen), in which Greek culture
set about to conquer the eastern world, and extended to Alexandria at the mouth
of the Nile, as well as to the important outposts in Antioch and Pergamum.

Above all, it was in Alexandria, which was the new foundation established by
Alexander the Great and which was the busy city on the border of the then known
three continents, that there arose under Ptolemy II, Philadelphos (285–247), and
Ptolemy II Euergetes (247–221) a sanctuary dedicated to the goddesses of *beaux
arts* and sciences, the *Museion*. Incorporated therein was the famous library, which
was under the direction of the leading scholars of that period, Zenodotus of
Ephesus, Callimachus of Cyrene,[7] Apollonius of Rhodes, Eratosthenes,
Aristophanes of Byzantium, Apollonius Eidographos and Aristarchus of
Samothrace.[8] The culminating goal of this scholarly academy of books was to gather
together all the cultural works of Greek culture that were available, to examine them
for their purity and completeness, to establish their author, and to draw up a clearly
arranged catalog of holdings. As marks of identification *(sillybos = index* or *titulus),*
strips were glued on the rolls themselves, along with the title and the number of
the row. These labels resulted in a list of holdings *(pinakes* = shelves or tablets)
that was arranged according to groups of poets, rhetoricians, or historians. They
contained allusions from biographies or from the history of scholarship.

This activity in collecting, and the scholarly description of the Greek literature,
was a unique example of caring for books on a grand scale, as well as of the cultural
and educational policy, which was replete with significant consequences for the
transmitting of cultural works; at the same time, it was an effective starting point
for a formal school of grammarians and philologists, which fashioned bibliology
anew from the ground up, and put a stop to textual degeneration. The writings of
a Homer, Hesiod, Pindar, Aeschylus, Sophocles, Euripides, Herodotus,
Thucydides, Xenophon, Plato, Demosthenes and Aeschines could henceforth more
safely confront their future chequered transmission.

Over and above this, Alexandria's library became a permanent shining example of wise provision for the world of culture. Always thereafter, where one reflected
on the significance and necessity for places where scholarly works are collected,
it was to Alexandria that one appealed; where one praised the patrons of the arts
and sciences, one mentioned in the first place the Ptolemies; when the fifteenth and
sixteenth century humanists glorified the newly achieved collections of books, they
always mentioned Alexandria as the typical model, so much had the Ptolemies'
foundation (which was one of the most brilliant phenomena in the entire Greek
world) become a most important conception, and an imperishable influence. Even
though the collection was destroyed in the years 48 to 47,[9] during Caesar's war
against the Egyptians, its name and its work have remained immortal.

Other princes of antiquity competitively sought, just as the Ptolemies did, to collect and transmit, such as, for example, the Syrian Seleucids in Antioch, and the Attalids, especially Attalos I (241–197) and Eumenes I (197–159) in Pergamum; indeed Pergamum became, as did Alexandria, an important center for the Greek literary tradition.

When the Greek-Macedonian Empire fell, and Rome entered upon the collapsing inheritance, many Greek book collections may have come to Italy. Thus it is reported that L. Aemilius Paulus has carried off the library of the Macedonian kings, along with the residue of Aristotle's possessions, to Rome. The defeated Greek world knew how to conquer culturally the victorious Roman Empire. Horace has expressed this superiority with the sentence: *Graecia capta ferum victorem cepit.* With the rise to political power, the cultural life flourished also in Rome. We hear of magnificent possessions of books, of special writings about book collections, and of a formal booktrade.[10] The author, Titus Pomponius Atticus (103–32), who was a trusted friend of Cicero's, put the writings of Varro, Cicero, and Catullus into circulation, and he was considered to be a trustworthy agent for books. The brothers Socius disseminated Horace's writings. Tryphon caused the works of Quintilius and Martial to be circulated. Even public collections of books were soon being mentioned. Tradition ascribes the first attempt in this respect to the highly educated orator and consul, Gaius Asinins Pollio (75–76), who erected a library in the Temple of Libertas in the vicinity of the Forum, and had it decorated with portraits of famous poets and authors.

With the leaders of its classical literature, Rome experienced its golden age: Cicero, Vergil, Horace, Catullus, Lucretius, Tibullus, Propertius, Ovid, Caesar, Sallust and Livy. Caesar Augustus, the founder of the Augustan Age, which was enveloped by the rays of art and science, has himself built two collections of books, one in the year 28 B.C. in the Temple of Apollo on the Palatine Hill and the other in the "Hall of Columns" that was named for his sister, Octavia. Among the later significant collections to be mentioned are the *Bibliotheca Pacis,* which was built by Vespasian, and the *Bibliotheca Ulpia* that Trajan (98–117) founded; there then developed a second flowering period of Roman literature; with Seneca, Lucanus, Martial, Persius, Juvenal, Quintilian, Pliny, Tacitus, and Suetonius, it significantly enlarged the world of books.

Most of the public libraries in Rome were connected with consecrated places, and they therefore had a sacred character, and enjoyed the same care as did the shrines. Initially protected here were only the notes, records, etc., which related to worship, and beyond that, the laws and public pronouncements; the scope subsequently came, however, to include the entire literature.

All the large and small book collections of antiquity, the buildings, as well as the rolls that were kept in them, have long since disappeared, having been totally destroyed by fire, by war and the storms of time. It is now seems odd that one of the forces that have destructively passed over the monuments of a foundering world, namely, the burying rubble, has, as if by a miracle, saved parts of this past. It was in the year 1752, when there was laid bare in the debris that buried the coastal city of Herculaneum with Pompeii and Stabiae on August 24, 79 A.D., the country house of the distinquished Roman, Calpurnius Piso Caesonius; he was one of the pupils and friends of the Epicurean philosopher, Philodemus. Also found was a rich treasure of unfortunately very charred papyrus remains with philosophical texts from the century before Christ; among them were writings of the aforementioned Philodemus, who was a contemporary of Cicero's. It was a well-arranged house library that came to light here, and one that its owner may himself have used on that terrible day.[11]

Just as here it was the mass of lava of Vesuvius that has wonderfully preserved these literary remains, so in Egypt, the dry desert sand not inundated by the Nile or its ground water have had the same preservative effect. Like a fairy-tale, from the rubbish heap there emerged a subterranean world, the ruins of houses and burial sites that at one time were abandoned, and villages that had filled up with earth, before the astonished people of the eighteenth and nineteenth centuries: the old world of Egypt, which since the founding of Alexandria had become a new home for Greek culture. In the year 1778 there were found in Gizeh (the old Memphis) several rolls of papyrus, only one of which was saved and published in 1789 by the Dane, Nicholas Schorr. The others have been burned by the fellaheen, who did not know what to do with them. Further finds came to light between 1815–1821 at Thebes, Tis, Panopolis, Sagguara, and on the Nile island of Elephantine (a valuable *Iliad* fragment was found here). Significant treasures were further revealed in the winter of 1877/78 in the field of ruins of the ancient Arsinoe in the Middle Egyptian region of Fajjum, as the farmers were digging there for clay and brick. Most of it came to Vienna, its value having been recognized by the Orientalist, Josef Karabacek. Significant theological papyrus discoveries have followed in the winter 1886–87 in the grounds of Akhmin (Panopolis).

Another important source of finds was discovered in the winter of 1889 by the English archeologist, William Matthew Flinders Petrie, in the Egyptian coffins at Madinet-Gurob, where numerous mummies' cases which had been constructed from pieces of papyrus, were found. Valuable fragments from the third century B.C. of the residue of Plato's works were found on this occasion; these are only 120 years younger than the original copies. Even greater interest was aroused when in the year 1890, there was found on the back of one of the accounts rolls acquired by the British Museum in London an unknown work of Aristotle's, the essay about the state of Athens; it was published by Frederick George Kenyon. The same researcher could in the same year edit a second valuable find, the *Mimes* of Herondas, one of the Greek poets who was from the island of Kios in the third century B.C. A further acquisition in London brought to light the *Odes* of Bacchylides, who was a contemporary of Pindar and Simonides; up to that time they had been lost. Since the winter of 1896–97, the "Egyptian Exploration Fund", established for systematic research into ancient Egypt, has undertaken regular digs at individual heaps of ruins at the ancient Oxyrhynchos (today's Behnesa), and has additionally brought to light about three thousand documents with three hundred literary items, among which were extracts from lost portions of the Roman history of Livy.[12] In old Aphroditopolis, the French scholar, Gustave Lefebure, discovered in 1905 an earthern vessel filled with papyrus rolls, along with a case that consisted of the scraps of a papyrus book of the fourth century B.C. containing the comedies of Menander. Germany has also undertaken excavations for papyrus treasures since the winter of 1898. The largest German papyrus collections are currently located in the State Museum at Berlin and in the National Library at Vienna.[13] The most valuable Berlin item is an almost complete roll of the *Persians* of Timotheos, a poet from the period of Alexander the Great.

Even though with these finds the scholarly world's quiet hope for a new jewel of world literature was not fulfilled, still the discoveries in Egypt in their totality did afford a tremendous view into a significant bit of ancient life, and they thereby brought to light inexhaustible contributions to the history of literary transmission with the unknown writings of Alkaios, Hypereides, Sappho, Korinna, Pindar, Bacchylides, Sophocles, Epicharmos, Callimachus, Kerkidas, Hierocles, Herondas, Timothy, and Menander.[14] Among other things, the preserved fragments allow us to recognize the great dissemination of Homer's works, and their (various) editions. A special new branch of classical archeology, papyrus research, is now attempting to sift the valuable finds, the epistolary and documentary ones, as well as the literary ones.[15] The essential thing is that in them the monuments of antiquity are directly preserved for us. Although no single book roll has been completely preserved, the residue can nevertheless give us a vital image of the way literature appeared at about the time of Plato. We know now that the form of the roll has dominated the world of writing and books from the sixth century B.C. until the fourth century A.D., and the especially suitable fibre of the papyrus has been the preponderant material for writing in ancient Egypt, as well as in Greece and Rome. Many of the mouments that have been found extend back into the third century before Christ, and thus into the peak period of the scholarship of the Alexandrian school, and thus into a period that has been of outstanding significance for the development of the ancient book. Many of the monuments, such as the Timotheos fragment found in a grave near Cairo, reach back into the fourth century B.C., into the period of Demosthenes and Aristotle. On commission for the artistic Pope Clement XIV (1769–1774), Raphael Mengs has decorated the library hall of the Vatican in Rome (which mostly preserves papyrus items that have come from Ravenna) with a parable of world history, on which we see a good genius carrying rolls, a symbolic representation of the significance of the roll.

To the protective soil that has preserved for us the precious papyrus rolls, we are also indebted for the saving of the vestiges of old library buildings, as in Herculaneum, Pergamum, Ephesus, and Rome; these give us at least an approximate picture of the rooms in which the literature of antiquity was publicly preserved. We enter into the area of the Temple of Pallas Athena at Pergamum. Surrounding the sanctuary is an open place, which in the east and in the north is enclosed by a hall of columns. The north hall is joined to a row of rooms, among which in the northeast is a room decorated with a statue of Athena, and on the walls of which are visible the slots for the hooks that formerly were for the papyrus rolls that were placed on the high shelves. We stand in the main hall of the famous library of Pergamum. One has discovered stones in the vicinity of the temple with inscriptions glorifying Greek literary figures such as Alkaios, Herodotus, Timothy of Miletus, and Homer;

these chance remains have apparently once decorated the rooms.[16] We have to imagine most public collections of rolls of the Hellenistic and Roman period like this:
amost always the lay-out was connected with a sanctuary and hall of columns, in
which the visitor could walk about, and it comprised as a center point the festive
room for the books, which was decorated with statue of Pallas Athena, the patron
goddess of scholarship, and sometimes also with the busts of famous poets and
authors. Symbolical figures such as Science, Wisdom, and Virtue served as
reminders to the visitor of the great powers of mankind's soul and spirit and they
sought to incline him toward reflection and sympathetic feeling.

2
The Literary Tradition of the Ancient World

In the area of the Mediterranean, antiquity's "world ocean" (Gregorovius) which washed the earth's three continents and connected the peoples and cultures, about a millenium had passed before the two gifted peoples on the peninsulas of Greece and Italy succeeded to a cultural flowering that was without peer. Past us march poets and thinkers, crowned with immortal fame: here, Homer, Hesiod, Pindar, Aeschylus, Sophocles, Euripides, Aristophanes, and there, Heraclitus, Herodotus, Democrites, Plato, Aristotle, Thucydides, Xenophon, Demosthenes, Polybius, Plutarch, Erathosthenes, Euclid, Archimedes, Strabo, and there, Lucretius, Catullus, Vergil, Horace, Propertius, Cicero, Sallust, Petronius, Tacitus, Plautus, Terence, Nepos, Caesar, Tibullus, Ovid, Livy, Persius, Juvenal, Seneca, and Suetonius. The whole of this precious legacy of the noblest humanity, filled as it was with the most mature ideas and the finest forms, and set down in fragile rolls, was exposed to the barbarians' mightiest assault, which threatened to bury every thing in its path.

What these works nevertheless preserved was the Great and the Immortal which filled them, and which ever and again inclined people to preserve them by copying them down and thereby consciously or unconsciously to cooperate in passing on this cultural treasure.[1] "The fate of many books is so odd, and how they survive is so extraordinary, that over them there watches, unmistakably, a providential genius. But with them the genius is no external force; it is rather an indwelling one: the special good, the peculiar excellence, and the existential necessity connected with it."[2] Plato's writings, to mention but one example, proclaimed such ideas as these; they were flashes from another world and wherever they fell into souls that were receptive, they caught fire. Still, never before has the force of the spiritual world, of the ideas of truth, beauty and goodness become such very triumphant reality as in Plato's ardent longing for the supernatural forces of life: truth, spiritualization, godliness, eternity and immortality. The cultural high points in the particular literary works and their evaluation among men will have played the chief roles in the selectivity of the tradition, many accidents notwithstanding.

A considerable number of Greek and Roman authors are still known to us only by name, while their writings have been lost. The span of time from Homer until the Persian Wars has handed on to us only the complete writings of Homer, Hesiod and Theognis; otherwise there are merely fragments from thirty authors. The period from the Persian Wars until the ascension of Alexander the Great (who was the effective forerunner in the Orient for the Greek cultural world) is represented by seventy-four complete writings and with four items that are remnants. In the Roman literature, Catullus and Ovid are preserved for us in extensive fragments, and Lucretius, Vergil, Horace and Prosper are entirely preserved.[3] The transmission of Cicero[4] and Vergil[5] has been the most zealously attended to, and this has contributed to their becoming the "two great forces of world literature" (Wissowa). In his *Divine Comedy*, Dante has chosen Vergil as the leader through the horrors of Hell and through the sufferings of Purgatory and thus has lent him a double immortality.

An especially important event for the preservation or the decline of the literature of antiquity took place when the texts were transferred from the papyrus rolls onto the more enduring form of the parchment book, a matter that will later be considered in some detail. This was the fateful time of selection, which determined the salvaging or annihilation of a work. Roman literary production found its last protector in the old knightly Roman families of the fourth century (as for example, families of the Nicomachi and Symmachi), which attempted to save the remnants of paganism from the progressing Christendom, and which were also concerned for good transcriptions. Caesar, Livy, Martial and Apuleius have apparently been thereby saved. The efforts of these last Romans on behalf of the literature of their fatherland and for the culture of antiquity are attested for us in several names that have been entered into such improved manuscripts.

The last grandsons of these families, among whom were officials in high position, we then encounter at the court of the Osthrogoth King, Theoderic (493–526), who was the first Germanic sovereign who strove toward a synthesis of the Roman and Germanic cultures; there they avidly protected the reconciled cultural heritage of Christianity and antiquity; they are the contemporaries of the statesman, Cassiodorus, who indeed, with quite other aims in view, also accepted the endangered cultural monuments of antiquity and tried to establish a close connection between them and the monastic communities. At the court of Theoderic (who was favorably disposed to education) has perhaps also originated the splendid manuscript of the translation of the Bible by Ulfilas, which today is located in Uppsala. The Roman statesman and philosopher, Boethius (480–525), held the highest position at the same court until he was imprisoned on account of his traitorous connections with the Byzantine court, and put to death in 525. During his imprisonment, he wrote his book of confessions; this work, which was significant in form as well as in content, was concerned with the solace of philosophy *(De consolatione philosophiae libri decem);* in the Middle Ages, it was read more than Vergil was, and it has been preserved in more than four hundred manuscripts. It has gone through seventy printings; in 1473 it has become the first printed work (in Latin and in German) of Anton Koberger in Nuremberg.[6]

Stronger than the attempts of the last Romans at preservation were the destructive periods that followed, and it indeed seems almost to have been miracle that from this time (which in Italy was the battlefield for both the declining and the conquering peoples), there are not greater losses to be deplored than the works (or fragments thereof) of Varro, Suetonius, Tacitus, Aufidius Bassus, Pompeius Trogus, Livy, Petronius, and Ammianus Marcellinus.

A better day dawned for Greek literature when it was sheltered by the flourishing Byzantium. Emperor Constantine had founded a library there in 354. Witnesses to that are the Theodosian Codex with a decree of Emperors Valens and Gratian of 372, according to which four Greek and three Latin classics experts in the Imperial Library of Byzantium were entrusted with restoring the older literature — a clear evidence for the fact that the enlightening example of Alexandria had still not been extinguished. Byzantium, too, has performed a highly important function as a significant locale for transmitting the literature of antiquity.[7] Emperor Justinian I (527–565) put together out of earlier Roman laws and works of jurisprudence an enormous book of laws, the *Corpus Juris Civilis*, which is an enduring classic and which has had an immense influence on the development of law in the West.

3
The Early Christian Period
and the Book

Greece and Rome had fulfilled their historical mission, the creation of a great culture, and a new longing was now permeating the world. Beside this world there commandingly arose the world beyond, and in Christendom it captured the thinking and willing of men. For the history of culture, Christendom's significance rests in this: that by its faith in a redeeming supernatural power, it bestowed a new meaning on life; with its calling to holiness, it gave to existence a fresh content, and as a spiritual reality it set itself in powerful tension with the heritage of the Greek and Roman antiquity. The Gospel wholly dominated the new movement's beginnings, but the tradition of the doctrine of salvation, and even more its definition, and the defense against heresy, were already necessitating the mastery of language and of writing, as well as the utmost exertion of intellectual power. It was again the book that assumed leadership of the great movement: the Bible, the book of revelation which was enveloped by cultic adoration and which was to become the all surpassing "world book" and the book of mankind for centuries beyond.[1]

Quickly associating itself with the new book was a rich literature with instructions for interpreting, for teaching, and for the liturgy. This earliest collection grew in quantity, as the struggle increased with the invading heretical doctrines. As the young church took over the grammar and rhetoric of antiquity for its clerical rescruits and for the Christian school, it thereby saved a good part of the pagan literature that had been passed on. There are no violent revolutionary periods that for their new building could dispense with the old building blocks of the past. It is only in this way that cultures survive. The transparent clarity of the highly polished Latin language in Roman literature was already, without opposition, drawing the leading classes among the Christians in its train, and was thus effecting the preservation of works. One did not want, above all, to dispense with the philosophical writings of antiquity, particularly those by Aristotle and Plato; for interpreting the world, these were quite inexhaustible; it has indeed meant already at that time what Victor von Scheffel had his Ekkehard say: "The Holy Scripture is for us the guiding star of our faith; nevertheless the classics shine across to us like the last red of a sun which still, even after its setting, radiates quickening reflection into mankind's mind."

Despite persecutions, the more Christendom spread and developed further, the more voluminous its literature became. There was already flourishing in Alexandria a very influential catechetical school, and it reached its zenith under Origen (185–254), who was the most significant scholar of the first three Christian centuries. The collecting locales for publications were equally increasing. Julius Africanus, the learned Palestinian from the third century, who was the founder of the Christian world historiography, and thus a forerunner of Eusebius, was already able to utilize rolls from Alexandria, from Nysa in Syria, and from Rome. He organized the library of Emperor Alexander Severus; Adolf Harnack has indeed called him the first Christian librarian that we know about.[2]

Around the year 220, we hear of a book collection of bishop Alexander of Jerusalem: it has later been used by Eusebius. The library of Caesarea, which was founded by Origen and expanded by Amphilius (d. 309), gradually came to be valued as the most significant Christian library; it was avidly used by Eusebius (265–340) and Jerome (340–420). Fifty Bible manuscripts were created here for Emperor Constantine; this was under the supervision of Eusebius; then, as a gift of the emperor, they were moved into the new capital city of Constantinople.[3] Jerome discovered in Caesarea the original text of the *Hexapla* of Origen; here, prior to 378, the difficult transcription of the papyrus rolls on to parchment manuscripts was already going on. When Jerome settled in Bethlehem in 385, in order to complete there the famous translation of the Bible (the so-called Vulgate), he already had numerous books in his possession. In him there appears for the first time the close connection of the contemplative monastic life with submersion in the book, a promising encounter between cultural forces that were essentially related, and on which has devolved an eminent significance for the life of books in the Middle Ages. Not without good reason has Jerome so frequently been portrayed with the roll or the book. Albrecht Dürer's wonderful drawings, "Jerome in His Study" and "Jerome in the Cell," are the most graphic of these representations. The close relationship of the old Christian monks and hermits with the book, Dürer has movingly observed and portrayed again a second time in his *Antonius* engraving, where the saint no longer knows anything of the world other than the book in which he is engrossed. Intelligent persons have already said much that is beautiful concerning the joys that a good book can give us. "Never, however, was the anthem to the book more purely intoned than in this small engraving." (Willy Pastor).

Spain has already in the fourth century produced two outstanding poets: Iuvencus and Prudentius. Iuvencus, who was influenced by Vergil, had composed the New Testament in Latin hexameters; Prudentius, in his 'Psychomachia', had presented the eternal conflict in the human soul between virtue and vice.[4] Both of these works were among the works most read in the Middle Ages and were not lacking in any library.

Paulinus of Nola had already arranged a suitable room in the Church of Nola where the faithful (as indeed an inscription bade them) could read the holy scriptures.[5] Tertullian (200),[6] Cyprian (230) and Lactantius (300) wrote in North Africa, and paved the way for the predominance of Latin in ecclesiastical literature. The popes in Rome were solicitous of church libraries, and Hippolytus and Novatius wielded the pen. Following the pattern since the fourth century (which gave

Christendom its freedom) were Ambrose, Jerome and Augustine among the Latins, and Athanasius, Basil, Gregory of Nazianus, and John Chrysostom among the Greeks; all of them were very prominent witnesses to a significant advance, in which the two great cultural forces of antiquity and Christianity strongly influenced each other in spite of the contrasts between them. Augustine (354–430) went so far in this accomodation that he considered the secular sciences of grammar, dialectics, rhetoric and the mathematical disciplines as being a necessary elementary schooling of human thought for penetrating into the divine truths. His is the most important mind of the Chrisitan antiquity that was now drawing to a close. His attempt to understand God and the world and life on the basis of a dominant set of ideas, the immense struggle between the city of God and city of the world (City of Man), has had a strong influence on the entire Middle Ages.[7] His unique *Confessions* (the earliest Christian autobiography)[8] is among the works of world literature.

The influence that this church father was still exercising even in later periods can be learned from the fact that in the sixteenth century, no less than thirteen complete editions of his writings (with ten of them being folio volumes) have been published. With the great authors of the church, Christendom was thus by this time in possession of its quite original body of writings, and so it had the responsibility to be concerned for its circulation. So intensely desired and read were Cyprian's writings that they followed directly on the distribution of the Bible. Of Jerome, John Cassianus thought that the writings of this monk radiated like divine light over the entire world. The eloquence of the four church fathers was compared with the four rivers of Paradise. Abbot Cosmos in the sixth century was exuberantly recommending Athanasius' works to his pupil, Johannes Moschus: "If you find some of the writings of the holy Athanasius and have no paper, then copy them on your clothing."

Just as the pagan libraries were connected with sanctuaries, so the Christian book collections also, with their total holdings (the holy scriptures and their exegeses, the works of the fathers of the church, the histories of the martyrs, the legends and sermons) all enjoyed the protection of the church, and in this connection, they were considered after the end of the fourth century as being an established institution of Christian congregations, until the peoples' migrations were again threatening to destroy everything.

4
Papyrus Rolls and Parchment Manuscripts

In the midst of the enormous cultural and political upheaval brought about through Christianity and the people's migrations, the externals of the book world of antiquity and of early Christianity were transformed from the ground up: the gradual transition from the fragile and troublesome papyrus roll to the durable and more conveniently used parchment manuscript. This involved transcribing the texts that had been handed down into the new form of the book and onto new writing material.

Quite noteworthy here is the fact that the material and the form have changed almost simultaneously. Again, significant practical experimentation and experience must have preceded the preparation of animal hides for the purposes of writing, until the parchment thus achieved combined with the tablet form.

The transformation came about within a lengthy temporal span. Possibly in the first century of the imperial period, the parchment codex emerged in gatherings of leaves put together; it gained acceptance in the second century, and prevailed more and more. In the excavations at Ilisos in 1904 there was found a grave stele from the end of the second century A.D., on which roll and codex are represented together. A bundle of rolls is visible at the feet of a young man; on his left forearm rests an open codex that is held by the left hand, while the right hand (which is holding the reed for writing), lies on the books.[1]

The form of the codex achieved its full domination about the year 400.[2] On a mosaic image in the Mausoleum of Galla Placidia (d. 450, a daughter of the Roman emperor, Theodosius I), the viewer sees several manuscripts, among which are four gospels that lie in an opened bookcase, while St. Lawrence is striding along with an open book in his hand. The new form of the book had already been prefigured in the wood tablet or the wax tablet, which for business uses had been placed together in pairs or in several layers, before it was applied to books. Its triumphant advance here was primarily due to its superior handiness and its inclusive unity. No more did the reader need (as was the case earlier) to hold the text with both hands; he could rather place the book conveniently on a desk or on a table and have the right hand free for writing. The utilization of both pages and the joining of the layers brought the text together now into a unified whole and abolished all the disadvantages of the earlier partitioning of the text in the rolls.

To be sure, the papyrus material should now have been adapted to the wood tablet and, in fact, individual examples of papyrus books have been preserved for us, as, for example, a fragment of the *Iliad* in the British Museum in London, a bundle of leaves with parts of the Septuagint in Heidelberg, and, in Munich, the Breviary written about 970 under Archbishop Peter VI of Ravenna, being from the properties held by the church of Ravenna. Sir Frederick G. Kenyon was still able to report in the year 1931 newly discovered Greek Bible fragments on papyrus in book form from the first five centuries. From these one can see that the codex form for Christian texts goes back until the middle of the second century, while the roll was preferred for the texts of antiquity until the fourth century. The decision factor in connecting the new form with animal material from the hides of sheep, calves and goats was that this material lasted longer and it was more stable. Pliny emphasized that the rolls lasted a hundred years; books of two hundred years he considered a rarity. The parchment book promised almost everlasting duration. One also wrote better on the new material. Besides, the papyrus material was brittle, and one could write only on one side of it, while parchment could be folded without harm and used on both sides. The new writing material offered a further advantage through the possibility of coloring with purple, while it also increased the splendor of the gold and silver script. Furthermore, at the time of the growth of Christian literature, the Egyptian papyrus bush appears no longer to have been sufficient in the rising market for writing material. The story goes that the kings of Egypt, out of jealousy, forbade the exporting of papyrus to Pergamum and would here have produced a countermeasure.

More apparent is the fact that in the center of the book production in the Hellenistic period, a vital trade in hide material developed quite of itself, and gradually this has lent to it the name, *Pergament* (parchment). With it, the Mediterranean areas have become independent of Egypt, and a new industry has been introduced into the economic life. In 301 there emerged the designation, "Membrana Pergamena," in an edict of the Emperor Diocletian. The church seems to have greeted and strengthened the triumphal march of the new book from the very beginning.[3] Soon after Pamphilus, the Martyr, had presented works of Origen and other ecclesiastical authors to the congregation of Caeserea, two clerics, Acacius (388–365) and Euzoius (376–379), endeavored to transcribe the sometimes damaged rolls onto parchment. St. Jerome, who in the fourth century communicated to us this and other valuable observations concerning the nature of the book, reports of his own book collection that it contained Christian and pagan manuscripts; on account of the secular works (among which were Cicero and Plautus) he begged forgiveness of his Savior since he had denied him.

It can scarcely today be determined whether, in connection with the transition to the new form of the book, there have been unavoidable losses in the total literary production that has been handed down. The gaps that now appear in the writings of Tacitus, Curtius Rufus, Diodorus, Varro, Livy, and other authors have hardly originated at that time. In contrast with the earlier period, the transmission of literature has changed only in respect to the writing material, not in the selection of what shall be transmitted. As before, one will have copied precisely only such rolls that, on account of their value, ought to be replaced. Certainly everything that has not been saved by being put on parchment has been destroyed with the papyrus rolls that were so fragile. But that would always have been the case with those materials, and the transcription can in no way be designated as the burying-place of the transmitted literature. On the contrary, the external transformation in all cases has to be valued as a significant advance in book production. The guarantee for the uninterrupted transmission of the most important literature was initially only given with the parchment manuscript, and with it the final form was achieved, which has not changed up until today.

It is no accident that from so early a period as the fourth century, there have been preserved for us only parchment manuscripts, such as the Plautus of the Amrosiana in Milan or the Vergil of the Vaticana in Rome, while from such early centuries we possess no papyrus roll at all. That the discovered rolls of Egypt have lasted even for centuries in the more secure earthen vessels is another matter. The farther we advance into the centuries, the more parchment manuscripts have been delivered from the storms of time. They now constitute the most treasured objects of value in our book collections, such as the famous three oldest Bible manuscripts in Uncial lettering: the one discovered in the monastery of St. Catherine on Sinai by Constantine von Tischendorf, which was preserved as the *Codex Sinaiticus* for a time in Leningrad, and is now in London, which comes from the fifth century and which, with its four textual divisions, reminds one of the arrangement of the writing on the papyrus rolls; then the no less famous *Codex Vaticanus* 1209, from about the same period; and the *Codex Alexandrinus* in the British Museum in London, which was presented to the English king, Charles I, by the Patriarch Cyrillus Lukaris of Constantinople.

Furthermore, there are these parchment manuscripts: a Parisian literary monument of the fifth century, with the written over fragments by Ephraim, the Syrian; the wonderful *Iliad* manuscript of the Ambrosiana in Milan; the *Genesis* in Vienna,[4] written with silver and gold on purple; likewise there is the Dioscurides manuscript, written for the Princess Juliana Anicia, granddaughter of Emperor Valentinian III and decorated with the famous portrait of the princess;[5] the Syrian Evangelary of the Laurentiana in Florence with the earliest known *Canones* frame, produced in 586 by the priest, Rabula, in the St. John monastery at Zagba in Mesopotamia; the Florentine *Biblia Amiatina* from the monastery, S. Salvator sul Monte Amiata, produced in the English abbey of Wearmouth-Yarrow for Pope Gregory II, one of the oldest of the manuscripts of the Vulgate;[6] the *Vergilius Vaticanus* with fifth century illustrations, the best of these pictures which go back to Roman painting, among them being Vergil with a purple roll in his hand, and beside him on the right and left a desk and a case that serves for storing the roll; the unique *Pandects* manuscript of the seventh century, which at one time in Pisa was revered like a relic, the world-renowned Medici Vergil from Bobbio with the marginal notes by the consul, Rufius Apronianus Asterius (494 A.D.), one of the oldest manuscripts of classical authors;[7] the gospel manuscript of the archepiscopal curia of Rossano in Calabria, which is written in silver and provided with magnificent illustrations; the *Codex Argenteus* in Uppsala,[8] which is written with gold and silver letters on purple-colored parchment and has fragments from the Gothic translation of the Bible of Bishop Ulfilas from the fourth century, all of them priceless antiquities, which project toward us like boulders from the end of the West Roman Empire and the tornado of the peoples' migrations. The art of reproduction had copied almost all of them and thus elevated them into possessions of the world that cannot be lost.

Further old monuments on parchment show the development of the art of writing in the oldest period, beautiful capital manuscripts with their epigraphically measured capital letters, some of them written with gold and silver on purple, such as the silver Vienna Luke and Mark gospels, or the manuscript of St. Germain in silver and gold, or the gospel manuscript of Vividale, which was produced with large uncial letters, and about which in the thirteenth and fourteenth centuries the legend was formed to the effect that the Mark gospel therein was the record in the evangelist's own handwriting.[9] Scholarship is indeed fortunate to have saved several fragments from this oldest period of European literary history, such as the few leaves of the St. Gall *Vergilius* with its wonderful capital script *(capitalis quadrata)* or the seven leaves of the *Vergilius Augusteus* in Rome and Berlin, so christened by Pertz, because he believed they stemmed from the Augustan Period.[10]

Individual manuscripts reveal their venerable age through valuable signatures as when in a parchment manuscript of the Archives of St. Peter in Rome, in which are located the writings of St. Hilary of Poitiers, the corrector makes it known that he has compared the text in the fourteenth year of the reign of the Vandal king, Transamund, (thus in the year 509), or when in a manuscript of Monte Cassino with a commentary of Paul's epistles a presbyter, one Donatus, communicates that he has read the writing during an illness in the third year after the consulate of Emperor Justinian, (and thus in the year 570).[11]

The splendid design of the handsome manuscripts the young Christendom adopted from the models of antiquity and applied them primarily to the Biblical text and to the liturgical books. The sacred nature of holy scripture, the unique monument of the new faith, derived from its being considered as divine revelation, and therefore no copy of it was worthy enough. Enjoying this same veneration were the liturgical books, which like all ecclesiastical instruments had sacred significance and became favorite objects of church art. The new form of the book also brought with it many changes in the way the illustrations were designed and integrated into books. The ecclesiastical book became the center of the early Christian and medieval book design. St. Jerome, as well as John Chrysostom, were already complaining about the increasing splendor of the holy books. But it was precisely the splendor of these monuments that has effectively protected the manuscripts from destruction.

The new form of the book brought with it another significant trend, the establishment and development of bookbinding. Precisely the better possibility for protection has doubtless contributed to the victory of the book's superior new form. The model for this protection became the Roman diptych, with wax-covered double tables out of wood or ivory connected by rings, which in simpler form were destined for accounts, for lists of names and other everyday records, or, artistically carved, were used by the consul as gifts upon entering his office and were therefore called consular diptychs. Such decorative ivory tablets were also introduced into ecclesiastical art, and had protected and adorned splendid manuscripts, as, for example, the sacramentary of Bp. Drogo (826–855), which at one time was in the Metz Cathedral, but is now in the National Library in Paris. Former consular diptychs were even used for binding ecclesiastical manuscripts; thus the diptych of consul, Rufinus Probianus (ca. 400 A.D.), which today is kept in Berlin, was used in the eleventh century at the monastery of Werden an der Ruhr for a liturgical biography of St. Ludger. To the extent to which the splendid liturgical manuscripts gradually developed, the binding was also decorated with precious ivory carvings, gold work, pearls and other jewels, and was valued as an accessory to the altar vessels. The principal representations on the exquisite covers were Christ, Mary, the apostles, the cross, or scenes from holy scripture. It was not the bookbinder, but the goldsmith and the ivory cutter who have created these wonderful book ornaments.[12] The oldest luxury binding is preserved for us in the cathedral of Monza. Both the covers have a gold metal overlay, and are separated into four fields by a cross trimmed with pearls and jewels. An antique cameo is set into each of these fields. An inscription reveals that the Lombardian queen, Theodelinde (d. 625), has dedicated this monument to the St. John basilica which was founded by her. The gospel that belongs in the priceless binding has been lost.

The victory of the parchment manuscript over the papyrus roll has also lent a new appearance to the preserving and collection of books, the form that has remained essentially the same throughout the entire Middle Ages: the books fastened to a desk, or they stand in presses and bookcases; from now on, only the rooms in which the books will be accommodated will change.

5

The Early Christian Period to the
Early Middle Ages

Up to the time of the waning of the Roman Empire and the people's migrations, it was primarily the learned Magnus Aurelius Cassiodorus (480–545) (who at one time was the influential chancellor for the Ostogothic Theoderic) who successfully attended to the endangered intellectual works of antiquity and Christianity. Cassiodorus had withdrawn from the business of state into the remote monastery of Vivarium in Sicily in the region of Bruttium, in order to live entirely for the salvation of his soul and for scholarship. Emphasizing the art of writing and learning as professional works that were well pleasing to God, he brought here something quite new into the monastic life, which had previously been fulfilled only through renunciation, contemplation and theological study. Even St. Benedict of Nursia (480–543), the contemporary of Cassiodorus and the founder of Monte Cassino, in his monastic rule had commanded only a zealous reading of holy scripture and of the works by the church fathers as an important component of the spiritual life. To the far-looking scholar of Vivarium, the matter had to do not only with a zealous care for holy scripture, but also with the secular disciplines (which were viewed as valuable means of assistance for understanding the holy scriptures), as well as with the copying of the literature that had been transmitted; in this respect, he was in agreement with the great church fathers.

In this challenge we see the beginnings of the monastic book world, which has played such a significant role everywhere throughout the whole of the Middle Ages. It was in Vivarium that the monastic scriptorium of the future obtained its first home and received its first attention. Care and attention were given there to the whole knowledge of that period. Cassiodorus had the greatest understanding even for medicine, and he zealously collected the writings of Dioscurides, Hippocrates and Galenus. He perhaps thereby had an effect on the encouragement of the science of medicine in the Benedictine monasteries, above all in Monte Cassino, and from there on the aspiring school in Salerno. Cassiodorus has thus created something of the highest significance in one of the important new epochs for the book, for scholarship and culture, and he has transmitted the philological interest of antiquity to the medieval monks and to the monastic life, as to the most favorable spiritual center at that time. Not incorrectly has he been called "The last Roman and the first Medieval man" (Fedor Schneider)—this man who has experienced two historical periods of world significance at their point of intersection.[1]

Cassiodorus' influence has to be estimated all the higher since the ecclesiastical circles of the time were strongly disinclined toward secular knowledge. He can only be compared with the life of his friend, Eugippius, the abbot in the Severinus monastery at Lucullanum (Castell dell' Ovo) in the Gulf of Naples (510–538), and with the successful activity of Isidore of Seville (570–630), which comes from a somewhat later period. The Spanish bishop, who attempted with such zeal to preserve the body of literature which had been transmitted in Spain, has himself assembled a valuable group of manuscripts, and in the much-read collective work, *Etymologiae* (which became an inexhaustible source of medieval learning)[2] he has tried to disseminate the whole of knowledge of his time. Attributed to him also were those famous library verses that celebrate in song the content in sixteen groups of a book collection, and mention the works that are required for it: the Bible, the church fathers, the Christian poets and authors, Prudentius, Avitus, Juvencus, Sedulius, Eusebius, Orosius, Gregorius, Leander, Theodosius, Paulus, and Gaicus. These verses have presumably been located originally in a library beneath the authors' portraits.[3]

It has to be accepted straightaway that books and libraries early received careful attention also in Rome, which was the seat of the highest ranking bishop. Pope Gregory I (reigned 590–604), who was himself an ecclesiastical author, and who founded a theological school of higher learning in Rome, can above all be shown by various witnesses to have been a patron of the churchly book. Papal Rome has soon become also an active center of the book business, from which ecclesiastical manuscripts, and later also the texts of antiquity, have gone out into all the world, but especially into England. Thus Pope Paul I in 757 communicated to the Frankish king, Pippin, that he had ordered into the Frankish Kingdom an antiphonal, the *Grammar* of Aristotle, the writings of Dionysius the Areopogite, and other treatises, all of them in Greek. Pope Hadrian I sent liturgical works to the emperor Charlemagne, and in return the emperor dispatched the psalter of his wife, Hildegard.

6

The Nature of the Book
in the Middle Ages

When different cultures encounter each other and mix, the culture that is more highly developed, according to an inner law, will invariably gain the upper hand. Thus, when the Germanic world had to confront the culture of Christianity and of antiquity—it was the most decisive hour for the subsequent development—it could not be otherwise than that the young Nordic peoples should be strongly affected by the leadership of the superior old cultures of the Mediterranean, as well as by the spirit of Christianity, and that the Nordic peoples should take from these cultures more than they gave. There is no doubt that language and literature, as the effective bearers of culture, also played a significant role. The Greeks and Romans had left behind them highly developed languages and an unexcelled literature. With its Bible and church fathers, Christianity was already in possession of a wealth of book treasures. And as a young people ready for assimilation, the Germanic races brought with them great cultural and moral forces at their incursion into the Roman Empire; they did not, however, bring with them a national literature that could have surpassed the intellectual creations of the south, which had been fostered through long ages.

Subjected to these new influences, the myths and the songs they brought with them were quickly lost. The oral traditions of supernatural ideas died away, no matter how impressively expressed they were in song and saga, as soon as they were confronted by superior ideas, expressed in artful language and in forceful writing. National feelings and intrinsic cultural values can become a possession of a people that cannot be lost only when they, besides being orally transmitted, are also put down in writing, and are thus protected when confronted by hostile accidents. It is only in literature—it is only in the book—that the cultural historical life of the peoples is securely anchored; indeed, as with the Greeks and Romans, it outlasts the life of the peoples themselves. Our search for the oldest original monuments from the period of the Germans' incursion into the Roman empire is thus abortive. Only the oldest historian of the Germanic tribes, a Jordanus, a Gregory of Tours, or a Paul the Deacon tell us a bit concerning the Germanic period. When those figures of heroic saga such as Hildebrand, Dietrich, Gunther, Hagen, Etzel, Kriemhild, Gudrun, and above all, Siegfried in the *Nibelungenlied*—when these became objects of an independent literature, the German heroic stories so entered into German life that they could not be lost.[2]

The period of the great peoples' migrations may not be presented as if it entailed the sudden collapse of empires and the political order; it rather has to be considered as having been a temporal span covering several centuries which were filled with transformations, additions, and fusings of all sorts. As in geology, so here also science has allowed the interpretation of catastrophic change to die away. Nowhere in all of history is there a total break; everything is ultimately a transition, a conversion. To be sure, much has fallen victim to the storms of the peoples' migrations — especially along the frequented main highways. But much remained that was saved: things that lay in sheltered sites in out-of-the-way hermitages, churches and monasteries.

Following the break-up of the Roman empire, which for a long time had been deteriorating, and after antiquity's world view, with its pessimistic ideas focused on decline, had foundered, the Greek and Roman cultural world had no home anymore. The Christian conception of life replaced the pagan one. Christendom now became the leader of the new world, and the church became the communicator of the culture transmitted from the ancient world; it became the future educator of the human race. Thus fate determined the age and the balance of power in that period. And Christian Rome, harassed by the Lombards, as heir of the idea of the Roman empire and as the seat of the papacy enjoying the protective power of the Franks, entered into that momentous connection which finally led to the Holy Roman Empire, in which the emperor with the worldly scepter, and the pope with the spiritual one, were supposed to lead the same united Christendom. An hour of historical necessity for the world was once again striking. In a broader temporal perspective, Jakob Burckhardt saw the significance of the Roman Empire for world history in the "creation of a common world culture, through which the extension of a new world religion became possible, both of them transmissible to the barbarian Germans of the migration period as the future coherence for a new Europe." The great triumvirate Antiquity, Christendom, and the Germanic peoples, was now illuminating the world. A new great idea of immeasurable responsibility and magnitude, the idea of the divine world order in the form of the empire and the papacy, the unity of the Christian sphere in the "Imperium mundi," henceforth engaged the Western world for centuries. The earth seemed to project forth into heaven, and heaven seemed to fall to earth; the world seemed everlastingly arranged until the end of time, even though this apparent everlastingness turned out to be a fullfillment for a time only of mankind's desire for a happier world.

As the spiritual and leading power, the Christian church took the book into its service in its broadest dimensions and, following Cassiodorus, the spiritual institutions, the monasteries, became the most important centers of the literature and book production in the entire Middle Ages that followed. Scattered throughout all the lands, these places constituted the most successful way for disseminating the book in ecclesiastical education and to a lesser extent they were also the best guarantee for a secure transmitting of literature. As established property of the permanent ecclesiastical communities, the book collections remained more secure there than anywhere else where they were kept, when faced with the possible destruction and decline; at the same time, they also exerted there a great appeal. Anyone else who personally owned books and desired to arrange for their safety after his own death, deliberately bequeathed them to a monastery or to a foundation; and in addition, he might also in his pious heart hope for a heavenly reward.

Quite special significance for the transmission of the literature should be assigned to the medieval monastic writing room, the *scriptorium*, an establishment that we can now scarecely anymore properly imagine. In almost every larger spiritual community that owned books, the scriptorium was the actual center of the ecclesiastical book production, where all the copying and the transmitting of written works, as well as the reproduction of the book, were primarily accomplished. Clerical libraries were in the main provided with their most necessary works from that source. Manuscripts were borrowed from other monasteries, in order to copy them and to incorporate the copies in one's own collection. Again, this arrangement could develop at its best only in foundations and in the monasteries, where a constant training of copyists and an insured transmission of the art of writing, in addition to the ties among the monasteries of a particular order, fulfilled together the necessary conditions. Only here could such significant success be aimed for, as has been exhibited in the famous writing schools of the Middle Ages. Work in the scriptoria has mostly concerned with accomplishing the renewal of texts that had been transmitted, and only rarely did it have to do with the recording of newly written work. Throughout the whole of the Middle Ages, the concern was almost entirely with transmission, or with the compiling, of older texts, and not with the increasing of knowledge.

The great cultural achievement of the medieval clerical scriptoria and collections of books which go beyond their own period and the immediate purposes of the church, consisted in the fact that they have saved and handed down to posterity the body of literature of antiquity and early Christianity, as well as the books of the Middle Ages, among which were precious art works of the scriptural schools. Everyone of the famous old monasteries and foundations of England, Italy, Spain, France and Germany has cooperated successfully in this very significant task and has preserved valuable works from destruction.[3] Thus, for example, the thirty-three books of Livy and the oldest Lucretius manuscripts have been saved by Mainz; by Corvey, Tacitus has been saved, by Hersfeld, Ammianus Marcellinus, books 41–44 of Livy which came to us fromt he fifth century, by Lorsch, the fables of Hyginus, by Freising, the *Argonauts* of Valerius Flaccus, by Fulda, and by St. Gall, the *Astronomica* of Manilius. Certainly it was a delusion when it was occasionally thought in the Middle Ages that one still owned the gospels in the original writing of the first centuries. No classicist's, no gospeler's own manuscript has been preserved for us; and yet, most of their writings have been saved all along the way of an uninterrupted tradition. The oldest known manuscript of the Aeschylus tragedies in the famous monument of the Laurentiana comes from the tenth century, and is therefore 1400 years younger than the original text. Furthermore, no more favorable star has protected the original writings of the Middle Ages; they are almost all of them lost. Only the original writings by Sedulius Scotus and John Scotus[4] from the ninth century, and such from the thirteenth century by Albertus Magnus and Thomas Aquinas, have been preserved. Even so, we do possess the valuable—especially for the history of Emperor Henry II—chronicles of the Saxon houses by Bishop Thietmar of Merseburg (975–1018) in their original writing, which Bishop Werner (1061–1091) has at one time given to the monastery of St. Peter in Merseburg; Georg Spalatine and Philipp Melanchthon have used them; they are now in Dresden.[5] Richer of Rheims, Leo of Ostia, Frutolf of Bamberg have likewise bequeathed to us their very own handwriting.[6]

To disentangle the current scattering of manuscripts, and to determine the center of certain lines of descent, will always belong to the most difficult, but also to the most fruitful, tasks of the history of medieval culture and tradition. Edward Norden has attempted to examine the basis of the reasons for the preservation of the motley plethora of medieval manuscripts, and he considers the fact that the *Annals* and the *Germania* of Tacitus have been copied in Germany, the books of Caesar from the Gallic War in France, Catullus in Verona, and the work of Frontinus concerning the water services in Monte Cassino (from whence one looked out over the artificially irrigated Campagna) as being based in external causes. For reasons of an internal nature, one preferred, for the schools, (besides the grammarians), especially Vergil, Terence, Sallust, Lucan, Statius, Persius, Juvenal, and for the imitation of historical works, Sallust, Suetonius, Livy, for speech, Cicero, for poems, Ovid, and for culture, Seneca, Cicero and Valerius Maximus. The most important sources of the history of tradition are, besides the actual remains that have been preserved, the numerous lists of manuscripts, which the careful librarians of the medieval monasteries and foundations have handed down even where the holdings in books have themselves to a large degree disappeared. Leibniz, Schannat, Pez and Angelo Mai have already published individual old book catalogs. It is only the modern period, however, provided as it is with better techniques, which has successfully opened up these valuable sources for medieval cultural history and, through publication, has again allowed (by means of catalogs that have been preserved) the former book properties of significant cultural centers such as Fulda, Mainz, Murbach, and Lorsch to be reconstructed.[7]

Let us imagine ourselves stepping into a medieval monastery library or a book room.[8] The impressive room, filled with desks and bookcases, serves not merely for preserving but also for using the books. Numerous works, primarily the thickest ones, lie on desks, most of them chained *(catenati)*,[9] and are only to be used here.[10] The chaining of books did not take place only in the monastery libraries. When the Palatine Elector Ludwig III presented books in 1436 to the Holy Ghost Foundation in Heidelberg, he stipulated "that in a library that one will prepare therein, one should place the same books and preserve them well and secure them with chains and keys, so that they remain there and not be taken, pulled out, or put in a house or under someone else's control, but whoever wants to study them or copy from them, should go into the library." Today in Zutphen, in Goldberg and in Leyden, one can still see these old forms of the library: about three hundred volumes lie in a chapel of the St. John Church in Zutphen on old oaken desks, with chains being fastened to iron posts. The smaller volumes are accommodated in cases. By the way, that the chaining of books did not always protect them from being removed, may be learned from an entry in a catalog of the Waldsassen monastery from the time of the storms of the Reformation, where it says once in the enumeration: *"Nota* that on these pages has previously lain the *Vocabula Papiae*, but it has been cut out, so that merely the boards (the binding) lie there and hang on the chains." The same is reported of a volume of Augustine. In later times, when one no longer knew the purpose of this form of safekeeping, one has attributed the chaining of manuscripts to all manner of legendary causes. Thus in Königsberg, it was believed that the manuscripts of the castle library chained there represented the library of the magician, Faust.[11] The difference between the library room as it once was and the ones we now have has been vividly described by Josef Andreas Schmeller, one of the best authorities on medieval books.[12] The desks, which for the most part, represented beautiful workmanship and the heavy volumes lying on them lent the medieval book room its impressive atmosphere.

Every place where that artistic affection for worthy books prevailed which shines toward us from so many glorious miniature paintings and beautiful scripts of the old manuscripts, there all the monastery's artistic powers also cooperated together in decorating the room for the books. Pictorial representations of the seven liberal arts, or the most important faculties of the spirit, were intended to dispose the visitor toward intellectual composure and elevation.

There one could see represented *Sapientia* as the leader of the virtues, and philosophy as the mother of the sciences. Most of the images were explained by inscriptions. Verses extolled knowledge and its particular branches. Tegernsee's industrious librarian, who cataloged the books of his monastery in 1504, also entered into his catalog the library inscriptions of Kaisheim, Wessobrunn, Benediktbeuern, St. Ulrich in Augsburg and Ebersberg. This widespread custom of salutation in the room for books, which was also a manifestation of love for books, probably goes back to the aforementioned library verses that derive from Isidore of Seville.

Catalogs that had numbers indicating where books were located made it possible to look for certain books. One consulted the catalog, read there beside the title the location AI or II, and so found the desired work on desk A or in the case A under number I or II; the work carried the same number on the cover. Since the labels that indicated shelf location were different in individual monasteries, these labels have great value today in that they frequently indicate the provenance of the manuscripts which have been preserved.

The books were mostly separated into three large groups: first, the holy scriptures and their exegeses, then the church fathers and the theologians of the time, and finally the secular literature: mathematical, astronomical, physical, medical, judicial, historical, philosophical writings, and works on natural science. The school books that served for purposes of instruction, were mostly in a special room, and the liturgical works were kept in the sacristy.

For borrowing, other books were frequently given in exchange as a pledge. When Abbot Wibald of Corvey desired to borrow a Cicero manuscript from the library of Hildeshein Cathedral, Prior Rainald (1159, Archbishop of Cologne), wanted a Gellius text and Origen's commentary on the *Song of Songs* as a counter pledge. But since Corvey owned no Gellius, Wibald sent a Frontius manuscript instead.

The main source for increasing the number of books was, besides gifts, the scriptorium, where industrious hands were indefatigably active in the copying of works. In an old plan of the monastery of St. Gall we see the scriptorium drawn in beside the church and below the library: it had six windows; in the middle is a large table, and seven tables for writing are at the walls. From somewhere else has been preserved for us a suitable benediction, in which the Almighty is implored that he may make the visitors of the scriptorium worthy, so that what they read and copy there, they may be able to comprehend properly and profoundly.[13] Little by little, the scriptorium came to be valued as an established component of the provisions in a monastery; this is expressed in the familiar quotation: *Claustrum sine armario est quasi castrum sine armamentario,* "a monastery without a writing room is as a fortress without an armory." The activity of writing was valued as work well-pleasing to God. Concerning the skillful monk, Marian, in Regensberg, a legend relates that three fingers of the left hand had once given light for him while writing, in place of the candle that he had forgotten.

The detailed regulations that the Byzantine abbot and saint, Theodore (759–826), has issued for his monastery, Studion, near Byzantium, yield a notable look into the life of a monastery library and scriptorium. Just as this successful reformer of Eastern monasticism has integrated the entire life of his monks through established rules, so the reading and writing were likewise ordered according to precise regulations. A signal that called the monks together into the library, given by the librarian, rang at fixed hours, which were free to work. There each monk received a book until time for vespers. Then he intoned the signal again, and the books had to be given back, clean and unharmed, according to the sequence in which they had been registered. Precise regulations obtained for the monk's writing activity.[14]

The color red played a significant role in the design of a medieval manuscript. The introductory letters of a text or section of a text were red, or they were set off with red lines. Sometimes the pages and the leaves of a text are parctically saturated with such decorations, which were supposed to delight the eyes as well as guide them. Besides red, blue is also encountered in a rich profusion. It is from the term for red *(minium)* that the entire artistic activity of coloring was designated as "miniare," and then the further decoration of manuscripts with colored pictures as miniature decoration. *Miniare* and *illuminare* are used interchangeably to refer to the decoration in color of a book. From the word *rubrum* (red), one formed the designations, "rubricate," and "rubric," for the setting off of individual letters or words by means of red coloring.[15]

The main stock of medieval catalogs of books consisted of Latin works. Only seldom does one find a German book cited. But such entries are not entirely lacking. Mentioned in the catalogs of the Reichenau monastery are the *Carmina theodiscae linguae,* Latin poems with German glosses; a survey of the monastery of St. Riquier from the year 831 enters a history of the passion of the Lord in the

German and Latin languages; Weissenau possessed a German gospel in the ninth century, perhaps the famous old Saxon epic, *Heliand*, or what is indeed more likely, Otfried of Weissenburg's rhyming gospels book, and in 1043 it had a German *Psaltarium*, which was probably Notker's translation of the psalms: Pfaffers listed in 1155 Williram's translation of the *Song of Songs*. Works of spiritual edification in German found protective care in the nunneries.[16]

In many monasteries there was a bookbindery associated with the library and the writing room; it was there that the manuscripts received their covers. Frequently used for this purpose were those parchment manuscripts that were incomplete, or which were considered as being superfluous. Thus on Mt. Athos, under Abbot Marcarius, a venerable uncial manuscript with the Pauline letters on them was used in 1218 as material for binding. The monks of St. Gall in about 1461 rebound manuscripts and used for the purpose such priceless items as the *Edictus Rothari*, with the earliest notes on Lombardian law, and an ancient Vergil manuscript. Valuable fragments have happily on occcassionally been preserved in the bindings. In was even worse when traders disposed of parchment manuscripts for industrial purposes, or when monks who lacked any understanding made bookmarks out of parchment leaves; as Gerhard Führer, the last abbot of the Cistercian monastery of Fürstenfeld, tells us, he had known a monk who, besides other manuscripts, cut to pieces the first necrology of the monastery and made out of it the so-called "Merkerle and Herzerle," bookmarks for choral books.

7
Important Places in the Early Middle Ages for the Transmission of the Cultural Tradition

Without being able to give a history of the medieval libraries in churches and monasteries, the following brief survey is intended merely to emphasize the several monasteries and foundations that have played an especially significant role in the history of transmission and which have bequeathed to our own time that which is valuable among what remains of their possessions.

It will hardly be possible today to ferret out all the connections that have proceeded from Cassiodorus and his founding of Vivarium. The Benedictine monasteries have surely been most effectively influenced—especially, Monte Cassino, which at one time had belonged to the learned Roman, Marcus Terentius Varro. A carefully nurtured creation of St. Benedict since 529, it was abandoned in 581 because of hostile invasions; rebuilt in 717, in the eighth century it was operating base for the Lombardian historiographer, Paul the Deacon. It was plundered again in 888, and then became once more an active cultural center and a secure home place for the literature that was handed down. It has saved for us valuable manuscripts which contain texts of Apuleius, Varro, Tacitus, Hyginus, and with these it has also presented us with priceless miniature paintings.[1]

Of more special significance for the resurgence of cultural life following its decline during the period of the peoples' migrations, as this has been so impressively portrayed by Gregory of Tours (540–594), were the Irish missionaries of the sixth and seventh centuries. They were attached by a pious zeal for conversion and a worldly wanderlust to distant lands with the aim of diffusing the faith and Christian morality. While the peoples' migrations on the Continent and in Britain had severely convulsed the old culture, Ireland—the old Hibernia—had remained protected from these storms. St. Patrick, the founder of Irish monasticism, had already proven himself a protector of the book and, under Pope Sextus (432–440), he had come back from Rome with relics and books. In the seventh century, in the monastery of Kells, there originated the gospel that was written with wonderful half-uncials and decorated with splendid illustrations; today it is the proudest possession of the library of Trinity College in Dublin.[2]

A series of monasteries—such as the foundations at Bangor and Armagh,

Clonmacnoise and Lismore—had been able to develop unhindered, so that, following the period of the peoples' migrations, they were successfully effective as the
starting points for a superior culture and of a richly developed world of books.[3] The
Irish literary monuments *(Libri scotice scripti)*[4] played a significant role in the oldest
catalogs of books in Bobbio, St. Gall and Reichenau; 150 such manuscripts can still
be authenticated today; to be sure, they are almost exclusively of theological content. In a Priscian manuscript of St. Gall, the writer (who was probably a monk from
Bangor) praises his activity in the forest with his much lined parchment; all around
him were the warblings of birds and the cuckoo's call; under the forest's roof one
writes a good hand.[5]

The Irish laid the ground work in England for that highly spiritual culture from
which have proceeded the Venerable Bede (672–735), the most significant scholar
of the early Middle Ages, Willibrod (d. 739), Winifried Bonifatius (680–754) (the
founder of the German church) and then, Alcuin, and Sturmi, Fulda's founder. A
legend tells us that the Friesians, following the murder of St. Boniface, could not
find any gold or silver in his belongings (as they had hoped); there were only books,
and three manuscripts from his possessions which are still shown there today;
among them is the one that the saint is supposed to have held as he was warding
off his pursuer's deadly blow.[6] Even now his letters give us good insights into the
vital trading in books that he carried on with various monasteries.

The Anglo-Saxons already had early and close connections with Rome, where
the college for theological education was situated in the seventh century. Thus Pope
Gregory the Great (590–604) sent manuscripts to the island, two of which have still
been preserved in the Bodleian at Oxford and at Corpus Christi College in Cambridge. From each of his trips to Rome in 661, 680 and 684, Benedictus Biscop
brought individual books to his Jarrow monastery, and on his death bed, he was
still commending the care of the library to his brothers.

In their long laborious operations on the Continent, the Irish and Anglo-Saxons
(besides Columban, Gallus and Bonifacius, there were also numerous other missionaries) scattered those seeds that turned out to be so fruitful under Emperor
Charlemagne: an increased receptivity on the part of the new generation to Christian doctrine and morality, as well as to the cultural works of the pagan, and early
Christian, periods. Under this influence, Luxueil, Fleury and the three monasteries
on the Somme (River) of Peronne, St. Riquier and Corbie, became significant
centers for transmitting the Insular literature. The Abbey of Gellone near Toulouse
has produced a famous sacramentarium in the eighth century, and indeed, it has
handed down this most artistically significant manuscript of the Merovingian
period; it is now in Paris.

One of the most important Irish plantations on the Continent originated in Upper Italy, when the Irish monk, Columbanus (d. 615) followed his Burgundian foundations of Anegray, Luxueil and Fontenay with a fourth settlement in 614 at the
foot of Mt. Penice, near the confluence of the Bobbio and the Trebia (rivers). Within
the lifetime of its founder, the new monastery at Bobbio was already receiving
valuable manuscripts, among them being items left from the library of Cassiodorus
from Vivarium, which presumably have been saved at the new educational

institutions by way of Pomposa. In these pre–Columbanian treasures we should see a significant connection to the legacy of Cassiodorus, and therewith a fruitful blending of Irish educational aims with the Vivarium spirit. Priceless portions of Bobbio's oldest possessions have been preserved until the present in the Ambrosiana in Milan[7]—such as the Medici Vergil manuscript of 494 (which was identified as such by Delisle), the Bamberg collective manuscript, with Jerome and Gennadius of Marseilles, and the Irish antiphony of Bangor.

Bobbio's treasures, and the writing school there, have already twice caused a stir in the scholarly world; the first time was in 1494, when the humanist, George Merula, reported valuable textual finds at the monastery, and the second time was in the nineteenth century, when sharp eyes detected under some texts a second one by an older hand, which had different writing. It seems that in the period from the seventh to the ninth century the monks of Bobbio have, by washing and scraping, blotted out the original older text of a number of their manuscripts, and they have written on the material that was thus again rendered serviceable. But since the initial writing was not entirely erased, the original characters still showed through, and these can be deciphered by means of special techniques, called in the Greek, *palimpsestas*, in Latin *codices rescripti*, and in German, *Schabhandschriften*, these literary monuments are among the most unique books of the early Middle Ages.[8]

As the entire Irish aim mainly had to do with spreading the faith on the Continent, so the Bobbio monks were also concerned primarily for ecclesiastical writing, in order to make use of it against Arianism. Those things in Vivarium's priceless legacy that were suitable to these aims were welcomed; what did not fit was used as writing material, so that it could be filled with Christian literature. Biblical texts and the works of Eusebius, Rufinus, Joseph Flavius and Cassiodorus remained unaltered as indisputably being the most valuable Christian holdings. Cicero's *Orations*, on the other hand, had to yield to the *Carmen paschale* of Sedulius, Cicero's work, *De republica*, to St. Augustine's commentary on the *Psalms*, Cicero's *Verrines* orations to a work by Cyprian, and fragments of Galenus and Dioscurides to the *Council Acts*, together with Isidore's *Etymologiae*. Where Lucan, Fronto and Symmachus, Gargilius Martialis, Palagionius and the *Codex Theodosianus* had been written, one was later reading grammatical treatises, acts of councils, the *Liber Pontificalis*, metrical elucidations, and Cassian's *Collectiones*. A unique palimpsest manuscript of the Munich State Library, which formerly was owned by the cathedral chapter in Freising (Cod. lat. 6333) contains in its top layer the writing of Jerome and Gennadius, *De viris illustribus*, while the work under it brings to light, among various texts, the royal letter of Emperor Charlemagne to Pope Hadrian concerning the appointment of Abbot Waldo of Reichenau to the bishopric of Pavia.[9]

Frequently with these transformed manuscripts the cause may have been the inferior items, or oddly written texts, which, for the monks, were of less importance. Priceless items of the first order now surfaced, such as Cicero's books on the state, which were written in large uncial script in the fourth century of our era, the letters and orations of Cornelius Fronto, and the letters of Emperor Aurelius Symmachus.

The first significant finds were made by the Italian Jesuit, Angelo Mai (1782–1854), librarian since 1813 of the Ambrosiana in Milan, and administrator of the Vaticana in Rome since 1819. Angelo Mai had opportunities in both of these collections to become acquainted with the chief items that were left from Bobbio, of which no fewer than seventy-one manuscripts had passed over in 1806 to the Vaticana; so did twenty-eight priceless items from the same collection twelve years later.

The valuable discoveries in Milan and Rome have led to further researches which have proven that not merely in Bobbio, but also in Verona (already since the sixth century a book center of the first order), in St. Gall, Autin, Fleury, Corbie and Orvieto, priceless parchment manuscripts have been written over. Niebuhr discovered in 1816 in Verona the *Institutes* of Gaius (which came from the eighth century)[10] under the epistles of St. Jerome; the elder Mone found in an eighth century Jerome manuscript from Reichenau, masses of the Gallican Church from the fourth century, and the younger Mone has found in the Benedictine monastery of St. Paul in Carinthia a manuscript written over three times from four different centuries.[11] Similarly, (as is the case with excavations), where the discovery of antiquities frequently brings with it the rapid decline of the treasures, the effort at reconstruction have also inflicted serious injury on palimpsests that have been discovered. Provided with finer instruments, the Benedictine monastery of Beuron[12] and the "Instituti Ferrini dei palinsesti" in Rome have devoted themselves in the most recent period to researching these manuscripts.

8
The Book in the Carolingian Period

Emperor Charlemagne's significance for the history of culture rests primarily on the fact that he consciously combined the great educational goal of Christianity with the cultural legacy of antiquity; that at this court in Aachen he created a broadly enlightening center for scholars from all countries, of Irishmen, of Anglo-Saxons, West Goths and Lombards; that he everywhere zealously espoused the cause of fostering education, and that with these efforts he established a great Western cultural life. His favorite book was St. Augustine's *De Civitate Dei*, and the godly state on earth was also the high goal of his striving. In his *Weltgeschichtliche Betrachtungen* ("Observations of World History"), Jakob Burckhardt thought that if Charlemagne's reign had continued in its full splendor for only a hundred more years, the world would have flowed into the full Renaissance, thus bypassing the Middle Ages.

A second Cassiodorus, but equipped with the plethora of power of a sovereign conscious of his strength, the king strove by all sorts of means for the reversal of the languishing culture; in his famous *Capitulary* of 789, he practically issued a curriculum, for he required greater care in the production of books for the church, he required the clergy to strive more zealously toward education and learning, he had the literal copy of the Rule of St. Benedict (the basic book of the medieval monastic life) brought from Monte Cassino, and he concerned himself just as enthusiastically with improving the Biblical texts as he did with the collection of the Germanic pagan songs,[1] and he entrusted outstanding men with the leadership of his palace school. Among them was the Lomabardian, Paul the Deacon, who had written the history of the Lombards in Italy and had brought several classical manuscripts with him into the Frankish kingdom.

The scholar who was culturally the most significant at the imperial court was the Anglo-Saxon, Alcuin (735–804). Alcuin had enjoyed a good education at the school in York, which was gradually becoming the most outstanding center of learning in England; he had seen Rome and the world, and in 766, he had taken over the school and library at York. In later years, he has still reflected on the copious collection that was there, in enthusiastic verses: everything that Italy and Greece, and that Hebrew education and Africa produced in cultural work, the works that Jerome, Hilary, Ambrose, Augustine and other church fathers, and which Pompey Trogus, Pliny, Aristotle, Cicero, Sedulius, Lucanus, Donatus and Priscianus have written—all those, and still other items besides, were to be found among the treasury of books in York. When Alcuin embarked on his great educational work in the Frankish kingdom, he first of all procured the requisite books from England. The items he handed out to be copied, he watched over with a conscientious zeal and he saw to the improvement of the neglected texts. He wanted a second Athens to arise in the Franconian kingdom, which in its significance would surpass the first one, since the teaching of Christ excelled all the wisdom of the Greek academies. The emperor finally secured in the Eastern Franconian Einhard, a gifted advisor who was as scholarly as he was statesmanlike. Einhard has dedicated the *Vita Caroli* (a biography influenced by Suetonius) to his sovereign following his death.

The influences that have radiated from the endeavors of Charlemagne and his court can now hardly be estimated too highly.[2] The book experienced a rich flourishing period in the cathedral and monastery schools. The texts that had been transmitted were examined and improved; with careful nurture, one saw to a clear, regular, legible and beautiful script in the so-called Carolingian miniscule, which was a graceful rounded lettering that would in time become the world's script. Lavish letters and initials were used; art was successfully put into the service of manuscripts, and all the possibilities were exhausted for increasing even further the magnificence of manuscripts, through purple coloring, with gold and silver, and with priceless bindings. The book was sunning itself, as it were, in the imperial favor, and in the high culture of the period, and it was itself the bearer and the symbol of this culture. Athens and Alexandria were revived. To be sure, the time for independent, intellectual creations had not yet arrived; for the new Western spirit, however, the period has become one of fruitful apprenticeship.

Almost our entire tradition of ancient literature goes back to the period from the ninth to the eleventh century. Only a very few classical manuscripts have come to us from the pre–Carolingian period. In this fact alone Charlemagne's significance for the transmission of the ancient literature clearly expresses itself. Many texts at that time were extant only in a few manuscripts, and some only in a single copy. The new tradition now connected to this extremely endangered residue. Had this process been known to the Italian humanists of the Renaissance period, they would not have been so surprised when they found so many ancient texts in the monasteries north of the Alps. It was primarily under this influence that Tours and Fulda became important centers of careful writing activity and the work of copying. From St. Martin in Tours have emerged such important manuscripts as the Parisian Lucan and Suetonius, the Berne Vergil, the Leyden Nonius Marcellus and Curtius; and from Fulda, the Vienna Avienus, the German Tatian and the Vatican Ammianus. Other Carolingian monasteries and foundations, however, such as Corbie, Fleury, Ferrières, Sens, St. Riquier, Péronne, Lyon,[3] Reims and Laon[4] in France, and Mainz, Hersfeld, Fulda, Seligenstadt, Lorsch, Winzburg, Murbach, Reichenau, Cologne, Trier and St. Gall in Germany have also distinguished themselves as important locales for the transmitting of texts.

The Carolingian period was also of the greatest significance for the artistic decoration of the book.[5] Those truly royal splendid manuscripts were created which are to be numbered among the most priceless pearls of medieval art and the most valuable book monuments of all time. As eloquent witnesses of a surprisingly high book culture, they must also not go unnoticed here.[6]

The new art movement proceeded from the immediate environment of Emperor Charlemagne, from the palace school in Aachen. Here developed into the highest flowering an exceedingly fine emotional empathy with the reawakened art of the ancient world; here there originated those wonderful evangelaries which are now kept as costly treasures in the Municipal Library in Trier, the National Library in Paris and the National Library in Vienna.[7]

Soon competing with the palace school in Aachen were the writing schools of northeast Franconia; promoted effectively by the court, the old sites of culture in Tours, Metz, Rheims, St. Denis, Corbie, and Orléans also produced outstanding works in the art of writing and in miniature painting. Alcuin's spirit continued to be effective for a long time in St. Martin of Tours. Under his successors, Fridugisus and Adalhard, the writing school there was successfully working out the unique application of the round and broadly shaped half uncial script for the introductions and beginnings of books. Investigation assigns to the older school of Tours the so-called Alcuin Bibles, which today are found in Zurich, Bamberg and Rome. The massive Bamberg Bible from the ninth century evidences by its verse on purple strips and by a three dimensional picture of Alcuin that it is surely a monument of Tours from the period soon after Alcuin.

Even more splendid are the creations provided by the younger school of Tours: The London Alcuin Bible, the famous Lothar gospel in Paris, which was copied for Emperor Lothar and decorated with his likeness; the most glorious of all the works of Tours: the Bible known throughout the world, which was copied by a monk of the monastery of St. Martin, and has been dedicated by Count Vivian to Charles the Bald, which is now also in Paris; the sacramentary that Abbot Raganaldus (Rainaud) of St. Martin at Marmoutiers had written about 845 in Tours, now in the seminary library at Autin; the evangelaries of Le Mans and Du Fay, which are kept in Paris; and finally, the Bamberg Boethius manuscript from the possessions of Emperor Otto III.[8]

The monastery of St. Martin aux Champs in Metz, one of the chief sites of Carolingian education, may boast of equally splendid manuscripts. Art creations of the first order proceeded from there: the gospel of the monk, Godescalc, 781–783, which was written for Charlemagne on purple colored parchment with gold and silver, and which is today in Paris; the gospel of the Municipal Library of Abbéville, from the monastery of St. Ricquier; the Ada Evangelary, written in gold on parchment and decorated with one of the imperial cameo from the fourth century, which is now in Trier; the magnificent evangelary from the Abbey of St. Médard in Soissons, which was presented by Emperor Ludwig the Pious at Easter 827 to the Abbey of St. Medardus, and is now in Paris; also there is the sacramentary, richly decorated with initials, which was written at the time of Bishop Drogo (826–855) for the Metz church.[9]

Since almost without exception, only liturgical books were produced in the Carolingian monasteries with such unprecedented sumptuousness, this was also the case in Rheims, where the evangelary has originated which was written under

Abbot Petrus of Hautvilliers for Bishop Ebo of Rheims (816–835), and which is now in the Municipal Library of Epernay, as well as two further splendid evangelaries;[10] and in St. Denis, an Iro-Scottish foundation, which has produced the so-called Evangelary of Francis II, in addition to the Bible destined for Charles the Bald, and the sacramentary for St. Denis (all three of these manuscripts are now in Paris) and, finally, the Evangelary of St. Vaast, which is today in the Library at Arras.

Chiefly attributed to the scriptorium of the Corbie monastery,[11] whose leader, Odo, was among the trusted advisors of Emperor Charles the Bald, are three splendid manuscripts which were produced for the emperor: the Paris Psalter, written with gold in capital script by a monk, Liuthard, between 842 and 869; further, the Emperor's prayer-book, which was earlier in the great minster at Zurich, and in now in the treasure room at Munich; and finally, the *Codex Aureus*, which was produced by the cleric, Berengar, in 870 (together with Liuthard) and decorated with the emperor's portrait. This was presented, together with its splendid binding that showed the enthroned Christ and was covered with stamped gold and pearls, by King Arnulf to the monastery of St. Emmeram in Regensburg; today it is in the State Library in Munich. Still to come were the most ornate of all the Carolingian manuscripts, the Bible produced for Charles III about 881 by St. Paul in Rome, the Paris Sacramentary of Hrodrardus, the Colbert Evangelary, which is also in Paris, and the Evangelary of Celestins, which is now in the Arsenal Library of Paris.

From the writing school of Orléans (which was affiliated with either the cathedral or with the abbey of St. Benedict) have apparently come the Bible that was written on commission from Theodulf, the learned bishop who, besides Alcuin, deserves the most credit for the improvement of the Biblical text, and a decorated manuscript especially rich in ornaments, which is now in the cathedral at Puy.

But the Carolingian period was not creative only in such splendid manuscripts; it also awakened a vital scholarly life on all sides. Hrabanus Maurus (784–856), the creator of the German school system, received his first instruction in Fulda, which itself was the most significant foundation of the apostle of the Germans (744). His teacher, Baugulf (799–820), a well-informed monk, who as an abbot was concerned with many things, had nevertheless copied Vergil's pastoral poems; for further education, he sent the gifted lad to Alcuin in Tours. Here the able pupil received the by-name of Maurus after St. Benedict's favorite. In the year 803, Hrabanus took over the monastery school in Fulda and rapidly made it Germany's foremost educational institution. In his tireless labor he found that he was successfully assisted by the monastery's rich library. With eloquent verses he proclaimed its fame; it contained everything that exists of spiritual and secular writings.

As abbot (822–842), Hrabanus likewise gave support to the book collection, and he was also concerned for the copying of the literature of antiquity. His pupil, Servatius Lupus, once apologized to the abbot of Seligenstadt, Einhard, for not having yet returned a borrowed Aulus-Gellius manuscript; Hrabanus held it back almost by force, so as to allow it to be copied together with Cicero's writing about oratory and with the commentary on Cicero. It is only from such a rich possession of books as Fulda maintained for him that Hrabanus could derive that broad knowledge which is expressed in his instructional books, and, above all, in his encyclopedia about the universe *(De universo libri XXII)*. His works have been speedily disseminated among the monasteries, and like those of Boethius, Cassiodorus, Isidore of Seville, and Bede, they are to be encountered in all medieval library catalogs.[12]

Among the places that transmitted the literature of antiquity, Fulda occupies an outstanding position; it is with its manuscripts that the textual histories of Cicero, Vergil, Columella, Vitruvius, Suetonius, Ammianus Marcellinus, Justinian, and Hegesippus are inseparably connected. But Old High German manuscripts also go back to Fulda: the *Hildebrandslied,* the oldest fragment in Old High German from the German heroic saga, with its representation of the tragic duel between Hildebrand and his son, Hadubrand, which was first written down about 780 and copied in the ninth century on the blank pages of a theological manuscript (it is one of our most precious national monuments and is now kept in the Territorial Library in Kassel); the Merseburg *Incantations,* which are entered in the tenth century in a clerical manuscript of the Merseburg Cathedral chapter; and the Kassel glosses.[13] Fulda has been no less significant a home for valuable artistic manuscripts from the Cartolingian and Ottonic periods, such as the famous sacramentary from Göttingen with its thirty illustrations, and numerous initials from the tenth century, and also the Bamberg sacramentary.[14]

One of Hrabanus' most outstanding pupils, the aforementioned later abbot, Lupus of Ferrière (842–862), became one of the most zealous book collectors of his time. One could simply call him the first early humanist, so eagerly do we see this remarkable man (who praised the renaissance under Charlemagne with Cicero's words) searching for the works of antiquity. Thus did he beg for Cicero manuscripts from Einhard; to Pope Benedict he sent an extensive wish list, which mentioned the *Noctes atticae* of Gellius, Cicero's treatment on oratory, Jerome's commentary on Jeremiah, a complete Quintilian manuscript, and the Donatus commentary on Terence. A cleric, one Adalgaud, copied Macrobius and other works for him; Archbishop Ursmar of Tours was besought to provide him with Boethius' commentary on Cicero's *Topica* from the library of St. Martin; he had Prüm send him the letters of Cicero; he begged the Abbot there to deliver to him the Fulda Suetonius manusscript, which was concerned with the lives of the emperors *(De vita Caesarum):* and he wrote to Reichenau to see if he might borrow Sallust's *Jugurthine War* and *The Conspiracy of Cataline,* Cicero's orations against Verres, and other manuscripts; and he sent his Livy to Archbishop Wenilo of Sens. Situated not far from Ferrières was Fleury *(Floriacum),* where there was a rich treasury of books in St. Benedict's monastery. There Lupus became acquainted with Valerius Maximus.[15] His letters, which have been preserved for us, are the best contemporary source for learning about the astonishingly highly developed book production in the Carolingian period.[16]

The Benedictine monastery of Reichenau on an island in Lake Constance, which was founded in 774 by St. Pirmin,[17] became a further thoroughly successful

locale for collecting the literature that had been handed down; the very learned
Reginbert (800–846) developed there a zealous activity in the copying of ecclesiastical and secular works. When on one occasion two Reichenau monks, Tatto
and Grimald, were sent to the Inda Abbey near Aachen, Reginbert commissioned
them to copy the *Regula St. Benedicti* from the manuscript of Charlemagne, which
goes back to the Italian standard copy; this copy is still kept today in St. Gall. The
Reichenau catalog of books of 822 is one of the oldest examples known to us of
subject arrangement. Bible manuscripts, church authors, lives of saints, law books,
historical works and geographies, medicine, liturgy, sermons, glosses on the passion narrative, grammars and poetry: the 415 volumes of the abundant library are
arranged in this sequence.

Another list records the books that have been copied in the monastery under
Abbot Erlebald (823–838). Among them are the writings of the church fathers and
Alcuin's treatises, but also secular works, such as Priscian, two works on
astronomy, Josephus Flavius' history of the Jews and the law book of the
Allemanians – thirty-nine items in all. Under Abbot Rundhelmas (838–842), nine
works have been copied, Vitruvius and Hyginus being among them. Most of the
old Reichenau manuscripts out of which Walafrid Strabo (809–849), the charming
portrayer of his little monastery garden *(Hortulus)*, has obtained copious
knowledge, are still kept for us today in the Territorial Library at Karlsruhe and,
within the context of literature and the history of writing, they are among the most
informative monuments of medieval manuscript lore.

Not far south of Reichenau there again developed an outstanding center of vital
cultural life and of the quiet pleasure in books: St. Gall, the foundation of
St. Gallus (d. 645), an Irishman and a pupil of St. Columbanus.[18] The library
there, which was founded by Abbot Gozbert (816–836), enjoyed its first flowering since the middle of the ninth century, when the Irishman, Moengal, raised
the monastery school to a higher plane, and Abbot Grimald (841–872), a pupil of
Charlemagne's court school and protégé of Ludwig the German, took over the
leadership of the school. The splendid creations of the St. Gall writing school,
among which was the psalter[19] of Folchart, (a ninth-century monk) provided with
unprecedentedly magnificent initials, and the golden psalter, of the ninth century
(the most significant master work of St. Gall) have become greatly renowned.
Among the books that the Abbot Hartmuot (872–883) wrote, or had copied, were
works by Isidore, Josephus, Priscianus, Solinus, Orosius, Martianus Capella, and
Boethius.

Several of the episcopal sees of this period also competed in their cultural activity with the monasteries. A catalog of books of the chapter in Freising cites several
grammatical and metrical writings, as well as the classics, such as Homer and
Vergil. From Freising also came valuable fragments of the Christian *Play of Herod*,
the first dramatic poetical work in Bavaria, and a valuable copy of the renowned
gospel harmony by Otfried of Weissenburg, (our first national poet) from the fifth
or sixth decade of the ninth century, the oldest German poem with end rhymes.
Under the Freising Bishop Arbeo, Arn grew up; he was the later founder of an imposing Salzburg collection of books, and he had close relations with the intellectual

leaders in France and had 150 manuscripts copied, among them being the works of his teacher and friend, Alcuin.

Regensburg had transmitted to us one of the notable manuscripts sent by Archbishop Adabraun of Salzbrug (812–836) to King Ludwig the German with a sermon of St. Augustine's, in which an inexperienced hand from the middle of the ninth century has entered the famous German *Muspilli* poem of the war of worlds and of the strife of the divinely sent Elias with the Anti-Christ. The marvels of language sound forth: "If the blood of Elias drops on the earth, so the mountains burn up, and not a single one of the trees stands in the earth; the water dries up, the sea swallows itself, it burns up in the flames of heavens, the moon falls, the *Mittilagart* burns, and not a stone stands securely anymore. Then the day of reckoning descends with fire onto the land to banish anew, then a relative can do nothing to help another in the face of the universal conflagration."

In Cologne, Archbishop Hildebald (789–819), a confidant of Emperor Charlemagne, had several manuscripts copied, twelve of which are among those kept until now in the Cologne Cathedral. One of them reveals *(Paraeneticus Fulgentii Ferrandi)* that it had been copied at the command of Bishop Wenilo of Laon for Hildebald from one of the books that Pope Leo has sent to Emperor Charlemagne.[20] One is again and again surprised concerning the lively trade in books of that period, with its quite undeveloped modes of transportation. In every direction, the book made its way, even the ones that contained classical and other secular literature. The list of holdings of the Cathedral Library in Oviedo of 882 enumerates forty-one manuscripts, among them being Vergil, Juvenal and Prudentius. The Passau Cathedral church lists in 904 the collection of books of the territorial bishop, Madalwinus, with fifty-six manuscripts: besides liturgical books and books for pastoral care, there are the *Capitularia* of Charlemagne, the laws of the Bavarians, of the Franks, of the Allemanians, and also Martianus Capella, Sedulius, Arator, Cato, Avienus, Plautus, Prosper, Prudentius and Vergil.

A map with all the locations of churches from which significant holdings in books are known to us, would show us that an entire network of cultural centers was situated all over Western Europe in the Carolingian period and the network has been effectively supported by treasures of books. It became a pious custom everywhere for men to bestow books on churches and monasteries. In a manuscript from Lorsch owned by the Vatican, twenty-three manuscripts are enumerated; the monastery has obtained these in 814 from the legacy of the Ghent abbot, Gewardus. This monastery of ancient renown, which owned precious classic manuscripts, such as Vergil and Livy with the books 41–45 (which have nowhere else been handed down), and further, an evangelary of the ninth century written in gold and bound with ivory tablets, has therefore drawn its holdings of books not only from Italy, Franconia and the Rhineland; this, again, is an example of the astoundingly mobile traffic in books of the period.[21]

Somehow, almost every significant monastery or foundation owned an especially priceless item: thus the Benedictine Abbey of St. Riquier had the Gothic history by Jordanes, which Alcuin has himself requested in 801; the Benedictine Abbey of St. Maximim in Trier, the famous *Ada* manuscript from the turn of the ninth century;[22] the Benedictine monastery of Corvey an der Weser had the *Annals* of Tacitus with the first six books, which have only been handed down here. The Benedictine monastery of Wessobrunn in Upper Bavaria secured a priceless Old High German literary monument from the beginning of the ninth century, in a manuscript (which is now at Munich) decorated with the most noteworthy pen and ink drawings, the *Wessobrunn Prayer* of ancient renown, and the song of the creation of the world, with its touching cries to God: "that I learnt among men as the greatest of wonders, that the earth was not, nor Heaven above, nor tree nor mountain, nor shone the sun, nor gleamed the moon, nor the mighty sea. When nought was there of ends or boundaries, there was the One, Almighty God. . . ."[23]

The Benedictine foundation of Benediktbeuern owned manuscripts that Charlemagne is supposed to have presented the monastery, among them being the *Rule of St. Benedict*[24] copied from the original of Monte Cassino; St. Emmeram in Regensburg owned the famous *Codex aureus*, which was written for Charles the Bald, and which King Arnulf has given to the monastery;[25] the Benedictine monastery of Schäftlarn preserved an evangelary decorated with miniature painting and pen drawings, which had originated in the commission of the Freising bishop, Anno (854–875). To the Benedictine monastery of Werden an der Ruhr belonged the work which is textually and historically so significant, the *Codex argenteus* of the Gothic Bible translation by Ulfilas, from the fifth or the sixth century.

Occasionally disclosed to us are especially remarkable glimpses into the book life of this period. Thus we learn that ecclesiastical supervision was already doing its duty concerning books. When, at the desire of Emperor Charles the Bald, John Scotus Erigena translated into Latin the work that went under the name of Dionysius the Aeropagite, *De coelesti Hierarchia*, Pope Nicholas, on becoming aware of the project, wrote the emperor about sending the book for examination by the church authorities. It was reviewed in Rome by the librarian, Anastasius, recopied, and sent back to the emperor.

9
The Period of the Saxon and Frankish Emperors (919–1125)

Under Otto I (who was himself an avid reader of the Roman writers), the royal court again became a focal point for cultural life as it had been in Charlemagne's time. Otto I's brother, Archbishop Bruno of Cologne, promoted knowledge and attracted outstanding scholars to the court; among them was the book expert, Gunzo of Navarre, who brought with him valuable manuscripts from Italy. Otto II, who was an enthusiastic bibliophile, occasionally obtained books from St. Gall. The learned nun, Hroswitha of Gandersheim (935–1001), the earliest highly educated German woman that we know of, composed Latin dramas and wrote a biography of Otto II in verse. The well-read monk, Widukind of Corvey, authored his famous Saxon history.

It was again in the monasteries where the priceless luxury manuscripts originated. Reichenau, for example, had the most famous painting school of the time. There, in the years 960–1016, about thirty outstanding liturgical and biblical books have been produced.[1] Among them were the pericope book of Archbishop Gero of Cologne, which is now in Darmstadt[2]; the Aachen Evangelary with its splendid dedicatory portrait in which the donor, Liuthard, paid homage to Emperor Otto I; the pericope book of Archbishop Egbert of Trier (977–933), which he had ordered in Reichenau on his return trip from Rome, and which was written by the monks, Kerold and Heribert, is one of the most significant monuments of the Ottonic art, and is now in Trier[3]; the psalter produced by Ruodprecht for the same archbishop, which was given by St. Elisabeth to Cividale[4]; or the Paris Evangelary, which has brilliant portraits of Henry I, Otto I and Otto II, all of them works in which the glory of the German imperial period is reflected. From Hildesheim, whence under Bishop Otwin (954–984) manuscripts have come from Italy, there came under Bishop Bernward (993–1022), the artistic teacher of Emperor Otto III, equally magnificent creations of miniature painting, among them being the priceless evangelary of Hildesheim cathedral with a beautiful dedicatory pictures, in which the bishop presents his book to the Mother of God.[5]

The active mutual relationships of the German territories to Italy, Burgundy, France and Constantinople again and again provided for fresh stimulation. The foundation schools of Cologne, Magdeburg, Liège, Hildesheim, Eichstätt and Regensburg developed to considerable heights. Outstanding in cultural activity

among the monasteries were Lorsch, Corvey,[6] Gandersheim, Quedlinburg, St. Emmeram in Regenburg, and Tegernsee. Otto III was taken to be a wonder of learning,
and he truly conducted himself as a princely patron of the book. The splendid
evangelary that he has presented to the monastery of Echternach, and which is now
in Gotha, and which has a binding with decorations of ivory, enamel and gold metal
set with pearls and precious stones, is at the same time a wonderful work of the
artistic handicrafts of the time. It has been copied for the sovereign in gold script
during the regency of Empress Theophanu (983–992).[7]

Otto's teacher, Gerbert of Aurillac, the later Pope Sylvester I (999–1003),
zealously collected manuscripts on his extensive trips through Italy, Belgium and
Germany, especially the works of the ancients such as Cicero, Caesar, Pliny,
Statius, Suetonius, and Symmachus. Gerbert's letters give valuable reports about
the traffic in books at that time. St. Emmeram in Regensburg under Abbot Ram-
wold (975–1001) owned over five hundred manuscripts, and among these were not
merely ecclesiastical and clerical ones, but even ones relating to grammar and
medicine, as well as classical ones, and copies of the Bavarian and the Riparian
Frankish laws. The monastery had perhaps already at this time acquired the poems
of the Gandersheim nun, Hrotswitha, which Conrad Celtes discovered there five
centuries later.

In St. Gall, the monk, Ekkehard, revived the Germanic heroic poem in his
Waltharius manufortis ("Walter with the Strong Hand") in Latin hexameter, after
the example of Vergil; the monk, Notker Labeo (950–1022), undertook the significant attempt to translate the books of antiquity into German, such as the works of
Boethius, Martianus Capella, and Artistotle. His translation of the Psalms has
become very famous; when Empress Gisela stayed as a guest in St. Gall following
Notker's death, she requested a copy of the Psalms as a gift. Invariably when the
discussion concerns the origins of the German language and poetry, the name of
Notker the German has also to be mentioned.[8] The enticing life of St. Gall in its
heyday Victor von Scheffel has vividly portrayed for us in his *Ekkehard*. Bishop
Abraham of Freising (957–994) had books from Toul and Metz copied for his
cathedral library. Posterity probably also owes to his collecting activity the important Munich manuscript with Liutprand of Cremona (Cod. lat. 6388),[9] and the no
less valuable Plautus codex, which, after an odyssey by way of Joachim
Camerarius, Heidelberg, Rome, and Paris, got back to Heidelberg in 1816.[10] At
the episcopal see city of Winchester, a successful church reform initiated that significant art school from which have originated the beautiful Benedictionale of
Bishop Aethelwold (963–984),[11] and the missal of Bishop Robert,[12] which is now
in Rome.

In Italy, at the mother monastery of the Benedictines, Monte Cassino, under
Abbot Desiderius (1058–1087) (the later Pope Victor III), a significant center of
learning flourished; here were copied, in addition to liturgical and clerical
books, numerous secular writings, such as Cicero, Homer, Terence, Horace, Ovid,
Vergil, Seneca, Tacitus, Varro, Apuleius, Donatus, Josephus Flavius, Jordanes,
Gregoary of Tours, and Paul the Deacon. The writing and art schools of Monte
Cassino played an important role in the history of manuscripts. Besides the unique

Lombard scriptural form, the whippet that is abundantly used as a decoration is especially distinctive. Also active under Abbot Desiderius was the learned Constantinus Africanus, who sought to communicate the copious Arabic medical writings to the Western world. As in Monte Cassino, so at the Benedictine monastery of Pamposa near Ferrara, the spirit of Cassiodorus was still quite influential; there are evidences for us in the letter of a cleric, Heinrich, of 1093, in which is portrayed for us how enthusiastically Abbot Hieronymous has been occupied with the monastery library. Added to this letter is a careful catalog of the fifty-eight books with an exact listing of all the parts. Abbot Hieronymous believed that he had specifically to justify the owning of pagan writings.

As Cassiodorus did in Monte Cassino and Pomposa, so has Isidore of Seville remained effective in the Spanish monastery of Ripoll; following the death of Abbot Oliva (1046), over 190 manuscripts were counted there; among them were writings of Gregory the Great, Cassianus, Josephus Flavius, Bede, Augustine, Isidor, Prosper, Eugippius, Cicero, Juvenal, Donatus, Priscian, Vergil, Sedulius, Arator, Prophyry, and Aristotle.[13] Bishop Gislibertus of Barcelona and his cathedral chapter in 1043 gave a Jew, one Remundus, a house and a field, in order to obtain in exchange a Priscian manuscript, which is still preserved in Barcelona. The Abbey of St. Martin at Tournay had enjoyed an especially zealous scribal activity in the eleventh century; upon entering the scriptorium under Abbot Radulfus, one could on occasion find twelve monks active at the desks with copies of the church fathers. In a Munich Orosius manuscript (Cod. lat. 10292), we have transmitted to us a rich catalog of books from the monastery of St. Èvre at Toul in the period of Abbot Wido (d. 1083). It lists 270 names, among which are many Roman classical writers.[14]

The eleventh century, with which the Old High German poetry ends and the Middle High German begins, has been a period of collecting and of recovery from the horrors of the Hungarian invasion, especially for the Bavarian monasteries, such as Niederalteich, Tegernsee, Benediktbeuern, and Ebersberg (where Abbot William, d. 1804, who was educated in Fulda, wrote his German paraphrase of the *Song of Songs.*) In Niederalteich were written the Altaich yearbooks, which were the most significant history works of the early Middle Ages. Under the Abbots Gozbert (982 until 1001) and Peringer (1003–1012) there originated in Tegernsee the abundant letter-copying of the monk, Froumund, who was fond of writing and who vividly disclosed for us the unusually vital cultural life of the monasteries, with their surprisingly widespread traffic in books, and further, the famous epic of the adventures of the nobleman, *Ruodlieb,* with its earliest portrayal of the courtly-knightly culture.

Under Abbot Eberhard II (1068–1091), the monk, Reginfred, upon his entrance into the monastery, gave (in addition to biblical and liturgical writings) numerous secular works, such as Vergil, Horace, Ovid, Dares, Curtius Rufus, Donatus, and with them, two world maps. Finally in Regensburg, miniature painting developed into the famous school that has produced the splendid evangelary of the Abbess Uta of Niedermünster (1002–1028) (for which a no less splendid case binding with the enthroned Christ in gold relief and precious stones and ivory was designed), as well as other sumptuous manuscripts. Arewold wrote in St. Emmeram; so did Otloh of Freising (1010–1070), who loved to write. On account of his zeal for writing, Wilhelm Giesebrecht has called him the first prolific German writer. Marianus Scotus, who founded an Iro-Scottish monastery in Regensburg in 1076, also had the pen ever in hand; Aventius still saw a Psalter written by him for the Abess Matilda in the year 1074 in Niedermünster, and the National Library in Vienna owns a manuscript of the Pauline letters completed by him in 1079.

A luminous center of especially exquisite book splendor we encounter at the episcopal seat of Bamberg, which was founded in 1007, and which was the favorite city of Emperor Henry II. Flowing together here were wonderful treasures from the entire kingdom that were presented by the generous emperor to his church there; originating there also were priceless monuments from the old cultural centers, and new creations of the most famous schools of painting of the period, from Liège, Fulda, Cluny, and above all, from Reichenau, the glorious home of the splendid manuscripts from the periods of Otto III and Herny III. One of the most priceless art works of the period, a *Canticum canticorum,* as well as the famous Bamberg *Apocalypse,*[15] come from there. Regensburg contributed the monastic rule book with the portraits of Emperor Henry and of the Abbess Uta of Niedermünster. Several of the sumptuously designed Bamberg manuscripts, over which hovers the glitter of the German imperial glory, are decorated with portraits of the sovereign. Thus in Gregory's commentary on Ezekiel (Bibl. 84), a monk hands the book over to the sovereign, and in an evangelary, as "Heinricus, rex pius," he offers the work, which was designed for worship, to the "Sancta Maria Theotokos," and a *pontificale* (Lit. 53) contains one of the best early Medieval portraits: the emperor with the world sphere in his left hand.

Two further priceless objects that were imperial gifts, the famous pericope book of Emperor Henry II (Cod. lat. Monac. 4452) with the representation of the sovereign couple being crowned by the enthroned Savior of the world,[16] and the no less valuable evangelary of the emperor, with its magnificent luxury binding, consisting of an ivory carving richly encrusted with enamel and gold decorations,[17] is now kept in Munich. Further imperial gifts are to be found in Bamberg: the much praised *Psalterium quadrupartitum* of Abbot Salomo III of St. Gall (Bibl. 44), the sacramentary from Fulda (Lit. 1) decorated with an ivory carving, an evangelary from Bremen (Bibl. 96), a copy of the *Remaclus* legend with old documents from Stablo (Hist. 161), a martyrologium from Malmédy (Lit. 1, 8), from Rheims, the outline by the monk, Richer, to the historial work recorded on commission from Gerbert (Hist. 5) and two important works of John Scotus (Philos. 2 u. Patr. 46) that are important for the history of texts. With these priceless objects, the new episcopal city was attracting the attention of the entire world.

Directly following the dedication of the Bamberg Cathedral in the year 1012, Abbot Gerhard of Seeon sent the emperor a manuscript with the rules of the saints Benedict, Columban and Marcarius (Lit. 143) ordered for the Michelsberg monastery; he praised the foundation of the sovereign as a glorious cultural center that could be compared with Jerusalem and Rome, with the Stoa, and with Athens. A commentary by St. Jerome on Isaiah (Bible 78), and presented by the Deacon

Bebo, recalls with praise the glittering festivities of the year 1020 which had just passed, in which Pope Benedict VIII had come to Bamberg to visit the emperor and had dedicated the new St. Stephen's Church. The sovereign desired to provide his Bamberg foundations (the cathedral, the St. Stephen foundation, the Michelsberg monastery) not merely with worthy liturgical works, but with scholarly learning. It was a fortunate accident that, on his Italian trip for this very purpose, he was able to acquire significant residues from the book collection of Otto III from Piacenza, which for their part go back to Archbishop Johannes Philogatos, the protégé of Empress Theophanu and the Anti-pope, Gregory VI.

From the priceless inheritance, a medical collective volume has been preserved, in which a confidant of Otto III has entered the total contents of the original purchase. Among them were works of Orosius, Persius, Fulgenitus, Boethius and Livy. Valuable remains of the Livy manuscript in old Uncial script from about the fifth century have been preserved in a binding of the fifteenth century, and these lead us back into the time when antiquity was in its decline.[18]

From the legacy of Otto III, Bamberg has handed down a second priceless literary monument, which is now preserved in Munich, the evangelary of Otto III (Cod. lat. 4453), which is set with pearls and precious stones, which has the famous picture of homage, where the sovereign of Christendom sits enthroned before a court and accepts the homage of symbolic females symbolizing Germany, Gaul, Rome, and the Slavic countries.[19] On his description of this splended image, Hubert Janitschek recalls those words with which Gerbert praises his imperial lord and former pupil: "Ours, ours is the Roman kingdom, we have the rich and fruitful Italy, we possess the warlike Gauls and the Germans, and the valiant kingdom of the Scythians serves us." It is here, as there, the song of imperial glory.

Out of the preference that the Ottos and their successors, Henry II, Conrad II and Henry III, had for princely splendid manuscripts, there developed (as it did also in the Carolingian period) a high flowering of miniature painting, to which we owe a handsome series of book monuments. The ultimate peaking of this art coincides with the reigning period of Emperor Henry III (1039–1056), the culminating point of the German imperial power. It is for him that the gospels manuscript *(Codex aureus)* of the Escorial Library, which was intended for the cathedral at Speyer, has been produced between 1033 and 1039, the origin of which is evident from the two dedicatory pictures with the portraits of Emperor Conrad II and Henry III together with their wives.[20]

Erasmus of Rotterdam was aware of the valuable item in the possession of the Queen of the Netherlands, Margaret of Austria; following her death, it came to her niece, Maria of Hungary, the sister of Emperor Charles V, and finally to King Philipp of Spain. A second splendid manuscript of Emperor Henry III, again an evangelary with two dedicatory pictures (Christ blesses the sovereign couple, and the Apostle Simon has accepted the offered book) is from the cathedral at Goslar (the silhouette of which is shown in the second dedicatory picture); it has come to Uppsala.[21] A third evangelary, which represents the king's family (Conrad, Gisela and their son, Herny III) in Echternach, is kept today in Bremen.

10
The Book in the High Middle Ages
(12th–14th Centuries)

The twelfth century was the proud period of the Hohenstaufens, and of the restoration of the imperial dignity through Frederick I Barbarossa, of the investiture struggle, of the Crusades, of St. Bernard of Clairvaux (1091–1153), of St. Hildegard of Bingen (1098–1179), of the historiographers, Otto of Freising (d. 1158), Rupert of Deutz and Gerhoh of Reichersberg, of the rising chivalry movement, of a new rejoicing in the world, and in chivalrous homage to women, and of the first foundations of the schools of higher learning; in this century, the world of books exhibits a maze of wealth of individual appearances as peaks in the development; nevertheless, since midway in its course, it was already pointing toward the flowering period of the courtly culture of the thirteenth century.[1]

While the earlier courtly art of the book was deteriorating, the ecclesiastical miniature painting was still quietly creating considerable works, such as Salzburg, where in the foundation of St. Ehrentrud, there originated the beautiful lectionary (Cod. lat. Monac. 15902), and in St. Peter, the antiphonary, with its pretty dedicatory pictures of the patron saints, Rupert and Wolfgang; in Tegernsee, where handsome liturgical works were produced[2]; in Prüfening near Regensburg, which showed significant creations of miniature painting, influenced by Salzburg[3]; in Helmarshausen an der Diemel, where the monk, Herimann, produced for the Corvey provost, Adalbert (1147–1176), a book for a fraternal organization with artistic illustrations and the splendid evangelary of Henry the Lion, with the patron saints of Brunswick[4]; in Zwiefalten, where artistic hands copied a passionale and Josephus Flavius and decorated them with unique initials.

In script, there developed under the influence of architectural style a transition from the Carolingian miniscule to the so-called Gothic script, in which the stems of letters are broken and marked off by beginning and closing strokes. The script, which soon spread over the whole of Western Europe, gave a new look to manuscripts.

A handsome bibliographic source unfolds for us in the epistolary of the Thuringian Benedictine monastery of Reinhardsbrunn,[5] from the period when Rudolf was in his office as abbot (1139–1141). There the monks requested manuscripts from outside, such as Rupert of Deutz's treatise, *De divinis officiis*, Hugo of St. Victor's writing, *De sacramentis fidei*, the *Gesta magni Alexandri*, the commentary by

Bishop Haimo on Isaiah, and then for their part, they lent to Paulinzella the prophets and the books of Kings and kept from there (Paulinzella) Augustine's commentary on the first forty Psalms with its beautiful accompanying words: *Nostra sunt vestra et vestra nostra* ("What is ours, is yours, and what is yours is ours").

The Michelsberg monastery in Bamberg shows us a stimulating life with books through the valuable sketches by the Benedictine, Burchard, who managed the monastery library under the abbots, Wolfram I (1112–1123) and Hermann I (1123–1147), and who compiled a careful catalog with the names of donors and patrons. As always, standing in the foreground are the liturgical, biblical and early Christian writings; we nevertheless encounter also the classical writers of antiquity, and other secular works from the fields of grammar, philosophy, music and chronology. In an Ambrosian manuscript, an artistic hand has quite nicely clarified the connection of the monastic life at Michelsberg with the book and the scriptorium through a pictorial representation (in several parts) of the preparations in the production of a book—how one cuts the pen, how one makes an entry on the wax tablet, scrapes off the parchment, how one prepares the cover, produces the signatures, stitches the book together, cuts the parchment, and then adds a fastening for the cover.[6]

Of works from antiquity, most often leading the lists of books in the period are the names of Ovid, Terence, Sallust, Vergil, Horace, Statius, and Persius. Vergil is the favorite, and indeed, the teaching master of the Middle Ages for grammar and rhetoric, and he is lacking in none of the larger collections of books. In two pen drawings, the abbot, Alto von Weihenstephan (1182–1197) is shown presenting the works of Horace and Vergil to St Stephen (Cod. lat. Monac. 21563) and he thereby hopes for heavenly reward. Cluny owned Josephus Flavius, Hegesippus, Suetonius, Lucanus, Livy, Justinus, Festus, Cicero, Juvenal, Terence, Statius and Ovid.

Nuns frequently participated also in the copying of books. Thus the hermitess, Diemut, in Wessobrunn, copied sixty-five works for the divine service and for the library. It was feminine learning that created the famous illustrated manuscript, *Hortus deliciarum* ("garden of pleasure").[7] The nun, Herrad of Landsberg, abbess of the Alsatian monastery of Hohenburg, brought together there everything worth knowing for the instruction of young females, and richly decorated the presentation with illustrations, among them being philosophy within the circle of the liberal arts.

It is to this age, literarily strongly influenced by France and its most significant court poet, Chrestien de Troyes, that German literature owes significant works, such as the *Song of Roland* of the priest Kunrat,[8] the imperial chronicle which courageously claimed Emperor Charlemagne for Germany, the heroic songs of King Rother and Duke Ernest, the world chronicle of Ekkehand of Aura, the Alexander song of the cleric, Lamprecht, which has been transmitted solely in a Vorau manuscript, the oldest edition of which has been destroyed (like the *Lustgarten* of Abbess Herrad) in the fire at Strasbourg in 1870, and the pretty love poetry of *Flore und Blancheflur,* the German adaptation of the story of Tristan and Isolde. Count Berthold von Andechs, Margrave of Istria, wrote between 1171 and 1186 to Abbot

Rudbert of Tegernsee, that he would like him to send the German book from Duke
Ernst for purposes of copying; it was supposed to be given back to him immediately.
The correspondence is remarkable as one of the few evidences in the Middle Ages
of concern with German language monuments.[9]

Gradually coming to the fore in the twelfth century (and still more in the thirteenth) were the patrons of secular German poetry. In the main, these were the
princely courts and circles of the nobility, which took care of the travelling singers
and welcomed their works as courtly and chivalric poetry, and at the same time as
manifestations of their worldview. To be mentioned here are the Guelphs, the
Ludolfingers, the Hohenstaufens, the Zähringens, the Babenbergers, and above
all, Hermann of Thuringia (1181–1217), whose *Dichterherberge* ("Hostel for poets"),
as his court was called, has generously received Heinrich von Veldecke, Wolfram
von Eschenbach, Walther von der Vogelweide, and Albrecht von Halberstadt. The
life at the Thuringian court has been portrayed in tradition through the famous
legend of the war of the singers of the year 1207, in which seven poets are said
to have participated in order to sing the praises of the prince – among these being
the legendary Heinrich of Ofterdingen, the epigrammatic Reinmar of Zweten,
Walter von der Vogelweide and Wolfgang of Eschenbach. The elaborate Stuttgart
Psalter has also been produced for him.[10] As an expression of the new shape of
life, the secular, life-affirming book grows in significance, and the German language
in its courtly mould applied to an aristocratic people experienced its initial flowering.[11]

The transition to the thirteenth century has given to us in three priceless
manuscripts the final conception of the *Nibelungenlied*, the great Middle High German folk epic, with its ideal of loyalty, its heroic songs of Siegfried and Kriemhild,
of Brunhild and Hagen, about the fall of the Burgundians in the land of the Huns.[12]
One of the three manuscripts, now in Munich, comes out of Hohenems; the second
one comes from St. Gall, and the third, which is now in Donaueschingen, again
comes from Hohenems.

The thirteenth century, which politically experienced the increasing decline of
the German Reich, together with its imperial dignity, brought about the foundation
period of the mendicant orders: the Dominicans, the Franciscans, the Carmelites,
the Augustinians, and the Servites; it developed the high flowering of Scholasticism
with the goal of uniting the doctrine of the faith with church dogma through
philosophy – to grasp, to prove and thus to comprehend together all that was known
about God, nature and the world in one great system of doctrine; it saw the rise
of the great leaders of this theological Scholasticism, Alexander of Hales (d. 1245),
Albertus Magnus (1207–1280), Thomas Aquinas (1225–1274), and Duns Scotus
(1265–1308); it experienced the radical effect of the mystic, Bonaventura
(1221–1274), the artistic creator of word and images, Gottfried of Strasbourg (d.
ca. 1220) with his polished Tristan epic, the fervent minnesong of Heinrich of
Morungen (d. after 1220) and Reinmar the Elder, the zestful writing and the singing
of a Walter von der Vogelweide (1165–1230) (who defined the purpose of art as
being the increase of joy in the world), the effect of a Wolfram of Eschenbach (d.
ca. 1220) and his *Parzival*,[13] and it brought about the high point of the chivalric

literature[14] and the victory of the Gothic architectural style in the cathedrals of Cologne and Strasbourg.

Hartmann of Aue (d. ca. 1215), with his tales, *Erec, Iwein* and *Gregorius auf dem Stein*, ("Gregory on the Stone") has introduced the flowering of German courtly poetry, and brought the Arthurian romance to Germany. His small verse narrative, *Der arme Heinrich* ("Poor Henry") has implanted itself deeply in German literary history; Chamisso has adapted it; Simrock has translated it, and Gerhart Hauptmann has transformed it into a drama. With the growth in secular education, knowledge was enlarged in the most diverse directions, and was pressing toward a conflict between the spiritual as over against this-worldly conceptions of life.[15] Added now as more secular teaching institutions to the church schools were the city school and the schools of higher learning. Bologna became the honored goal for law students, Salerno the focus of medical science, and Paris, with its Sorbonne, the broadly beaming light of theological teaching. A proverb was coined: to the Germans the *Imperium* (empire), to the Italians the papacy, and to the French, study.

In Paris, the scholarly Dominican, Vincent of Beauvais (Vencentius Bellolvacensis, d. ca. 1264), wrote down his *Speculum universale,* one of the most powerful medievel conceptions of human knowledge about God and the world. The comprehensive work falls into four parts: the *Speculum nationale* (God and nature), the *Speculum doctrinale* (science and art), the *Speculum morale* (virtues, sins and the last things), and the *Speculum historiale* (world history); it has became the most important educational medium for the century that followed. Dante also used this work, and the earliest printing was still issuing out several editions of it in spite of its mammoth size, until Scholastic thought finally exhausted itself.[16]

In the northern latitudes, around the thirteenth century there were gathered the famous Icelandic *Edda* songs, together with the songs from the Nordic mythology, and the heroic sagas that go back to the time between the ninth and twelfth centuries.

To the world of books, which, with the secular municipal school and the schools of higher learning, was extending itself into ever wider circles, the century brought as its most important gift the introduction of paper, the art of preparing it having apparently come into Europe out of Arabia. We find the first European paper mills in Italy and Spain. The paper mill built in 1390 in front of Nuremberg's city gates by the patrician, Ulman Stromer, has to be considered as having been the oldest such German establishment; it goes back to Italian modes.[17] The newly introduced material, made from rag fibers, was of immeasureable significance. Today we can scarcely anymore establish just what influence the use of the new, cheaper and infinitely more producible material for writing has exercised on the arts of reading and writing in daily life, and on the exchange of letters in the lawyer's office. In any case, in monastic scriptoria, and everywhere that books were produced, there gradually came about a great transformation, which in many ways changed the appearance of books.

Parchment and paper still continued alongside one another for a long time. Where one attached great importance to festive and enduring garb (as with liturgical books) one used parchment for the most part, just as before; paper, on the other hand, was used for other kinds of works. The new writing material became very valuable, especially for the young schools of higher learning, where overall a voluminous traffic in books developed within the context of the scholarly school operation, and professional traders *(stationarii)* were active in the sale or in the lending of books. The cheap book was a vital necessity for this school operation. The actual shining hour for paper, however, came only with the discovery of printing, when printing found in paper its most powerful ally. In both cases technology has decisively intervened in the development of the book.

Miniature painting, especially in France, underwent a noticeable upsurge in this century. The center of this movement (which then spread also into Burgundy, England and the Rhineland territories) was Paris and the royal house, the lavish court of which redowned also to the good of the book. Louis IX (1226–1270), the saint, loved manuscripts and he encouraged those decorated with color, in which funny little designs *(drôleries)* pursued their high-spirited play. His psalter is decorated with a rich plethora of illustrations in which the Gothic style is already prevalent.[18]

In addition to the psalter (which above all was prized by the noble women), the illustrated Bibles were very beloved in the noble French society; they are to be considered as being forerunners of the later books of hours. Gradually, the range of the book decoration was extended: in addition to Bibles, ecclesiastical and devotional books, chivalric poetry, folk books, didactic poems and chronicles were enclosed within borders and decorated with illustrations. Designed in an artistically pleasing manner, the French book became especially prized and cared for in courtly circles.[19]

The Parisian scholarly world of books about this time discovered a new center in the Sorbonne, which was the foundation of the chaplain, Robert de Sorbon. Here, already forty years after the foundation (1250), there wre over one thousand books, chained and at the disposal of the college. Duplicates of the works were located in the so-called small library and were lent out *(libri vagantes)*. The leaders of the Sorbonne have missed a favorable opportunity for significant growth when King Louis' (Saint Louis) rich book collection, which according to tradition has been administered for a long time by the learned Vincent of Beauvais (the aforementioned author of the encyclopedia, *Speculum universale)* went to various monasteries after the sovereign's death, and thus was lost by the Sorbonne. It has been more fortunate, however, in the subsequent legacies of the poet and chancellor of the church of Amiens, Richard de Fournival (1201–1260), one of the inspired bibliophiles, to whom we owe one of the earliest theories of the library ("Bibliomania").

The lists of books of the century evidence no essentially altered image from that which obtained earlier. A Vergil manuscript of the Court Library of Schönborn at Pommersfeld contains a list of the School Library of St. Pancras in Hammersleven with 106 works, among which are Priscianus, Plato, Orosius, Aristotle, Sallust, Ovid, Boethius, Prosper, Sedulius, Prudentius, Homer, Aesop, Statius and Cicero. These are works that we encounter in all the monasteries that were connected with schools and which had served especially for learning the Latin language.

We encounter a lively trade in books at the court of the Passau bishop, Otto von Lonsdorf (d. 1265), who himself owned 150 manuscripts, and who lent several times to chapter canons and monastery abbots, as for instance, St. Florian,[20] Niederalteich, Lambach, Aldersbach, Garsten and St. Nicola, and on the other hand, received manuscripts with Seneca and Jerome from the monastery of Reichersberg.[21] In the Benedictine monastery of Scheyern in Upper Bavaria there originated under Abbot Conrad (1206 until 1225) a beautiful *Matutinale* (cod. lat. Monac. 17401), with pen-and-wash drawings and unusual illustrations of legends.[22] In Benediktbeuern, hands that were fond of writing inserted in a book the famous *Carmina Burana*, the high-spirited Latin and German vagabond songs, and they decorated them with small illustrations, among which was a lottery wheel with inscriptions.[23] Abbot Berthold (1200–1232) in Weingarten had manuscripts written and some of them were provided with artistic miniature paintings.

In the same century in which the sophisticated works of the great Scholastics dominated scholarly literature, there could then still arise, out of the Germanic past, the law books known as *Sachsenspiegel* and *Schwabenspiegel*[24]; the *Sachsenspiegel*, was authored in Latin in 1220 by the Anhalt knight, Eike von Repgow, the "first German law instructor." It was then the oldest law book of the Middle Ages translated into Low German; the same is true of the *Schwabenspiegel*, which originated in, and was directed at, Germany.[25] Both of the works were later diffused by means of many manuscripts and printed works. The mystical book of the Begine, Mechthild of Magdeburg, *Vom fliessenden Licht der Gottheit*, ("Of the Flow of God's Light") could kindle the hearts and give rise to the creations devoted to courtly love by our great Middle High German poets.

This period, so fond of song, has at about the turn of the thirteenth to the fourteenth century given us that wonderful *Manesse* manuscript of songs, the richest collection of Middle German songs, and one of the most precious creations of the German past. "Sang ist ein gar edles Gut" ("Singing is indeed a noble good") are the words with which it is prefaced, with which the poet, Johann Hadlaub gratefully extolled therein the Zurich patricians, Rüdiger and Johann Manesse, father and son, because they did not allow the minnesong to perish and they collected the songs with such great zeal. This solicitude brought everlasting fame to the two Zurich men and forever connected their names with the priceless manuscript. The work is unequalled in its copiousness of content and in the sumptuous quality of its design; in the world of books it is a pearl. Karl Zangemeister judged that with its 140 individual poets, and its richness of songs, it contains the equivalent of a whole Middle High German library. Many of its memorable illustrations, especially the one of Walther von der Vogelweide sitting on a stone, have become, as have scarcely any other illustrative matter, the established representations of the first flourishing period of the German art of poetry.

The history of the manuscript reads like an epic, so full of complexities is it. It lead us to the ancestral castle of the *Hohensax*, to Augsburg to Ulrich Fugger, to Heidelberg into the Electoral Castle, and then again into Switzerland until the manuscript, at Marquard Freher's insistence, returned in 1607 to Heidelberg.[26] Brought into a secure place during the Thirty Years' War in the face of the threatening conquest of the city, it landed in all probability in the French town of Sedan, in order then to succeed to the Hague in the possession of the banished Palatine Elector Frederick II. From there it came to the librarian, Jacques Dupuy (Puteanus), with whose book collection it then came on July 4, 1657, to King Louis XIV, and later in to the National Library in Paris. The great embezzlement of books, *Libri Barrois*, finally brought about the return of the precious manuscript to Heidelberg. It was exchanged on February 23, 1888, for twenty-three stolen manuscripts from Tours (which by arrangement of the Strasbourg bookdealer, Karl J. Trübner,[27] had been acquired at the cost of the German Empire from the Ashburnham collection) and, on April 10, 1888, it was transmitted by Emperor Friedrich III to the Grand Duke of Baden. It was henceforth united with the rest of the priceless German monuments of the old Heidelberg Library; indeed, it was the proudest one among them, and a shining example of great significance, which can approach being the single book to serve as a symbol of past culture, and as a priceless national possession.[28]

From the beginning of the thirteenth century, there came two further famous manuscripts with German poetical works, which are today kept in Berlin: that of the priest, Werner of Tegernsee, "Lieder von der Maget," with old-fashioned designs, and the *Aeneid* which was completed in poetic form before 1190 by Heinrich von Veldeke, the first real court poet. He was praised by Gottfried of Strasbourg: "He implanted the first sapling in the German tongue."[29] Provided with well-done outline drawing, these are two of the first German poetical works decorated with illustrations. At about the same time there appeared in the literature the *Welsche Gast* ("Italian Guest") of Thomasin von Zerclaere, a favorite didactic poem, which has been handed down to us in eighteen manuscripts. The majority of them are decorated with pen drawings.[30] The poem is one of the earliest of the monuments of literature that has an established title.[31] It represented practically an encyclopedia of courtly education. The aphoristic poem, "Bescheidenheit" ("Modesty"), which was composed by Freidank about 1229, and is the greatest didactic poem of the Middle Ages, has been revived through the early printing in the revision by Sebastian Brant and in the period between 1508 and 1583, has gone through eight editions. Hugo von Trimberg (1235–1313), the learned schoolmaster of Bamberg, who has collected two hundred books, has become known through his didactic poem, "Der Renner."

From the initial flowering period of our German poetry there has developed — stimulated by the Romantics — an entire discipline, Germanistics, with numerous critical restorations of texts and an enormous literature; this is again a significant evidence of the effect of the book lasting over and beyond the centuries.

The fourteenth century gave to the world the greatest poetical revelation of the Middle Ages, Dante's (1265–1321) *Divina Commedia*,[32] the powerful poetical world judgment concerning the past and his own period. Carlyle was of the view that, in Dante, ten silent Christian centuries had found a voice. Living and writing within the same time frame were our great German mystics, who sought, as over against the hierarchical thought structure of Scholasticism, for the direct connection of the individual person with God: Meister Eckart (1260–1328), Heinrich Suso

(1295–1366),[33] Johann Tauler (1300 until 1361)[34] and John Rysbroek; in Avignon, the temporary site of the papacy (1309–1378), there arose a new center of the stimulating life of books,[35] and further in Italy with Petrarch and Boccaccio, there was a preparation for the significant intellectual movement of the Renaissance, which will still be portrayed in more detail.

The chief sources for our knowledge of the library holdings of the fourteenth century are again the lists of books that have been preserved, which make clear not only the possessions, but also the total life of books in the period. Thus in 1347, the Benedictine monastery of St. Emmeram at Regensburg inventoried its holdings with 280 volumes and thirty-two desks, and added to it the lists of books of the Regensburg Dominicans, Franciscans, and Augustinians, as well as those of the Benedictines in Prüfening and the Carthusians in Prühl (these were two neighboring monasteries); this was one of the earliest examples of a regional general survey and of the methodical arrangement of books. An informative description of the Cisterians' library is given in the list of books of the monastery of Fürstenfeld from the year 1312.[36] First there are enumerated the seventy-nine manuscripts of the general library *(commune armarium)* in the usual order, and then the books of the smaller library *(in minori armario)*, which contained almost exclusively the literature for instruction, and thus clearly evidences itself as the school library of the monastery.

In the Benedictine monastery of Admont, the monk, Peter of Arbon, drew up catalogs of the library in 1370 and 1380, and in the foreword thereto he elaborated about the foundation of a properly administered collection of books: it has to be steadily increased, it must be protected from fire and water, and be regularly improved and provided with good catalogs. The Cathedral Library in Münster in 1362 was maintaining an extensive set of library regulations, according to which the keeper of the books had to display the manuscripts to his superiors (the cathedral dean and chapter) once a year on the day before the feast of St. Martin, and by means of the good condition that the books were in, he had to demonstrate that he was qualified for his work. In the Benedictine foundation of SS. Ulrich and Afra at Augsburg, Abbot Marquard (1316–1334), in order to guard against pressing financial embarrassment, had to mortgage to the Dominicans of the city a greater number of the more valuable manuscripts, among them being an extensive *Papias* volume, which Abbot Heinrich had copied in the year 1175. The books were again redeemed under his successor.

There were clerics everywhere in monasteries and in foundations who took care of the books that had been entrusted to them with a special devotion. Heinrich von Ligerz (d. 1360) considered the treasures of his Benedictine foundation of Einsiedeln quite as his own; he marked important places in the texts, he entered notes about the historical period, he lent the books out for a pledge, and with this mutual assistance he saw to it that records were kept in good order. When, for example, he gave out a manuscript to the Salem monastery, he wrote very carefully in the book: "Iste liber est monasterii Sanctae Mariae de Heremitis et debet restitui Fratri Henrico de Ligercio Thesaurio euisdem monasterii" ("This book belongs to the monastery of St. Einsiedeln and is to be given back to the librarian there, Heinrich von Ligerz"). Under that, the Salem monks wrote what for their part they had received as pledge.[37] The historical value of many of the lists of books that have been preserved has been enhanced through the valuable statements concerning the provenance of possessions. Thus the Netherlands abbot, Egmond, in addition to other parts of the holdings, lists nineteen manuscripts that have been presented at one time by Archbishop Egbert of Trier (977–993).

The literary history of this period has a famous bibliophile of whom to boast, the Englishman, Richard de Bury (1287–1345), since 1344 the Chancellor and the keeper of the Great Seal for King Edward III; de Bury was a contemporary of Petrarch's, whom he had come to know in Avignon. He loved books passionately, and he wrote one of the most beautiful glorifications of love to the book *(Philobiblon seu liber de amore librorum)*. It has become world famous, being the oldest literary exhibit of bibliophily that is known to us. We know forty-six manuscripts of it and thirty printed editions and translations.[38]

11
The World of Books in the
Early Renaissance

The word "Renaissance," as it is employed in the history of culture, we tend to associate with the idea of a double rebirth and of a fresh vitalization of humankind in the declining period of the Middle Ages: first, in the environment of Italy's zestful city culture that was bursting with vigor, in contrast with the Middle Age's basic world denial, and in powerful tension with its transcendent orientation, the entirely submerged humanity that was oriented toward this world again comes alive – the humanity that, in keeping with an eternal mandate of this world, ardently craves the beauties and the goods of this world, and in an intensified self-consciousness, strives for mankind's highest development and conceives of the meaning and purpose of life as being in life itself; secondly, in Italy, in a radiant brightness and viewed as its own past, there emerges out of the towering ruins and from the transmitted cultural works this age of a grandiose world of culture, wherein one believes he can already see fulfilled his own desire for beauty, for a complete education for humanity, and the mastery of the educational world of Greek and Roman antiquity. A new world view, a new image of man coming of age, of man suffused by a feeling of strength – all at once these stood before the mind and held their ground, despite the warning call of that grim despiser of the Renaissance, Savonarola.

It was one of the most powerful cultural movements of human history, this decisive turning back to the world of beauty and the mind set of a period that was past, and it is no accident that it found such a brilliant historical representation as Jakob Burckhardt has given us.[1] Great historical phenomena always call for deeper sensitivity and for artistic patterns and they find their masters to fashion them.

As the most vital residue of that golden age, the cultural works of Greece and Rome took on a newly enhanced significance. The book of antiquity, which even in the Middle Ages was never quite dead, now experienced its renewed hour of greatness and it became the center and the bearer of the desired educational goals. Passionately and with love, the literature of the past was sought out, read, collected, and it was perpetually copied again and again. As Konrad Burdach has portrayed it, the book, in its spirit and in its form, became a vital nerve center of the Renaissance.

Thus Francesco Petrarch (1334–1374), one of the great discoverers of the world of antiquity, was a passionate bibliophile and a collector of books. He counted it as one of his most beautiful experiences when in 1345 he found in the Cathedral Library at Verona a very old, and almost destroyed, manuscript with the letters of Cicero, and he was able with his own hand to copy it; and with the same pride, he might call his own Homer and Plato, Augustine, and Ambrose; he sought in books a vital connection with great men, with Seneca, Cicero, Quintilian, Livy, Horace, Vergil, and Augustine; and he valued Pisistratus and Ptolemy amidst their book treasures as being greater than the rich Crassus with all his tremendous wealth. He owned Homer, and revered him as a saint, although he could not read him since he was ignorant of Greek, indeed suspecting that there lay an entire cultural world—the soul of Greece—that was closed to him. There is a nice legend that Petrarch had one day been found dead, with his head on top of an open manuscript.[2]

From books there has arisen for him a new order and valuation of life. His letter to Dionisio da Borgo San Sepolcro of April 26, 1335, is famous: in it he describes the climbing the mountain Mont Ventoux. Moved as he was, he afterwards depicted the deep impression that the unique natural spectacle of the summit made on him; he continues, "While I was looking at the details, now lowering my eyes to the valleys, and now raising them and the spirit heavenward, when involuntarily I withdrew from my pocket Augustine's *Confessions*, a book that I always carry with me, because in spite of its small size, it is of an infinitely rich content, and upon opening it, I immediately encountered the place where it says: So do people go and wonder at the peaks of mountains, the enormous waves of the sea, the wide river beds, the breadth of the ocean, the spheres of the stars, but on account of those they forget themselves. At these words I was frightened; I closed the book and was as angry at myself because of my having gazed at earthly things, since I could still long since have learned even from the heathen philosophers that the spirit ought to be the great thing, the thing to be admired, so I silently left the mountain and I turned my attention from the external to my inward nature."[3]

Petrarch's passion for books has been transmitted to all the humanists. As Giovanni Boccaccio (1313–1375), the first inspired forerunner of Dante's *Divine Comedy* (which was the new unsurpassed world book for all humanity) saw in the venerable old Monte Cassino a Tacitus with the last books of the *Annals* and the beginning of the *Histories*, but also mutilated manuscripts, and when he learned that the monks had cut out parchment so as to produce devotional books with it, he wept on account of the pain and the indignation that he felt. His own most famous work, the *Decameron*, which he regretted when he became older and which he condemned, has won for him an established place in world literature as the linguistically polished declaration of a significant new epoch. Paolo Giovio, on the other hand, was already of the view two centuries after the composition (when the Latin writings of Boccaccio were scarcely managing to survive) that the charming *Decameron* ought to be translated into the languages of all peoples and never become extinct. Boccaccio's book possessions were transferred to the Augustinian Eremites of St. Spirito in Florence and were accommodated there in a worthy manner by Niccolo de'Niccoli. In the light of a list of books of 1451, research still believes it is able to authenticate eight Florentine manuscripts (among them Apuleius, Statius and Ovid) as being the former property of the poet.[4]

Once the enthusiasm for the cultural work of antiquity was awakened, it quickly embraced the Italian upper class in its entirety. The learned Florentine statesman, Coluccio Salutati (1331–1406) proudly called himself a slave of his books, zealously sought out Pompeius Trogus, Curtius, Quintus Ennius, Varro, Catullus, Tibullus, and Propertius, fervently read Cicero's letters to his family, had Margrave Jobst of Mähren report to him about an allegedly discovered Livy manuscript in the diocese of Lübeck, worked indefatigably for the improvement of texts which had been trasmitted with errors, and he quickly welcomed those subscriptions in the textual monuments of the fourth, fifth and sixth centuries as valuable verifications of original writings and transcriptions.[5]

A welcome opportunity for extending their manuscriptural inquiries beyond the borders of their own country was afforded the Italian humanists in the church councils in Constance (1414–1418) and Basel (1431–1449), where in the company of clerical and secular princes, a whole group of doctors, chancellors and poets showed up and were able to indulge their scholarly inclinations during the extended discussions. Both councils thus became vital centers of the book trade and of the search for manuscripts. The monk, Thorirus Andreae, from the Scandinavian monastery for Vadstena, who stayed in Constance on account of the canonization of Brigitta, bought several manuscripts there, of which four can still be authenticated; manuscripts have even been dispatched to Frauenburg in Ermland.[6]

The sophisticated ambassadors of Italian humanism, who had believed that they were the sole heirs of the Roman cultural world, were quite surprised to find old libraries in the northern countries with numerous works of antiquity. They now were arrogantly feeling as if they were the saviors and liberators of the imprisoned treasures. When the Florentine citizen, Poggio Braccolini (1380–1459), who, in addition to Giovanni Aurispa, was the most successful discoverer of the literature of antiquity,[7] entered St. Gall in the year 1416 with his friends, Bartholomeo de Montepulciano and Agapito Cenci de'Rustici, they believed they were hearing the plaintive voice in the library: "O ye men who love the Latin language, do not allow me through neglect to be entirely destroyed here; save me from these chains!"

From Constance visits were made to Reichenau, Weingarten, Langres, and Cluny; and one returned with rich booty. Poggio extended his voyages of discovery as far as Fulda, Cologne, Paris and London. The *Argonautica* of Gaius Valerius Flaccus, fragments of Lucretius, the commentaries on Cicero of Asconius Pedianus, the complete text of Quintilian that had been sought for the longest time, the *Silvae* of Statius, the *Astronomicon* on Manilius, the *Architectura* of Vitruvius, the book of Vegetius about the nature of war *(De re militari)*, the treatment of Pompeius Festus about the meanings of words *(De significatione verborum)* – these, quickly copied and also occasionally carried off, were the most important discoveries of the Italian humanists in the northern monastery libraries.[8] Poggio found in Cluny a priceless manuscript with Cicero's orations for Sextus Roscius of America and for Murena, and he sent them to Florence to Guarino and Barbaro; eight further orations of Cicero he copied in Langres on the Marne.

As was the case with the council of Constance, so the church council in Basel also became not only a stimulating center of the book traffic with the trading and exchange of manuscripts, but also a favorable locale for the discovery of books near and far. Giovannni Aurispa (1370–1459) found in Basel an important Tertullian manuscript, and in Mainz, the Latin Panegyrics with the encomium of Pliny to Trajan and the Donatus commentary on Terence. After his return from England, Poggio continued zealously his researches into manuscripts at home: in Rome he became the leader of tireless searches for unknown texts. Rumors about alleged Livy and Tacitus manuscripts in Hersfeld brought much anxiety to the enthusiastic disciples of antiquity. A Hersfeld monk has played a mysterious role with these reports.[9] In the year 1429, Poggio stayed in Monte Casioo and was there allowed to borrow for copying the Frontius manuscript concerning the Rome water administration. When the bishop of Lodi was seeking for documents in the cathedral there in 1422, he discovered an old collective manuscript with items from Cicero, among which were three complete books, *Of the Orator*, the *Brutus*, or concerning the famed orator, and the *Orator*, addressed to Brutus. The Italian humanists became ecstatic over the find and they quickly made copies of the texts. All of Italy soon owned the new book and so preserved it, since the discovered manuscripts of Lodi were soon lost.

A standstill ensued in about 1430 in the discovery of the unknown writings of antiquity; the first great period of discovery was at an end, but its effects remained.[10] Out of the devoted love for the old cultural works there issued forth a vital refreshing of the scholarly spirit; a renewed concept of the significance of public libraries came about, the saving of the Roman and the Greek literary stock developed; so did the new science of antiquity. Rediscovered from the dust of libraries, the ancient book remained the main vehicle for the new cultural movement.

It is out of such zeal for the world of antiquity that Florence—a second Alexandria— has blossomed forth; here also the idea of the public collection of books as the center of cultural life has been newly awakened. Niccolo de' Nicoli (1363 to 1437), the bookish Florentine,[11] was the driving force behind the increased vitality of books in the city on the Arno. He stood in closest connection wtih Ambrogio Traversari (d. 1439), the General of the Order of the Camaldolese, whose letters and records bring us valuable reports concerning the libraries he visited. His most significant deed was that he transferred his book collection to the city of Florence as an official possession, and his greatest success was that he found in Cosimo de Medici (1389–1464) a truly princely executor of his legacies. The liberal patron of the arts and sciences brought the gift into an artistically designed room of the Dominican monastery of San Marco and he increased it with many Greek and Western manuscripts. In the year 1444, in which the books were set up in their entirety, they were already numbering four hundred Latin and Greek manuscripts. The foundation may indeed be designated as the first public library of the modern period. That it was attached to a monastery need not surprise us; public life then possessed no other possibility for the treasures of books entrusted to it. The collection that was soon richly increased is supposed later to have formed the substantial basic stock for the famous Laurentiana in Florence.[12]

Cosimo de Medici, the ever generous bibliophile, also presented other monasteries with books, as, for example, the Canons Regular in Fiesole, the Minorities of S. Francesco del Bosco in Mugello outside Florence, as well as the Benedictines of S. Georgio Maggiore at Venice, who had hospitably taken him in during his banishment. For these foundations the learned Tommaso Parentucelli, the later Pope Nicholas V and the new founder of the Vatican Library sketched an outline that was supposed to show what a monastery library would contain: the Bible, the church fathers, the great theologians of the Middle Ages, the philosopher, Aristotle and his commentaries, the works of Plato, of the most important Roman prose writers, and of the poets, Ovid and Horace. The Medici designed for himself a sumptuous house library, engaged book copiers, whom the book dealer Vepasiano da Bisticci, had to supervise[13]; and he twice sent the Greek scholar, Janos Lascaris, to the East to acquire Greek manuscripts.

Under Casimo's uncle, Lorenzo de Medici the Magnificent (1448–1492), and through the accession of newer manuscripts elaborately decorated by the artists, Antonio del Cherico, Attavante, Gherardo, Monte Giovanni and Boccardino, the collection became the most famous possession of books in all of Italy, until the Medici had to flee in the year 1494 and the chequered fate of the family itself also overtook the library.[14] The salvaged residue thereof was carried off to Rome in 1508 by Giovanni de Medici, the later Pope Leo X, and afterwards given back again to the Florentines in the year 1522 by Cardinal Giulio de Medici, the later Pope Clement VII; in 1571 it was accommodated in the handsome building that Vasari had completed on the basis of a design by Michaelangelo.[15]

Vespasiano da Bisticci (1421–1498) is inseparably connected with the distinguished Florentine book life of the period; he was the aforementioned famous bookdealer of the Renaissance period, who, in a fortunate connection of an excellent business sense with a good acquaintance with books, recognized the demands of the time and in well equipped scriptoria produced beautifully written and exquisitely designed manuscripts for almost all the Italian bibliophiles, especially for Cosimo de Medici and Duke Federigo da Montefeltro in Urbino. On occasion he maintained forty-five copyists for Cosimo de Medici and completed two hundred books in twenty-two months. Later, when the art of printing was already spreading, the clever bookdealer wrote down modest memoirs of his contemporaries and thus left to us in these works a valuable historical source for the cultural and artistic life of Florence in that period.[16]

Soon there were other Italian library foundations that were competing with the possessions of books in Florence. In 1452, the apostolic vicar, Ghismondo Malatesta, had an exquisite basilica built in Cesena with a double row of Corinthian columns and he filled it with beautifully bound books on artistically designed desks, in order then to present the entire facility to the Franciscans of the city and to provide for its support with a hundred ducats. Pompeo Randi, an artist of Forli, has celebrated the dedication of the library in a mural painting.[17] United with the municipal library, the magnanimous gift still lives on today under the name of Malatesta.

In Urbino, Raphael's birthplace, Duke Federigo de Montefeltro (1422–1482), one of the most ostentatious of the Italians shaped by the Renaissance, planned a large book collection and, in connection therewith, he put between thirty and forty copyists to work. Successfully assisting him in this matter was Vespasiano da Bistici. Under his leadership there originated between 1476 and 1478 the magnificent Bible manuscript which today reposes in the Vaticana, and which on account of the relationship of its illustrations with the frescoes in Siena has been called the Bible of Pinturicchio. A second sumptuous manuscript in the Vaticana from Urbino, which was completed for Duke Federigo between 1444 and 1452, contains Dante's *Divina Commedia* with 122 illustrations and has been marked several times by the scribe, Matthäus de Contugiis from Florence, with the name and arms of the duke. Illustrations from antiquity, from the Middle Ages and the Renaissance period decorated the room for the books. One saw Plato, Artistotle, Cicero, Seneca, Homer, Vergil, Euclid, Ptolcmy, Hippocrates, Solon, Moses, Salomon, Jerome, Augustine, Ambrose, Gregory the Great, Bartolus, Thomas Aquinas, Duns Scotus, Albert the Great, Victorinus da Feltre, Peter of Abano, Dante, Petrarch, Popes Pius II and Sixtus IV and Bessarion. Verses at the entrance of the library showed the visitor the way to the special collections.[18]

Already soon after the founding of the library, Urbino owned the list of books of the Vaticana, of the collection of San Marco in Florence, of the Visconti Library in Pavia, yes, even that of the college in Oxford, and so it could establish that its own properties, insofar as the number of writings was concerned, exceeded all the rest of the collections. Pope Alexander VII has acquired the valuable collection in the year 1658 for the Vaticana. It has been set up here in a special collection.[19]

In Naples, where already under King Robert (Petrarch's patron) an interesting court culture had been created, King Alfonso of Aragon (1401–1458) enthusiastically collected manuscripts[20] and in the midst of his beloved books had Livy explained to him by Antonio Beccadelli in the presence of the humanist, Lorenzo Valla; the Livy manuscript had been presented to him by Cosimo de' Medici. This library was swept (as was the one in Florence itself) into the whirl of political events, and it was mortgaged under King Ferdinand (1458–1494), along with the crown and pearls, to the Florentine businessman, Baptista Pandolfini, in exchange for his monetary assistance against the Turks.[21] Again freed from its banishment, a portion of the collection ultimately came into the power of King Charles VIII of France, and the remainder into the possession of George d'Amboise, the archbishop of Rouen.

The largest possession of Greek manuscripts on Italian soil was acquired by the scholarly archbishop of Nicea and later Cardinal, Johannes Bessarion (1395–1472), that culturally distinguished prince of the church who is to be seen as one of the most effective ambassadors of Greek culture. In his titular church of San Apostoli in Rome one saw in one corner of the vault around the Redeemer the four evangelists with a Latin and a Greek church father each at his side. The uniting of the two great churches was the most ardent goal of his life. And as he did in the world of faith, so also on cultural grounds he strove for reconciliation and for a blending of the West and the East. An outstanding connoisseur of Greek cultural treasures (primarily of Plato), he zealously collected old Greek manuscripts, especially in the Basilian cloisters, such as in the monastery of the Order of St. Nicolas at Casoli in Apulia (Pugli); among the ones he collected were Aristarchus' Scholia of the *Iliad*, and copies were produced by Greek scribes, such as Johannes Rhosos, Michael Apostolios, and Johann Argyropylos. An enthusiastic admirer of Plato, he brought the Greek philosophers into close contact again with the West and in 1469, he had an apology for Plato reproduced by the German printers in Rome. The most effective thing he did for the salvaging of the Greek literature was when, filled with the pure Renaissance spirit, he decided to hand over his manuscripts to the public domain. Vacillating for a time among Florence, Rome, and Venice, he finally considered the Benedictine monastery of San Giorgio Maggiore in Venice, but he then chose San Marco in Venice because the island mon-ʾ mastery seemed to him too difficult to reach at high tide.

On May 31, 1468, Bessarion wrote from Viterbo to the Doge, Christoforo Moro, that he was already during his lifetime bequeathing his treasure of books to the city of Venice as a permanent possession, in order to assist in the saving of cultural works. When in the following years the priceless collection, with its 745 manuscripts (among which were 482 Greek ones) in forty-eight cases arrived in Venice, the grateful city presented the noble donor with four hundred ducats.

Bessarion died on November 19, 1472, in Ravenna, but his handsome legacy had an imperishable permanence and it became the center of the Greek Renaissance in Venice. The first ones really to make it known, as well as its initial beneficiaries, were destined to be Aldus Manutius and the scholarly circle that gathered around him. The collection was placed in 1553 in the building where it is today, which was built by Jacopo Tatti, (called Sansovino), and which was decorated with columns, with statues and paintings by such famous artists as Guiseppe Salviati, Andrea Schiavoni, Paolo Veronese, Giovanni Zelotti, Giovanni de Mio, Battisa Franco, Giulio Licinio, and Titian. For over two centuries the famed Marciana was effective as the inexhaustible treasury of sources for the literature of Greece, until, at Napoleon's command, it was transferred to the great hall of the ducal palace.[22] Later it was again returned to its old location. Still kept there today, as a priceless reminder of the noble legacy, it is the catalog presented by Bessarion; the arms of the cardinal, of the doge, and of Pope Paul II – together with the lions of San Marco – decorate the memorable document in beautiful miniscule script.[23]

The most famous Italian book collection of the following centuries was destined to become the Vaticana in Rome; newly created by Pope Nicholas V (1447–1455), it became again a pure Renaissance library, going back to the cultural environment of Florence.[24] Its new founder has already been mentioned as the scholarly advisor of the Florentine Cosimo de'Medici. Already from early on, Tommaso Parentucelli (so had the Pope previously been called) had been an enthusiastic book collector. When he became the supreme ecclesiastical head of Christendom, it became his favorite goal to elevate Rome to the status of a second Florence, to a new Alexandria, to an effective collecting point for the world of books, and to make the library, which was built upon what Pope Eugene IV had left behind, accessible to all scholars.

The new pope expressed his concern for Greek letters through his plan for disseminating the whole of Greek literature by means of Latin translations. At the suggestion of the humanist, Theodorus of Gaza, he ordered the acquisition in Constantinople of the manuscript of the eight books of Origen directed against Celsus and offered a reward for the translation of the work into Latin. The valuable copy from which one derived all the rest of the drafts of the text, is today to be found in the Vatican (Cod. 386); it is on the basis of it that Christoph Persona has published the first Latin translation in 1481. Lorenzo Valla received five hundred gold ducats for his Thucydides translation; the manuscript contains an initial in which Valla presents his sword to the Pope. Nikolaus Perottus likewise received an estimated five hundred gold ducats for a Polybius translation. The same Perottus transmitted Greek manuscripts to Rome from Trapezunt on the Black Sea, through Bessarion's mediation. Pope Nicholas V eagerly occupied himself with collecting all of St. Augustine's writings. Augustine stands in the most visible position among the Latin and Greek doctors of the church; Fra Angelico of Fiesole (1387 to 1455) has decorated the chapel of San Lorenzo at the Vatican with his portrait.

When the rumor spread in Rome that a complete Livy manuscript been found in Denmark or Norway, the Pope on April 30, 1451, sent the humanist, Alberto Enoch from Ascoli northward with the commission to search in the church and monastery libraries of Scandinavia, and on the banks of the Weichsel and the Pregel, for old manuscripts. The Königsberg Archives still preserves the papal credentials presented to the grand master, Ludwig von Erlichshausen. Among the treasures that the ambassador brought to Italy there was a valuable Tacitus manuscript. But since the pope had died in the meantime and his successor, Calixtus III (1455–1458), had no interest in the acquisition, the discoverer tried to find another place for it. Aeneas Sylvius Piccolomini, who afterwards became Pope Pius II, later acquired it. Jovianus Pontanus copied the Tacitus manuscript in 1460; the copy currently kept in Leyden has been made accessible through George Wissowa's transcript.

When following the death of its founder, Pope Calixtus III had the library cataloged by the Spaniard, Cosmas Montserrat, he counted 795 Latin and 414 Greek manuscripts. A later section will report concerning its significant development under the librarian, Giandrea dei Bussi. His successor in the administration of the library, who as a scholar was known also as Bartolomeo Platina (d. 1481) and who was appointed by Pope Sixtus IV, has become famous through a mural of the grand master, Melozzo da Forli (1438–1494): Pope Sixtus IV ceremoniously hands over the office to the humanist.[25] The beautiful painting, which was originally located in the room of the Latin manuscripts and is currently preserved in the Vatican's painting collection, expresses in a fascinating manner the close connection between the papacy and the book and scholarship. We are even still able to leaf through the list of users which the librarian, Platina, has designed in the year 1475. It is a handsome volume in which are entered year by year cardinals, humanists, scholars, among them being Johannes and Isaac Argyropylus, Mathias

Palmieri, Pomponius Laetus, Johann Philipp de Lignamine, and also the German scholar Johannes Tolhopf, who is listed in the entry January 18, 1485, under the next librarian.[26] Most of the receipts are drawn up in Latin, although individual ones are also in Greek, Italian and French.

Another attractive view from the Vaticana comes to us from Platina's library accounts, which had also been preserved. We encounter expenditures for the bookbinding and materials for the bindings, for paper and ink, for copyists and illuminators, for nails and keys, for parchment and brushes for the dusting of the books, and for gifts presented to the scholars who have dedicated their books, such as the German astronomer, Nicholas Germanus, who once received two hundred gold florins. For a long time onward, the Vaticana has had no such loving treatment extended to its collection as it did under these popes, Nicholas V and Sixtus IV, in whom the book has found its first great patrons and guardians at the papal court.

Although it anticipates the actual temporal period a bit, a brief survey of the attention given to the world of books by the succeeding popes will be given here. The Italians, Albertini and Bembo, report that Pope Julius II (1503–1513) had the storage room for his own collection of books changed into an artistic jewel, decorated with paintings and statues. It is on the basis of this report (which has nowhere else been transmitted to us) that Franz Wickhoff has based the supposition that Julius II had created the famous *Camera della Segnatura* (with the Raphael murals that are known the world over) for his collection of books. The pictures speak for that theory: theology is represented by Augustine, Ambrose, Jerome and Gregory, poesy by Apollo, Muses by Homer, Dante, Vergil and Sappho; philosophy, by Aristotle holding *Ethics* in his hands, by Plato carrying his work *Timaeus*, by Ptolemy, Boethius, Euclid and Diogenes; Justice, with the presentation of the books of Roman and canon law. "There is," so Wickhoff maintains, "no second work of the fine arts in which books play so great a role, in which everything issues from books and everything is referred back to them."[27] This explanation has encountered opposition that has some basis, since the Segnatura has always served for the judicial decisions of the popes and not for storing the books of the library; but it is not impossible that, originally, the room was designated for the library.

Both the Medici popes, Leo X (1513–1521) and Clement VII (1523–1534), divided their love for books between the Vaticana and their respective families' house libraries. Leo X, whom Raphael has represented as he was holding the magnifying glass in readiness to examine a richly decorated manuscript, had the first five books of the *Annals* of Tacitus printed in 1515 by Filippo Beroaldo of the firm Stephen Guilleretus in Rome on the basis of a manuscript taken from the monastery at Corvey, and which is now in the Laurentiana. At the conclusion of the edition one reads in Latin under the papal arms the works, "In the name of Pope Leo X, imposing rewards are promised to those who hand over to him old works that have not yet been published." The Abbey of Corvey was presented by the pope with a beautifully bound copy of the printed edition and he consoled them for their loss with an indulgence together with a reference to the publication's usefulness.

When the Liège cleric, Johann Heitmerts, travelled in 1517 with papal commissions to Germany, Denmark, Sweden, Norway and Gotland, he obtained special credentials addressed to the spiritual and secular princes of the North for the acquiring or borrowing of manuscripts from them. For the discovery of valuable book treasures, (it says in this letter) the pope, since the beginning of his pontificate, had spared neither effort nor cost. In the letter to Archbishop Albrecht of Mainz from November 26, 1517, there is even a reference to the Mainz Livy manuscript that had been found shortly before then, and for which 147 ducats were offered. As evidence of the proper use for the old literary monuments, the published Tacitus edition is pointed to; the Corvey monastery was richly compensated for surrendering it. In another papal brief to King Christian II of Denmark on November 8, 1518, the pope reports that he had become aware that the Roman classics had been preserved at Kallundborg Castle; he begs the king to send them along with other manuscripts to Rome—for a receipt.

While the great library foundations of Florence, Cesena, Urbino, Venice, and Rome remained permanently preserved in Italy, the collection of the dukes of Milan in Pavia enjoyed only a brief flowering. Founded by the family of Visconti,[28] very richly enlarged by the Sforza family, and singled out for praise by the humanist, Uberto Decembrio, in his translation of Plato's *Republic*, the library was among the largest collections of the Renaissance period and among its priceless items it could show several manuscripts that had been owned by Petrarch. Giovanni Visconti, Petrarch's patron, was already assembling book treasures, just as were his nephew, Galeazzo II (d. 1378), who was the actual founder of the library, and his son, Gian Galeazzo (1378–1402), the builder of Milan cathedral and of the Certosa at Pavia. The enterprising Lodovico Sforza il Moro (1451–1508) directed the Milanese ambassador in France, Erasmo Brasca, to acquire rare or unknown manuscripts in France. Brasca in fact forwarded reports about the libraries in Marmoutier, of St. Hilary in Poitiers, and of St. Martin in Tours, and he hoped to acquire copies of texts. The entire book treasures of Pavia were ultimately carried off to France—like the collection of the Arangon kings—by King Louis XII.

The princely house of Este in Ferrara also assembled a typical Renaissance library. Under Leonello (1441–1450), Borso (1450–1471), Ercole (1471–1505), and Alfonso I (1505–1535), the consort of Lucrezia Borgia, there originated art works of book illumination which can hold their own beside the most exquisite creations of the period. The Borso Bible in two volumes, illuminated mainly by Taddeo Crivelli and Franco Russi (it is the most splendid of all the Este manuscripts), was decorated with about a thousand illustrations and small pictures. The twenty-two great choral books donated by Duke Borso to the Carthusian monastery of Ferrara and four volumes of the Bible are still today among the famous items worth seeing at Ferrara. On March 30, 1466, Duke Borso has presented a hundred gold florins to the German astronomer, Niccolo Germanico (Nicolaus Germanus), for one Ptolemy manuscript, and he has followed this in April with a further thirty florins for a Tacitus text. We already know from Platina's account that the same German scholar has been supported also by the papal court. The Ulm printer, Lienhard Holle, in an initial letter of the Ptolemy edition of the year 1482 has figuratively represented him as he hands over the book to the pope. Outstanding among the later developments from the exquisite Este books is the missal of Cardinal Ippolito I from the beginning of the sixteenth century.[29]

As the last of the splendid Renaissance libraries to be mentioned, there is the beautiful possession of manuscripts of the Duke Andrea Matteo III Acquaviva (1458–1529). His collection has not remained intact for long. Johannes Sambucus, on his trip through Italy about the middle of the sixteenth century, was already able to take nine richly decorated classical manuscripts (that had come from the scattered legacy) with him across the Alps. They have come to Vienna at a later time with his collection of books.[30]

The beautiful book has thus been valued in the courts of Italy as an essential constituent part of Renaissance culture. This new enthusiasm for the book also expressed itself in the beautiful rooms that were built in Florence, Cesena, Urbino, and Rome for the manuscripts that had been assembled there. One of the most brilliant such rooms Francesco Piccolomini (who in 1503, as Pius III, for scarcely a month reigned as pope) had built in the cathedral of Siena as a memorial to his uncle, Pope Pius II. He had it decorated by the painter, Bernardino Pinturicchio, with ten colorful representations from the life of the pope, among them the event of his being made poet laureate at Frankfurt by Emperor Frederick III.[31]

Commissioned by Pope Sixtus V (1585–1590), the architect, Domenico Fontana, produced in the years 1585 to 1588 in the Belvedere court of the Vatican, a handsome new building (with the famed "Salone Sistino") for the increased treasury of books: here the books (mostly manuscripts) were kept invisible in cases and were protected from the light, while a series of portraits all around pointed to them: Bonaventura, the church fathers, Cicero, Livy, Pythagoras, Euclid, Aristotle, Justinian, Xenophon, Ptolemy, Zeno, Donatus, Vergil, Boethius, Plato, and Peter Lombard. The walls are decorated with colorful representations from the history of the popes and the great libraries such as the one of Pisistrades in Athens, the Museion in Alexandria, the library of Augustus on the Palatine Hill in Rome, the ancient Christian libraries at Jerusalem and Caeserea, and the book collections of the popes. An oil painting of the Vatican Library shows Sixtus V sitting on an easy chair and surrounded by his nephews, Michele Peretti and Montalto, as well as by the Cardinal-librarian, Antonio Carafa, and a few officials of the library (among them being Federigo Rainaldi) as he accepts Fontana's plan for the proposed library building. The beautiful room was the first Italian hall-type library.

The aforementioned foundation of Bessarion recalls another magnanimous bequest which the Canons Regular of San Antonio di Castello in Venice received when the Cardinal Domenico Grimani (1463–1494) awarded them his priceless collection of Greek, Hebrew, Chaldean and Armenian manuscripts, which were partially from the possessions of the philosopher, Govanni Pico, count of Mirandola (1463–1494). The distinguished Bible scholar, Agostino Steuco, obtained the position of leader in the new library, which was declared to be public property. Celio Calcagnini on January 13, 1525 wished his friends luck in this enterprise, and requested for himself a catalog of the library's holdings. The German humanist, Jakob Ziegler, visited the collection three years later in the company of his faithful companion, Martin Richter; the listing of the Greek manuscripts incorporated into this collection is still currently held at the Marciana in Venice. The collection itself has now been scattered in all directions; significant residues of it are still to be found in Udine, in Munich, and Holkham. Grimani has become world famous through its splendid breviary, a priceless artistic creation of a Netherlands master; the wonderful work has become one of the last great monuments of the dying art of miniature painting.[32]

Again in Venice, the distinguished historian of the republic, Pietro Bembo (1476–1547) assembled a valuable scholarly library; he was the same one who administered the foundation of Bessarion between 1530 and 1543.[33] Priceless items such as the original text of the poetry of Petrarch (which was used for the Aldine edition of the year 1521), a famous Vergil manuscript from the legacy of the humanist, Jovianus Pontanus, and an equally valuable Terence copy, are included in the handsome collection. Following the Cardinal's death, the possession has again been scattered; part of it has been acquired by Fulvio Orsini.

The rich library, consisting mainly of Greek manuscripts, of Cardinal Niccolo Ridolfi (d. 1550), who was one of Pope Leo X's nephews, had passed in large measure to Marshal Strozzi, and then to Catherine di Medici, the consort of King Henry II of France and, following their deaths, into the library in Paris. This was the third library that France obtained from Italy!

The splendor of these new court collections of books in time relegated the ancient Italian book centers almost completely into the background. Only on occasion did the glitter of the venerable centers of culture again shine forth, when, for example, the humanists, gladdened by their discovery, unearthed priceless manuscripts from this or that monastery. One of the most famous finds of this sort was the manuscript discovered in the monastery of Bobbio in the year 1493.[34] Duke Lodovico il Moro Sforza had in 1482 called the learned Giorgio Merula to Milan as teacher of Greek and Latin; at the same time he had entrusted him with the task of writing a history of the ducal house. With the expanded searching for historical sources, Marula's assistant, Georgio Galbiato, came upon the forgotten manuscript of the Bobbio Abbey. On December 31, 1493, Merula reported exuberantly to the duke concerning the find, and he promised to present the wonderful treasures to the scholarly world, but death overtook him on March 18, 1494.

In the year 1497, Galbiato published the work by Terence, De litteris, syllabis et metris Horatii, and reported there concerning the treasures that had been discovered. A printing license of the duke added thereto mentions five further grammatical works that have been found in Bobbio: those of Fortunatianus, Velius Longus, Adamantius, Probus and Cornelius Fronto. The complete list of the treasured lifted from Bobbio, a German in the papal curia in Rome, one Jakob Aurelicus von Questenberg, has sent to Bishop Johann von Dalberg. It numbers twenty-five titles that are distributed among fifteen manuscripts; seven of these can still be identified; the rest have been lost. Aulo Giano Parrasio has probably carried off the majority of them.[35] A priceless Agrimensor manuscript,[36] retrieved by Tommaso Inghirami from Bobbio, has gone by way of Erasmus of Rotterdam and Jan Laski to Wolfenbüttel, and thus has gone through all the vicissitudes of the

Wolfenbüttel library, even including being carried off to Paris and being returned again in the year 1814.

With its own collections of books, its inexhaustible deliveries to the rest of Europe, and its later innumerable printed works, the Italy of the Renaissance period may be considered the country of the world in that period that took the greatest delight in books; it was also the one richest in books, just as, in the same period, it has attained the very highest pinnacle of art with the names of Leonardo da Vinci, Raphael and Michelangelo. Florence, Rome and Venice can claim the lion's share of this indisputable fame.

The emperors', kings' and princes' love of ostentation has also for the most part redounded to the good of the book. The French royal house of the Renaissance period offers an especially vivid example of that. The love of ostentation and ambition went hand in hand with the increasing plenitude of power enjoyed by the French kings. The book also entered into this service. Most conspicuous in this respect was the extravagant provision of books with dedicatory pictures, arms and bindings. Several artists' workshops were established that devoted themselves professionally to the production of such exquisite books. The contents (of a book) have retreated considerably before the book's external design. Since Louis the Pious it was no longer just the liturgical and other spiritual texts, but above all the chivalric novels and translations of the classical authors, that were artistically written and adorned; Livy and Valerius Maximus were given special preference. The lengthy, scarcely interrupted series of French kings who enjoy books was initiated by John II, the Good (1350–1364). He bequeathed his own joy in books also to his four sons: King Charles V, Duke John of Berry, Duke Louis of Anjou as well as his nephew, René, and Duke Philipp the Bold of Burgundy. The collection of Charles V the Wise (1364–1380), to which Léopold Delisle has devoted an investigation,[37] was placed in the year 1368 in the Louvre Castle and it already included a long series of French translations. An entire army of copyists, translators and illuminators have been occupied with their production. Augustine, Sallust, Suetonius, Seneca, Vegetius, Ovid, Lucan, Valerius Maximus, Aristotle, and Petrarch were represented with their main works.

A new kind of book and type of book ownership was emerging—one that went beyond the courtly and liturgical splendidly designed book of an earlier period, and which wanted to dispense to the lay world of the court and the nobility instructive and entertaining items of literature in the vulgar tongue; for the most part, to be sure, they were only translations. Elaborate dedicatory pictures decorated the manuscripts and depicted the king as he was accepting the gift book from the artists, say from Jean de Vaudetar and Raoulet d'Orléans, or from the translators, such as Raoul des Presles, Jean Golein, or Nicole Oresme. Pierre Bohier admiringly compared the collection, which ultimately numbered over nine hundred volumes, with the treasures of Alexandria. Even the poetess, Christine de Pisan, who was living at the court, praised the treasures, which were accommodated in a worthy room.

King Charles VI (1380–1422) enlarged the splendid possession, but he still permitted the manuscripts to serve as a veritable supply house for gifts to princes, to well-known personalities and courtiers—yes, even for purposes of instruction for the princes and princesses. Today we are acquainted with a mere 104 manuscripts; they have been scattered in all directions. An especially priceless item of the once so majestic collection, the Psalter of Queen Ingeburg of Denmark (d. 1286) which Louis the Pious had already owned, is currently kept in the Musée Conde at Chantilly. Also turning up there has been the valuable residue of those books of hours that were decorated with an inexhaustible richness of pictures and which were produced for Jean, the duke of Berry (d. 1406), who was the brother of Charles V, and the collector of the royal family who took the greatest pleasure in splendor.[38]

With Philipp the Bold (1363–1404), who was King Charles V's third brother, the Burgundian collateral line of the House of Valois also began to care for the splendid book. Philip the Good (1419–1467) and Charles the Bold (1467–1477), took skillful illuminators into their service such as Jean de Pestivien, Willem Vrelant, Jean Miélot, Jean de Tavernier, Loyset Lyédet, and Jean Hennecart, and paid out considerable sums of money for the purpose. Indeed, outside King Charles V, no prince has received so many splendid manuscripts dedicated to him and decorated so abundantly with his own image as has Philip the Good.[39] The duke has once, in a Brussels manuscript, been portrayed as he enters with the scribe, David Aubert (who, oblivious to the world about him, sits at the writing table), while outside a battle is raging—a highly characteristic reflection of the appeal that the beautiful book had. Active also as an enthusiastic collector of splendid manuscripts was the duke's son, Anthony of Burgundy, who was called le Grand Bâtard de Bourgogne; to his castle, La Roche in the Ardennes, he brought an imposing number of splendid books; they have now been scattered in all directions.[40]

A further branch of the French royal house that was enthusiastic for books sprang up among the dukes of Orléans, when King Charles VI (1380–1422) awarded the sovereign territory of Orléans in 1391 to his brother Louis, the Count of Valois (1370–1407). Not only did he, but also his son, Duke Charles of Orléans (1391–1465) (who was famous as a poet) collect illuminated manuscripts[41] and bequeath them to the son and grandson, Louis, who, as Louis XII (1498–1515), ascended the royal French throne in 1498 and married the following year his predecessor's widow, who was the enthusiastic bibliophile, Anne of Brittany, and whose favorite painter, Jean Bourdichon, has created a wonderful book of hours for her[42]; the new king, as the grandson of Valentina Visconti (who was consort of his grandfather, Louis), laid claim to the duchy of Milan and victoriously carried off the Court Library of Pavia from there. Inasmuch as he then united it in Blois with the likewise captured holdings of the king of Naples and the court's own scattered possessions, as well as with those of the enthusiastic collector, Louis of Bruges, (Sieur de La Gruthuyse), he became the actual founder of the French Court Library, which from then on advanced rapidly.

The first German prince of the Renaissance period who displayed by his enthusiastic attention to books the courtly love of splendor was Emperor Charles IV (1347–1378), the scholarly friend of art and patron of Petrarch, who, influenced by France and Italy, especially elevated Prague (the capital of his patrimonial dominion of Bohemia) into a favored center of courtly and cultural life. The cathedral of Prague, the castle of Hradschin, and the University of Prague (the oldest one in the German countries) have become eternal monuments of this concern. This new attention paid the book was induced through the double influences of the Italian Renaissance and the French courtly splendor.

The cultural leader of the Prague Court circle became the highly educated chancellor and Bishop of Olmütz, John of Neumarkt, an enthusiastic admirer of Petrarch's and of the Renaissance. With the latter he shared the joy he felt in beautifully decorated books: artistic monuments such as his travel breviary *(Liber viaticus)*, which today is in the museum in Prague, the missal of Nicholas of Kremsier, the missal of John of Troppau and the missal that is named after himself — these have all been produced through his commission.[43] When in 1368 he went with the emperor to Italy, he left behind his books (in all twenty-seven manuscripts, among which there were several classical works and a Dante text which may well have been the first copy of Dante on German soil) in a special cabinet at the St. Thomas monastery of the Augustinian Eremites and he provided that, in case of his death, the monastery should receive the collection as a legacy.

The generous emperor supplied the *Collegium Carolinum* of the University of Prague in the year 1366 with the most needed books; four years later he added to his foundation the legacy of the Dean of the Wysehrad, William von Hasenberg, with its 114 theological, juristic and theological manuscripts.

Once the love of books was awakened at the imperial court, it had its effect also on Emperor Wenzel (1378–1400), who had a concern not merely for scholarly works but for German poetry as well. At his bidding, outstanding splendid manuscripts came into being — such as the German Wenzel Bible in six volumes, the priceless William of Orange manuscript, an exposition of the psalter by Nicholas of Lyra, a richly decorated copy of the Golden Bull of Emperor Charles IV — and still others besides. They can be recognized at the first glance by the unusual border decoration with its ever-repeated bathing maidens.[44] Several of the manuscripts designed for the king contain instructions for the illuminator, as to where and how he was to have the proposed images interposed. These entries make it clear that the script and the illustration in the manuscripts do not always originate from the same hand. As in the French courts, the splendid items of King Wenzel have solely and alone served the curiosity and splendor of the court. Following the emperor's death they went to his son, Sigismund; then in a constant exchange of possessions they finally went to the Archduke Ferdinand of Tyrol at the Ambras Castle, and came in 1665 to Vienna.

Lasting effects of the courtly concern for books in Germany have issued only from the Palatine courts of the Rhineland; the love they had for books was bequeathed from generation to generation and this has gradually led to excellent results. King Rupert of the Palatinate (1352–1410) and Palatine Count Louis III (1410–1436) were the first German princes after Emperor Charles IV who provided their schools of higher learning with books. Elector Friedrich I, the Victorious (1451–1476), strongly influenced here by the South, favored humanistic bibliology and had an effect also on his sister, Mechthild (1418–1482), who collected books industriously at Rottenburg am Neckar; incidentally, she was one of the first German princesses to do so. The letter of honor to her is famous, in which Jakob Püterich von Reichertshausen (1400–1469), who himself was an enthusiastic collector of old chivalric books, has communicated in 1462 to her a list of his 162 German manuscripts, among which were works by Hartmann von Aue, Gottfried of Strasbourg, and Wolfram of Eschenbach.[46] There we hear of over eighty manuscripts of the Countess Palatine, but we learn the titles of only twenty-three works that the letter writer did not own. For the most part these are German translations of French and Dutch novels of the fourteenth and fifteenth centuries. The love of books, which since Philipp the Just (1476–1508) has turned its attention to the Middle High German and French literature, has remained an excellent tradition of the Palatine house and has provided the foundation for the later Heidelberg riches in books.[47]

From the estate of Jakob Püterich, the Bavarian State Library in Munich is the owner of two German prayerbooks, which their one-time owner has bequeathed to the Munich Püterich nunnery (Doc. germ. 305 and 306). The prayer books were still being read from in 1512 and it has been noted in them that the contents are "indeed beautiful to listen to."

The last great book collection of the early Renaissance came about at the court of the Hungarian king, Matthias Corvinus (1443–1490), at Ofen, which is called the Corvina after its founder.[48] Thanks to the prince's generosity, the foundation rapidly grew from nothing to an unprecedented excellence, and as a positive wonder of the world, it imbued its contemporaries with a respectful astonishment. But following the death of the king, it nevertheless fell into a decline just as quickly, and was scattered in all directions. The speedily acting king had been stimulated to collect books by his teacher, Johann Vitéz of Zredna,[49] the scholarly friend of two famous contemporaries, Georg Peurbach and Johann Regiomontanus; but the love of books had come no less from his own consort, Beatrix, who was the highly educated and luxury-loving daughter of the King of Aragon and Naples; she was same princess to whom Jacobus Philippus de Bergamo had dedicated a book decorated with pictures of pretty women entitled *De claris mulieribus* ("Concerning famous women"); it was printed by Laurentius de Rubeis in Florence in the year 1497.

The Renaissance moved into Ofen with the princess. "It will constantly remain as Matthias' claim to fame that he followed up – as the first and the last one outside Italy to do so – on the ideas of Petrarch and Niccoli." (Voigt.) His librarian was the humanist, Bartolomeo Fontio. Research has established ten Corvinus manuscripts, eight of which are currently held in Modena, all of them having been colorfully decorated by the Italian artist, Attavante degli Attavanti.[50] The raven *(Corvus)* (the king's armorial device), steps out from a silver heart-shaped escutcheon, while the background in other manuscripts is blue. Florence is considered the chief locale for the great book production of the Hungarian royal court. There were Bibles, the church fathers, theologians, classical writers, medical, geographical, architectural, and mathematical works which have been copied. The idea that the king rejected printing as being inferior to the manuscript is unfounded, even if he has indeed loved spendidly finished books more than works that were merely printed.[51]

When the prince died on April 6, 1490, everything was over so far as his commissions went. Only with effort were the manuscripts completed that had been begun, in order thereupon partially to succeed into the hands of the Medicis and partially into the Marciana in Venice. Soon one or another of the Ofen manuscripts was leaving the library as either a gift or for use, especially by members of the learned Danube Society in Vienna, members of which were more than once seen as visitors in the library rejoicing there in some discovery. The humanists, Johann Cuspinian, Joachim Vadian, George Tannstetter, and Johann Gremper, repeatedly reported in their letters concerning Ofen manuscripts, which in the second decade of the sixteenth century have been lent to Vienna. On May 1, 1520, the scholarly Francesco Masser told Giovan Batista Ramusio about his visit to the Corvina, and he complains there bitterly that almost all the valuable books have disappeared. Only a very old Vergil in Lombardian script, and an Aelianus as transmitted by Theodor Gaza, struck him as being valuable. He had also seen there a handsome manuscript with Cicero's work, *De Legibus*. With the Greek manuscripts in their water-damaged and rotten bindings he was not able to do anything, because he did not understand Greek. A quite good Pliny manuscript had come to Girolamo Balbi.[52] Still more grievous was the loss when King Louis II (1516–1526) died on August 29, 1526, in the battle near Mohacs against the Turks, and the collections were now robbed of any protection.

A vivid report concerning the further fate of Corvina has been handed down to us in the Salvianus edition of 1530, in which the publisher, Johann Alexander Brassicanus, expatiates in detail concerning the significance of the book collections for the scholarly disciplines, and as a brilliant example of it, he praises the Hungarian king. The library, which the Turks plundered relentlessly and which now possesses only the names of its former glory, had imploringly besought him to publish its fame abroad. He had come years before to the King Louis' court in the company of the imperial ambassador, Wilhelm von Eberstein, and by the good services of Queen Maria, had gotten a glimpse of the Corvina. For the splendor and glory of the Latin and Hebrew treasures there the enthusiastic humanist did not know how to find sufficiently laudatory words. The king has acquired priceless manuscripts from Greece; others had been copied down in Florence. Finally, Brassicanus has enumerated a series of Corvina manuscripts; he deplores very deeply the destruction of the collection, and he finds consolation only in the fact that he owns several Greek manuscripts that King Louis had given him, and which he would soon have published.

The library, captured by legend, has frequently been overestimated in its significance. The main part of the holdings have been composed from fifteenth century copies that have no supreme significance for the textual tradition. The value of these treasures chiefly rests in their artistic design which demonstrated to the world the art of writing, book illumination and the splendid bindings of the Renaissance period as perhaps only the Medici collection in Florence would otherwise have done. Besides these younger manuscripts, however, the Corvina also owed some individual priceless items from the earlier period. Eugen Abel, one of the most knowledgeable authorities on its holdings, reports in detail concerning their significance: "In Vienna there is a Corvina Codex from the twelfth or thirteenth century containing Chrysostom's homilies; in Erlangen and Vienna there are manuscripts of the *Cyropedia* by Xenophon from the thirteenth and fourteenth century that belong to the Corvina; the church history of Nikephoros Kallistos is preserved for us only in a single manuscript that formerly belonged to the Corvina. It is with the help of a Corvinian Zonaras Codex that Hieronymus Wolf initially filled numerous gaps in our Zonaras texts; it was at Ofen that Cuspinianus has found the last five books of Diodorus Siculus; the *Aethiopica* of Heliodorus was first published from an Ofen manuscript."[53]

Today there are about 156 manuscripts that are known for certain to be Corvinian; they are divided among more than forty libraries. Of a small group of the missing items from Ofen the Ansbach gymnasium director, Vincent Obsopäus, tells us in his *Heliodorus* edition of 1534, that following the disastrous battle of Mohacs, a soldier from France (who by vocation was a dyer) had, because of their glittering gold decorations, taken them with him and carried them off to Ansbach. Obsopäus and Camerarius were able to use them there. Of these manuscripts that were carried off, three are still known: they are today in Wolfenbüttel, Erlangen, and Munich.

A period such as the Renaissance, which was so devoted to splendid books, felt compelled also to create wonderful rooms for its treasures. The brilliant hall-type rooms of Cesena, Urbino, Rome, Siena, Venice, and Florence we have already encountered. Oftentimes their embellishments harked back to concepts in the intellectual sphere as these had been established in the instructional life.[54] There the seven liberal arts were still exerting their influence from the Middle Ages: the *Trivium* with grammar, rhetoric, dialectics, and the *Quadrivium* with arithmetic, geometry, music and astronomy. Figuratively, one assigned these knowledge areas to their most famous teachers; thus Donatus or Priscianus represented grammar, Cicero rhetoric, Zoroaster or Boethius dialectics, Pythagoras arithmetic, Euclid geometry, Tubal music, and Ptloemy astrology.[55] The faculties gradually assumed places within the liberal arts: philosophy, theology, jurisprudence, medicine.

In the famous Castello del Buon Consiglio at Trent, which was erected in 1539 by Bishop Bernhard Cles, the main wall of the room for books showed the Madonna with Child and before her St. Vigilius with the kneeling cardinal. On the walls one saw the four church fathers, Augustine, Gregory, Jerome, and Ambrose, and on the ceiling were Plato, Demosthenes, Aristotle, Socrates, Pythagoras, Hippocrates, Galen, Euclid, Boethius, Parmenides, Ptolemy, Albert the Great, Thomas Aquinas, Duns Scotus, Averroes, Justinian, Quintilian, Priscian, Pliny, Cicero, Vergil, Ovid, Lucan and Horace.[56] Thus in the pictures of the bookroom of this humanistic prince of the church, antiquity, early Christendom and the Middle Ages have found themselves amicably together.

12
The Perfecting of the Book in Printing

As a conscious public form of communication, literature bears within itself the desire and the impulse to address as many as possible–indeed, in the final analysis, to speak to all the people. It therefore fulfills its meaning if it finds the broadest dissemination. Reproduction provides the means. Centuries and indeed, millennia, had, with their innumerable laborious copying, endeavored to fulfill the book's purpose and at the same time they thereby saved for posterity selected cultural works from the past. And then, all at once, about the middle of the fifteenth century, a Bible was issued from an obscure workshop in quiet Mainz in a hundred folio copies, and there was thus proclaimed to the world the wonder of the book's perfecting and its fulfillment in almost unlimited reproduction and through mechanical means.[1] For the book there was achieved a new sphere of infinite extent–one with unparalleled possibilities.

It is not quite the case, as one can frequently hear, that the discovery of printing was due to the increase in education and to the need for books which was at that time in the air, and that all that was required was a head to discover it in order to fulfill a pressing demand of the time. If that were the case, the discovery would then have been successful a long time before, or Italy (the most culturally advanced country of the time) would have had to have been the home of printing, as in fact it has become the most eager sponsor of the new art. For Germany, there would have to have been demonstrated evidence of an apex of cultural life with stimulating demands for the book. Such a growth, however, apart from the towering figure of the philosopher, Nicholas of Cusa (1401–1464), is nowhere to be established, not even in Mainz, which at that time numbered only about three thousand inhabitants.

Cause and effect should not be confused. If one examines the oldest printed works for their contents, one must rather state that the environment for the new work was, culturally speaking at least, quite unprepared, and that everything must have been left to the accidental effect of the printer himself. The period was not itself rich in cultural works, and it lived almost exclusively on the tradition that it had inherited. It is still entirely the Middle Ages, with its quite spiritual character, which we here encounter: the Bible, theology, canon law, the school and instruction in conformity with tradition, and which are now only carried forward in the new form of the book. Thus in its initial phases, printing was more a technical matter and a matter of the book trade, than it was a wholly culturally motivated event.

It is only from this observation and consideration that the immeasurable significance of Gutenberg and the universal effect of his discovery for the period which then followed upon it, can be properly seen and evaluated. Only the cultural movement of humanism, penetrating from Italy, and its best helper, the art of printing, have brought to pass in Germany that great cultural upsurge at the end of the fifteenth and the beginning of the sixteenth century, which Ulrich von Hutten has summarized in the spirited words: "O, what a century! Studies flourish, the spirit is awakening; it's a joy to be alive." If the increased educational stimulus of the period had been the main impetus for the new revolutionary discovery, this would then have had somehow to have been associated with the center of the cultural life or of the book trade—perhaps with an outstanding place of scholarship, with the spritual or secular courts of princes, with a monastic scriptorium or with a bourgeois copier's workshop. But it had nothing to do with any of these. The colophon of the *Catholicon* of 1460, one of the oldest monuments of printing, expressly emphasizes that it had been printed and completed under the protection of the Almighty, according to whose will the tongues of babes had been made eloquent and who had often revealed to the little ones things hidden from the wise.

No, it was not the stimulation of a scholar or of a school of higher learning, it was not an especially inspired cultural or educational life, it was not the quiet monastic cell, it was not the Brothers of the Common Life, (who took such pleasure in writing), it was not the painter of letters or the calligrapher who have presented mankind with the greatest art, but it was rather the highly developed metal technology, and an outstanding mind such as Gutenberg's, who understood it creatively so as to be able to master it. To be sure, the idea of reproduction had already been in the air for a long time. But here also Nietzsche's word holds true: "In every discovery, it is the accidental that does the essential; but most people do not encounter this accident." Technology has indeed often gone way off the beaten path and has then often accelerated mankind's development by a powerful jolt forward. In music, the production of instruments had lent the human soul the possibility of expressing its inexpressible feelings, and has extended the richness of sound infinitely, as well as refining it. This time it was the inroads in the workshops of copyists and artists of letters, and in the world of books, with external effects which Gutenberg himself could not have foreseen in the least.

Only if one understands what a powerful change has occurred since Gutenberg's time (which was still, even in the printed works, determined by the Middle Ages) until about the time of the death of Albrecht Dürer, may one be able to grasp Gutenberg's great significance and the enormous meaning of his new discovery. With it, there began nothing short of a new age, the age of the idea of the book conceived of completely, the book raised to its full effect.

And indeed in this second half of the fifteenth century there was one marvel after another. Scarcely had the discovery of printing opened up for mankind an infinite expanse for the exchange of ideas, when a few decades hence, the discovery of a whole new part of the earth disclosed to the same age possibilities that were completely unheard of.

Both events, the discovery of the art of printing and the discovery of America, belong fatefully together. Deeply impinging on human development, they stand on the threshold of two ages, the Middle Ages and the modern period. Basically, Gutenberg still belongs, just as Columbus does, to the Middle Ages. Gutenberg, with his decisive technical experiments, was hardly thinking of a cultural revolution. He was only devising a new technical way to a more effective book production and he obtained it through hard work. Columbus was likewise still living entirely within the geographic conceptions of the Middle Ages, and he was only trying to find a new way to East India. When on October 11/12, 1492, he landed on the Bahama Islands, he fancied himself to be in East India, and even his further sea voyages did not alter this belief. Both discoverers were parted from their work without imagining that, with their great successes, they had found new worlds. Also in this respect their fates are similar, in that it was only a later posterity that accorded them the fame that was due them. Concerning Gutenberg, his name has hardly been known any more following his death, and the part of the glove discovered by Columbus has not been called after him, but rather for the more fortunate seafarer, Amerigo Vespucci.

At this point no history of the discovery of printing need be given[2] – only its significance for the book's development and its effect are to be briefly depicted. The essential matter in the discovery is the reproduction of script, borrowed from goldsmithery and the metallic art of dies and seals of the types cut and cast on cones of equal size, which can be put together and dismantled. Stamp printing, copper engraving and woodcut[3] (all of which are also modes of reproduction) had already been discovered. "But to see this existing ability and knowledge in a great new and surprising connection, to think of them together with the intent of reproducing books, that was Gutenberg's achievement, and his own cultural property."[4]

It is as if the prophetic master had once more lived through the entire creation of script and its letters which were assembled as artistic symbols of speech, and in his own way, he had recreated so as finally to solve the reproduction of script and the preparation of the book through metallic, technical ways. "This book," stated the aforementioned colophon of the *Catholicon* edition of 1460, "has been printed and completed, not with the help of the quill, of the slate pencil or the pen, but through the wonderful harmony, relationship and measure of the punches and forms."[5]

As brief as his own testimony is, the reality clearly expressed therein has transformed the book and the world. Now past is the tiresome copying of books, and the lack of books is over. The new art takes the pen out of the hands of the monk and of the professional copier, and gives easily hundreds, yes, thousands of copies of a work to the public, and, with duplication, the production of books is made cheaper by about a fifth, and its marketability increases into infinity. Immeasurable ways are opened for making the book attractive. Something quite new was beginning. The clear, separable new script, moving at the same intervals of letters and lines, will, on account of its incomparable legibility, make the art of reading (this important presupposition for all cultural progress) into a common good, and thereby achieve results which, through their easy attainability, the cheap reading materials will reinforce even further.

Special professions will arise and devote themselves to the book: the typecaster, the printer and setter, the bookdealer, and the publisher. The book will become profitable merchandise, rewarding capital outlay, and a valuable economic good. The new art will busily engage thousands upon thousands of people, and whole generations, and it will support them. It will create new foundations for cultural life, generate other forms of ideas and instructional means, it will send forth the pamphlet into the world, it will develop the journal as an offshoot of the book, it will announce the happenings of the time first, by the once only, then in the weekly and finally, in the daily newspaper, and in the one issued several times a day, it will eventually originate new wonders of technology in typecasting, machine composition, quick press, and the rotary machine.

Without his contemporaries being able to foresee and grasp these things, the Mainz citizen Johann Gutenberg prepared his great undertaking, the 42-line Bible.[6] New researches have shown that the small items formerly considered to be the earliest Mainz attempts[7], especially the so-called astronomical calendar of 1448,[8] the Turkish calendar of 1455,[9] the so-called Sibyl book,[10] the German *Cisiojanus*, the blood-letting and laxative calendar for 1457, the Turkish bull from the end of 1456,[11] have originated only about 1455–1458, and with their conclusion, namely the 36-line Bible, belong to another workshop than that of Gutenberg.

The 42-line Bible appeared about 1456 following long attempts at printing; it is the handsomest and the most memorable printed work of all times, a masterwork of typography without equal. Problems relating to the types and the scriptset are here ideally solved, the beauty of the handwritten manuscript is completely equalled, and its legibility is unsurpassed. Gutenberg's creativity has here attained something incomparable.

Like the manuscript, the book begins immediately with the text (without title), in St. Jerome's letter introductory to his Latin *Vulgate* translation. In dependence on the manuscriptural tradition, the heading of St. Jerome's letter has been printed in red; it is the initial attempt to duplicate the emphases in color which was deemed to be necessary, an attempt which was to play a big role in the further development of printing.[13] But the matter has been carried through actually only on the first page and even then only in individual copies; otherwise an empty space had been left in which the heading can be subsequently added manually, in order to alleviate this later job, several printed form leaves (the so-called rubric tables) were produced; these gave the rubricator a clear compilation of all the headings to be produced by hand. This supplementary matter (the 36-line Bible also had such a supplement)[14] became superfluous in the very moment that the forms had been entered into the book in color and by hand. So only a few copies of this memorable device have been preserved. The Munich item has a remarkable entry in one passage. The typesetter has forgotten to indent the text in the Bible, at the twenty-second chapter of Matthew's Gospel, and thus to allow a place for the manuscriptural addendum. So now it says in the rubrics table: here the space for the chapter number has been left out; therefore before the beginning of the text a rubric sign and the number twenty-two on the border are to be added. In the Munich copy of the Bible, this direction has in fact been carried out. The memorable entry in the rubrics table indeed goes directly back to the environment of Gutenberg. Easier than the headings were the initials that were to be added manually before the individual chapters.

The printing of the Bible itself consists of strong and dark black Gothic types in large missal script, which is skillfully composed of main and connecting forms, after the letters that have extensions toward the types that follow, the simplified auxiliary form without the initial points follows.[15] This strictly executed law of script results in an equal distance of the columns of letters, which are now arranged as column on column in a row and thus gives a wonderfully finished image of the script. The printed block-like surfaces, which are also geometrically marked off and sharply delineated around the wide margin, stand out in relief on strong paper or parchment. Of the forty-six copies of the Bible that have been preserved, twelve are on parchment, and thirty-four are printed on paper. Of these, the German speaking countries today own eleven, and thirteen copies are in America. In all, 150 paper and thirty parchment copies may have been published. Of the majority of the oldest large printed works, a portion of the copies have been published on parchment. There must have been bibliophiles who did not mind paying larger costs if they thereby obtained especially beautiful, and artistically decorated, printed works. Gutenberg research has estimated the sale value of the Bible at that time to have been forty florins for the paper type, and fifty florins for the parchment copy.

When, as a result of the First World War, the Austrian monasteries were impoverished, the Melk monastery allowed its Gutenberg Bible to go in 1925 to America; there on February 15, 1926, it brought 430,000 DM and was later presented as a gift to Yale University. St. Paul in Carinthia sold its parchment copy in 1926 for 800,000 DM; it finally (for over a million marks!) came to the Library of Congress in Washington, and is solemnly kept there in a room by itself. The Bibliothèque Nationale in Paris owns the most notable copy of the Gutenberg Bible; in it, the Mainz vicar, Heinrich Albech, called Cremer, has entered the valuable information that he had rubricated, illustrated and bound the Bible from the 15th to the 24th of August, 1456. This entry gives us an important temporal starting point for the origin of the undated Bible. Dom Maugérard has carried off the priceless Paris monument from Mainz in 1789.[16]

With this 42-line Bible is associated the second Bible edition, the so-called 36-line Bible. It presupposes the 42-line Bible as model, and is printed with a type with which the earliest Mainz minuscules have been produced. It may be considered that their typographical conclusion had been published about 1459 or 1460 – in 1461 at the latest. From then on the Bamberg printer, Albrecht Pfister, used the type. Whether he has also produced the 36-line Bible can be surmised, but it cannot be proved conclusively. The two memorable Bibles have definitely been produced by two different masters.[17]

Following soon after the Mainz Bible, which was perhaps planned by Gutenberg, is a splendid monument of printing, the Mainz Psalter. It is the first printed work that in its colophon gave precise statements concerning the time of its origin and its provenance. The beautiful work has been published on August 15, 1457, by Johann Fust and Peter Schöffer. All of the ten copies still preserved are printed on parchment, an evidence for the fact that the maker wanted here to produce a really fine work for the divine service. Everything in fact has been done here to create a worthy monument, which in its impressive types and the multi-colored initials could be a match for any manuscript, so far as beauty is concerned. Especially do the initials again and again awaken our admiration; they are models of metal cutting. In another way, too, this book has come to be of the greatest significance for the whole further development of printing. In the exquisitely printed colophon of the work, not merely is the outstanding design of the Psalter extolled, but its title is also mentioned, and besides, we learn the names of the Mainz producers, Johann Fust and Peter Schöffer, just as we also learn the publication year of 1457. Both masters placed this important statement at the end of the book, and this has become standard practice for the several decades remaining, until the title page (which the Mainz men had not yet thought of) took over this statement. But we should be grateful indeed to both the masters, that they have so amply identified their work and have thus broken through the impenetrable obscurity which until then prevailed in the early printing. The Mainz Psalter has thus become one of the most important historical monuments of printing.[18]

If the two aforementioned printed works as sumptuous books make use of the big, impressive types, so two further works, the *Rationale divinorum officiorum* of Guilielmus Durandus of 1459, which was an expostion of the church's worship, as well as the Latin dictionary, *Catholicon* of Johannes Balbus of 1460, which was famous for its colophon, represent attempts by two other Mainz publishers to produce comprehensive texts with a small working-type script.[19] Therein, in fact, rests the significance of the two works for the history of printing types. With these four printed works the new art has shown that it was capable of fulfilling all the tasks of book production. The further modifications and changes in the design of books had only incidental significance; they were only developmental phases that arose out of the continuing experiences and considerations of the day.

Externally, the oldest monuments of printing follow entirely the manuscripts of the waning Middle Ages. Their types are shaped like the hand written scripts of the time, the columns are broken and they tend to end in angles, and in their pattern they are related to the Gothic architectural style. Sometimes the construction is solemnly measured, as it was in the Bible, and in the Psalter, sometimes there was a flowing movement like the cursory lines of the hand—so it was in *Durandus*, and in the *Catholicon*. The common Gothic script, on account of its flexibility, made for extremely rich variations and thus generated an almost unmanageable variety in fifteenth century type forms. Almost every printery had its own foundery, its special script, and its own style that was influenced by its geographical locality. The oldest printing also here reproduces the variety of the medieval book, which was written by hand. Where the manuscript has interspersed colored ornamentals, such as red headings, various colored initials or otherwise emphasized marks (rubrics), the older printing left space free for manuscriptural additions. Just as faithfully does it adopt the abbreviations and the connections among the letters,[20] although this runs entirely contrary to its technology. It desires everywhere to do just like the manuscript and to show thereby that the new reproduction method is equal to — indeed, has overtaken the manuscriptural one.[21] This effort has generated an interesting transition from the written to the printed book, which allows us to speak of a manuscript period of the very oldest printing. This character lasts so long until the progressive development of the new art uses (in place of the decorating colors) the red print, the bold type and printed initials, until it decorates the beginnings of the text with borders,[22] uses wood cut pictures, abandons abbreviations, introduces signatures, sheets, numbers of leaves or pages, and until the title page (which in the earliest printing was still unknown) develops into a permanent arrangement. Through all that, the book becomes more standardized, clearer and more legible. Above all, it is wholly reproduced, and entirely finished, from the printer's workshop. The first developmental stage of the art of printing, the period of incunabula, is then closed. In the meantime, the trends traverse the boundaries into the sixteenth century.

Yet to be mentioned are more of the initial ambassadors of the new art, who have gone out into all the world from Mainz as successful recruiters for, and preparers of the way of, the new book. Scarcely have the initial successes been achieved through Gutenberg, Fust and Schöffer, that printing soon finds a market in Strasbourg, the first place of Gutenberg's activity, where in about 1460 Johann Mentelin brings a Latin Bible onto the market; in 1466, the first German Bible translation, in 1471 (as a surprisingly modern enterprise), a printed book announcement with Vergil, Terence, Valerius Maximus; in 1477, Wolfram von Eschenbach's *Parzival* and *Titurel*, as the first printed editions of Middle High German poetry, which were already in the formal style of divided verse lines, as these have become poetry's prerogative.

Roughly contemporaneous with Strasbourg, Bamberg also obtains its printer; since 1460, Albrecht Pfister prints there with the types of the still mysterious 36-line Bible, the twin sister of the oldest Mainz Bible, and what is its special merit, combines (as the first printer to do so) the woodcut with the book, and publishes German books with woodcut pictures in them.[23]

Soon after Strasbourg and Bamberg (it is the year 1465) we see two German masters active in Italy, Konrad Sweynheym and Arnold Pannartz, who opened up their workshops first in Subiaco near Rome, and then in Rome itself. We would so like to know what it was that lured the two printers to Italy at a time when Augsburg and Nuremberg still did not have one printery. Did they know that the high level of the Italian culture at that time promised quite especially favorable conditions for their work? Did they have the idea that Italy would enthusiastically greet the new art as did no other country and people? Their successful work in publishing the church fathers and the Latin classics has yet to be described.

In Cologne, in 1465, Ulrich Zell ushered in the long series of printers who have since been active without interruption in the episcopal see city.[24] Cologne has been the first German university city to have made printing its own.

In Eltville, where the Mainz Archbishop Adolf of Nassau held court, the Mainz men, Nikolaus and Heinrich Bechtermünze, settled as printers; in the years 1467–1468, however, they produced only a few printed works, among them being the Latin dictionary, *Vocabularius exquo*, in several editions. Eltville nevertheless belongs among the towns where printing was practiced while Gutenberg was still alive.[25]

Augsburg followed in 1468 with Günther Zainer, the publisher of numerous German popular books decorated with pictures, and the first illustrated German Bible; further, Basel with Berthold Ruppel, who has participated in the Mainz proceedings of Fust against Gutenberg; Ruppel was a witness for Gutenberg.[26]

While the new art was already expanding to the most varied places, its great discoverer, Johann Gutenberg, died as a lonely figure on February 3, 1468. The economic breakdown of his enterprise had at the last moment robbed him of the success of his great historic deed. Whether the successful developments in Mainz, Strasbourg, Bamberg, Cologne, and Augsburg have perhaps become known to him, we do not know; they at least might have been a source of wistful satisfaction.

Just as Rome, so has Venice (which would soon become the most significant locale for printing) also obtained printing through a German master. He arrived on the scene in the person of Johannes de Spira. His first printed works (two editions of Cicero's *Epistolae familiares* and the *Historia naturalis* of Pliny, and thus editions of Roman classics) bear the publication date of 1469. On September 18 of that year, the Council of Venice tendered him a five year printing privilege; for us it is the first known letter for the protection of the printing trade. When the enterprising master died during the printing of a work by St. Augustine, the master's brother, Vendelinus de Spira, carried on the business and, in addition to classics and law books, did editions of Petrarch's *Canzoniere* and the *Divina Commedia* of Dante. The German masters, as the first printers on Italian soil, have therefore not merely printed Romac classics, but also Italian poetry. In the colophon of the *Panormitanus* edition of 1473 the home of the Venetian printer is celebrated by the sentence: "To him, your proud son, you Speyer, owe as much as Mantua owes its famous Vergil."

Each year in the decade 1470–1480 has become important for the extension of printing into Western Europe. In 1470 in Nuremberg, the capable master, Johann Senseschmidt, began to print law books especially in association with the legal scholar, Dr. Heinrich Rummel. In 1473 he joined with Heinrich Kefer, a former assistant of Gutenberg's, in order to publish with him the great volume of the *Pantheologia* of Rainer de Pisis.

In the same year of 1470, France obtained in Paris the first printing shop, when Guillaime Fichet and Johann Heynlin (two scholars of the University of Paris) induced three German printers, Ulrich Gering, Martin Crantz, and Michael Friburger, to settle in the French capital and to build a printery at the Sorbonne. The humanistic edition of the *Epistolae* of Gasparinus Barzizius Pergamensis appeared as the first work printed there.[27]

In Ulm, Johann Zainer developed a successful line of work, especially in the production of German woodcut books. His printery is the first German workshop known to us, which entered into association with a scholar, the Ulm city physician, Heinrich Steinhöwel, in order to bring on the market several significant German popular books, among which (as the most successful of them) was the 1477 edition of Aesop which was decorated with woodcuts; it served as the pattern for numerous copies. His first printed work with a firmly established date is Heinrich Steinhöwel's *Regimen sanitatis* of January 11, 1473; his first book decorated with pictures was Boccaccio's work, *Of Famous Women.*

Printing came to Lübeck in the year 1473. The master, Lukas Brandis, published there in 1475 the *Rudimentum novitiorum*, an extensive world chronicle that had one of the first world maps ever printed; this book was also decorated with many excellent woodcuts.

The new art was also extended in 1473 to the Netherlands, where Nicolaus Ketelaer with Gerland Leempt in Utrecht (Holland), and Dierk Martens with Johannes de Westphalia in Aalst, all began to print; and further still, the art went to Hungary, where the German, Andreas Hess was active for a short time in Ofen, and published the *Chronica Hungarorum.*[28]

The year 1473 can also be seen as the beginning of Spanish printing. Research has established its founder as having been the German merchant, Jakob Vizlant, a member of the Ravensburg trade society; he has founded a printers' association in Valencia.[29]

In 1474 at Cracow in Poland there was printed by an unnamed master an edition of Turrecremata; in all probability, the printer was Kaspar Straube from Saxony. England got its first printer in 1476 in William Caxton, who had learned the new art in Cologne, in order then to build a printery near Westminster Abbey, from whence issued numerous important printed works in the masterwork of the English language and literature, among them being the English medieval poet, Geoffrey Chaucer's *Canterbury Tales.* Caxton was among the few older printers who has cared more about the popular indigenous literature than for the scholarly Latin writings. Of Caxton's approximately ninety printed works, over seventy have been composed in the English language. The Roxburghe Club has erected a monument to him in St. Margaret's Church next to Westminster Abbey.[30]

The first northern printer was again a German, Johann Snell; he wandered from Lübeck to Rostock as a wandering printing master; he first introduced printing in 1482 in Odense in Denmark, and in 1483 in Stockholm, Sweden.

This fleeting survey of the extension of the new art may be enough in order primarily to illustrate the alacrity with which printing took over the production of new books in all the countries of western Europe. The survey has also already mentioned individual works of the first important places of printing and thus attempted to show which kinds of books were the first among the hundreds of issues to make their victorious way through the countries. A detailed survey of all the printing locales of the fifteeth century would have to emphasize (besides the connection with the most important trading streets) the fact (surprising for us) that the current centers of the German booktrade (Berlin, Leipzig, Vienna, Stuttgart, and Munich) have, in the oldest incunabula period, played no role or, as with Leipzig, none approaching the one played later; even Frankfurt am Main had not come into prominence at that time.

That there were German masters also in foreign lands (in Rome, Venice, Paris, Valencia, Cracow, Ofen, Odense, Stockholm) who have introduced the victorious discovery and disseminated it, is a special glory of German printing history.[31] Particularly in Italy and Spain do we encounter German masters at the most varied locales: in Foligno, Naples, Mantua, Padua, Santorso, Vicenza, Lucca, Perugia, Capua, Palermo, Aquila, Siena, Saragossa, Barcelona, Seville, Burgos, Toledo, Lerida, Tarragona, Perpignan, and Montserrat. Especially to be emphasized among these printers active in foreign lands (besides the already mentioned ambassadors) is the Augsburg citizen, Erhard Ratdolt. He began to print in 1476 in Venice with Bernhard Maler and Peter Loeslen, and he soon was among the most competent and enterprising masters of the city. The decorations of this books still today excites our admiration. It continues to be remarkable that it is a German printer who has introduced the Renaissance ornamentation into the Italian book. His ornamental borders and initials are among the most beautiful book decorations of the fifteenth century. We may assume that Ratdolt's collaborator, Rernhard Maler of Augsburg, was the artist of these splendid items.[32]

The *Appianus Alexandrinus* edition of 1477 is quite a wonderful book. In much of it the master has been completely innovative in his art. In liturgical works he applied the color wood cut by means of several printing plates, experimented with gold printing for the remarks in the dedicatory preface, in his Euclid edition of 1482, he reproduced[33] (as the first one to do so) geometric figures, and published a proof-sheet with his entire type stock, which was the first of its kind. Geography and astronomy were among his chief interests. Johannes Regiomontanus found him to be a tireless advertiser for his works.

Ratdolt published in Venice in 1476 a calendar in the German language of this great astronomer. It is the first book in the German language printed in Italy, famed above all for its beautifully decorated title page, with two very fine vignettes; it was one of the earliest title pages to be fully perfected. In 1483 Ratdolt had a second German book follow in Venice – the *Buch der Zehn Gebote* ("Book of the Ten Commandments"). In Johann Engel's *Astrolabium* of 1488, he expressed himself concerning the earlier, not very successful efforts with the sciences, and he alleged that the main cause for this was the lack of printers who could have disseminated the most important works. That would now be otherwise, because the art of printing was bringing forth from day to day ever more books, so that nothing valuable could any more be lost. Ratdolt returned to Augsburg in 1486 and here developed a quite exciting activity in the production of beautiful liturgical printed works.[34]

The Hamburg citizen, Steffen Arndes, has also followed a course of life similar to Ratdolt's. He printed since 1470 in Italy, at first in Foligno, and then in Perugia. After 1486 he was again active in Germany, first in Schleswig and then in Lübeck, where his most beautiful printed work, (a Bible in Lower Saxon dialect, with wonderful woodcuts) was published in 1494.[35] He was among the printers who, with an unrivalled freedom to move about from place to place, wandererd about and set up a working place wherever fortune smiled on him.

Among the most mobile of these restless wandering printers was the Mainz citizen, Johann Neumeister, who, just as Arndes, first emerged in the Umbrian town of Foligno and there in 1472, together with Emiliano Orsini, prodcued the first edition of Dante's *Divina Commedia,* and then returned to Mainz, publishing there two small printed works, until he went to France, where at Albi in the Lanquedoc, and then at Lyons, he produced magnificent missals for the French churches.[36]

The German masters, Valentin Fernandez from Moravia and Nicolaus de Saxonia, brought the new art to Lisbon, the capital of Portugal, in 1495; in the same year they published the first book printed in the Portuguese tongue, Ludolf of Saxony's *Vita Christi,* in four volumes.[37]

Therein lay a special significance of the transformed book production, in that it made possible a wide dissemination of the indigenous literary monuments, and thereby in Germany, as well as in the other civilized countries, contributed essentially to the establishment and cultivation of the national languages. Dante's *Divina Commedia* had already been printed three times in 1472, and in the fifteenth century it still went through twelve more editions. Within the same time frame, Petrarch's *Canzoniere* appeared in thirty-one printings, and Boccaccio's *Decamerone* in eleven. There then followed valuable contemporary works in the sixteenth century: in 1516, Lodovico Ariosto's *L'Orlando furioso,* which was printed by Giovanni Mazzocchi in Ferrara at the expense of Cardinal Ippolito d'Este; in 1528, at the Aldus printery in Venice, Baldasarre Castiglione's famous educational writing, *Il cortegiano;* in 1532 at Antonio Blado's in Rome, Nicolo Machiavelli's political work, *Il principe.*

William Caxton published the first book in English in 1475 at Bruges: *The Recuyell of the Historyes of Troyes,* by Raoul Lefèvre; the same printer then had (as has already been mentioned) numerous works published in his mother tongue that are of great significance for the history of the English language and literature. Active in Spain was above all the German printer, Paul Hurus, who already had printed in Barcelona in 1475 an edition of *Fueros y Ordonanzas* in the service of the indigenous literature. In Paris in 1476 the Master, Pasquier Bonhomme, produced the first printed work written in French: the edition, in three volumes, of the *Grandes Chroniques de France.* Holland has to thank the printers, Jacob Jacobssoen van der Meer and Mauricius Yemantszoen, for its first book in the national language; it was a translation of the Old Testament, which was published in 1477. The following year the German printer, Adam Steinschaber, brought out at Geneva the first book in the French language to be decorated with pictures, the *Histoire de la belle Melusine.*[38] The first printed Danish language monument, the *Dansk Rym-Kronike,* was published in 1495 at Copenhagen from the workshop of the Netherlands printer, Govaert de Ghemen.

Contemporaries (and among them, especially the Italians) gradually recognized the significance of the new art and they praised it in the most extravagant words. We mention here only several of these encomiums. Lodovico Carbo, in his Pliny edition of 1471, greeted the new period with its flowering of science, which above all is indebted the German discovery. Nicolaus Gupalatinus, in the dedication of the Venetian Mesue edition of 1471, writes of the discoverer of the new art: O thou excellent German spirit, that you first should have discovered this wonderful art that is worthy of the highest praises of man! You have yet shown the way, the easiest way, to attain and preserve all scholarly undertakings. On January 1, 1472, the Paris professor, Guillaume Fichet, the enthusiastic patron of the first Paris printers,

wrote to Robert Gaguin: The generation of the new printers has brought a new light
to studies, which Germany now, like the Trojan horse, sends forth everywhere.
Sebastian Brant, the poet of the *Narrenschiff* ("Ship of Fools"), said of the use of
printing in 1498:

> What otherwise at one time only the rich and the king owned,
> Is now found everywhere, even in the cottage—a book.
> Thanks therefore first of all to the gods—yet a proper thanks also to the printers,
> Because it is to their spirit that this direction has been shown,
> One that escaped the wise Greeks as well as the ingenious Romans,
> This discovery that stems now from within the German spirit.[39]

Finally the Italian humanist, Richard Sbrulius, sings at the beginning of the sixteenth century:

> Exactly so much, O Germany, as you are indebted to the Roman language.
> Should the Roman mind give back in gratitude to you;
> It has long taught you to speak in refined forms;
> You gave it eternal being, dedicating it for the first time to print.

Besides the uniqueness of its origin and design, the Mainz Bible still evidences
a further significance which was of decisive impact for the entire subsequent
development of the book business—the participation by outside capital in the production of books. Considerable money was necessary for executing so great an
undertaking as the Bible, and Johann Fust lent the money, while Gutenberg completed the work. In this first relationship of capital and work, we have heralded
already the later pattern of the production of books: the increasing formation of
companies (as these strongly developed especially above all in Italy but also in
Basel), the separation of production and distribution and of printing and publishing.

Printing still was in the forefront, and it sought to retain all the processes of
the work in its hands—but we still rarely learn the names of those who gave commissions, while already for a very long time, printing had been performed on that basis;
in the wider development, however, the future belonged to the division of the work
of the wholesale business, and the name of the publisher was patently more and
more coming to the fore. And a third work force was soon inserting itself into the
distribution of books: the "booktrader," the bookdealer, who in the future had an
especially important task to fulfill, the most expedient distribution of the
book.[40]

The discovery and development of the art of printing contained yet something
else of value, namely, the possibility of improved editions and impressions. This
assistance to scholarship has a great significance, one that indeed can scarcely be
estimated highly enough. One has only to consider the progress in the various text-
editions of the ancient classical writers, or the modern and improved reworkings
of scientific handbooks, encyclopedias and all the other large and much-used
reference works. These account for a goodly portion of scholarly development.

13

The Flow of Books in the Incunabula Period

If Gutenberg's work was to be of lasting success, strong cultural and economic forces had to combine with the technical discovery, so as to pave the way through the world for the happily reproduced book, whether it was the ordinary book useful for daily life, or a school book intended for instructional purposes, or devotional writing for the pious Christians, or works for education and scholarship. The moment the book left the printers' workshop in hundreds of copies, it became an economic item of a new and unique sort, an item of merchandise that anticipated wages and sales. Related to marketed goods were such matters as the utility and quality of the object for sale, as well as appropriate price and related matters. The usefulness of the first printed works must have been clear to every observer at first glance.

Price setting also had a powerful advantage over the earlier period's manuscripts, which took such effort to produce and were therefore quite expensive. The most important presupposition for the marketability of books and their sale depends on how stimulating the content is. Here from the very beginning supply and demand stood in the most favorable relationship imaginable. The past of antiquity and the Middle Ages had stored up cultural works in stupendous dimensions; but they had always been expensive and were thus too little disseminated. But the world had already been hungering for books. Now the opportunity arose of meeting this need, indeed of satisfying it on a grand scale, and added to this factor was another favorable accidental one, that the economic forces of the time could accept the growth of new goods on the market without much difficulty. Especially did the educated classes of the secular and religious clergy, which were dispersed in all the countries, possess to a remarkable degree the two most important preconditions for extensive book acquisitions, the cultural and volitional readiness to accept them, as well as the economic capacity to do so. The numerous courts of princes and the bourgeois world in like manner promised to the growing urban economy a vital relationship with the book. With their concentrations of wealth, the cities and their trade relationships were destined to become the main centers in the production and distribution of the book industry.

So the new art did not have to fear for the future, but only had to supervise carefully how the new cultural and economic merchandise was added to the existing cultural and economic life. Who at that time would have conceived that, when at a later time the world was after five hundred years celebrating the anniversary of the discovery of the book, Germany alone (the natal land of the new art) in a single year would produce 35,000 books in about seventy million volumes with a value of around two hundred million marks? And yet the germ of this powerful growth already lay within the essence of the discovery itself, and it awaited only further dvelopment—cultural, industrial, technical and economic. With Gutenberg a new age began for the book and for the book trade—one with great, never completed tasks.

The altered situation for the book since the middle of the fifteenth century was by now such that there came into being almost overnight the completely new profession of printer and publisher, which devoted itself with all its might to reproducing and distributing publications,[1] so that the work of printing became an object of capital and of enterprise, promising as it did, a profit. For the book, that meant an unparalleled expansion of its power.

How much there was waiting for the march through the world![2] Waiting were the ordinary books useful in church and school, and with these, the whole enormous learning of the Middle Ages; standing ready for dissemination was Christian antiquity, with its great church fathers; reporting in at just the right time was the rediscovered antiquity with its rich Roman and Greek cultural treasures; so there was a great cultural harvest of centuries of millenia to usher in—to which there yet was added what its own period had to say. An assignment was thereby given to the regenerated book, which in its grandeur was standing there unrivalled in history. It was like the extremely rich yielding harvest of a blessed year.

First, church and theology, and with them, the leading ranks of the clergy, raised enormous demands which at that time included: the Bible together with numerous excerpts and expositions, further the works that provided Christian instruction for introducing people to the teaching of the faith, for the edification of the faithful, and further, the "Epistles and Gospels for the Sundays and Feast days fo the Church Year," also called *Plenaries*, and the witnesses to the desire of the time for the word of God in the mother tongue, the legends,[4] the little books for confession, the lives of the saints, lives of the ancient fathers (eremites), the little books that listed relics,[5] the Rome guide *(Mirabilia Romae)*, and finally the liturgical books in the broadest sense. With their market, these groups were already placing an enormous demand on the new book production.

Thus Anton Koberger, the most significant bookdealer of the incunabula period, published the book of sermons, the *Quadragesimale* of the Franciscan, Johann Gritsch, alone in five editions, and the collection of legends, *Historia Lombardica (Der Heiligen Leben)* of James of Voragine (1228–1298) in six editions. This book of legends has become one of the most widely read volumes and has gone through a hundred editions before the Reformation period; each edition numbered about a thousand copies. If we can assume that all the editions have been sold, the book was distributed in 100,000 copies around the turn of the sixteenth century, while previously there had been at the most a few hundred manuscripts. Only the Latin Bible had so large a distribution.

Of the *Imitation of Christ* of Thomas à Kempis, one of the most widely disseminated publications in the world, ninety-nine editions were brought out already in the fifteenth century, the collection of pericopes and postils (often with pictures),[6] with the prayers and portions of the holy scripture used at mass, came to a hundred printings, the guide for pastoral care, *Manipulus curatorum* of Guido de Monte Rocher came to sixty in all, and the sermon collection, *Sermones aurei*, to forty-three printings. The printer had an especially difficult task in coping with theology proper, because demanding their rights here were the great church fathers, Ambrose, Jerome, Augustine, Gregory the Great, Athanasius, Basil, Gregory of Nazianus, John Chrysostom, and further the most significant theologians of the Middle Ages, such as Bernard of Clairvaux, Peter Lombard, Thomas Aquinas, Albert the Great, Vincent of Beauvais, John Duns Scotus, and John Gerson. It was indeed quite an enormous undertaking; thus the Augustine edition published by the printer Johann Amerbach of Basel, contained 2200 items in eleven folio volumes.

Also making for rather considerable difficulties were the books (much requested by church and clergy) of canon law with their expositions, which had the sentences of commentary to be added around the text; the addition of remarks under the text was not yet known. Fust and Schöffer were already publishing such law books since 1465; these were among their earliest undertakings. Finally, the books designed for worship, such as missals, breviaries and psalters, posed the greatest typographical challenge. These assignments too were mastered, and they produced pieces of work that are among the best of the early printing. Within these typical groupings, whole printeries came about that provided the dioceses over a wide territory with the requisite liturgical works. Over nine hundred mass books (missals), over 520 breviaries, and over 250 psalters have been produced in the final decades of the fifteenth century.

Within the professions with a demand for books, the clerics are followed directly by the legal profession, which especially requested the law books of the Roman and canon law together with their commentaries, further the introductions to law and finally, the dictionaries of jurisprudence and the books of formularies. Here also Peter Schöffer led the way in 1468 with an edition of the *Institutes* of Emperor Justinian, and the legal profession soon found itself surrounded by a great quantity of specialized books.[7] Italy, which is the home of Roman law, had the chief share in distributing this scholarly legal literature. The Venetian printer, Baptista da Tortis, has devoted himself almost exclusively to the publishing of law books. In one of his borders for the title page one could find pictured all the more significant past teachers of the law: Abbas Panormitanus, Johannes Andreae, Bartholus, Baldus, Alexander, P. de Castro, and Jason. The observer of the title page thus had portrayed before him a genealogy of the "fathers" of his scholarly discipline.

A no less strong demand issued from the school, especially from those learning the Latin language, at that time the language of education, and the international tongue.[8] Above all, it was grammars and dictionaries that were required. The *Grammar* of Aelius Donatus has been published (as one of the first printing monuments of Mainz) in several editions. Following shortly thereafter was the weighty dictionary, *Catholicon,* of Johannes Balbus; in the next decades it went through twenty editions. Still much more frequently requested was the *Doctrinale* of Alexander de Villa Dei; it is a teaching book of Latin grammar accompanied by memory verses; of this work no fewer than 228 medieval manuscripts and 279 printed editions from the incunabula period, have been listed. It has properly been said that three centuries have learned their Latin from it.[9] Of the much used *Vocabularius breviloquus,* twenty-five printed editions have been issued during the years 1476 until 1500.

Becoming the most widely distributed historical work of the incunabula period was one that was condensed, the world chronicle of the Carthusian, Werner Rolevinck, *Fasciculus temporum;* in the period between 1474 and 1500 it was brought out in over thirty editions.[10] The *Chronica pontificum imperatorumque* of Johannes Philippus de Lignamine, which was published in Rome in 1474, offers one of the earliest reports concerning the discovery of the art of printing and it names Jakob (!) Gutenberg and Fust in Mainz, and beyond them, Mentelin in Strasbourg, as the first masters who with their metal types may have daily produced three hundred printed sheets. Thus there were already being published here and there — if still timidly at first — contemporary reports concerning particular significant events, as, for example, about the election of Maximilian to the Roman throne at Frankfurt am Main on February 16, 1486, about Maximilian's crowning at Aachen on April 12 of the same year, about Emperor Friedrich III's funeral at Vienna on December 7, 1493 and about the investiture of the German prince at the Worms Diet on July 14, 1495.[11]

The Middle Ages had taken its knowledge of science and medicine primarily from antiquity. Thus the printers, already early in their work of publication, tried their hand at desired works of the ancient world. The German printer, Johannes de Spira, published for the first time Pliny's *Historia naturalis;* it was the fundamental natural history for the entire earlier time; de Spira published it in Venice in 1469. There were already fifteen editions with at least three thousand copies before 1500, while only about two hundred manuscripts of this work from the fourteenth and fifteenth centuries are known.[12] Peter Schöffer published the first herbal book printed, a Latin *Herbarius,* in Mainz in 1484; he decorated it with numerous pictures of plants in woodcut. The first hygiene book, entitled *Hortus sanitatis,* was published in 1485 by Schöffer and was essentially supplemented in 1491 by Jakob Meydenbach in Mainz.[13]

The most handsome medical printing monument of the fifteenth century is the work of Johannes Ketham, *Fasciculus medicinae,* which is embellished with several anatomical woodcuts; it was published in 1493 in Venice by the printers, Johannes and Gregorias de Gregoriis.[14] We find already quite advanced illustrations in it: how a doctor holds counsel, how a corpse is cut up, how someone infected with the plague is confined to his bed. These — and all the other scientific and medical printed works of the fifteenth century — are not only important evidences of the advance of printing in ever-widening spheres of knowledge; they are also valuable sources for the development of reasoning and observation in the natural sciences during the waning Middle Ages.[15] In all of these works, the woodcut has performed outstanding service and has effectively supported the word.

It was a German printer, the already mentioned Konrad Sweynheym in Rome, who prepared for its first publication a further important scientific work of antiquity, the *Geographia* of the Alexandrinian mathematician, Claudis Ptolemy (106–178 A.D.); to it he had affixed twenty-six engraved maps—ten for Europe, four for Africa, and twelve for Asia. As he died during the arduous undertaking, his compatriot, Arnold Bucking fortunately brought it to a conclusion in October 1478. In the dedication to the pope, the tiresome preparations are recalled which had been necessitated by the comparison of the Latin manuscripts with an ancient Greek text, and the artistic engraving. If in the colophon the beautiful printed work has been lauded as an eternal artistic and cultural monument, that is a value judgment that is entirely justified. The work of both the German masters, the first printed atlas of the world, was in fact of immeasurable significance for geography, and for knowing about the various countries, (one should consider that it was fourteen years before America's discovery), it was simply a revelation; it represented an extension of a quite special sort for the broadening range of the book. The next Ptolemy edition was published in 1482 from the printing shop of the Ulm master, Lienhard Holle; the accompanying maps in woodcut are designated as being products of the artistic blockcutter, Johann Schnitzer of Arnheim; to the earlier maps five new ones (with Spain, France, Scandinavia, Italy, and Palestine) have been added. The further Ptolemy editions of the incunabula period,[16] had important geographical functions too, and above all, later had to bring the newly discovered lands closer to contemporaries. Quite soon there were appearing printed reports (authored by explorers of the new continent) concerning the lands of wonder, and these paved the way for the promising literature about America.[17]

Like all periods, the Middle Ages had attempted also in large surveys to comprehend the total knowledge of the time. Printing took to these books, and published, for example, no fewer than twenty-five editions of the work, *De proprietatibus rerum* of Bartholomaeus Anglicus, within the years 1470–1500; among them were French, Spanish and Dutch translations.

The publication work of Anton Koberger (the most significant bookdealer and publisher of his time) in Nuremberg, gives us a good picture of the enormous flow of books in the incunabula period; with his various enterprises, he spanned the entire scholarly literature of the waning Middle Ages and he supplied all of Europe with them.[18] His approximately two hundred works from the years 1472–1500 represent the well-known late medieval writing of the clergy and of Scholasticism. At the pinnacle stand numerous Bibles and Bible expositions, and added to that, the multi-volume Bible work of St. Hugo; there then follow the church fathers, Ambrose, Augustine, and Jerome; the Scholastics, Peter Lombard, Alexander of Hales, Thomas Aquinas, Bonaventura, Duns Scotus, Raymundus de Sabunde, and James of Voragine; the encyclopedias of Vincent of Beauvais and Rainer de Pisis; the comprehensive *Summae* of Antoninus Florentinus, Astesanus, Angelus de Clavasio, Baptista de Salis, Johannes de Friburg, Nicolaus de Ausmo, Johannes de Bromyard; the innumerable sermons with these well-known names: Homilarius,

Paratus, Dormi secure, Meffreth, Johann Gritsch, Petrus de Palude, Johann Herolt, Hugo de Prato, Nicolaus de Lyra, Leonhard von Utimo, Bernardinus de Bustis, Heinrich Herp, Alphonsus de Spira; and as they are usually are called, the theological works, which at that time found an almost unlimited capacity for acceptance, and still today comprise the main holdings of our large collections of incunabula; further, the philosophical writings of Boethius and Walter Burlaeus, the grammars of Alexander Gallus, and Johannes de Balbis; the *Corpus juris civilis* and the *Corpus juris canonici.*

On the other hand, Koberger's publications in the German language can be counted one hand: one Bible, the lives of the saints, Albrecht von Eyb, Brigitta in Latin and German, Hartmann Schedel's *World Chronicle* in Latin and German, Ortolff von Bayerlandt's book of medicine,[19] Stephen Fridolins' *Schatzbehalter (der wahren Reichtümer des Heils)* ("Collection of Treasures of the True Riches of Salvation"), and the *Reformation of the City of Nuremberg.* The *Himmlische Offenbarungen der h. Brigitta* ("Heavenly Revelations of St. Brigitta"), which was published at the request of the Bridgettine Order in 1502, has been warmly supported by King Maximilian. The classics and the humanistic writings have been represented even more sparingly in the Nuremberg publisher's listing: Poggio, Aeneas Sylvius, Platina, Marsilius Ficinus, Cicero, Juvenal, and Vergil. We see that the Middle Ages are still quite at home in Koberger's stock—only a few German books and humanistic foreigners appear here. And thus similarly do we, in fact, have to imagine the entire period of Gutenberg.

They were mostly weighty volumes that were produced in the workshops of Koberger and the printers who worked with him.[20] The Basel masters, Johann Amerbach and Johann Petri, worked for the Nuremberg publisher no less than five years (1498–1502), in order to complete the Latin Bible with Hugo's postils in seven large volumes. Eighteen manuscripts from Cologne, Lübeck, Heilsbronn, Nuremberg, Maulbronn and other locales were sent from Nuremberg to Basel. On one occasion the entire text was assembled for the printing of a volume, when Heilsbronn[21] demanded to have its manuscripts back and would not allow them to be given to the printery. So the text in question first had to be copied and compared with the original. All this work, however, has been well worth it; the tremendous completed work was sold within a short time. Koberger's market was the whole world of that time; it was supplied by bookstores in Milan, Venice, Ofen, Cracow, Lemberg, Lübeck, Antwerp, Paris and Lyons.

It was a remarkable coincidence that, not long before the Gutenberg's discovery, the cultural world of antiquity had set out on a new triumphal march through the ages. Printing and the ancient world now found themselves together in activity that spanned the entire globe. Fust and Schöffer were already publishing Cicero's *Officia et Paradoxa* in Mainz in the year 1466. That was, however, only an interlude that was not immediately continued. It would also have been odd if Italy, the home of the reawakened antiquity, had not by means of printing, taken up the renewal of the Roman and Greek cultural works. But there were still two German masters, the already mentioned clergymen, Konrad Sweynheym and Arnold Pannartz, who from their workshops gave to Rome the church fathers and the

Roman classics for the first time in great numbers; and in connection with the learned later librarian of the Vaticana, Giovanni Andrea dei Bussi (1417–1475)[22] (who was a second Cassiodorus!), quickly published between 1468 and 1472, one after another of works of Augustine, Jerome, Apuleius, Aulus Gellius, Caesar, Cicero, Lucan, Livy, Strabo, Vergil, Quintilian, Lactantius, Pliny, Suetonius, Cyprian, and Ovid.

Valuable publishers' prefaces increase the significance of these printed Roman works and reveal to us in a compelling way those aims in which we can discern the initial cooperation on a grand scale of scientifically inspired scholars with the great German discovery. In the second volume of the Jerome letters of 1468, the publisher complained about the endless effort of preparing the text, until the punctuation had been figured out, for instance. And yet in this respect a properly arranged book performs the same as the teacher who, by analogy, lectures. Now the work is finished, and the fathers are able to purchase it for their studying sons, and the sons should read it. There is no greater silliness than to have cases filled with beautifully bound books and thus to show off, but all the while be bristling with ignorance.

In the preface to the Livy edition of 1469, the merits of Pope Paul II in promoting printing are effusively praised. Among the popes (according to the Jerome edition of 1470) God, besides his other gifts to Christendom, has granted the favor that the poor could now also obtain cultural treasures for little money. Or is that to be only a lesser glory for the popes, that volumes, which previously cost about a hundred florins, were now to be hand for only twenty, or even fewer, and in good editions? That which earlier had been lying in hidden corners with dust and spider webs, was now pouring through the entire globe, thanks to the Germans' incomparable discovery. Truly, a more glorious discovery has indeed not been made, either in ancient or in modern times. Germany deserves the glory and the greatest esteem, Germany, where this art of the highest utility was discovered! If Nicholas of Cusa has once wished that this new art might come to Rome, this wish is thus now fulfilled.

Still during the preparation to the Nicholas of Lyra edition, the printer (who ran out of the large-sized paper for it) came to Bussi and requested a text suitable for a smaller size of paper. The hard-pressed scholar quickly came up with a copy of the Cyprian letter which he had from his student days in Paris, and in the shortest time the two masters had a copy ready for printing. The insertion of explanations to the Gellius edition of the text is excused, in that the printer held it to be impossible to print the glosses on the border. The indefatigable publisher groaned repeatedly about the corrupted text of the work as it had been transmitted. He was soon also having to complain about the economic failure of the great undertaking. In the Nicholas of Lyra edition of 1472, he extolled the services of the two German printers to learning and to libraries, made reference to their previous thirty-six editions with 12,745 copies, and he begged the new pope, Sixtus IV for the support of both the masters, whose house was full of books, but was empty of the necessitites. From documentary reports we know that the pope has responded with the prospect of clerical benefices.[23] We also do not want to forget that the brave assistant of the two German printers, the admirer of Bessarion's and of Plato, has accompanied the German, Nicholas of Cusa, in the winter of 1451–1452 on a trip through Germany, in order later to enter into his service (1458–1464), and to whom he has dedicated a worthy obituary in the Apuleius edition.[24]

The first German scholar who has recognized and applied the significance of printing for scholarship was the famous astronomer, Johannes Regiomantanus. With the support of the wealthy Nuremberg citizen, Bernhard Walther, he built in the Franconian imperial city a workshop for astronomical instruments, as well as a suitable printery, in order to publish therewith the most important retrospective astronomical works, as well as his own calculations.[25] An announcement printed in 1474 of the planned publications as stipulated comprised over forty titles, and shows on what a grand scale this unique publishing activity had been conceived and prepared. Only ten of the works, to be sure, have been published, as a result of the scholar's early death; among they are the work of Georg Peuerbach concerning the movement of the planets and the *Astronomicon* of Manilius. Among the astronomer's own works (who, following the call from Rome, soon died there), his *Ephemeriden* have been most successful. Containing in tabular form the astronomical reckonings by decades and provided with a wide border, this book format of a perpetual calendar was extraordinarily appealing, and contemporaries have liked using it for diary records. It is indeed to be seen as a forerunner of the engagement calendar.[26] The most beautiful book honor was accorded the German astronomer through the wonderful woodcut with its figures of Ptolemy and Regiomantanus, added to the Regiomantanus extract from Ptolemy by the Venetian printer, Johann Hamman in 1496.

Beside its other services to the book, early Italian printing may likewise lay claim to the inital concern for reproducing Greek literature.[27] The manuscripts had already found safe and protective locales in the library of the Medici at Florence and in the Marciana at Venice. The first Greek book came out in the year 1476 in the compendium of Constantine Lascaris, which was printed by Dionysius Paravisinus of Milan. The co-publisher, Demetrius of Crete, went into a detailed exposition in the foreword concerning the difficulties that had been encountered in producing the type and the diacritical marks.[28]

Likewise at Milan in about 1480, there came out in print (in Greek and in Latin) the fable collection of the legendary Greek poet, Aesop; it was published by Bonus Accursius.[29] Up until the year 1500, over a hundred editions of this book (in about 20,000 copies) have come on the market; before this the name had scarcely been known! Gradually the work has become a favorite book of the world and it has exercised a significant influence on literature. The first Homer edition was issued in 1488 in Florence; it was prepared by Demetrios Chalkondylas, and was an event of the first order – the luminous emergence of the beauty of Greece. We cannot imagine any more today what it meant for the world of that time when Homer or Dante appeared in print for the first time. Deserving of the most credit, so far as the dissemination of the Greek literature is concerned, is the Venetian printer, Aldus Manutius,[30] who was successfully supported by the Greek scholar, Marcus Musurus. Manutius effectively took on the Greek cultural works, and he presented to the world no fewer than thirty-one first editions of antiquity. Constituting the high-point of this enormous achievement were the large editions of Aristotle and Aristophanes from the year 1498. The five weighty volumes of Aristotle can indeed be designated as the greatest literary and typographical undertaking of the fifteenth century. It was a sign of unparalleled success when in the same year the active printer was able to publish a book notice with a proud catalog of his published Greek works.[31]

Aldus complained in the Euripides edition of 1503 about the loss that accompanied the destruction of the library of Alexandria; by means of the art of printing, God had provided for the salvation and the dissemination of the residue that was still preserved. The printer praises Venice as the second Athens in his collection of Greek rhetoricians completed about 1513. Together with Aldus, the Cretans, Zacharias Calliergi and Nicholas Blastos (Vlastos), have founded an exclusively Greek workshop in Venice; in 1499 they have published the gigantic *Etymologicon magnum* in a beautiful presentation.

Printing has, in fact, become the savior of Greek literature. Homer, Aeschylus, Thucydides, Xenophon, Aeschines, Demosthenes, Plato, Aristotle, Plutarch, Theocrites, Sophocles, Euripides, Aristophanes, Herodotus, Pindar, Dioscurides, Suidas, Strabo, who up to this time had scarcely been known (or, if known, only in Latin translation) – all these were now disseminated in hundreds of copies. The house of the inspired friend of things Greek, Alberto Pio of Carpi, was compared by Federicus Asulanus in his Galen edition of 1575 with the residence of an Athenian, because it was so replete with Greek manuscripts and printed works. Under Aldus, Venice ruled the book market over a wide territory indeed. Heinrich Glareanus wrote from Basel on October 19, 1516, to Ulrich Zwingli: Wolfgang Lachner (Johann Frobens' father-in-law) was just ordering a wagon full of classics in the best Aldine editions; the friend should quickly send his commissions and the appropriate money. With each such shipment, thirty buyers would be standing there for one item, and they fought over the books. Demands for these treasures was like a madness, and it overtook people who surely have had no use for these books. Especially were there strong demands for the handy and cheap editions of the classics (such as Vergil, Horace, Lucan, Juvenal, Persius, Catullus, Tibullus and Propertius) which had been issued in the space-saving cursive type since 1501 and which ushered in something entirely new in the life of books. The designer of this type is mentioned for us in the Vergil edition of 1501 as being Francesco Griffo of Bologna.

Even though Aldus required an appropriate privilege for his projects, his editions soon became imitated in Lyons. The Venetian printer cautioningly pointed out, in a broadside of his own, the differences between his editions and the imitations; in these, the printer's note and the printer's mark were lacking; the paper was bad and it had an unusual smell; the script followed a particular design that had ugly large letters and the separated smaller type, while with him, the letters, the consonants and vowels were one with each other, just as they were in the manuscripts. Aldus published one of the most beautiful Italian woodcut books in 1499 with the Latin love story, *Hypnerotomacia Poliphili* by Francesco Colonna.[32]

Still especially prominent among the Venetian early printings was the earliest Italian translation of the Bible from the pen of the Camalduense monk, Nicclol Malermi (GW 4317) It has been published on October 15, 1490, by Giovanni Ragazzo for Lucantonio Gianta; it has charming small pictures with delicate outlines.

Of the approximately five thousand works that have been published in Italy in the fifteenth century, Venice alone could claim 2800. In the city of the lagoons, with its extensive commercial traffic, the book has found a base of support the likes of which it had nowhere else.[33]

He who would represent the plentitude of books in the incunabula period, and that even only in fleeting outline, may not forget an especially helpful and faithful aid to the new art, the woodcut, which has essentially contributed thereto by making the book into a valuable eidetical means as well as a civilizer, with heightened attractiveness. Especially has the German woodcut book a claim to our greatest attention.

Already at the beginning of the fifteenth century, (still prior to the discovery of printing) the professional production and distribution of popular German manuscripts has set in; these especially consisted of devotional books and beyond that, of the edification literature and the literature of entertainment. Enterprising illuminators' and copiers' workshops, which otherwise kept themselves occupied with the trade in holy pictures, playing cards and other small sheets, had attempted to extend their activity through manuscriptural reproduction of transmitted texts which they decorated with tinted pen and ink drawings.[34] There were available, for instance, the edifying *Speculum humanae salvationis* ("Mirror of Human Salvation"),[35] the *Biblia pauperum*, the *Legenda aurea*, the *24 Ancients* of Otto of Passau, and besides those, fables, wise sayings concerning health, *Parsival, Titurel, Tristan, Wigalois, Wolfdietrich, the Trojan War*, the *Gesta Romanorum*, the *Wälsche Gast, Freidank, Lucidarius, Schachzabel*, and the *Seven Wise Masters*. They were not priceless luxury books on parchment, but unassuming paper manuscripts that did not cost much and which attracted the eye through their multi-colored pictures. For the most part, buyers have been princes, nobility and patricians, and thus from the secular circles.

From a catalog of manuscripts we are acquainted with one of these workshops that was situated in Heidelberg; it is recommended there in the words: "What materials one likes in pretty books, large or small, spiritual or secular, and painted prettily, one finds all of them at Diabolt Lauber, the scribe at Hagenau."[36] The origin of these popular manuscripts falls approximately in the period from 1427 to 1467; over fifty of them can still be authenticated.

It was in such workshops, in which a business-like reproduction of books was therefore already taking place, where one could have expected the earliest attempts at mechanical production. But the earliest ideas of reproduction in print form have emanated not from the book, but rather from pictures. The picture in simple outline is related to the stamp and as such is easily reproduced, because the printing has to happen only from a single outline. For these reasons, block printing with woodcut, metal engraving, and copper engraving has arisen earlier than the printed book, which was composed from many letters, and therefore from numerous individual outlines. In contrast with the book, the picture is producible without high costs and so it can therefore count on large sales. The printer has thus gradually developed from the painter. Pictures of saints and playing cards seem to have been the earliest block printing. It was in the course of development that the printer added to these little pictures, where it seemed desirable, subscriptions (such as the names of saints, or a short prayer, and textual citations) which could be cut into the block or into the metal plate and printed from these.

A further step led to picture books, in which the pictures printed with blocks and the pages of text were integrated with each other in the form of the book. Doubtless already before printing there were such individual block books or block printings, and their production may (as did the whole of block printing) have exercised a certain influence on the discovery of printing, even though the majority of the block books which have been preserved are younger than the oldest printing. The *Chronica von der hl. Stadt Köln* ("the Chronicle of the Holy City of Cologne"), which was published in 1499,[37] reports that printing, "pre-conceived" in the Netherlands, had, on the contrary, first really been discovered in Mainz. This narrative is (if it can be supported by facts at all) intended to explain that block printing was being pursued in the Netherlands, but on the other hand, it is in Mainz that printing has actually been discovered. That the block book has in no case generated printing directly is already to be seen in the fact that the oldest monuments of printing connect neither with the workshop of a metal cutter not with the subject matter of the block books.

For some time the block book and printing existed side by side. With the block printing the matter has always had to do with a few voluminous productions from small establishments of painters and metal cutters. They belong to the most unique form of the book and they afford us a glance into the pictorial tradition of the waning Middle Ages.[38]

The picture book has still always been an indispensable means of assistance for instruction and for edification, and even the manuscript period has known the use of a series of pictures for instructional purposes. The painters needed only to transfer them into the woodcut. Such traditional series of pictures were intended especially for the lower clergy and were meant to present the truths of the faith. The so-called *Pauper Bible (Biblia Pauperum)*,[39] with its illustrations from the Old and New Testaments, then attempted to depict the work of redemption in its promise and fulfillment, in an again-and-again varied cycle of pictures that goes back to the ninth century. Individual explanations of holy scripture are used to make a visual impression: the book of *Kings (Liber regum)*, the *Song of Songs (Canticum canticorum)* with the canticle of the Virgin Mary, and the *Revelation of St. John.*

Absorption in Christian doctrine further served the interpretation of the *Our Father (Exercitium super Paternoster)*, the symbolizing by pictures of the twelve articles of faith *(Symbolum apostolorum)*, the representation of a blessed death *(Ars moriendi*, the art of dying),[40] the cues of the gospel narratives *(Ars memorandi)*, the *Mirror of Salvation (Speculum humane salvationis)*, the *Little Clock* (book of hours) with the information concerning what one should pray for and observe at every hour, the seven deadly sins, the defense of Mary's Immaculate Conception

(Defensorium), the *Salve Regina*, legends of Meinrat and Servatius, the Sybilline proverbs, the *Confessional Mirror*, and the *Endchrist*, that is, the history of those who deny God, and the fifteen signs. Prints on secular subjects are very much in the minority. In the first place we find an introduction to Latin grammar, which is named for Aelius Donatus; it was the school book and the book of daily instruction for the Middle Ages.

Other favorite secular items are the *Acht Schalkheiten* ("Eight Pranks"), the book of the planets, the calendar of the astronomer, Johannes de Gamundia, the palmistry of Johann Hartlieb, the *Totentanz* ("Dance of Death"), which is also abundantly represented in great art, the spiritual and secular Rome *(Mirabilia Romae)*, and the *Fable of the Sick Lion*. Text and illustration are connected in these unassuming books so that they constitute an integral whole, and their concise quality lends the editions unique attractiveness. Still known to us are thirty-three such wood block printings in about a hundred copies; some of the especially rare editions have been reprinted.

If printing did not want to renounce an important circle of customers and didn't wish to yield the picture book to the painters and metal cutters, sooner or later it had to try to combine the picture with the new book production, and thus create a new form of book, the block book. The earliest printers who saw this possibility for the development of the book and created the first popular German books, with which the picture has to serve as an essential and complementary component for the imagination of wider circles, was Albrecht Pfister in Bamberg, the master whom we have already encountered as one of the earliest printers. His first printed work decorated with pictures is the powerful medieval didactic poem *Gespräch des Ackermans von Böhmen mit dem Tode* ("Conversation of the Peasant of Bohemia with Death"), a discussion within which the ultimate questions of existence are treated.[41]

Following this intial attempt, which probably stems from 1460, were *Das Buch der vier Historien von Joseph, Daniel, Esther, und Judith* ("The Book of the Four Stories of Joseph, Daniel, Esther and Judith"), with sixty-one pictures, Ulrich Boner's collection of fables, *Edelstein*, ("Jewel") a Latin *Biblia Pauperum*, and finally, the *Belial* of Jacobus de Theramo. The most remarkable and comprehensive work among them is Boner's *Edelstein*; it is also remarkable for its colophon, which is the oldest printing notice in the German language. Lessing has exhaustively discussed the block book in the Wolfenbüttel *Beiträge* ("Contributions") and the Graphic Society has photocopied it in 1908. Pfister has won a place in the history of German literature with his *Ackermann aus Böhmen* and Boner's *Edelstein*. Like all the oldest woodcuts, his pictures represent applications of craft—not artistic works, but simple artless outline sketches that had to be subsequently tinted.

The picture—as over against script—has the advantage of having a direct effect on the eyes. Language and writing—these are mental, not sensual; the picture is real; it is concrete. We are able in a book to comprehend the pictures, even if we do not understand the language of the book, just as a child can become absorbed in a picture book even when he is not yet able to read. Today we can scarcely any more properly imagine the effect produced by early woodcut books, in which for the first time pictures have come before the reader on a large scale. The Bamberg printer appears to have been thoroughly aware of this significance of the picture. Perhaps Pfister has moved on from letter press and metal cutting to printing and thus has integrated the two artisitc proficiencies.

It is probably not accidental that the next publisher of block books came from the scribal and metal-cutter professions. This activity of Pfister's is unique in the history of printing and only after many years has it been taken up in Germany; whether the next oldest block book, which has been published in Rome in 1467 by the German printer, Ulrich Han (it contains the *Meditationes vitae Christi* of Cardinal Johannes de Turrecremata), has been subject to Bamberg influence, cannot any more be established. In any case, Albrecht Pfister may claim a position of honor within the history of German popular books and block books.

The wealthy Swabian trading city of Augsburg became the first home of the German block books. There, soon after the new art had been introduced, enterprising printers have supplied the citizenry with popular books. So especially Günther Zainer after 1470 issued one German popular picture book after another from his workshop, and he therewith developed for printing a new and enduring category of material, with unlimited markets. From then on, the German block book was a much desired and sought after item on the book market.[42]

Zainer was already able in 1471 to advertise on a printed sheet, besides four Latin books, the following German publications: "Whoever wishes to purchase several German and printed works, of which the names are hereafter written, he should come into the smith's house to Günther, named Zainer von Reutlingen; there he finds them, and he will be given them for a fair amount of money: one little book of seven German psalms, vespers, vigils, and masses for the soul and many of the other prayers of worthy sacraments, the history of the life of a king from Tyre and Sidon, called Appolonius, a letter drawn from Francesco Petrarch and translated into German, of a virtuous woman called Griselda, etc."[43]

Soon coming on the scene was a second Augsburg printer, Johann Bämler, who was successful in competing with Zainer, and who likewise advertised numerous German popular books that were decorated with pictures. A third Augsburg printer, Anton Sorg, could boast in a leaflet of thirty-five German books with entirely new titles: *Der Heiligen Leben mit allen Figuren* ("Lives of the Saints with Pictures"); the gospels and epistles; the imperial law of the land, called *Schwabenspiegel* ("Swabian Mirror"); forms and rhetoric for writing letters; Otto von Passau's book called the *24 Alten von der liebhabenden Seele* ("Elders of the Loving Souls"),[44] the lives of the holy ancient fathers; Suso's material on the seven deadly sins; an exposition of the *Our Father;* of the childhood of Christ; the *Mirror of Sinners;* Ulrich von Richenthal's book on the council of Constance, with all the participants . . . You also find therein their arms painted according to their order; Aesop with his figures, Ovid on love, translated by Hartlieb; how the city of Troy was destroyed; the history of Duke Wilhelm of Austria; the history of Duke Gottfried; Johannes de Montevilla, *Reisen* ("Travels"); Conrad of Mergenberg's book of nature; Brigitta's *Offenbarung* ("Revelation")' *Melusina*[46] (which is very amusing to read), with pictures; Ortlof's medical book; Schrick, *Von den ausgebrannten Wässern ("Concerning the Waters*

That Have Dried Up"); the little book, *Lucidarius*[47]; a beautiful passion; a little wine book; a pretty little book of a young noblewoman, Sigismunda; a little prayer book for the seven times of the day.

The printer thought he had to defend the German translation of Nider's *Buch gennant die 24 guldin Harfen* ("Book called the 24 golden harps") with the hope that the reader might be attracted more by the truth of the contents than deterred by the roughness of the style.[47]

Most of these German books consisted of older writings from the Middle Ages, or translations of ancient and modern French works. Preferred above all else was the medieval didactic poetry; the *Minnesang* meanwhile remained neglected, and the *Heldenbuch* with Ortnit, Hugdietrich, Wolfdietrich, and the large and small *Gardens of Roses* were published only twice in the fifteenth century, and *Parzival* and *Young Titurel* only once (1477); the *Nibelungenlied* got no chance at all. Freidank's *Bescheidenheit* ("Modesty") was printed about 1487 in Leipzig, and then in 1508 it was renewed by Sebastian Brant. Often one had simply, without thinking about it, been taking over texts which had German language forms of a time long since passed, although the linguistic obscurity must have stood in the way from the beginning of the dissemination of works. Even the first printed German Bible translation rested on an old textual pattern that was hard to understand.[48]

Wolfram of Eschenbach's *Parzival* and the *Titurel* (held to be Wolfram's work) likewise were scarcely intelligible in the first Strasbourg edition, and probably for this reason they did not have a second edition. Lacking everwhere were the forces that would have linguistically transformed the transmitted texts and made them palatable. There was not yet a fully formed German language for writing. Printing also had here an enormous function to fulfill, and the gradual development of a common German langugage is connected with it in the closest way. The German language has been primarily promoted in the books that were decorated with pictures, and this factor can certainly not be overestimated. Only through the picture did the German book really become a reading book that penetrated a wider circle.[49]

In the *Spiegel menschlicher Behaltnis* ("Mirror of the Human Behavior") of 1476 the publisher wrote: "I hold nothing to be more necessary or useful in this present life than that a man should know his Creator and his own nature. This knowledge may be had by the learned from literature; the unscholarly, however, should be instructed through books for the laity—that is, by the pictures. And for the praise and glory of God and the instruction of the unlearned I want, with God's help, to make a books for laymen!"[50] In a similar way the translator of the *Vier Historien von Joseph, Daniel, Judith und Esther* ("Four Stories of Joseph, Daniel, Judith and Esther"), which was published with pictures by Albrecht Pfister in Bamberg, justified his transcription into German. The German Bible translation has also taken on this high evaluation of the picture. It was always decorated ever more richly with pictures and became still in the fifteenth century one of the most beautiful block books of the time. Even Luther (who was, generally speaking, not very disposed towards pictures) has recognized and utilized the attracting power of the illustrated Bible.

In the older German block books, printing had first to create for itself the necessary aids – the artistic as well as the linguistic ones. For us today, it is astounding how few names of authors or publishers of their own period we encounter in the first half century of the incunabula period – and how quickly they are listed, such as Heinrich Steinhöwel, Albrecht von Eyb, Hans Neithart, Niklas von Wyle, Johann Hartlieb, Stephan Fridolin, Marquard von Stein and a few others. And most of them were active not as independent authors, but only as the translators of old literary items. Frequently the contemporary scholars (who were all Latinists) have initially, through the strong demands for the printing of German books, come to translations, and in this roundabout way, to the actual shaping of the German language. "Eigen gedicht wer mir zu schwer, latein zu teutschen ist min (be) ger" ("A poem of my own is too difficult, Latin to translate into German is my desire,")[51] says Heinrich Steinhöwel in his first attempt at translation.

One can trace precisely the groping of the printer of new attractive materials, as they looked beyond the edification and pious books for other cultural nourishment. Little by little there were published descriptions[51A] of the Middle Age's most significant traveller, Marco Polo, of Montevilla, Breydenbach, Tucher, & Schildberger; published also were the chronicles of Lirer, Rolevinck, Schedel, the lawbooks of the Saxonian *Spiegel* as well as of the Swabian *Spiegel*, the golden *Bull* of Emperor Charles IV, the municipal laws of Nuremberg and Worms, and the regulations of the Supreme Court of Justice. Also coming out were scientific and medical works, such as Konrad of Merseberg's *Buch der Natur* ("Book of Nature"), the *Herbarius*, the medical book of Ortolff of Bavaria, the *Regimen sanitatis*, which is about regulating health, and the book on surgery by Hieronymus Brunswig.

In addition to Augsburg, the imperial city of Ulm early became a busy center of the German block books. It was above all Johann Zainer, Leonhard Holle and Konrad Dinckmuth who looked out for the new types of books and who, through consultation with good artists, knew how to develop the woodcut successfully from the purely outline designs to more independent black-white effects.

Johann Zainer's *Boccaccio* of 1473 and the Aesop edition of 1477,[52] (with the famous picture of Aesop), both of them translated by the Ulm physician, Heinrich Steinhöwel, the book of wisdom of the old masters attributed to an Indian sage, of 1483, with 126 beautiful woocuts,[53] and printed by Leonhard Holle; Konrad Dinckmuth's edition of the *Chronicles of Swabia* of Thomas Lirer (1486), and the *Eunuchus* of Terence, from the same year[54] (translated by the councillor Hans Neithart), who received twenty-eight bound copies and thirty-nine more copies of the *Chronicles of Lirer* – all these are among the most appealing block books that the incunabula period has presented to Germans in that era.

An artistically especially distinguished wood cut book was published toward the end of the seventh year in Cologne: the Cologne Bible that was probably produced by the printer, Heinrich Quentel. With its bold woodcuts, it has influenced all the picture Bibles that followed it until Dürer and Holbein. Only a significant artist could have created such figures.[55]

One of the most progressive books (in terms of both its contents and its pictures) of the fifteenth century was published on June 24, 1486, in Latin and German at

Mainz, in the publishing house of the artist, Erhart Reuwich: the trip to the Holy
Land of the Mainz Cathedral dean, Bernhard von Breydenbach; it has quickly gone
through twelve editions and translations. In the preface, with its dedication to Archbishop Berthold, the author reports that he had applied special diligence on the
trip to research and experience all things differently as there would be a need so
to know them, and he also took with him a good painter, "who depicted the notable
places on water, land and especially the holy places, and also actually painted
Jerusalem, so that the resulting book that describes such a trip would be more
enjoyable, and so through its writing it would serve reason and through its figures
it would serve sight." Numerous woodcuts represent Venice, Jerusalem and other
cities, or they reflect previously unknown peoples, and also pictures of animals from
the East. The work is the first German block book which gives us the name of the
artist.

Erhard Reuwich, the travelling companion and draftsman, has also been the
publisher of the beautiful book in which the woodcut has already attained artistic
effects through rich cross-hatching, and for the first time the picture refers to nature
itself. Significant also is the splendid title wooduct. In its upper part it shows rich
foliage filled with roses and holly trees, with children climbing in them. These putti
which are here represented for the first time in a German woodcut have certainly
come from Italian book decoration and they will also in the future play a significant
role in German decoration. The artist may have become acquainted with the motif
in Venice during the course of his trip to the Holy Land.[56]

In the hands of good artists, the power of expression in the German block book
quickly attained the high point of its development. The Nuremberg printer, Anton
Koberger, in 1491 published Stephan Fridolin's *Schatzbehalter oder Schrein der
wahren Reichtümer des Heils und ewiger Seligkeit* ("Treasury or Shrine of the True
Riches of Salvation and Eternal Beatitude") with outstanding woodcuts; it is among
the finest accomplishments of the Nuremberg picture decoration. In the beautiful
printed work there are sixteen pictures, (in which are a variety of sacrificial animals,
there as a prefiguration of the passion of Christ, such as cow, lamb, ram and dove)
and with them, the following pretty printed indication (which was, due to the composer's negligence, printed by mistake): "And if one wishes to distribute the colors
among the named animals, then the cow should be painted red." The colors were
therefore stipulated still for this beautiful book—a further evidence of how forceful
had been the tradition of the old enjoyment of color.[57]

The most richly decorated illustrated work of the fifteenth century is Hartmann
Schedel's *Weltchronik* ("World Chronicle") of 1493, a tremendous volume that contains over two thousands woodcuts, which mostly shows small realistic representations of events, cities, buildings, and sculptures, and more than once employs the
same picture for various representations. Dürer's teacher, Michael Wohlgemuth,
has designed the drawings, along with his stepson, Wilhelm Pleydenwurff; Sebald
Schreyer (a well-to-do Nuremberg merchant) has, with Sebastian Cammermeister,
taken over the publishing; and Anton Koberger has executed the printing of the
work. It was an enormous undertaking, and the completed work has become the
most famous book of the fifteenth century. Especially have his representations of

cities (they were the first of this kind of thing) excited great attention, and even today they are no less a delight to those who are interested in them. The representation of Passau, with the beautiful rendering of the inns, the cathedral and castle, is one of the handsomest of these pictures to be observed.[58]

With a significant artist (whom research has designated as a "double" of the young Albrecht Dürer) have originated the beautiful woodcuts in the *Buch des Ritters vom Turn von den Exempeln der Gottesfurcht und Ehrbarkeit* ("Book of the Knight of Turn of Examples of Piety and Respectability"), which is the translation of a didactic poem about good and bad women, and was intended to lead to virtue and a reverence for God; it was published in 1493 by the Basel printer, Michael Furter.[59] The second edition of the handsome book, published in the year 1513, is quite remarkable on account of the borders on the title page; it is among the first of the German title frames in the Renaissance style.

The most popular block book of the fifteenth century is Sebastian Brant's *Narrenschiff* ("Ship of Fools"), printed in 1494 by the Basel printer, Johann Bergmann of Olpe, and decorated by an outstanding artist with 114 pretty pictures. It is the first printed German literary monument in which one who was knowledgeable in the language of the time has worked together with a capable artist for a significant book creation. Composed in popular, picturesque language, couched in catchy verse, filled with delightful drawings, the work (which was translated into several languages) has become the most widely read book of the period. Everyone could see himself represented here without being offended, due to the comforting word that stood written on the ship's pennant: "That's how it goes. For he who sees himself as a fool is soon made into a wise man." The author was thereby also ridiculing the book fool, who knew his favorite works only from the outside and watched over them so carefully so as to keep the flies off of them. The fine little picture of this ridicule – the book fool – has become famous.[60]

Just as the fifteenth century book as a whole was, in its search for new forms, constantly in flux, so the design of pictures was groping for new expressions. The woodcut ran through all the developments from the simple outlines of primitive picture-prints up to the painterly effects that it borrowed from copper engraving. Strasbourg went the most decisively in this direction; it was perhaps influenced by Master E.S. or by Martin Schongauer. Here the leader– the master–is Johann Grüninger, who could not do enough with such artistically effective additions. Terence and Vergil of 1502, with 214 fine woodcuts, which introduce us to the world of the Roman poets in the garb of Strasbourg citizens and Alsatian peasants, are the oldest examples of such book decoration. In Sebastian Brant printing has found a well-informed and also artisitic counselor, who was filled with understanding; hence, in Strasbourg there has developed from the earliest period, a fruitful relationship between the city's scholars and its printers, following Basel's example.

Also among the consequences of Gutenberg's discovery was the fact that in the book there emerged a broad field of activity for the artist. And the artists gladly seized the opportunity and developed the woodcut deriving from the book into its highest flowering.[61] The variety of the works created here is inexhaustible. Lübeck has also contributed significantly thereto, and has given to contemporaries an impressively designed *Totentanz*[62] and a picture Bible as well, which was one of those published by the printer Steffen Arndes in 1494, which in its expressive power remains unsurpassed.[63] In 1498, Lübeck has dedicated to the Low German literature a translation, decorated with pictures, of *Reynke de Vos*. The animal fable, which comes from an essentially older period, has gradually become part of world literature. Goethe has recreated it, and has praised it as "the unholy world Bible" with the verses: "Did a poet sing this centuries ago? The material is, yes, of yesterday and today."

The culmination of the artistic development in the block book was attained in Albrecht Dürer's picture supplement to *Offenbarung des hl. Johannes* ("Revelation of St. John") of 1498, where the woodcut has been developed into an independent art. The lines have here experienced a growth in their effectiveness that will not ever be surpassed. The representations themselves have become definitive for the German apocalyptic imagination. As with the picture of the Man of Sorrows, so here has Dürer become exemplary, too.[64]

So has the art of woodcut, grafted onto the book, known how to shape artistically the inexhaustible rich materials. And vice versa, the book has, by this relationship with the woodcut, been significantly elevated — its attractiveness has increased, and its readership has been extended.

In order to distinguish and embellish textbooks and school books in the incunabula period, the practice was adopted of supplying the title page with a woodcut, which represented a teacher with his pupils, instructing them. Often there has been added to the picture the inscription: "Accipies tanti doctoris dogmata sancta" ("You will receive the holy teaching of an important teacher"). The representation has thus received the designation of *"Accipies* woodcut." It appears that the Cologne printer, Heinrich Quentel, has been the first to introduce the little pictures and has applied them in about eighty of his printed works. Numerous variations of the woodcut in the fifteenth century are a good aid in determining those printed works which tell us nothing about their origin.[65]

Printing meant an essential advance for the book in the German language. If one compares the period shortly before Gutenberg with the decades that followed him, only a relatively few manuscripts in the German language are to be found, while the period around 1500 A.D., in spite of the ascendancy of the Latin literature, was already exhibiting six hundred editions of books. If we set the number of copies for an individual book at only a hundred, 60,000 copies of books in German had been issued.[66] Even if the printers could not sell their stock, the German book was thus already disseminated in considerable range throughout the whole of Germany. One was now reading considerably more and in a wider circle than was the case before Gutenberg. Printing penetrated into the people, the actual soil within which every healthy literature must make its root. Even if this harvest brought with it much that was absurd, this increased dissemination of the German literary stock in any case had one consequence: the German language grew with it, it gained expressive power and richness in words, as well as uniformity.

We certainly cannot overestimate these efforts of the masters of the new art concerning the German book, if we consider how difficult it was for them to find German texts in intelligible language and form. Latin had its long development behind it — yes, in the models of the classical writers it was now experiencing a new flowering period and in this renewal was enchanting mankind. There were here sufficient people who could select the text, examine it and proofread it during the printing process.

The German language, on the other hand, was still completely undeveloped; as yet, it had no rules for grammar, for correct writing, or for a beautiful style. There scarcely existed outstanding texts for distribution. The printers were here searching entirely in the dark; they just had to make up the rules, to arouse those forces that would assist them; they had to recruit new circles of readers. And they had success on their side. The scholars increased in number who became interested in the first rediscovered German literature, and in Emperor Maximilian I there soon arose a powerful protector, who with the *Theuerdank* made the German block book presentable at court, and thus lent it an increased valuation. Therein is to be seen the great mission and meaning (relative to the history of the book) of these works that were printed by the court. The book represented an effective incursion of the German language then experienced in Luther's Bible translation and his pamphlets.

There is no doubt that Luther had read the old German books with pleasure, especially the Bible translations, and that he learned a lot from this. Even the humanist, Joachim Camerarius (who was completely preoccupied with Latin), acknowledges in his preface to the Psalter translation of his friend, Johannes Claus on December 24, 1541: "Although I indeed have not used my days in particularly industrious exercise of the German of my native tongue, yet in my youth I have undertaken to read old German books and at times also to write German, and I have therefore in a certainly not superficial experience come to speak of the quality of this language, the meaning of the words and its patterns." For a humanist, that was lot to say. On the other hand, we hear what Johannes Cochläus, another spirited humanist, writes concerning the German language in 1523 in his work, *Gloss und Comment auf 154 Artikel, gezogen aus einer Sermon Doctor Martin Luthers von der hl. Mess* ("Gloss and Commentary on the 154 articles, drawn from a sermon by Doctor Martin Luther on the holy Mass"): "Say to Luther: the German language? How long has it been written? Show me a German book that is six hundred years old — yes, that is four hundred years old. For every leaf I'll give you a florin." Many other humanists of the time thought like Cochläus.

The fact that ushered in here was a powerful revolution of the way things were conceived, the German language owes not merely to the leader of the new church movement, but also to the cooperation of the German printers. The humanist, Johann Altensteig, was already writing in 1523 in his *Unterricht, was ein Christenmensch tun oder Lassen soll* ("Instruction on what a Christian should do or leave undone") that he would write in German, "so one wants it more and will read it, than is the case with Latin." Lorenz Fries defended himself in 1530 against his opponent, who had found fault with him, maintaining that he had written German in his *Spiegel der Arznei;* ("Mirror of Medicine"). "It also seems to me that the

German tongue is no less worthy for all things to be described in it than are Greek, Hebrew, Latin, Italian, Spanish, and French, in which one finds everything translated. Should our language be any less? No, it should indeed be much more. Because it is an original language, not assembled by begging from Greek, Latin, the Huns and Goths, as is French; and it is also more regulated." Other scholars also, such as Simon Minervius, Valentin Boltz, Sebastian Franck, and Wilhelm Holtz, attended to the dissemination of the German language in books.

It is impossible in a few pages to demonstrate the whole enormous creation of printing workshops of the waning Middle Ages—even only the most important monuments among them. As in Germany, so also in Italy, in France, in Spain, and in the Netherlands, outstanding book creations appeared, in which especially script and illustration were integrated to produce an impressive effect. Still, several significant foreign printed works might be least be mentioned. The much admired block book of Robertus Valturius *De re militari*, which was printed in 1472 at Verona by Johannes Nicolai, and embellished with beautiful pictures by the hand of the Veronese artist, Matteo de' Pasti; several printed works of the German master, Nicolaus Laurentii (who was active at that time in Florence) that were decorated with beautiful copper engravings, such as Antonio Bettinis' *Monte Santo di Dio* of 1478, the Dante edition of 1481 and the geography of Francesco Berlinghieri of about 1481,[67] the *Totentanz* edition, *Danse macabre* of the Parisian printer, Guy Marchant, of 1485; the *Compost et Calendrier des bergers* of the same master, from 1491, which was decorated with scary representations of the punishments of Hell; the most famous French block book, *Mer des histoires* of 1488, which was printed by Pierre le Rouge, and decorated with wonderful initials; the *Chevalier déliberé* of Olivier de la March from 1486, which was to influence later the *Theuerdank*;[68] the Terence by the Lyons citizen, Johann Trechsel of 1493, which was the most significant block book in Lyons. Revealing itself in all of these works was an increased power of expression in the book decorated with pictures that was without precedent.

Among the Spanish printed works, an externally insignificant work (but one that an account of its contents was of the highest significance) ought to be mentioned: the report of the seafarer, Columbus, concerning the discovery of the supposedly western islands, which really represented a new continent; it was printed for the first time in 1493 by Pedro Posa in Barcelona.

The marvelous radiance streaming from Gutenberg's handsome Bible has extended to the whole of printing in the decade that followed. The incunabula period belongs forever to the typographical high points in the history of printing. The worthy designing of books was the most serious concern of all involved; in its production during the period there had to be assumed at the same time the expression of the increased refinement of life generally, and of the feeling for beauty, which the economic growth of cities had generated. An immense joy in books—in the content of them as well as in their form—ruled the men of that time. Bibliophily indeed knew no bounds. In 1507, the humanist, Christoph Scheurl of Wittenberg (where he had shortly before moved as a professor at the new university) travelled to Bologna, in order to pay old book debts from his student days there; after a short while he has returned to Wittenberg—with new books and new book debts!

And there were truly already enough books. When about fifty years had passed since Gutenberg's discovery, and one was writing about 1500, there were already in Western Europe about thirty thousand printed works in thirty million copies, the majority of them in folio volumes. Whole houses were already preparing themselves to serve, through long generations, the production and distribution of the book. After a hundred years, the family of Aldus Manutius could look back on a total performance amounting to 1049 printed works, among them being 628 classical authors.[69]

Since this many books had to bound, there resulted also a significant stimulation of the bookbinding industry. As had already been the case with manuscripts, with the oldest printed works also the wood boards covered with leather constituted the most common protection for the book. The leather cover was decorated with all sorts of ornaments that were stamped into it: for this purpose one made use of individual stamps, or later, of larger metal plates, and also of rolls. Everything was enlisted that there was in the stock of ornaments, beginning with animals (the lion, eagle, stag, dog, hare) and plants (the rose, the lily) and going on up to the pious representations of Christ, of Mary and of the Lamb of God. The plates were filled with all sorts of images, of all the holy figures; there were also garlands of leaves. It was an excellent craftsmanship that was here applied; it was connected with the effort to lend a decorative appearance to the protective covering.

If one still wanted to shape the binding in an especially unique way, one would cut with a knife an artistic ornament into the leather that came from the plant and animal world; and thereby one effectively made the covers more interesting. These are the much admired leathercut bindings, which are among the greatest treasures of the old binding art.[70] For the protection of the bindings, the covers were frequently furnished with metal mountings, and in the middle of the covers a hump was placed, on which the book rested when open. Clamps or braces were supposed to protect the interior of the book from dust and from the full light of day. On occasion, the clamps were added; with these the bindings could be fastened to the post of the desk *(libri catenati)*.

In many cases, the stamps that had been pressed in divulged the names of the individual book binding master and therewith offered valuable organizing clues for retrospective research into book covers. The bookbinding stamp of the Nuremberg Dominican, Conrad Forster, from the period of 1433–1456, is famous. Its peculiarity consisted in the fact that it was composed not as a single piece, but out of individual letters and it therefore allowed the printing of moveable letters. Other names of bookbinders that are known from their stamps are: Johann Richenbach from Geislingen from the years 1467–1470, Ambrosius Keller and Andres Jüger from Augsburg, Jorg Wirffel in Ingolstadt, Johann Rucker in Eichstätt, Johann Hagmeyer in Ulm, and Franz Staindorffer in Nuremberg. Several bookbinder stamps, with the names or arms of monasteries, such as Tegernsee,[71] Rebdorf, Ebersberg, Benediktbeuern, and St. Emmeran, show us that numerous monasteries of this period had bookbinderies.[72]

14
The German Book Possessions
of the Waning Middle Ages

Printing has completely transformed not only the externals of the book; it has also altered entire collections of books, whether these were in scholars' rooms, in the vaults of monasteries, or in the rooms of universities. A brief survey will attempt to show through several examples the destinies and the radical changes in this transitional period from the manuscript to printing.

Four hundred fifty books, manuscripts and printed works were purchased for about 1100 florin at the Benedictine monastery of Tegernsee in the period from 1461 to 1492 under Abbot Konrad Airnschmalz.[1] A catalog of the year 1484 contained 1130 items, and a second one of 1494 was already listing 1738 items; within a decade, therefore, the total holdings had increased by about 635 works. The monastery compiled a new list in 1500, and in 1524 it contained over 1800 titles. The manuscriptural admonition concerning use by the librarian is remarkable; he was concerned for the salvation of the reader's soul. Instead of Vergil, the monks are rather to read Sedulius, and instead of Ovid, Alcuin; instead of Propertius, Lactantius, instead of Statius, Arator; instead of Catullus, Prosperus; instead of Tribullus, Juvencus; instead of Horace, Prudentius; instead of Marital, Hermann von dem Busche; instead of Lucan, Gualther (Burleaus); and instead of Juvenal, Baptista Mantuanus. None of the numerous book collections which have wound up in Munich following the dissolution of the monasteries at the beginning of the nineteenth century has contained so many and such well maintained incunabula (abundantly provided with rare pamphlets) as Tegernsee; these were a worthy supplement to the same monastery's priceless manuscript collection (numbering up to two thousand).

An equally vital cultural life was dominant also in the Benedictine monastery of SS. Ulrich and Afra in Augsburg.[2] The learned abbot, Melchior von Stamhaim, had a library room built there in 1471, and in the following year he built a monastery printery; during the hours when they were not praying, the monks were supposed to be active here with writing, correcting, printing, rubricating, and binding; and through the exchanging of books they were supposed at the same time to enrich the library. The undertaking was intended to revive in modern form the scriptorium that had been suspended. The books printed at the monastery were given away, or they were exchanged for other works. But at SS. Ulrich and Afra the quiet writing activity blossomed also. The artistic Leonhard Wagner began in 1489 to write a *Graduale* for the choir; it was executed in wonderful letters on parchment; for a few years he (together with his pupil, Balthasar Karmer) was released from singing in the choir in order to be able to produce two psalters. He had become best known for his specimen of type, which was dedicated to Emperor Maximilian I,[3] and his portrait has been drawn by no less a figure than Hans Holbein.

In the monastery of Michelsberg at Bamberg, Abbot Ulrich II Haug (1475–1483) had the library richly increased, and in 1481 he called the Nuremberg printer, Johann Sensenschmidt, to the post of provost at St. Getreu in Bamberg in order to have him print a Benedictine missal in five hundred, and a *Collectarius* (an exposition of the Psalms) in a hundred, copies. It was undoubtedly this task that induced the printer to set himself up entirely in the episcopal see city and to transfer his interests wholly to liturgical printing. To the industrious scribal activity of this monastery under Abbot Andreas Lang (1483–1502), we owe not merely significant monuments of an excellent scribal school, but also knowledge of the book holdings in this collection from the year 1483; it then had 510 volumes. Abbot Ulrich has inserted into his own monastery history valuable old book catalogs from the period of Abbot Wolfram I (1112–1123) and Hermann I (1123–1147), according to which it can be established (among other things) that the initial preparation of the great *Weltchronik* ("World Chronicle") did not originate from Ekkehard or Aura, but rather from the Michelsberg monk, Frutolf (d. 1103). The same source also transmits to us the catalog of the bookbindery that belonged to the monastery. As in Tegernsee, Ebersberg, and Scheyern, artistic monks in Bamberg have also bound the books themselves. Entries and accounts for the purchasing of red-colored leather, brass mountings, nails for books, buckles and other materials for book covers, have likewise been preserved for us from the Benedictine monastery of Liesborn (near Lippstadt).

It almost seems as if the Benedictine monastery of this period had consciously attempted to take over little by little the prominence that the mendicant orders enjoyed in scholarship. The intensified cultural life lay in the direction of that significant renewal of the monasteries which was associated with the church council at Basel, and which had become especially effective and successful in the Bursfelde congregation. The same active enthusiasm that there was in Tegernsee, Augsburg, and Bamberg is also to be observed in St. Emmeram at Regensburg, in Ottobeuren, in Sponheim, at St. James in Mainz, and in Melk an der Donau. In St. Emmeram, Dionysius Menger carried through a new organization of the library in 1500 and, in connection therewith, he separated the books into groups of parchment volumes, of paper manuscripts, and printed works.[4] That the monastery knew well how to value its treasures and to protect them is made clear from the visit by the humanist, Conrad Celtes. He had to bring two civil attestations with him, in the time of Abbot Erasmus Münzer, when he wanted to borrow the manuscriptural poems of the nun, Hrotswitha.[5] Although Celtes carelessly handed over the precious manuscript (it is the best transmission of the text) to the printers' workshops, so that still today it shows red chalk marks, it has nevertheless been returned to the monastery and is now kept in Munich (Cod. lat. 14485).

Following the example of SS. Ulrich and Afra in Augsburg, Ottobeuren has also built a monastery printery in 1509. Abbot Leonhard Wiedemann, in his foreword to the first work printed there (an edition of Alcuin's writings on the Trinity), praised work as a blessing, and he cursed laziness as the source of all depravity. It was in order to guard his flock from this deadly pest that, at great cost, he had founded a printery, which should give to the brothers of the Order a noble and useful undertaking. This work, which was initiated with such hope, has, it must be admitted, soon been given up again.[6]

The abbey of Sponheim in the Hunsrück surpassed in eminence all the clerical book collections of the declining fifteenth century. It served as the temporary operating base for the scholarly abbot, Johannes Trithemius (1462–1516), who was one of those best acquainted with the book world of the time, as well as with the sources of German history. Through indefatigable collecting, he gradually assembled two thousand volumes which were, in fact, the principal sources for his scholarly history of the literature of ecclesiastical authors *De scriptoribus ecclesiasticis.*[7] The abbot, who was devoted to books, could show his proud collection to many prominent visitors such as Celtes, Reuchlin, Cuspinian, Dalberg and Wimpfeling. Since 1506 abbot of St. James monastery in Würzburg, Trithemius had the knowledgeable monk, Paul Lang, search for German history sources in numerous mansteries, such as Lüneburg, Halberstadt, Erfurt, Andechs, and Groningen.

The example of Sponheim has not remained without influence. That is evidenced by the competition of St. James monastery at Mainz, where the Benedictine Wolfgang Trefler, a scholarly friend of the abbot of Sponheim, carefully catalogued the books of his monastery in 1512, and in close connection with Trithemius, provided brief biographies, with bibliographical reports.[8] A brief survey of the development of the library, along with the supplmentary old book lists from the years 1186 and 1444, have enhanced the value of these catalogs, which are unique combinations of catalog and literary information.

Among the Cistercian monasteries of the waning Middle Ages, it was especially Altzelle in the time of the scholarly abbot, Martin von Lochau (1493–1522), that made a good start toward a stimulating cultural life. The book list of the year 1514 listed 960 works that were lying on small desks. For purposes of designation, the individual disciplines carried various colors: theology was red, jurisprudence was black and medicine, green. A manuscript of the eleventh century that was acquired in 1500 (Claudianus Mamertus' treatise on the condition of souls, or, *De statu animae)* the humanist, Petrus Mosellanus, took as the basis for his first edition of the year 1500. Abbot Martin himself published the sermon of St. Bernard, *Stabat iuxta crucem Jesu mater,* in 1516, and he emphasized in the preface thereof that the monastery library had been zealously searched. In the year after that, the monk, Michael Smelczer, who with numerous copies eagerly contributed to the library's increase, followed up with a printing of an introduction to music by St. Bernard which was taken from one of the monastery's manuscripts.

Numerous accounts of the fifteenth century from Klosterneuberg (the Augustinian Canons' foundation at Kahlenberg near Vienna) reflect the activity of the writing room there with the expenditures for writing or copying, for parchment, for the illustrations, for bookbinding, and for chains and rooms, have been preserved.[9]

Individual Carthusian monasteries also owned handsome libraries.[10] Johann Heylin, called *a Lapide* (d. 1496), whose name is inextricably associated with the introduction of printing at the Sorbonne in Paris, made a gift to the Basel Carthusians of 165 valuable manuscripts and printed works, among them some valuable items of French provenance. The monastery had a close relationship with the Basel printer. A remarkable rule book from the monastery's library from 1509 is known to us.[11] In another Carthusian monastery, the foundation of St. Bruno, La Grande Chartreuse near Grenoble, an enthusiastic German bibliophile, the Ermland canon and historiographer of the Knights of the Teutonic Order, Laurentius Blumenau, has retired in 1475, so as to be able to dedicate himself wholly here to his books and to a life of piety. The monastery received through him as a present the printed Mainz Catholicon, among other things. The residue of his possessions, above all the law books (among which were ten Bartolus prints, and further, two manuscripts containing Vergil and Orosius), still bear his bookmark, and are now preserved in the Municipal Library of Grenoble.

According to listings of 1457, the manuscripts (three hundred in all) in the Cathedral Library at Chur lay on eight desks in this sequence: canon law, secular law, the sentences and theologians, Bible manuscripts, Bible exegeses and sermons, collections of letters, chronicles, philosophy, medicine and poets.

Unusual manuscripts, forty-two Hebrew texts presented by Duke Albrecht IV of Bavaria, most of them items from the Talmud and Talmudic expositions, came into the Dominican monastery at Regensburg in 1476; there they were catalogued by the scholarly citizen of Inglostadt, Professor Petrus Nigri, with the help of the Jewish rabbi, David, from Eichstätt.[12] They were supposed to serve in combatting Judaism. The year before, Nigri had dedicated to the Regensberg bishop, Heinrich IV, of Absberg, a writing of his against the Jews; it is one of the oldest anti-Semitic printed works.[13]

We must still consider the Brothers of the Common Life, that spiritual brotherhood of pious priests founded by Gerhard Groote (1340–1384) and Florentius Radewin (1350–1400). The Brothers considered (in addition to prayer) the writing of spiritual (above all, liturgical) books as being a vocation pleasing to God, and they supplied churches and monasteries with their copies for a small payment. When printing put a stop to their activity, they transferred to the new modes of copying and they founded printeries in various places, such as in Deventer, Zwolle, Gouda, Herzogenbusch, Brussels, Louvain, Marienthal,[14] and Rostock;[15] still, they were not very successful. From the same circle there has been issued in that period the significant work, *The Imitation of Christ*, which, translated into all languages, has become one of the most widely read books in the world. Gerhard Groote, or the mystic Thomas à Kempis, may be claimed as its author; the latter died on July 25, 1471, as sub-prior of the monastery on the Agnetenberg near Zwolle. Up until the year 1500, fifty-three text-editions of the work and thirty translations (six German, four French, fifteen Italians, four Spanish) had already been published.

Today there are over three thousand editions and transcriptions of this contemplative book of devotion.[16] "It is the final achievement in which the old-fashioned Christianity speaks to all, and can say something to all." (Rud. Eucken.)

Among the institutions within the cultural life of the late Middle Ages that were most capable of development were the universities; they have originated after the twelfth century, first in Italy (Bologna, Salerno, Padua), in France (Paris) and in England (Oxford, Cambridge). Germany followed with Prague (1348), Vienna (1365), Heidelberg (1386), Cologne (1388), Erfurt (1392), Leipzig (1409), Rostock (1419), Greifswald (1456), Freiburg (1457), Basel (1460), Inglostadt (1472), Tübingen (1477), Wittenberg (1502), and Frankfurt an der Oder (1506). Where (as here) science, professionally considered (and not merely theological knowledge) was taught, the book also found a favorable environment. Bookdealers *(stationarii),* copiers, preparers of parchment and book decorators settled down, and as members of the higher schools, they were endowed with rights and with liberties. Smaller or larger book collections were soon being assembled in close connection with the individual colleges and faculties. Here we find the initial approaches to a new book industry that, even though it is also dependent on the medieval world view like the monastic collection of books, has nevertheless extended beyond them as well as into wider circles. The beginnings of the future university library are here. Emperor Charles IV bestowed on his university foundation the most necessary books immediately from the beginning. The scholarly physician and mathematician, Johann Sindel (d. 1443), has given it two hundred manuscripts by bequest.[17]

When the holdings of the University of Heidelberg were catalogued in 1396, the following groups of books were already present there: 215 theological, juristic, natural historical, and philosophical manuscripts from the legacy of the Worms dean, Conrad von Gelnhausen; 114 theological, natural-historical and philosophical manuscripts acquired from the faculty of arts, forty-six of them being volumes presented by the Master, Gerhard von Emelissa, and 235 books encompassing all areas of knowledge, given by Prof. Dr. Marsilius von Inghen.

The school of higher learning in Erfurt obtained a valuable collection when the professor of medicine, Amplonius Ratinck, who founded the *Collegium Amplonianum* (it was named for him) for the education (free of charge) of fifteen students, gave to it in 1412 his library of 635 medical, mathematical and theological manuscripts.[18]

Dr. Heinrich Rubenow donated to the newly founded University of Greifswald all his books on November 11, 1456. They were supposed to be designated by his name and only to be lent out within the compass of the city itself—and then only with the surrender by the borrower of something as a pledge. This eager collector also proposed a library for the faculty of arts and donated books for it.[19]

When, on April 30, 1460, the first rector of Freiburg, Matthäus Hummel, spoke at the opening of the university concerning the bad neglect of the books, he indeed was only speaking words based on the *Philobiblon* of the Englishman, Richard de Bury;[20] he was nevertheless the cause of a stimulating interest being given to the books from the beginning. A special library room within the faculty of arts can be authenticated as having existed in 1462. In the oldest regulations of the library, it is stipulated that only the less important (and unchained) books might be lent. On March 17, the dean summoned all the masters to an investigation concerning whether good Aristotle manuscripts should not be acquired. After 1470, we regularly encounter formal requests for handing over keys to the library; the purchases from estates, or from the book trade, increase in number. On October 31, 1495, the well known humanist, Jakob Locher, obtained a Pliny text; when he took the book with him to Inglostadt without getting permission, the faculty admonished him on June 8, 1499, to return it. A world map was acquired on September 7, 1495; there later followed a Ptolemy edition, which was acquired for seven florins.[21]

An Aristotle manuscript was purchased for four florins in 1476 at the university in Ingolstadt (founded 1472); four years after that, the Arts faculty installed a book room in the Avicenna lecture room. Several presents followed after 1481; these were from the possessions of the Regensburg canon, D. Johann Tröster; among them were manuscripts that had been acquired in Rome and Florence and which contained Plautus, Curtius, Plutarch, Cicero and Boccaccio.[22] Each book bore the arms of the arts faculty with a picture of St. Catherine and the signature of the university notary.[23] In 1496, the faculty obtained books for 110 florins from the Augsburg bookdealer, Johann Rynmann: the seller added to the lot a Baldus edition, as his gift. When the contentious humanist, Conrad Celtes, applied for entry into the arts library on May 1, 1494, the faculty did indeed hand over a key to him, but it made him promise to conduct himself becomingly toward faculty members.

Participation by the universities in the production of incunabula has been surprisingly small. It was primarily the advancing humanism, especially in Leipzig, which entered into association with printing. In the history of incunabula, the schools of higher learning have played as good as no role at all.

The philosophical faculty of the University of Cologne in 1474 constructed a catalog *(Tabula)* in the form of a broadside of their book holdings, which were accommodated on twelve racks. Thanks to a special bit of good fortune, the catalog has been preserved on front papers that a bookbinder has used for covers.[24]

Just as the university library followed upon the founding of the higher school, so in the cities, the municipal library came subsequent to the increase in education. There are the secular disciplines (and especially the works of jurisprudence and medicine) that these libraries covered, and they were supposed to serve professional life. The users of these new institutions were city scribes, legal assistants, city physicians, and school masters.

In Regensburg, the legal scholar and canon of St. John, Conrad von Hildesheim, willed eight valuable manuscripts to the city in 1430. The State Library in Munich still owns four of them.[25] At about the same time, the dean of the Regensburg cathedral and the Nuremberg pastor of St. Lawrence, Dr. Konrad Kunhofer, bequeathed priceless manuscripts to the city of Nuremberg; these were put with the basic stock of the Municipal Library in Nuremberg.[26] Transferred in the year 1430, the collection two years thereafter found accommodations in a room beside the office quarters and were placed under the authority of two city clerks. One of the first users was the legal scholar, Gregor von Heimburg; he had to be admonished in early 1440 to return three law manuscripts. The bequest consisted of 151 works, among which were ninety-three theological, thirty-eight jurispruden-tial, and twenty medical manuscripts. In June, 1487, the holdings comprised 371 volumes on thirty-three desks. To each desk there was attached a small tablet with the title and number of the group concerned; a large parchment double tablet cited the totality of the collection. The books themselves bore a small parchment label with the title. In the years 1486–1488, the council spent 483 florins for library pur-chases, for binding and the rubrication of 179 works. The bookseller, Michael Paul, was paid the chief sum (with 182 florins) for printed works which he had delivered.

In Ulm, the heirs of the minster pastor, Heinrich Neithart (d. 14 July 1439) built, in keeping with his last will, a library in the minster's tower, on July 5, 1443. It held five hundred books which were intended for public use. In case the family died out, 150 volumes were to go to the city itself, and the other 150 were to be sold to provide dowries for needy daughters in the city. The building of the family chapel was begun in 1444 at the northeast side of the minster, and in connection therewith, a room for the library was built around the chapel. Students of both types of law might keep the books they borrowed for eight years. After the family had died out, the foundation devolved to the city in 1658.

The municipal libraries of Brunswick, Frankfurt am Main, Leipzig, Hamburg and Lübeck also go back to the fifteenth century. In these beginnings, it was sometimes a matter of church libraries which have been supported by the city ad-ministrations. When the Brunswick pastor of St. Andrew's, Johannes von Ember, bequeathed to his presbytery a considerable book collection in 1422, an agreement was reached, according to which the congregation was responsible for the building of the room, and the pastor for attending to the library itself. The building that was then erected, a picturesque brick creation at the side of St. Andrew's presbytery which is still standing, and it may be reckoned as being among the oldest library rooms that have been preserved.

Rich holdings from the dissolved church and monastery libraries have then re-dounded in the Reformation period to particular municipal libraries.

15
The Book World of Dürer's Time

Like rings in a tree that show its years, the historical turns of the centuries are indications to human memory of the development of everything that is and that happens within easily comprehended limits; they are the organizing ranks, as man has need of them in order to be able rightly to find himself within infinity and its representation of time, and in order to gain concrete ideas from the flow of events. If we think on the sixteenth century, firmly delineated images of the period arise before us. Immediately we see at the beginning of the period the enormous increase in art and science, and of the great artists, Leonardo da Vinci, Raphael, Michaelangelo, Dürer, Grünewald, Holbein, and added to these there is Erasmus of Rotterdam, the towering leader of a surprisingly brilliant cultural life. Following then is Martin Luther, the destroyer of the world's medieval unity, and the founder of the Evangelical faith. We experience, as it were, the Peasant's War, the colliding of the territorial principalities with the imperial dominion in the Schmalkald War, the Augsburg religious peace, with its final unfortunate division of the German people, the renewal of the old church and the vigorously advancing Counter-reformation.

In addition to Erasmus, we encounter in the intellectual life of Europe: on the Italian soil, Lodovico Ariosto (1474–1533), with his significant epic poem, *Orlando Furioso* (1516 and 1532);[1] Torquato Tasso (1544–1595), with his much-read poem *Gerusalemme liberata* (1581); Count Baldassare Castiglione (1478–1529), the author of the widely disseminated treatise *Il Cortegiano* (1528); the statesman, Niccolo Machiavelli (1469–1527), with his much-praised, and much-reviled political publication, *Il principe* (1532); the defender of, and martyr to free thought and inquiry, Giordano Bruno (1548–1600), who in his farewell to Wittenberg praised as the three great Germans, Nicholas of Cusa, Copernicus and Paracelsus, who had opened up new paths in philosophy. In France, the satirist, François Rabelais (1495–1553), wrote his novel (which later influenced Fischart), *Gargantua et Pantagruel* (1532/35),[2] and Michel de Montaigne (1533–1593) wrote his brilliant *Essais* (1580/85). In England, the statesman and humanist, Thomas More, writes his eternally valuable novel of world improvement, *Utopia*, which his friend, Petrus Aegidius, published in Louvain in 1516; and William Shakespeare begins his immortal career. In Germany, the linguistically adroit Franciscan, Thomas Morner, (1475–1535), applies himself to the satire against the Wittenberg reformer,[3] *Von dem grossen lutherischen Narren, wie ihn D. Murner beschworen hat* ("Concerning

113

the great Lutheran fool, as conjured up by D. Murner") (1522); the surgeon, Philippus Aureolus Theophrastus Paracelsus (1493–1541), who was striving for a universal world concept, glorifies the human soul as the microcosm and as the prototype of the world, and rejects the ancient medical models, Galenus and Avicenna, as well as book learning, and leaves behind only four books, none of them medical; the popular poet, Hans Sachs (1494–1576), treats the whole of life in his verses, as well as the follies in his time; the popular books, *Eulenspiegel*, of Doctor Faustus, and about the *Schildbürger* are produced; the satirist, Johann Fischart (1545–1590) hurls his *Flöhatz* (1573) ("Fleahunt"), his *Jesuiterhütlein* (1580) ("Little Jesuit hats") and other satires against the papacy, or the world's absurdity; the Franciscan, Johann Nas (1534–1590), who was an eloquent writer, continues Thomas Murner's struggle against Lutheranism. With its increased eloquence and distribution, the book now assumes a vital role in all the affairs of public life, as well as in the intellectual movements (such as Humanism, the Reformation, the Counter-Reformation), and with its daily publications, it is also a participant in political events.

If setting the limit of the incunabula period at the turn of the century (around 1500) is something that has been gradually introduced, so this separation (although, like all temporal division, it doesn't occur precisely in the year itself) still has a certain justification in the considerable change that the book underwent about this time. What the book brings in terms of the culture's total intellectual assets has already essentially changed. Medieval Scholasticism, which is entirely dominated by theology, is threatened and superseded by humanism, which to a large extent controls the market for books. Standing in the foreground are the classic authors, the church fathers, the contemporary humanistic literature—the expression of a newly awakened need for literary communication. The physical form of the book has also changed markedly. More and more it consciously and decisively takes leave of the manuscriptural character of the early period of printing; it frees itself from the fetters of the supplementary colored ornamentations, the functionless abbreviations, the unnecessary connection between the letters, and becomes more flexible, more unified and clearer.

The most important achievement of the advance of printing is the title page, which already had been introduced here and there in the last two decades of the fifteenth century, but which now for the first time is generally prevalent and becomes an established part of the modern book. It is one of the many peculiarities of all human productions, that the greatest difficulties are often solved easily, while quite simple questions, on the other hand, require many years for their solution. Two of the oldest Mainz printed works already had regular titles, even if no actual title page as yet carried them: the *Türkenbulle* ("Turks' Bull") and the *Mahnung der Christenheit wider die Türken* ("Warning of Christendom against the Turks"). This very functional designation of the contents of the book has remained sporadic for a long time. It may have been just as it is today in villages, where one knows exactly who lives in each house, even though it is not written on the door. It is only where there was settlement in crowds, in the city, that the house sign becomes necessary. Thus the increasing abundance of printed works has called for the book label, the book title, and the title page. That all began about 1475. Executing the matter was not easy.

In line with the feeling for form that was taken over from the manuscript, early printing loved the closed block type, which filled the pages like rows of columns. How was this rule supposed to be applied to the title page? This difficulty has doubtless frustrated for a long time the firm establishment of the clear and visible designation of the book—something that in and of itself was desirable—just as even still today the functional and pleasing layout of the title page is among the most difficult questions for the designing of books. Early printing often had recourse to the underscoring the title with a woodcut illustration, which block-like, had to fill the title page and link it together. With the same purpose in mind, one occasionally fashioned the entire title page with title heading and picture, or where there was no picture, the superscription on one wood block, and through decorative design of the script (which could be kept as large as one liked), brought about quite wonderful title pages, as, for example, the shaping of the title for Albrecht Dürer's *Apocalypse* of 1511.[4]

The most functional integration of the title into a formal framed picture one then found in the decorative border, which printing needed only to take over from the much used frame of the manuscript of the Renaissance period, and to transfer it to the title page. The book extracted a double profit from the border: for one, the block format of closing off the title within a white field of paper, and after that the decorative frames, which simultaneously worked as an advertisement. The new arrangement quickly gained favor, and in the first decades of the sixteenth century it became the main design for the book, to which the period matchlessly devoted itself with care and love.[5] Well-known artists, such as Urs Graf, Daniel Hopfer, Hans Wechtlin, Hans Weiditz, Lukas Cranach, Hans und Ambrosius Holbein devoted themselves to the book and decorated it with exquisite creations of the finest small artistic work. The impinging Renaissance forms added still significantly to the number of these forms. The beautiful frames designed in about 1516 by Holbein with nine puttos, of which two bear the title frame, and two others the printer's sign of Johann Froben's (Butsch: Taf. 41) is one of the earliest Renaissance ornamental borders, and from the aspect of art history, it is additionally remarkable, in that it assigns the name of the artist. Beginnings of the insertion printer's information on the title page one also already finds occasionally, but generally speaking, this designation of the origin of the book is still reserved for the conclusion of the book until well into the sixteenth century; for such a long time afterwards, the printer's colophon of Fust & Schöffer in the Psalter of 1457 was still effectively determinant.[6]

As with the book as a whole, so also with the type design, a significant transformation occurred at about the turn to the sixteenth century. The preceding period had been one filled with an enormous wealth of forms. In this mass of book publications of the fifteenth century there is set before us an incomparable technical and aesthetic achievement. The leading forms were the strictly Gothic type, the half-Gothic rotunda, the Gothic cursive script, and the wide *Schwabach;* all of these forms again changed countless times; they were now more pointed, and then more angular, and now more fluid and connected; so do these Gothic and half-Gothic forms lend a mobile character to the page, rather like the highly individualized "play" of the manuscript in an immense number of variations, and they evoked that charming character which lends to early printing its unsurpassable vitality and puts the seal of outstanding artistry on this craftsmanship. To these Gothic types were added from Italy the rounded arch type, the Carolingian miniscule renewed by the veneration of the ancient world, and in which the humanists imagined the script of the Romans reflected. Carried along by the humanistic movement, this form (called, after its alleged origin in antiquity, *Antiqua*) was quickly disseminated and, together with the italic (a "reclining small form") that was introduced by Aldus Manutius, it was destined to become the world type of the future. The Frenchman, Nicholas Jenson, who was active in Venice, has given to it its initial, beautiful design.[7]

Influenced by the humanists, the German printers took over the Antiqua for the classic authors and for humanistic publications, and then gradually for all the works in Latin; for books in German, however, they held fast to the broken type in a decided feeling for the form with its beauty of the mobile line, and they developed these further in the same direction. The most significant creations of this development were the two publications of the prayer book (1513) and the *Theuerdank* edition (1517), which were created for Emperor Maximilian I. From these two splendid publications of the imperial chancellery there then emerged about 1525 the small but no less artistic *Fraktur* of the Nuremberg citizen, Johann Neudorfer, which Hieronymus Andrea (called *Formschneider*, or metal cutter), who was the technical collaborator of Albrecht Dürer in woodcut, artistically converted into types. With a thoroughly lively play of lines and finely structured decorative type, it was to become the German printing script of the future.

Albrecht Dürer's writings on art theory are among the earliest printed works in this script; it is through these that the new script received its special inspiration. Its pleasing form doubtless contributed to the fact that the German printers continued to prefer the broken script for the book in the German language, and they employed the *Antiqua* as something foreign for them, and only for the Latin language. Thus the year 1525 (in which the Nuremberg *Fraktur* entered upon its triumphal march) has become of the greatest significance for the history of German printing and for the German book. "It would not look well if one were to write the German language with Latin letters," the Nuremberg writing master, Wolfgang Fugger, asserted in his *Formeln mancherlei schöner Schriften* ("Forms of Many Beautiful Scripts"), and thus he gave clear expression to his period's insistence on form.[8]

Like the types, the initials also (the decorative letters of the early period of printing), which were likewise influenced by manuscriptural tradition, enjoyed as careful attention as they had scarcely enjoyed in any other period. As an established component, they had also had belonged to the sphere of the book since the end of the fifteenth century, when the woodcut was sufficiently developed to reproduce the small formations of the letters. Infinitely multi-patterned forms have been spread over the pages of books, covered all around by vines, foliage and strap-work, filled with small pictures from the life of the law or of the school, decorated with images of Ambrose, Jerome, Augustine, and Aristotle, and enlivened by children, trees and animals. Significant artists produced this work—Hans Springinklee in Nuremberg, Jörg Breu in Augsburg, Urs Graf and Hans Holbein in Basel, and Anton Woensam in Cologne. This significant small-scale artistic work experienced its highest flowering in Holbein's children's alphabet and his *Totentanz* letters.[9]

With the printer's device, the printers introduced a new book decoration. Sometimes it appeared as the printer's sign, and sometimes as the designation of the publisher. It is primarily to be seen as a manifestation of professional pride, and beyond that, as a decorative and indicative sign of the specific printer's or publisher's house. As with the initials, Fust & Schöffer had also here set the example in the beautiful double marks in metal engraving, with which they decorated their Bible of August 14, 1462, as well as further printed works. Even if it is associated with the colophons of the manuscript, where frequently the name of the scribe is found cited, the printer's device is still positively to be considered as an independent custom of printing. Again, artistic hands, such as Urs Graf, Hans Wechtlin, Hans Holbein, and later Jost Amman, Tobias Stimmer, have participated successfully in this designing of the book. The chief goal of their devices, the obvious marking of printer's and publisher's works according to where they originated, the more significant publishers and printers of that period have attained in fullest measure: the dolphin with anchor in the works of the Venetian printer, Aldus Manutius, Johann Frobern's snake and doves, the lily of the Giunta House in Florence, the printery depiction of the Paris master, Josse Bade, the fruit tree of the printers, Robert and Henri Estienne, the "Fama" of the Frankfurt publisher, Sigismund Feyerabend, Christoph Plantin's compass and his motto, "Labore et constantia"—these have become known the world over.[10]

Just as the contents of the book and book design have undergone remarkable changes in the beginning of the sixteenth century, so about the turn of the century there was a visible transformation of the working process by which books were produced and distributed: the publisher, who did not himself print books, but rather passed on his commissions, came more and more strongly to the fore. Anton Koberger at Nuremberg had commandingly presented this new phenomenon in the history of printing already at the end of the fifteenth century. Now we learn even more frequently in the printed works themselves, not merely the name of the printers, but also that of the publisher who has covered the costs of production and accomplished the book's distribution. Beside the printer's sign the publisher's device appears more and more, and proudly announces the book's originator. Among the most active of these publishers were the brothers, Leonhard and Lukas Alantsee (1505–1522) in Vienna, who printed over a hundred books (mostly with theological content) in Basel, Schlettstadt, Strasbourg, Hagenau, Tübingen, Nuremberg and Venice; Johann Rynmann (1498–1522) in Augburg, who produced 150 printed works in Augsburg, Basel, Strasbourg, Nuremberg, and Hagenau; Gottfried Hittorp and Franz Birckmann, who administered their commissions from Cologne, and who sold their books over a wide territory and even in England.[11]

A nice acknowledgement of this work is found in a quite hidden place in the dedicatory address of the Nuremberg mathematician, Johann Werner, to his Vienna publisher, Lukas Alantsee, of January 11, 1522, in the publication about curves and other mathematical objects. Werner indicates there that all educated persons owe a great debt of gratitude to the bookdealers, that there should be no more lacking in the indispensable means of assistance to study. "What do we not have to thank you for," the author more or less continues "You care for the literature and you scour the libraries, to see whether or not valuable works of old are perhaps lying in obscurity. But you even look after the author who has lived until a short while ago no less than you do those who are still living. It must seem amazing that, if it comes within your hearing, there is in any nook and cranny of Germany a man who occupies himself a bit in his leisure hours with philosophical matters, and who is quite unknown to you, you leave your house and seek out that man. So you have even come to me, in order to inspect my work."

A period which was so inspired the book—that loved it so passionately—as the age of Emperor Maximilian I and Albrecht Dürer, required of its own accord a worthy and decorative appearance for the book and with entire enthusiasm it was devoted to its care. We now enter the flowering period of the German book design.[12]

With the *Apocalypse* of 1498, Albrecht Dürer indisputably reached the pinnacle of the block book. Further picture volumes followed it in the year 1511: *The Great Passion, The Life of Mary,* the *Small Passion* and the second edition of the *Apocalypse.* In the title page of the wood-cut *Passion,* with the world's redeemer seated on a quarry-stone and sunken down in pain, Dürer has represented the pattern of the Savior's suffering quite as being the incorporation of the suffering of mankind and has thus determined the way the redeemer's humanity was conceived for centuries to come. It has become a title page significant for the world's history.

On account of their *Fraktur* types, Dürer's writings on the theory of art have attained great significance for the development of the German printing script. His name is also assigned to several woodcuts and title page borders in Nuremberg printed works, such as the title page border with the arms of Willibald Pirckheimer, the beautiful crucifixion woodcut in the Eichstätt missal of Hieronymous Höltzel of 1517, the strap work design and the Johannes frame of the printer Friedrich Peypus. The monogram of Dürer's can be affixed only to the woodcut of St. Jerome in the work translated by Lazarus Spengler, *Beschreibung Eusebii von dem Leben und Sterben des hl. Hieronymus* ("Eusebius' description of the life and the dying of St. Jerome") of the year 1514. Added to this in the copper engraving is the portrait of Elector Albrecht of Mainz in the little Halle sanctuary book of 1520.

Such first-rate blockbooks as these in the fifteenth century, Nuremburg has never seen again. Nevertheless at the beginning of the new century, there did appear book works that were still outstanding, such as the publications of the humanist, Conrad Celtes, whose own poems *(Quatuor libri amorum)* and the poems of Hrotswitha (both of them editions provided with beautiful dedicatory pictures), and further, the already mentioned *Himmlische Offenbarungen* ("Heavenly Revelations") of St. Brigitta, which the imperial proto-notary, Florian Waldauf, had printed in 1502 with Anton Koberger, at the wish of Emperor Maximilian I. Ulrich Pinder published a more extensive and beautiful blockbook in 1505 in the pious work of edification, *Beschlossener Garten des Rosenkranzes Mariae* ("Enclosed Garden of the Rosary of Mary").[13] Following it was the splendid Passau Missal of Jobst Gutknecht of 1514, the equally worthy Eichstätt Missal of Hieronymus Höltzel of 1517, the *Reformation der Stadt Nuremberg* ("Reformation of the City of Nuremberg") which was printed in 1522 by Friedrich Peypus and decorated with a beautiful set of arms in woodcut, Luther's Old and New Testaments by the same printer in the same year, and the *Wahrhaftige Beschreibung des andren Zugs in Österreich wider des Turcken, vergangene 1532. Jahres beschelen* ("A True Account of the other Campaigns Austria Against the Turks That Happened This Past Year, 1532"), which was produced in 1539 by Hieronymus Formschneider, with Michael Ostendorfer's presentation of Count Palatine Friedrich in full armor on horseback and with two large depictions of battles. Dürer's pupils, Hans Springinklee, Erhard Schön, Wolf Traut, and Hans Sebald Beham, worked as skilled minor artists in the ornamentation of the Nuremberg printed works with pictures, initials, and ornamental borders. Hans Sebald Beham decorated the *Papsttum* ("Papacy"), which was printed in 1526, with exquisite representations of Roman Catholic clergy, which stamped the book as practically an "encyclopedia of the clerical dress" of the period.

Memorable scholarly printed works proceeded from Nuremberg, effectively sponsored there by the councillors in the years 1529–1531, with the four volumes: the Greek text of the Roman law with the digests, the *Institutes*, the *Codex Justiniani* and the supplements, all of which had been prepared by the legal scholar from Zwickau, Gregor Haloander (1501–1531), on the basis of the manuscript. According to Willibald Pirckheimer's judgment, the Nuremberg Council considered it to be a glory of the city, to make known the strictly guarded law books, which until then had been kept only in Florence; in connection therewith, the city gave the publisher printing quarters for the time being, and his board in St. Giles' monastery, and it added three hundred gold florins honorarium. The printer, Johann Petreius, received four hundred florins in advance. When the city soon thereafter delegated an envoy to Emperor Charles V, they gave him the four volumes decorated with many colors and mounted with silver gilt. The present was handed over in Piacenza to the imperial chancellor for his lord. The design and preparation of these volumes had cost over seventy-seven florins.[14]

In addition to Nuremberg, Augsburg also remained for a long time in the sixteenth century a preferred city for books, in which printers and artists cared devotedly for the book. That the then emperor, Maximilian I, played here an outstanding role, and was the creative mover behind such books as the prayer book and the *Theuerdank*, is something we shall depict elsewhere. The enlistment of the Nuremberg and Augsburg artists in the decorating of these works has increased quite essentially the value given the book generally.

Year after year the Augsburg printers brought selected beautiful books on the market, such as Johann Otmar's edition, *Pomerium de tempore* of 1502, with an effective copper engraving looking like a pastel drawing on black background, which shows the author, Pelbartus de Themeswar, sitting at his writing table, or Ulrich Tengler's *Laienspiegel von rechtmässigen Ordnungen in bürgerlichen und peinlichen Regimenten* ("Lay Mirror of Legal Ordinances in Civil and criminal Laws"), of 1511, with its beautiful dedicatory pictures that represent the entire kindred of the author; further the valuable *Taschenbüchlein aus dem Ries* of 1512, or Henry Suso's *Geistliche Lehren* ("Spiritual Doctrines") of the same year, which was decorated with twenty-two woodcuts. Hans Schönsperger in 1520 decorated the attractive *Büchlein, genannt der Gilgengart* ("Little Book called the Gilgengart"), with a uniquely convoluted type, which thereafter was christened "Gilgengart script."[15]

A great music work, Ludwig Senfel's *Liber selectarum cantionum, quas mutetas apellant*, was published in November 1520 with the masters, Sigismund Grimm and Marx Wirsung; it had beautifully colored woodcuts and the arms of Cardinal Matthias Lang. The two printers wished to carry out two further large projects, and so they planned to publish Petrarch's *Von der Arznei beiden Glücks* ("Of the Medicine of both Fortunes") and the German version of Cicero, with many woodcuts. But they were thereby undertaking too much. Wirsung left his companion in 1528, and Grimm had to surrender the totality of his belongings to the creditors.[16] Filling the gap was Heinrich Steiner, and in 1531 he published the German translation of Cicero with ninety-seven woodcuts. The success was far beyond expectations. In the next few years, six subsequent editions were quickly published, one after the other. Steiner followed in 1532 with the German Petrarch edition; it had 159 woodcuts; therewith he gave to the German people one of their most beautiful books, in which German life is extensively viewed and portrayed as it scarcely is anywhere else.[17] Steiner further published in German translation Polydorus Vergilius, Justin, Plutarch, Xenophon, Demosthenes, Flavius Vegetius, and Boccaccio, which were decorated richly and randomly with pictures and ornamentation; with these, he put himself in the forefront of those printers who have promoted the German popular book. Following his economic breakdown, numerous wood blocks went to Christian Egenolf in Frankfurt and were used here as book decorations for a long time.

Book decoration with title page frame, publisher's devices and initials was cultivated especially in Basel, the city that for a long time held the leadership role in the publication of scientific books, especially the numerous classical authors, and the church fathers. The guiding master of this book ornamentation was Hans Holbein, who bespangled Basel books with borders and initials and sometimes has inserted the Sermon on the Mount, John the Baptist, God the Father, Peter and Paul, and at times, Homer (the king of poets), the exploits of Mucius Scaevolas, the history of Tantalus, Aristotle and Phyllis, Hercules and Orpheus. His initials exude, as in the children's alphabet, the carefree and playful life of children or—as in the *Totentanz* letters, the transitoriness of everything earthly.[18] Holbein's best creation in book ornamentation, his famous Bible and the *Totentanz* pictures, have first been published in 1538 at Lyons in the printery of the brothers Trechsel, Melchior and Caspar.[19] With their fine drawings and lines, they represent the high point of the German art of illustration in that period. "In his pictures of death Holbein has brought to an artistic conclusion the cultural work of centuries." (Carl von Lützow.)

Basel had the good fortune to have in Hans Lützelburger an outstanding metal cutter. Holbein and Lützelburger, Albrecht Dürer and Hieronymus Formschneider, Hans Burgkmair and Jobst Denecker — they must be named together as pairs, when the discourse concerns the flourishing period of the sixteenth century German woodcut.

It goes with the indigenous quality of early printing that each region, indeed each locality, possessed some specialty which by its products distinguished it from others. Thus the Strasbourg book of this period too has its own "face." The chief representation of book production in the dawning sixteenth century is Johannes Grüninger, the enterprising printer and publisher of numerous German block books, who in Sebastian Brant (the author of the *Narrenschiff*) had an informed advisor at his side. Evidence of this close connection is the Vergil edition of 1502, which was decorated with 214 outstanding woodcuts, and appeared much like the editions of Horace, Caesar and Terence; it showed how humanism has tried to capture the world of antiquity imaginatively. The Strasbourg artists strove as much as possible to shape the woodcut artistically through corresponding divisions of light and shadows, and to obtain the power of expression of copper engraving. Grüninger delighted in the decoration of his books. Thus in his Ptolemy edition of 1572 he was lavish with pictures of all sorts, and in a short afterword he took much pride in himself for it. The bookdealers, he believed, would wish for the greatest possible variety of pictures, frames and other decorative items on the back sides of maps. An entire book of pictures opened up before the viewer, with all kinds of wonders of the world, with representations of the morals and customs of other peoples.

When Grüninger lavished the Ptolemy edition of Willibald Pirckheimer of 1524 with equally rich decorations, the publisher resisted it with sharp words and referred to Albrecht Dürer's disapproving judgment. The scholarly publisher finally resolved his dilemma in a colophon to the effect that he could be responsible only for the text of Ptolemy and the explanations by Regiomontanus; all the rest had been added with consideration of the bookdealers, who would expect better sales. One achievement, however, Grüninger can be entitled to: through extended use of pictures he contributed to a strong increase in the demand for the book. The much honored works of Hieronymus Brunswig that are so richly decorated with pictures evidence that also: the *Buch der Chirurgia* ("Book of Surgery") and the *Buch der rechten Kunst zu destillieren* ("Book of the True Art of Distilling"). Excellent artists, such as Johann Wechtlin, Hans Baldung Grien, Urs Graf,[20] and Hans Weiditz, participated successfully in this rich life for books which there was in Strasbourg, just as linguistically gifted authors such as Johann Geiler von Kaisersberg, Hans von Gersdorf, Otto Brunfels, Thomas Murner also did.

The art of German translation was also industriously attended to in Strasbourg, especially somewhat later by the preacher, Casper Hedio, who was the same one who, seeing far beyond his own time, has proposed to the Palatine Elector, Otto Heinrich, a library for the people. Augustine, Ambrose, Chrysostomus, Eusebius, Hegesippus, Sabellicus, Cuspinian, and Platina issued from his pen in German, and these became books that were much read by people in the cities. In the foreword to Hedio's translation of the *Chronica* of Johann Cuspinian (1541), Phillipp

Melanchthon praises the translating activity of the Strasbourg scholar with warm words.[21]

A remarkable little book that was widely effective was published in 1507 in the little town of Saint-Dié in Lorraine; it was a short introduction to geography entitled, *Cosmographaie introductio*, and it was authored by the geographer, Martin Waltzemüller (Walseemüller) (in the Greek, Hylacomilus). At one place where, without mentioning Columbus, the talk is of the four discovery trips of the seafarer, Amerigo Vespucci, it says it this way: "Yet another fourth continent has been discovered by Americus Vesputius and I can't see why anyone could prevent this land from being called after its discoverer, the far-looking Americus, Amerigen, as it were the Land of Americus, or America."

On a small map of the globe appended thereto (and on large world map as well) for the new part of the world, Waltzemüller has in fact inserted the designation "America" and thus has become the originator of that name.[22] Columbus and Gutenberg have therefore undergone a similar fate of displacement in posthumous fame. Waltzemüller has to some extent made good his oversight when in the world map of the Strasbourg Ptolemy edition of 1513, he has properly designated Columbus as the discoverer of the new part of the world *(Terra incognita)*. The name of the countries as "America" has, however, remained.[23]

The learned Carthusian, Gregor Reisch, with Johann Schott published in Freiburg in 1503 a concise summarization of the knowledge of that time under the title *Margarita philosophica;* it had numerous pictures. Particularly valuable in this beautiful book is the added world map.[24]

Appearing in 1509 in Wittenberg was the little book of relics, printed probably by Simphorion Reinhart; it was decorated with woodcuts by Lukas Cranach, and entitled *Zeigung des hochlobwürdigen Heiligtums der Stiftskirche Allerheiligen zu Wittenberg* ("Exhibit of the highly praised relics in the Collegiate Church of All Saints at Wittenberg"). Introducing the little book are a copper engraving with the double image of Electors Rudolf and Friedrich, and a woodcut with a depiction of the collegiate church. One hundred nineteen further pictures represent the relics themselves.[25] The same printer in 1512 published a little work that was likewise significant for the history of art: *Ein sehr andächtig christlich Büchlein aus heiligen Schriften und Lehrern, von Adam von Fulda in deutsch Reimen gesetzt* ("A very devotional Christian little book taken from holy Scripture and the doctrines, set in German rhyme by Adam of Fulda.")[26]

Still richer in pictures than the little relics book of Wittenberg was the Halle one, which was published in 1520 by Cardinal Albrecht of Mainz. Its main decoration consisted of the famous engraving by Albrecht Dürer, "The Little Cardinal." Following it was a double woodcut image with the donors to the church treasury, the collegiate church itself and the patron saints. Over 230 illustrations of relics accompany the description of the shrine.[27]

An unusual man is closely associated with the life of books in Ulm in this period (which compared with the earlier considerable growth, was severely diminished at the end of the fifteenth century); he may on the one hand claim a place in the history of the book as one of the first and most significant German authors, and on the other hand, as a printer and dealer in books: Sebastian Franck (1499–1543). Ill-disposed to the church-bound Christendom, he was an eccentric recluse of those days who focused on the inner illumination through God's Spirit. As a popular German author, Franck has made a name for himself primarily through two great works: through the one published in Strasbourg in 1531, *Chronika, Zeitbuch und Geschichtsbibel* ("Chronicle, Annals and History Bible"), which was the first universal history in the German language, and through the *Weltbuch* ("World Book"), which was printed in Tübingen in 1534, the oldest of the German descriptions of the world. As an opponent of both churches, the ostracized man repeatedly had to move from Evangelical locales; as he once wrote, "If one now does not subscribe in all articles, in all things to the churches where he is, be he wheresoever he wills, he has there less peace and freedom to believe and speak than were he among the heathen and the Turks." With his wife and children, he was even exiled from Ulm, where Franck had built a printery and a book trade, on January 6, 1539, because of his writing for the press and his printing activities. The school superintendents had, however, to acknowledge in their complaint that God had lent him "special gifts as a layman to assemble and to describe many things industriously and painstakingly," and that "as a layman," he had a special gift "for putting and presenting a matter in German." On May 22, 1539, he wrote from Basel to Eberhard von Rümlang in Bern, that he was searching for a new home, most preferably in Switzerland, since in Ulm he could get no paper. He wrote he had a beautiful printery with ten kinds of type, which he was only able to use a little in Ulm. "I would also have a beautiful shop with books of all sorts and on all questions; I still have about 250 florins worth of books at Ulm, where I've also had a shop." Bern might well be too far removed from Frankfurt and the fair there, but Basel already had twelve printers and ten bookshops. The hard-pressed scholar has finally found lodging with the Basel printers, Nikolaus Brylinger and Bartholomäus Westheimer.[28]

The scholars, Johann Huttich and Simon Grynaeus, published in Basel in 1532 at Johann Herwagen's a significant compilation of travel descriptions of the most recently discovered lands and islands, with woodcuts and a world map by Sebastian Münster. A German translation followed a year later in Strasbourg.[30]

A special quality in the book production of those days is evidenced in the small town of Simmern, the capital of the principality of the same name. Here Hieronymus Rodler, the secretary of Prince John of Palatine-Simmern, maintained a printery between 1530 and 1533, which issued several small (but richly provided with woodcuts) German works, among which in 1530 were Georg Rixners' famed and notorious (because full of falsifications) tournament book, which was one of the oldest of this kind of book; further, two popular books from the epic cycle on Emperor Charlemagne: the *Fierabras* and the *Geschichte von den vier Söhnen Haymons* ("History of Haimon's Four Sons"), to which was added the amusing poem, *Das weltlich Klösterlein* ("The Secular Little Monastery"). The printed works of Simmern are among the earliest books produced with pronounced Fraktur types.[31]

Intended for daily life was a handsome little book, the *Rechnung mit der Linie* ("Accounting with lines"); authored by Adam Riese (who in time has become proverbial), it was printed in 1525 by Mathes Maler in Erfurt. The title page of this first German account book presents the author in a fur-lined robe sitting before a table covered with computing instruments. The little publication, which is the basis of our multiplication tables, has gone through numerous editions.[32]

With the sixteenth century and its increasing expressiveness, publications on current events also came to be used heavily. The previous period was still thoroughly sparing in words, yes, it had been silent.[33] It was rare when brief reports were published concerning the events of the time. The trivial works of the painter and metal cutter had mainly consisted of pictures and pictorial sheets. That changed quickly when more and more small printeries were established and they brought cheap pamphlets and leaflets on the market. The Reformation movement with its churchly and political struggles then generated a real flood of this literature to the market. It is astonishing how quickly here the world had changed. Even if these small printed items had been written only for the day obtaining and most of them had disappeared with the day's passing, their value for the period should nevertheless not be underestimated. They went from hand to hand, and they were read aloud, and invited again to be read. It was through them that the art of reading became extraordinarily demanded, that participation in events was strongly awakened, and the public's attention was turned to the book. The *Neue Zeitung* with its short reports concerning individual events or natural phenomena, had the widest distribution. Nor was the degeneration of this journalistic literature wanting from the beginning. Above all there were the innumerable astrological publications, frivolous offspring of the growing astronomical science, the prophesyings and the miracle stories.[34] For the year 1524, the astrologists predicted in numerous pamphlets, on the basis of the planets under the sign of the fish, a flood and deluge. All of Germany, alarmed, expected the feared, unfortunate month of February; many fled with their provisions for living to the high mountains, in order to secure themselves. Up to a hundred pamphlets embarked on a debate for and against the evil prediction. When February arrived, nothing happened, and indeed there was a beautiful and fruitful year. God, so each astrologist now said, had had mercy on mankind and his wrath had turned away from them. And then they got themselves ready again for the next year's predictions.[35]

The liturgical books (that is, the ones provided for divine worship) constituted an unusual group among the printed works of the fifteenth and sixteenth centuries. In line with their purpose, one sought, as with the medieval manuscripts, to make them as beautiful as possible. The most outstandingly designed works for divine worship are Johann Fust's and Peter Schöffer's Mainz Psalter of 1457, which was a master work of the new art, and the similarly designed *Canon missae* of 1458. At the summit of the missals stands the celebrated, mysterious *Missale speciale*, which, printed with a type related to one of the small Psalter types of Peter Schöffer, belongs among the earliest liturgical printed works.[36] For a time the experiments with the difficult liturgical printing ceased, until in 1474, primarily on Venetian soil, (the future main home of the books for divine worship), whole workshops adapted themselves to producing the much sought-after breviaries, missals, and psalters. In Venice it was especially Peter Lichtenstein, Nicholaus de Franckfordia and Lucantonio Giunta, who sent out, far beyond the borders of Italy itself, the variously designed breviaries and missals for particular dioceses, to Brixen, Gran, Zagreb, Prague, Salzburg, Chiemsee, Augsburg, Freising, Passau and Würzburg. The content of the books called for a special sort of decoration, which manifested itself in the numerous small pictures of saints in the breviaries, as well as the presentations of the crucifixion and of the patron saints in the missals.

In Germany, Peter Schöffer in Mainz (1457–1516), Johann Senschmidt in Bamberg (1488–1491), Georg Stüchs in Nuremberg (1484–1517), Peter Drach in Speyer (1477–1502), Georg Reyser in Würzburg (1479–1499), Konrad Kachelofen in Leipzig (1493–1513), Johann Winterburg in Vienna (1499–1519) and Edhard Ratdolt in Augsburg (1478–1522) distinguished themselves through their splendid missals. Deserving of special mention are Bartholomäus Ghotan in Lübeck, who printed missals for the northern church dioceses of Strengnaes, Upsala, Abo, and Lebus; Johann Haller in Cracow, who supplied church books for the dioceses of Breslau, Plocz, Gnesen, Posen, and Cracow; and Edhard Ratdolt, who sought to heighten the significance of his illustrative contributions to the missals through the colored woodcuts, and created such magnificent leaves such as in the black, red, yellow, olive and blue printed crucifixion picture of the Augsburg missal of 1491, and similarly artistically, the patron saints for the missal of Aquileia, with Mary and the saints, Ermachoras and Fortunatus. Significant artists such as Michael Wholgemut, Hans Brugkmair, Jorg Breu, Hans Baldung Grien, Urs Graf, Wolfgang Traut, Lukas Cranach, and the Master D S, played their part in the decorating of missals. Artistically skilled type designers created outstanding types which, in their expressive power, are among the most beautiful script forms of all times. Also in Paris and Lyon there appeared numerous breviaries and missals for France; and likewise for the German and the English dioceses. In the main there seems to have been no boundaries by country for the liturgical book at all. In the *Graduale* that was produced by Nicolaus Prevost in Paris in 1528 for the English diocese of Salisbury, it says that it was to be obtained from the bookdealer, Franz Birckmann (therefore, a German) in the court of St. Paul's church in London.

An astounding mobility in the book trade is everywhere a peculiarity in the printing of the liturgical books. Thus Georg Stüchs in Nuremberg created breviaries and missals for the dioceses of Regensburg, Salzburg, Prague, Olmütz, Gran, Cammin, Naumburg, Magdeburg, Hildesheim, Minden, Brandenburg, Meissen, Lübeck, Havelberg, Skara, Melk, Linköping, and entire editions have been delivered to the specific ordering locale.

When the Reformation was gaining ground in Germany, the flourishing period of the liturgical book had also passed.[37] At the suggestion of the Council of Trent, Rome under Pius V standardized the books for divine worship according to the Roman breviary and the Roman missal, and thereby blocked the previous development of the liturgical printing. At the same time, there was a typographical transformation going on: the Latin type superseded the Gothic, and the copper engraving replaced the woodcut. Christopher Plantin in Antwerp became the chief printer.

Corresponding to the official liturgical printed works that were intended for the clerics were the devotional books for the laity, which also have been carefully provided for. In Strasbourg, Mainz, and Nuremberg especially did one richly provide the "little garden of souls" *(Hortolus animae)* with ornaments of all sorts. The most beautiful editions have been printed by the Koberger House in Nuremberg, by Johann Clein at Lyons, and Johann Stüchs and Friedrich Peypus at Nuremberg. Erhard Schön and Hans Springinklee decorated them with small pictures and ornamental borders. They were often printed on parchment for bibliophiles and were handsomely painted. For the painting of sixty-one pictures, the Nuremberg patrician, Anton Tuohor, paid the artist, Hans Springinklee, five gold florins; the parchment proof-sheets meanwhile had itself cost only two florins.[38] Among these prayer books there is also to be reckoned that German breviary which the knight, Christoph von Frangipani, produced during his imprisonment at Venice in the year 1518, with the printer there, Gregorius de Gregorios; he had it decorated with numerous woodcuts, among them being his own likeness and that of his consort, Apollonia. The book, which is beautifully designed, is one of the few printed works of that period produced in the German language in Italy.

The home of all these handsomely designed books of devotion is France, their forerunner being the *Livre d'heures*, the book of hours, which, in connection with the exquisite manuscriptural books of hours of the waning Middle Ages, has been most enthusiastically fostered, especially in Paris. Their main publishers were Simon Vostre and Antoine Vérard, the latter being a master who also otherwise has taken special care for the beautifully decorated printed work on parchment.[39]

Characteristically, these pious books, extravagantly decorated as they were with borders, initials and small pictures, and frequently printed on parchment and colorfully fashioned, are charming gems and signs of pampered taste such as could thrive only in a society luxuriating in beauty and a refined art of living. The book is also here again the unmistakable symbol of the confident lifestyle of that period.[40]

The increased love for books and the joy in more beautiful designs also passed over into individual governmental publications. Thus there arose at Bamberg in 1507 the Bamberg criminal court order, which was printed at Johann Pfeil's on commission from Bishop Georg of Limburg; it was highly significant—not only artistically, but for the history of law as well. The beautiful work has become the precurosor of the *Peinliche Halsgerichtsordnung* ("The Capital Criminal Court Order") of Emperor Charles V.[41] In Munich, the court painter, Casper Clofigl, decorated the *Buch der gemeinen Landgebote in Ober- und Niederbayern* ("Book of the Common Land Laws in Upper and Lower Bavaria") of 1518 and the *Reformation des bayerischen Landrechts* ("Reformation of the Bavarian Land Law") of 1518, with beautiful portraits of both the ruling Bavarian dukes, Wilhelm and Ludwig.[42] Also the *Stadtrechte und Statuten der Stadt Freiburg im Breisgau* ("City Laws and Statutes of the City of Freiburg im Breisgau"), printed by Adam Petri in 1520 in Basel, have been decorated with on outstanding illustration of the arms and the city's patron saints—two woodcuts that were probably sketched by Hans Holbein.

The idea of reproduction did not rest until it had mastered all the possibilities of book production.[43] The difficulties of printing musical notes were soon also overcome, and music books were published. The German master, Ulrich Han, in Rome, was already utilizing printed notes for the choral music in his 1476 missal, and the Venetian printer, Ottaviano dei Petrucci (1466–1539), was likewise doing the same for the florid counterpoint in his *Odhecaton* of the year 1501. Just as with the liturgical printing entire workshops have directed their energies toward producing works for divine worship, so publishing houses appropriately equipped for it have also been active in musical printing, as, for example, Antonio Gardone in Venice, who between 1538 and 1571 published no less than 112 mostly voluminous musical works. Erhard Oeglin at Augsburg, Peter Schöffer the younger at Mainz and Strasbourg, Matthias Apiarius at Strasbourg and Bern, Hieronymus Form-schneider, Johann Petreius, Johann vom Berg and Ulrich Neuber at Nuremberg, and Georg Rhau at Wittenberg—all of these also printed with music notes. In Paris, Pierre Attaingnant, Robert Ballard and Adrian le Roy were successfully engaged in this respect. Outstanding in their musical printed works in the second half of the sixteenth century were Adam Berg at Munich, who was the printer of Orlando di Lasso, and Christopher Plantin at Antwerp, the enterprising publisher of great mass works. It had still not been a century since the discovery of printing, when already countless sprirtual and secular books of songs, advancing the art of singing and cultivating the popular song, were going from hand to hand, and large volumes of missals lay in the choirs of churches, and numerous musical works of the great masters, such as Orlando di Lasso, Cyprian de Rore, and Ciovanni Perluigi da Palestrina, were being disseminated in large editions. They contributed effectively to the increased attention that was being paid to the art of music.

A detailed survey of the extra-German printeries of this period would have to mention a world of workshops and their creations; only several highly significant masters can here be emphasized: the Venetian printer, Daniel Bomberg from Antwerp, who in the period from 1517 to 1549 published numerous Hebraic works, among which was the first complete edition of the Babylonian *Talmud* in twelve volumes; the Paris printer, Josse Bade d'Asc (Jodocus Badius Ascensius), who has printed up to seven hundred works, among which were numerous Latin and Greek classical authors, and also the writings of Erasmus of Rotterdam, and who for France has become what Aldus Manutius was for Italy and what Johann Froben was for Germany;[44] further, and likewise in Paris, Simon de Colines, who, being active from 1520 to 1546, produced over seven hundred decorated printed works, among which were several works with borders and the initials of the artist, Geoffroy Tory;[45] the printer from Antwerp, Wilhelm Vorstermann (1504–1543), who brought outstandingly designed books into the trade, among which were the Netherlands Bible translation of 1528, which had woodcuts by the artist, Jan Swart of Groningen and Lukas van Leyden;[46] after that, the Spanish master, Arnao Guillen de Brocar, who, summoned by the learned Cardinal Ximenes de Cisneros to Alcala de Henares (Complutum), (the birthplace of the poet Cervantes), published there between 1514 and 1517 the famous Complutensian Polyglot Bible, which was the first edition of Holy Scriptures fashioned in several languages, and the most extensive printed work of that period;[47] the Vaticana in Rome still today possesses the parchment copies of six of the large volumes, as the one-time beautiful present in return for the Vatican's having sent over to Spain the priceless Roman Bible manuscripts during the reign of Pope Leo X.[48]

If we look around us for forces that have helped to bring about the ever increasing expansion and dissemination for the book, ever and again to be mentioned in the first place is the woodcut, which with the reproduction of pictures gained continuously widening circles for the book. Its discovery is therefore not merely to be seen as a more significant continuation of the idea of reproduction and therewith also of the concept of printing, but no less than an essential reinforcement of the total effectiveness of the book. The book and the picture have, in their association with each other, become intensified forces that served to advance culture. In the book, the woodcut could vividly bring to the reader the entire human environment—the plants,[49] the animals, the heavens and earth—within a range that, until then, was quite unanticipated. It even included the activities and the daily pursuits. Thus already coming from the printing shops were early art books,[50] sample block books,[51] lace-work books, sports books,[52] cook books,[53] manuals for the art of writing,[54] technical books[55] and other kinds of introductions into the daily life of that day and time, and all of them represented significant extensions of the book's effectiveness into ever broader circles. From Roman antiquity Ovid has, above all, had a stimulating effect on the layout of books with mythological representations.[56]

The enjoyment of the use of color in books—still operative as an aftereffect from the manuscript period—had the printers and the metal cutters again and again devising ways and means of decorating books with many pictures in color. The aforementioned artistically finished woodcuts in color of the Augsburg master, Erhard Ratdolt, are therefore already of special historical significance (so far as the history of art is concerned), because they are doubtless connected with the artist, Hans Burgkmair.

If these colored woodcuts posed the difficulty of lining up plates in several colors printed side by side, so the color effect was achieved with another technique, through over-printing. That was the chiaroscuro cut whose black line plate had to provide outlines and shadows, while the over-printing color plate was supposed to provide coloration and highlights. Johann Schönsperger the Elder in Augsburg and Johann Schott in Strasbourg tried their hands several times in this art, since they overprinted title page, pictures or title page borders in red. Yet these attempts have enjoyed no greater success. Only Schott's Ptolemy edition of 1520 evidences an excellent title page frame with the Judgment of Paris, which is overprinted with a brown tinting sheet, and works quite effectively. We know that, at the same time, renowned artists—such as Lukas Cranach, Hans Burgkmair, Hans Baldung, Hans Wechtlin, and Albrecht Altdorfer, have published single artistic sheets with colored woodcuts and chiaroscuro cuts. One has only to recall Burgkmair's portrait of Emperor Maximilian I (reproduced by Lützow, p. 132/3), of Hans Paumgartner and of Jakob Fugger's (see Lützow p. 170–171), Wechtlin's skull (see Lützow, pp. 1676–7), Mary in the garden (see Lutzow, pp. 168–9), and Altdorfer's "Schöne Marie" ("Beautiful Mary") with six plates (see Lützow, 176/7).[57]

The book cover of this period proceeded almost unaltered in the forms of the incunabula period (which had been taken over from the medieval period). Still prevalent was the wooden board covered with leather. The single stamping on it is enriched by the print of the metal rools, filled with Biblical, mythological and allegorical representations made possible and successfully meshed with the panel stamps for larger illustrative representations. In keeping with the spirit of the time, there increased on the stamps and panels the pictorial borrowings from the world of antiquity, interspersed with likenesses of the princes and famous personages of the time, primarily Erasmus, Luther, Melanchtohon, Emperor Charles V, King Ferdinand, Elector Johann Friedrich of Saxony, and Count Palatine Ottheinrich.

The book being an easily movable item, which occasionally is also borrowed, connected with it from of old has been the ownership entry, which shows to whom the book belongs, whether it be a monastery, a foundation, a princely court, or some other type of owner. Even here printing (of books and pictures) soon took up the reproduction of such ownership notices and created exciting book plates *(Ex Libris)* with arms, symbols and ornaments of all kinds. Artists such as Burgkmair, Holbein, Cranach and the minor masters of the Dürer school have successfully assisted with this matter. These leaves pasted in the volumes are charming indications of the personal care that there was for books.[58]

16
The German Humanists and the Book

It was an enormous cultural wave that, with humanism (the zeal for the reawakened world of antiquity), penetrated in the fifteenth century from the South into the German territories and, without opposition, took hold of the leading ranks of the German people, It is not as if in the life of peoples that, at the turning points of time, there always stand certain guideposts that a people need only observe, in order immediately to find for themselves the most appropriate and most beneficial direction; it is rather that most of the time a people must tirelessly seek its way so as at the end to prove whether the choice was correct or not. For German destiny, antiquity and Christendom have alike been mysterious temporal turning points, enticing challenges, forces that impinged like natural powers, now advancing, and now checked, and finally, in spite of all the detours and wrong tracks, and in spite of many items becoming overwhelmingly controlled by foreign influences, they yet redounded to the final enrichment of the German nature. That was what won the Germans to the reawakening of the world of the spirit and forms of antiquity – that the movement, despite its strong Southern element, was still not an exclusive matter solely for the Italian people, as the successors of the ancient Romans, but that it was the fresh renewal of a high goal for humanity, with life immortal and a powerful renewal of intellectual endeavor.

Even if it were a momentary challenge of the period, the humanistic goals of cultivation and education were a force that rested in eternal values, a vital concern for the entire world of culture that was thereby destined to become an inheritance of mankind that could not be lost. With cultural rebirths, invariably it comes in the end to the inspiration (*Begeisterung:* the word comes from *Geist,* spirit, intellect) with which an overwhelmed period summons the eternal powers to help toward the renewal of a numbed world, and, in its own way, makes vital connection with it. In the observation of divine and human affairs, transformations occur from time to time, as soon as a concept of the world is exhausted. History is itself an eternal transformation. To be sure, we cannot spare humanism the one reproach, that on account of its preference for the fashioned harmony of the Latin style, it has ominously reinforced the supremacy of this alien power within German literature. The omnipotence of the langauge of the world and the persuasive feeling for form have shut off the sounds of the mother tongue, which at that time were little developed.

With full inspiration, the German humanists gave themselves to the new reality. Whole bands of students and scholars were attracted to the schools of higher learning in the South and, spiritually transformed, all of them returned to Germany. And as it was in Italy, so it was also in the German countries, that the book became the chief carrier of the new movement, the inexhaustible source of a flowing rich material for cultural formation, the connecting link of the humanists who were eager for knowledge.

That victorious intellectual breakthrough filled the books, (which were its carriers) not merely with new content and new speech patterns, but also altered the book's external appearance, such as changing the form of the title and the title page, creating its own decorative forms, and giving to the entire literature a definitely unique external character. Humanism dislodged the whole Scholasticism of the Middle Ages, and in its place it put the works of classical antiquity, and it shaped its own literature thereto in the sense of the new educational goals, as in the effectively enlisting letters of famous men to Johann Reuchlin,[1] or the broadsheet, *Dunkelmännerbriefe.*[2] The great common leading ideas of the new educational goals lent to the entire humanistic literature an unprecedented drive and impetus. Ulrich von Hutten expressed this new feeling of strength and of proud cultural consciousness in the already mentioned paean, and in his Maximus-Tyrius edition of 1519, the printer, Johann Froben, summoned the readers of his announcements to his new publications: "Be glad that you have been born in this century, in which not merely the Latin, Greek and Hebrew tongues have again been revived, but also all the noble disciplines, beginning with theology and philosophy; celebrate their rebirth."[3] The author's self-confidence awakened, because he knew, that through the reproduced, militant and already victorious book, disseminated in hundreds and thousands of copies, he could achieve as well as confer, fame.

This new relationship of author and publisher to the book, which was effected through printing and the dissemination of printed works, was strikingly expressed in communicative prefatory remarks, in dedications to patrons or friends, and in commendatory accompanying verses by pupils and by those who were likeminded. When in 1516 an historical work *(Memorabilium omnis aetatis chronici commentarii)* by Johannes Nauclerus appeared, Erasmus of Rotterdam and Johann Reuchlin (the "two eyes" of German humanism) therein praised with high words in scholarly forewords the author and the Tübingen printer, Thomas Anshelm, to whom scholarship was so indebted for the publishing of excellent works in Latin, Greek and Hebrew (and additionally in beautiful types)[4]; or when Erasmus and Ulrich von Hutten introduced the Mainz Livy-edition of 1518 with flattering words, it meant the most effective recommendation for the introduction of this book. The prefaces, the dedications and the friendly commendatory poems are established phenomena of the humanistic book, and they eloquently express the increased status-consciousness of the new period.[5]

Added to this were the obvious transformations in the externals of the humanistic book. Italian humanism transferred this presumably old Roman form from the manuscript originals of the ancient texts that were frequently in the Carolingian miniscule forms, and with them it founded the prospective world-wide dominion of the Antiqua. Even the German printers yielded to the pressures of the humanists and adopted the round script, together with the slanted cursive, for the

ancient and the humanistic literature, and extensively for all their publications in
Latin. When the Basel printer, Johann Bergmann de Olpe, published in 1498
Johann Reuchlin's *Scenica progymnasmata,* he pointed out with a truly humanistic
pride that the book was not printed with barbaric, i.e. Gothic, type, but rather with
Antiqua type *(non barbaro quidem, sed antiquo canactere).* Thus the Antiqua type,
under the influence of humanism in Germany, became the script for the Latin
language, while the broken form has been maintained—even for the future—for
German texts.

Finally, the title-page border, an established custom of the book since the turn
of the sixteenth century, took on all the wealth of the ancient notions concerning
illustration. We thus encounter the triumphal chariot of Humanitas, which was
given a shove by Vergil and Cicero, drawn by Demosthenes and Homer, or Athena
with the helmet and shield, and Apollo with lyre and bow, the graces with Minerva
and Mercury, and scenes from the history of Mucius Scaevola. Very beloved are
the half-length portraits of Roman authors, such as Vergil, Horace, Pindar, Ovid,
Valerius, Maximus, Quintilian, Sallust and Cicero. In a border by Johann Bebel in
Basel we see assembled small portraits of almost all the authors of the ancient
world: Aristotle, Plato, Aristides, Demosthenes, Lucian, Plutarch, Socrates,
Pythagoras, Homer, Hesiod, Euripides, Aristophanes, Theocritus, Pindar, Cicero,
Quintilian, Pliny, Aulus Gellius, Titus Livius, Sallust, Vergil, Horace, Ovid, and
Lucretius: in the panel below, Homer draws from Castilian springs and is crowned
by Calliope in the company of eight Muses.[6] Two title-page frames of Ambrosius
Holbein are famous: on the one is the battle of Varus and the slandering of Apelles,
the other represents court life based on Lucian's description. The scenes in these
borders are often filled with a whole number of figures from the myths of the gods
and heroes of antiquity. Thus shown in the upper panel in a border of the
Strasbourg printer, Wolf Kopfel, is the sun-like Apollo, in front of him Mercury hur-
ries to Juno, and behind this, Jupiter is enthroned with his sceptre; the right panel
depicts Venus and Mars, Vulcan and Mercury; in the decorative piece to the left,
Homer plays on the harp, and below that, Odysseus and Penelope are sitting at a
banquet, in addition to Demodocus with the harp; in the quarter panel below that,
Odysseus rises to Ithaca with three companions; on the left, Tantulus, standing up
to his knees in water, tries to reach a tree branch. It certainly didn't hurt, if in
Erasmus' Latin paraphrase work on the gospels and epistles,[7] (and thus in a
thoroughly Christian book), no less than five frames with purely antique figures
(among them being Apollo and Daphne, Pelops and Tantalus, Mercury and Jupiter,
Julius Caesar and Hector, Venus and Cupid, Nemesis and Amor, Humanitas with
Vergil, Homer, Cicero and Demosthenes) were inserted.

The antique world of the gods on occasion also returned in independent
representations in the humanistic book. Thus a music book of Petrus Tritonius
(Melopoiae sive harmoniae tetracenticae super XXII genera carminum) of 1507 contains two full page woodcuts, one the Parnassus with Apollo and the Muses, who
bear with them all sorts of instruments, then Jupiter and the company surrounding
him: Phoebe playing on the harp, Mercury to the right, Pallas on the left, and
Pegasus on the feet (again surrounded by the Muses, who are playing on their

instruments). In Arnold Schlick's *Tabulaturen etlicher Lobgesang und Liedlein auf die Orgeln und Lauten* ("Tabulation of sundry praises and little songs on the organ and lutes"), printed in 1512 by Peter Schöffer the Younger in Mainz, Euterpe (the Muse of lyrical song) plays the flute, and at her side a swan listens and musical instruments lie at her feet.[8]

The printer and publisher were even proud to belong to the community of humanists; like the scholars, they translated their names into Latin or Greek, and they expressed this spiritual fellowship frequently in their devices, which were often designed with ancient symbols and with inscriptions in three languages. Johann Oporinus in Basel used Arion and the dolphin, Philipp Ulhart in Augsburg Pegasus with the music-making Muses, as well as the temples of Helicon and Parnassus.[9]

This book, filled as it was with new spirit and transformed into new forms, the German humanist loved and cared for with enthusiastic spirit. This devotion is expressed in all the letters and printed works of the time: the talk there is always of new publications, of manuscripts that have been discovered, of books sought for and borrowed, of advising with printers, of visits to libraries, and of open or closed doors. The whole of Germany appears to have been transformed into a vast scholarly society, the connecting bond of which was the humanistic book. All the disciples of the victorious cultural movement have become enthusiastic bibliophiles, whether they owned manuscripts or printed works: from Petrus Luder, Samuel Karoch, Sigismund Gossembrot,[10] Felix Hemmerlin, Gregor von Heimburg, Nicholas of Cusa, Rudolf Agricola, Conrad Celtes, Heinrich Bebel, and Jakob Wimpfeling up to the great book collectors, Hartmann Schedel, Konrad Peutinger, Beatus Rhenanus, Willibald Pirckheimer, Johann Jakob and Ulrich Fugger.[11]

In order to get to know such a humanistic library, we look in now on the Castle of Ladenburg am Neckar, three hours from Stuttgart. There the Worms bishop, Johann von Dalberg (1482–1503),[12] a lively aesthete and friend of art and science, has built an attractive library. In keeping with the humanistic education in three languages, stored there in great numbers are Latin and Greek and Hebrew manuscripts, as well as printed works. But also among the manuscript treasures are Middle High German linguistic monuments; the two *Rosengarten*, the *Schwanenritter* of Conrad of Würzburg, German translations of Latin romances such as the *Trojanische Krieg* according to Guido of Columna, Lucius Apuleius' *Goldene Esel*, or contemporary poems such as the songs of Hermann of Sachsenheim. The bishop, who took pleasure in books, readily placed his possessions at the disposal of his guests. Johann Trithemius, Sebastian Murrho, Johann Reuchlin, Andreas Stiborius, Conrad Celtes, Rudolf Agricola, and Johannes Vigilius used the collection and sang its praises. The humanist, Jakob of Questenberg, who knows books well, copies manuscripts in Rome and sends them, in wonderful script, to his patron, Johann von Dalberg.

Hartmann Schedel (1440–1514), the famous author of the *Welt Chronik* ("World Chronicle"), the book of the incunabula period that was richest in pictures, has received his passionate love for books from his older cousin, Hermann Schedel, a notable physician and humanist who has turned to good account his changing residences and the stimulating connections he enjoyed with the representatives of the older humanism, through the devoted collecting of manuscripts. The younger cousin is indebted to him not merely for his suggestion of the very profitable stay at the University of Padua, but also his inheritance from him of fifty manuscripts. Hartmann Schedel now became one of the first book collectors who devoted himself to printed works with the same love he had had for manuscripts. He knew how to give to all his books (through colorful inscriptions, woodcuts and copper engravings—today they are of the highest value—that were pasted in, and also miniature paintings, drawings by hand, and other kinds of ornamentals) a thoroughly personal attractiveness, which still exercises an irresistible charm, even today. His collection demonstrates especially clearly the possessions of books from the period of the transition from the manuscript to printing—from the period that still existed wholly under the influence of the colorfully designed manuscript and hence also loved to sprinkle the new printed works with birght colors. The Munich State Library, the later fortunate heir of the handsome collection, still today owns Schedel's own hand copy of his *Weltchronik*, with its multicolored painted woodcuts, its pages with red and blue inscriptions, its manuscript designs that have been inserted, and ten rare leaflets which have been pasted in, and that have been partially preserved only in these pieces. One can only imagine Schedel with his pen and pencil in his hand over his books and their leaves, so saturated are his books with ornamentals, and so numerous are his copies. Much of it has come down to us only through him and therefore has significant value as source material, among which are the famous fragment from the Greek diary of the traveller, Cyriacus of Ancona, with the drawings of Mercury and Arion stepping on the dolphin, which Albrecht Dürer has afterwards used as sources for hand drawings. In 1552 all the valuable items went from the ownership of the last Schedel (for about five hundred gold florins) to Johann Jakob Fugger, and again later (with his entire collection) to Duke Albrecht V of Bavaria.[13]

No other German city of the sixteenth century has become such a locale for books as the Swabian imperial city of Augsburg. For evidence of that, one only needs to recall the many painters of the city, or the names of Konrad Peutinger, Johann Jakob and Ulrich Fugger, or the growth of the municipal library there. The valiant city clerk, Konrad Peutinger,[14] may claim fame as the one who has shown the way to such enjoyment in books. He was not himself a creative spirit, but a thoroughly learned man and the vital center of Augsburg's humanistic circle; in his considerable and multifaceted collection of books he expressed the close understanding there was with the entire education of his period. The numerous manuscriptural entries in them tell us that he did not merely collect and love his books, but that he has also read and worked through them. His learned daughter, Konstanze, has written him very nicely on April 20, 1521, to the Reichstag in Worms about how his books missed him; she was the same one who has woven the laurels that Emperor Maximilian awarded to the humanist Ulrich von Hutten.[15] The versatile humanist obtained special merit through his methodical collecting of German historical works of the Middle Ages. He owned the writings of Reginald of Prüm, of Otto of Freising, of Liutprand of Cremona, of Paul the

Deacon, of Jordanes, of Widukind of Corvey; not only did he collect these texts, but he also attempted to give them a new vitality when in 1515 he published the history of the Goths by Jordanes and the *Deeds of the Lombards* by Paul the Deacon, with their valuable statements concerning the sagas of the heroes and the songs of the gallant people.

From Conrad Celtes, Peutinger obtained that world-renowned map with the military roads of the West Roman Kingdom that is still called *Tabula Peutingeriana*, and which is among the most valuable monuments of antiquity. Peutinger desired to publish the map, and in 1511 he included it, with Emperor Maximilian's permission, in his Jordanus edition, but he did not complete the project. In 1587, Marcus Welser found two pieces of the first section which Peutinger had had traced for the impression, and he published them in 1591 through the Aldus printery. When the original copy again emerged a short time thereafter, it was published in 1598 by Ortelius at the Plantin printery. The map itself remained in Peutinger family until 1714, when it was purchased by Prince Eugene of Savoy and came with his rich collection into the National Library in Vienna in 1738.

To Peutinger's collecting activity we likewise owe the obtaining of one of the oldest monuments of printing, the pamphlet, *Ein Mahnung der Christenheit wider die Türken* ("A Warning of Christendom Against the Turks"), which is now known only in "Peutinger's copy." One of the most valuable books of the Augsburg humanists was the famous prayerbook of Emperor Maximilian; it was decorated with miniature paintings, among which were the arms of the Peutinger and Welser families. Today it is in the Vaticana in Rome, being one of five copies that have been preserved for us; the most splendid of these is the world famous one with the border drawings by Albrecht Dürer and other artists.

As a counselor to Emperor Maximilian, Peutinger was already very closely connected with the book world of his time. Not only did he take part in the projects of the Emperor himself,[16] but he also arranged for the bestowal of imperial privilege for publishers and printers; he supported the publications of the Augsburg society of scholars; he joined eagerly in the publication of the Ursberg *Chronicle* and of Procopius by Beatus Rhenanus; and as one of those who knew books best, he counselled his friends. With his far-sighted evaluation of original sources, with his enthusiastic collecting of manuscript documents, inscriptions and coins, Peutinger's work stands (as Erich König has emphasized) in the first rank of those scholarly efforts to which scholarship later owed the *Monumenta Germaniae historica*, the *Corpus inscriptionum latinarum* and the *Regesta imperii*.

Peutinger's library, which ultimately amounted to about twenty-one hundred volumes (among them being 170 manuscripts), devolved by inheritance to the family following the death of the founder, until the deacon of Ellwangen, Desiderius Ignatius Peutinger, left the possession in 1718 to the Jesuits in Augsburg. Following the suppression of the Order, the treasures have partly come into the Augsburg State and Municipal Library, and partly into the Munich State Library.

Several humanists have already during their lifetimes provided for the security of their books in safe places. Conrad Celtes left his collection to the Arts Faculty in Vienna; only the Roman travel map did he award to his friend, Conrad Peutinger.

Johann Reuchlin, the founder of the Greek and Hebrew language study in Germany, who owned (among other items) a Hebrew Bible given him by Emperor Friedrich III, stipulated St. Michael's foundation in his native town of Pforzheim as the heir of his handsome library.[17] The books of the Alsatian humanist, Beatus Rhenaus, went to the community of Schlettstadt. Finally, St. Gall still owns the valuable estate of Joachim von Watts (Vadianus), who had bequeathed his books several months prior to his death (April 6, 1551) to the city where he worked. There also rests his enormous correspondence, which is one of the most important historical monuments for humanism as well as for the Reformation.

If a whole host of valuable humanists' libraries have been preserved for us – at least so far as their chief components are concerned – up to the present day, so also have important collections nevertheless been scattered. Already in his lifetime, Erasmus of Rotterdam has relinquished his books to Johannes Laski (1499–1560), for two hundred florins; Laski was a learned humanist, who later became a leader in the Polish Reformed Church. Following Erasmus' death, it was taken away to Cracow, and the collection has gradually been wholly dispersed.[18] The valuable library of the humanist and patrician, Willibald Pirckheimer (1476–1530), which for a time was kept in Nuremberg, and which contained especially numerous printed works in Greek, has been carried off in the seventeenth century by Thomas, Duke of Arundel; what is left of it is today owned by the Royal Society at Launceston in Cornwall.[19] Concerning the rich book possessions of the Schlettstadt humanist, Jacob Spiegel, we know only that they were transferred in 1542 to the Strasbourg bishop, Erasmus of Limburg; but they had later been dispersed.[20] Through Conradus Mutianus, the belletristic leader of the Erfurt circle of humanists, we know that books have been the indispensable bases for his peaceful conception of life *(Beata tranquillitas)*. He has been associated in a brisk trading of books with Trithemius, with Spalatin, with Aldus Manutius in Venice, with the Amploniana in Erfurt, and with the Frankfurt Fair; nothing more is known of his possessions.[21]

The commanding center of the humanistic book world was Erasmus of Rotterdam,[22] the most significant of the Nordic humanists, the brilliant master of the Latin language, the sage of Basel, who, as Cassiodorus did to his monks, and as Charlemagne did to his Franks, now gave mankind his great goal of education and piety. In him, the "man himself," an entirely new type of scholar has gone across the world's stage, a phenomenon that has been matchlessly portrayed by Hans Holbein, meditating, inquiring, and surrounded by books; as the carriers of the spiritual, by them his whole existence was dominated, and his life fulfilled; they were the successful ambassadors of his passionate vocation to the essential education into human being; they signified his consuming interest. That which we so significantly encounter in the incunabula period in Rome and Venice, the close cooperation of printing and scholarship – we have on Germanic soil in the even more brilliant equivalent of the beautiful bond that existed between the Basel printer, Johann Froben, and Erasmus. When Froben died, Erasmus expressed his pain in words to the effect that everyone who loved scholarship should wear black. It was when it was associated with Erasmus that printing manifested itself in in Germany for the first time as a powerful force in the service of scholarship and of public opinion. There was again an "intellectual" Europe. In Albrecht Dürer's engraving of Erasmus, he is likewise completely surrounded by books.[23]

Just as Holbein has matchlessly depicted the scholar with the paint brush, so also Johannes Oecolampadius, the linguistically gifted collaborator in the Greek edition of the New Testament, has portrayed him in the midst of his books, as he proofreads and compares the Latin and Greek manuscripts, or as he had submitted the manuscript of the printery. From St. Paul's in London, from Mecheln, from Brussels, from Ghent, from St. Agnesberg near Zwolle, from Corsendonk near Turnhout, manuscripts came in as valuable complements to the book possessions that he had in Basel and Constance. Erasmus also knew how to obtain manuscripts from near and far for his other textual editions. In his Augustine edition of 1529 he asserted that it should be the official duty of princes, bishops and abbots to have texts produced which have been carefully prepared by scholars (especially the holy books) and to preserve them in public libraries. The provision of reliable texts — something that Erasmus demanded repeatedly — his printer Froben also has made his own. Erasmus was here for Basel, and indeed for all of Germany, the successful instructor in the art of editing, and Basel, as a city of books, could consider that it was on a par with Venice and Florence.[24]

Erasmus had spent eight months with Aldus Manutius in Venice in creative work and in giving counsel. In the House of Froben he was the intellectual leader of an unprecedented activity in printing, one that indeed presented to the world amost the entirety of the riches of the literature of antiquity and of the ancient Christian writings. All that Erasmus published is hardly to be grasped: the Greek New Testament,[25] Plautus, Terence, Seneca, Cicero, Pliny, Livy, Suetonius, Demosthenes, Ptolemy, Aristotle, Plato, Cyprian, Jerome, Arnobius, Hilary, Irenaeus, Ambrose, Augustine, Chrysostom, Epiphanius, Lactantius, Basil, and Origen. One can indeed assert: Erasmus has mastered the intellectual work of centuries.

Erasmus has moved the world also as the author of his own works, and the book has become his widely-heard herald. The collection of proverbs, *Adagiorum opus*, printed in 1500, was a small selected treasury of the most profound wisdom; it has been through thirty-four editions that were much read, and it has been distributed in about 34,000 copies. Even to a greater extent his chief publications, such as, *Enchiridion militis christiani* (which addressed itself against becoming alientated from the Christian life), the *Encomion moriae*, which, dedicated to the gods of foolishness, was a biting satire on daily life and human pretenses, or the spirited and brilliantly written *Colloquia familiaria*, were in the hands of all educated persons within the European cultural orbit. Erasmus has become the first great author who has called upon the immense possibilities for effectiveness that to an unprecedented extent were present in the book, and who has won the entire western world as his readers. "His name," says the contemporary Swiss, Johann Kessler, in his *Sabbata-Schrift*, "has been transformed into a proverb. Whatever is artistically, carefully, scholarly and wisely written is — one says — "Erasmian," that is, complete and without error."

While Erasmus of Rotterdam was assembling the intellectual works of antiquity as well as the stock of ideas of the ancient Christian world, in a previously unattained fullness and extent, and together with his own rich interiority, was forging in a totally new sense, those magnificent educational goals that were fulfilled through an unshakable faith in Christian philosophy and in the effective power of the human spirit (which was also in the world of antiquity), he was heard extensively—he, who was greeted as the inspired re-awakener of the highest cultural forces of the world, the last great proclaimer of an inwardly renewed common cultural community of Europe, just as the contemporary emperor, Charles V, has become the last great emperor of the Holy Roman Empire and of Christendom. The western world now had to see how it might rightly find its way within the new which was breaking in upon it, and how perhaps in distant times it would win a new unity on the basis of transformed foundations.

When we are speaking of the publications of the great humanists, we should not forget an exquisite book monument, which once more shows us Erasmus and Holbein associated together, the *Lob der Torheit* ("Praise of Folly"), in a copy of the Froben edition of 1515 from the possessions of the *Magister,* Friedrich Myconius.[26] Myconius (or so tradition has it) read the work together with his friend, Hans Holbein, and has induced him to do all kinds of drawings on the margin of the text, while he himself has written several elucidations thereto. The artist later took the book with him and decorated it with further sketches. The unique book today rests in Basel's Municipal Museum, and through a faithful reproduction, has been made accessible. When on Epiphany, 1516, Erasmus viewed the larger portion of the eighty-two drawings (among which was his own handsome portrait) he, amused, expressed the opinion to Myconius that: "If I still looked so young, I'd marry immediately." The word gave to the witty artist the occasion to draw a further small picture that has Erasmus paying so much attention at the appearance of a beautiful woman, that he steps into the egg basket of a market woman and, to her dismay, breaks the eggs.

It is a witness to the farsightedness of the German humanists that they devoted themselves not merely to antiquity in spirit and in form, but that they also inquired into the literary monuments of their own past, and set the great deeds of the Germanic peoples over against the heightened feeling for fame that was present among the Italians. The humanist, Heinrich Bebel, in his publication praising Germany, established the claim of the German medieval imperium to the world leadership with the vital strength of the German people, which is visible everywhere. A strange dispensation of fate willed that the reawakening of the Roman antiquity also reproduced for the Germans their past (which was as good as forgotten) as this has been portrayed so concretely and gloriously in the records of the Romans, and especially in Tacitus. Tacitus had been almost entirely unknown in Germany when his *Germania* was published for the first time in 1470 by the German printer, Vendelinus de Spira, at Venice and then at Nuremberg in 1473. The first six books of the *Annals* of the same author, with the significant report about Arminius, were published in 1515 at Rome, at the suggestion of Pope Leo X. Both the editions did much to increase the self-confidence of the German humanists, and to stimulate them to make their own inquiries into, and editions of, the cultural monuments of the

Germans.[27] Thus in 1501 at Nuremberg, and in a volume provided with handsome dedicatory pictures, Conrad Celtes published the Latin poems of the Gandersheim nun, Hrotswitha (955–1001); he had discovered them in the Benedictine monastery of St. Emmeram at Regensburg.[28] Soon thereafter the humanist, who loved to wander about, found in the Cistercian monastery of Ebrach near Bamberg a second medieval poem, the ten songs of Ligurinus concerning the deeds of Emperor Friedrich I, and had them printed in 1507 in Augsburg. The manuscript itself is now lost.

Other scholars have soon followed the examples of the German "arch-humanist." Thus in 1508, on the basis of a manuscript of the cathedral chapter at Speyer, Gervasius Soupher published the medieval heroic poem about the war of Heinrich IV against the Saxons; as already mentioned, Konrad Peutinger in 1515 published the historiographers, Jordanes and Paul the Deacon; so did Johannes Cuspinianus publish in 1515 (from a manuscript of the Vienna Scots monastery) the important historical work of Bishop Otto of Freising (1115–1158), which had described the deeds of Emperor Frederick Barbarossa; thus there appeared in 1512, published by Hermann von Nuenar, the life of Einhard, and the deeds of Emperor Charlemagne, and in the same year, the annals of the Prüm monk, Regino, published by Sebastian von Rotenhan; further, in 1525, Lambert of Hersfeld's *Historia Germanorum*, in a textual version supplied by Kaspar Churrer from a manuscript of the Augustinian monastery in Wittenberg; and in 1532, Martin Frecht's collection of sources, with Widukind, Einhard, Liutprand, and the biography of King Henry IV from a Widukind manuscript at the monastery of Eberbach am Rhein.

One of the most zealous researchers into the native sources for history became the Bavarian historiographer, Johannes Aventinus, who, with covering letters from the Bavarian dukes, Ludwig and Wilhelm, moved from monastery to monastery during the years 1517 and 1518, and from church to church, in order to prepare a history of the land of Bavaria for its princes. He found the biography of Henry IV in St. Emmeram at Regensberg, and he published it in 1518 in Augsburg. He was one of the four humanists who also gave his attention to the German language monuments and valued them as concerns of the German nation. As he wrote on one occasion: "Of these matters and things there are still be many old German rhymes and master songs present in our foundations and our monasteries, because such songs alone are the old German chronicle, just as with us it its still the custom with us for the mercenaries to make up a song about their battles." And from the German heroic poem he mentions: "King Lareyn, of whom we yet sing and say much — there is still present a whole book full of rhymes of him, set in poetic style."

The learned Beatus Rhenanus (1485–1547), one of the humanists best informed concerning books and a successful counselor to the Basel printers, Johannes Amerbach and Johann Froben, found in 1515 a very old manuscript of the *Historica Romana* of Vellejus Paterculus (it was hopelessly torn) in the Benedictine monastery of Murbach.[29] He had it copied by a friend, and then he wanted to compare the text with one of George Merula's manuscripts which he had discovered in Milan. But because the persons around him, who were very curious on account of its reports concerning Varus' conflict with Arminius, were pressing for the work's publication, Rhenanus had the text printed only on the basis of the Murbach copy. Prior to the publication, his friend Albert Burer, by comparing with the Murbach original, established that the copy, as well as the reproduction, had come out very defective; so it had to be accompanied by five full leaves of textual corrections. Such experiences with copying and printing have not been unusual at that time and have been a source of much annoyance to the publishers.[30] In his edition of the church historians *(Augores historiae ecclesiasticae),* for which he was able to utilize a Greek Theodoritus manuscript of the Dominican monastery in Basel, Rhenanus expressed the desire that the clerical dignitaries in Rome might provide improved editions of the church fathers; in the ecclesiastical capital, there could be a lack neither of old manuscripts nor of scholars. In the elucidations to Pliny of 1526 he was already establishing the progressive principle that, in reproducing texts, one should go back to the most important, to the oldest, manuscripts. In the Cathedral Library at Freising, the humanist, who rejoiced in making his discoveries, came upon the rhymed poem, "Liber evangeliorum in Teodiscarm linguam versus;" it was Otfried's book of the gospels, which is now kept at the Munich State Library. In his German history he described in detail the valuable manuscript and rendered several examples, the first printed lines of Otfried's poetry.[31]

It was a book event of the highest significance when in 1518 the Mainz printer, Johann Schöffer, published a Livy-edition prepared by Wolfgang Angst and Nikolaus Carbaach with new textual sources form a parchment manuscript of the Mainz Cathedral Libray.[32] That Ulrich von Hutten and Erasmus of Rotterdam introduced the publication with enthusiastic words must have excited the greatest sensation. If already (so highly does Hutten speak about the merits of printing) Ptolemy Philadelphus, who founded in Alexandria a great and rich (but still only a single) library, should be blessed with unceasing praise, how highly then should those be praised who with their printed works were the first to give us, with their printed works, entire libraries in all languages and disciplines? With these words, Hutten has rightly seen and proclaimed the significance of printing in the service of the book and of cultural life generally.

The works of the pupil of Erasmus, Johannes Sichardus (1499–1552),[33] who through many years advised the Basel printers, Johann Bebel, Andreas Cratander, and Adam and Heinrich Petri, and during the years 1526–1530 managed no less than twenty-four editions of texts (among them being Caelius Aurelianus and the publication, *Laus Pisonis,* which we are acquainted with only from these publications, their manuscripts having been lost), give us a valuable view into the humanistic publication activity.

Nowhere else has so profound an understanding of the functions of the scholarly book combined with the printers' workshops as in Basel. Andreas Cratander, the distinguished publisher of the leaders of medicine in antiquity, Claudius Galenus, or Johannes Oporinus, (the printer of Vesalius) were themselves highly educated and they executed their work in a spirit that was conscious of its responsibility. Ancient manuscripts, or copies of them, were constantly lying around their houses, ready for printing. They maintained the closest relationship with the university libraries. With this trade things sometimes went very curiously. On August 2, 1542, Oporinus wrote to Theodor Bibliander, to whom he had insidiously sent a Koran of the University Library for a new edition, that Bibliander might soon send the book back, and if he were asked whence he had the manuscript, he should say, Andreas Karlstadt had sent it to him; he alone had held the key for a long time. One may as well lie of the deceased who himself always devised lies even against honest and upright people. The publication of the Koran certainly turned out to be a dangerous project. On August 30, the Basel council seized the sheets of the Latin translation of Bibliander that had been printed up to that point and put the printer, Oporinus, in prison. It was only with Luther's intercession that the printer and the book regained their freedom.

When the Franciscan, Peter Crabbe, published at Cologne in September 1538 his collection of the acts of church councils, and dedicated it to Emperor Charles V, he was able to point with pride to the fact that he had searched for sources in more than five hundred libraries. The Cologne Cathedral Library alone proffered him thirteen manuscripts. Thus did printing successfully open up for us the monastery libraries which up to that time been dusty, and it brought fame to these collections, since they were mentioned in the publication of their treasures. Research into manuscripts and the comparison of texts had everywhere established themselves as the indispensable requirements of publishers and printers.[34]

The Cologne publishers distinguished themselves also in other ways—through the publication of new or improved texts and, in connection therewith, they successfully made use of the rich book treasures of the Rhineland monasteries. The printer, Eucharius Cervicornus, obtained manuscripts from Cologne, from Heisterbach, from Siegburg and from Gladbach. The printer, Johannes Gymnicus, once recieved from the abbot of Springiersbach not merely a manuscript, but also a contribution to the costs of printing. The humanist, Friedrich Nausea, praised Cologne with its libraries as an outstanding center that even surpassed Alexandria.

In the person of Franciscus Modius we encounter one of the most vital searchers for manuscripts. Born August 4, 1556, near Bruges, he was friendly with the master of philology, Justus Lipsius. After wandering for quite some time, he became librarian of the zealous collector of books, Erasmus Neustetter (called Stürmer), and was subsequently active as a corrector with the Frankfurt printers; he finally was knocked about anew by Fate until he died at Aire on June 23, 1597.[35] Factors that secure him a place in the history of the book are: his astounding acquaintance with manuscript treasures, his indefatigable searching for texts that as yet were not known, and his valuable reports concerning the visits he made to monastery libraries. Several trips between 1575 to 1578 took him through the libraries of his Belgian homeland. Especially significant for him was his sojourn in Cologne, where he got to know the book treasures of the city and of the neighboring monasteries of Siegburg and Heisterbach, and likewise, through repeated visits, of the Fulda library. Several of the utilized manuscripts, such as the Justinian codices of Fulda and the *Silius Italicus* of Cologne, are lost today, and thus the mostly rather scarce notices concerning their use are all the more valuable. The Munich State

Library possesses the autographed diary of the humanist from the years 1581 to 1587, with valuable explanations about the visit in Fulda, and concerning the activity with the Frankfurt publishers, Feyerabend and Wechel.[36]

Traces of their having been in printers' workshops can still today be established in several manuscripts that happily have been preserved, such as the Hrotswitha-manuscript which was published by Celtes (it is now in Munich), in the Fulda Philo-manuscript that is now in Kassel, in the *Breviarum Codicis Theodosiani* at Bern, in the Bible manuscript at Basel which was used by Erasmus, and which contains numbers inscribed with red chalk pencil for the instruction of the typesetter.

It was an enormous mass reproduction of old texts which the fifteenth and six-teenth centuries experienced. The fact that some valuable manuscripts have thereby disappeared has its basis mostly in the publisher's carelessness, but fre-quently also in that of the original owner. The manuscripts have repeatedly gone directly to the printery and occasionally they have not been returned. The far-seeing imperial court historiographer, Nikolaus Mameranus, in his Paschasius edi-tion of 1550, censured those monks who believed that once a text had been printed they didn't need to keep the manuscript any more and thus it could be handed over to traders, chemists, goldsmiths, bookbinders and to the preparers of parchment. The old manuscripts, even when they had been printed a thousand times, had to be preserved most conscientiously, and protected as a valuable treasure. Their venerable age, and a proper respect for the past, required that. Seeing surprisingly far into the future, Mameranus was already demanding a public protection for the manuscriptural monuments, so that the old monastery manuscripts might not be so easily wasted, and the salesmen of manuscripts might not undetake any acquisi-tion without there being an official examination beforehand.[37] The losses that have come about in the process of reproduction, however, probably have been richly outweighed through the recovery and the growth in books that have flowed to the world out from numerous printers' workshops.

The learned sons of the Augsburg house of Fugger belong to the later great humanisitic bibliophiles. Endowed with rich, but certainly not inexhaustible, means, the highly educated and linguistically gifted Johann Jakob Fugger (1516–1575) strove to bring together an all-encompassing collection of books, in-cluding the entire literature of his period. With the library of Hartman Schedel, he acquired the entirety of the literary stock of the past generation almost, as it were, in one fell swoop. If, along with that, he eagerly collected Greek and Hebrew manuscripts, he was only paying homage to the humanistic preference for attending to the goal of the three languages – something to which each disciple in this move-ment devoted himself if he wanted to claim the name of "humanist." Since the old Greek parchment manuscripts were becoming rarer and rarer, he had to be satis-fied with copies that were not always without error. These mostly came from Venice, the inexhaustible market for books, with which Augsburg constantly stood in vital connection.

One can indeed directly designate the Swabian imperial city as being the chief buyer at the Venetian bookstores. Several of the older Hebrew manuscripts of Fug-ger came from the possessions of Cardinal Dominico Grimani, that enthusiastic collector of books who has bequeathed his treasures to the monastery of S. Antonio di Castello in Venice. A Cilician monastery has contributed a precious Armenian manuscript of 1278. In his Claudius Aelianus edition of 1556, Konrad Celtes indeed could not speak highly enough of all that was owed to the scholarhsip of the Augsburg bibliophile, who was in competition with Pisistratus, Ptolemy, Eumenes, Tyrannius and other book collectors. With a sense of satisfaction, Gesner mentions the great libraries of his own time (the Vaticana in Rome, the Marciana in Venice, the Medici collection in Florence, and the foundation of the kings in Paris) in order finally to praise the collection of his patrons as being one of the most outstanding.

Even Johannes Oporinus, the scholarly printer of Basel, in the Cicero commentary of 1553, made known his praise of Fugger. He thought that Fugger in his library not only offered protection to the living, but to the dead as well: for there were stored up in a well-organized way countless old and new manuscripts and printed works in the most diverse tongues, both sacred and secular ones without distinction, in the proper recognition that even the most negligible work could have a value of its own. The enormous sums that the purchases and the copying devoured from year to year meant the loss for Fugger of such financial resources that the passionate collector was finally faced with economic breakdown. Stepping in then at just the right time in the interests of the threatened collection was Duke Albrecht V of Bavaria, the generous patron of the arts and sciences. Already for a long time associated with the Bavarian court, Fugger after 1562 was obtaining one sum after another in advance, until the library in 1571 passed as security into the possession of the Bavarian duke, and Fugger was accepted among the duke's secret counsels with a compensation of a thousand florins. Counselling and encouraging, he was even now still able to devote himself to his "wards" until he died on July 14, 1575, not quite sixty years old.

A strange accident of fate arranged that in the same year of 1571 a second great Fugger collection, the library of Ulrich Fugger, has gotten into another princely court—the one at Heidelberg. Or was it by no means accidental (but only consistent) that in Munich the Catholic duke, and in Heidelberg the Evangelical duke, as leaders of their faithful, wanted to obtain enticing book possessions in order to be able to accomplish their ecclesiastical political goals also with cultural weapons? As the older borther of Johann Jakob, Ulrich Fugger (1526–1584) had inherited his pleasure in collecting from the father, Raimund Fugger. In the effort to get the Greek literature in valuable older manuscripts, Ulrich was more fortunate, because better relationships connected him with Italy. On October 6, 1553, he was able to acquire seventy-three valuable Greek manuscripts from the estate of the Vatican humanist, Giovanni Battista Egnazio, who was one of the most distinguished publishers of the ancient authors.[38] Fifteen manuscripts from the possessions of a Greek priest, Nathaniel, succeeded to him in 1559.[39] Again from Italy came a third significant acquisition, the exquisite collection of the Florentine statesman and humanist, Giannozzo Manetti (1396 to 1459), who had originally intended his possession of books for the Augustinian Hermits of S. Spirito in Florence. Now the treasures (among which was also the precious *Joshua* roll, a significant illuminated manuscript of the sixth to seventh century) got into the Swabian imperial city.[40] There the new master ruled over his possession like a prince. Freely he assisted the disciples of scholarship; he associated with scholars near and far, he attracted as his librarian the Scot, Henry Scrimger, who was publisher of the Emperor Justinian novellas, and so fully did he support the scholarly printer, Henricus Stephanus, that in several of his printed works Stephanus gratefully designated himself as Ulrich Fugger's printer. Contrary to his brother, Johann Jakob, Ulrich converted to Evangelical doctrine, collected the manuscripts of Evangelical preachers, as well as publications by Luther, and he finally put himself and his possessions under the protection of the Evangelical elector, Friedrich III of the Palatinate (1559–1576). The handsome collection, which at its removal to Heidelberg numbered over a thousand manuscripts (mostly Greek and Latin), was set up in 1571 in Holy Ghost Church and officially cataloged by the imperial notary, Ludwig von Schwechenheim. The charter with the attested seal is now kept in the Vaticana in Rome.[41] The collection initially remained in Ulrich Fugger's possession; he had taken up his permanent residence in Heidelberg.

Two new acquisitions yet accrued to him in 1583, the book treasures of the Augsburg city physician, Achilles Pirmin Gasser (d. 1577), and those of the Heidelberg councillor, Justus Reuber. Following Ulrich Fugger's death in 1584, the handsome collection ultimately was transferred into the possession of the Palatine elector and it enriched the Heidelberg library by about a third of its total holdings. The chief value of the significant increment lay in the Greek[42] and Latin manuscripts; there were also there, however, unique German literary monuments, such as the oldest known illuminated manuscript of the *Sachsenspiegel* ("Saxon Mirror") (Pal. Germ. 164), the old High German history of the gospels of Otfried of Weissenburg (Pal. lat. 52) and apparently also the famous *Manessische Lieder* manuscript, the brilliant treasure of the *Minne* singers, with its seven thousand strophes and 371 illustrations. A French translation manuscript with Wilhelm von Tyrus' *Histoire de la Guerre sainte* (Pal. lat. 1358) may boast an especially prominent provenance; it has once belonged to the Norwegian queen, Isabella (d. 1358); she was the consort of King Erik II Magnusson. When Jacques Bongars was preparing his edition of *Gesta Dei per Francos* in 1598, he needed to borrow the manuscript from Heidelberg; the corresponding directive of the electoral chancellery to the librarian, Paul Melissus, is today still attached as a loose leaf.

The *Joshua* roll attracted the special attention of the new caretakers of the collection, and it was listed as "an old Hebraic (!) tablet written on parchment, many feet long that unrolls on two rolls, doubtless belonging to Judaism."[43] The poet, Paul Melissus, had the pleasant task of immediately incorporating the Fugger treasures into the great Heidelberg collection. Friedrich Sylburg (d. 1598), the most significant German Hellenist of his time, set himself up in Heidelberg in 1591 mainly to sift through the valuable Greek items with the help of the scholarly printer, Hieronymus Commelinus.[44] Still more successfully did Janus Gruterus,[45] the most knowledgeable of the German researchers into antiquity, utilize the Heidelberg Library and spread its fame into the entire scholarly world. In Heidelberg (as in Augsburg), printing and book collecting have together made for more valuable scholarly activity, have opened up important texts from the old manuscripts, and have thereby have fulfilled a difficult as well as rewarding assignment in caring for books.

One of the last valuable humanists' libraries to be preserved up until current times originated with Dean Erasmus Neustetter, called Stürmer (d. 1595), who worked in Komburg bei Schwäbisch-Hall, as dean of the chivalric foundation there and who devoted himself completely to an aesthetic style of life.[46] One of his most valuable book acquisitions was the priceless collection of the Bavarian nobleman, Oswald von Eck (d. 1550), who was in considerable debt.[47] Among them were excellent books of Dietrich von Plieningen, whose widow Leonhard von Eck had married, and further priceless residues from the estate of the Bavarian historiographer, Johannes Aventinus, such as the fair copy of the *Annals*, and the *Bavarian Chronicle*. Nikolaus Cisner could publish in 1580 the *Bayerische Chronik* ("Bavarian Chronicle") according to the Komburg manuscript, and, commending him, could mention that his patron had acquired the library of Eck, with Aventinus' legacy, at great cost, and had handed over to him the manuscripts. When in 1590 Neustetter was writing down his last will, he wrote in the abbey of Komburg as the heir of the collection (valued at over two thousand florins), which had been praised by Conrad Gesner, Johann Posthius and Franciscus Modius, on condition that two thousand florins had to be set up as a foundation by the beneficiaries for maintenance. After the institution was dissolved in 1803, the handsome collection of books has come to Stuttgart, and into the Territorial Library there.

17
The Reformation and the World of Books

When on October 31, 1517, Martin Luther posted his ninety-five theses on indulgences to the Castle church in Wittenberg, and when on December 10, 1520, before the Elster Gate he threw the papal bull (which threatened him with excommunication) and the books of canon law into the blazing fire, those fateful hours were striking also for the book world, which would radically reshape the literature of the time. Humanism was already waging an assault on medieval Scholasticism and barbaric Latin. Humanism's authors, however, were scholars, its language was Latin, and its readers were only from the educated class. Its announcement of combat had directed itself not against the foundations of the church, even though the ridicule directed at secularization in the church and ignorance among the clergy did have a profound effect, and the church's diminishing prestige had been sensitively hit. The decisive thing with Luther was that he, out of deep religious emotion, and a passionate and incomparable power of speech, summoned the entire German people to struggle against the old church, and that in the German pamphlet literature he acquired a weapon of irresistible force. "What Luther said," Herder once asserted, "one had long known; but now Luther said it."

All forms of the summons: the sermon, the circular, the comforting word, the exhortation, the speech of judgment, the condemnation, the invective—for him these because impressively formed pamphlets and they went out into the world in hundreds and thousands of copies. Luther was thoroughly conscious of the power of these things, and of their effect as well. [1] Thus he said in the dedicatory preface to his 1520 publication, *Von den guten Werken* ("Concerning Good Works"): "And although I know full well and hear every day that many people think little of me, and say that I only write little pamphlets and sermons in German for the uneducated laity, I don't let that stop me. Would to God that in my lifetime I had, to my fullest ability, helped one layman to be better! I would be quite satisfied, thank God, and quite willing to let all my booklets perish. Whether the making of many large books is an art, and of benefit to Christendom, I leave for others to judge. But I believe that if I were of a mind to write big books of that kind, I could perhaps, with God's help, do it more readily than they could write my kind of small discourse."

The distribution of Luther's pamphlets was truly incredible. the *Sermon von Ablass und Gnade* ("Sermon on Indulgence and Grace") was published in the years 1518–1520 in twenty-two editions. The publication, *An den chrislichen Adel deutscher Nation von des christlichen Standes Besserung* ("To the Christian Nobility of the German Nation on the Reformation of the Christian Estate"), was published in August 1520 by the Wittenberg printery of Melchior Lotter in four thousand copies—perhaps the largest edition that a printer up to that time had released. A second edition was already following after only one week, and within the shortest time, the publication was distributed in fifteen editions and printings. The rousing call to awaken, *Von der Freiheit eines Christenmenschen* ("Of the Freedom of a Christian Man") (1520) has gone through eighteen editions. This publication represents the high point of Luther's publicizing work, which the Reformer himself designated with the apposite words: "As can be seen from the paper, it is a small book, but still there is comprehended in it the whole *summa* of the Christian life, as the meaning of this is (commonly) understood." Luther's best troops were the printers and the booksellers, and they dispersed his publications all over Germany, as well those of his comrades in arms. "Printing made it so that, through the Luther of the first public years, all of Germany for the first time stood under the influence of a single man." (Lortz).

When on May 26, 1521, Emperor Charles V formally declared Luther under imperial ban from Worms, and in his edict he also forbade his writings, it was already too late. The German people and public opinion stood on Luther's side, and actually carrying through the imperial ban was all the less likely, as the emperor himself left Germany for almost a decade and Luther found a powerful protector in his Elector, Frederick of Saxony. Luther's pamphlets were stronger than the imperial edict, the attack more effective than the defense. From the period of Luther's greatest influence until the people's alienation following the Peasants' Wars, one can count up to two thousand editions of the Reformer's publications. Reprints had their initial flowering, and Luther's repeated invectives against it had as good as no success at all. His publications were eagerly sought out, and the printer offered them in countless authorized, as well as unauthorized, editions.

Just at Luther's burning of the books had already challenged medieval literature, so in his publication *An die Rathern aller Städte, dass sie Christliche Schulen aufrichten sollen* ("To the Councillors of all the cities that they should erect Christain schools"), the Reformer was yet once more thundering against the "foolish, useless, shameful monks' books: *Catholicon, Florista, Grecista, Labyrinthus, Dormi secure* and similar asses' dung that have been introduced by the Devil," and . . . in his complaint delivered to the City of Nuremberg on September 26, 1525, concerning the reprinting of his publications there, he wrote: "I am also well aware that many books remain lying around at Koburger's,[2] as well as at other printers. But what can we do? Are we supposed to suffer for it, we who with our books have not tried to harm them; God, however, disposed that these should pass away and be demolished, as it goes also in other trades." That was Luther's attitude to the Scholastic world of books in the period that was past, and his word soon became public opinion. "Previously," said Johann Eberlin in 1521, *"Dormi secure, Thesaurus novus, Postilla Guilhelmi,*[3] *Discipulus, Pomerius,* etc, yes, Gabriel (Biel), Oliverius (Maillard), *Summa predicantium,* etc., were good books; now, one doesn't care for them; it is now said that the teaching of such books should be, and that it is, wrong."

That Luther's movement, which initially was a purely religious one, gradually grew into a national one, was especially effected by the contentious humanist and crowned poet laureate, Ulrich von Hutten, who, consumed by an unbounded hatred of everything papal and monastic, took his stand with Luther and was soon likewise flinging among the people (in the German language) fiery secular challenges to Rome and the clergy. "I have written in Latin before/ That which wasn't known to each and everyone/ Now I cry out to the Fatherland/ The German nation, in its own tongue/ To bring down vengeance on these things." Invariably he had his pen in his hand, and a printer at his side. In 1519, he wrote to his brother-in-law, Sebastian Rotenhan: "I am amazed that you would that I have something to write about, or at hand to poeticize, just as if you had not found me writing, even when I still was in the middle of gathering and commotion." And in the margin one reads: "Hutten is always writing something."

Never again in German history has the pamphlet attained such significance as it did in the Reformation movement of the years 1520–1525, a period that can be virtually designated as the pamphlet's classical period. The pamphlet dominated the daily publications, the printing workshops, the book market, and public opinion. It developed an eloquence that was without equal. It was as if, all of a sudden, the tongues of men had been loosened. This growth of language and this art of publicity were already expressing the new form of communication in a variety of titles. We here encounter the *Unterrede* ("Conversation"), das *Gespräch* ("Talk"), the *Dialog,* the *Sendbrief* ("Circular") the *Antwort auf den Sendbrief* ("Answer to the Circular"), the *Weggespräch* ("Talk Along the Way"), the *Büchlein* ("Little book"), the *Mandat,* the *Lied* ("Song"), the *Anrede* ("Address"), the *Pasquillus* ("Lampoon"), all of them very effective addresses to the reader. The titles have frequently been accompanied by pictorial representations.

In *Gespräch* or *Dialog* there appear for the most part men of the people, such as a canon or a farmer, a mendicant monk and a countryman, a priest and a weaver, a strawcutter and a wood cutter, a pastor and a mayor, a monk and a baker, or the speakers with their names before the reader as if they were real, as if they were old acquaintances, such as Cuntz and Fritz, Hans and Heinz, Hans Tholl and Claus Lamp, Hans Schöpfer and Peter Schabenhut. Luther mingled with the professions and the trades, in order to get people to confirm the language. He said in the sermon on the Kingdom of Christ and Herod, "A strike of a thresher in the barn is as valuable before God as a psalm sung by a Carthusian." Concerning the papists it is stated in the *Sermon zu Erfurt:* They "feed the sheep, just as the butcher does on Easter Eve." And a master who rules according to his foolish head and discretion, is compared (in the publication, *Concerning Good Works)* with a driver "who with horse and wagon runs on through the bushes, the hedges, ditches, water, mountains and valleys, unsafe paths and bridges, who will not drive for long before it goes into ruins." And the Reformer asserts about himself: "I have been born in order that I may get at loggerheads with devils and hordes of robbers, and wrestle in the field with them; therefore my books are, many of them, stormy and militant. I must eradicate the stumps and the roots, cut off the thorns and the hedges, fill up the puddles, and I am the rough wood cutter who prepares and fixes the path." His environment is an inexhaustible source for the powerful shaper of language.

In *Grosser Sermon vom Wucher* ("Great Sermon on Usury") it is complained that always an interest drives the other like water does the mill wheel. Marriage and chastity are for him two equally valuable ways of living, "just as when two walk to a city, one may go on the pavement, the other on the highway itself, as it seems best to him." Luther gladly took animals as illustrations in order to heap ridicule on an opponent. Of Hieronymus Emser he says, "Emser fits with St. Paul like the ass does with the nightingale." Of Augustine Alveldt he asserted: "I indeed see that the ass does not understand lute music; before him the thistle has to be put;" and another time, "I beg you that whoever will oppose me should arm himself with the Bible; what does it help that a poor frog has puffed himself up? Even if he bursts, he will still not become an oxen." The man who wants to be saved through good works alone, loses his faith, "like the dog who carries a piece of meat in his mouth and snaps after a reflection in the water, and so loses the reflection and, with it, the meat." Luther mocked his opponent, Karlstadt, with the comparison: "Perhaps he likes to hear himself talk as gladly as does the stork hear his beak clack." Luther also augments his treasury of words and images from natural events. "You should know," he appeals to the councillors of all the cities and towns, "that God's Word and grace is a cloudburst that doesn't come again, where it once has been."

This rich treasury of word and speech of Luther's has to be illustrated with several examples, because it belongs to the essence of the Reformation pamphlet, and it helps to explain the enormous effect it had on the German people. Shown here for the first time in the most powerful effect is what popular publications and printing are indeed capable of, if they be coupled with stirring thoughts in a language that is appealing.

The second great influence of Luther's on the development of the book world consists of his German Bible translation. It did not merely have an incomparable religious significance, but it was also of the greatest linguistic consequence and, in the Reformation movement's turning back to primitive Christendom, it became the principal book of that movement.[4] To be sure, fourteen High German and five Low German translations had previously been issued by the most varied printeries, partially decorated with beautiful woodcuts; but with their difficult language, these had not spoken to the people, the 1520 Halberstadt one perhaps being excepted. Only Luther has become THE German Bible translator, and so has he remained for centuries. The Reformer here has clearly recognized his task and he has pursued it consciously. "I have," he writes in an epistle from the interpreters, "striven in translation to render a pure and clear German. And we have indeed often looked for a word for fourteen days, or for three or four weeks, and nevertheless sometimes we have not found it." Luther and his fellow workers have often sat together in the Reformer's dwelling in the old Augustinian monastery before the evening meal, Luther himself with his German and Latin translation, Melanchthon with the Greek, Cruciger with the Hebrew and Chaldaic, and Bugenhagen with the Latin text. "Anno Domini 1543, on January 24" – so goes Johann Stols' report concerning the final session before the completion of the entire Bible – "thoughtful gentlemen have undertaken anew to correct the Bible throughout, and have in many areas rendered the same into German plainer and clearer than it previously was. They have especially had trouble with the prophets in order to render them accurately into the German language. Jesus Sirach has especially required a lot of effort, before he was expressed in a clean, good German." Because of this searching and formulation, Luther's Bible translation has become a linguistic master work.

Luther's Bible translation thus had exceptional success in the book market, such as had never been seen before. The first edition of the New Testament came out in September, 1522, with the woodcut title, *Das Newe Testament Deutzsch*. Neither the publisher nor the printer is named in it. Only the indication of the place as Wittenberg divulged the origin of the printed work. We know now that the painter, Lucas Cranach, and the goldsmith, Christian Doring, had published the book with five hundred copies at their publishing house. It has been printed by Melchior Lotter The Younger in Wittenberg. The decorative illustrations, twenty-one woodcuts of the Apolcalypse, come from Lucas Cranach. The dragon in chapters 11 and 16, and likewise the Babylonian woman, belligerently wear the papal tiara. A second edition was following already in December of the same year—this time with Luther's printer's device. The tiara is here reduced to a simple crown. As with the pamphlets, the printers had their hands full in satisfying the demand for the New Testament, as well as for the other parts of the Bible translation that quicly followed, one upon another. The New Testament came out in the years 1522–1534 in eighty-five editions; counting the individual parts, the number climbed, until Luther's death, to over four hundred editions. The first entire text appeared in 1534 in the publishing house of the Wittenberg bookdealers, Moritz Goltz, Bartel Vogel and Christoph Schramm; it was printed by the Wittenberg master, Hans Lufft, Luther's chief Bible printer. Luther has played a big role in the book's illustrative layout. Christoph Walther, the printer's corrector, expressly reports that the Reformer had "to some extent assigned the figures himself, and how they were supposed to be cut." As a man of the people, Luther took pleasure in the Bible woodcuts. "What harm would it do," he said in his preface to the *Passionale* of 1530, "if someone portrayed one after another of all the prominent stories of the whole Bible as a little book, that such a little book would be a layman's book? Indeed, one can't hold up for the common man the word and work of God too much or too often." The electors of Saxony and Brandenburg, as well as the princes of Anhalt, had the whole Bible decorated in 1535, with special title pages and their own arms; the bust of Elector Johann Friedrich of Saxony has been added besides. In individual copies the Wittenberg reformers entered album verses. As a result, Luther's Bible translation has become the most read religious book of Evangelical Germany.

Luther's table talks, which were recorded and published by the friends and table companions of Luther, have introduced a new form of publication; these talks can be compared with Goethe's conversations with Eckermann.[5]

Not much has been preserved from the books that Luther himself owned.[6] Most of this material consists of Luther's works with manuscriptural entries made by the Reformer. The *Schmalkald Articles* in Luther's original text are in Heidelberg.[7]

Luther's brilliant words concerning the freedom of the Christian man have only too quickly gone throughout the world or been subject to adulteration. In his own way, the author was influenced by that publication storm that in the spring of 1525 swept over all of Germany in twenty-five editions, and openly challenged the peasants to a common struggle against oppression by the authorities. On the title page it is stated: " The basic and legitimate main articles of all the peasants and small farmers (to) the spiritual and secular authorities, by whom they are oppressed." In the introductory sentences the reproach that the new gospel leads to disobedience and agitation is refuted. Since the basis of all the articles of the peasants should be to hear the gospel and to live by its as if by a "yardstick, how then can the anti-Christians call the gospel a source of revolt and disobedience?" The further programmatic publication of the initially moderate movement was entitled: "Matters, articles, and instructions, which have been taken up by all the gangs and crowds of peasants, to which they have bound themselves together."

A second edition of the publication, in misjudgment of the feelings in Wittenberg, called as umpires between the peasants and lords, first of all, Elector Friedrich of Saxony, Martin Luther, Philipp Melanchthon, or Johann Bugenhagen. The revolutionary development of the peasant movement under Thomas Münzer's leadership, and the other passionate enthusiasts (and to no less extent, Luther's curse of the peasants) have all finally transformed the entire folk movement in to a bloodbath. Of the numerous editions of the *Hauptartikel aller Bauernschaft* ("Main Articles of All the Peasants"), which were issued with so many hopes, only a few copies have been preserved, so that today one has to draw on fourteen libraries, in order to obtain the editions all together. The considerable diffusion of pamphlets, in which is to be seen one of the most memorable political protests in German history, has contributed not a little to the swift spreading of the peasants' movement.

With the peasants' attacking the monasteries and castles, numerous clerical and nobiliary treasuries of books have also been destroyed, along with other properties. In sad rememberance of the beautiful monastery library that was destroyed, Georg Truchsess of Wetzhausen, the abbot of the monastery of Auhausen, cried out in indignation: "A valuable library of twelve hundred books in all disciplines, which have cost the blessed Dean of Eichstätt and me over fifteen hundred gulden, the Devil's children have torn into several parts, have spoiled and cut to pieces, and burned and thrown in to the wells." The entire library was a heap of ruins. Things have not gone much better in the monasteries of St. Blasien, Roggenburg, Maihingen, Maria-Mai, Maulbronn, Ochsenhausen, Ebrach and others. Seventy monasteries have been plundered in Thuringia alone. From Reinhardsbrunn, only several manuscripts which had by chance been lent out have been preserved.[8]

The wars of the Reformation has also been disastrous for several printers, and especially so for the minor masters, who out of their own inclination, or in order to increase their incomes, have made common cause with the emerging religious enthusiasts and the Anabaptists. Thus Hieronymus Hötzel in Nuremberg was called to account in 1524 because he had printed the writings of Andreas Karlstadt, as well as the work directed against Luther, *Hochverursachte Schutzrede und Antwort Thomas Münzers wider das geistlose, sanftlebend Fleisch zu Wittenberg* ("Highly occasioned supportive speech and answer of Thomas Münzer against the stupid, soft living flesh at Wittenberg"); the Nuremberg Council also intervened, with punishments, against the printer, Hans Hergot, on account of other pamphlets by Münzer which he had printed. The same printer had to pay still more dearly for the sale of the provocative publication from the year 1526, *Von der neuen Wandlung eines christlichen Lebens* ("Concerning the new transformation of a Christian life"), which promoted the communal ownership of property. The bookdealer was arrested in Leipzig and at the command of Duke Georg of Saxony, he was beheaded on March 20, 1527, the first offering in blood known to us that the printed pamphlet literature has demanded.[9]

It was a turbulent period. Even the treasuries of books in the numerous monasteries and foundations came to feel the force of this tempestuous time, and frequently they were dissolved. With the rejection of ecclesiastical ceremonies, and the whole of the medieval tradition of theological learning, the death sentence was also pronounced over the totality of the liturgical, theological and canon law books. With the dissolution of numerous monasteries in the Evangelical cities and territories, their book holdings were for the most part scattered, pilfered or obliterated. Heinrich Bullinger specifically reports to us how only a few of the books in the Great Minster of Zurich were kept, and how all the others had been destroyed, or sold for a pittance. In the catalog of the minster of 1525 there is listed "Caroli des Kaisers Betbuch, mit Gold gefasst" (Charles the Emperor's prayerbook, bound with gold). For a long time forgotten about, this handsome prayer book of Emperor Charles the Bold surfaced again in 1580 and came to Duke Wilhelm V of Bavaria. The text was printed in 1583 in Ingolstadt *(Liber precationum)* and was decorated with picturesque reproductions of parts of manuscripts, which are indeed to be seen as the first attempts at manuscript reproduction.[10] A German translation followed in the next year, and in 1585 a French one. The manuscript itself was first placed in the Munich Court Library, and later in the treasure chamber. The earlier binding, embellished with gold, silver, and precious jewels, had long since disappeared.

In the confusion of the Reformation period, several of the libraries of dissolved monasteries have been completely ruined; their possessions are now as good as lost. One thus searches in vain for what is left of the books of Amelungsborn, Corvey, Walkenried, Riddagshausen, and Lehnin.[11] It was fortunate when the famous library of Lorsch was abruptly carried off by Count Palatine Ottheinrich to Heidelberg and thus saved.

The initial (but certainly not very effective) thrust toward the new building of the Evangelical book world Luther gave in his admonition of the year 1524, "To the Councillors of all the cities in Germany, that they should erect and conduct Christian schools." Since the Reformer here primarily had in mind, among the institutions required, the scholarly schools of higher learning for educating the clerical and secular leaders of the people, so he was demanding school libraries and scholars' libraries as important assisting means thereto; they were not popular libraries, as one can occasionally read. "My advice," writes Luther, "is not to heap together all manner of books indiscriminately and consider only the number and size of the collection. I would make a judicious selection, for it is not necessary to have all the commentaries of the jurists, all the sentences of the theologians, all the *Questions* of the philosophers, and all the sermons of the monks. Indeed, I would discard all such dung, and furnish my library with the right sort of books, consulting with scholars as to my choice." To the most necessary possessions of a library must belong the holy scriptures in as many languages as possible, and the best interpretations added to them; further, books that serve the purposes of knowledge of languages, such as poets and orators (whether they be Christian or heathen), and besides that, the literature from the liberal arts, law and medicine, and finally, but not least, the chronicles and histories—the ones that are useful for knowing the course the world has taken as well as for governing—and also for seeing God's wonder and work.

The regulations of the new faith were to a certain degree effective in this direction, in which the significance and the necessity for collections of books is expressly referred to. Thereupon everywhere in the cities and towns, church and school libraries were built that gradually developed into collecting sites for the more valuable gifts of the councillors, the school men and the clerics, and which attempted to carry out the functions of the earlier monastic libraries. Many of today's church, municipal and gymnasium libraries go back to them.

Where the dissolved monastery libraries were not totally destroyed, what was left of them found shelter in the already existing secular book collections, or in new ecclesiastical ones.[12] The book treasures came off best when they were given to universities, as in the Duchy of Saxony, where the University of Leipzig received valuable parts of the holdings from dissolved monasteries of the territory, especially from Leipzig, Altzelle, Pegau, Chemnitz, Salza, Buch, Pirna, and Lauter-Berg, there being about fifteen hundred manuscripts and four thousand printed works in all;[13] or in Basel, where in 1559 the valuable Dominican library with valuable possessions of Cardinal Johannes von Ragusa, as well as a larger part of the Cathedral Library, were united with the books owned by the university.

We do not know much about the achievements of the Evangelical church and school libraries. Wolfgang Büttner, the author of *Historien von Claus Narren*, in his historical excerpt, *Epitome Historiarum* of 1576, praises the Count of Schwarzburg, who had founded a copious book room for the church at Sonderhausen; through the intervention of Christoph Helmreich, he was allowed to see it.

Most of these church libraries suffered heavily under the difficulties of the time. When the Strasbourg preacher, Martin Bucer, had to report in March, 1547, to the Newburg printer, Hans Kilian, concerning his attempt to elicit interest in his printed works in Strasbourg, he had dejectedly to write: "I have inquired everywhere at the German libraries; unfortunately all book sales in these troubled times are quite depressed; they could give me no hope with my sales."

As in Germany, so also in the other Evangelical countries, in England, Sweden, Norway, and Denmark, the church and monastery libraries came to an end through the introduction of the new doctrine. In the confusion of the time, the rich university library at Oxford was so completely destroyed that as good as nothing was left, and therefore even the book shelves were auctioned off. England's scattered book treasures found an understanding protector in the Archbishop of Canterbury, Matthew Parker (1504–1575), who brought together a rich collection of manuscripts. The main residues of it are preserved today in Corpus Christi college at Cambridge.[14]

The libraries of Cluny, Fleury and Micy near Orléans fell as victims to the religious wars in France. The most significant of them was the very ancient book collection of the Benedictine monastery at Fleury, which goes back to the seventh century, and is also called St. Benoit-sur-Loire. Its mark of ownership, "Liber Sancti Benedicti floriacensis" has become quite famous. Following the monastery's being stormed by the Huguenots in 1562, Peter Daniel, the abbey's counselor, was able to appropriate valuable manuscripts through the favor of Cardinal Odo Colingy, sire of Chatillon, the monastery's secular abbot, and a zealous Huguenot; from his possessions, these have partially come in 1603 to Paul Petau (Petavius), and later to Queen Christine of Sweden, and then finally to the Vatican; and partially they have come to Jacques Bongars, with whose books they have further come to Bern.

The second pioneer of the German Evangelical book world after Luther became Philipp Melanchthon, the savior of the endangered education in Evangelical Germany, the learned humanist, who sought to connect the gospel with scholarship, and the doctrines of the new faith with a humanistic education.[15] His *Loci communes*, the first Evangelical book of doctrine and ethics, was among the most widely distributed books of the Protestant publications. His most famous publication is the *Augsburg Confession*, the confessional document of the Evangelical Lutheran Church; it was handed over on June 25, 1530 to the Emperor and Empire with the signatures of the imperial estates who accepted the new faith.

Besides Luther and Melanchthon, a still younger theologian of the Reformation period who intervened in the Evangelical book world was Matthias Flacius from Illyricum, who therefore is called Illyricus (1520–1575). The most aggressive theologian of the period, he was the founder of the first Evangelical church history, which because of its origin and arrangement, is called the *Magdeburg Centuries*.[16] One of the most industrious promoters of the great church history undertaking was Kaspar von Nidbruck, King Maximilian's influential counsel, with whom Flacius was associated in an exchange of letters.[17] Nidbruck himself collected manuscripts and, while being counsel to the king, had easy access to other collections. He readily placed his books at Flacius' disposal. In order to arouse no suspicion in Vienna, Regensburg was chosen as a harmless locale for the exchange of books, which could be easily reached from Vienna by way of the Danube. In Magdeburg, the chief site for the collaborators, the collegium of five (Matthias Flacius, Johann Wigund, Martin Copus, Matthäus Judex and Gottschalk Prätorius) had to be responsible for punctually giving back materials that had been lent; in Regensburg, the Evangelical city council took the guarantee.

Following these preparations, numerous manuscripts and printed works were assembled in Magdeburg and Regensburg.[18] In Regensburg, there was above all Marcus Wagner, one of the most enthusiastic collaborators in the project; he was active from September 1556 to the summer of 1557 in working through the treasures of books sent there.[19] Through Nidbruck's mediation, Wagner received letters of recommendation for other collections of books; the letters were issued by Bishop Urban of Gurk; in them it is stated that the bearer (of the letters) had been dispatched to search for old treasuries of books, and chiefly for the historical sources for an imperial Germany history. It was a severe blow for the project, when Nidbruck (who was scarcely over 30 years old) died on September 26, 1557. On October 22, 1559, King Maximilian gave thanks for the first century of the Magdeburg church history; but he simultaneously demanded the return of the manuscripts which had been sent back to Regensburg. The lawyer, Georg Tanner, searched in Italy for useful sources of Madgeburg.[20] We encounter him in Venice, Padua, Florence, and Rome.

The now already experienced Marcus Wagner successfully toured in England and Scotland and returned home with especially rich booty from St. Andrews and Edinburgh. His stories about the dissolved monastery libraries there induced Flacius to issue the famous challenge to Matthew Parker, Archbishop of Canterbury, on May 22, 1561, to purposefully transfer the endangered treasuries of books in dissolved English and Scottish monasteries into public ownership, because such were for the whole country and the church; they were not individual property, but a public possession.[21] If Flacius had also raised his voice in Germany in this way many book treasures would thus have been saved. He himself searched church and monastery libraries whenever he had opportunity, and he primarily found an entree where the monastery was in process of disintegration. Exiled from Jena, he had scarcely obtained shelter in Regensburg in 1562, when he immediately visited the monasteries of the area, and on February 23, he also put in at the Benedictine abbey of Reichenbach im Regentale. The monastery, which belonged to Palatine-Neuburg, was already facing total decay; the abbot, Michael Katzbeck, had become Evangelical and had married. Soon Flacius was returning with twelve old manuscripts. His patron, the Regensburg superintendent, Nikolaus Gallus, posted a regular borrowing slip with the short titles of the manuscripts and assumed the bond for them. At least three of the items lent can be traced today to the Wolfenbüttel Library, which was the heir of Flacius' library; they have thus not been returned to Reichenbach.[22] Flacius was even able to get manuscripts out of Fulda. Elector Ottheinrich put the book treasures of Heildelberg at his disposal, and where he was able, he supported the work of the *Centuries*. The second book of the first *Zenturie* has been dedicated to him and to Elector August of Saxony. Within the context of this activity with the literary monuments of the Middle Ages, Flacius became one of the best and most knowledgeable authorities on manuscripts in his period, and in his collection of books he accumulated one priceless item after another. It was on the basis of a Heidelberg manuscript that he published the chronicle of Sulpicius

Severus in 1556; on the basis of an original text from Minden he published Julius Firmicus Maternus' work, *De errore profanarum religionum,* in 1562.[23]

We are further indebted to him for the first publishing of the oldest of the larger Old High German language monuments, the famous book of the gospels of Otfried of Weissenburg. The Augsburg city physician, Achilles Pirmin, had already copied the text from Ulrich Fugger's manuscript, and sent it for printing, together with a glossary, to Conrad Gesner in Zurich, but in August 1563 he received it back with the answer that no printer in Zurich wanted to undertake the work, because no one understood the language. Now Flacius managed it so that the beautiful poem appeared in 1571 at Basel. For Flacius it was an important evidence that holy scripture had already been transmitted from the ancient time into the German popular tongue. Two lower Rhineland assistants of the *Centuries,* Georg Cassander and Cornelius Wouters, have found another significant language monument, the Gothic Bible translation of Ulfilas, the oldest textual transmission in the development of the German language, about the year 1554. They discovered it in connection with their search for old texts in the West German abbey of Werden an der Ruhr among the most valuable of the manuscripts preserved there, the world famous *Codex argenteus.*[24] The manuscript has later come into the possession of Emperor Rudolf II and has been carried off to the North by the Swedes during the Thirty Years' War. It is now in Uppsala.

When Flacius died, his heirs found themselves confronted with a rich collection of priceless manuscripts. It was fortunate that they found a patron in Duke Heinrich Julius of Brunswick; he obtained the entire possession for his court library for 1095 thalers in 1597. The treasures are thus now preserved in Wolfenbüttel. There are among them quite unique priceless items, such as the Aachen *Capitulare* of Charlemagne from 789, the famous *Capitulare de Villis,* the *Lex Alamannorum* from the eighth century, and Vergil's *Aeneid* from the twelfth century.

What Flacius meant for the Evangelical church historiography, Johannes Sleidanus, the historiographer of the Schmalkald Federation, meant for the representation of the political history of Evangelical Germany: through his contemporary *Commentare über den Zustand der Religion und des Staates unter Kaiser Karl V* ("Commentary on the Condition of Religion and of the State under Emperor Charles V") he has achieved such fame that he is considered to have been the first historiographer of the Evangelical faith movement.[25] The work, which was based on pamphlets and acts of the state, was published in 1555 for the first time by the Strasbourg printer, Rihel; it was printed again and again in eighty editions, used in Protestant gymnasiums as an instructional book, and it is still regarded today as being one of the most important sources for our knowledge of the Reformation period.

A remarkable episode in the Evangelical book production took place in Württemberg, when the Carniolan primate, Truber (1508–1586), an enthusiastic dispenser of Evangelical doctrine in the south Slavic regions, with the help of Duke Christoph of Württemberg and of the baron, Hans Ungnad von Sonneck, printed in the years 1550–1564 several Evangelical publications in the Slavic and Croatian languages with Cyrillic and Glagolitic types, and distributed them among the population of Carniola and Croatia.[26] The bindings of these works are mostly decorated with pictures of Truber and his collaborators, Stipan Consul and Anton Dalmation. In this form, the Tübingen and Urach printings are among the most unusual German book phenomena of the sixteenth century.

Even in the northern countries, and in the Baltic Sea states of Latvia, Lithuania and Estonia, printing and the Reformation had their special functions and significance, since in these territories they distributed the Bible and Evangelical publications in the native languages and thereby fostered the national languages of these countries. The Evangelical faith-movement has frequently brought there the first printed national monuments of printing. Becoming the main centers of this dissemination were Wittenberg, Königsberg and Danzig. When Michael Agricola of Wittenberg returned in 1539 to Finland, he was entrusted with translating Luther's Bible translation into Finnish. Agricola is therefore not only the church reformer of his fatherland, he has also become the founder of the Finnish literary language. Or one fetched a German master into the country, such as Ludwig Dietz of Rostock, who on commission from King Christian III, produced the great Danish Bible translation in three thousand copies in 1550 at Copenhagen. Apart from the printer, the king also called on the Lübeck bookbinder, Paul Knobloch, with the commission to bind two thousand copies of the Bible in his capital within a year; for each item he was provided with free lodging and rewarded with two Danish marks for each item.[27] Dietz had become known through his Low German Luther Bible, which was published with beautiful woodcuts in 1533–1534.

Just as the Reformation did, so also has the Catholic counter movement deeply impinged on the history of the book. One needs only here to refer to the *Index librorum prohibitorum* and its consequences for the book world.[28] According to the ecclesiastical stipulations, the monasteries and all the faithful had to destroy the publications of all definite heretics, such as Luther, Zwingli and Calvin, and following that they had to "purge" those works which in themselves were permissible, but which, on account of their prefaces, or the names of their heretical publishers, were suspect – that is, they had to clean them up through the removal of all suspected passages. The scholarly Spaniard, Arias Montanus, on commission from King Philip II of Spain and the Duke of Alba, published in 1571 with the Antwerp printer, Christoph Plantin, his own *Index expurgatoribus librorum*, with regulations for managing the index, and especially for prescriptions related to expurgation.[29]

A concrete illustration of such censure measures is given in the books of the Munich Jesuits which today are held in the Munich State Library, and which have been purged in 1578 of all suspicious passages by the famous Peter Canisius and a second Jesuit, Gerard Massetus. Books that were actually heretical were locked up. All other works had to be inspected and their orthodoxy tested. Those works that came from Catholic publishing locales could for the most part be allowed to pass unopposed. Everything, on the other hand, that issued from Evangelical printeries, whether they were fathers of the church, or classical authors, or other secular works, had to be purged. The names of the heretical authors were blacked out, pasted over, or in other ways extinguished. Things went no better with the printers and publishers; even their names were made illegible. Since the Roman

Index of Pope Paul IV of 1559 had produced its own list of all the heretical printers, one could easily go by it. Several examples can be given. The Basel Greek Basilius edition of 1532 was textually harmless; nevertheless, the name of the publisher, Erasmus of Rotterdam, and its origin in the printery of Froben, were partially pasted over and partially torn out; Erasmus' preface likewise fell victim to the censors. With a collective volume that contained various works,[30] the Catholic portion thereof was left inviolable; on the other hand, the collective writings of Bucer and Latomus which preceded it, being heretical, were bound together with cords, and thus rendered useless; the title page was pasted over, and the passages glued together. With the Basel Epiphanius edition of Johann Herwagen of 1544, the printer's device on the title page, and the dedicatory preface of the publisher, Johannes Oporinus, to the Strasbourg bishop, Erasmus of Limburg, have been removed, and the printer's device in Greek at the end has been blacked out.

The Ingolstadt edition of the Bavarian *Annals* of Johann Aventinus of the year 1554 has especially had havoc played with it, even though Hieronymus Ziegler, a Catholic author in a Catholic printing locale, has published it with a dedication to Duke Albert V, and with the printing privilege of Emperor Charles V.[31] The name of the author has been everywhere glued over, or removed by other means. The letters to Aventin that precede the text itself have been partially glued over, and partially removed entirely. There are numerous passages in the text that likewise have been glued over, or stricken out, glued together, or entirely excised. All the books of library were examined in this way, and numerous works (among which were many volumes form the legacy of the Orientalist, Johann Albert Widmanstetter that had been kept in the monastery of Duke Albrecht V) were brutally disfigured and mutilated.[32] In the entire operation we have before us the model example of a comprehensive purgation of books, as such events were everywhere commanded, but which already, for lack of proper personnel, could not be easily accomplished.

The Bavarian State Library nevertheless preserves numerous mutilated printed works (also from holdings previously owned by others) which demonstrate that the purging of the library has at least been taken in hand in many monasteries. In the Irenaeus edition of the Basel printery, Hieronymus Froben and Nikolaus Episcopius of 1560, everything suspicious has been removed; the striking out of the printer's name in the colophon, however, has been overlooked. In the accompanying volume, a Clement edition of 1556, the name of the printer, Isingrin, has been erased, while the printer's sign, the palm, remains. The volume stems from the Baumburg monastery (2 P. gr. 297). The name of the printer on the title page and in the colophon has been cut out (2° A. lat. a 194) in the Paris Plautus edition of 1530. Especially does the treatment in a copy of Johann Adelphi's collection of facetiae (L. eleg. m. 130), published in 1509 in Strasbourg, seem strange to us. That one would not tolerate the various offensive anecdotes in a monastery is entirely understandable; but that one does not completely remove the book, but rather only cuts out the worst concluding portion of the text, leaving the paper margins as a kind of frame, is quite remarkable.

In Christoph Rudolf's *Rechnung mit der Ziffer und mit den Zahlpfennigen*

("Calculation with the digit and with the counters") (Math. P. 485) the names of the author and printer are deleted, just as they are in Josias Simler's *Regiment löblicher Eidgenossenschaft* ("Regiment of laudable confederacy") from the printery of Christoph Froschauer in the year 1576 (Helv. 657). In Heinrich Pantaleon's *Deutscher Nation Heldenbuch* ("Book of the Heroes of the German Nation"), which was published in 1567 by Nikolaus Brylinger in Basel, all three parts of the names of the author and the printer have been blacked out, while the author's portrait has been left inviolable, and only the name of the biographee has been covered over (2 Biogr. c. 65). The ecclesiastical demand of the purging (of books) rests on the conception of the Inquisition, that the heretic may be tolerated nowhere, and thus not even in books. It is therefore the book which—in place of the authors, the publishers, and the printers, who were also responsible—has suffered the punishment for their revolt.

Acquisitions of the monastery had to be adjusted to the *Index* regulations. Duke Albrecht V of Bavaria printed his own catalog of tolerated books in 1566,[33] and purposely in 1569 the Tridentine list of forbidden books; at the same time he gave guidance as to how a Catholic library collection could be built and purged of its dangerous publications. Primarily recommended are the church fathers, the great theologians of the Middle Ages, and the guardians of the doctrines of the Catholic faith. The classics, philosophy, legal science, and medicine could still be represented with the best works (in each such discipline). Monastery directors would do well to obtain their books only from Catholic printeries and thus from all of Spain, Italy and Belgium; care should, however, be exercised with France, so that no Calvinistic books would be smuggled in. The publications that the Sorbonne in Paris and the Royal printery in Paris produced should be considered as free of objection. In Germany the publishing localities of Cologne, Freiburg im Breisgau, Mainz, Munich, Ingolstadt and Dillingen guaranteed the contents of their works.

Concerning the rest of the printing locales there was no certainty. Just the single city of Basel alone had already occasioned great mischief with the corrupted editions of the church fathers which were published there. Duke William V was still more zealous (in this matter) than his father was. An augmented edition of the Trent Index was published in 1582 in Munich. It was introduced by the papal nuncio, Felician Ninguarda, and it contained over three hundred more names from the Frankfurt Fair catalog. Under the new duke, the monasteries even had to be provided with their books by the ducal chancellery in Munich. Thus in 1583 the Augustinian Canons' foundation of Beyharting obtained thirty-one publications, chiefly theological and school books, among which were several in more than one copy, and they had to pay forty-seven and forty-five kreutzer for them. The duke likewise arranged for the Rottenbuch monastery on May 18, 1585, to accept books for pastoral care and for the school, for about eighty-two gulden.[34]

A religious Order such as the Jesuits, which considered its main goal to be defense of the Catholic church and contending with erroneous teaching, had to apply special attention to literature and the book. Besides the numerous publications of their own by those who belonged to the Order, a chief concern was the directing of the enormous book collections, which especially Peter Canisius advocated.[35]

Many of these collections quickly grew to considerable proportions. Thus the library of the *Collegium Romanum* at Rome, which was entrusted to the learned Possevino, was soon among the most significant book collections in Rome. The Jesuits also on occasion tried to take printing into their service as an activity of their own. What dissuaded them from this course were the necessary commercial matters connected with book publishing. Even when Emperor Ferdinand I wanted to connect a printery with the Jesuit College in Vienna, Rome was against it; the refusal order, however, only arrived in Vienna when the printery was already built.[36] Theses, lists of lectures, school books, and the first edition of the famous *Exercises* of Ignatius of Loyola (1563) ever printed in Germany, issued from the workshop. On account of bad business experiences, the order again soon ceased its operation, and the equipment was sold on January 11, 1578, for about five hundred florins. Later similar attempts in other locations, such as in Dillingen (1620), Braunsberg (1697), and Breslau (1705), turned out just as unsuccessfully. Of considerable significance, on the other hand, were the numerous mission printeries that the Jesuits built in foreign countries in order to enable them to distribute the necessary books for pastoral care, and the church books in the language of the people who had been converted.[37] The catechism of the Jesuit, Peter Canisius, in the German and Latin languages, which was promoted by Emperor Ferdinand, was vigorously disseminated. The first Latin edition has been published under the title *Summa doctrinae christianae* in 1555 by Michael Zimmerman in Vienna.[38]

It was an adverse providence which willed that Luther's faith movement, becoming rigid in the course of the sixteenth century, and the opposition to it that set in among the persevering Catholic powers, gradually divided the German people into two hostile groups. Even the German book world, too, went along this path. The Evangelical book speedily gained the upper hand. The most significant of the old centers of the book market, such as Augsburg, Nuremberg, Strasbourg and Basel, embraced the Protestant book with almost all the printer's workshops and added to that, as important shipping points, were especially Wittenburg, and later Frankfurt am Main.[39] One knows that this ever increasingly unhealthy splintering of the church has been no blessing for Germany from the very first. It was also bad for books. The farther things proceeded after Luther's death, the more the general nature of the German book situation seemed to be in trouble. Especially was this so with the theological literature, which everywhere stepped overwhelmingly into the foreground of public life, and went on a rampage in opposing disputes, even within its own ranks. The German people have scarcely in any other period consumed their intellectual powers so fruitlessly as in the continuing sixteenth century, with its everlasting strife over the right faith, its abusive publications without number, and its hateful squabbling by the theologians — in which even Melanchthon himself could scarcely escape. The medieval theology had just been renounced, and one was now again in the midst of a new, and perhaps even more unfruitful, theology which, in its intolerant power, struck at everything. Seen from the aspect of the history of culture, not only has the century of the Thirty Years' War been the most cursed time for Germany — the second part of the sixteenth century must already be seen as a bad forerunner thereto.

18

The Book and the Princely Courts
of the Sixteenth Century

After the re-awakening of the classical ancient world (especially in Italy) and the discovery of the art of printing had generated significant growth in the whole of western culture, as well as a new valuing of the book, the rest of the princely courts in Europe could not unconcernedly ignore the altered attitude toward cultural life and the book.

The first German prince who found a close relationship with the printed book was Emperor Maximilian I, the culturally stimulated patron of the humanists, who freely crowned his scholars with the laurel wreath and graciously received the dedications of their books. In 1502 Conrad Celtes dedicated to him his amatory poems and he had the book (the printing costs of which the prince assumed) issued with a beautiful dedicatory illustration that presented the sovereign in his full honors, with scepter and orb, as he was accepting the opened book from the kneeling poet. In the German Livy edition of 1512 there is again a splendid ceremonial illustration in which King Maximilian, with all the symbols of his power and surrounded by the seven electors, is presented the book by the translator, Bernhard Schöferlin. In similar fashion is the dedicatory illustration in Petermann Etterlin's *Chronica von der Eidgenossenschaft* of 1507. One of the handsomest dedicatory illustrations, which indeed is drawn by Hans Schäufelin, is to be found in Ulrich Tengler's *Laienspiegel* of 1511; again the king is enthroned there within the council of the electors, and the author, with the book in hand, kneels before him, surrounded by his quite numerous kinsmen. From Hans Burgkmair, the most competent of the Augsburg artists, comes the lively woodcut in Wolfgang von Mäns *Leiden Christi* ("Passion of Christ") of 1515; within the beautiful Renaissance border the emperor sits under the canopy, and he bows to the kneeling author, who hands over the book. Two publications of the abbot of Sponheim, Johann Trithemius, have similar presentations. Finally, Dietrich von Plieningen presents the emperor with his Pliny translation of 1515 under the auspices of Duke William of Bavaria.

These surprisingly numerous dedicatory illustrations demonstrate concretely the close relationship that existed between Emperor Maximilian and the book.[1] The printed book has now become socially acceptable—yes, more than that, it enjoys the emperor's favor and thereby grows in the estimation of contemporaries. In order to prove itself worthy of this favor, it is designed with handsome garb, it is handsomely designed, and it includes woodcut illustrations. Thus we again encounter here an emphasis on courtly splendor and consciously chosen attention to the exquisite book.

The pinnacle of this close connection we observe in the open-minded emperor's own book creations, primarily in the world-famous prayerbook, filled as it is with psalms, hymns and texts of the gospels, and which, printed on December 30, 1513, by the Augsburg printer, Johann Schönsperger, with new and wonderful types on parchment, was intended for the knights of the Order of St. George.

According to a letter of Conrad Peutinger's to the emperor on Octber 5, 1510, "ten little prayerbooks on parchment" were ordered in Augsburg; six copies are still known to us today. A copy of a printed work with red lines and adorned with flourishes (thus giving the effect of a handsome manuscript) the most famous artists of the period, on commission from the emperor, had decorated with marginal drawings, which perhaps were later to be reproduced by woodcut, or indeed, what is more probable, were supposed to constitute a specially handsome property of the emperor. Individual signatures of this one edition were apportioned out to Albrecht Dürer, Hans Burgkmair, Hans Baldung Grien, Jörg Breu, Lucas Cranach, and Hans Dürer for decorating with fine free-hand drawings. In such decoration the glorious book has been preserved for us as one of the most priceless book monuments. Particularly did Albrecht Dürer provide quite wonderful drawings, in which spiritual and secular images are interwoven in a mutli-colored variety: Christ as the Savior of the world, the sorrowful Mother of God, the annunciation, Mary decorated with ears of wheat, the saints Maximilian, Michael, Augustine, Barbara, Andreas, Sebastian, Mathias, Antonius, George and Apollonia, then again battling mercenaries, peasants who fight against the knights, a woman who has gone to sleep at the spinning wheel, the wife of a burgher who is coming from market, musicians, knight and death, an Oriental with a camel, the fox and a crowd of hens, sea monsters, only loosely (or not at all) connected to the book's pious Latin text. That so much of a secular sort could be added, proclaims the full freedom which the client had yielded to the artist's imagination. When Goethe discovered Dürer's marginal drawings in the imperfect lithography of Strixner of 1809, he was enchanted by them, even in this form.[2]

Among the Emperor's further book projects, only the *Theuerdank* with the title *Die Gefährlichkeiten des löblichen streitbaren und hochberühmten Helden und Ritters Theuerdank* ("The Perilous Ventures of the Laudable, Valiant and Quite Famous Hero and Knight, Theuerdank") was completed and printed in 1517 again by Johann Schönsperger. Since the publisher, Melchior Pfinzing, resided in Nuremberg, the printing was also done there. The work was not released immediately, but it was kept in trunks, so it would be distributed only following the emperor's death as a memorial to him. Only a few men will have seen the work prior to the year 1519, besides the emperor himself. In the text, the emperor portrays his experiences in allegorical form and struggles with the demons, Fürwittig, Unfallo, and Neidelhart while on his wedding trip in the Burgundian countries. Exquisite woodcuts by Leonhard Beck, Hans Schäufelin, Hans Burgkmair and Erhard Schön, most of them cut by Jobst Denecker, illustrate the contents of the verses.

The types, which were decorated with flourishes, and designed by the Imperial court secretary, Vincent Rockner, were intended to reproduce entirely the strokes of a handwritten manuscript, as the prayerbook type did. Equally, the woodcuts in the preferred parchment copies are artistically decorated in order to give the effect of miniature painting.[3] According to the will of the enterprising emperor, who took pleasure in the project, there were still two further woodcut works planned as encouragements for the grandson: *Der Weisskunig* ("The White King"), with a portrayal of Maximilian's life and reign and the *Freydal*, with its representation of the knightly proficiency of the emperor. At the death of the emperor, 236 woodblocks of the *Weisskunig* were in hand, but there were only a few from *Freydal*; they have been reprinted only in later centuries and have provided us still with outstanding woodcuts of Hans Burgmair, Leonhard Beck, Hans Schäufelin, and Hans Springinklee.

The unstable nature of the court life of Emperor Maximilian corresponded to the gradual dispersion of the Hapsburg book possessions in Vienna Neustadt, in Innsbruck, and in Vienna. And the books that were here assembled – among them were valuable Burgundian manuscripts from the legacy of the first consort of the Emperor, Maria of Burgundy, or the priceless *Heldenbuch* ("Book of Heroes"), written down about 1515 on commission of the prince with poems in Middle High German – were kept entirely within the limits of a hobby. A better future seemed to ensue for the collection when the humanist, Conrad Celtes, got the administration of the books transferred to him. On March 1, 1504, Celtes reported to his patron that he had established that the library indeed did not evidence any great holdings, but it was already showing valuable Latin, Greek and other works. When Celtes died on February 4, 1508, the matter appears again to have been forgotten.[4]

One of the first German princes who tried to work toward libraries that would really be used, was Elector Frederick the Wise of Saxony (1486–1525), the founder of the University of Wittenberg (1502), the princely patron of scholars, to whom Petrus Ravennas, Conrad Celtes, Andreas Karlstadt, Beatus Rhenanus, Christoph Scheurl, Philipp Melanchthon, and Petrus Mosellanus have dedicated works. The humanist, Georg Burkhardt from Spalt (called Spalatin) (1484–1545), undertook the administration of the new collection of books. An account that we still have from 1512 evidences the handsome sum of 202 florins for the purchase of books. The University Library of Jena owns a book catalog of 1514 with individual lists of eight monastery libraries. Spalatin has probably drawn up the catalog to help with making the lists of desired book additions. On December 1, 1512, the Elector wrote to Aldus Manutius (the Venetian printer) that he wanted to build a library for the general use of all instructors and students of his school of higher learning, and thus he requests him to send publishers' catalogs. Luther and Melanchthon have been industrious users of the library.[5] Spalatin has himself not experienced the break-up of the electoral house following the Battle of Mühlberg; the Wittenberg library had moved to Jena on June 14, 1548.[6]

In the German East, in Königsberg, Margrave Albrecht, the first duke of the former territory of the Teutonic Order, Prussia, has founded a library for the scholars and clerics of his new court and country, and the books were acquired for him by Lucas Cranach and Crotus Rubeanus. On the bindings of his collection were found the ducal arms with Latin verses, which admonished users to be grateful for the use of the book and to return it unharmed. Since the end of 1534 the Netherlands refugee, Felix König (Polyphemus) managed the treasures.[7] In the year 1540 the collection, which numbered about fifteen hundred works, could be declared ready for use. Decorating the room was a portrait of Erasmus of Rotterdam. The prince maintained his own chamber library for himself and his consort, Anna Maria (born Duchess of Brunswick and Lüneburg), who loved exquisite things; it has become famous under the name of "Silver Library." It included a series of Reformation works, all of them decorated with valuable silver plates on beech book-boards. Portraits, arms, scenes from holy scriptures, symbols with inscriptions, rich decorations with strap work designs—these are themes of the artistic silver work.[8]

The principality of Anhalt maintained in Dessau an unusual Evangelical book collection through Georg III of Anhalt (1516–1553), who was active as the provost of Magdeburg Cathedral, was a friend of Luther's and Melanchthon's, and who himself authored Evangelical publications. What he collected was all theological literature, decorated with beautiful bindings. In him, the Evangelical book has found its first princely protector.[9]

Palatine Count Ottheinrich, prince of the younger Palatinate (an artificially and quickly assembled small territory on the upper Danube and in the Nordgau, also called Pfalz-Neuburg, with the little town of Neuburg an der Donau as its seat of government) became one of the distinctive princelings of the Renaissance. The young Palatine Count was already devoting himself to the favorite Renaissance pursuits such as the collecting of books, coins, tapestries and foreign animals, until the overwhelming need for money forced him on August 22, 1544, to cede his sovereign territory to the country's estates. Since then he was living in Heidelberg or Weinheim; he gave himself over to his zeal for collecting. When his uncle, Elector Friedrich of the Palatinate, died on February 26, 1556, the Palatinate as well as the electoral office devolved to the nephew. Fate has given him only three years—yet just enough time that he was able to build the Ottheinrich's palace in Heidelberg—and then on February 12, 1559, he died.

If initially the Palatine Count had taken pleasure at the castle at Neuburg in beautiful and venerable old books, so, following his conversion to the Evangelical faith, the Strasbourg preachers, Martin Bucer and Caspar Hedio, made him aware of how he could put his collection activity at the service of the Evangelical cause. On November 1, 1554, Bucer wrote to Heinrich Bullinger in Zurich, that his friend should try to provide him, through Conrad Gesner, with the galleys of his *Bibliotheca Universalis* for Count Palatine Ottheinrich. The prince wished to plan a library, and he wanted to know from Gesner's catalog the books that were deserving of purchase.

Two years thereafter, Caspar Hedio dedicated to the Count Palatine his German translation of Platinas *Historia von der Päpste und Kaiser Leben* ("History of the Life of the Popes and Emperors"), and with it, he contributed two lists of recommended books, with the following remarkable elucidation: "So now your princely graces are, out of Christian and princely design, to build a library of books of the holy scriptures, jurisprudence, medicine, and all kinds of histories, and you wish a list of such books. I have in the accompanying list designated the names of the foremost books, and also where and in which locales you can get them. And thus, as the Christian library work commences, one may augment it from day to day and in each period at the Frankfurt Fair. Meanwhile, however, beside the library of Hebrew, Greek and Latin books, a work that is useful for all should be considered, namely, having a German library in an publicly accessible area for pious God-fearing citizens and laymen in an electoral, princely or otherwise honorable or imperial city, so that young persons—even the young apprentices— might have open access on Sunday and on holidays, so that the time in which other- wise they would use up in wine and beer houses, on the ninepins or in places of games, or otherwise waste in dishonorable places, they would apply to the improve- ment and salvation of their souls; and so that they may themselves read in German books (or hear them read), I have also designated a number of German books, among those that I have liked in the twenty-two years I have preached at Strasbourg—and even several that I have liked so much that I have myself translated them into the German language."

In a further place of the dedicatory preface, Hedio gives a short survey of the most famous library foundations, and he raises vehement objections against the despicable soldiers who have destroyed so many books, or as lately, have laid waste at Rome. Hedio had several years before impressed strongly on the chaplain who was to accompany the troops against the Turks, to hold the soldiers off from plundering the libraries of the Hungarians, the Thracians, of Greece and especially those of Constantinople.

The Strasbourg preachers did not deceive themselves, when they were also ex- pecting from the Count Palatine's bibliophily some profit for the Evangelical cause. Ottheinrich is among the first princes who have consciously and zealously promoted pamphlet materials against the old church. He supported numerous authors of Evangelical publications, among whom were also later Matthias Flacius and Johann Sturm; he willingly accepted dedications, and in 1544, through his accountant, Hans Kilian at Neuburg, he had his own printing workshop erected at Neuburg, which was also supposed to serve the struggle against the papacy. The *Psalter deutsch*, which was printed there in 1545, has been introduced in a special preface by Martin Luther; this was in accord with the Count Palatine's wishes. When Neuburg was conquered in 1546 by the imperial forces, the printery was also destroyed, and it was not rebuilt until 1556, and then was active for only a year. In spite of his constant need for funds, the Count Palatine was able gradually to obtain a great number of valuable manuscripts and printed works. The most valuable booty was the library of the monastery of Lorsch before it was dis- solved.[10]

Among the treasures was also found a formula for an oath, written in Greek on papyrus material. A specially valuable manuscript of the Speyer Cathedral library with the *Itinerarium Antonini,* the famous list of the streets of Rome that comes from the fourth century, the Count Palatine was finally able to appropriate, despite the opposition of the careful cathedral chapter. Little more than a double leaf has been preserved of the valuable manuscript today. Also, three old parchment manuscripts out of the Speyer Carmelites' library came into Ottheinrich's possession. The Neuhausen foundation near Worms gave him a parchment manuscript of the tenth century that had the Ambrosian commentary on Luke's gospel. The Basel printer, Hieronymus Froben, presented a Greek parchment manuscript that came out of the Basel Dominican monastery and that was once used by Reuchlin and Erasmus; it contained Hippolytus' commentary on the Apocalypse. It was a handsome collection of about eighty manuscripts and 250 printed works, which the Count Palatine had for his own chamber library. Following his death, the collection came to the Count Palatine Wolfgang von Zweibrücken and it again found its way back to Neuburg. There it was soon suffering severe damage and it was finally scattered completely. More favorable was the fate of the other collected rich book treasures which Ottheinrich united with the large Heidelberg library in the Holy Ghost church. Shortly before his death the Elector urgently commended to his successors the collection that had been so richly increased by him "as a specially dear treasure of the Electorate." The collection was to remain in the Palatinate electoral office and in Heidelberg, where the university was, and was to be increased with useful books.

The elector has been very well advised, when in this last publication of his will, he desired to see the Electoral Court Library inseparably connected with the University of Heidelberg. Most of the rest of the electoral library foundations in Germany were exclusively court collections, and they have been more admired than they have been actually used. The Heidelberg book possession, on the other hand, was rated as being nothing short of the territorial library, and it thereby achieved a greatly extended range for its effectiveness. Increased in the year 1584 with Fugger's priceless gift, the library became the successful point of departure for numerous publications connected with scholars with well-known names.

Elector Ottheinrich has very effectively provided for the lasting fame of his book treasures through the bindings, with which he had numerous manuscripts and printed works furnished in one of his own court bookbinderies. They bore his arms, and also had the motto, M(mit) D(der) Z(Zeit) ("Up to date") and the year when they were acquired, and frequently even the likeness of the prince. Over one thousand such "Ottheinrich volumes" have been scattered through the entire world.[11]

Just as the Evangelical preachers in Strasbourg have aroused the interest of the Palatine Count Ottheinrich in book collecting, so as at the same time to place in his hands cultural weapons as the protective sovereign of the Evangelical faith, so did the Jesuits in Munich have an influence on the Catholic Duke Albrecht V, in order to arm him (as the protective sovereign of the Catholic movement) with books. Following their counsel, the Bavarian duke acquired in 1558 the collection (which was especially rich in Eastern manuscripts) of the scholarly Orientalist, Johann Albrecht Widmanstetter, and placed it extensively at the disposal of the

Jesuits. Found among the treasures was a priceless Greek collective manuscript with Alexander of Aphrodisias' commentary on Aristotle, wherein is to be read in Widmanstatter's clear script that he had obtained the manuscript in 1533 as a present from Pope Clement VII, when he explained to him Copernicus' teaching on the movement of the planets in the Vatican gardens in the presence of two cardinals and their entourage.

Succeeding Widmanstetter's beautiful collection in 1571 was the already mentioned, and still more significant, collection of books of the Augsburg patrician, Johann Jakob Fugger—a strange play and counterplay between Munich and Heidelberg, where in the same year Ulrich Fugger's valuable collection (he was the Evangelical son of the Fugger House in Augsburg) moved in, in order after his death to fall completely to the Electoral Library. With the book collection of Johann Jakob Fugger, numbering over ten thousand volumes, Duke Albrecht at the same time got the valuable library of the humanist, Hartmann Schedel, incorporated into it. The prince proclaimed his love for beautiful books by commissioning exquisite music works, the motets and penitential psalms of the music masters, Cyprian de Rore and Orlando di Lasso, brilliant creations with elegantly colored pictures by the Munich artist, Hans Muelich, in whom the courtly miniature painting was running its last course.

Like his cousin, Ottheinrich, Duke Albrecht also fostered printing; he had Johann Aventin's *Bavarian Annals* published in 1554, in 1557 he had the twelve volume *Historien der Heiligen Gottes* ("Histories of the Saints of God") of Laurentius Surius printed in German translation, he published in 1558 the *Bayerische Landtafeln* ("Bavarian Land Register") of Philipp Apian, and in 1568, Hans Wagner's *Beschreibung des hochzeitlichen Ehrenfestes Herzog Wilhelms und der Renata* ("Description of the Festival Honoring the Marriage of Duke Wilhelm with Renata"), which was engraved with fifteen copper plates.[12] Priceless items of the first order are now held in the Munich Court Library or in the *Kunstkammer* there, such as the jewel book of the duke and his consort, Anna, who was the daughter of Emperor Ferdinand I, with the pretty pictures of the ducal pair playing chess, the fencing book of the Augsburg council clerk, Paul Hector Mair, with pictures of the artist, Jörg Breu the younger, the French Boccacio with the illustrations of the miniature painter, Jean Fouquet,[13] the papyrus manuscript, *Codex traditionum ecclesiae Ravennatis*, which was composed in the tenth century and decorated amply with pictures, and also the Dioskurides manuscript from Monte Cassino. The handsome collection had the good fortune of remaining almost entirely unharmed for centuries, and it still today proclaims (in spite of the damage sustained in the last World War) the fame of its founder and preserver, who took pleasure in books.[14]

Elector August of Saxony (1526–1586) has begun his collecting activity (which for Dresden has a significance equal to what Albrecht V's collecting enthusiasm meant for Munich) at approximately the same time in the summer castle of Annaburg; decorated with the likeness of the sovereign, the nicely bound books of the elector (whose numbers grew to 2300 in the year 1580) represent the distinctive collection of a prince who was pursuing books as a hobby. Constituting essential items in the choice collection that was ordered primarily in Paris from Hubert Languet,[15] were the priceless bindings done in gold and silver or in velvet and silk, and decorated according to Italian and French models, with strap work in gold; they represented significant artistic works of the excellent Augsburg master, Jakob Krause and his assistant, Caspar Meuser, and they are among the most beautiful bindings of the German Renaissance.[16]

Elector August's son and successor, Christian I (1560–1591) had the valuable possession set up in the Dresden castle in 1586 and increased through significant purchases. Following his death, a lengthy standstill in the development of the collection ensued; it was not until in the eighteenth century (through the acquisition of the great Bünau and Brühl libraries) that it received a new and significant wealth of material.

With the quiet enthusiasm of a scholar, Duke Julius of Brunswick had collected in his castle at Essen manuscripts and printed works, especially French chivalric romances, and in July 1567 he acquired a rich book possession from the legacy of the Nuremberg syndic, Michael Kaden, when fate called him in 1568 to the leadership of his territory. Transported to Wolfenbüttel, the collection received valuable enrichment from the book holdings of the Brunswick and Hildesheim monasteries that were dissolved in 1575 – especially from Amelungsborn, Wöltingerode, Steterburg, Heiningen, Georgenberg, Lamspringe, and Marienberg. In 1577 there was acquired from Johann Aurifabers's estate at Erfurt a valuable collection of the manuscripts of Luther and other reformers. While the princely owner treated his books most devotedly, he seems to have dealt rather harshly with his librarians. The *Magister*, Leonhard Schröter, who was installed on December 30, 1572, and was required to sing in the choir, could not bear with him for even a quarter of a year.

Under the next duke, the dramatist, Heinrich Julius (1589–1613), one of the most significant scholarly libraries of the time was incorporated into the Wolfenbüttel collection, the already cited possession of the theologian, Matthias Flacius, with its priceless old manuscripts. But Friedrich Julius, the next heir of the collection, which then numbered five thousand volumes, considered the priceless treasure to be a pressing burden, and in 1618, retaining the property rights, he transferred it to the school of higher learning at Helmstedt, which had been founded by Duke Julius. It is from there that the most valuable portion was first returned to Wolfenbüttel at the beginning of the nineteenth century.

In Hesse-Kassel, Landgrave Wilhelm IV (1532–1592), was called "The Wise" due to his being a learned astronomer and mathematician. He enthusiastically provided for the building of a court library, which was primarily supposed to accept old manuscripts.[17] On January 20, 1582, he dispatched to his brother, Ludwig, a long list of books that he desired to have sent out from the holdings in Marburg. The request, to hand over to him old manuscripts in exchange for newer useful books, has been fulfilled in Marburg without objection.

In addition to the Munich court, King Maximilian (the later emperor) in 1558 also had an eye out for the already mentioned library of Johann Albrecht Widmanstetter. The impetus toward the king's collecting of books seems to have been given by the councillor, Kaspar von Nidbruck, the same scholar who has eagerly provided the author of the Magdeburg *Centuries* with church history manuscripts. It was also due to him that his sovereign has commissioned the imperial ambassador to the Turkish court, Ogier Ghiselin Busbeck, to purchase books in Constantinople. What Kaspar von Nidbruck then no more lived to see, the building of a court library, became the task of the learned librarian, Hugo Blotius, whom Emperor Maximilian II (1564–1576) has entrusted with the direction of the library situated in the Minorite monastery of Vienna.[18] In a speech of April 24, 1576, which has become famous, the new director summarized his work in the following guiding principles: the task ought to be to enter into successful competition with the libraries of the Vaticana in Rome, of the Medici in Florence, and of the French kings at Fontainebleau. One needed only time, money and space in order to be able to dig up the treasure that still lay hidden from the world.

To the first of the larger Vienna acquisitions belonged the beautiful collection (numbering two thousand volumes) of Johann Dernschwam,[19] who travelled in the East, and the valuable estate of the imperial court historiographer, Wolfgang Lazius. Two further large accessions followed under the government of Emperor Rudolf II (1576–1612): the 262 Greek manuscripts that Ogier Ghiselin Busbeck had brought from Constantinople, and the rich book treasures which came from the estate of the imperial court historiographer, Johann Sambucus (1531–1584); he had been born in Hungary.[20]

On August 2, 1578, Sambucus had offered to the emperor his valuable items for three thousand ducats; the emperor has finally acquired them for 2550 ducats. Among the items were exquisite manuscripts from the earlier possessions of the dukes of Acquaviva and of the Aragonic kings of Naples; further, a notable fragment of the synodal acts of the third council of Constantinople from the year 681, which was written on papyrus material and sold in 1553 to Sambucus by Torquato Bembo; a Greek evangelary from the tenth century; Aristotle's works on natural science, copied in the year 1547 by the Cretan, Johannes Rhosos; the tragedies of Seneca, which were produced in the years 1419–1422 for King Charles VII of France; the erotic letters of Aristainetos, which were published in 1566 by Christopher Plantin in Antwerp on the basis of this single manuscript preserved for us by Sambucus. His priceless possessions, which were chiefly acquired in Paris and Italy, often came from well known ancestors and Sambucus had already previously freely put them at scholars' disposal; Sambucus is praised in Gerhart Falkenburg's *Momus* edition of 1569 as the owner of a rich book collection which is accessible to all, and as one who, in contrast to others knew how to promote the publication of his treasures, and even how to stimulate printers by means of considerable patronage. With the old holdings of the house and the new enormous acquisitions, the Vienna Court Library might indeed claim a place for itself (as Blotius had dreamed) on the same level with, and at the side of, the largest European libraries.

The French kings had become bibliophiles already in the late Middle Ages. King Louis XII had left considerable book treasures to his cousin and son-in-law,

Francis I (1515–1547); among them were valuable manuscripts that Charles VIII had carried off from Naples, the chief parts of which lay stacked up in Blois. From the collection of Prince Eugene of Savoy, the Vienna national Library owns a catalog from the pen of the Dominican and later bishop, Guillaume Petit (d. 1536), which assigns Blois ownership from the year 1518, and it gives introductory descriptions of the individual monuments. Thus is communicated there the word-for-word entry of Petrarch's from an Augustine manuscript of Pavia, according to which Petrarch has obtained the book on April 30, 1355, in Milan, from Giovanni Boccaccio of Florence.[21] This basic stock was united in 1544 with the collection of Greek manuscripts of Fontainebleau, and thus it became one of the richest collections of books of the time. The collection found its way to Paris toward the turn of the century, and there it constituted an especially brilliant attraction of the French royal court.

At about the same time, when the courts in Munich, Heidelberg and Vienna were beginning, or extending, their book collections, King Philipp II of Spain (the son of Emperor Charles V) also commenced the foundation of a rich courtly collection. Here also, the original goal was for a splendid court library. Already in the first years of the government of the young king, the Spanish historiographer, Juan Páez de Castro, was working on an official opinion concerning the proposed foundation. For situating the new collection, (which was supposed to be open for general use), Valladolid, which was an outstanding center of cultural life, was recommended. In a special section, it was considered how many valuable book holdings could be acquired. One had here to keep in mind Rome, Venice and Florence, the most important markets of the book collections that were already in existence. Certain valuable books even from the Levant were offered as soon as it became known that the king of Spain wanted to build a large library. Further, there were in Sicily and the Italian region of Calabria old Greek manuscripts the owners of which no longer used them, and these could easily be acquired in exchange for new printed works.

In the meantime, in El Escorial, a solitary village in the province of Madrid, there was rising that gigantic structure (growing ever larger and more massive, set as it was in the midst of the solitary mountains) in which the king, who was as pious as he was loving of splendor, had vowed to St. Laurentius in thanksgiving for the victory accomplished on the saint's feast day in 1557 at Saint-Quentin. At once a palace and monastery, church and presbytery, the favorite residence for the kings, and the eternal resting place of Spanish sovereigns, a collection of paintings, works of sculpture and goldsmith works, but now also a shelter for intellectual works – all these the towering king's palace was supposed to be. The new goal of the book collection therefore became something other than the original plan had projected. In the judgment of the historiographer, Ambrosio de Morales, in the goal of the new collection of books, there is reference to the example of the Vaticana in Rome, the Marciana in Venice, the Laurentiana in Florence, and the library in Fontainebleau, and a comprehensive collecting in all disciplines and languages for the benefit of the intellectual life is called for; so the Escorial was supposed as the same time to become a *Studium generale*, a sort of school of higher learning in the service of scholarship. After about 1566 there was now initiated a zealous collecting in keeping with the new high goal.

What the king already owned as property of his house consisted essentially only of a few, but also valuable, manuscripts from the legacy of his father, Emperor Charles V. One of the first acquisitions was the collection that stemmed from Gonzalo Pérez, which was especially outstanding on account of its splendid manuscripts; that had come from the possessions of the Aragonic kings of Naples. There was a special significance in the royal project, in that now there was a collection locale for all the deserted book treasures of the country and that, with this undertaking, there was created a significant national center for the cultural life of Spain. Not easily anywhere else has the national literature of a country been so zealously gathered together at so early a period as was the case in Spain under King Phillip II. It was not only the works of Isidore of Seville, nor the manuscripts of Spanish councils, such as those of the council of Albelda (976) with their rich pictorial decoration, and other priceless items from the medieval scriptoria of Spain; it was not merely the numerous works which King Alphonse X[22] (the most significant sovereign of medieval Spain) has himself written, or caused to be written; moving into the Escorial also were all the other venerable old scriptural monuments written in the language of the country, in so far as they were available, so that they now, united, constituted a proud monument of Spanish intellectual history.

Among the most successful ambassadors of the king in collecting was Benito Arias Montano; in 1568, during his stay in the Netherlands, he was successful in acquiring forty Greek manuscripts from Andreas Darmarius, as well as valuable parchment manuscripts from Netherlands monasteries, especially from Breda and Hooghstraeten. The reports concerning them give a concrete picture of the condition of the Netherlands monastery libraries in that period of political and ecclesiastical confusion.[23] The scholars had at the same time obtained a commission to supervise the printing of the Complutensian polyglot Bible (a project induced by the King himself) that Christopher Plantin of Antwerp has produced in the years 1569–1572. Of this enormous work in eight volumes, thirteen copies were issued on parchment, for which 16,263 animal skins were utilized; six copies came to the Escorial, one each went to the pope and to the Duke of Alba, and five went to the Duke of Savoy. Duke Albrecht V of Bavaria, who also wanted a parchment copy, had to be satisfied with one of ten further copies specially produced on wide-bordered paper. As we have already mentioned, Arias Montano intervened yet a second time into the world of books, when in 1571, on commission from his king and the Duke of Alba, he has published with the same printer, Plantin, the notorious *Index expurgatorius librorum;* in the intention of the Council of Trent this included exhaustive regulations for purging the books that were condemned by the Catholic church.

The Escorial's book collection obtained further valuable growth from the library of the learned Juan Páez, who had already been working as an advisor on books to the King. Páez had primarily been collecting zealously during the Council of Trent. When Ambrosio de Morales had to comment on the estate, he especially praised the Greek manuscripts and the printed works that were becoming more and more rare. Outstanding among the fifty Greek, sixteen Latin, thirteen Spanish and sixteen Arabic manuscripts that were then acquired, was the Dioscurides manuscript; Andreas de Laguna has based his Spanish translation on it (Antwerp 1555), further a publication of Emperor Constantine Porphyrogenetos with unpublished texts (an item often mentioned in letters of contemporaries), of which Vulcanius and Höschel have published items; both manuscripts were lost in the fire of 1671.

While in Spain it was primarily the secretary of the king, Antonio Gracian, who was leading the comprehensive collection activity, in Italy it was the Spanish ambassador, Don Diego de Guzman de Sylva, who was setting everything in motion, in order to procure for his king the catalogs of the most important libraries of Italy and such valuable treasures as the possession of Greek manuscripts of the learned book trader, Antonios Eparchos, or the Greek collection of the Plato admirer, Franciscus Patricius.[24] With a fine understanding for old manuscripts, the enthusiastic adviser pointed out the old bindings of the priceless items of Eparchos, which inspite of their bad state of repair, should be preserved as historical monuments; unfortunately, this intelligent counsel has not been observed. Eparchos had brought his treasures with him from Greece, whence he had been sent by Popes Marcellus II and Pius IV.

Ambrosio de Morales travelled in 1572 through all the monasteries of the northern Spanish regions of Leon, Galizia, and Asturias, and he came back with priceless acquisitions. Princes of the church and the prominent people of the kingdom everywhere contributed manuscripts.

It was a significant moment when King Philipp II on May 2, 1576, transferred his book treasures (among which were over eighteen hundred manuscripts) through the master of the treasury, Hernando de Briviesca, to the monks of the Escorial monastery of San Lorenzo, the sons of St. Jerome.[25] Vainly had the voices, confronted with this solution, warned and expressed the fear that, in the Escorial the treasures would find, instead of their resurrection, their grave. The king had insisted on having his way and he now experienced the satisfaction of seeing his favorite palace, a monument of the eternal Spain, equipped also with excellent scholarly treasures in all languages. In the same year he also acquired the priceless possession of Greek manuscripts of the Spanish humanist, Don Diego Hurtado de Mendoza, and ten years later, the valuable estate of Archbishop Antonio Augustin (Augustinus) of Tarragona (d. May 31, 1587). Like Mendoza, this passionate bibliophile had collected primarily in Italy, but he had also visited several libraries in Germany and, little by little, he brought together 272 Greek and 561 Latin manuscripts, to which were added a thousand printed works. The catalog of the collection, which was published in 1586 by the Canon Martin Baillus, is among the best cataloging works of the sixteenth century.[26]

Among the reports on the arrangement of the acquired monuments, the essay of the later archbishop, Johann Baptista Cordona is outstanding; he required good and generally accessible catalogs, in addition to which, copies of the holdings lists of all the great libraries of the world (and therefore a kind of union catalog and survey of world literature); he wanted hospitality to be extended in the monastery to all worthy scholars and users of the treasures; he insisted on the printing of the catalog and he set up surprisingly progressive principles for the description of manuscripts. The king assigned the leadership of the collection to his protégée, Arias Montano. The library was arranged according to languages, and within this, by manuscripts and printed works, and then according to their content. The hall for the books, which was built by Herera and was one of the first Baroque library halls of Europe, had (after the example of the Sistine Chapel) a ceiling painting executed by the Italian Pelegrino Tibaldi, with the seven liberal arts, as well as the philosophy and theology groups, which looked down on the book treasures in the room. A lightning strike in 1671 has unfortunately destroyed about four thousand manuscripts of the unique collection.

To enhance the brilliance of the courts with exquisite book treasures in competition with other princes was the main motive for founding the princely library; this was an idea that had come from the Renaissance. As with the entire courtly collecting situation, however, the effects of owning books extended far beyond the original intent. Closely connected with the princely houses and their territories, these collected treasures of books, like the monastic libraries, carried in themselves something lasting and eternal. They became the glorious forerunners of the later territorial and national libraries, and, enlarged by new influxes of books, they developed into valuable common properties of the entire people until another power, namely, the state, officially undertook the task of maintaining them.

The Collections of Greek Manuscripts in the Renaissance Period

As the whole of Western culture is quite closely bound up with Greek antiquity, so has the Greek literature of pagan and Christian antiquity (and likewise that of the early Middle Ages) won domiciliary rights within Europe as a whole. The Paris National Library alone reckons 4800 Greek manuscripts among its holdings; the Vaticana in Rome has 3600, the Laurentiana in Florence a thousand, the Marciana in Venice a thousand, the library at Oxford a thousand, the British Museum in London over seven hundred, the Munich State Library over six hundred and the collection in the Escorial five hundred Greek manuscripts. Frequently we find the names of Thucydides, Xenophon, Plato, Demosthenes, Aeschines, Aristotle, and Homer in golden letters shining down on the rooms of libraries. When King Louis I of Bavaria was erecting the stately building for the Court and State Library in Munich, in the front of this temple of books he had statues of Aristotle, Thycydides, Hippocrates and Homer set up as symbolical figures. The designations of library, bibliography, catalog, paper and parchment recall for us no less urgently the Greek spirit's protective sovereignty within the world of books, as indeed do also almost all the conceptual designations for the fields of knowledge: ethics, eros, plastic, problem, tragic, idea, physics, philosophy, mathematics, epic, lyric, tragedy, comedy — all of these go back to the world of ancient Greece, to that initial magnificent period of thinking and knowledge about humanity and the world.

The most important locales for the transmission of Greek literature in the Middle Ages have been the Byzantine Empire with Byzantium, Mt. Athos, and the Greek colonies in the south of Italy.[1] Byzantium, since the year 330 the new capital city of the Eastern Roman Empire, was called on in later centuries as was no other place in the world to save the Greek cultural works of antiquity. What this New Rome has here accomplished chiefly rests in the gathering up of the works that had been handed down by means of large collective works as these especially have been designed in the ninth to the twelfth centuries. The emperor and the princes of the church shared in the service of this work of deliverance. Archbishop Arethas of Caeserea in Cappodocia (900), the author of an exposition of the Apocalypse, whose works recall Cassiodorus' activity in Vivarium, had transmitted to posterity significant treatises such as the literature of Plato, Dion, Aristides, Lucian, Pollux, Philostratos, Pausanias and the older Christian apologists.[2]

A considerable number of manuscripts have been copied in the years 888–932, among them being the Plato manuscript Clarkianus 39; dating from 895, the priceless manuscript was later carried off from the St. John monastery on Patmos by Samuel Clark; it is now kept at Oxford. Significant encyclopedists such as Photius, Eustathios, and Acominatos were felicitously able to connect Christian intellectual property with that of antiquity. Emperor Konstantinos Porphyrogenetos (912–959) had comprehensive extracts from the ancient Greek literature produced, which clearly bring to our consciousness the numerous losses in the original writings. The Byzantium of this century became a vital center of the reawakened Greek spirit, the almost inexhaustible source of a stream of manuscripts, which in a later period has flowed toward the West. Among the famous monuments in this time period one would perhaps name the world famous *Iliad Codex Venetus A* of the Marciana in Venice from the tenth century, with its valuable scholia (commentaries), or the invaluable *Codex Laurentianus* in Florence, which comes from the eleventh century and which has the best texts for Aeschylus, Sophocles, and Apollonius Rhodius. Through faithful reproductions, priceless Byzantine items have been made available to us today.

If in radiant Byzantium it was the great men of the world and of the church who provided for the extension of Greek literature, so within the narrow compass of quiet Mt. Athos the simple hermits and monks in their hermitages and cells handed down from one generation to the next the books of the church and of theological learning. This enchanting spot of earth in the eastern foothills of the peninsula of Chalcidice, with its 1900 m high elevations and its lonely places, extending far out into the Aegean Sea, is a strange land of books and of world-weary souls devoted to the service of God. After the tenth century an entire network of hermitages and monasteries gradually encompassed the world-denying mountain. What developed here in valuable Greek manuscripts (most of them having Biblical and theological content) came mainly from the eleventh and twelfth centuries. The strangeness of the landscape and the peoples' belief in miracles also have influenced the world of books. Just as foreigners were there looking for the greatest priceless items, so did the monks even observe many of the old manuscripts with a holy reserve; they believed a gospels manuscript produced with golden script at the Chiliantari monastery and coming from the fourteenth century was a direct souvenir of St. John Chrysostom, or in a psalter of the Dionysius monastery they thought they owned a copy of St. Melania, who according to legend, is supposed to have copied books. But the same monastery transmitted that important manuscript which has preserved for us in Greek an ancient Christian work, the *Shepherd* of Hermas, who was one of the so-called apostolic fathers. The mountainous land today still owns numerous (mostly Biblical, theological and liturgical) manuscripts.[3]

St. Catherine's monastery on Sinai has also sheltered within its walls precious manuscripts since the ninth and tenth centuries, such as the valuable gospel of 955 and two Bibles from the ninth century.[4]

Ecclesiastical literature found secure places of refuge in the famous St. John's monastery on the island of Patmos. In 1201 there were counted there 267 parchment and sixty-three paper manuscripts, of which 114 are still extant.[5]

In Lower Italy, in the remote mountainous areas, there were again industrious and pious monks, members of the Order of St. Basil, and quiet monastery places such as Rossano, Santa Maria del Patio, Santa Severina, Castanzaro, and Casole, which owned very ancient Greek manuscripts; they were copying them time and again and so transmitting them to posterity. Everywhere that the praying and penitent sons of St. Basil settled, especially at Grottaferrata, following after them were valuable manuscripts which reached back into the tenth century.[6] Out of such a monastery may also have come the Greek gospel manuscript of the cathedral of Rossano in Calabria, which has been described by Oscar Gebhart and Adolf Harnack, a priceless work of art of the sixth century that is written in Greek uncial letters with gold and silver on purple, and decorated with splendid pictures that are among the oldest known monuments of miniature painting coming from the transitional period between the ancient Christian and Byzantine art.[7]

There are two presuppositions that are associated with the successful penetration by a cultural power in a foreign land and among foreign peoples – on the giving side, there must be an irresistible inner strength, and on the receiving side, a relaxed capability of acceptance of the impinging new reality. For the Greek literature both of these held true; after Constantinople's capture by the Turks on May 29, 1453, the world of Greek culture had to flee into foreign lands, but under the influence of the reawakened antiquity, Italy greeted the Greek cultural world with open arms as a needed supplement to the new goal of education.

Already in ancient times the Romans had brought to Rome the book treasures of Aristotle and the defeated Greeks have become the cultural teachers of their conquerors. Lower Italy and Sicily throughout the whole of the Middle Ages had cultivated vital lines of communication with the world of Greece. Fleeing, this cultural power now victoriously penetrated into Italy, so as from here to become an important component of the Western Euorpean education. In the large collections of Rome, Florence, Venice, Naples, Turin, and Milan, Italy owns even today as many Greek manuscripts as does the rest of Western Europe put together, the collections of which came also from the Apennine Peninsula. Thus already through the external property relations there comes clearly to expression Italy's surpassing significance for the triumphal procession of Greek literature. The stream of manuscripts flowed in two ways, once through the direct wandering of old manuscripts out of the East, and then through the untiring scribal activity of numerous Greek refugees, who found a new vocation, as well as a means of livelihood, in the copying of their native literature. The discovery of printing did its share in promoting the successful diffusion of Greek cultural works through extensive reproductions.

A complete survey of the diffusion of Greek literature in Italy would have to go into the numerous translations from the Greek at the court of Pope Nicholas V (1447–1455), and into all the meanderings of the Greek manuscripts, above all into Francesco Filelfo (1398–1481), one of the most active ambassadors of the Greek cultural world,[8] into the collecting activity of the Medicis, into Bessarion (the chief communicator of the Greek spirit in the fifteenth century), into Venice, which with Bessarion's bountiful gift became an extremely significant center of the Greek tradition, into the Vaticana in Rome,[9] to which little by little a great treasury of Greek manuscripts have streamed, in the sixteenth century above all into the holdings of Cardinals Cervini, Sirleto,[10] and Carafa, and finally into those of Cardinal Alessandro Farnese, who was the nephew of Pope Paul III and a passionate collector.[11] Here it may suffice to indicate approximately the ways the Greek literature has proceeded in its journeyings from the East into the West, in order to find more secure places of refuge within the collections of the Western Europe.

Already several decades before the fall of Constantinople, individual scholars who were fond of travelling, especially Ciraco de Pizzicolli from Ancona (1391–1450) and Giovanni Aurispa (1370–1459), have brought Greek manuscripts from the East to Italy. Cyriacus of Ancona is the great traveller of the *Quattrocento:* he called Vergil and Homer his teachers; he was filled with an everlasting restlessness; he wanted to see the wide world; he had his eyes open everywhere for all the monuments of antiquity; in 1425 he stayed in Chios and in Adrianople, always seeking for manuscripts; on a second trip he ventured to Egypt to the pyramids, and then he travelled through Dalmatia and Greece; he acquired a Plutarch manuscript that is now kept at the Vaticana; on all his trips he zealously kept a diary and also described there the manuscripts he had seen. Half adventurer and half ambassador of knowledge, he earned his place also in the history of the transmission of Greek literature.[12]

In 1423, the Sicilian Aurispa, (the same one who, on his way from the Basel Council, discovered the Latin Panegyric in Mainz, Pliny the Younger's enconium of Emperor Trajan and the Donatus commentary on Terence) has brought to Venice an entire collection of 238 Greek manuscripts from Constantinople and thus saved them in the face of the destruction that was threatening them. One need only name such priceless items as the Florentine Codex, with Sophocles, Aeschylus and Apollonius Rhodius, the Venetian Homer manuscript A, Demosthenes, Plato, Xenophon, Aristotle, Strabo, Diodorus, Plutarch, Arrian, Lucian, and Athenaeus,[13] in order to put in its proper light the great significance of this carrying off of books. "It was in fact the planting of an entire literature on a new and fruitful ground." (Voigt) Even from Emperor Manuel II Aurispa has obtained two manuscripts as gifts, the great history work of Procopius and the little book of Xenophon on horsemanship. Following the death of the owner, the handsome collection went into the most diverse hands. An Archimedes manuscript from the collection has become especially famous, because the only transmission of the text rests on it.[14] For a while it was in the possession of the humanist, Georg Valla, the distinguised translator of the Greek literature and an enthusiastic collector (d. 23 January, 1500); he owned numerous, mostly later, manuscripts. When Angelo Poliziano was eagerly searching out manuscripts in 1491 for Lorenzo de' Medici, with the help of his friend, Niccolò Leoniceno, he was successful in obtaining permission to copy several manuscripts of Valla, among which was the Archimedes one. Following Valla's death, his collection came, for eight hundred ducats, to Alberto Pio of Carpi, in 1530 to Rodolfo Pio, in 1564 to Latino Latini,[15] and finally into the library of the Este at Modena, where some sixty manuscripts from Valla's possessions are still kept today. The Archimedian manuscript, however, is not among these. Copied the last time by Chrisoph Auer in about 1544 on commission from the French ambassador, Georges d' Armagnac, for the library at Fontainebleau (Cod. Paris 2361), it has since then disappeared.

The earliest Greek manuscripts on German soil were in Basel, when in 1443 Cardinal Johannes Stoikovic of Ragusa left his valuable library to the Basel Dominican monastery in thanksgiving for the hospitality he enjoyed there during the Council of Basel, on the condition that the collection be accommodated within a room of the monastery to be constructed at his cost.[16] The scholarly prince of the church had spent a while in Constantinople in the years 1435–1437 and had obtained valuable old Greek manuscripts there. The treasure, which at that time was still unique in Germany (previously there had scarcely been any Greek manuscripts there) soon excited the attention of the scholarly world. In 1488, Johann Reuchlin obtained from Basel a Greek manuscript on the New Testament coming from the tenth century: it was lent to him for as long as he lived; following his death, it was returned. A second Greek literary monument with an Apocalypse commentary, likewise used by Reuchlin, and then by Erasmus of Rotterdam, was later (as we have already mentioned) presented by the Basel printer, Hieronymus Froben, to Count Palatine Ottheinrich. A third item, which formerly belonged to the cardinal and with a Ptolemy text, had been written down during the Basel Council and handed over by Johann Gast to the Basel printer Johann Herwagen; it ended up in Zurich and Tübingen, where it was used by Martin Crusius; now it rests in the Vaticana in Rome.

When a three day plundering followed the capture of Constantinople in May 1453, over 120,000 manuscripts are supposed to have been destroyed, as this has been related by Cardinal Isidor of Russia, Archbishop of Kiev, the same one to whom Pope Calixtus III, following the death of his predecessor, Nicholas V, had transferred fifty-one manuscripts of the Vaticana for his lifetime. The destruction of numerous works has also been attested from other sources. Just as one has dreamt in later centuries of the scattered book collection of King Matthias Corvinus, that like some enchanted treasure, the books are still resting in some corner of the Hungarian capital, so also since the eighteenth century, men's imagination has woven legends around the one-time treasury of books in Constantinople to the effect that the old library of the Palaeologi, the last Byzantine emperors, lies hidden and dormant in the castle of the sultan and that it would once again be resurrected.[17] Both stories have turned out ot be illusory.

Of Italy's later numerous ambassadors of the books of the East there deserves to be named in the first place the Greek, Janos Lascaris, a refugee; at one time, he was taken in as a friend by Bessarion, and following his death, he was allied with Lorenzo de' Medici in Florence in purchasing manuscripts. Later active in Paris, after 1503 he was the French emissary in Paris; in 1513 he was called to Rome by Pope Leo X; he was again in Paris in 1518, in order to cooperate there with the famous Hellenist, Guillaume Budé (Budaeus), in the building of the library in Fontainbleau. It can be authenticated that in 1534 he was once more in Rome, and after 1535 he was no longer alive – such was the fate of the Greek refugee who had no home and no fatherland. In the study of manuscripts, Lascaris deserves our attention as the indefatigable wanderer who has seen many libraries, brought hundreds of manuscripts out the East to Italy, and, just as Cyriacus of Ancona did, has left valuable reports concerning the collections that he visited. His most significant trip came in 1491 and in 1492; it led him to Ferrara, Padua, Venice, Corfu, Salonica, Galata, Sosopolis, Athos, Apulia, Corigliano, and Monte Sardo. A Vatican manuscript (Codex Vat. Graec. 1412) contains lists by his own hand of manuscripts he has seen as well as those he has acquired, and also of the works that he was looking for, among them being several writings probably listed by Photius. We also therewith get to know the forty-four manuscripts that Lascaris has purchased for Lorenzo de' Medici at Candia on April 3, 1492, from Niccolò Giacomo da Siena, at a cost of about 405 ducats; among them is the oldest known parchment manuscript of the so-called surgeon's collection of Greek writings with surgical content (Codex Laurentianus LXXIV). Another of his acquisitions from the East, the most complete transmission of the Demosthenes *Orations* in uncial script of the tenth century, has come by way of Cardinal Niccolò Ridolfi and Queen Catherine of Medici to Paris, and has been faithfully reproduced by Omont.[18]

A host of Greek scholars, writers and traders would have to march past us if there should be mentioned all those disseminators of Greek literature who have transformed Italy into a second cultural Greece. Most well known among them are: Theodoros Gaza, the author of a Greek grammar whose beautifully written *Iliad* for Francesco Filelfo, (which at one time Bessarion sought in vain to acquire) today reposes in Florence; Constantine Lascaris, whose valuable collection of books fell to the town of Messina, in 1679 came to Palermo and was later carried off to Spain[19]; Marc Musurus, the trusted counselor of the Aldus printery; Nicolaos Sophianos, who was active for the book collection of Cardinals Marcello Cervini and Niccolò Ridolfi and, for Hurtado de Mendoza, visited Greek monasteries in the East (especially Mt. Athos), and acquired three hundred manuscripts on this trip; Johann Rhosos from Crete, who after 1447 stayed alternately in Rome, Florence, Bologne, and Venice, and has written many manuscripts for Cardinal Bessarion, for the papal proto-notary Gaspar Volaterranus, for Demetris Servius, and for Lorenzo de' Medici—of which over forty items can be documented today in the collections at Venice, Paris, Florence, London, Gotha, Moscow, and Naples; Angelos Vergetius (Bergites) from Crete, one of the cleverest Greek calligraphers, who between 1535–1568 completed an immense number of manuscripts, produced a catalog in Fontainebleau of the Greek manuscripts there, and provided a script pattern for Greek printing for Robert Estienne (Stephanus); Constantius Paleocappa, a Greek monk, who stayed on Mt. Athos from 1539 to 1543 and then later participated in the drawing up of the catalog of Fontainebleau.[20]

Antonios Eparchos, from Corfu (1492–1571), in 1544 printed in Venice a plaintive obituary on the decline of Greece, and in the following years disseminated a list of manuscripts that were fore sale, which itself led to successful transactions with the city of Augsburg, and in the year 1550 offered the famous Spanish statesman, Antoine Perrenot de Granvella, a new collection of Greek manuscripts, and was sent to Greece by Popes Marcellus IV and Pius IV to acquire books[21]; Matthäus

Devaris, who in 1562 was called by Pope Pius IV to the Vatican in order to improve defective Greek manuscripts: Nicholas de la Torre, who was active in 1564 in Constantinople (and later in Paris and Venice), and since 1573, for King Phillip of Spain. Finally, Andreas Darmarius, the indefatigable and prolific writer from the Lacedemonian Epidaurus, who in the years from 1560 to 1587 traversed half of Western Europe, offering everywhere his glittering (to be sure, they were not always gold!) wares, who found many buyers in 1562 and 1563 at the Council of Trent (among whom were the Spanish bishop, Antonio Agustin), spent a longer time in Spain beginning in 1570, and was living in 1584 in Strasbourg and Tübingen, where he found an influential protector in Martin Crusius, and in Duke Ludwig of Württemberg a generous patron.[22]

The most ambassadors for the Greek world have been provided by the island of Crete. From there came the scribes, Georges Manuel, Johannes Gregoropoulos, Johann Rhosos, Michel Damascenus, Angelos Vergetius, Marc Musurus, the most significant promoter of Greek printing, Demetrius, who supplied the first Greek types for the Milan printer, Dionysius Paravisinus, and Zacharias Calliergi and Nicolaos Blastos, who themselves have built in Venice in 1499 an exclusively Greek printer's workshop. Among the copiers we once encounter even a German, Christoph Aure, who at Rome in the years 1541 to 1548, has copied about twenty-five Greek texts for the French bishop and legate, Georges d'Armagnac.[23]

To the most enthusiastic buyers of Greek manuscripts on Italian soil belonged the already mentioned imperial legate and scholarly humanist, Don Diego Hurtado de Mendoza from Granada (1503–1575): he was one of the most brilliant Renaissance figures of Spain and a passionate book collector. He used his long stay in Italy for the most successful augmenting of his treasure in books.[24] Through Greek refugees, such as Nicolaos Murmuris from Nauplia, Johannes Mautomatis from Corfu, Nicolaos Marulos, Nicander Nucius from Corcyra, he had numerous manuscripts copied in Venice and Florence; twice he dispatched the Greek Nicolaos Sophianos to the East, and acquired priceless old manuscripts, among which was a valuable literary monument of the eleventh century from St. Athanasius' monastery on Mt. Athos, and he even obtained a gift of manuscripts from the Turkish sultan, of which a Bible from the possessions of Cantacucenus is still preserved for us today.

Associated with him for a long time in his book acquisitions (1538 to 1546) was the scholarly Belgian, Arnoldus Arlenius from Herzogenbusch, the distinguished publisher of Josephus Flavius of 1544 and of Lycophron in 1546; he was one of the best book connoisseurs of the period, and this knowledge has been praised even by German scholars such as Georg Tanner and Conrad Gesner.[25] The Spanish collector was liberal in making his treasures available. Conrad Gesner was able to take out several manuscripts to Zurich; for that he dedicated to the envoy his Greek-Latin lexicon and, for eighty-eight titles of his famous *Bibliotheca*, he listed Hurtado de Mendoza as the owner of the texts concerned. Arlenius, for his Josephus-Flavius edition, drew upon three manuscripts of his patron, and in his dedicatory preface he praised his contributions to the production of the first complete text. Cardinal Marcello Cervini was able at his own discretion to make use of the entire of the entire collection during the Council of Trent, and he even procured valuable manuscripts for his friend, Gentianus Hervetus, for publishing the work of Zacharias Scholasticus of Mytilene against Ammonius. Following the death of the owner, the handsome collection on June 15, 1576, went over into the library of the Escorial, in connection with which King Phillip II took responsibility for the debts of the estate. The fire of 1671 caused heavy damages here, too; of the original 260 Greek manuscripts, only ninety are evident in the current holdings.

Even before receiving the priceless collection of his envoy, King Phillip II has already acquired other Greek manuscripts from the possessions of the learned philosopher, Franciscus Patricius (1529–1597), and on June 26, 1575, he has had them transferred to the Escorial, along with the rest of the initial gifts. There were seventy-four volumes which their owner had acquired from the monasteries of the county while he was doing administrative work on Cyprus in the years 1563–1568. The sale to King Phillip was originated by Don Diego de Guzmann de Sylva, the Spanish envoy in Venice, the same one who organized the inflow of Greek manuscripts form the possessions of the trader, Eparchos; of those treasures that Patricius has personally brought to Spain, only twenty-two are still remaining.[26]

So many Greek works accrued to the Escorial from the possessions of Andres Darmarius, Juan Páez, Antonio Agustin, Matteo Dandolo and Niccolò Barelli, that one can speak of a veritable stream of Greek manuscripts from Italy into Spain.[27]

A second great transfer of Greek manuscripts from Italy has gone to France. Primarily to be named here is Bishop Guillaume Pellicier (1529–1568), the leader of the Renaissance movement in Montpellier, who spent a time from 1539 to 1592 as the French ambassador in Venice, during which period he was able to acquire numerous Greek manuscripts.[28] He is held in high esteem among researchers into Greek manuscripts. He traded enthusiastically in Venice with Antonios Eparchos and he mediated between him and King Francis I, who on October 2, 1541, remitted to him a considerable sum of money for Greek manuscripts, a contract according to which a relatively large number of Greek manuscripts were transferred to Fontainebleau and into French ownership.[29] Pellicier wrote on October 8, 1540 to Pierre du Chastel, the librarian of his king, that a foreign trader would procure for him the library of the Palaelogi in Constantinople. This remarkable passage from the letter evidences that the French ambassador had his hand everywhere where there were Greek manuscripts to be acquired for himself, or for the court; but it also shows that at that time there were already bold swindlers who were trying to take advantage of the passion for collecting characteristic in that period. Pellicier's manuscripts for the most part have later come, by way of Claude Naulot, into the possession of the Jesuits in Paris, and there have shared the fate of the *Bibliotheca Claromontana* until the majority of them have ultimately come into the State Library at Berlin. A catalog of the original possession located in Paris, with 239 items (among which were sixty Greek manuscripts) has been published by Montfaucon.

The interest of King Francis I (1518–1547) in Greek manuscripts has been engaged through Janos Lascaris and Guillaume Budé. The new foundation was supposed to have its seat in Fontainebleau and deliberately to enter into competition with the Vaticana, the Marciana and the Laurentiana. Venice and Rome became the focal points of acquisitions and the envoys, Jean de Pins, Georges de Selvi, Georges d'Armagnac and Guillaume Pellicier, made arrangements for sales. Henry II (1547–1559) successfully continued his father's efforts. Under him the Greek calligrapher, Angelos Vergetius, spent a while in Fontainebleau and, together with two other Greeks, Constantine Paleocappa and Jakob Diassorinos, he designed the catalog. The young collection was already numbering 546 Greek manuscripts in 1552. Palaeocappa alone copied twenty-six manuscripts in Fontainebleau, but frequently he corrupted and falsified the texts. Diassorinos later participated in a plot and in 1563 he was executed on the island of Cyprus. With what is currently the Paris manuscript Graec. 3064, one possessed in Fontainebleau not only the catalog of its own collection, but also lists of the possessions of Bessarion, Guillaume Pellicier, Jérome Fondule, Antonios Eparchos, Aldus Manutius, and well as an excerpt from the list that Agostino Steuco (as librarian of the Vatican) had sent in 1540 to Ippolito d'Este. The French library once more obtained a valuable enrichment from Italy in 1599, when King Henry IV (at the urging of the scholars, Jacques Auguste de Thou and Pierre Pithou) had seized, following her death, the Greek holdings of Cardinal Niccolò Ridolfi (the nephew of Pope Leo X) which Catherine of Medici had taken over from Marshal Pierre Strozzi. The treasures of Fontainebleau have been very closely connected with the flowering of Greek studies in France as well as with the founding and the leadership of the entire movement in Guillaume Budé (1468–1540), Adrien Turnèbe (1512–1565), Isaac Casaubonus (1559–1614), of whom Budé and Casaubonus have personally administered the library.[31]

Venice was the most important point of departure for the meanderings of Greek manuscripts; we hear about two valuable lending lists of the Marciana from the years 1545–1549 from which it emerges that numerous manuscripts at that time have been passed to envoys and scholars in exchange for a borrowing ticket and pledge. Many more recent copies, most of them incorporated into the Escorial collection, can be traced back to these Venetian texts and can be determined according to those lists.[32]

Germany was also to obtain rich Greek treasures out of Italy—above all, the city that was most vitally connected with Venice and which has perhaps contributed most strongly to the increasing competitiveness of Germany in book collecting—the proud, rich Augsburg, where (as already mentioned) not only the brothers Johann Jakob and Ulrich Fugger brought together valuable Greek manuscripts that later found their way to Munich and Heidelberg, but where the city also acquired a priceless treasure. In 1544 there was issued in Venice a list (transmitted to us in the Vienna National Library) of one hundred Greek manuscripts, most of them being texts of the church fathers, which Antonios Eparchos (already mentioned as the trader from Corfu) desired to sell on account of his lack of money. As it expressly says in the announcement, there were among them no less than forty-five parchment manuscripts, and thus they were priceless old literary monuments. That signified an unusual offer, which may have been cause for no little sensation among the Venice book collectors. Then something happened that was rather unexpected.

It was not someone such as Mendoza or King Francis I who acquired the tempting collection, but rather Phillip Walther, the plain, relatively unknown merchant and representative of the city of Augsburg, who carried the proud booty across the Alps. It is a rare event in the history of the book: a German municipality, which up to this point has scarcely owned more than the usual book collection composed of theological and juristical works, tenders a sizeable small offer (it was over a thousand gold gulden) in Venice for a possession of Greek manuscripts, which, as we now know, has been among the most valuable offers of the market at that time. Concerning the significant event, the Augsburg city account contains the following entry: 937½ florins paid in cash to the Burgomaster Welser for Venice for Greek books; 38 florins' expense to send the Greek books from Venice to Augsburg; 163 florins, 21 *Keruzer*, 4 *heller* paid also on account of the Greek books, kept back in Venice and paid to Phillip Walter and accounted for by him.

On April 21, 1544, Gereon Sayler sent the remarkable communication to the two Augsburg burgomasters, Georg Herwart and Simprecht Hoser, that Emperor Charles V had turned his attention to the Augsburg book treasure. In the name of Landgrave Phillip of Hesse, Sayler gave the advice to refuse the request and to respond that the books were first supposed to be printed. If this excuse also achieved nothing, then one should say that the books had already been spoken for by the Hessian landgrave; the prince will know how to deny the emperor his wish.[33] In fact the imperial court counselor of Speyer had already on March 27 given to Augsburg from Speyer instructions for the take-over (by purchasing) for the emperor.[34] That one has been on guard in Augsburg is evidenced in a letter of the English embassy secretary, Roger Ascham, from the year 1551, in which it is reported from Augsburg that sixty of the best manuscripts have been hidden, in order to secure them in the face of the emperor and the people of his court, who perhaps could be covetous of them.

The acquisition brought high honor to the city and it bore rich fruit. Already in 1545 Nicholaus Gerbel was jubilating in his Polybius edition over Augsburg's service to knowledge, and even the later textual editions that were gradually issued from the priceless possession carried the fame of the city into all the world. Following a somewhat unfortunate publication by Sixt Birk, the systematic disclosure of the Augsburg treasures began when the scholarly philologist, Hieronymus Wolf, the former librarian of Johann Jakob Fugger's, became rector of St. Anna in Augsburg in 1556, and with this post, took over the administration of the Municipal Library. In 1562 the holdings were transferred to St. Annenhof and arranged in a hall decorated with pictures of Augsburg and portraits of the church fathers. Hieronymus Wolf authored the inscription for it and in a Latin poem he praised the work. Seven small towers crowned the roof of the hall: They were supposed to remind viewers of the seven liberal arts. In 1575 there appeared under the title *Catalogus Graecorum librorum manuscriptorum Augustanae bibliotheca* a short catalog of the Greek manuscripts: the unnamed publisher is again to be sought in Wolf. The list may boast of being one of the first printed manuscript catalogs.

Following Wolf's death, (1580), stepping into his place initially was Georg Henisch, and then since 1593, David Höschel (1556–1617).[35]

By order of the city trustee, Marcus Welser, Höschel published a new complete catalog of the Greek manuscripts in Augsburg in 1595. With Welser at the head, a special scholarly society was founded, which was to make use of the treasures of the library and was primarily supposed to publish editions for which no publisher could be found. A special printery, named for its symbol (the pine cone of the Augsburg city council's coat of arms), *Ad Insigne pinus* ("At the Sign of the Pine"), was supposed to carry out the production of the proposed editions. It was a lively, gay life that was pursued within this interesting Augsburg circle; at its head was the versatile patrician, Marcus Welser, who raised lovely Dutch flowers and plants in his garden, observed the constellations, loved and collected books, published important Bavarian historical works, rediscovered the Peutinger table which had been forgotten, and exchanged friendly letters with Ortelius, Lipsius, Casaubonus, Scaliger, and Goldast; the indefatigable David Höschel, who quickly published one after the other, Philo, John Damascene, Maximus Margunios, Athanasius, Basilius, Andronikos, and Gregory of Nyssa, and with his Photius edition of 1601, enjoyed the assistance of the philologists, Janus Gruter, Konrad Rittershausen, Isaac Casaubonus, Joseph Justus Scaliger and Justus Lipsius; and finally, in neighboring Munich, the Bavarian chancellor, Georg Hoerwarth von Hohenburg, a kindred spirit, to whom Höschel in 1600 dedicated his publication of minor Greek geographers, and who had printed in 1602 a list of the Munich Greek manuscripts, in exchange for sending it to Augsburg he received Höschel's proofs for a new Procopius edition. This exciting scholarly life in the sixteenth century has found its counter part (on German soil) only in Heidelberg. This upsurge of scholarly activity in both the cities goes back to the Greek manuscripts that were acquired from Italy.

Added to the great Greek collection of the sixteenth century in the Escorial, in Fontainebleau, in Augsburg, in Heidelberg, and in Munich was Vienna, the gate to the East. It received its first treasures from Constantinople, the city which, like Venice, constituted an inexhaustible market for Greek books. Again it was an ambassador who was the successful mediator; Ogier Ghislen von Busbeck,[36] who between 1555 and August 1562, remained (with only brief interruptions) in the Turkish capital as the envoy of Emperor Ferdinand I, and zealously collected Greek manuscripts there. He purchased no less than 262 valuable monuments, and shortly before Emperor Maximilian II's death, they came to Vienna. Rudolf II had the manuscripts appraised and he offered the owner a thousand florins. Busbeck accepted the sum as a present in return (not as a sale price), and with his treasures he gave the court library a basic Greek stock that was scarcely to be equalled in the entire world. Many of the manuscripts originated in Greek monasteries, and several came from the possessions of a Greek monk, one Mathusalas; the priceless holdings are still today almost entirely to be found in Vienna; only two of the manuscripts have come to Paris, having been carried off by the French in 1809.

Busbeck had also learned in Constantinople of the famous Dioscurides manuscript, with its portrait of the aunt of Emperor Valentinian III, Juliana Anicia, and he sought to acquire it for Emperor Ferdinand I. Aurispa had already spotted the monument once at the monastery of St. John Praecursor in Constantinople; it then belonged to a Jew, the son of a Turkish court physician. Because the owner was demanding a hundred ducats of Busbeck, the deal came to nought. But Busbeck still seems then to have acquired the manuscript with his own money, and to have made a present of it to the emperor. As one of the oldest of its literary monuments, it still today constitutes what is perhaps the most valuable treasure of the Vienna library. Enlarged by the significant collection of the imperial court historiographer, Johannes Sambucus (384 Greek and 113 Latin manuscripts), under Hugo Blotius, the young foundation was speedily augmented, and could be considered as being the most comprehensive collection of Greek manuscripts.

Not so grandiose an operation, but still an attractive cultural-historical symbol of the enthusiasm for Greek literature was also taking place about this time at the University of Tübingen. Situated in the center of the Greek studies there was Martin Crusius, a scholar not unknown in the history of antiquarian scholarship. At his suggestion, the Tübingen (Evangelical) theologians, Jakob Andrea and Jakob Heerbrand, undertook the audacious attempt of winning over the Greek patriarch, Jeremiah II, of Constantinople, for a union of the churches, and for an Evangelical league against the papacy. The adventurous undertaking took on tangible form when the envoy of Maximilian II to the Sublime Ottoman Porte, David von Ungnad, Baron of Sonneck and Preyburg, entered into the proposal and in 1573 he took with him as the embassy preacher to Constantinople the Tübingen collegiate church chaplain, Stephan Gerlach (1546–1612). Here Gerlach resided for almost a full five years, from August 1573 to June 1578; furnished by Crusius with exhaustive directions and lists, over and above his ecclesiastical assignment, he zealously concerned himself with acquiring of Greek manuscripts. In a diary published by the grandson, Samuel Gerlach,[37] he has fully portrayed his experiences, among them being those with books. He found several Greek manuscripts in Galata in October, 1573, but they had no special value. In October 1575 he inquired at the patriarchate in Constantinople, but he learned nothing further than that there were several manuscripts at Mt. Athos that one perhaps could have copied against payment. In September 1576, he presented a ducat to the departing protonotary, Theodosius Zygomalas,[38] (who wanted to visit old libraries during an official trip in Patmos, Pisidia and Caesera) for which sum the man pledged himself to seek zealously for old books. In May, 1577, Gerlach saw a book written in "very beautiful Persian," with gold and leaf work, the binding of which had cost fifty thalers. On May 22, 1577, he attended a cerremony at the festival of the Jews in Constantinople. "The Five Books of Moses, inscribed on parchment and fastened to two rods, someone lifted out a case and showed it to the people, who bowed before it."

Gerlach finally got to see the patriarchate's library in June 1577. "Today," he wrote, "I have seen the patriarchal library and found bad books. Only Chrysostom is almost complete, and several of those of Athanansius, of Epiphanius, and concerning John; otherwise there are very nearly no outstanding church doctors. Overall, the books come to 150; they are lying full of dust in a vault, and there is no one reading. The patriarch did not want to lend me any of the books; but I could read in the patriarchate itself; their rule permits that." At about the same time, Gerlach also visited the library of the Trinity monastery on the island of Chalki near Constantinople, and he copied the catalog. Another time he reported that there were only a few bookdealers and therefore there were also only a few manuscripts to buy or borrow. Busbeck had taken away several cases with manuscripts, and so had Karl Rimmus, Ungnad's predecessor in the ambassadorial post. Gerlach gives a vivid report about a book auction in Constantinople. On May 24, 1578, he was able to see the library of Antonius Cantacucenus and obtain a catalog for it.

When Gerlach returned to Tübingen in June, 1578, not only did he bring with him copies of catalogs from Greek monasteries, but also seventeen valuable Greek manuscripts that came to Duke Ludwig and to Martin Crusius. In the present day Munich manuscript collection Cod. gr. 266, one reads a postscript of Gerlach's, according to which he had obtained the volume on March 6, 1575, in Constantinople, at cost to Duke Ludwig of Württemberg. On January 10, 1579, there subsequently arrived a Greek chronicle from Constantinople that was sent by the protonotary Theodosius Zygomalas; it is now in Paris. Crusius has published it in his 1584 description of Turkey. A new acquisition opportunity arose in Tübingen when on August 30, 1584, the bookdealer, Andreas Darmarius, turned up with fifty-four Greek manuscripts and remained until September 10. On May 12, 1584, the Augsburg preacher, Georg Mulius, wrote that the Evangelical college in Augsburg had purchased twenty-five manuscripts from Darmarius. This report may have aroused the people in Tübingen to emulation. At Duke Ludwig's command, Gerlach and Crusius bought eight Greek manuscripts from the bookdealer for thirty-five Italian crowns for the castle library in Tübingen.[39] Again, the most enthusiastic user of the new acquisitions was Crusius.[40] He frequently wandered up to the Tübingen castle and borrowed the Greek manuscripts from the castle overseer, Johann Hermann Ochsenbach. The industrious perusal of the treasures one can still today follow by means of the entries that the Tübingen professor made in the manuscripts.[41] Without any qualms—yes, it was even with a certain pride—Crusius has entered into the manuscripts in the Greek language the borrowing and the duration of his working through the manuscript. Most of these Tübingen manuscripts have later come to Munich as war booty to the Elector Maximilian I of Bavaria.

How strong the interest of Western Europe in the Greek treasures of Constantinople had gradually become, is evidenced also by a strange Strasbourg work, from 1578, *Bibliotheca siva antiquates urbis Constantinopolitanae*, which was published by the Freiburg professor of Greek, Johann Hartung;[42] in the main, catalogs of books are here reprinted; these are supposed to show how many priceless treasures of the Christians were lying imprisoned in the plundered city that was now under the sovereign power of the Turks. The title of eight collections were, however, not always suitable for inspiring confidence. They list disappeared treasures, such as the comedies of Menander and Philemon, the histories of Ephorus and Theopomp—priceless items that therefore cause one to suspect that these lists only partially related to items actually possessed, and for the rest, they contain works passionately searched for, which were only imagined as being in Constaninople, or which were being promoted by cunning dealers. A far greater significance may be claimed for the list of books printed in 1598, and which the Dutchman, Georg Dousa, had brought with him from Constantinople in the previous year.[43]

Turkish Istanbul has also remained for the future the center of an expanding trade in manuscripts.

The acquisition of Greek manuscripts through Italy's example, and the still persisting outflow from Greece, had became a passion for collecting which included the whole of Western Europe and continued throughout the entire sixteenth century until the supply was bought up and the manuscripts were in firm possession. The amateurs seem to have been motivated by the desire to acquire the unique and the different in the literature that was newly discovered, as well as in possessing texts that were as yet unpublished. Greek literature has thus experienced its turbulent manuscriptural and incunabula period late in the sixteenth century — an excellent example of the irresistible attraction of a significant world of books over the centuries, and at the same time a valuable social witness to the cultural history of the Renaissance movement.

20

The Second Flowering of the World
of Books in the Later Sixteenth Century

Stimulated by the world of antiquity, and fully receptive to the beauty of form, the power of the waning Middle Ages (which was the final moment of an integrated way of life as this has scarcely again been experienced in such unity) had flowed over onto the world of books. The decline of this culture also ended the great flowering of the book. In the initial ecclesiastical and political confusion of a world that was collapsing and being rebuilt, concern for books could not properly prosper any more.

To be sure, the preservative powers were initially still strong enough, in spite of the descent from the earlier cultural heights, to issue in a second flowering of book design, which is distinguished by the more secure sovereignty of the decorative forms in woodcut and copper engraving, which in an earlier period would have involved painstaking struggle. And we nevertheless still encounter significant books on all sides also in the second half of the sixteenth century. What the new period, however, no longer exhibits is the earlier unity of the German – and yes, the European – book market, the care and attention formerly given to all parts of the book, in paper, title page, typeface, binding, illustrations – that is to say, to the book's total layout.

Conspicuous in Germany on account of the artistic energies that they spent on the book were Hans Sebald Beham, Virgil Solis, Hans Brosamer, Jost Amman, and Tobias Stimmer. A new center of stimulating book production developed in Frankfurt am Main, which in a speedy rise was soon to become the principal site of the German book trade. The first native printer there became Christian Egenolf (1513 until 1555), who produced an impressive number of richly decorated books, and for them took into his service the clever Nuremberg artist, Hans Sebald Beham, but who also, without any qualms, had used old woodcuts for his pictorial decorations, items he had acquired from Heinrich Steiner in Augsburg.[1]

That Frankfurt underwent so quick an upsurgance as a book city it owed chiefly to its enterprising printer and publisher, Sigismund Feyerabend (1528–1590), who with unprecedented expenditures published book after book, richly furnished with woodcuts, and who became (just as Anton Koberger had once been) Germany's most significant publisher.[2] For the decorating of his publications he drew on the artists Virgil Solis, Jost Amman, Robias Stimmer, and he laid out considerable sums for the purpose. We are told in one account that has been preserved for us that "to draw and cut the figures to Vergil, to Adam Reissner's Jerusalem, Ovid, and *Fabulis Aesopi*, 790 florins" have been disbursed; in order to draw all the figures to the Bible, and cut them, 949 florins; for figures to Livy together with the form and two borders, 152 florins; to draw and cut figures and borders in *Chronika Aventina*, 30 florins." Feyerabend oversupplied his works with book decorations as Johann Grüninger once had. On June 17, 1559, Feyerbend's business associates, the printers (who were related to him by marriage), David Zöpfel and Johann Rasch, had borrowed 990 florins from the Holy Ghost Hospital in Frankfurt by mortgaging their houses, in order to be able to print all the more handsomely their new work, which was a large German Bible. This Bible appeared in the following year with likenesses of the Palatine electors, Ottheinrich and Friedrich III, in unprecedented splendor. Virgil Solis had the entire volume practically covered with pictures and borders.[3]

For those less well off, the publishers issued these illustrations in a separate special edition as "Biblical figures." Scarcely had the two editions appeared when the Wittenberg Bible printers were heavily inveighing against it. Christoph Walther, the proofreader at the Lufft printery, published in 1563 a report of his own against Frankfurt: *Bericht von Unterschied der Biblien* ("Report of the Difference among the Bibles"), and in it he chiefly opposed the layout of the Frankfurt Bible. "The figures in the reprint Bibles" it says there, "are quite small, and what is of such importance for the text, they are almost unrecognizable. Around the figures, however, they have had painted much foolish work, puppet work, and devil's work. They have put several borders around the figures, because they are so small, with such foolish fantasies as devilish faces, hoot-owls and other filthy ghastly faces and monstrosities. And they have designed and set borders around the figures, ones that would suit much better for the Marcolfo than they do in the Bible, next to God's Word." Walther further upbraided the Frankfurt printers, that they also otherwise stressed the externals by having the Bible bound in velvet and silk and mounted with gold and silver, and then gave them to the princes and high ranking gentlemen as a gift. The attacked publisher now issued a second edition of the Bible with a new series of pictures—this time by Jost Amman[4]—and he omitted the borders on the grounds that they had displeased so many.

Feyerabend's large picture books have given much stimulation to contemporary crafts; frequently, as with Ovid, Aesop and Alciato, especially, they have been used as genealogical registers. In the dedicatory preface to Johann Bocksberger's and Jost Amman's *Neue Biblische Figuren des Alten und Neuen Testements* ("New Biblical Figures of the Old and New Testements") from the year 1569, Feyerabend praises the painters and illustrators who, with their images, represent holy scripture for those who can't read, or for those who enjoy the pictures or find them stimulating—that is, the painters, the goldsmiths, or the other art lovers. Leonhard Fronspeger's military book, the Tournament Book of 1566[5], and the *Eigentliche Beschreibung aller Stände auf Erden* ("Actual Descriptions of all the Professions on Earth") of 1568, with verses by Hans Sachs and Jost Amman's representations of the professions among which were the typesetters, the drawers, the metal cutters, paperers, printers, miniaturists, and bookbinders, may be counted as being among the books most in demand in this period.

Very special, and indeed unique, and at the same time an evidence of Feyerabend's publishing output, were his large collective works, in which he brought together texts that had already been published and read with pleasure, such as the *Heldenbuch* ("Book of Heros") of 1560 with the transmitted heroic sagas, the *Neue Welt* ("New World") of 1567,the *Buch der Liebe* ("Love Book") of 1578 with the various popular romances, the *Reysebuch des heyligen Lands* ("Travel book of the Holy Land") of 1584, with its eighteen descriptions of trips, the *Theatrum Diabolorum* of 1569, which brought him a court complaint from the printer, Nicholas Basse, who charged that Feyerabend had reprinted eleven of his devil's books in this collection. Feyerabend decorated most of his large published works with splendid title page borders, and also with his device (a figure of *Fama* as a symbol of the good reputation), with which his house has in fact achieved a worldwide reputation. In order to lend popular devotional books a festive garb, he liked to draw frames around on all the sides, employing various ornamental forms. The high number of these framed books, as these richly decorated devotional books were called, clearly expresses the great popularity of such book publications. The Munich State Library owns a collective volume with four printed works from the year 1579 (4 Asc. 601), the pages of which are all framed with decorative borders. That the publisher has been conscious of his significance in the service of the book, is indicated by his numerous dedicatory prefaces, in which he expresses himself chattily and self-confidently concerning the goal and the success of his work.

A remarkable little book that would later play a significant role in the history of German literature came out in 1587 at the Frankfurt printery of Johann Spies: *Historia vom D. Johann Fausten, dem weitbeschreyten Zauberer und Schwarzkünstler, zum schrecklichen Beyspiel, abscheulichen Exemple und treuherziger Warnung zusammengezogen und in den Druck verfertigt.*[6] ("History of D. Johann Faustus, the widely renowned magician and necromancer, put together as fearful fables, odious examples and candid warning and composed in print"). An unknown friend in Speyer, (so reports the printer in his foreword) had the stories, legends and shocking tales of D. Johann Faust, (which were inquired about "in all guest companies and societies") collected and printed in Frankfurt. The printer possessed sufficient experience, and an enterprising spirit, so that he considered the half-weird, half-frightening, but ever piquant combination of legends to be a surely marketable book. Thus did the oldest Faust book come about, in which there is portrayed how the necromancer associated with the devil and his fellow, Mephistopheles, as magician, astrologer, doctor, and philosopher, who took to himself eagle's wings, and who would explore "all ground on heaven and earth," and do his mischief, until the devil threw him from one wall to the other and, hurled out onto the manure heap, he died.

Among the older places for printing, Basel was still also maintaining a significant position in the book trade of the period—the later sixteenth century.[7] Thus (to name only several of the most outstanding books published there) the printer, Michael Isengrin, published the *Neue Kräuterbuch* ("New Herb Book") of Leonard

Fuchs in 1542 in Latin, and in 1543 in German, with 515 fine plant illustrations throughout, and then he added the likenesses of the author and of the contributing artists, the painters, Heinrich Füllmaurer and Albercht Mayer, as well as of the metal cutter, Veyt Rudolf Speckle.[8] And so did Johannes Oporinus, one of the most highly deserving printers for the life of books in his period, publish in 1543 the anatomy, *De humani corporis fabrica libri VII* of Andreas Vesalius with wonderful woodcuts, among them being the likeness of the author and a representation of a post-mortem examination[9]; drawings for it are thought to have been designed by the Italian artist, Johann Stephan von Calcar, a pupil of Titian's. The most disseminated book from Basel in this period was Sebastian Münster's *Cosmographica*, which was initially published in 1544 with Heinrich Petri, in order then to be reissued almost in every year.[10] It was supposed to be a popular book which as the author wrote "will please our descendants four hundred years from now." For the same reasons, Münster composed it in German and intended that no one should turn up his nose at it, for the representations had been taken from the best sources.

The work had an enormous success, despite its large dimensions. No less than forty-six editions, in six different languages, have been published. The work, which is of the highest value in the history of culture, is inexhaustible. Who, for example, would look there for the *Our Father* in the Latvian language? But there it is in the 1550 edition. Münster has received the text as imparted by the Hessian, Johann Hasentöter, who has been in Riga in the period from 1547 to 1548. The publisher did all he could to satisfy peoples' curiosity to see. Picture after picture, and one ornamental border after another filled the pages and leaves: maps, representations of cities, pictures, foreign people, animals and plants. The author had exerted a great deal of effort with the city views.[11] Letters had gone out to numerous princes, scholars and cities requesting pictures of particular locales. The author reports in the finished work that good representations of cities had come in above all from Italy, out of Rome, Naples, Venice and Florence—but also from the German cities and towns, from Trier, Sitten, Solothurn, Baden, Rufach, Colmar, Weissenburg, Landau, Speyer, Worms, Lindau, Freiburg, Nördlingen, Ulm, Strasbourg, Vienna, and from Frankfurt an der Oder. The princes of Pomerania had sent depictions of the cities of Stettin and Stralsund, with a description of the entire duchy and the Palatine Count Johann had submitted a representation executed by himself, of his residential town of Simmern, together with a copper engraving of it.[12]

Also not lacking, however, were the refusals, most of which were based on the want of suitable painters, and also disapproving and critical judgments of the finished work. Thus Count Palatine Ottheinrich, who had sent in a view of Heidelberg for the first edition, was indignant that the author had unnecessarily and deceitfully published his work for the third time, and had written of the Lorsch monastery that an emperor was buried there and that a book was present there which Vergil had written with his own hand, both of which were not true—"Therefore indeed considering how badly mistaken he is about matters close at hand—how does it go with the matters which are far off?"[13] On October 15, 1554, there came before the Basel city council a deputation of both the Engadines complaining about an abuse of the

Engadines by Münster, who was supposed to have said the inhabitants there "were greater thieves than the gypsies." The Basel councillors declared that were the author still living, they would make him take responsibility; but those insults were in no way to be considered harmful and injurious to the reputation and honor of those insulted. The printer had to apologize.[14]

One of the most important scholarly works of the entire sixteenth century the printers, Heronymus Froben and Nikolaus Episcopius, published in 1556: the large collective work by Georg Agricola, the founder of petrology and mining (as a study or discipline), concerning his researches in the Saxon mines. The work, which was dedicated to Duke Moritz of Saxony as patron of the local mines, has also appeared in an Italian translation in Venice in 1550,[15] and for two centuries it was the technical "bible" of mines throughout the whole world.

The Basel printer, Peter Perna, who was born in Italy and was a successful book trader between Italy and Germany, published a further significant printed work in the years 1555–1557. It was a reissue of the portraits of famous men from the collection which the deceased bishop of Nocera, Paolo Giovio, had compiled, partly in originals, and partly in copies, in his native city of Como. On commission from the printer, a particular painter (probably Tobias Stimmer) had gone to Como and there had painted sixty-two portraits of scholars, and twenty-eight of generals, so they could subsequently be transferred to woodcuts. This beautiful work of portraiture, *Elogia virorum illustrium*, has for the first time made accessible the unique collection in Como and made it famous in all the world.[16] The beautiful work generated a series of similar projects which all set themselves the task of bringing to the attention of their contemporaries, in pictures, the leading men of the past, as well as their own period. This represented a new possibility for the book's effectiveness, and one that was closely connected with the picture.[17]

Likewise in Strasbourg there were published several important and much requested works, such as the 1545 herbal book of Hieronymus Bock, which was decorated by David Kandel with plant drawings, and came from Wendelin Richel's printery; or Nikolaus Reusner's collection of portraits, with its fine woodcut drawings of Tobias Stimmer; it was published in 1587 in the house of Bernhard Jobin, who was the son-in-law of Johann Fischart. The editions of portraits, eloquent testimonies to the intensified emphasis on the personality, were enjoying an increasing popularity.

As if by a fortunate circumstance, Nuremberg had already become the printing locale of the most famous book of the time, the *Theuerdank* of Emperor Maximillian I, so there was published there in 1543 yet a second significant work, which was connected with the city only in a formal way: the revolutionizing publication of the Frauenburg canon and founder of the new astronomy, Nikolaus Copernicus, concerning the movements of the heavenly bodies, *De revolutionibus orbium coelestium libri sex*. The Nuremberg scholars, Andreas Osiander, Georg Joachim and Johann Schöner had it printed just before the death of the distant author by Master Johannes Petreius. The work, which was looked after by the German cardinal, Nikolaus Schömberg, and dedicated by the author to Pope Paul III had, as is well-known, lifted the earth (as did the discovery by Columbus) out of its previous position and instead put the sun, encircled by the planets, in the center of the universe.[18] The publication of the work has had a remarkable fate. In the long years of his researches, the learned Frauenburg canon had, through hard work, obtained the foundation to his new world system. News about it had already gotten into the wider circle of those who were excited about astronomy, and even to Rome; here we already encounter Johann Albrecht Widmanstetter as an adherent of the new astronomical teaching. Even the young professor of mathematics, Georg Joachim in Wittenberg (who after his home province, Vorarlberg, was called Rheticus) had heard the marvelous tales, and through them, he was induced in May 1539 to seek out Copernicus in Frauenburg, in order to become more precisely acquainted with his work. He was already writing in September to his teacher, Johan Schöner at Nuremberg, concerning his encounter with Copernicus. The report printed in the following year of 1540 in Danzig gave to the world for the first time exact information on the new world system, which was causing such a stir.[19] Soon thereafter Joachim encouraged the canon, who was still hesitant, to publish the results of his research, and in fact he got the manuscript dispatched by a friend to the bishop of Kulm, Tiedmann Giese. It was printed in Nuremberg in 1548. Copernicus died shortly thereafter.

Outstanding among the further works printed in Nuremberg, were Walter Rivius' publication of 1547 about architecture and his German Vitruvius translation of 1548; both of them were richly decorated with woodcuts.[20] The two works have been essential contributions in spreading the appreciation for the forms of the Italian Renaissance.

The heraldic book of Virgil Solis and Wenzel Jamnitzer's, *Perspectiva*, was published with plates in 1555. With very scanty expenditure, the printer, Leonhardt Heussler, published in the years 1558–1561 the poems of the shoemaker who enjoyed verses, Hans Sachs; there Sachs portrayed the whole life in his time with didactic rhymes and struggled against the world's foolishness and its infirmities. Georg Willer from Augsburg, the publisher of the work in several volumes, the same one who has become famous in the history of books through his Frankfurt Fair catalog of 1564 (which was the first of its kind), praised in his exuberant preface the Nuremberg master singers as the greatest poets of the German people, worthy to be compared with Homer and Vergil. The Nuremberg metal cutter, Hans Weigel, had a good idea when in 1577 he published a costume book with 219 full-page woodcuts; it was one of the earliest of this pictorial series that has speedily achieved an established place for itself in the world of books.[21]

Outstanding books have also come from Zurich, where the leading printer was Christoph Froschauer, the diligent printer of Ulrich Zwingli and the indefatigable publisher of well designed Bibles.[22] One of his most significant books is Johann Stumpf's *Schweizer Chronik* ("Swiss Chronicle") of 1548[23], which is decorated with over 2500 illustrations and for which he spared neither efforts nor costs. Thus on November 24, 1544 he reported to the author concerning the artist who had designed the work: "As I wrote to you fourteen days ago concerning Vogtherr[24], he came the same day; he had cut the tenth plate and now has begun the sixth one, which is of the Zurich district, and which he will have finished in a week.

Accordingly he still has Europe and Germany to do in fourteen days. What you still have to make in the way of plates, make them, and do them on thin paper; if you have none, I'll send it to you; it is very bad for him that you have used such thick paper. The thinner the paper is, the better he can see through it; because he has to cut everything from behind on the wood." And on January 18, 1545, the printer wrote to Joachim Vadian: "I have now since St. Martin's Day the best painter, who now lives with me now at the house, where I give him two *groschen* every two weeks, and food and drink; he does nothing but cut figures for the *Chronika;* half the figures may be cut by the time Fall begins; to that end no costs will be spared."[25]

When in 1586 the author's son, Johann Rudolf Stumpf, was preparing a second edition of the *Chronicle,* the design of the work was restricted for the following reasons: "So that the size of this book and the cost may be reduced, not only have we taken a smaller set of letters and used more supple paper, but we have also eliminated many countless imaginary and unnecessary figures, with which the entire work previously had been filled and indeed had been clogged, and we have allowed to remain only those plates with maps and the depictions of cities, of battles, of notable persons and their arms."

With the same printer, Froschauer, there also appeared the natural history of Conrad Gesner[26], the founder of modern zoology[27]: the quadrupeds with eighty-two illustrations in 1551, the amphibians in 1554 with fifteen woodcuts, the birds with 217 pictures in 1555, and the aquatic animals[28] in 1558 with 737 woodcuts. These works were all in Latin and German editions; they were copied from good illustrations, and the editions were accomplished with the cooperation of numerous scholars. Gesner also once mentions an artist, the Strasbourg painter, Lukas Schan, who copied for him most of the birds from life and has also furnished descriptions, a man who was as knowledgeable in paintings as in bird catching. Gesner would have preferred to print the images in their natural colors; but because this was not possible, the printer subsequently had a number of copies painted according to the colorful originals for such buyers who were not put off by the high price. Zacharias Ursinus on July 27, 1561, wrote from Zurich to the medical doctor, Crato von Crafftheim at Breslau,[29] that Froschauer had put Gesner's works up for sale at the Frankfurt Fair, with and without the colors. The price for the quadrupeds unpainted was two florins, and painted, four florins; for the amphibians unpainted, seven shillings, and painted, one florin, and ten shillings; for the birds unpainted, one florin and ten shillings, painted, seven florins and ten shillings. One could even have the illustrations by themselves painted or unpainted. Valuable sources for becoming acquainted with the production of scientific works of that period are revealed to us in this letter.

Gesner has also done pioneering work in other directions. His *Bibliotheca universalis* will be mentioned in the section relating to bibliography. His pamphlet about milk and pasture economy[30] is one of the oldest statements of Alpinism. The author expresses himself enthusiastically concerning the excitement of mountain climbing. He had intended to scale a summit every year in order to get to know the alpine plants and at the same time to relax.

A likewise splendid woodcut work was published in 1559 by the Zurich printer, Andreas Gesner: Jakob Strada's collection of imperial portraits decorated with a beautiful ornmental border of Christoph Schweytzer and with excellent portraits by Hans Rudolf Manuel, called Deutsch. Peter Flötner's wonderful decorations, which have the effect of goldsmithery, constitute an outstanding decoration of the book – a special quality in addition to the designating of the artistic works with the monograms of the master, along with which even the woodcutter is mentioned: Rudolf Wyssenbach.

Following his conversion to Evangelical doctrine in 1540, the Brandenburg Elector, Joachim III, called the Wittenberg printer, Hans Wiess, to Berlin, and there he published several official works, such as the *Reformation Churfürstlicher gnaden zu Brandenburg* ("Reformation in the Electorate of Brandenburg"), *Camergerichts zu Cöln an der Sprew* ("Law Court at Cöln an der Sprew"), and the *Kirchenordnung im Kurfürstentum der Marken zu Brandenburg* ("Church Order in the Electorate of the Mark of Brandenburg"). The two printed works therefore stand, surprisingly late, at the beginning of the Berlin publishing house, which was afterwards so successful.

Vienna in 1549 brought a significant work of great effort to the book market: the description of Russia from the pen of the scholarly statesman, Sigmund von Herberstein's *Rerum Moscovitarum commentarii*. The work was formulated on the basis of the author's own observations on a trip into Russia, which then was almost unknown; in 1557, he translated the book into German for the many "who do not know Latin and yet are eager to learn about these things." Among the accompanying woodcuts from the hand of the artist, Augustin Hirschvogel, are (besides the map of Russia) especially the portrayal of a sleigh trip made by the author, and, additionally the representation of the bison and the aurochs that have become famous; as is well known, the aurochs have soon died out. Within the shortest time span, five Latin and four German editions of the beautiful work have been published, in addition to a translation into Italian.[31]

The abbot of the Benedictine monastery of Tegernsee, Quirin Rest, had a printery built in his monastery in 1573 by the master from Dillingen, Sebald Mayer, and in addition to numerous printed works of an edifying nature, produced a beautiful choir breviary in 1576, and in 1577 the *Reitkunst* ("Horsemanship") of Hans Friedrich Hörwart von Hohenburg, which was decorated with many woodcuts. After advancing again under Abbot Petrus von Guthrath, the workshops published two significant historical works, Gottfried Bessel's *Chronik von Göttweig* ("Chronical of Göttweig") in 1733 and in 1766, Magnus Klein's *Urkundenbuch des Kosters Lorsch* ("Recordbook of the Lorsch Monastery"). Tegernsee occupies one of the first places among the German monastery printeries.[32]

It is one of the most stimulating tasks of the history of the book to trace the ways in which the ever larger expansion of the enterprises relating to the book have gone in the most diverse directions during the incunabula period. Thus we find a series of art and architecture books which, being richly provided with pictures, were intended to give handy instructions and pattern drawings to architects, stone masons, painters, goldsmiths, and joiners for their professional activity. It is primarily in

Italy (the homeland of Renaissance art) that several such books have appeared. Already the famous *Hypnerotomachia Poliphili* of Francesco Colonna of 1496 was containing pretty drawings of imaginary ancient buildings. Further art and architecture books were inspired above all by Vitruvius, the outstanding master of Roman architecture. The Italian translation of Vitruvius, printed by Gotardo da Ponte in 1512 in Como, together with the elucidations of Cesare Cesariano, was especially effective. It has also become the basis of the aforementioned German translation of Walther Rivius, with its numerous woodcuts.

Jean Gazeau produced the first French translation (from the pen of Jean Martin) in 1547 in Paris, which also had many woodcuts. Several architects were stimulated by Vitruvius to publish independent architectural books, such as Sebastiano Serlio in 1537, Antonio Labaccos in 1538, in 1559 Jacques Androuet du Cerceau, in 1561 Philibert de L'Osme, Jacopo Barozzi da Vignola in about 1563, and Vincenzo Scamozzi in 1583. Elector Ottheinrich of the Palatinate, the founder of the large Renaissance wing in Heidelberg castle, has owned several of these architectural books in his library and has been guided by them. Going along in the shadow of these architectural books were several small booklets for all kinds of arts and trades. Hans Sebald Beham's *Kunst-und Lehrbüchlein* ("Booklet of Art and Instruction in Art") has gone through eight editions in the years 1546–1608. Heinrich Vogtherr, Hans Brosamer and Jost Amman have likewise been very successful with their publications.[33]

The later sixteenth century has also become the period when the atlases originated – those comprehensive collections of maps of sea and land in book form. The name came from the Titan Atlas, who as a punishment for his participating in the assault on the Titans on Olympus has been condemned to carry the firmament. A later myth has Atlas transformed into the Lybian king, who was an astronomer and who is supposed to have produced the first celestial globe. The earliest naming of the map works according to this figure of myths was in the large atlas of the Jülich scholar, Raumold Mercator, the son of Gerhard Mercator, who was the most famous geographer of his time. The atlas was printed in 1595 at Düsseldorf by Albert Bussius. The title page of the first part shows the king enthroned and busy producing the celestial sphere; over the columnar construction are the two attendant figures who are carrying a completed celestial globe.[34]

The friendly relations amongst people made for a book form that, from the viewpoint of the history of culture, is an exciting one: the album intended for manuscriptural entries by acquaintances and friends. One set up such "friendship" books in such a way that pretty small printed works were bound with empty leaves or had empty paper inserted. Especially suited for this purpose were the Emblemata editions[35] of Andrea Alciato (since 1531), of Nikolaus Reusner (1591), and of Isaak and Theodore de Bry of 1593[36]; they contained maxims and symbols, which then harmonized well with the testimonials of friendship entered there. It was primarily students, the scholars, the nobility and the patricians who planned such albums. One entered his name, his place of residence and his motto, and if one could, one painted his arms or a likeness of himself. Resourceful printers put this custom successfully to use and published genealogical and arms books (or albums) that they had themselves created; among them are woodcut works of Jost Amman and David Denegker, both from the year 1579.[37]

We get a good insight into the book situation of a travelling book dealer from the second half of the sixteenth century in reports which have been transmitted to us from the Frankfurt bookdealer, Michael Harder, concerning the success at the Lenten Fair of 1569.[38] Five thousand nine hundred eighteen books were sold, many of them in numerous copies; most were works of a popular nature. Chivalrous epics, popular books, didactic narratives – these were especially in demand. This is a list of the most desired books in the sequential order of their sales. The *Geschichte von den sieben Meistern* ("History of the Seven Masters") attained 233 sales, Appollinaris' medicine book, 227, Paulis' *Schimpf und Ernst* ("Insult and Injury"), *Fortunatus, 196, Die Schöne Magelone,* 176, *Die Meerfee Melusine,* 158, Adam Riese's *Rechenbuch* (an arithmetic textbook), 150, *Ritter ("Knight") Pontus,* 147, *Ritter Galmy,* 144, Albrecht's *Rechenbuch* (Arithmetics), 138, *Albertus Magnus,* 135, *Octavian,* 135, Hans Wilhelm Kirchhoff's *Wendunmut* 188, Jörg Wickram's *Goldfaden* (Golden Thread), 116, Paris, 108, booklets on the planets, 108, and practical farming, 106. Already emerging were all sorts of dubious books, especially the joke books that did not belong in everyone's hands. Johann Baptist Fickler was complaining in 1581 about the malevolent influence of such writings "as *Die Centonovelle, Gartengesellschaft* (of Martin Lindener), the booklets for rest and for the night (of Michael Lindner and Valentin Schumann), and many more of the same, more than we can relate here, are being sold here and again in the bookshops, to the corruption of good morals and community standards." Even Luther's tabletalk, the Catholic speaker continued, was purchased with pleasure, and likewise the translations of Spanish and French publications, such as the *Amadis di Gaula.* Luther's sermons were also widely distributed. "Irrespective of these," it further states in the complaint, "At the court day at Frankfurt, that has been held in 1577, I have heard from the mouth of a leading printer at that time that the *Amadis di Gaula* has brought in more money than Luther's sermons.[39] The bookdealer, Feyerabend, could indeed not issue sufficient sequels of the *Amadis* novel.

In the Netherlands, the book found its most successful attendant in the printer, Christopher Plantin at Antwerp, who may be designated as the most significant publisher of his time. He or his son-in-law regularly visited the Frankfurt Fair, in order to sell their books there. Six barrels went to the Lenten Fair of 1579 by way of Cologne to Frankfurt, with 567 works in 5212 copies. One thousand eight hundred nine florins were taken in. Plantin's chief work is the polyglot Bible in eight volumes, which he produced in fourteen hundred copies from 1569 to 1572, on commission from Phillipp II of Spain. It was a tremendous work and it has established the house's worldwide renown, the fame of which yet lives today in the Musée du Plantin in Antwerp, which is a unique museum of the book.[40]

Venice, which long since as forfeited the significance it had earlier enjoyed, had something of an upsurge in its book trade with the rise of the Italian belletristic literature. This was primarily fostered by the Venetian printers, Gabriel Giolitto de' Ferrari,[41] Vincenzo Valgrisi, and Francesco Marcolini,[42] the printer of Pietro Aretino and of Sebastiano Serlio. The works of Pietro Aretino (1539), Boccaccio (1542), Dante (1544), Antonio Francesco Doni (1552), Dolce (1553) and Ariosto (1543) were put out in handsome editions.

In Florence, the Fleming, Lorenzo Torrentino, who was called there by the Grand Duke Cosimo de' Medici, developed an exciting printing activity in the years 1547–1563. Of his projects, to be mentioned above all are the first edition of Vasari's *Vite* (1550) and the *Historia di Italia* of Guicciardini (1561).[43]

In Rome, the enterprising master, Antonio Blado, published the significant Roman work of Bartolomeo Marliano, *Antiquae Romae Typographia,* and the handsome fencing book of the fencing master, Camillo Agrippa, with fifty-five outstanding copper engravings (1555). This work, repeated two more times, has contributed a great deal to the revival of the art of fencing in Italy.[44]

The illustrated book was more and more placing itself in the service of the natural sciences. Making its appearance in Bologna in the years 1599–1603 was the significant work in three volumes, *Ornithologia,* by the natural scientist, Ulisse Aldrovandi; it had numerous woodcuts by Christopher Coriolano. This work is one of the first of the bird books that were so popular later on.[45] Aldrovandi has kept a painter employed for thirty years in producing pictures.

Paris became the effective center of activity of the publishing family of Estienne *(Stephanus).*[46] Robert Estienne, the learned publisher of the *Thesaurus linguae latinae* and the king's printer for the folio edition of the Greek New Testament, which was published in 1550 with the new Greek types (Grecs royaux = ½ Grecs du Roi)[47] that were designed by Angelus Vergecius, and cut by Claude Garamond; due, however, to his inclinations toward Calvinism, he had to leave Paris and settle in Geneva. His son, Henri, became even more famous through the numerous editions he did of the Greek and Latin classics, above all, through his *Thesaurus linguae Graecae* (in four volumes) of 1572. In a sharp bill of indictment of the year 1569 relating to the text he appropriately rebuked the printers who were poorly prepared for their vocation while bestowing all kinds of praise on his scholarly professional contemporaries, among whom were the German masters, Johann Froben and Johann Oporinus.[48] He gave expression to his close connection with Germany in 1574 through a nice description of the Frankfurt Fair, in which he was enthusiastic concerning the city's favorable situation, the amiable behavior of the people of Frankfurt, the pleasantness of his stay there, the impartiality of the judges, and the enormous trafficking that there was with the bookdealers and printers among the professional authors, poets and scholars; and finally, he praised the art of printing as being the most meritorious of the German discoveries.[49] The Frankfurt council has given him a golden goblet on April 10, 1574, in response to his sending them a pamphlet.

Jean de Tournes published in 1557 at Lyons an outstanding handsome Ovid edition, *Le metamorphose d'Ovide,* with attractive woodcut illustrations and ornamental frames from the hand of the artist, Bernard Salomon, the successful counselor of the printing house.

Among the French printing types coming from the middle of the sixteenth century the *Lettre de civilité* had become the best known; it was designed in 1557 by

Robert Granjon, a skilled Lyonnaise typecutter and printer. It was supposed to be a faithful example of the French writing script of that time, and at the same time a master script for school instruction; but it did not prevail. It then found an entree with the Antwerp printer, Christopher Plantin, as well as with Aimé Tavernier. Utilized by them for the French translation of Erasmus of Rotterdam's work *La civilité puérile*, it seems in that way to have gotten its name.[50]

Throughout the fifteenth and sixteenth centuries, the woodcut has been the faithful helper and accompaniment of the book; in the last decades toward 1600, it had gradually to yield to the copper engraving. Enterprising printers had already been employing the copper engravings in the fifteenth century for pictures and for maps, as Colard Mansion at Bruges did in 1476 for his French translation of Boccaccio, or Nikolaus Laurentii at Florence, for his Dante edition of 1481[51] and for the *Geographia* of Berlinghieri; and so also have Conrad Sweynheym and Arnold Bucking for their Ptolemy edition of 1478, George Reyser at Würzburg for the choir breviary of 1479, and Michel Topié and Jacques Heremberck in 1488 at Lyons for a French translation of Breydenbach's travel description.[52] The flourishing period of the copper engraving first began at the end of the sixteenth century, when the altered concept of taste was requiring more conspicuous forms of expression – especially splendor and pomp – than the simple, strong language of lines in woodcut, and this gave the advantage to copper engraving with its picturesque tone values. It was primarily the title page, the main arena for the new book decoration, that was richly supplied with symbols of all sorts.

Thanks to its capabilities for expression, thanks to the enterprising tendencies of the entire engraving workshops, and to the success of the great pictorial series, the copper engraving gradually developed into a new form of the book – one that deliberately put the picture into the foreground, the printed text contributing only elucidation. This new function of copper engraving, the brothers Johann Dietrich and Johann Israel de Bry advocated in the edition (which appeared in 1609) of their "Oriental travels" (Latin: *Collectiones peregrinationum in India),* which was filled with pictures. There they referred to the responsibility that people have to serve God according to their gifts by active work, and thus even through the art of painting and copper engraving.[53] The apparent success of such large and expensive works shows us what we can also find proclaimed abundantly in the history of the book, that it primarily depends on the clever insight and the enterprising spirit of the editors and the publishing houses, in order for new paths to be opened again and again for the book.

The development of copper engraving reached its zenith when the geography of countries and localities made use of it in increasing measure and added maps, city views, and other representations to their works for the purposes of demonstration. The most stupendous copper engraving work of this sort came out in the city views that the Cologne Cathedral dean, George Braun (together with the engravers, Simon Novellanus and Franz Hogenberg) published at Cologne after 1572 under the title, *Civitates orbis terrarum* ("Description and Likenesses of the most Prominent Cities of the World") in six parts, with 370 plates.[54] Until then, people had not seen anything of that kind. At most the work can be compared with Schedel's

Weltchronik ("World Chronicle") of 1493, or with Sebastians Münster's *Cosmographia* of 1545, but what enormous progress there was within this span of time! It was an immediate success, as the publisher was able to report already in the second part that the initial installments were sold out. He closed his preface with an urgent invitation to the reader for assistance: "Whoever does not find in these two books his ancestral and native town, I would beg the same in a friendly spirit that he should depict the same from life and send it to me and I would have such drawn by means of the artful Francis Hogenberg–like manner, and place it, with a proper announcement, in the first, or in this book, or otherwise hold it for the third book."

Several sample books with copper engravings served the functions of applied art, as, for example, Wendelin Dietterlin's *Architectura* of 1593, the "basic book of the German Baroque style" (von Lützow) with over two hundred engraved plates, mainly intended for carpenters. Other copper engraved works reproduced paintings of famous artists, or the architectural monuments of the ancient world. One of the most famous of these is the one by the Roman copper engraver, Antonio Lafreri, which was published in the year 1574: *Speculum Romanae Magnificentiae;* in it, ancient Rome is supposed to have been resurrected. There thus developed expanded workshops and publishing houses which devoted themselves almost exclusively to the producing and distributing these much desired copper engraved works–a development that found its continuation and growth in the seventeenth century.

As the period of the Renaissance had so devotedly attended to applied art in its totality, so great attention also came to be paid to bookbinding. Through the gilding stamps and platens, cover decor was intensified; new decorative motifs flowed from Oriental ornamentation and from the treasury of forms of the Renaissance, with its strap work and garlands. Particularly in Italy and France applied art works of the first order originated; covered with gold and colors, they are outstanding evidences of the loving care that was given books. The names of Jean Grolier,[55] Viscount d'Aguisy and Thomas Mahieu (Maiolus) have become famous as the subscribers and the owners of such Renaissance volumes, which were influenced by Oriental forms. The German students, Nikolaus von Ebeleben, Damian Pflug and Ulrich Fugger, brought to Germany from Italy and France beautiful hand-gilded art volumes that they had ordered during the time when they were studying in Paris and Bologna in the years 1541–1548.[56] We have already come to know Elector August of Saxony as an enthusiastic friend of the splendid Renaissance volume. But it was in France that the Renaissance volume found by far its most careful cultivation. It was primarily the ostentatious binding, however, that the French kings loved: Louis XII and Francis I, but especially Henry II, with his consort, Catherine of Medici, and also the king's mistress, Diana of Poitiers.

Book Promotion and Bibliology in the Incunabula Period

The book has not only to be reproduced; it has to be disseminated; it has to be read. How does the book get noticed by its environment? How do printers and bookdealers find buyers for their books? In the early period of printing, these questions (which are now as good as solved) were among the most difficult ones for a successful book trade.

The earliest promotion that we encounter in printed books is in Fust's and Schöffer's *Psalterium* of 1457, where, in the colophon, the unique layout, with its wonderful initials and clearly arranged divisions, stands out proudly. Then there follows, as the first independent page of advertising, the purposive prospectus of Schöffer of 1470 for his edition of the letters of St. Jerome, which were to be more complete, clearer and more reliable than those issued earlier; the reader of the page is asked to wait for the edition and not to buy any other.[1] About 1469, the same printer issued a catalog of books that had already been published, in which are mentioned quite significant Mainz printing monuments, such as the *Psalterium* of 1457, the *Canon missae* of 1458, the *Catholicon* edition of 1460, and the Bible of 1462. The famous sheet concluded with a proudly emphasized sample of the types of the Psalterium *(Hec est litera psalterii)*. Schöffer's prospectus to the *Decretum Gratiani* and the *Decretals* of Gregory IX of 1472 and 1473 refer to the lucidity of the carefully prepared typeset of the commentary and the elucidations of which are arranged around the text; further, the printer's mark is emphasized as a trademark.

Wandering booksellers were already early advertising the items they had brought with them by means of printed pamphlets. Thus a bookseller (of whom no more is mentioned) solicited for his stock of books, where there were Venetian editions which, due to their beautiful printing and their careful layout of the text, should be preferred by all; but a part of his stock also were Mainz, Nuremberg, Cologne and Basel editions, as well as those from elsewhere. The remarkable advertisements of books in the fifteenth century in the German language have already been mentioned,[2] and also the 1474 prospectus of the astronomer, Johannes Regiomantanus, for his projected works.[3] In his own advertisements, the publisher, Anton Koberger, has recommended Hartmann Schedel's famous *Weltchronik* ("World Chronicle") of 1493, because of its rich layout and the engravings of all the significant men and all the large cities in Europe. In order to avoid the many inquiries concerning his published works, the Venetian printer, Aldus Manutius, published three sheets in the years 1498 to 1513 which are of significance in the history of Greek literature; in them the previously published texts (among which were the most important editions of the complete Aristotle, besides Aristophanes, Theophrastus, Demosthenes, Plato, Pausanius, and Homer), are listed together with their prices. A notable sample of his Netherlands *Melusine* edition the printer Geraert Leeu decorated in Antwerp in 1491 with an enticing picture of Melusine in the bath.[4] On a promotional sheet of the English printer, William Caxton in Westminster, which was for a set of liturgical rubrics for the Diocese of Salisbury in 1477, one is requested to allow the bill to be posted (supplico, stet cedula) – a reference that tells us that the sheet, like all such promotional items was intended for public notice.

A special kind of book prospectus in functional connection with the announcements of lectures was developed at Leipzig in the decade after 1500; there the school of higher learning (as the earliest of all the German unversities) came upon printing in its common tending to the needs of those who were studying. Thus the Master Georg Arnoldi announced in a sheet about 1500 a lecture on Seneca's work, *De mundi gubernatione*, and the printer, Konrad Kachelofen, recommended at the same time the printed edition of the work, with the declaration that he would sell copies of the improved text in Aristotle Hall. At about the same time, Johannes Honorius was communicating in a printed pamphlet that instead of lecturing about Statius and Ovid, he would lecture on the *Doctrinale* of the grammarian, Alexander de Villa Dei, which for a small amount of money was to be purchased in Kachelofen's shop. We are already here hearing about the bookshop, which in the history of the book had yet such a significant function to fulfill. On another occasion, Master Andreas Propst made it known that he would lecture about Horace, and that the text was to be had at the printer's, Jakob Thanner. Johannes Honorius mentioned the same master for his Horace lecture, and the College of St. Bernhard as the place for selling.

An entire bundle of such advertisements has been preserved for us of the printer, Martin Landsberg. He had available a *Logic* of Magnus Hund, a letter specimen-edition of Paul Niavis, a Lucanus text for the lecture of Professor Petrus von Windsheim, a further edition of Valerius Maximus for the expositions of Professor Johannes Honorius, a Juvenal for Master Benedikt Teyl and the *Ethics* of Aristotle for Professor Franz Richter. The editions of these texts are mostly printed double spaced, so that the students would write their instructor's elucidations in the spaces between the lines. We still find in libraries that contain old holdings numerous such printed college books that are covered all over with handwritten glosses. These kinds of books also appear preponderantly to have been fostered in Leipzig, and they may be evaluated as important historical sources for getting to know the operations of the schools of higher learning in this period.[5]

Ingenious authors, or printers also, soon knew how to take advantage of the title page for promoting the book. Through the composition of the title, the reader could already be encouraged to take a look at the book. If one wished to stimulate the viewer further to purchase a publication one then poeticized eloquent verses for it, and added them to the title.

It was especially the pamphlet, which was addressed to the broadest audience, that liked to make use of catchy rhymes in order to motivate the reader to purchase; as a pamphlet of 1511 proclaimed on its title page: "He who would know how things stand/ At the moment in Württemberg Land/ He buys and reads the text at hand/ It is called the poor Conrad."[6]

Comprehensive publisher's catalogs have also soon appeared. Thus in 1559 there was the *Academia Veneta*, which had been established in Venice at the suggestion of Nobile Federigo Badoaro under the patronage of Cardinal Michael Ghislerius, the later Pope Pius V, in order to publish exemplary editions of old and new works; it offered to the public a surprisingly progressive publisher's catalog. The learned society put its hopes also in Germany on sales and exchange, and therefore it had its own decorated list printed (with the pretty publisher's mark of *Fama*) of the publications that were going to the Frankfurt Fair.[7] This prospectus may be considered a formal forerunner of the later Frankfurt Fair catalog.

The advancing significance of Frankfurt am Main as a leading city for the book trade is also illustrated in the *Vezeichnuss aller Potentaten, Chur- und Fursten, geistlich und weltlich, auch derselben Gesandten, item Grafen, Freyen und deren von der Ritterschaft, so auf der Römischen Königlichen Majestät Wahl und Krönung zu Frankfurt a.M. persönlich gewesen sind.* ("List of all potentates, electors, and princes, clericals and secular officials and also ambassadors of the same, likewise counts, freemen, and those of the knighthood, who have personally been in Frankfurt at the election and coronation of His Royal Roman Majesty"); it came out in several editions in 1562. The following special group of participants listed there surprises us: "Scholars who have written books and have been ascertained at this time at Frankfurt from booksellers and the courts of princes." We read the following names with their approriate designations: Johann Agricola, Georgius Wicelius, Johann Brentius, Abdias Praetorius Gottschalk, Melchior Kling, Franciscus Hottomannus, Christoph Ehem, Nicolaus Cisnerus, Simon Schardius, Michael Beutherus, Johann Voerthusis, Samuel von Quickelberg, Laurentius Scharderus, Johann de Franckolin, Heinrich Millius, Johannes Sturmius, Cyprianus Volemius, Michael Toxites, Andreas Rapitius, Johann Posthius, Martinus Kuberus, Johannes Taisnerus I.V.D., Orlandus de Lassus." It was therefore quite an illustrious scholarly society that assembled for the election of King Maximilian in Frankfurt am Main, and that was therefore accessible for literary inquiries, as well as for business connections with printers and publishers. Frankfurt has already very early been a popular rendezvous for all those circles that participated in the life of books.

Among the German printers, the masters from Zurich, Basel and Frankfurt chiefly published abstracts of their published works on broadsheets or in pamphlets. Thus Christoph Froschauer in 1562, announced his publications in a pamphlet of sixteen leaves: the items have been ranked one after another in a Latin and a German group according to subject. Johannes Oporinus and Heinrich Petri proceeded similarly in Basel.[8] The Frankfurt publishers, Feyerabend and Egenolf, had pamphlets issued in 1579, with listings of their stock of theological, jurisprudential, medical and historical books; they were divided into language groups. In the prospectus of Sigismund Feyerabend, in which there publicly emerges for what may well be the first time the German designation *Buchladen* ("bookshop"),[9] especially cited are the publisher's numerous collections of the opinions of legal counsels. In a promotional sheet from the same period of the Egenolf house, uppermost are the theologians, Lukas Lossius and Erasmus Sarcerius, and further the legal scholars, Melchior Kling and Johann Oldendorp. The publisher's prospectus of the house of Gerlach in Nuremberg lists numerous musical works with grand names such as Orlando di Lasso and Jakob Regnart.

An important renewal in promoting the book was brought about by the enterprising bookdealer, George Willer, with his catalog, which appeared in 1564; it listed all the books he had bought at the Frankfurt Fair, which for the first time gave a selective survey of the book market to booksellers as well as to the buyers of books. The value of this new device was yet essentially enhanced, in that the list was prepared anew for each fair and thus appeared twice in the year, and in that the Frankfurt printer, Nikolaus Basse, published in 1592 a comprehensive compilation based on the listings of publications for the years 1564 until 1594. The first fair catalog *(catalogus universalis)*, which was published by the Frankfurt council came on the market in 1598.

The fair catalog that the Leipzig bookdealer, Henning Grosse, published (using the Frankfurt Fair catalog as a basis) for the Leipzig Michaelmas Fair in 1598 was to become even more significant. This Leipzig fair catalog was at the same time a testimony to Leipzig's growth as a city of the book trade; it was yet to have a great future.[10]

If all these catalogs served primarily the business promotion of the book for booksellers and publishers, so the enormous increase in printed books, and the growing numbers of readers, and book collectors, were demanding literary surveys of the publications appearing on the book market. Already in 1494 the Benedictine abbot, Johannes Trithemius, who was well informed about books, was publishing a catalog of ecclesiastical authors (based on examples for the ancient church and the Middle Ages) at the Basel printer's, Johannes von Amerbach[11]; authors of secular works were also accepted into this catalog. The publication has been much read and has gone through new editions as late as 1531 and 1546.

Representing an incomparable advance as over against this first history of literature was a work that can be designated as the first bibliography: Conrad Gesner's *Bibliotheca universalis sive Catalogus omnium scriptorium*, which was published in 1545 by Christoph Froschauer in Zurich.[12] The scholarly author, a native of Zurich, first professor of Greek in Lausanne and then professor of physics and medicine in Zurich, had been acquiring a rich knowledge of books since the twenty-fifth year of his life from the catalogs of the Vaticana in Rome, the Medici library in Florence, the St. Salvator monastery in Bologna, the Marciana in Venice, the Municipal Library in Augsburg and the book collections of Erasmus of Rotterdam, Konrad Peutinger, and Diego Hurtado de Mendoza; and he gave to his own time a unique reference work that was soon wanting in no major book collection. In the dedicatory preface to the imperial councillor, Leonhard Beck von Beckenstein, he reported concerning the old lost libraries which today are little more than legend. Even the more recent period, he said, had heavy losses for which to commiserate, such as the famous Ofen Library, which, with its rich Greek and Hebrew manuscripts, was no more. He meant his work to be a guide for the founding and growth of collections in libraries, which alone handed down to posterity the intellectual properties in writing. His sources for the work, he reported, were publisher's lists, library catalogs, and listings of literature. With the printed works that were cited, he added the printer's name, by which the purchaser knew where to turn. With the manuscripts the places where they were discovered, along with brief descriptions, were supplied as indications for the printer, should they perhaps desire to publish the texts. Through the possibility of manuscriptural insertions of the shelflist notations, Gesner felt the work could also be used as a catalog for each library. The work served everywhere as a welcome guide through the literature. In a supplementary subject catalog of 1548 and 1549, *Pandectarum sive partitionum universalium libri XVI*, Gesner devoted individual sections to the most outstanding printers of his period, and he simultaneously provided remarkable appreciations of their attainments. Of individual publishers – such as Aldus Manutius, Sebastian Gryphius, Johann Frellonius, Johann Gymnicus, Christian Wechel and Froben – he reprinted the publisher's lists that they had published.

Konrad Lycosthenes published an extract *(Elenchus)* from the *Bibliotheca universalis* in 1551 in Basel; he added an asterisk to those items that were supplementary to Gesner's works. Gesner, who had not been made aware of the project, now urged his friend, Josua Simler, toward an improved and enlarged edition of the abbreviated handbook. The edition was published in 1555, with a dedication to the Count Palatine Ottheinrich. In his preface to the 1561 publication of Josua Mahler's *Die deutsche Sprach* ("The German Langauge"), Gesner expressed the desire that there might also be published a German *Bibliothek* ("Library"), with the names of all the writers in the German language and their works; he himself would gladly make his rich collection available for such a purpose.

The second edition of the *Bibliotheca univeralis* of 1574 was also published by Josua Simler, and dedicated to the Count Palatine Ludwig VI. The significance of libraries is made clear by examples from the ancient world, as well as from more recent times. The fame of the Medici (Library) remains immortal – the library that had granted hospitality to the books and scholars that were banished from Greece. If anyone would now say that the best authors had been cheaply printed and that therefore the princes did not need to maintain expensive libraries anymore, since everyone could lay out for himself a book collection in keeping with his taste, in response to them it is to be replied that the old works, especially those in Greek and Hebrew, had been neglected by the printers, because such items were not much requested; even very good books would not see the light of day, if the princes did not themselves support scholarship. And however large the mass of printed books might be, it nevertheless remained necessary for textual comparisons that there be public research libraries with old manuscripts and first editions.[13] Simler, boasting in the reader's preface, emphasizes the cooperation of the assistant,

Matthäus Dresser, who had forwarded to him a listing of manuscripts of old libraries in Saxony and Thuringia. Johann Jakob Fries (1547 to 1611) followed with the third edition in 1583; in accompanying words he refers to the special assistance he got from the head of the Imperial Library in Vienna. Hugo Blotius had shared with him the greater part of the Vienna catalog and thereby significantly enriched the author list with titles of manuscripts and old printed works that had been tucked away there.

In keeping with the author's suggestion, Gesner's *Bibliotheca universalis* was often used as a catalog of libraries; one noted in the margin the items that were owned by the library. Thus the director of the Court Library in Munich cut apart two copies of the abbreviated Simler list of the year 1555, glued the strips on wide paper and noted there the holdings of his own collection. The Vienna National Library owns Gesner's *Bibliotheca* from the year 1574, with handwritten supplementary note slips which cite additional holdings from the book collection of Philipp Eduard Fugger. When the Spanish archbishop, Antonio Augustin, had to present proposals for the library of the Escorial to King Phillip II, he also referred to Gesner's work, which had only to be purged by the Inquisition, in order to constitute a means of assistance in the building of the new collection of books.

The book world of the sixteenth century had thus already created valuable resources for its book trade and literature, which served to benefit equally the printers and publishers, the book collectors and scholars. These beginnings have been the forerunners of an immense succession (which extends to the present day) of surveys of books, of publishers and booksellers lists, and backlists.

22
The Seventeenth Century Book

The first half of the seventeenth century has been filled with the noise from the weapons of the war among brothers, the fateful Thirty Years' War, and the second half, by the domination and the overpowering influence of the Sun King, Louis XIV (1643–1715). The year 1648 brings the unhappy Westphalian Peace, and the terrible year of 1683, the siege of Vienna by the Turks. In western cultural life, a new conception of the world, one that is increasingly detached from domination by antiquity and ecclesiastical connections, is embarked on; the "Scienza nuova" makes it appearance: philosophical thought with its new questioning, the natural sciences, political science and natural law, and history and geography are demanding their rights. Paris becomes the center of a brilliant courtly culture which radiates over all of Europe.

Determinative of literature in England are the great dramatist, William Shakespeare (1564–1616), the first complete edition of whose works is among the most significant books of all times), John Milton (1608–1674), whose epic *Paradise Lost* is one of the most widely read works of the period and has strongly influenced Klopstock's *Messias*,[1] the philosopher, Francis Bacon of Verulam (1561–1626), who with his memorable survey concerning the value and the progress of the sciences *(De dignitate et augmentis scientiarum,* 1623) tosses into the world's arena the weighty words, "Knowledge is power," Thomas Hobbes (1588–16789), John Locke, the leading spirit of the Enlightenment (1632–1704), the great scientist Isaac Newton (1643–1722), the discoverer of general gravitation, which holds the heavenly bodies together and directs their courses. At work in France are Pierre Corneille (1606–1684), with the widely disseminated drama, *Cid* (1635), Jean Baptiste Molière (1622–1673), Jean Baptiste Racine (1639–1699),[2] Jean Lafontaine (1621–1695), whose tales and fables fill up the bookshops for a long time, the philosopher, René Descartes (1596–1650), with his famous words, "Cogito ergo sum," Blaise Pascal (1623–1662), Pierre Bayle, whose *Dictionnaire historique et critique* (1696) becomes one of the most successful strongholds of the coming Enlightenment, the significant pulpit orators, Jacques Bénigne Bossuet (1627–1704) and François Fénelon (1651–1715), the brilliant author, François Larochefoucauld (1613–1680).

Conspicuous in Spain were the celebrated national poet, Miguel de Cervantes Saavedra (1547–1616), with his *Don Quixote* (1605 to 1612),[3] Lope Felix de Vega (1562–1635),[4] and Don Pedro de Calderon (1600–1681); in the Netherlands,

Hugo Grotius (1583–1645), who with his chief work, *De jure belli et pacis* (1625) (which became all of Europe's textbook on the natural law)[5] becomes the founder of the general political law and of jurisprudence, and further of the pantheistic philosophy of Baruch de Spinoza (1632–1677); in Italy, the physicist and astronomer, Galileo Galilei (1564 to 1642); in Germany, Johann Kepler (1571–1635), the founder of modern astronomy and the discoverer of the laws of the movements of the planets, the indefatigable inquirer into nature, Otto von Guericke (1602–1686) and the great philosopher, Gottfried Wilhelm Leibniz (1646–1716). In France, which under the absolutism of its kings and the influence of its great statesmen, Richelieu (1585–1642) and Mazarin (1602–1661), experienced an enormous political and intellectual advancement, the French Academy *(Académie française)* is founded in the year 1635; it becomes the determinative authority for all matters of language and style, as well as the great example for the later large learned societies in the rest of the countries. England is following already in 1661, with its Royal Society for improving natural knowledge.

In 1609, Germany introduces a new form of the daily literature: the continually appearing newspaper for the speedy announcement of the most important events of the day. France tries to outdo Germany with the equally valuable establishment of the first newspaper, the *Journal des Sçavants*, which was founded in 1665, and reports mainly concerning the most important book publications and about events in the scholarly world. In great art, there develops from the offshoots of the High Renaissance the exciting, elaborate Baroque style, which was adorned with flourishes and tended toward the exalted and fervent — and that dominant art form immediately extended also into the book, while it influences the style of language and the external design of the book, especially the title pages, which are still, even more than before, filled with splendid constructions and with rich allegories.

Conspicuous in the Netherlands were the great artists, Rubens and Rembrandt, and in Spain, Velazquez and Murillo.

Following the Thirty Years' War, Germany was the most unfortunate country of Europe: devastated, robbed, politically and ecclesiastically torn, split into a southwest German Catholic, and a northern German Protestant, cultural circle. At the very time when it had to be rebuilding its destroyed culture, an enormous upheaval in the intellectual world was already occurring everywhere in the rest of Europe.[6] New and enduring universities originated in 1607, in Giessen, and 1694, in Halle. The latter institution was to become the first modern school of higher learning.

Among the most welcome phenomena within the German world of books in this period was the increasingly conscious concern that there was for the German language, which had scarcely made any progress at all under the past centuries when Latin was ascendant. The progress made under Luther had lasted only too briefly. Language societies, such as the "Fruchtbrigende Gesellschaft" ("Productive Society") of 1617, were now constituted according to the example of the *Academia della crusa* in Florence, with the goal of freeing language and poetry from the overwhelming hegemony of the Latin language, and of purifying the sounds of the mother tongue from foreign words. It was in this sense that Martin Opitz

(1597–1639, the founder of the first Silesian poetry school) published in 1624 the *Buch der deutschen Poeterey, in welchem all ihre Eigenschaft und Zugehör gründlich erzehlet und mit Exempeln ausgeführet wird* ("Book of German poetry, in which all its properties and things pertaining to it are basically related and introduced with examples"). The book consequently went through ten editions and elevated the author to the status of being Germany's most famous professional writer. Germans for almost a century thereafter endeavored to teach people how to write poetry, thus forgetting that poetry is an art and a grace, and is not a teachable skill. And the gifted poets had not yet been given to the German people. But we may as little forget gallant Opitz' struggle for the German language which he wanted to push through as the ordinary speech even of scholars and educated people)[7] as the publication of the *Lied auf Anno den Heiligen* ("Song of St. Anno") by Chancellor Emperor Henry III according to the single transmitted manuscript, which has now disappeared.

Very soon coming on the scene were successful patrons and shapers of the German language and of the German book. They immediately created a new world of books with enormous results. The success showed that profound effects of the book could proceed from significant individual works, as well as from the totality of an elevated world of books. Then there was published the *Geistige Andachten* ("Spiritual Devotions") with its oft-sung songs, "Nun ruhen alle Wälder," "Nun lasst uns gehn und treten," "Befiehl du deine Wege," "Die güldne Sonne, voll Freud und Wonne," which quickly were in everyone's hands; they were the work of Paul Gerhardt (1607–1676), the most significant poet for Evangelical church song.

The poet of spiritual songs, Friedrich Spee (1591–1635), then created his *Trutznachtigall* (1649) and composed the tender *Trauergesang von der Not Christi am Ölberg in dem Garten* ("Sad Song of the Need of Christ at the Mount of Olives in the Garden"), with its plaintive beginnings: "Bey stiller Nacht zur ersten Wacht ein Stimm sich gund zu klagen" ("In the quiet of night at the first watch a voice groans deeply"). Then Johann Michael Moscherosch (1601–1669), in his *Wunderliche und wahrhaftige Gesichte Philanders von Sittewald* ("Wonderful and True Stories of Philander of Sittewald") (1642–1643) was able to provide a powerful image of the morals and suffering of wartime.[8] Johann Balthasar Schupp (1610–1681), in his *Schriften* ("Writings") (1663) courageously took up the cause for a higher evaluation being again put on things Germanic, and he sharply contended with the modish contemporary period, with morals, with the clothes and the linguistic Leviathans, which were essentially foreign.

Johann Scheffler, called Angelus Silesius (1624–1677), attained wide influence as a mystic and singer of the *Cherubinische Wandersmann* (1674). One was hearing here sounds not ever heard, such as the verse: "Die Sonn erregt das All, macht alle Sterne Tanzen, Wirkst du Nicht auch beizeit, gehörst du nicht zum Ganzen" ("The sun stimulates everything; it makes all the stars to dance; if you don't cooperate with it, you do not belong to the whole"), or "Rein wie feinste Gold, steif ein Felsenstein, Ganz Lauter wie Kristal, soll dein Gemüte sein" ("Your nature should be pure as the finest gold, strong as a rocky stone, and as clear as crystal"). Paul Fleming (1609–1640), was the most significant lyrical poet of the Silesian school. His warm poem, "Ein getreues Herze wissen, Ist des höchsten Rhumes Preis" ("To know a faithful heart is the praise of highest fame"), have become folk songs. His song, *In allen meinen Taten*, ("In All My Deeds") may be reckoned as being among the best church songs. Georg Philipp Harsdörffer (1607 to 1658), founder of the Pegnitz Order (1644) has achieved a name for himself through his *Poetischer Trichter* (1647–1653) ("Poetical Funnel"), which seeks to bring the art of poetry within established rules and through his *Frauenzimmer Gesprechspiele* 1641–1649) ("Women's Conversation Plays"), which attempted to put forward instructively the whole secular educational material in that period. The lyrical poet, Simon Dach (1605–1659) has endeared himself to us all through his song, *Der Mensch hat nichts so eigen* ("Man has nothing so much his own"). Friedrich, Baron von Logau (1604–1653), the author of German short satirical poems (1657) and epigrams, has given us the beautiful verse in the German language: "Kann die deutsche Sprache schnauben, schnarren, poltern, donnern, krachen, / Kann sie doch auch spielen, scherzen, lieben, kosen, tändeln, lachen" ("If the German langauge can snort, snarl, rattle, thunder, and explode / It still can also play, joke, love, caress, fiddle-faddle, and laugh." Johann Jakob Christoffel von Grimmelshausen (1625–1676), the most successful poet of the century, in his great portrayal of the world, *Der abentheuerliche Simplicius Simplicissimus* ("the Adventurous Simplicius Simplicissimus") (1669) (which was published by Wolf E. Felssecker in Nuremberg under the publisher's fictitious designation of *Mompelgart bei Johann Fillion)* has movingly and graphically portrayed his period for us, with its needs and hope.[9]

Grimmelshausen's novel is one of the first prose works in which poems are interspersed—an art form that Goethe in his *Wilhelm Meister*, and further the Romantics (especially Brentano and Eichendorf), have so effectively applied. Andreas Gryphius (1616–1664) authored the comedy, *Herr Peter Squentz* (1647) and *Horribilicribrifax* (1655), which is numbered among the best dramatic poems of the entire century. Heinrich Anselm von Ziegler und Kliphausen (1663–1696), in his love story, *Die Asiatische Banise* (which was inspired by the wonders of East India), created a much-purchased popular book of the period. In his delightful parody, *Schelmuffsky. Curiose und sehr gefährliche Reisebeschreibung zu Wasser und Land* (1696), Christian Reuter (1665–1710) ridiculed the boasting and deceitful travel descriptions of the time, and with his impressive manner of speaking, has exerted strong influences on the slogans of the day. Ulrich Megerle, called by his monastic name of Abraham of Santa Clara (1644–1709), who was a linguistically gifted popular preacher and scoffer, was heard and read with equal enthusiasm. His publications, and especially his chief works, *Judas der Erzschelm* ("Judas, the Archrogue") and *Etwas fur Alle* ("Something for Everyone") (1699) still have much to say to us, both linguistically as well as from the aspect of cultural history.[10] The Capucin, Martin von Cochem, achieved unusual success with his deeply felt and stirringly fashioned *Leben Jesu* ("Life of Jesus") (1691). The work has remained for a long time the best Catholic devotional book.

Those are perhaps the poets whose books are to be valued as being the determinative and essential ones of the century; they are not great intellectual works, but still they (and especially Grimmelshausen's stirring representation of the period) are considerable forerunners, and, as it were, bridges to the coming great period; above all, they are eloquent sources of information regarding the increased sharpness of the sense for sound and accent in the German language, the valiant guardians and indeed the champions of the German spirit.

Jakob Böhme (1575 to 1624) came to be of considerable influence on questions of education and worldview, with his publications of theosophy and mysticism; he was perhaps the profoundest creative German of the Baroque period; proceeding from his inward view of God, he progressed to surprising philosophical recognition of the true reality of things and he understood how to present his mystical ideas with an uncommonly rich fullness of language, especially in his *Aurora oder Morgenröte im Aufgang* (1612). Likewise influential was the theologian, Johann Arnd (1555–1621), whose linguistically clever devotional work, *Vier Bücher vom wahren Christentum* (1609), ("Four Books Concerning True Christendom") was disseminated to an extent that was unheard of up until that time.

There was also the influential educator, Johann Amos Comenius (1592–1670). In his works, *Didactica magna* and *Orbis sensualium pictus* (1657), even Goethe and his sister have been instructed by their father; in them Comenius sought to capture the entire world in pictures, and to solve the confusing variety of appearances in a final unity in God; also, the pedagogue, Wolfgang Ratich (1571–1635), who warmly espoused the cause of the mother tongue as the organ and first object of scholarly linguistic pursuites;[11] again, there was the pious founder of Pietism, Philipp Jakob Spener, who, as over against the deadly literalistic faith, preached a piety of the heart that was active in works and in moral holiness and who, with his writings, *Collegia pia* (1670) and *Desideria pia*, gave to an entire cultural movement the name that has been deeply embedded in German thinking; also, the pietistic theologian, Gottfried Arnold (1661–1714), who in his *Unparteiische Kirchen- und Ketzerhistorie* ("Impartial Church and Heretic History") blamed the church because again and again she presented pure faith as being something formal, while he sees the deep truths of religion as being vitally preserved only in those spirits that the church judges to be heretical. The work has had a lasting effect on Goethe.

From scholarly circles, perhaps to be named as special promoters of the book world are the polyhistor, Melchior Goldast (1578–1635), the indefatigable publisher of German historical sources *(Alamannicarum rerum scriptores aliquot vetusti,* 1606) and laws of the Empire, a prominent connoisseur of Old German language monuments, who wanted already to publish the famous Manesse *Lieder* ("Songs") manuscript; also the versatile Kiel professor, Daniel Georg Morhof (1639–1691), who with his *Unterricht von der Teutschen Sprache und Poesie* ("Instruction in German Langauge and Poetry") (1682), founded German literary history, and with his work, *Polyhistor sive de notitia auctorum et rerum commentarii* (1688), authored practically a history of world literature with an accompanying treatment of information about the book and the library; also, Johann Schilter (1632 to 1705), who for the first time published the Old High German *Ludwig* song celebrating the victory of Ludwig III over the Normans in the year 881, an item that was discovered by Jean Mabillon in the northern French monastery of St. Armand, and who prepared for publication numerous older German texts that, after his death, were published from 1726–1728 in Ulm in three folio volumes, under the title, *Thesaurus antiquitatum Teutonicarum*, and which contained Otfried's *Evangelienbuch* ("Book of Gospels"), William's paraphrase of the *Hohe Lied* ("Song of Songs"), Notker's *Psalmen*, Kero's Old High German interlinear version of the Benedictine Rule, and the Song of Roland by Conrad, the priest.

Deserving of credit for his research into the German language is the legal scholar, Justus Georg Schottel (1612–1676); in both his works, *Teutsche Sprachkunst* ("German Language Art") (1614) and *Ausfürliche Arbeit von der deutschen Haubt Sprache* ("Introductory work on the German Main Language") (1663), he expressed a warm devotion to the mother tongue and a deep sadness concerning Germany's disruption, but at the same time entertained a strong hope in a coming ascent of its fortunes.[12]

Before the century came to a close, desires and proposals of individual scholars were heard about embarking on a comprehensive history of Germany's past. Thus, inspired by the medical doctor and polyhistor, Christian Franz Paullini,[13] there came into being the so-called historical imperial college, *Collegium historicum imperiale*, which as a preparatory work wanted initially to produce and print a catalog of the most important historical sources with the locations where they were to be found; it was in connection with this that the deserving work of Michael Hertz, *Bibliotheca Germanica* (1679), was basically planned. In an inspired speech, the Leipzig librarian, Joachim Feller, celebrated the establishing of the project in January 1691; Leibniz actively took up the cause; research trips were undertaken; Johann Ulrich Pregitzer was already travelling in Switzerland, Upper Swabia, the Alsace, and the free duchy of Burgundy.[14] Finally, however, the work which had begun with such promise—indeed it was a memorable forerunner of the *Monumenta Germaniae historica*—ran aground on inadequate financial resources. One can see here how much is involved in bringing a great book idea to a successful ending.

Among the men of the period who have attained great merit for German scholarship, a still further prominent one is Hermann Conring (1606–1681), the founder of German juristical history, the first instructor in a school of higher learning who had held lectures concerning the German legal history, and has published a significant work about it *(De origine juris Germanici commentarius*, 1643).[15]

So, approximately, does the intellectual compostion within the literature of the Baroque period present itself to us.

So far as book design is concerned, the degeneration that we have already portrayed went relentlessly farther. Of concern for books as the expression of a refined culture one can finally scarcely speak any more.[16] Something that had been advancing already in the sixteenth century—namely, the penetration of books by copper engraving—came to its full development in the new century under Italian and Dutch leadership. Copper engraving was now dominating the field almost exclusively, whether it bore an individual image in the volumes, or as a title page was supposed to decorate the book, or whether in hundreds of sheets it was integrated into one of the large illustrated works. Like the woodcut, it proved to be a true assistant to the book and its advancing goal of reflecting the whole of life in word and picture. Above all, the large illustrated works that often encompassed many volumes, which now were reproducing in a confused manner architectural and art monuments, and then cities and country landscapes, and then again scientific models, may not be overlooked if we wish to become familiar with the main trends in the seventeenth century book.

The House of Merian at Frankfurt am Main attained the pinnacle of the art of topographical representation in its famous topographies. Founded in 1642, by Matthäus Merian (1593–1650), the son-in-law of the copper engraver, Johann Theodor de Bry, and directed to the end by the sons, Matthäus the Younger and Kaspar, these works ultimately consisted of thirty-one parts with ninety-two maps, 1482 plates and 2142 views.[17] As Sebastian Münster, Abraham Ortelius, and Georg Braun had already done, the publishers of the topographies relied also on submitted presentations[18] and sought to obtain original pictures of a locality if it perhaps were still lacking, "that such this work may incorporate, so that finally it may be quite complete." In that way the enormous work of illustrations, with its representations of architectural works that later were remodelled more than once or that have disappeared, has taken on significant value as a source work. The sheet on Heidelberg, may, for instance, be designated as the best of the older pictures of the city on the Neckar. Just as Georg Braun's *Beschreibung der Städte der Welt* ("Description of the Cities of the World") did, Merian's topographies also had the chief aim of portraying the beauty of the cities (especially the German ones) and of representing the accomplishments of the citizenry. Thus the work is even still today a monument to German power and accomplishment from a period when fate was weighing down heavily on the struggle to rebuild German culture.

The abilities of the family of Merian were also transmitted to the daughter of Matthäus Merian the Elder, Maria Sibylla (1647–1717), who has published several nice books of flowers and insects.[19] In 1699, the artist undertook a trip (for research into insects) to Surinam in South America, and as a result published in 1705 a work of plates with sixty copper engravings.[20]

The topographies of Merian almost surpassed the *Theatrum Europaeum*, a pictorial chronicle in grand style that in a certain sense was already the forerunner of the later *Illustrierte Zeitung* ("Illustrated News"); begun by the same house in 1635, within three generations it wound up with the twenty-first volume in 1738.[21]

Besides Frankfurt, Augsburg and Nuremberg especially had large copper engraving workshops, from whence comprehensive volumes of plates have also appeared. Thus the engraver, Dominic Baltens (called Custos, 1550–1612) published in Augsburg in 1593, the portraits of the house of Fugger *(Fuggerorum et Fuggerarum effigies)*, and the pictures of the princes of the Spanish Room in the Ambras Castle. Through his marriage with the widow of the Augsburg goldsmith, Balthasar Kilian, he had the opportunity of introducing Kilian's sons, Lukas and Wolfgang Kilian, to the Dutch manner of art as well as to skilled copperplate engraving.[22] The family of Sadeler was active in Munich. Raphael Sadeler supplied Matthäus Rader's

Bavaria pia et sancta (1615) with numerous copperplate engravings. In Nuremberg in 1603, there appeared the tremendous botanical work, *Hortus Eystettensis,* of Basilius Bessler, with 360 large copperplate engravings of Wolfgang Kilian and other artists; in a later decade (1675–79) there followed Joachim von Sandrart's significant *Teutsche Akademie der Bau, Bild- und Malerei-Künste* ("German Academy of Building, Picture and Painting Arts"). Not only was it one of the prettiest printed works of the period; it is also the first German history of art.[23] A further outstanding work emerged at Nuremberg 1605–1609, with the famous *Wappenbuch* ("Book of Arms") of Johann Sibmacher (d. 1611); one could find here the arms of princes, generations of the nobility, and of cities.

The project, which enjoyed good fortune despite its considerable range, had a great success, and went through new editions again and again. The Nuremberg art dealer, Paul Fürst,[24] took over the work about the middle of the century and brought it out in five volumes in the years 1655–1667. In his foreword of September 1, 1654, the new publisher supplied the locations to which one could send his arms for inclusion in the continuing work: "either here to Nuremberg, or in market time to Leipzig to the *Bilderhaus* in Auerbach's court, or to Frankfurt at Fair time in the Barfüsser-Kreuzgang, or have for sale in market time at Vienna, or have for sale at the market in Linz outside on the water; or to be inquired about in the Graz market time at H. Sebastian Haubt." Sibmacher's book of arms is, in it revision, currently still as vital as it was in the time when it originated, and it can be designated as one of the most successful publisher's undertakings of the seventeenth century. In the actual book trade, Nuremberg has especially distinguished itself through the lively house of Endter, which had published a series of significant printed works, among which are (1) the famed Electors' Bible of the year 1640, which bears its name from the accompanying portraits of the Saxon electors and is also called (after its commission-giver, Duke Ernst I of Saxe-Gotha) the Ernestine Bible and (2) further, the 1658 instruction book, *Orbis pictus* of Johann Amos Comenius; it was often reprinted and imitated.[25]

Within the compass of the German book world of the century, time and again it was the scholarly literature in the Latin language that dominated the field. The main buyers and the readers of books were still (as they had earlier been) the scholars, and above all, the clergy and the lawyers. Heavy folios filled the cases in scholars' rooms, and the thousands of volumes frequently threatened to burst the house asunder. Public libraries were still scarce, and thus for the scholar, a considerable possession of books was among the most necessary household effects; it was indeed his pride and joy. The Leipzig Easter catalog of 1650 lists 314 Latin and 131 German books; of the German ones, seventy-three belong to theology, thirteen to history, eleven to belles-lettres, five to geography, seven to medicine, and two to jurisprudence. Gradually, however, under the influence of the German poets and of the language societies, the German language in books successfully progressed, and toward the century's end, it attained equal weight, as over against the Latin literature. What here came on the market were mainly (besides the poets) popular books, story books, legends, commonplace books, books of dreams and riddles, calendars, sermons and occasional printings.

In 1602 the *Kurze Beschreibung und Erzählung von einem Juden mit Namen 'Ahasverus'* ("Short Description and Narrative of a Jew with the name 'Ahasverus'") came out; it is the story of the everlasting Jew, who would not let Jesus rest on the way to Golgotha, and on that account, has to wander until the end of the world. As the first editions (they have gradually increased to seventy) would have it, Ahasverus is supposed to have been seen in Hamburg in 1542, in 1572 in Madrid, and 1599 in Danzig.

In the German booktrade, the double dominance of the two book fairs of Frankfurt am Main and Leipzig continued for a long time until the emphasis shifted more and more in favor of Leipzig, which since about 1680 had evidenced great enterprising publishing houses as Thomas Fritsch, Johann Friedrich Gleditsch, and Moritz Georg Weidmann, while under the influence of the Thirty Years' War, Frankfurt's significance as a former international center of the book trade receded more and more with the passage of time. With the rebuilding of the German book world, the north German and Evangelical book moved, with Leipzig, into the foreground. Frankfurt am Main, Cologne, Augsburg, Strasbourg and Basel fell back, and individual south German towns dropped out almost entirely. Prior to the outbreak of the war, the year's average of the German book production amounted to 1587 items; during the war, it fell back at times to 660, in order only to attain the old level again around the middle of the following century.

Even if its days of actual vitality were already past, the valuable book remains a treasured commodity for scholars and collectors, or it takes shelter in the quiet rooms of a public library, and there awaits history's judgment. Now and then it turns up on the market as an item in the antiquarian trade, which, following the enormous growth of the world of books in past centuries, brings once more into the trade the books that were set aside or left behind. Advancing knowledge increasingly requires the older books for research, and the scholar enthusiastically collects the earlier books in his discipline. The numerous scholar's libraries of the period thus became the great reservoirs that accepted the books of the market, in order later to send them out into all the world. This lasting value and circulation of the book stimulated not only the antiquarian market;[26] due to it also are the significant catalogs and book descriptions, such as the lists of the great antiquarian booksellers, as, for example, Bernard Quaritch, Sotheby & Co., and Maggs Brothers; also it secured for itself a second outlet in the book auction, which, beginning in Holland,[27] became a custom that continued throughout the course of the seventeenth century.

On German soil, the Leipzig booktrader, Christian Kirchner, carried through the first book auction in the year 1670, despite strong opposition from the rest of the book dealers; in an announcement of April 16, 1671, he mentioned that he had already auctioneered twice according to the Dutch style, and in this act had "broken the ice," and bought and sold libraries "in which there are still to be found at times quite rare books that otherwise indeed would remain entirely in obscurity or would have been devoured by the mice." The new form of distribution has become an important outlet for the sale of numerous large scholarly libraries of the seventeenth and eighteenth centuries.[28]

The comprehensive survey of the scholarly corrector, Georg Draudius,[29] meant a big step forward in the opening up of the German book market beyond the fair catalogs;[30] for his catalogs he used not only the fair catalog but also manuscript lists of the holdings in stock (or the inventories) of numerous booksellers. The bulky work, which was first published in 1610, had a second edition in 1625 that went back into the sixteenth century; for a long time, it was the most significant reference work for the books being published.[31] In 1717, there was already emerging in Leipzig the significant words for the future: *In allen Buchläden zu finden* ("To be found in all bookstores").

The leadership role in the European book market in that period Germany did indeed have to concede to the Netherlands. After they had been freed from Spanish dominion, the Netherlands, with their own political ascent, experienced a great efflorescence in the arts and sciences, which also redowned to the good of the book world. The first place in printing and in the book trade, the large publishing firm of Elzevier in Leyden and Amsterdam, the Hague and Utrecht, was able to secure through several generations, with perhaps two thousand published works spanning the entire world. The secret of this success was a new entrepreneurship that thought through the leadership of the business down even to the individual, and understood the book as a profitable commodity until it was finally used up. Most famous here have been the so-called "Republics" of the years 1625–1644, inexpensive and handily decorated descriptions of the various states and countries, with pleasing title pages.

The small volumes have become of far-reaching significance for the extension of the book market. The versatility of this publishing house's undertakings is illustrated in the names of authors such as Caesar, Pliny, Vergil, Terence, Boccaccio, Rabelais, Hugo Grotius, Molière, Corneille, Descartes, Bacon of Verulam, Comenius, Milton, Hobbes, Larochefoucauld, and Galileo.[32]

Bibliology had paid special attention to those works that have appeared with fictitious names of authors, publishers and printers. Among the numerous falsified names of printers, one of the best known ones has been the frequently repeated publisher's mark, *Cologne chez Pierre Marteau.* There has never been a Cologne printer by this name. The designation first surfaced in 1660 in the printed work of the House of Elzevier; since the end of the seventeenth century, it was also used by several other printers and publisher for endangered publications of religious refugees, or for dubious publications of an erotic nature.[33]

Successfully active in Antwerp was the House of Moretus—above all, Christopher Plantin's uncle, Balthasar Moretus (1574–1641), who was a friend of the Flemish artist, Peter Paul Rubens, who painted portraits for him and sketched designs for title pages. These ornamental borders have been fashioned very much in the spirit of the time; of splendid construction, they would not only please the eye but likewise symbolize the book's content, in order thereby to put the reader into the frame of mind for what the author desired to communicate. Thus the title page to Franciscus Haraeus' *Annals* of the Princes of Brabant from the year 1623, contains a representation of the temple of Janus with the bust of the god and the symbols of tumult round about it. The wild figures of hate and discord have torn asunder the gates to the temple, the curtain of which bears the title of the work. On the ground the many-headed Hydra rages against the symbols of order. The representation would serve to illustrate the opposition of Belgium against Spain, and with it to introduce symbolically the book's contents.[34]

European renown came also to the Amsterdam publishing house of Blaeu and its daring founder, Willem Janszoon Blaeu (1571–1638), who owed the bases of his astronomical and geographical knowledge to the astronomer, Tycho de Brahe, in the Castle of Uranienborg on the island of Hveen, where the astronomer had built a printery *(Officiana Uraniburgica),*[35] and, since 1597 in Amsterdam, had published great map works, in addition to maps for ship voyages and longitudinal tables. His *Theatrum orbis terrarum* has been published in four languages. His son, Johann, completed as a principal work in 1662 the *Atlas Major,* with eleven volumes.[36]

The first significant Parisian printing monument was the polyglot Bible in ten volumes; it was produced at the expense of the legal advocate, Guy-Michel Le Jay, in the years 1628–1645, with an enormous extravagance of expenditure. Its printer was Antoine Vitré, the royal printer for oriental languages. The display of splendor of the French royalty put its stamp also on the Royal Printery (Imprimerie royale) at Prais; it had been founded about 1640 by King Louis XIII and Cardinal Richelieu. Great works, such as the Latin Bible of 1642 in eight volumes, enormous scientific editions like the *Concilia* (1644), with its thirty-seven volumes, the *Scriptores historiae Bycantinae* (1648) with twenty-nine volumes – these carried the fame of the Paris printery far beyond the borders of France itself.[37] The book was again entering into the service of the court and it had to enhance the princely glory. The *Dictionnaire* of the French Academy of 1694 has been decorated with a small picture in which the graces crown the bust of King Louis XIV with the laurel. For future heirs to the throne, *(in usum delphini),* King Louis XIV had prepared after 1617 at his own cost about forty-two unobjectionable classical editions – such as Florus, Ausonius, and Ovid – with instructive explanations. From the viewpoint of cultural history, these volumes possess a certain charm, and are readily collected.

Working in Rome as the leader of the significant copper engraving workshop was the antiquarian of the Pope and Queen Christine of Sweden, Pietro Santo Bartoli (1635–1700); he published large works of plates with Roman antiquities, and also the pictures of the Vatican's Vergil manuscript; also working there was Pietro Aquila, who mainly published picture books of the sixteenth and seventeenth centuries, such as those by Raphael, Annibale Carracci, Pietro Berrettini, and Giovanni Lanfranco. In these great works of copper engraving, art history and archeology have attained valuable aids to their research, just as this is now provided by photographs and the reproductive arts.

In London in 1623, there was issued with the printers, William and Isaac Jaggard, the first edition of Shakespeare's *Works,* with eight dramas (which up to then had not been printed); it was prepared by the friends of the poet, John Heminge and Henry Condell, and it was decorated with the author's portrait by Martin Droeshout; typographically it was no masterwork, but culturally it was the most significant event in English printing and publishing history at that time. Of the works, 172 copies can still today be established, of which 106 are in Great Britain, three are in British colonies, sixty-one are in America, and only two are on the European Continent.[38]

Further of significance was the London polyglot Bible which Brian Walton, bishop of Chester, published in 1635–1657 in six folio volumes, with the support of Oliver Cromwell: it was the fourth polyglot Bible, and it excelled the earlier polyglot editions in scholarship, and even contained Persian and Ethiopian translations. Thomas Roycroft, the most significant of the masters of England at this time, has printed the work; Wenzel Hollar had decorated it with a copper engraving title page.

If we cast only a fleeting glance on the bookbinding of the period, we see in the everyday books the heavy wood cover that was covered with leather being gradually replaced by the less heavy leather and cardboard volume. The binding is lighter and has become less expensive. There is a concern at the courts for the splendid binding—especially in France, where in a continuation of the *Fanfare* style, they now like to apply stamps with golden spirals on red leather, the lines of which are set together from small points working in the manner of filigree *(fers pointillés);* there later follow fan and cone designs.

Frequently associated with the binding was something that had already been introduced in the sixteenth century, the *Super Ex libris*, the external designation of ownership, which was externally pressed on to the cover of the binding and which chiefly consisted of the arms with the names and motto of the onwers, or also the number of the year of the impression. These adorning designations of ownership have above all settled permanently (as it were) in the monasteries—but also at the courts, and with numerous book collectors.[39]

Approximately two hundred years following Gutenberg's discovery, printing was also introduced into the British colonies of North America. In 1640, there was published *The Whole Book of Psalms.* It was printed by the English immigrant, Stephen Daye, at Cambridge (Massachusetts). The work, which was translated and elucidated by Richard Mather, may be designated as the first "New English" book. Otherwise, there were initially issued only almanacs, catechisms, sermons and minor printed matters. More significant was John Eliot's printed translation of the Bible in the language of the Indians in 1663. There was published in Boston in 1677, Hubbard's *Narrative of the Troubles with the Indians in New England,* with a map of the country; it was printed by one John Foster. Philadelphia (1685) and New York (1693) followed with small printers' workshops. The immigrants and the inhabitants of this colonial period brought with them from home their literary "household effects." As it was, the efforts of each day did not leave much time for being occupied with intellectual matters; and, after all, the colonial people felt themselves to be entirely connected with British literature and culture. The period of the independent American "world" of books was still a long way off.[40]

23

The Seizure of Books in the Thirty Years' War

In the history of the modern period, it was not the first time that books, which had been highly treasured since the days of the Renaissance, were pilfered (their indissoluble connection with the homeland notwithstanding) by the victors as valuable war booty. Thus the French Kings Charles VIII and Louis XII had already carried off the court libraries of Naples and Pavia to France. In its extent, however, the confiscation of books during the Thirty Years' War has found a counterpart only in the Napoleonic period.

Following the defeat in 1620 of the Bohemian "Winter King," Frederick V of the Palatinate, (who was the leader of the Protestant league) on the White Mountain near Prague, heavy clouds were gathering over Heidelberg, the capital city of the defeated Palatine princes, who had secured within their walls the costly book treasures of the Palatine House and of Ulrich Fugger; this was a seductive attraction for the plundering leaders and their troops. The escaped Elector wrote from Gravenhage in October 1621 to his chancellor, Johann Christoph von der Grün, that the archives and library, and especially the manuscripts, should early be brought into security. On October 26, the apparently less concerned councillors answered the prince at Amsterdam, to the effect that the library could not yet have been hidden on account of its size. A relative of the prince, Marshal Henri de La Tour d'Auvergne (1555–1623), declared on February 11, 1622, that he was prepared to accept the most valuable manuscripts in his Sedan castle, which was protected.

Now on June 26 the Palatine chancellor had a portion of the most valuable items removed from among the holdings, in order to bring them into security. Kaspar Schedius, the assistant of the librarian (who was Paul Melissus), drew up a document (which was later carried off to Rome by Allaci and is now in the Vaticana) according to which all the Greek, Hebraic and Latin manuscripts from the Fugger possessions had been hidden. Schedius expressly mentions manuscripts of Livy, Cicero, Horace, Juvenal, Lucan, Martial, Plautus, Sallust, Seneca, Statius, and Vergil, and then an old German book of rhymes, probably the *Manesse Song* manuscript, a very old Vergil (that well might be from Lorsch), a *Psalterium* in the "Lombardic" script, a Livy (apparently the one kept currently in Vienna, which stemmed originally from Lorsch), the famous uncial script manuscript published by Simon Grynäus in 1531, a Greek-Syrian Testament, a Basilius manuscript, an Hebraic Bible, an Ethiopian *psalterium*, an Arabic book, Hebrew manuscripts out of the Palatine Library, besides the bird book of Emperor Frederick II, a Greek Testament which the Apostle Paul "is supposed to have written," an entire Latin Bible, a Danish book, and finally, Sylburg's list of Greek manuscripts. Finally Schedius announced: "It has been assembled and sealed. Witnessed sincerely and honestly with his own handwriting: Caspar Schedius Francus. Everything occurred on June 26, *anno* 1622." These precautionary measures, however, apparently had no success, because the majority of the manuscripts mentioned here have nevertheless fallen into enemy hands, and only a few precious objects (among them probably being the Manesse Song manuscript) have been carried off in time from Heidelberg. In the meantime, Johann Tserclaes, Count von Tilly, (1559–1632), had beaten the opponent near Wimpfen am Neckar, and likewise near Höchst am Main, and on September 16, 1622, had taken Heidelberg, Covetous eyes had already fallen on the Palatine city's main booty, the Electoral library. Sebastian Tengnagel, the administrator of the Vienna Court Library, had written to Emperor Ferdinand II, that a concern ought to be communicated through instructions to the field marshals that the Heidelberg Library (to which almost all of Germany had contributed priceless manuscripts) should be treated with consideration by the troops; the Imperial Library could perhaps be enriched by it. According to martial law, Duke Maximilian I of Bavaria would indeed have had the main claim on the Heidelberg library; he was the leader and victor of the Catholic League. But then a third claimant, Pope Gregory XV, (advocated by Cardinal Lodovico Ludovisi), came forward.

Much has already been written concerning why the Bavarian duke let the handsome collection get away, since it was to be carried off from Heidleberg.[1] The past can scarcely be made entirely clear anymore. The pope has later expressly praised the duke as a true son of the church who has seized a perilous weapon from the Calvinist heretics.

Political and economic reasons have also played a role. At the restitution negotiations in December 1815, Cardinal Consalvi explained that yielding the library to the pope was not actually a gift, but had been much more an appropriate compensation for papal subsidies. Be that as it may, the seizure of the Heidelberg library is, and remains, one of the worst German losses of the Thirty Years' War, and the bitterness is relieved only by the thought that the priceless collection has at least been spared plundering and destruction.

In Rome, Leone Allacci, the scholarly librarian of the Vaticana, was designated to take the booty away.[2] He recieved precise instructions on October 23, 1622, that, above all, he was to seize the entire library and everything related to it, so as to get back even the books that had been lent out or that otherwise had been removed. In order to bring the treasures safely to Rome, he would have to protect the boxes (which should not be too large or too heavy) against water by lining their sides with pitch and waxed linen, and against blows or bumps by ropes at the sides. In order to lessen the weight, he was supposed to have the wooden covers taken off – only the valuable bindings with their ornaments, coats of arms and

and inscriptions, should not be removed. All the reports that could serve the history of the collection must also be saved.

On October 28, 1622, Allacci departed from Rome, in order to hurry to Munich by way of Florence, Ferrara, Venice, Treviso, and Innsbruck. He arrived there on November 26, and obtained already here seventy-three relinquished Greek and 101 Latin manuscripts. On December 13, he arrived in Heidelberg and was hospitably accommodated by Count Tilly. The papal envoy was not so happy when it was established that a whole number of manuscripts had been lent outside the city—among them being items lent in Wittenberg to Professor Erasmus Schmidt, in Augsburg to Marcus Welser and David Höschel, in Lyons to Thomas Erpenius, in Vienna to the librarian, Sebastian Tengnagel, in Breslau to Petrus Kirsten, in Cologne to the book trader, Antonius Hierat, and in Heidelberg, especially to the printer, Hieronymus Commelinus, who like the Electoral adviser, Marquard Freher, had a whole supply of Greek manuscripts with him.

On February 14, 1623, fifty heavily freighted wagons moved into the streets, under military cover, towards Neckarsulm; for the cognizant observer it was a shameful sight: The proud German Heidelberg collection is carried off by a foreigner out of the heart of Germany. The train of wagons arrived in Munich on February 27, and the contents were put into lighter containers. For the collection, the elector had had produced by the engraver, Sadeler, for about 300 florins, 4300 larger, and 4500 smaller bookplates with the superscription: *Sum de bibliotheca, quam Heidelberga capta spolium fecit et P.M. Gregoria XV trophaeum misit Maximilianus utriusque Bavariae dux et S.R.I. Archidapifer et Princeps Elector.* Allacci continued his journey on April 26, 1623, and he arrived on August 5, in Rome, wherein the meantime Gregory XV had died, and Urban VIII (1623–1644) had become pope. That the Vaticana's new acquisitions obtained a separate room, so as to come into their own, externally considered, was owing to the Bavarian elector's efforts; on May 10, 1623, in possibly a certain nationalistic change of heart, he expressed to Cardinal von Zollern his clear displeasure with the intermingling he had observed with the Vaticana collection, that he certainly did not find it expedient "that this famous Heidelberg *corpus*, by such planning and effective incorporation elsewhere would have to be allowed to drift, and quite lose in so short a time the great name it has previously had both in and out of Germany." He would rather recommend that the library be arranged separately as a perpetual memorial to the victory over the enemy of the Catholic name, as well as to the pope's assistance and of his (the elector's) obedient fidelity, and that it should receive the name *Bibliotheca Gregoriana.*

The Heidelberg collection did in fact remain together and it constituted one of the most valuable parts of the holdings of the papal library, which is so rich in priceless items. Allacci had brought to Rome over 3,500 manuscripts, among which were 430 Greek, 289 Hebrew, 846 German, and thirty-one French ones— that is to say, the entire old electoral collection, together with the personal property of the librarian, Janus Gruter, had fallen into his hands. The scholar, Zinkgref (who was ordered to protect the treasures in Heidelberg) has written that the sight could move a stone to tears.

Elector Karl Ludwig later sought to regain the collection, but it was in vain; his emissary, Ezechiel Spanheim, had to return again from Rome in 1663 empty-handed. Perhaps it was fortunate for the priceless property, since it would doubtless have been destroyed in Heidelberg in 1693, when the troops of King Louis XIV, under the leadership of Field Marshal Louvois, mercilessly plundered the entire Palatinate and Heidelberg. At that time even the Heidelberg University Library, renovated by Karl Ludwig, has been destroyed. In 1760, Elector Karl Theodor of the Palatine sent his librarian to Rome, in order to have the library searched thoroughly for historical reports. Several transcriptions produced at that time and attested to by the papal librarian, Elias Baldus, are still today in the Munich State Library. Like the mysterious collections of Constantinople and Ofen, the Heidelberg treasure has also been adorned by legends. "One hoped to find here several thousand manuscripts of the Old German poets and among those, perhaps even the grammatical and poetical works of Charlemagne." So Friedrich Adelung was reporting in his *Nachrichten* ("Reports") of the year 1796, wherein the scholar was seeking to disperse the various erroneous suppositions.

Thus while almost without effort, papal Rome succeeded in possessing one of the largest German book collections, the leader also of the opposition party – King Gustav II Adolf of Sweden (1611–1632) let no opportunity go by to enrich his country, and especially the University of Uppsala (a favorite foundation of the king) with German books that had been taken as booty.[3] The victorious prince had set his designs primarily on the Jesuit libraries, in order thus to do injury to Protestantism's most dangerous opponent; but he also unscrupulously confiscated other collections. When Würzburg had surrendered on October 15, 1631, the city lost not merely a significant part of the holdings of the Jesuits' library, but also the castle library of the prince-bishop, Julius Echter von Mespelbrunn (1573–1619).[4] The plundered books of the Jesuits later fell again into the hands of the imperialists and got back to their owners.

The grateful Jesuits had bookplates of their own glued into the repossessed books, so that the users might recall the magnanimous deed of the giver, the prince-bishop, Franz von Hatzfeld. Several manuscripts and printed works from Würzburg have found their way to Gotha; they are there as booty of Duke Ernst the Pious, who from 1632–1645 administered the Duchy of East Franconia for his brother, Bernhard of Weimar.[5] The main holdings of Würzburg Cathedral Library (which was rich in valuable old manuscripts) had, however, been removed and hidden just in time, to be again discovered only in 1717 by the cathedral dean and later bishop, Christoph, Baron von Hutten, just as the collection of books kept in Prague of the learned Bohemian knight, Wenzel Wrzessowitz (died July 19, 1583), was also thought for a long time to have been robbed by the Swedes, until it was discovered in 1780, well-packed in an out-of-the-way vault. But the cathedral treasure of Würzburg was not totally spared; the university library in Oxford owns forty-six priceless manuscripts from it, which Archbishop William Laud of Canterbury has presented to it from the booty in 1635.[6]

In Mainz, King Gustav Adolf, following the occupation of the city on December 13, 1631, commissioned his physician, Jakob Roberthonius and the court preacher, Johannes Matthiae, to seize all libraries and books in the castle, in the colleges, schools, monasteries and abandoned houses. The formal charge is still to be found in the University Library in Uppsala. It was easy to silence legal objections. For the most part, the confiscated book treasures were carried off to Sweden; sixty-nine manuscripts of the cathedral have (supposedly as a gift of the King to Bernard of Weimar) come to Gotha. The Mainz book treasure was plundered for the second time in February 1635, when the Swedish chancellor, Axel Oxenstjerna, appointed a young scholar from Västeras, Johannes Terserus, to the office of "bibliothecarius" and entrusted him with further confiscations of books for the cathedral churches in Västeras and Strengnäs. This second Mainz booty of books has (according to a credible tradition) sunk in the Baltic Sea.[7]

On the way to Mainz, the Swedes have also taken into their possession the Cistercian monastery of Eberbach im Rheingau and plundered it. Numerous manuscripts from there have gotten into England. Thus over fifty of them are in Bodleian Library at Oxford as a gift of William Laud, archbishop of Canterbury; several from the collection of Thomas Howard, Earl of Arundel, (d. 1646), have later gotten into the British Library in London.[8] The Foundation Library of Fulda, rich in valuable manuscripts, has likewise come to an end in the chaos of the war of this terrible time.

Further robberies in Ermland,[9] Moravia and Bohemia have soon followed this Swedish seizing of books form the Western part of Germany. The collections of books of the Jesuits in Riga and Braunsberg, of the cathedral chapter in Frauenburg, of the episcopal see in Heilsberg, of the cathedrals and the monasteries in Olmütz and Prague, of the castle in Prague and the monastery in Posen—they all (and still others) have come as booty to Stockholm and Uppsala, and into individual school libraries newly established by Gustav Adolf. Among them were valuable monuments of the intellectual life of those countries, such as the books of the Leipzig professor and Ermland canon, Thomas Werner, who in 1499 had willed the main part of his copious library to the Franciscans in Brunswick;[10] so, too, the items left by the famous astronomer and canon of Frauenburg, Nicholas Copernicus, following his death; numerous letters of the Ermland bishop, Johann Dantiscus; the book possessions of the nuncio and cardinal, Stanislaus Hosius; and then from the Prague Art Chamber, the so-called Devil's Bible, which is an enormous manuscript *(Gigas librorum)* on parchment that was (according to legend) copied one night in the thirteenth century by a monk of the Benedictine monastery of Podlazic with the Devil's assistance, and is decorated with illustrations of the Devil and Hell; finally, as the main piece of booty of the Field Marshal Hans Christoph von Königsmark, the Bible translation of the Arian bishop, Ulfilas, which was written with gold and silver on purple parchment, which at one time was carried off from the Werden monastery to Prague, and later taken away by Isaak Vossius (the librarian of Queen Christine) to Holland, and finally bought back by the Swedish imperial chancellor, Magnus Gabriel de la Gardie, and which is now the item of greatest value in the library in Uppsala.

When the victorious Swedes marched into Munich in May 1632, the manuscripts of the Court Library, packed up in barrels, had indeed been brought into security at Burghausen; instead, however, the unprotected treasures of the art chamber had to be surrendered to the enemy. Although Gustav Adolf had issued orders to protect the princely collections from plundering, Duke Wilhelm of Weimar still had the priceless manuscripts of the art chamber carried off.

The Gotha Territorial Library,[11] which in other ways has realized valuable benefits from the booty of books of the Thirty Years' War, still owns fifty pieces of booty from Munich, among which are the Bible of Palatine Count Ottheinrich, which is decorated with colorful pictures by the artist, Martin Gerung, two manuscripts with the *Weltchronik* ("World Chronicle") of Rudolf von Ems, and with Thomasin von Zerklaere's *Der Welsche Gast*, thirty volumes of the work on coins of Jacobus de Strada, which at one time Johann Jakob Fugger had ordered for Duke Albrecht V. The herbal book of Leonhard Rauwolf, which likewise was carried off by the Swedes from Munich, has later come to Isaak Vossius, and then to the Leyden University Library. Displeased by the enemy's plunderings in his capital city, Elector Maximilian I immediately considered compensation through the confiscation of a foreign collection of books, and it was with this in mind that he wrote on June 20 to his court counselor that one ought to establish how many books had been robbed, because "even we have to consider how profitably to make such a loss good, we would perhaps also like to come into a library and be able to take revenge for the damage that has been done." The court counselor responded that two thousand works were missing.

The exasperated elector issued the order on October 6,1632, from Bamberg to the counts of Pappenheim: since Duke Wilhelm of Weimar is the one which played havoc in Bavaria and in the capital city of Munich by plundering, burning and pillaging, and has even plundered in the Art Chamber (something from which even the Swedish king abstained), in Weimar the field marshal should burn as much as possible to the ground. A favorable opportunity for compensation Elector Maximilian found already after a short period, when on September 24, 1634, Hohentübingen fell into the hands of the Catholic League. Maximilian immediately took the necessary steps to seize the library of the Evangelical dukes of Württemberg, which was kept in the Tübingen Castle. He at first wanted only to have those books replaced which he had lost; but since comparing of the lists was taking too long, in an agreement with Duke Charles IV of Lorraine (the commander-in-chief of the League) on May 26, 1635, through his fully authorized representatiave for the war, Wolf Jakob Ungelter, and despite the oppostion of the ducal librarian, Thomas Lansing, he had the entire collection seized and the greatest part thereof conveyed to Munich.

Among the perhaps six hundred volumes taken as booty there were priceless items, such as the Hirsau *Chronicle* of the abbot, John Trithemius, the Greek manuscripts (most of which had been acquired at one time by Duke Ludwig of Württemberg), a parchment copy of the Wittenberg Bible printing of 1561 with Lukas Cranach's miniature portraits of Elector August of Saxony, Luther and Melanchthon, which was inscribed by Philipp Melanchthon, and which has an autobiographical note by Martin Luther.[12]

These enormous seizures of books are only one part of the fate that this terrible German religious conflict has brought on the book treasures of the empire. What additionally has been destroyed by fire, we do not know; it would not have been little.

24

Concerning Seventeenth Century Libraries

Among the eloquent witnesses to the increased esteem in which the world of books was held is the establishment of two new great book collections in the first decade of the new century, which are reckoned as having been among the earliest examples of modern public libraries; these are the university library in Oxford and the Ambrosiana in Milan, both of them being institutions that have initially issued from generous bequests.

The university library at Oxford was destroyed in the religious confusions of the sixteenth century; for its glorious renewal it has to thank the scholarly diplomat, Sir Thomas Bodley (1544–1613), whose name it still bears today. Bodley had scarcely withdrawn from political affairs, when he embarked on restoring the library at Oxford, and on February 23, 1597, he made known to the university's vice-chancellor that this was his purpose. Not only did he everywhere purchase books for the collection; he also oversaw the building of the rooms. His assistant, the book trader, John Bill, travelled extensively on the Continent and obtained manuscripts and printed works at Rome, Padua, Florence, Venice, Milan, Paris and Frankfurt am Main. A large gift book with gilded bosses, which bore the arms of the founder as well as those of the university, recorded the names of patrons. The memorable opening of the collections, which was already numbering 2,500 works, took place on November 8, 1602.

The new establishment was called a public library *(publica bibliotheca)* and in contrast with the collections in the colleges was accessible to all members of the university community. On June 20, 1604, King James I (1603–1625) stipulated that the institution should be named after its founder and he honored Bodley by elevating him to the knighthood. In the year 1606, the Earl of Sackville, who at that time was chancellor of the university, presented the bust of the founder, a memorial that is preserved in the library to this day. In 1605, Thomas James published the first printed catalog of the collection, along with an historical introduction about its founding. Bodley died on January 28, 1613, but his work has made him immortal. It was great day for his library when in 1610, the scholarly administrator of the royal collections, Patrick Young (Junius) delivered the works of the king at his bequest to the university and, officially presented them in the university church. The volume found its place in a bookcase of priceless items between the two breviaries of Henry VII and of Queen Mary.[1]

That which was significantly new in the Bodleian lay not so much in the zealous collecting of books, as in the willing exhibiting of its holdings. It has to be considered as one of the first public book collections of the world. It is inextricably connected with the history of England as a glorious monument of the economic and intellectual revival of the Elizabethan age. It was also significant as a reservoir for circulating large collections; thus in 1629, there were obtained over 240 Greek manuscripts of William Herbert, the earl of Pembroke; in 1634, the valuable English manuscripts of Sir Kenelm Digby's, and finally, the priceless collection of the legal scholar, John Selden, which included about eight thousand Greek and oriental manuscripts. Significant manuscripts and rare printed work still today constitute the special pride of the Bodleian.[2]

The collecting of books more and more became a sign of good taste among the leading classes of English society. Thomas Howard, the earl of Arundel, (1586–1646), assembled one of the largest collections; in it were even parts from the estate of the Nuremberg patrician and humanist, Willibald Pirckheimer. The grandson, Henry Howard, presented the main part of the property to the Royal Society in 1667; from there the manuscripts came into the British Museum in 1831; the rest of the collection was auctioned off in 1925, and scattered.

The Ambrosiana in Milan also owes its rise from nothing to an individual man's determination: it was Count Federigo Borromeo (1564–1631), the highly educated nephew of Cardinal Carlo Borromeo. Around the turn of the century, the count, as archbishop of Milan and cardinal, was founding a great instructional institution in his see city, the *Collegium Ambrosianum,* and in connection with it, a scholarly library. Among other things, he purchased manuscripts for the Milan cathedral chapter from the property of the Archbishop Francesco Picciolpasso (1433–1443). His agents travelled the whole of Italy, the Netherlands, France, Germany, Spain, the East with its islands, and Syria, and they came home with rich booty. Thus was acquired the priceless library of the Genoese, Gianvincenzo Pinelli (1535–1601), which contained 268 Greek manuscripts, the famous illuminated manuscript of the *Iliad* being among them[3]; thus successful in Rome were purchases of Petrarch's Vergil manuscript from the library of Antonio Agustin and thirteen Greek manuscripts from the collection of Franciscus Partricius. The St. Basil monastery in South Italy sold seventy-five priceless manuscripts.

Of celebrated origin were, further, twenty-four manuscripts from the earlier possessions of George Merula and forty literary monuments from the collection of the legal scholar, Cesare Rovidio. The most valuable acquisition consisted of the very ancient manuscripts of the Bobbio monastery, which came to the cardinal in the year 1606. The new collection could be opened as a generally accessible library on December 10, 1609. Accommodations for the treasures were in thorough correspondence with their internal value; the room represents one of the first Baroque halls for books without pillars, with a high vaulted ceiling, and under which there was a gallery running along the hall; the gallery, however, did not disturb the broad spaciousness for which the builders were also striving. When the founder of the library died on September 21, 1631, acquisitions began gradually to recede; only the year 1657 brought with it still a specially priceless gift of the Count Galeazzo Arcomati: the famous volumes of the original texts of Leonardo da Vinci.[4]

In Germany it was still primarily the court libraries that tended to the world of books with a more or less great success even in this terrible century. Under Duke Wilhelm V, the Munich Court Library had two valuable enrichments: once in the treasures of the Augsburg senator, Johann Heinrich Hörwart with their rare musical printed works, which were acquired in the year 1585; and then in 1592, in the rich holdings form the properties of the Augsburg canon, Johann Georg von Werdenstein, who in 1587 had already given the duke an elegant evangelary coming from the second half of the eighth century; it had earlier belonged to the Augsburg bishop, Hanto (809–815). Duke Wilhelm's son, who afterwards was Elector Maximilian I (1597–1651) had already been an enthusiastic promoter of Bavarian historiography when he was the ducal heir, and in March 1595, he had charged the court librarian, Andreas Promer, to support the historian, Marx Welser, through lending him manuscripts.

Welser had then in fact borrowed a whole series of historical works from the Munich Court Library, and used them for preparing his Bavarian history. At his suggestion, Maximilian instructed the monasteries and foundations of his country, on March 30, 1595, to compile lists of their manuscripts and documents, and to forward them to the ducal chancellory. For the printed works, it was hoped they could manage with the libraries of Munich, Ingolstadt and Augsburg. The summons was repeated to the monasteries in 1610. The lists that were submitted have been preserved for us until now, and they afford us valuable insight into the book holdings of the Bavarian monasteries at that time. Abbot Benedikt of Benediktbeuern reported on June 11, 1595, that Johannes Aventinus and Kaspar Bruschius once borrowed manuscripts from there; but they had not returned them. The abbess of Niederschönenfeld wrote that everything in their nunnery had been destroyed in the Bavarian war. Our Lady's Foundation in Munich explained that it owned only liturgical books. Following the submission of the lists, numerous manuscripts and documents from thirty monasteries were called in and copied. Also solicited were historical works (or information concerning them) from Komburg, Fulda, Regensburg, Cologne and other locales. Submitted from Bamberg was the original text of Aventin's *Chronik* ("Chronicles") and the *Annalen* ("Annals"). Marx Welser in his proposal had above all pointed to Fulda and St. Gall as two very old monasteries that had considerable treasures.

Duke Maximilian had the Greek manuscripts of the court library published in a catalog in 1602 – the first example of all the printed catalogs of princely libraries. The prince oversaw book acquisitions personally. When the Frankfurt Fair catalog arrived in Munich, the chancellor or his official representative submitted it to individual scholars for their expert opinions. The list of selected books, guided by the librarian, then found its way to the censors, to the chancellor, and finally to the prince, who made the decisions about acquisition; books from foreign lands were acquired through the bookdealer in Ingolstadt, or as the opportunity presented itself. All the books in the library obtained their bookplates with the ducal arms glued in the years 1618 and 1619; for this purpose, some 10,300 engraved slips were needed.

When Maximilian succeeeded to the electorate in 1623, the ducal arms were replaced by the electoral ones and the new bookplates were glued in over the old ones. The cost alone for the addition of the 18,200 items came to forty-six florins and twenty farthings. The entire library numbered 17,046 books, 275 Greek, and 723 Latin manuscripts. During the time when Maximilian I was ruling, 5881 florins and 57 farthings were expended for the purchase of books, in addition to the numerous honoraria for book dedications and costs for closed collections.

In the imperial Court Library at Vienna,[5] Hugo Blotius was followed by Sebastian Tengnagel, a scholarly Orientalist, whose knowledge was especially beneficial in disclosing the library's holdings through his valuable editing of texts. Tengnagel's own collection of books passed into the possession of the Court Library and there, with its valuable Oriental manuscripts, it was helpful in providing a foundation of the Oriental department. The next librarian, the canon Matthäus Mauchter, a good library connoisseur, who had visited several large libraries in France, Italy and Germany, obtained six hundred florins from the court chamber on March 27, 1655, for an important trip to Augsburg, where he was supposed to inspect the library of Count Albert Fugger. The result was that, for 15,000 florins, Emperor Ferdinand III (1637–1657) bought the collection, which had been founded by Raimund Fugger, and which had been richly augmented with 14,000 volumes by Philipp Eduard Fugger (among them being the famous Fugger journals);[6] Mauchter then had the materials sent to Vienna in fifty-two large barrels on five rafts and a ship down the Danube. With that, the third of the great Fugger collections was saved from dispersion.

Perhaps the most fortunate period that the imperial Court Library experienced was under its scholarly director, Peter Lambeck (1662–1676), who is reckoned as being among the most significant book connoisseurs of that time. In Vienna, he had the rare fortune of finding a sympathetic bibliophile in his master and emperor, Leopold I (1658–1705). The association of the inquisitive emperor with his librarian who was so rich in knowledge – this is one of the most charming pictures in Viennese library history. During the fourteen year period when Lambeck was active, hardly a month went by without his being visited by his imperial master. The skilled connoisseur of books became an indispensable counselor and conversationalist in the emperor's leisure time. The fate and arrangements of libraries often constituted the object of their learned conversations.

It did not even annoy the emperor (who was eager to learn) to read the dry work of Jan Lomeier concerning libraries. It is amusing to see how the hard-presed librarian became desperate if he didn't immediately find suitable works for fulfilling the multifarious imperial wishes, or was vainly seeking for some particular book. There must have been no small excitement on April 11, 1671, when the emperor announced the visit of the empress and ordered the keeper of the treasures to have especially exquisite items laid out for inspection. In 1665 Lambeck had the chance to accompany the greatest part of the handsome Ambras collection (which had fallen to the imperial house after the extinction of the Tyrolean line), with its 6,449 volumes, on a ship to Vienna, and he had to incorporate it into the Court Library. The 583 priceless manuscripts partially came from the old Habsburg house properties of Emperor Wenceslas IV, Friedrich III and Maximilian I, partially from the valuable collection of the counts of Zimmern, with its priceless German manuscripts, among which were the so-called glosses of Hrabanus Maurus from the ninth century, Notker's *Psalms* and William's *Hohes Lied* ("Song of Songs")– treasures which Count Wilhelm of Zimmern had given Archduke Ferdinand of Tyrol, in the year 1576.[7] On March 8, 1666, the Vienna librarian, as a consequence of an imperial mission, was able to have a look at what remained of the famous Corvina Library. There he found barely four hundred volumes, most of them printed works; they were in disarray, covered with dust and lying on the floor. He was able to take three manuscripts for the Court Library as a gift of the Turkish grand vizier. In the same year, there was the imperial chamber library (in which there was the splendid psalter manuscript that Charlemagne at one time had given to Pope Hadrian as a present) to be catalogued, and the printing of the *Österreichische Ehrenspiegel* ("Astrian Mirror of Honor") to be supervised.

Lambeck could point to unique accomlishments in his final report of February 21, 1676. There was, above all, his list of ten thousand manuscripts, which had been done by his own hand. There was also available for users a printed description of the Court Library in eight folio volumes; abounding in scholarship, it was a veritable instructional work in paleography, and an everlasting monument of fame to the Vienna collection.[8] We find in the voluminous work, among other things, several minor Old High German literary monuments, and additionally, valuable notes interspersed about the Vienna Otfried manuscript and the Ambras version of the *Psalms* of Notker. The author of this work could justifiably claim that from then on, the imperial Court Library (which previously was unknown even in Vienna and was, indeed, almost dead) had received new life, through which it not only compared favorably with its contemporary libraries throughout the whole world, but even surpassed them. With the increasing growth of large libraries, in which their administration was more and more considered as being a full-time occupation, there had developed among professional librarians a new and dynamic fostering of the book. Peter Lambeck could be considered as being among the oldest and most successful of these new patrons of the book.[9]

To be seen as one of the most significant events in the history of German book collecting in that period is the founding of the Electoral Library at Berlin in 1661; thanks to the insightful decisions of the great elector, Friedrich Wilhelm (1640–1688), it was developing quickly already in the first decade of its existence, and in 1687, when Christoph Hendreich, in officially reporting on the new collection, had already counted twenty thousand volumes.[10] The further development of the foundation experienced the same fluctuations in its fortunes that all libraries did in this period and would hardly suggest that Germany's future greatest library would be rising here. In 1688, a librarian was successful in pushing through the idea (which he thought would be a credit to the collection) that all its volumes should receive the same backs, and decorative symbols were put above the book cases. As was so frequently the case in courtly collections, it was aimed at the visitors who took pleasure in looking, since the proposal began with the sentence: "The sameness of the volumes as likewise of the paintings or plaster ornaments only promote the external appearance of the library—of which the strangers (who come to look at the library) often make more than they do of the books themselves." In spite of Hendreich's opposition, in the years from 1690–1698, more than twenty thousand volumes have been provided with gilded backs and with the signature of Elector Friedrich III.[11]

Perhaps the most passionate princely book collector of the seventeenth century in Germany was Duke August the Younger of Brunswick, who set up a new library in 1644 in Wolfenbüttel, in place of the one carried off to Helmstedt in 1618. In 1661, the new library owned over 28,000 volumes and two thousand manuscripts.

The prince, who was a real book enthusiast, attended to his books himself, listing his acquired treasures in four comprehensive volumes and keeping the books in proper order. For the more convenient use of the large catalog he had a carpenter produce (according to his own specifications) a revolving desk, which has been preserved to this day. As always in agitated times, there were good opportunities, both during and following the confusions of the Thirty Years' War, for acquiring books of all sorts that had been carried off. Thus at that time, the handsome missal, with the likenesses of Emperor Maximilian I and Duke Albrecht IV of Bavaria, has gotten to Wolfenbüttel. From Holland there was acquired a portion of the collections of books of Peter Scriverius, among which was the priceless *Codex Arcerianus*, an uncial manuscript of the Roman surveyors from the seventh century which the Bobbio monastery had owned at one time. In his final testamentary disposition, Duke August of Brunswick was able to recommend the collection to his successors with proud satisfaction as an "immeasurable treasure of the country."[12] Even though, after the prince's death, the personal care for the handsome collection had itself come to an end, there were still valuable enrichments to some extent; above all, there were the hundred priceless manuscripts of the Benedictine abbey of Weissenburg in Alsace, which at one time had been carried off by the Swedes. Baron Heinrich Julius von Blum had acquired them in Mainz, when they were supposed to be sold to the goldbeaters in Frankfurt am Main, and from Prague they were offered to the Vienna librarian, Peter Lambeck, for the Imperial Library for three thousand florins. When the negotiations with Vienna miscarried, the priceless items were acquired in 1689 by Duke August's sons for Wolfenbüttel.

A remarkable property exchange within the range of the clerical book collections occurred in June 1630, when the Benedictine monastery of Weingarten near Ravensburg (which already owned priceless items, such as the oldest of the three famous *Minnesänger* manuscripts and the psalter of the Landgrave Hermann of Thüringen), under Abbot Franz Dietrich, acquired from the cathedral chapter in Constance 172 parchment manuscripts and numerous printed works for about three hundred florins. Thus has Weingarten, in the midst of the war, become one of the most significant monastery libraries in Germany.[13]

The fact that, already in this period, libraries were being considered as objects worthy of being seen, can be demonstrated for us in a travel report of the

Dutchman (who was a good connoisseur of books), Constantin Huygens (d. 1697). Huygens accompanied Prince William of Orange to Berlin in 1680. Here the librarian, Christoph Hendreich, guided him through the Electoral Library Hall and showed him several priceless items, among them being the *Codex Wittechindeus*, which at that time was still set with jewels, and further, several of Luther's manuscripts and a manuscript of the gospels with notes in the margins made by Erasmus of Rotterdam. David Hanisius showed the traveller in Wolfenbüttel manuscripts from the Corvinus library. In Helmstedt, the professor of medicine, Hermann Conring (1606–1681), was supposed to lead him through the library; but since there was no more time for it, the visit was omitted.[14]

Of libraries outside Germany in the seventeenth century primarily to be mentioned are the Vaticana in Rome, which in this time period has grown enormously through three large collections, the Orsini Library, the Heidelberg treasures, and the items in the legacy of Queen Christine. Fulvio Orsini, a true son of the late Renaissance (1579–1600), had acquired (in addition to books) cameos, paintings, inscriptions, drawings, marble busts and coins. His book collection consisted primarily of valuable manuscripts which, abounding (as they did in several cases) in important marginal notes by scholarly humanists, are to be seen as significant indications of the Italian Renaissance movement. With this concern to find works of famous provenance, Orsini has to be evaluated as one of the first scholars who understood how to treasure the significance of such origin for the history of antiquities. Thus he did not quit before he had wrested from the son of Cardinal Pietro Bembo (d. January 18, 1547) his most valuable bequest. Negotiations with Torquato Bembo lasted for a full decade, until Orsini had in his possession almost all the priceless items, among which were a Terence *Bembinus* and a Vergil manuscript in large letter script, and then two valuable Greek literary monuments with Pindar and Dionysius of Halicarnassus; further, the original text of Petrarch's *Canzioniere*, according to which Aldus Manutius had published the text in 1501, the work of Boethius, *De consolatione philosophae*, in Boccaccio's copy, Petrarch's *Rime* and Dante's *Commedia* copied by Pietro Bembo, the pastoral poetry *(Bucolicum carmen)* and the philosophical treatment, *De ignorantia* in Petrarch's copy done by his own hand, and finally, Dante's *Divina Commedia*, copied by Boccaccio and presented to his friend, Petrarch.

One also encounters in Orsini's possessions other famous names of the Italian Renaissance. Thus Cyriacus of Ancona was represented with a memorable Plutarch manuscript, in which one could read valuable reports about the famous traveller's experiences; and thus reported several names of the earliest collectors and patrons of Greek literature, about their successful efforts in respect to the endangered intellectual treasures of antiquity: a Manuel Chrysoloras, Theodore Gaza, Michael Apostolios, Marcus Musurus, Constantine Lascaris, Janos Lascaris, Matthäus Devaris; thus did priceless manuscripts exhibit the humanisitc zeal of a Poggio, Philelphus, Barbaro, Laetus, Politianus, Panormita, and Colocci. Orsini initially thought about selling his collection to King Philipp II of Spain; Pope Gregory XIII finally decided to grant the owner an income of two hundred ducats, in order to oblige him to leave his book possessions to the Vaticana. Orsini died on May 18,

1600, and his book collection was integrated with those of the Vaticana.[15] In 1623, the Orsini collection was followed by the priceless Heidelberg library, about which we have already reported.

In 1690, there again came into the Vatican a collection of books from a foreign country, the book holdings of Queen Christine of Sweden (1626–1689.) The highly educated daughter of Gustavus Adolphus had at one time gathered together in Stockholm a significant circle of scholars, such as the Dutchmen, Isaac Vossius, Nikolaus Heinsius, Hugo Grotius, and the French Salmasius, Daniel Huet, Rene Descartes and Gabriel Naudé. An enormous book collection had been added, which on account of her father's war booty was so extended that it became Sweden's largest library. In October 1648, there arrived from Paris for her the library of the legal scholar, Hugo Grotius; three years later there followed the collection of the parliamentarian, Alexander Petau, with its many French manuscripts, and the libraries of President de Mesme, and of the Orientalists, Christian Ravius, and Gilbert Gaulmin. But this splendid period in Stockholm lasted only ten years (1644 to 1654). When Christine abdicated the throne on June 6, 1654, and withdrew to Rome, her collection went with her. In spite of large losses, even in Rome the library still amounted to one of the most significant book collections in the city and, in Lukas Holste, it found an appreciative leader.[16] Following the Queen's death, the valuable possession fell to Cardinal Azzolini, and it was transferred in 1690 to Pope Alexander VIII for eight thousand piasters. It was ultimately incorporated into the Vaticana as "Bibliotheca Alexandrina," and with the unique portions of its holdings, it provided valuable supplementation for the Vaticana. Numerous volumes bear the Queen's signature and the Swedish crown in gold on the binding.[17]

It was primarily the cardinals who contributed to the augmentation of the remaining book possessions in Rome. Thus Francesco Barberini (1597–1679), a nephew of Pope Urban VIII, mainly collected manuscripts in his palace at Rome and had them administered by scholars who were book connoisseurs.

The library's catalog, which was printed in 1681, numbered forty thousand printed works and 3,500 manuscripts. Mabillon ranked the collection among the libraries of Rome just behind the Vaticana. It has been acquired for this library (the Vaticana) in 1902. The cardinal, Girolamo Casanate (1620–1700) Vatican librarian since 1693, gifted his rich book collection in 1698 to the Dominican monastery of St. Maria sopra Minerva at Rome, together with a considerable annual allowance that permitted the regular purchasing of books for the monastery— something that was granted only a few libraries in that time. The collection still exists today as state property.

Since the French kings had led the way in the successful tending to books, it was considered as being among the duties of the leading social classes to participate in the nation's cultural life by enthusiastic patronage of the arts and sciences. Among the numerous book collectors in France's golden age, three statesmen of the country towered over all the others with their rich libraries: Richelieu, Mazarin and Colbert.

Armand Jean du Plessis, duke of Richelieu, (1585–1642), the omnipotent leader under King Louis XIII, maintained permanent book buyers in Italy and Germany and bequeathed a handsome library to his grand nephew, Louis François Armand (1696–1788); it has finally fallen to the Sorbonne in Paris.

Jules Mazarin (1602–1661), the much abused regency advisor of King Louis XIV, was ambitious to transform his property in books into a public establishment, and he enthusiastically proceeded with the accomplishment of this project.[18] His advisor in book affairs was Gabriel Naudé (1600–1653), who at first had been librarian with Cardinal Bagni in Rome, and then with Francesco Barberini (also at Rome), and finally with Richelieu. Once again there met two men who were zealous in their concern for the world of books, with rich results for the book. Mazarin's first large acquisition was the estate of the canon, Jean Descordes of Limoges, with its six thousand volumes. With holdings of twelve thousand volumes and four hundred manuscripts, the collection was handed over the public in 1643. Renaudot reported in his *Gazette* of January 30, 1644, that Mazarin's house stood open each Thursday between 8–11 and 1–5 o'clock to all scholars. Only three libraries in the world, the Ambrosiana in Milan, the Bodleian in Oxford and the Angelica in Rome might boast such a similarly easy access to their treasures.

As Richelieu had dispatched his Jacques Caffarel and Johann Tileman Stella to buy books, so did Mazarin send out his Naudé[19] for the enrichment of his favorite foundation. With his influence he succeeded in procuring acquisitions that otherwise would scarcely have befallen mortals. Thus in 1646 he was able to carry off books from the library of the bishops of Speyer which was maintained in Philippsburg. Naudé had already brought together 45,000 volumes, decorated with the cardinal's arms, when ruin closed in over all the glory. Because the Fronde faction knew that the destruction to his library would especially severely affect the learned cardinal, the collection, despite the abundant opposition of its librarian, was officially put on the market by an act of Parliament on January 6, 1652. The attempt of Queen Christine of Sweden to acquire the entire collection failed; but Naudé followed her call to Stockholm. Following the re-institution of his master, he wanted to return to Paris, but he died on the way back to France at Abbéville on July 29, 1653. Mazarin bought his library, in order therewith to supplement his own renovated (even if also plundered) collection. To the Duke August of Brunswick in 1659 he sent works which had been printed in Paris in gratitude for the fact that the prince had refused to acquire books out of the confiscated property. In about 1660, the library was again entirely renovated, and was annexed to the "Collège des Quatre Nations," which had been founded by the cardinal under the condition that it would be open to all scholars twice a week. When its founder died on March 9, 1661, it was among the best administered, and the most utilized, of the Paris libraries. Thus the glorious and eventful foundation continued (as its founder had wished) under the supervision of the Sorbonne until in the year 1791, when it was declared to be state property. It still bears today the name of the bibliophilic cardinal.

Jean Baptiste Colbert de Torcy (1619–1683), finally, the significant leader of the state under Louis XIV, the deserving founder of the Paris Academy, understood in 1676 how to acquire priceless manuscripts, such as the chief treasures of the

Metz Cathedral, among which were the famous psalter and the no less priceless Bible of Emperor Charles the Bald, and also through his librarian, Etienne Baluze (1630–1718),[20] who was himself a zealous bibliophile, had purchased portions of the correspondence of Nikolaus Ellenbog (a scholarly Benedictine from Ottobeuren),[21] as well as entire collections (thus in the year 1680 the valuable property of the Paris Parliamentary president, Jacques August de Thou)[22] and spent considerable sums of money acquiring the Oriental manuscripts which were offered him by Jean Michel Wansleben and M. de Monceaux (who travelled in the Orient). Following his death, the statesman's heirs had the printed holdings, with sixty thousand volumes, auctioned off, while the 15,000 manuscripts were acquired by Louis XV for the Royal Library for 100,000 ducats.

The fate of dispersion has also befallen the significant collection of the parliamentary counselor, Nicholas-Claude Fabri de Peiresc (1580–1637).[23] It consisted primarily of Greek manuscripts, among which were twenty-three items copied by Darmarius, which Peiresc had purchased from Julius Pacius in 1629. The new owner unselfishly yielded them to Lukas Holste in Rome for his use, but they were not published. Six manuscripts that Holste had not immediately given back have come with his estate to Hamburg. Pieresc has obtained from Cyprus an important Greek parchment manuscript with extracts from Polybius, Diodorus, and Nicholas Damascene; Henri de Valois has published them in the year 1634. The hope to have obtained in the manuscript, which is now situated in Tours, an item owned by Emperor Constantinos Porphyrogenetes has proven illusive. In the spring of 1618, Peiresc borrowed from London the famous Cotton *Genesis*, in order to utilize the text for the planned Septuagint edition of the Sorbonne in Paris. At the same time the illustrations of the manuscript were supposed to be issued in copper plate engravings. When the English sender was impatiently demanding the loan back after some time, Peiresc responded in bad temper that if this rare residue from the ancient world should once be lost or destroyed without being published, the guilt would fall more on London than on Paris. The shrewd warning has been cruelly fulfilled when the manuscript (together with the priceless pictures) has been destroyed for the most part in London in the fire of 1731. The Parisian copies have been preserved in the Bibliothèque Nationale. Following Peiresc's death his possession has been sold by his heirs.

Yet to be mentioned among the other Paris libraries, is the collection of the abbey of Ste. Geneviève, which in 1675 obtained a new type of splendid hall, in which perhaps for the first time it was consciously recognized that books themselves, with their handsome bindings and compactness, can effectively influence the spatial pattern of a book room — a recognition that would give the library buildings of the next century their special features.

Italy, always one of the countries of Europe richest in books, also became the country of the most advanced bibliography; there was especially successful work of this sort in Rome, Milan, Venice and Florence. One of the best connoisseurs of the libraries in Rome, the Augustinian Eremite, Angelo Rocca (1545–1620), whose name the former library of the monastery of S. Agustino still carries ("Bibliotheca Angelica"),[24] had already published in 1591 a valuable description of the

Vaticana.[25] Another significant inquirer into books, the Jesuit Antonius Possevinus, published in three volumes of his scholarly collective work, *Apparatus sacer* of 1603, a series of manuscript catalogs; he was acquainted with manuscripts from all over the entire world. A successful archeologist, the learned Hamburger Lucas Holste (Holstenius), who for a time was the head of the Barberini Library, and then of Queen Christiane's collection, and finally of the Vaticana, had gathered texts for the publication of the so-called minor Greek geographers from the libraries of England, France and Italy, and for drafting he has used texts of the later Pythagoreans, Demophilos, Democrates and Secundus, as well as one Vatican, one Barberini and one Parisian manuscript. He published the Arrian pamphlet concerning the hunt from the important Heidelberg manuscript in 1644.[26] As director of the Vaticana, among the numerous visitors at one time he could even greet the English poet, Milton. He showed him the Greek palimpsest manuscript of the Vaticana as an especially priceless possession.

To the most significant bibliographical works in Italy there further belong the descriptions of the manuscripts of Padua (1639) and Venice (1650) from the pen of the canon, Jacopo Filippo Tomasini, who, encouraged by Gabriel Naudé and Leone Allaci, compiled brief lists of all available manuscripts and understood how to organize them usefully through a well arranged index. In Venice, he had to describe no less than twenty-seven collections, among which were the manuscripts of Jacopo Barozzi, which were put up for sale in 1617 and succeeded a decade later to Archbishop William Herbert, the Earl of Pembroke, and finally to the Oxford Library. Alvise Ferdinando Marsigli (1650–1730), the liberal founder of an enormous scientific institution in Bologna, which, like the *Collegium Ambrosianum* in Milan, gradually integrated several collections, acquired primarily Oriental manuscripts and printed works, and published a catalog for them in 1702. The most famous connoisseur of books and the collector of the century in Italy was Antonio Magliabecchi (1633–1714), the well-known Florentine librarian who found in the Grand Duke Cosimo (1670–1723) a sympathetic patron of the book treasures entrusted to him. He had the Court Library to administer, but he also zealously collected for himself, and he was thoroughly taken up with the world of books. His knowledge of books has become proverbial; even Leibniz has made use of it when he was investigating the house of Brunswick. Magliabecchi bequeathed his own book collection to the city of Florence; thirty years after his death it was opened to users, and it still bears today the name of the memorable bibliophile.[27]

In France, Paris, with its learned directors of the Court Library, Isaac Casaubonus, Nicolaus Rigault, Pierre and Jacques Dupuy, and Nicolaus Clément, had the leadership in bibliography. Manuscript research obtained an especially exciting center in the Benedictine congregation (founded in 1621 by Pope Gregory XV, and protected by Richelieu) that was called (after St. Maurus, Benedict's favorite pupil) the Maurist congregation. For the furtherance of their scholarly studies, the Benedictines built a handsome library in the Paris monastery, St. Germain des Prés, and connected with it a kind of academy. In their well ordered procedure, they provided a remarkable example of significant scholarly division of work and the effective concentration of all the faculties. With Benedictine industry (which had become proverbial), they embarked on great undertakings: editions of the church fathers, the *Acta Sanctorum ordinis* of St. Benedict (1668–1701), the *Collection Recueil des Historiens des Gaules et de la France* (1738–1833), and the comprehensive work, *Gallia christiana.*[28]

Of the bibliographical scholars of this circle, deserving of mention especially are Dom Jean Mabillon (1632–1767) and Dom Bernard de Montfaucon (1653–1741). Mabillon assisted in the years 1684 and 1685 with the cataloging of the Latin manuscripts of the Paris library, and for this purpose he kept a series of manuscripts from the Royal Library that were entrusted to him; lits of these are still preserved today. The Rheims archbishop, Charles Maurice Le Tellier, who had the catalog of the Paris library renovated by a whole staff of co-workers, sent Mabillon, together with a brother of the Order, Michel Germain, on scholarly trips to Italy to work through the manuscripts. In Rome, Mabillon had a memorable conversation in July 1685, with the leader of the Vaticana, Schelstrate, and with Bellori, the librarian at Queen Christine's, concerning the age of the famous Vatican Vergil manuscript, 3225. Together with his companion, he brought together for the library of the French kings four thousand printed works and forty-five manuscripts in Turin, Milan, Venice, Rome, and Florence.[29] In 1687 there appeared in Paris his *Museum Italicum,* in which he reported concerning the book collections they visited, their history and their treasures. The substantial work belongs among the first descriptions of the scholarly travels, and it has been of great influence on later reports of a similar nature. By the unusual knowledge of manuscripts that Mabillon gained in the midst of the Paris treasures, he founded paleography, and through his chief work, *De re diplomatica* (1681), the theory of diplomatics.[30]

Because since the days of the Renaissance, Italy was generally regarded as the promised land of manuscripts, Bernard Montfaucon, with his fellow Order member, Paul Briois,[31] set out in 1698 for Italy so as to become acquainted with as many transmissions of the texts as possible for the edition of the church fathers that was planned; they were commissioned by the Maurists. From Rome, Montfaucon reported on October 7, 1697, to the Abbé de Louvois (the leader at that time of the Royal Library in Paris) about his experiences in the book collections of Milan, Modena, and Venice; he praised the Ambrosiana in Milan, which was then being administered by Muratori, as one of the richest manuscript collections of Italy, but which was lacking in the important more recent printed works; he complained about the impeded access to the Marciana in Venice, and he submitted titles of books that were supposed to be compared with the Parisian holdings.

Excursions were undertaken out from Rome to Subiaco, Monte Cassino, Naples, Grottaferrata and Siena. In Naples, the tireless searcher came upon a French history manuscript that stemmed from Spain and was now for sale. He wrote to Paris that if one wished to have the enormous manuscript copied, it would cost just as much as its owner, Valette (who presided over one of the most handsome libraries of Italy) demanded for it. When he was with the Augustinians in Naples he had seen a very beautiful Dioscurides manuscript; he was enclosing a list of the other manuscripts of this monastery. Since the travellers were supposed to be again in Paris toward Easter, they would have to limit themselves overall to the most pressing tasks for copying. Three days in the week they were going into the Vaticana, and they worked there from early in the morning until evening. On the days that remained, they looked through the manuscripts of the Ottoboni Library. Following the death of his fellow traveller, Briois, on February 10, 1700, Montfaucon continued searching alone and he arrived in Paris again on June 11, 1701, with rich results.[32] The most famous work of the remarkable connoisseur of manuscripts became the *Palaeographia Graeca* of 1708, which rests on accurate investigations of thousands of manuscripts, and can still be successfully used today. Very valuable also is the description of manuscripts that Montfaucon in 1715 devoted to the *Bibliotheca Coisliniana olim Segueriana*, the collection of the Metz bishop, Henri Charles de Cambout, Duke of Coislin (1664–1732), that was founded by Chancellor Pierre Seguier.[33] The magnanimous owner in 1732 then bequeathed the priceless treasures, with four thousand valuable manuscripts and twenty thousand printed works, to the monastery of St. Germain-des-Prés, in the hope that they would be best preserved under the care of the Benedictines. The catalog of Montfaucon may be seen as the first example of a manuscript catalog provided with specimens of handwriting. A further large project that was supposed to bring together all the lists of manuscripts, did not get beyond the first two volumes.[34]

While the Benedictines in France were thus dedicating themselves to scholarship, in Belgium scholarly Jesuits led by Heribert Rosweyda and Johann von Bolland (therefore called "Bollandists"), were taking on a great project that today has not yet been completed—the *Acta Sanctorum* (1643), which, resting on enormous researches in manuscripts and arranged according to the days of the month, contains the history of the saints, and with its sixty-five folio volumes it belongs to the oldest scholarly team efforts, and to the greatest book projects.[35] Also, this enormous work is based on the accurate searching through of innumerable collections of books and their manuscriptural treasures.

25
New Literary Forms in the Journal and Newspaper

Among the most significant results of Gutenberg's deed was that it accelerated enormously the circulation of ideas and, with that, mankind's whole experience. Following the great discovery of printing, the book world initially made its way slowly. People had time to print and to assimilate the literature of a lengthy past. And then, all at once, movement came into the usual course and with this, the shaking off of that part of the works just created that was felt to be a burden. And peoples' ideas again moved more quickly. The pamphlet captured the printers' shops and quickly made its way through the countries. Peoples' participation in current events increased further. The book was not keeping in step with the life of that day. Taking its place was the "Neue Zeitung," which comprised only a few pages. And the development went further and further. The urgency of communication, the increase in literacy and in the demand for reading, progress in transportation, the enterprising spirit of individual printers — all of these together, by the application of the regular recurrence of the advertisements which had initially been carried in the Fair catalogs — helped to bring about something new, the journal, and following it the newspaper; these were projects that were of an unforseeable future significance for public, as well as for cultural, life.

"Zeitung." All of a sudden the word was there that would gradually signify an entire world in itself. It entered the printed literature for the first time not as a main title, but only as a superscription, "Newe zeytung vom Orient und auffgange" ("Newspaper from the Orient and rising") above a report of the Doge Leonhard Lauredan, which had been written down on December 4, 1501 and translated into German; it dealt with the reconquering of the island of Lesbos by the Venetians and the French in 1501. During the course of the sixteenth century, the *Neue Zeitung* ("Newspaper") quickly became the most popular form of the report that was made about the events that concerned the public, about campaigns, battles, natural occurrences such as floods, lightning strikes, mirages, parhelions, comets, eclipses of the sun and moon, earthquakes, the swarming of locusts, deformed children and animals, and also about murderous acts, executions and the burning of witches.[1]

In addition to the designation, *Neue Zeitung*, ("Newspaper"), we encounter similar superscriptions such as "Report," "Notions," "History," "Herald." Its derivation from the manuscriptural newsletter reveal designations such as *Copia,* "Copy," "Letter," "Impression," "Missive," "Epistle." Whoever was capable of composing good titles immediately moved the event being related into the foreground and wrote: "Of the new island in the lands, thus as has been discovered a short time ago," or "The battle of the king of Poland with the Muscovites," and he who understood advertising announced a "genuine," a "terrible," a "good," a "fortunate" *Neue Zeitung* ("newspaper"). In addition to the individual reports, collective reports gradually came about: these treated several events. One such was issued already in 1523 as the *"Newe Zeitung* from the Netherlands. From Rome. From Naples. From the new towns. From Austria." Again, later on, there emerged continuations of the reports concerning certain events, such as a "sixth," "seventh," and "eighth" new *"Zeitung* from His Imperial Majesty's field camp in Hungary," concerning the war with the Turks in the year 1566. So did the new *Zeitungen* ("Times") gradually become constituent parts of current literature, which still continued to use the book format. Authors were clericals, scholars, booksellers—in a word, they were people who could learn something of the world outside and who were skilled with the pen. Such utilization of the individual report for a one-time publication remained the pattern for a few decades.

A momentous further development of *Neue Zeitung* ("The Journal") occurred from the scholarly side through Michael von Aitzing, a zealous historian. Stimulated by an enthusiastic participation in the happenings of the day throughout the world, he utilized in a fortunate way the Frankfurt Spring and Fall Fairs for publishing regularly recurring reports every sixth month concerning the most important events of the recent period. *"Nova historica relatio*—that is, a new historical description of memorable affairs and histories," this new undertaking was designated; it quickly caught on after 1583, and it was soon being imitated.[2] One of these reports, called *Frankfurter Messrelation* ("Frankfurt Fair Relations"), was continued until into the nineteenth century.

It was not a big step from the *Relation,* issued every six months, to the monthly; still, it took almost three decades before the Strasbourg publisher, Johann Carolus (who apparently was the first to do so) published his *Relation aller fürnemen und gedenkwürdigen Historien, so sich hie und wieder in diesem 1609. Jahr verlaufen und zutragen möchten* ("Relation of all eminent and memorable stories that have come to pass in this year 1609.")[2] The word *Zeitung* turns up in this *Relation,* in which indeed the first real *Zeitung* is to be seen, only it is in front of the reports about the individual events, and not in the title itself. A sister *Zeitung* that was apparently published in Wolfenbüttel or in Helmstedt in the same year carried the title, "Avisa, Relation or *Zeitung.*"[4] Both the publications competed with one another for the fame of being the first continuing *Zeitung* of the world.[5] The publishers of both the *Zeitungen* could not have dreamt that their projects would become the first ones to develop into the great daily and world newspapers. The year 1609 is consequently to be seen as having been the natal year, and Germany, printing's homeland, is likewise the native land of the continuing *Zeitung.* Externally considered, these monthly *Zeitungen* were still attached entirely to the book; they were basically nothing more than reporting chronicles.[6] The new—and certainly the overall significant and decisive—thing was that they were issued in installments. The way to the continuing *Zeitung* was now embarked on, and soon it led to numerous foundations both domestic and foreign. The Leipzig bookdealer and printer, Timotheus Ritzsch, took a big step forward; on January 1, 1660, he published the first *Zeitung* that appeared daily, the "new continuing report of war and of world affairs," and he entered into a close connection with the postal service, an alliance that gave the *Zeitung* the possibility for further successful development and distribution. Ritzsch may therefore claim the fame of having published the world's first daily newspaper.

The more the *Zeitung* developed (and it certainly did so only hesitantly and slowly) the more independent it became of the book, and the more autonomously it went its own way. Reference to it will be made in the pages that follow only insofar as, going beyond the service of reporting and the political sector, it gradually attempted, with its entertaining and generally instructive representations, to have some effect on cultural life, and so entered into competition with the book and the journal.[7]

The weekly reporting newspaper, which has quickly evidenced its effectiveness, was soon followed by the scholarly journal, a consequence of the constantly more richly developing world of the books and of scholarship, which were more and more requiring regular surveying. The increasing book publications, the developing scholarly life in the schools of higher learning, the most important changes in the scholarly world—all of these, as well as the general need for reporting, were pressing toward regularized reports. The initial great undertaking of this kind was the Parisian *Journal des Scavants*, which, under the leadership of the parliamentary counsel, Denys de Sallo, began to be published on January 5, 1665. At first it came out weekly, but later it was issued every fourteen days, or even in longer time intervals.[8] A varied mixture of reports concerning scholars, of reports about scientific experiments and discoveries, of descriptions of books and communications about learned societies—this was its content. Still in the same year there followed in London the *Philosophical Transactions*, in Rome in 1668 the *Giornale de' Letterati*, in 1682 in Leipzig (published by Otto Mencke) the *Acta eruditoram;* composed in Latin, it continued for a century and from its inception it had men such as Leibniz and Thomasius for collaborators.[9] The first scholar who had the courage to publish a journal in the German language was Christian Thomasius (1655–1728); he is the same one who in 1688 delivered for the first time a formal lecture in the German language, and opposed anyone who was of the opinion that "our language was only be useful in the affairs of the common life, or if it so happens, when it comes to the highest things, to nothing more than little stories, and to write newspaper reports on them, but not for presenting the philosophical, or the higher faculties' teachings and basic principles." It was in this sense that, after 1687, Thomasius was issuing in the German language the "ideas, light and serious, reasonable and simple, on all sorts of pleasureable and useful books and questions."

Quite soon then one journal was following upon another, and already in 1718, Heinrich Ludwig Götten, in his *Gründliche Nachrichten von den französischen, lateinischen und deutschen Journalen, Ephemeridibus, monatlichen Extracten oder wie ie sonsten Namen haben mögen* ("Basic reports of the French, Latin and German Journals, ephemerals, monthly extracts or what other names they may have") was complaining, while recognizing the advantages of the journal, about the outright mania that everybody wanted to write for a journal.

Like the newspaper, so the journal also—the second significant offshoot from the book—gradually received a strong impetus and became an enduring establishment of public life.[10] Even when, in many respects, it was pursuing other goals than those of the book, goals that were at variance with the book, it still remained (in contrast with the newspaper which, fully independent, went its own way) closely associated with the book, and also with book publishing and the book trade. It likewise shared the same development present in all public communications toward an ever larger extension of its subject field and classes of buyers. Since it was quite soon extending beyond the actual world of scholars, it was creating unlimited possibilities for its own development. The enhanced readiness to accept an enormously enlarged class of readers accommodated itself increasingly to the content, which was extended into instruction and entertainment, and this factor also became of the greatest significance for the distribution of books.

In the centuries that followed, the book, the newspaper and the journal were the three complimentary forms of communication for the public, until the human spirit discovered a fourth one, the radio, which, for its wonderful effects, surpassed in many respects everything that had come before.

26
Leibniz and the Book World of His Time

That a man such as the philosopher, mathematician, legal scholar and statesman, Gottfried Wilhelm Leibniz (1646–1716), who embraced the whole of knowledge in his time and who was sympathetic with all public matters concerning Germany, should also think of himself as being intimately associated with the German world of books lay already within the entire nature of such an all-encompassing spirit. External factors in his life and avowed goals were still bringing him closer to the book. Leibniz appeared in his intellectual life to make up for everything which Germany for almost a century had been neglecting[1]; for him, the highest goal was constantly to make knowledge serve life. He was the first great German herald of the enlightened goal of culture, consciously to shape the world and life itself in keeping with a propitious progress. There would often be more truth and utility in a book concerned with agriculture or with cabinet-making, Leibniz once wrote, than from an entire library, more in ten years' worth of newspapers than could be had from a hundred classical authors. In 1673, he was complaining from Paris about the unprofitable filling of the library with books that would not be used. Only two types of books would he allow to come into a library: first, such books as contained discoveries, demonstrations, and experiments and secondly, those that contained political and historical documents, chiefly from the contemporary period, and the descriptions of states. Such a library would not cost much, and yet it would be immeasurably rich for the purposes of instruction. He himself had brought with him from London the best of the English book world, for which he paid forty thalers. That this commanding intellectual figure, in spite of this idea about the use value of a book (it was one-sided and quite conditioned by time), still possessed so comprehensive a view that he also recognized the everlasting value of the world of books, was shown when Duke Johann Friedrich of Hanover named him as his counselor in 1676, and also as head of the new Court Library in Hanover, and at the same time he entrusted him with writing a Guelph history. In 1691, the dukes, Rudolf August and Anton Ulrich of Brunswick, also named him director of their library at Wolfenbüttel. Leibniz clearly expressed how highly he regarded the significance of great book collections in a letter to the chief marshal of Brunswick.

The entire world knew, he once wrote, what a gem the incomparable Wolfenbüttel library was for this princely house and for the whole country, and so it was seldom that a scholarly person or a person with curiosity (from inside or outside the country), travelling in this area, would not seek the opportunity of seeing it. Because a library could maintain itself not merely by keeping in good condition the stock that it currently owns, but would, like the fire, have to experience constant growth, so it should acquire not only new items, but it should also fill out the gaps of not a few years. "Because otherwise it must soon be said in the world, that here is an old, now run-down library that is not specially continued or augmented, and which should not in fact have the name 'August' anymore." Leibniz, with a perceptive eye, was here alluding to the sorest point that governed princely book collections, which as a rule were planned for show. As a scholar, Leibniz knew that not much could be done with mere occasional acquisitions. So, with a far-seeing eye, he tried to draw the Wolfenbüttel library beyond the narrow circles of the court, and to associate it closely with publicness. Thus he proposed to his prince the consideration of whether the library might not be more closely connected with the academy, so that the praiseworthy inhabitants of the region might also contribute to the preservation of this jewel; not only would such a library bring renown to the entire country, it would also be useful, because everyone could draw both pleasure and the knowledge they needed from it.

One has to search extensively in library history to see this demand (it was far in advance of the actual development) for a systematically augmented territorial library even being made, let alone being met. The actuality was indeed denied even the Wolfenbüttel librarian, and his wishes were not fulfilled. Still, at least in his proposal of 1710, the valuable collection (which was rich in manuscripts) of the Danish state adviser, Marquard Gude (1635–1689), was acquitted for Wolfenbüttel for 2240 thalers. Duke Anton Ulrich decided in 1705 to rebuild the library, which, following its completion, represented one of the first separately standing library buildings; from the handsome dome there hung a shining, gilded celestial globe.[2]

Visitors at the Wolfenbüttel library seem not always to have found in Leibniz the courteous director that they might have wished him to be. The youthful collector of books, Zacharias Konrad Uffenbach,[3] was indeed received in 1710 in a friendly manner, but he was not guided into the library; this had not yet been organized – or so the refusal read. Leibniz had certainly encountered similar experiences as a user of foreign libraries. While book collections in Rome readily opened to him, on the occasion of his visit to the Munich Court Library in 1687, the collection remained firmly closed to him in spite of Electoral consent, just as Jean Mabillon, the famous French Benedictine, had also not been allowed to enter there in 1683. While Leibniz was staying in Vienna in the years 1712–1714, the court librarian, Johann Benedikt Gentilotti, approached him in a friendly manner, but he nevertheless refused his guest's desire to be allowed to use the manuscripts outside the library on the ground that he absolutely held "that in case someone desired from the Wolfenbüttel collection, (the chief inspection of which Herr von Leibniz conducts) several *ineditos codices*, he would surely not advise that they were being handed over." The highest court office likewise expressed its opposition, because the applicant could copy the manuscript and have it printed; in that case, the reputation and rarity of the Court Library would be diminished, or perhaps something that would be prejudicial to the religion or prerogatives of the emperor or of the other authorities might be published.[4]

Leibniz had already quite early been busy with the question of how the languishing world of books should be reorganized, so that it could better fulfill its main purpose of promoting life and the state. He especially planned to establish a journal that would list every six months the new publications brought to the Frankfurt Fair, with brief descriptions of their content and value.

The second goal that Leibniz pursued was the reorganization of the higher leadership of the German book world. Instead of the Frankfurt Book Commission, the Electorate of Mainz office of the archchancellory was supposed to step in as director of the German book world and take all the appropriate measures in order to regulate the relations of book acquisitions, to administer censorship, to create an imperial book trade order, and to regulate the relationship among authors, bookdealers, correctors (editors) and printers. No books should be printed anymore in which the author did not announce in a stipulated place what sorts of new uses the book would bring to the community.

All these plans of his Leibniz set forth in a memorandum, and in 1668 he wrote his own *Meditation über die beste Art, das Buchwesen zu reformieren* ("Meditation concerning the best way to reform the world of books").

Leibniz further strove to found an association, a learned society *(Societas eruditorum)* for the whole of Germany, which would be engaged in cooperative activity through the exchange of letters, communications and reciprocal aid, and with its united energies would cultivate, order, and control the vast field of knowledge. Associated therewith was the indefatigable reorganizer's desire to free scholars (through the founding of subscription societies and patronal societies) from the shackles of the book trade, "so that," as he opined in 1715 in his design for the founding of an imperial academy in Vienna, "the scholars would not become (to the shame of scholarship) the hired workers of the bookdealers."[5] It was the first, and not the last, time that serious opposition between scholarship and the book trade has been publicly reported.[6]

Most of these proposals, which to some extent were quite forward-looking, and to some extent (certainly from hindsight) impracticable, have not been carried through. Only the planned scholarly society has experienced its fulfillment in 1700 in the founding of the Royal Society of Sciences in Berlin. In the same year, Johann Georg von Eccard (1674–1730), the same one who in his publication in 1729, *Commentarii de rebus Franciae*, has published for the first time the *Hildebrandslied* ("Hildebrand's Song") with facsimilies from the manuscript, has issued, as a scholarly aid to philosophy, the *Monatliche Auszüge aus allerhand neu herausgegebenen nützlichen und artigen Büchern* ("Monthly Extracts form the Newly Issued Useful and Artful Books") in which, quite in the sense of the cultural founders, there were published reports about the books noted and their authors, as well as *Neue Zeitungen von gelehrten Sachen* ("Newspapers of Scholarly Matters").

The first and final goal of the energetic scholar was the rebuilding of the proscribed arts and sciences in Germany, a goal toward which, by means of his creative cultural work, Leibniz has effectively worked as has no other German.

In Hanover, in the place where Leibniz has managed for forty long years his office as librarian and a writer of history, there lies his inexhaustible literary legacy, with its two hundred folio volumes, together with over 15,300 letters. It is a visible witness to the enormous efficiency of labor of this German cultural giant of the seventeenth century.[7]

In his relationship to the book, Leibniz stands at the decisive turning point of an era. He has freed himself from the past, and he strives for something new, for the utmost use of the book in the interest of the happiness and welfare of mankind. He is already sensing the power of the period which is coming — the great Enlightenment movement.

27
The Enlightenment Period and the World of Books

In the eighteenth century, it is the political events that stand out, the most momentous of these being the Seven Year's War (1756–1763), the North American struggle for freedom against the English motherland (1775–1783), and finally, the French Revolution with the Revolutionary Wars that followed it (1789–1815); the eighteenth century was at the same time an age of enormous cultural reconstruction. Again, the stimulating question of the meaning and purpose of life, of mankind's position in respect to the secular and to the divine—this question is raised and answered otherwise than it formerly was. The heritage of the Middle Ages, which was breaking up in an infinite number of places, with its still predominant goal set in the Beyond and its commitments, suddenly fell completely under the soaring of the natural sciences and of philosophy, which sought to fathom the whole world and its laws, and victoriously there arose something new: the power mastering the whole of life—the power of reason, of knowledge, of enlightenment, of progress, and of order: a happy culture built up entirely on "this life," this present existence. For the Enlightenment, the world is no longer considered as being the consequence of original sin; it rather rests in the divine order of reason. No longer has revelation the leading role in scholarship; such leadership is no more given to tradition, but rather to research; the world view is no more determined by theology, but rather by the natural sciences, and by philosophy, which itself bans all obsolete prejudices, and all superstitions. A boundless belief in an imagined omnipotence of reason, in the creation of intellect, fulfills people, and it allows them almost to forget that the faculties of thought and reason by themselves are not enough to rouse all the powers of soul and will, nor sufficient to subdue life's questionable quality and its abysses, to bring to fulfillment or to silence the soul's mysterious dreams and ideals, or to master one's own inadequacies, human nature's demonic dimension, or also destiny, beset as it is with constant dangers and threats to one's existence.

But the Enlightenment period has always been considered as a turning point of immense magnitude for the whole of the new thinking, especially also for scientific penetration of the world and of life, which is a chief mainstay of modern culture. Kant, with his essay in the *Berlinische Monatschrift* of 1784, "What is Enlightenment?" has given this slogan its enduring effectiveness.

As with each great cultural movement, so also with the Enlightenment's

upheaveal, the book, as the most effective carrier for new ideas, has been of surpassing significance. One has only to recall the rousing works that have gone out
in that period from France into all the lands—Voltaire's *Henriade* (1728),[1] Montesquieu's *Esprit des lois* (1748), the *Encyclopédie* of the enlighteners, Denis Diderot
and Jean le Rond d'Alembert (1751 to 1780).

For German cultural life,[2] the eighteenth century means even more than
merely the Enlightenment and the loud opposition resulting from it, of the world
of feeling as over against reason's sole sovereignty, a renewed pietism and the
Sturm-und-Drang ("Storm and Stress") movement; it signifies the great event of the
German cultural awakening, the high flowering of the German language as the eloquent harbinger of the eternally awakened German soul, the speedy rise of German
poetry, of philosophy, of music—a unique peaking of artistic culture. Klopstock,
Lessing, Goethe, Schiller, Kant, Bach, Handel, Gluck, Haydn, and Mozart created
their works, and regained for the German people its leading cultural position in the
world. A miracle has taken place: the German people have found the style suitable
for them; they have discovered their language and cultural integrity.

Faithful to our aim of showing the books with particular tendencies of a period
in their most significant manifestations as measures of the book's efficacy, we cite
the most important publications of the Enlightenment period in which there was a
concern for new expressions of belief, or for revived patterns of language, which
have had an effect far beyond their own day and time.

The literature of the Germans had formerly centered overwhelmingly on
scholarship and in the Latin language. Simultaneously with a new world of ideas,
the German language was now victorious. It was just as it was in Luther's time; the
Reformer then had to speak the people's language if he wished to win over the German people. Christian Wolff and Christian Thomasius were the first philosophers
who proclaimed the new world view in the German language, in order to be able
to carry it into wider circles. "Reason, virtue and happiness are the three foremost
things for which man should strive in this world;" it was with these words that Christian Wolff (1670–1754), the philosophical teacher of the German people, began his
chief work (which quickly came out in six editions), *Vernünftige Gedanken von Gott,
der Welt und der Seele des Menschen, auch allen Dingen überhaupt* ("Reasonable
Ideas of God, the World and the Human Soul, also all the Main Things") (1714).
Taken as a whole, Thomasius may be designated as the arch-enlightener. Through
his essays and journals, he consciously attempted with the Germans to create a
great educational community that was needed to attain the new goal of progress,
and with it, mankind's desired happiness.

Also the German book again now had a great function to fulfill: it had something
to say which was of concern to all and that spoke to them in a language which
everyone understood. And taking its place beside the book was also the journal,
especially the moralistic weekly, which in popular form gave the widest circulation
to the new ideas. In addition, the German language (mainly after Klopstock)
discovered sonorous words which it earlier had not known; book and journal were
therefore filled with new content and new style; they won readers to an extent that
they never had before.

As in nature there are fruitful years as well as the ones less blessed—years in which everything thrives, and again years to which are denied the fructifying rain or the sun that brings things to maturity—so also in cultural life there are periods that yield poorly and periods in which the yield is rich, according as Fate wills it. At that time, the Enlightenment, the world was enjoying a culturally blessed period.

Through valuable books of life, the poets competed with the philosophers in the struggle to rebuild the German cultural life to a point commensurate with a great and gifted people. Barthold Heinrich Brockes (1680 to 1747), in his poetically eloquent collection of poetry, *Irdisches Vergnügen in Gott* (1721) ("Earthly Pleasures in God"), sought the goal that corresponded with the new philosophy of poetically representing the greatness and goodness of God in the inner purposefulness that there is in nature.

Johann Christoph Gottsched (1700–1768), the head of the *Deutschliebende poetische Gesellschaft* ("Poetical Society of Lovers of German"), the founder of the new German drama, was striving in his *Versuch einer kritischen Dichtkunst für die Deutschen* (1730) ("Attempt at a Critical Poetic Art for the Germans") to yoke poetry within fixed rules; but he was also able in his *Beiträge zur kritischen Historie der deutschen Sprache, Poesie und Beredsamkeit* ("Contributions to a Critical History of the German Language, Poesie and Eloquence") (1732–1744) to awaken an understanding for old German poetry. In contrast with Gottsched, the Swiss Johann Jakob Bodmer (1698–1783), Milton's inspired admirer and translator, emphasized the power of presentation and the gift for invention as being most important in the poetic art. He received the Manesse *Songs* manuscript, sent to him from Paris, and from it he issued his *Sammlung der Minnesinger* (1758) ("Collection of Minnesongs"). The pietism that was still effective from the past century found unique and impressive soundings in the founder of the Brethren community at Herrnhut, Nicholas, Count von Zinzendorf (1700–1760), and in his *Sammlung geistlicher und lieblicher Dichter* (1775) ("Collection of Spiritual and Popular Poets"). His concept of godliness grounded in a spiritual harmony is expressed in the beautiful words: "Christianity depends on very little, and it can be written down on an octavo sized page." The unhappy poet, Johann Christoph Günther (1695 to 1723), was skilled in singing love songs that charmed hearts all over.

Christian Fürchtegott Gellert (1915–1769) was among the poets who had the richest influence in this period; his *Fabeln und Erzählunger* (1746–48) ("Fables and Tales") and *Geistliche Oden und Lieder* ("Spiritual Odes and Songs") were perhaps the most read books in those days. Gellert has been one of the few German poets whom the German people of all social strata have read. Johann Wilhelm Ludwig Gleim (1719 to 1803) celebrated in song the heroic spirit of the time in his *Preußische Kriegslieder von einem Grenadier* ("Prussian War Songs of a Grenadier") (1756–57). Johann Peter Uz (1720–1796), in his charming poem, *Versuch über die Kunst, fröhlich zu sein* ("Essay on the Art of Being Always Happy") was so able to capture the spirit of the time that the little work was translated into several languages. Also read again and again was Albrecht von Haller's famous canticle to the world of the mountains, *Die Alpen* (1729), which revealed to mankind the beauty of the mountains, and worthily opened up the later Alpine literature; Ewald Christian von Kleist's (1715–1759) portrayal of nature, *Der Frühling* ("Spring") (1759) was likewise read. The vital temper of the Rococo period Salomon Gessner (1730–1788) was able to bring to expression in masterly language and charming etchings in his *Idyllen* ("Idylls"). Of Friedrich von Hagedorn (1708–1754), the creator of the German social song, the poem, "Johann der Seifensieder," has been especially lasting. Matthias Claudius (1740–1815) presented his contemporaries with contributions in prose and poetry in the *Wandsbecker Bote* (1775–1812). A genuine national treasure, among these are his deeply-felt songs of nature and his cheerful drinking songs. Gottfried August Bürger (1747–1794), creator of the German ballad, achieved an enormous success with his moving "Leonore" (1773). No less a figure than Walter Scott has translated him into English. He has been considered the founder of the German ballad, that form of poetry which has given to us such glorious creations as the ballads of a Goethe, a Schiller, Uhland, Hebbel, Liliencron, Münchhausen and Droste-Hülshof.[3]

Johann Heinrich Voss (1751–1826) impressed himself deeply into the hearts of his numerous readers through his lovely idyll, *Luise* (1795), and he influenced Goethe to write his poem, *Hermann und Dorothea*. Voss has also had great effect on German cultural life with his Homer translation. Ludwig Christoph Heinrich Hölty's (1748–1776) poems have first been published following the poet's early death, but have thereby lost nothing in their effectiveness. Johann Karl August Musäus (1735–1787) enriched the book world of that time in the years 1782–1786 with his *Volksmärchen der Deutschen* ("Popular Fairy Tales of the Germans") in five volumes; it was one of the most successful works that, in numerous editions, remained vital until after the middle of the nineteenth century.[4] Further, the novel, *Anton Reiser*, by Karl Philipp Moritz (1757–1793), was much read; so was Johann Heinrich Jung-Stillings' (1740–1817) *Lebensgeschichte* ("Life History"), the favorite book of quiet people everywhere (Goedecke); it was highly treasured even by Nietzsche.

Out of Enlightenment ideas, and the heightened sensitivity of the period, our great German poets, Friedrich Gottlieb Klopstock (1724–1803), Gotthold Ephraim Lessing (1729–1781), Christoph Martin Wieland (1733–1813), Johan Gottfried Herder (1744–1803), Johann Wolfgang Goethe (1749–1832), and Johann Friedrich Schiller, (1759–1805) have then created in a perfected style their revelations of a new struggling and conquering humanity. It began with Klopstock's *Messias*, the powerful world poem on the glories of the godly life, the first part of which was published in the *Neue Bremer Beiträge* ("New Bremen Contributions") of 1748; with this creative work, which was jubilantly greeted by his contemporaries, German literature's marvelous ascent to dignity and to greatness has begun.[5] Herder thought of Klopstock: "When in 1748 the first three songs of his *Messias* first appeared, it was as if not only a new language, but at the same time a new soul, a new heart, a purer poetic art had been discovered."

At the same time, the classical period, with its fullness of spirit, has reached a culminating point in German linguistic and literary artistry, the likes of which can scarcely be found anywhere.

The climax is attained in Goethe's lyrics. "It is a long way to the simplification and the deepening of a feeling, or of an experience up to true poetry. The language has to be millennia old before it develops to 'Über allen Wipfeln ist Ruh' (Rudolf G. Binding) ("Overall the treetops it is quiet"). But it is the book that is the bearer of this development.

With the literature of the eighteenth century has come an entirely new world of books borne up by a new generation of quite gifted poets and authors, who were read by the broadest strata of society. The thinker, the poet, and the writer achieved a public acclaim not previously known; he becomes socially acceptable.[6] France possesses its Voltaire who, like Erasmus of Rotterdam, is a European cultural great power; in the years 1750–1752, he associates with Frederick the Great almost as if he were his equal; he is honored like a prince by Elector Karl Theodor of Palatine in 1753 in Schwetzingen, where works by him are enacted in the summer theatre. *Robinson Crusoe*, by the Englishman, Daniel Defoe, captivates the entire world in the shortest time, and attains over three hundred editions, besides its countless revisions. Of the German imitations, the recastings done by the pedagogue, Joachim Heinrich Campe, (1779) issued in 120 editions.[7]

From several recollections of youth, we mention only Karl, Baron von Klöden, and Bogumil Goltz; we know what a deep impression this book has made on youthful hearts. "Eleven times," says Karl von Klöden, "have I read the book one time after the other, without missing a syllable, and I can almost repeat it from memory. Besides the Bible, no book has worked so powerfully on me; none has been of such essential benefit in my area of ideas." Even Johann Georg Schnabel's *Fata einiger Seefahrer* ("Fate of Several Seamen"), later generally called *Insel Felsenburg* ("Island of Felsenburg") (1741–1743), has, as an eloquent expression of a mood of the time, of a longing for a life close to nature and directed solely by reason on a lonely island in the middle of the sea, found an enthusiastic acceptance everywhere; Goethe has read the book in his youth. The Boston Public Library owns a *Robinsonade* library with thirty thousand volumes. In Germany, Klopstock, as our first great poet, is dominated by a greatly increased will to achieve status; he feels (as once already Leibniz has) the dependence of author on publisher as being unworthy of cultural performance, and he tries to escape these shackles by way of subscription; but it is without success. At his solemn burial at Ottensen near Hamburg on March 28, 1803, the entire German people, deeply stirred, have participated.

The burial has been illustrated for us in a painting of the artist, J.W. Tappe, and subsequently in a mezzotinto page of J.F. Feidhof's; girls clothed in white strew roses and myrtles on the coffin on which lies the *Messias*. Lessing felt himself to be a professional writer who, as a researcher, critic and poet, wanted to influence not only individuals, but the whole German cultural life, and the whole world, because he was conscious of having something unique to say in the most polished language to his contemporaries. He also resisted the dependence on publishers and, together with Bode, he tried to become independent through the "Dessauische Verlagsbuchhandlung für Gelehrte und Künstler" ("Dessau Publisher-Book Business for Scholars and Artists"); but it was without success also.

The members of the Weimar Court of Muses, Goethe, Wieland, and Schiller, ultimately made their way to the pinnacles of fame and, already during their lifetimes, they were the uncontested cultural leaders of the German people. Goethe's novel, *Die Leiden des jungen Werthers* ("The Passion of the Young Werther") became the favorite book of the world and generated a true frenzy of *Weltschmerz*, the "Werther fever." Even England[8] and France had a *Werther* literature. A diluted *Werther* imitation, Johann Martin Miller's novel, *Siegwart*, has also had countless readers. "So much has scarcely been cried on printing paper as is the case with *Siegwart*" (Edward Engel). Even Schiller has been moved to tears by the sentimental monastery history. "For hours long he could sit at the lonely barred window (of the Stuttgart Academy), with lilies that he grew in flower pots, raving about the book of the Ulm preacher."[9]

For the first time since the discovery of the art of printing, there is the writer in the actual sense. To achieve a large circle of readers, which is the necessary prior condition for the possibility of being effective, the unconditional presupposition is the widest distribution of the book. Printing has created this for the first time. In the moment when the printed book could put itself in the service of a great cultural movement, there was also commencing the first great period of the professional literary authorship. There was Erasmus of Rotterdam, who was effective as the celebrated leader of humanism; there was Martin Luther, effective as the boasted hero of a faith movement that was proceeding in new directions. The period of the Enlightenment brought the second flowering of the importance of the writer; in this period the book again prepared great ideas concerning the matters and questions of life in forceful language; it brought the period of the classic writers, in which enormous poems in complete form went through the country.

The increased diffusion of the book transformed the relation also to the poets and of authors to the publisher, and basically to the book trade as a whole. The increased sales elevated the social status of intellectual creation and its self-awareness, increased the economic value of the achievement formulated in books, and it led to a new relationship of power as over against the world of the publisher. The interplay among literature, the world of readers and the book trade belongs to the most interesting inquiry of bibliography. The world of reading often comes off poorly in its considerations, and yet it is of decisive significance. The best fashioned, the clearest written, most beautifully printed, and most expediently distributed book has no great effective power if it be unwanted, or is not read. A corresponding economic situation, a greater market capacity for absorbing new materials, a quite positive cultural attitude on the part of the people – these are the indispensable conditions that are decisive concerning the increase, the flowering or decline in the world of books.

The eighteenth century shows that the German people, in spite of all the anguish of a difficult past, in spite of the political powerlessness of their own period, still had remained a civilized nation which was not only capable of producing classic writers (and composers) in poetry and music as its cultural leaders, but that it also possessed the power to appropriate to itself the great works of art, and to incorporate its everlasting cultural properties. Just as the inner values of these creations and the beauty of their language represent the actual essence of their worth, so are the receptive and inspired readers also still infinitely important as the heralds of these great cultural accomplishments, as their notary with letter and seal. Even so, the German people had never previously read so much as they did in the second half of the eighteenth century. The book trade had a good share in this transformation of the one-time cultural property into an everlasting educational possession for the German people. The publisher was cognizant of the time, as well as his function in it, and he offered his hand to the poet and the professional writer for common work in the service of the book. There arose the fruitful relations of friendship between Herder and Hartknoch in Riga, who has also been Kant's publisher, among Wieland, Schiller and Göschen in Leipzig, and among Schiller, Goethe and Cotta in Stuttgart.

The market's capacity to absorb new materials, and the literary needs of the German reader, were gradually increased sufficiently to be able to include even foreign intellectual properties, above all works in English.[10] Of the works most distributed at that time there should perhaps be mentioned: Jonathan Swift's (1676–1746) poetical satire, *Gulliver's Travels* (1726); the frequently translated poem, *The Seasons* (1730) of James Thomson (1700–1748), the poet of the British national anthem, *Rule Britannia;* and finally the novel, *The Vicar of Wakefield* (1766) by Oliver Goldsmith (1728–1774). They have all been translated into German several times.[11] Also Samuel Richardson (1689–1761), James Henry Lawrence (1713–1768), Edward Young (1683–1765),[12] Alexander Pope (1688–1744), Henry Fielding (1707–1754),[13] Lawrence Sterne (1713–1760), and Thomas Percy (1720–1811) have acquired numerous German readers. With his philosophical works, Anthony, Earl of Shaftsbury (1671–1713) has strongly influenced the arts education of Lessing, Herder, Goethe and Schiller; Adam Smith (1723–1790), the Scottish founder of modern national economy, with his work, *Inquiry into the Nature and Causes of the Wealth of Nations* (1776) has strongly influenced the German concept of the basic sources of national riches.

If the poetic art of the century gave the German people especially priceless gifts, still there flowed yet from other quarters further essential books in impressive number. Johann Joachim Winckelmann (1717–1768), the founder of the classic German prose, the inspired discoverer of Greek art, wrote his *Geschichte der Kunst des Altertums* ("History of the Art of Antiquity") in 1764; it had a deep effect on classicism. Johann Georg Sulzer (1720–1779) created in his *Allgemeine Theorie der Schönen Künste* ("General Theory of the Fine Arts") (1771–1774) the long-valued reference work for aesthetics. "This book," Gottfried Keller says in his *Grüner Heinrich* "must had had in its time an immense diffusion, for one finds it in almost all old bookcases, and it appears at all auctions and can be inexpensively purchased."

Immanuel Kant, (1724–1804), the perfecter and conqueror of the Enlightenment, published in 1781, in his work, *Die Kritik der reinen Vernunft* ("Critique of Pure Reason"), the first great philosophical work that was conceived and written down in the German language. Johann George Hamann (1730–1788), the passionate opponent of the Enlightenment, the prophet of *Sturm und Drang* ("Storm and Stress"), again put into his works the power of the soul, the miracle of feeling, and in poesie he saw the human race's mother tongue.[14] Justus Möser (1720–1794), the valiant champion of the German people who was highly treasured by Goethe, collected his contributions to the Osnabrück *Intelligenz-Blatt* under the title, *Patriotische Phantasien* ("Patriotic Fantasies"), and with them he essentially contributed to a heightened assessment of the German peasantry and of the peasants' customs.[15] One of the most famous book works of the period became Johann Kaspar Lavater's *Physiognomische Fragmente zur Beförderung der Menschenkenntnis und Menschenliebe* (1775–78) ("Physiognomic Fragments to Advancing Human Knowledge and Human Love"). Designed with 343 copper plates and 488 pictures within the text itself, this book monument, which attempts on the basis of one's appearance and shape of the head to determine the psychic characteristics of people, belongs among the period's most memorable publications, so far as the history of culture is concerned. It has brought the author into association with the most outstanding of his contemporaries, even with Goethe,[16] who is represented by several silhouettes.

Working successfully in educational ways were Johann Bernhard Basedow (1723–1796), the founder of the Philanthropine, who published in four volumes his much read *Elementarwerk* in 1774, with a view to reforming the German educational system; Heinrich Pestalozzi (1746–1827), who attempted to arouse spontaneity in children, in opposition to the dead, "mechanical" type of learning, and in this sense he wrote his successful books, *Lienhard und Gertrud* (1781–1785) and *Wie Gertrud ihre Kinder lehrt* (1801) ("How Gertrude Teaches Her Children"). Both educators have been powerful influences on Jean Jacques Rousseau (1712–1778), the great revolutionary and herald of a new human happiness, who made an assault on his entire age and in his upsetting books, *La nouvelle Héloise* (1759), *Emile* (1762) and *Contrat social* (1762) demanded that in place of empty reason there be a return to the condition of nature, with its originality of life and development, and the completing of natural tendencies toward the unfolding of a free personality — ideas and educational goals that became enormously influential also in Germany, and even had an effect on Kant, Goethe, Herder, Schiller, and Fichte. Rousseau's *Confessions,* the first self-description of the modern period based on philosophical foundations, has further been effective on the literary form of voluntary confession. "I begin," says Rousseau, "a project which up to now is without example and which will find no imitators: I want to show my fellows a man in his whole natural truth (dans toute la verité de la nature) and this man I shall be myself."[17]

Under the stimulation of the new educational teaching, the children's book came to be newly created for the first time. There appeared 1775–1782, in twenty-four volumes, a work that enjoyed a large distribution, *Der Kinderfreund* ("The Friend of Children") of Christian Felix Weisse (1726–1804), the poet of the familiar song, *Schön sind Rosen und Jasmin* ("Roses and Jasmine are beautiful").

There followed the same author's *Lieder für Kinder* (1779) ("Songs for children"), with the children's poem, *Kinder geht zur Biene hin* (1765) ("Children run to the Bee"), Basedow's *Kleines Buch für Kinder aller Stände* (1771) ("Little Book for Children of all Classes") and Rochow's *Bauernfreund* (1776) ("Peasants Friend"), with tales for children of the village. Most successful was Joachim

Heinrich Campe, active as a writer for young people and publisher of the *Kleine Kinderbibliothek* ("Little Library") with contributions by Hölty, Hagedorn, and Claudius.[18]

How fruitfully the idea of the Enlightenment has worked according to the most varied aspects can be seen from Rudolf Johannes Becker's *Not-Hilfsbüchlein für Bauersleute* ("Little Emergency Aid Book for Farming People"), which, as the house and family book of German farmers, was supposed to provide for "the most outstanding physical and spiritual needs of the country man and to advance his secular condition, as well as his sense of being content with God and the world." The work, which was published in 1788 by Göschen and provided with forty-nine woodcuts, became with one fell stroke one of the most widely read books in Germany; it was soon sold in 30,000 copies, and in 1791 had already appeared in eleven editions. It has certainly also been the cheapest book of the period. Authors and publishers learned from it that if good books come on the market, there are always readers for them. "Who could suspect, before the moralistic weeklies, how many people would read moralistic weeklies; who before Klopstock and Gellert could suspect how many people would read *Messias* and fables; and who before Becker's little emergency aid book could suspect what enormous sales such a work could have in the country?"[19]

Added to all the works mentioned were the old and new popular books, the robber novels, the Robinsonades, the almanacs and the calendars. Even they belong to the literature of a period and they stamp the cultural face of a people. "Goethe and Vulpius," says Gustav Roethe, "Faust and Rinaldo[20] have at the same time become favorites of the nation. The modish type should not be lacking within the total picture, beside the work that is individually significant. It is not only the moving and the moved that interest the historian, but also the hindering and that which is at rest."[21] With the rise of the educated classes, there now set in the "paper age," properly speaking, in which writing as well as reading increased, the reading societies[22] and the lending libraries were formed, and the book trade received an enormous impetus.

The scholarship of the century contributed the enormous works that even now arouse our admiration, the huge reference works of the most varied fields, and the large collections of sources for history and archeology. No history of the sciences, not even any survey of the most important scientific books, can be offered here. Only several references and names may serve to illustrate the kind and character of the scholarly publications of that period. There emerged the enormous collections of documents and laws by Johann Christian Lünig, among which was the *Deutsche-Reichs-Archiv* with twenty-four folio volumes (1713 to 1722), which contained all the imperial laws, final decrees of the *Reichstag*, peace settlements, alliances, and all kinds of documents in addition. We encounter there the *Allgemeine Gelehrten-Lexikon* ("General Scholarly Lexicon") of Christian Gottlieb Jöcher in four parts (1750/51) (it is still much used today), with the later continuations and supplements by Johann Christoph Adelung and Wilhelm Rotermund (1810–19), or Georg Christoph Hamberger's *Gelehrtes Teutschland* ("Scholarly Germany") in the fifth edition, with twenty-three volumes (1776–1806). There comes forward the *Oekonomisch-technologische Encyklopädie*, which was devoted to the applied sciences, and which the scholarly phsyician, Johann Georg Krünitz, has published since 1773 with seventy-eight volumes; it is an inexhaustible reference work that has eventually grown to 242 folio volumes. Of the various attempts at making known history sources we know of new editions of the older collections of Schard, Pistorius, Urstisius, Freher, and in addition, new projects such as the *Scriptores rerum Brunsvicensium* of Leibniz in three volumes (1707–1711), and further, the publications of Joh. Georg Eccard (1732), Joh. Burkhard Mencke (1728–1730), Johann Peter von Ludewig (1720–31), and Heinrich Christian Senckenberg (1734 to 1741). The attempts to make public the whole of the German history sources, such as those that Johann Christoph Gatterer, Johann Christoph Krause, and Johann von Müller embarked on, for the most part collapsed already in their beginning stages, and it was only in the nineteenth century (under the leadership of Baron vom Stein) that they materialized.

More successful at that time in publishing the historical sources relating to the German fatherland has been Italy, where Lodovico Antonio Muratori in the years 1725–1750 published in twenty-five volumes the medieval historiographers of the country *(Rerum Italicarum Scriptores ab anno 500 ad 1500)*, and therein published valuable reports on the use of manuscripts, a project that has become of far-reaching significance as well as inspiration for other countries.

Italy also gave to scholarship the significant dictionary of medieval Latin of Egidio Forcellini in four volumes *(Totius Latinitatis Lexicon,* 1771) and the voluminous Italian literary history of the Modena librarian, Girolamo Tiraboschi (1782). The copper engraver, Giovanni Battista Piranesi (1720–1778), devoted himself to the pictorial reproduction of what is left from ancient buildings, with his work in four volumes, *Le Antichità Romane,* and with the numerous (gradually becoming sixteen) volumes filled with leaves of copperplate engravings. His son, Francesco (1758–1810), had a further thirteen volumes follow them.

Of more special significance for the great common scholarly projects was the founding of the learned academies and societies, besides Berlin (1700) in Göttingen (1732), Munich (1759) and Mannheim (1763). In connection with these societies, a form of scholarly publishing that was independent of the book trade was constituted.

Friedrich August Wolf (1759–1824), the "greatest classical scholar of Europe" (Raumer) at that time, has renewed classical studies; above all, his *Prologomena* to Homer (1795) has become famous. The English philologist, Richard Bently (1682–1742), had enriched his discipline with a standard edition of Horace (1711).

As did historical research, so also did the German philology search for the sources of the past, in order especially to uncover medieval poetry. Christoph Heinrich Müller (1740–1807), from Zurich, who at that time was a teacher at the Joachimsthal Gymnasium at Berlin, published in 1784 a copious *Sammlung Deutscher Gedichte aus dem XII, XIII, und XIV. Jahrhundert* ("Collection of German poems from the XII, XIII, and XIV centuries"), with the Nibelungs, Veldeke's *Eneide,* Wolfram von Eschenbach's *Parzival,* Hartmann von Aue's *Armer Heinrich,*

Gottfried of Strasbourg's *Tristan,* Konrad Fleck's *Flor und Blanschflur,* Hartman's *Iwein,* Friedank's *Bescheidenheit* ("Modesty") and Conrad of Würzburg's *Trojanische Krieg* ("Trojan War") and distributed therewith an unknown wealth of medieval German poems; the great significance of this work cannot be diminished, even by Frederick the Great's disapproving judgment.

Holland has devoted an admirable monument of undaunted scholarly diligence to its great son, Erasmus of Rotterdam, through the edition (not even surpassed today) of the total works of the famous humanist, which the refugee from Geneva, Jean Leclerc (Johannes Clericus) offered the world in (1703–1716), in ten enormous folio volumes, together with the busy printer and publisher, Pieter van der Aa. The same book dealer about 1729 put on the market the pictorial and map work (provided with over three thousand engravings), *La Galérie agréable du Monde.*

Although the public research libraries were still leading a rather obscure existence, they were already willingly placing their book treasures at the disposal of serious enquirers who applied to them for the publishing of texts. When the learned Hellenist Johann Jakob Reiske was preparing in 1770 a critical edition of the Greek orators, Andreas Felix Oefele sent him from the Munich Library a Demosthenes manuscript, Lessing passed on to him a Helmstedt Aeschines codex, and the Augusburg Municipal Library offered him four further manuscripts. Reiske was also able to employ manuscripts from Munich, Augsburg and Wolfenbüttel for the edition of Libanius, the Greek sophist.

Of the century's ever more numerous journals with general content, the so-called moralistic weekly publications were of the greatest significance. They undertook the task of carrying the philosophical and scientific understandings of the period into a wider circle and, in the sense of the Enlightenment, of aiding in mankind's search for perfection and happiness.[23] In spite of an abundance of superficiality, they undoubtedly contributed effectively to the rise of a large educated class that became capable of participating in the coveted cultural progress of the period, as well as in the literary life. Its homeland is England, where the poet Joseph Addison (1672–1719) and the author, Richard Steele (1672–1729) were after 1706 publishing the journals, *The Tatler, The Spectator,* and *The Guardian,* and dealing there with all the questions of life in an entertaining and interesting form. The influence of these weekly publications surpassed all the previous effects of literature. The most varied imitations were being distributed in no time all over Europe. The moralistic weeklies practically became the authoritative literature of the period. In Germany, Johann Mattheson was publishing at Hamburg in 1713 the journal, *Der Vernüftler* ("The Reasoner"). To the most important further publications of this sort belonged *Der Patriot,* which was published in Hamburg 1724–1728, the *Discourse der Maler* ("Painters' Discourse) (1721–23),[24] which was edited by Johann Jakob Bodmer, and Johann Christoph Gottsched's journal, *Die vernünftigen Tadlerinnen (1725–26)* ("The Reasonable Female Critics"). Like the English models, the German imitations also aimed at a pleasing, stimulating manner of writing, and they successfully cultivated the essay, the presentation of something in a briefly concluded treatment. This stylistic carefulness was of the greatest profit for the development of the German language.

The evident progress was already recognized by contemporaries. Thus it says in the *Bairische Sammlungen und Auszüge zum Unterricht und Vergnügen* ("Bavarian Collections and Extracts for Instruction and Pleasure") of 1764: "We do not need to recall that nothing is more powerful for the stimulation and diffusion in a country of good taste in letters, but especially of elegant writing and linguistic art, than the scholarly journal. Experience has indeed verified this; is there anyone who is not aware that, since the Hamburg journal, *The Patriot,* has arisen and become a fecund father of the Bremen contribution, the *Maler* ("Painter"), the *Jüngling* ("Youth") and other excellent weekly and monthly publications, the German language has obtained the greatest part of its current beauty and sophisticated elegance? Even those do not err who ascribe the perfection of the English language—which now appears to have reached its zenith—to the moment when the famous *Spectator* came forward in England."

The number of the moral weekly publications swelled enormously. Gottsched's journal, *Das Neueste aus der anmutigen Gelehrsamkeit* ("The Most Recent Issues of the Attractive Scholarship") published in 1761 a *Verzeichnis der in deutscher Sprache herausgekommenen sittlichen Wochenschriften* ("List of the Moral Weekly Publications Issued in the German Language"), and for the period 1713–1761, it introduced no fewer than 178 titles. In all, there were over two hundred English and five hundred German moral weeklies. With their educational goal, they also appealed to the women's world, and attempted to introduce them to the new educated class. Gottsched, who wanted to win women not merely to poetry but also to scholarship, in his preface to the journal, *Die vernünftigen Tadlerinnen* ("The Reasonable Female Critics"), expressed as the goal of his project "to bring into the hands of the German women a sheet that would serve them as a pleasant entertainment, and yet in its content would be more useful and more instructive than the usual novels." Education and enlightenment were therefore intended also for the world of women, whose conquest was yet to become of the greatest significance for the increasing effectiveness of the book. With its increasing dilution and exhaustion, the moral weekly publication—like the entire literature of the Enlightenment—gradually suffered the loss of its significance, until finally frequently being jeered at, it was ripe for succumbing.

To the journal of the future there belonged poetry, literature, zeal for the beautiful, already also art.[25] It was also here again Gottsched who, with his witty and critical discussions concerning art and literature, showed the way, and with his *Beiträge zur critischen Historie der deutschen Sprache, Poesie und Beredsamkeit* (1732–1744) ("Contributions to a Critical History of the German Language, Poetry and Eloquence") created the first German literary sheet.

In the year 1744, there followed (edited by Karl Christian Gärtner) the significant *Neue Beiträge zum Vergnügen des Verstandes und Witzes* ("New Contributions to the Pleasure of Intelligence and Wit"); for the locale where it was published it was briefly referred to as "Bremer Beiträge." Here (in this journal) were published in the early part of 1748 the first cantos of Klopstock's *Messias;* it is the earliest example of the very close connection of the German poetry with the journal format, which was to follow. The further development of the critical literary journal is chiefly associated with the bookdealer and writer, Christoph Friedrich Nicolai, who, with Lessing, first published the *Bibliothek der schönen Wissenschaften und der freien Künste* (1757–1760) ("Library of the Belles-Lettres and the Liberal Arts"), and since January 1759, the *Briefe, die neueste Literatur betreffend* ("Letters Concerning the Most Recent Literature"), and then, especially since 1765, the *Allgemeine deutsche Bibliothek* ("General German Library"), one of the most outstanding journals of that time; it held forth until 1800, and reached 208 volumes. Great significance was also achieved by Wieland's *Deutscher Merkur* (1773–1810) ("German Mercury"), in which the poet's *Abderiten* and *Oberon,* and further *Die Götter Griechenlands* ("Gods of Greece") and *Die Künste* ("The Arts") of Schiller, and also Goethe's *Aufsätze* ("Notes") were published. Attempts by Schiller and Goethe in the *Horen*[26] and *Propylaen* to lead their contemporaries out of the troubled political depths to pinnacles of truth and beauty, so as to allow them to forget the ugly present, failed. Both the journals again quickly went under. Germany at that time would have needed other challenges; but these remained denied to both of the great poets, who perceived German nature too exclusively in terms of the refined personality and the cultural character of the nation.

As a certain species of the journal, the annually-appearing almanac,[27] the pocketbook, and the yearbook have established themselves. Initially utilized by Perthes in 1763 in his genealogical calendar,[28] this interesting publication format, which was closely connected with the calendar, has quickly taken hold of a wide subject area, especially poetry, history and the general entertainment. Among the historical almanacs, the most famous is the *Historische Calender für Damen* ("Historical Calendar for Ladies"), which since 1790 has been issued by Göschen with engravings; it was edited by Archenholz and Wieland.[29] Seven thousand copies of it were sold in the shortest time. Schiller's *Geschichte des Dreißigjährigen Krieges* ("History of the Thirty Years' War") began to appear in its second annual volume. Wieland inaugurated the third volume with a significant patriotic preface.

The almanac of Muses devoted itself to the actual belles-lettres literature, especially poetry.[30] Following the example of the almanac of Muses, which since 1765 was published at Paris by Delalain, Heinrich Christian Boie published in Göttingen after 1770 the Göttingen Muses' almanac, which through light societal pieces was supposed to awaken devotion to the Muses even in remote areas and to provide opportunity to young poets to make themselves known, besides accepting good old ones of an entertaining and pleasing character.[31] With its valuable contributions, the project has become part of the history of German literature.

Hölty, Claudius, Voss, Friedrich Leopold, Count zu Stolberg, and Bürger have published songs here; Gluck and Philipp Emanuel Bach have contributed compositions. Voss had the leadership from the third year onward. Of no less significance has been Schiller's *Muses' Almanac* (1797–1800),[32] which was published by Cotta in Tübingen. Goethe, Herder, Hölderlin, Kosegarten, Langbein, Mattissan, Pfeffel, the two Schlegels and Tieck, were collaborators in it, and its contents included important first editions: in 1798 there appeared there the ballads of Goethe: *Die Braut von Korinth* ("The Bride of Corinth"), *Der Gott und die Bajadere* ("God and the

Bayadere"), *Der Zauberlehrling* ("The Magician's Apprentice"); by Schiller, *Der Taucher* ("The Diver"), *Der Ring des Polykrates* ("The Ring of Polycrate"), *Die Kraniche des Ibikus* ("The Cranes of Ibicus"); in 1799, there followed Goethe's metamorphosis of plants, Schiller's *Bürgschaft* and the *Fight with the Dragon;* in 1800, Schiller's *Song of the Bell.* Goethe wrote about the significance that Schiller's Muses' almanac had had for him on January 11, 1829 to Friedrich L. Schultz: "I do not really know what would have become of me without the Schiller stimulations. If he had not needed the manuscripts for the *Horen* and the Muses' almanacs, I would not have written the *Unterhaltungen der Ausgewanderten* ("Conversations of the Emigrants"), I would not have translated Cellini, I would not have authored the collected ballads and songs, as the Muses' almanac printed them; the elegies would not at least have been printed at that time, the *Xenien* would not have hummed and in general, as well as in special aspects, many things certainly would have remained different."

Mostly decorated with small ornamental copper engravings, and covered in pleasing jackets, the almanac represented a pretty type of the book of the Rococo period, which was affectionately and infinitely cared for, and that affords nice insights into the formation of taste in the society of that period. Added to that is its frequently rather considerable intellectual content, which with its numerous first editions of the more significant poems elevates it into a valuable source for the history of literature.

About the turn of the new century, the Muses' almanac succumbed to inner exhaustion, until it again gained a fresh vitality in the period of the Romantics.

A cultural movement such as the Enlightenment, which summoned the entire existing world to the sharpest feuding, could not maintain itself otherwise than in embittered struggles against the persisting powers. Even the world of books of the Enlightenment encountered on all sides a warding off and persecution. In Austria and Bavaria several lists of forbidden works were issued. Thus there appeared in 1770 in Munich the *Catalogus verschiedener Bücher, so von dem Churfürstl. Büchercensur-Collegio teils als religionswidrig, teils als den guten Sitten, teils auch als den landesfürstlichen Gerechtsamen nachteilig verboten werden* ("Catalog of various books that are forbidden by the Electoral Collegium-censor of books, partly as being religiously adverse, partly as being injurious to good morals, and in part as being also damaging to the princely privileges"). The catalog mentioned as being among the outlawed works, publications by Rousseau, Bayle, Lamettrie, Jakob Böhme, and Voltaire.

In a further *Katalog der von dem kurfürstl. Bücher-Censur-Kollegium in Müchen 1790–1792 verbotenen Bücher* ("Catalog of the Electoral Book Censor-Collegium in Munich 1790–1792 of forbidden books"), practically everything is rejected that is even distantly reminiscent in a slight degree of the Enlightenment; mentioned are by name, Montesquieu, Rousseau, Voltaire, Spinoza, Kant, Herder's *Briefe zur Beförderung der Humanität* ("Letters for Promoting Humanity"), Friederich the Great, Knigge's *Briefe* ("Letters") and *Über den Umgang mit Menschen* ("Concerning Relations with People"), Rochow's *Kinderfreund* ("Friend of Children"), Kotzebue, Swift, Goethe's *Leiden des jungen Werther* ("Sufferings of the Young

Werther"), *Schiller,* the folk tales of Musäus, Ovid's *Metamorphosis* and Vergil's *Aeneid.* [33]

One has already reflected much over how periods are to be explained that are especially richly blessed by human genius, such as the Periclean Age, the Augustan Age, the Renaissance flowering with Leonardo da Vinci, Raffael and Michaelangelo, and the Goethe period. Indeed, even certain years appear to be especially favored. With justification, Richard Benz, for example, mentions 1762 as having been extraordinarily favored: One must know that in the year of Gluck's *Orpheus,* the first German translation of Shakespeare also appeared, and the first translations of Homer and the Songs of Ossian enchanted mankind; at the same time, Winckelmann discovered and revealed the pure Greek art, the noble simplicity and the quiet greatness of antiquity. The year 1781 was a similarly memorable one: "The year of Lessing's death, at the same time the year in which Kant's *Kritik der reinen Vernunft* ("Critique of Pure Reason"), Schiller's *Räuber* ("Robbers"), Pestalozzi's *Lienhard und Gertrud,* and Johann Heinrich Voss' *Odyssey* translation appeared." (Friedrich Paulsen). We do well to receive gratefully such mature harvesting periods (in Goethe's sense), and to honor them. If there be such a time, the second half of the eighteenth century belongs very definitely to the blessed times. The book also had fortunate days here, and it has contributed quite essentially to the period's cultural growth.

28

Book Design, the Market for Books and Bibliography in the German Classic Period

France, the home of the *Imprimerie Royale* in Paris, of the famous printing house of Didot,[1] and of the gracefully decorated Rococo book, has attained the leadership in the designing of the eighteenth century book.

Among the printed works of the *Imprimerie Royale* (since the outbreak of the French Revolution called "Imprimerie de la République") especially deserving of mention is the *Histoire naturelle générale et particulière* of the natural scientist, Georg Louis Leclerc Buffon (1707–1788); it was a work that penetrated deeply into cultural life. It appeared in thirty-six volumes between 1749–1788, and it had a large circle of readers, especially among the prominent. France's most famous printer became Françoise Ambroise Didot (1730 to 1804), who successfully devoted himself to typecutting and produced splendid antiqua types that aroused admiration generally. Printed works such as des Lognus' *Pastoralia de Daphnide et Chloe* of 1778, or Torquato Tasso's *Gerusalemme Liberata* of 1782 are among the most handsome typographical achievements of the period. His son, Pierre Didot l'Aîné, produced the so-called Louvre editions, among which was Racine in three volumes between 1801 and 1805; ajudicators declared it to be the most consummate creation of all times. The favorite book of the overly-refined culture of France became the Rococo book; it was richly decorated with full-length pictures and ornaments of all kinds (especially with head vignettes and colophous) and it was charmingly bound; with these books, design was everything and the content was of little significance.

There were mainly editions of the life-affirming classical authors of antiquity and of the more recent period: Horace, Ovid, Theocrites, Anacreon, Catullus, Vergil, Longus, Boccaccio, Ariosto, Tasso, Lafontaine, Molière, Corneille, and Fénelon, all of them poets who glorified the cheerful art and the love of life. They stood in the foreground of this light-hearted literature. The title page is richly encircled by flowers and wreaths; figures of children and little amoretti bustle about among them. Among the most outstanding books of this sort are: the splendid edition of Molière's works of 1734, in six volumes, with over two hundred vignettes and the famous thirty-three full-length pictures of the adroit artist of form, François

Boucher, or Boccaccio's *Decameron* of 1757, with its graphic contributions by Boucher, Cochin, Eisen, and Gravelot; also Ovid's *Metamorphoses* of 1767, in which a whole host of artists have collaborated, and not least, the Molière edition of 1773, which was Moreau's chief graphic work.

As compared with the splendid French books of the Rococo period, the contemporary German literature (which, in relation to its content, was in full flower) goes along only very scantily clothed.[2] There were certainly skillful book artists also in Germany who knew how to sprinkle books successfully with little pictures and ornaments. Georg Friedrich Schmidt (1712–1725) designed Frederick the Great's poem, *Palladion*, (1749) which was produced in the castle (au donjon du chateau) at Berlin in twenty-four copies and today is preserved only in a single copy in the Hohenzollern Museum at Berlin, and likewise in 1751 the king's *Brandenburgische Memoiren* ("Mémoires pour servir à l'histoire de la maison de Brandenbourg") which was rich with pictures and small decorative items; beside their French prototypes, these stand up well. The artist, Adam Friedrich Oeser (1717–1799) in Leipzig, who made friends with Winckelmann, was chiefly active in the service of the publisher, Philip Erasmus Reich;[3] Oeser decorated Gellert's collected works, Moritz August Thümmel's *Wilhelmine* (1766) and Wieland's *Grazien* (1770) ("Graces") with vignettes. The etcher, Johann Wilhelm Meil (1732–1805), contributed pictures and decorative pieces in the service of the publishers, Nicolai and Voss, to Lessing's *Writings* (1753) and to the *Hamburgische Dramaturgie*, ("Hamburg dramaturgy"), to Kleist's *Poems* (1756), Ramler's lyrical anthology (1774), Goethe's *Schriften* ("Works") of 1775 and Göschen's edition of 1787.[4]

Daniel Chodowiecki (1726–1804),[5] the most significant book artist of his time and the most successful illustrator of the German classics, decorated Lessing's *Minna von Barnhelm* in the Berlin *Genealogische Kalender* for 1770, Friedrich Nicolai's novel, *Das Leben und die Meinungen des Herrn Magister Sebaldus Nothanker* ("The Life and Opinions of Master Sebaldus Nothanker") (1773–1776) Gellert's *Fabeln* ("Fables") (1775), Hippel's *Lebensläufe nach aufsteigender Linie* ("Life's Progressive Ascent") (1778–81), Goethe's *Hermann und Dorothea* in a pocketbook for women of 1798, and numerous other works and alamancs with fine little pictures. These were his strongest points and they impressively reproduced the German life of the time, the German bourgeoisie, and family life; at the artist's death, Gleim could say without exaggeration: "Chodowiecki was!/ He was! If he hadn't been/ So indeed a host of books/ would have remained unread." Bürger, Campe, Gleim, Goethe, Hölty, Klopstock, Kotzebue, Iffland, Lavater, Lichtenberg, Matthisson, Nicolai, Pestalozzi, Pfeffel, Schiller, Stolberg, Voss and Wieland have been illustrated by him.

One of the most priceless little pictures is the vignette to *Wether's Leiden* ("Werther's Suffering"): Lotte is in ball dress, as she slices bread for the children standing around her. Quite captivating also are the copperplates to the *Elementarwerk* ("Elementary Outline") of Basedow, for instance a musical society (Illustration in Lützow p. 263). Salomon Gessner (1730–1788), the kindly Zurich poet and painter, master of the poetic idyll and of landscape painting, primarily did the layout for his own works. He was especially effective in the quarto edition of

1772–78, with its shepherds, nymphs, puttos, flowers, and garlands, but also in the editions of Wieland's *Schriften* ("Works") and with Eschenburg's translation of Shakespeare of 1775, with its exciting vignettes which August Wilhem Schlegel praised, commenting that "each little figure lives and his character is made known." Egid Verhelst (1742–1818) finally beautified (among other things) Desbillon's translation of Aesop's fables quite in the spirit of the French rococo; in Müller's *Adams erstes Erwachen* (1778) ("Adam's First Awakening"), however, as well as in Matthisson's *Gedichte* ("Poems") (1781), he was able to put his own stamp on his work. But the total picture of German book design is rather modest, in spite of such artistic collaboration, and it manifests little homogeneous book art.

The publications of the classic period inform us in several ways concerning their former fortunes. When Gellert offered his *Fabeln und Erzählungen* ("Fables and Tales") to the publisher Breitkopf, he got a refusal. Johann Wendler, who took over the book in 1746 and embellished it with copperplate engravings by Johan Heinrich Meil, became a rich man and the work itself was soon translated into almost all the European languages.

Gottfried August Bürger's *Gedichte* ("Poems"), which were published in Göttingen by Johann Christian Dieterich in 1778 and 1789, has been decorated with a handsome title page and with two full-page illustrations by Johann Wilhelm Meil, as well as with the poet's portrait and illustrations by Chodowiecki; among the latter is a representation of *Lied vom braven Mann* ("Song of a Good Man"), which was printed on bad paper and has thereby lost a great deal in comeliness. In a foreword, the poet rails sharply against the reproducer and against the purchasers of such fraudulent works, for whom it is a matter of gaining a half or a whole florin. "Such a profit is indeed worth honoring and blessing in gratitude to the national benefactors, Schmieder[6] and their consorts. Amen."

Klopstock's *Messias,* the earliest of the chief works of classical literature, has appeared with the first cantos in 1748 in the *Bremer Beiträge* ("Bremer Contributions") and was issued in book format in 1751 by Carl Herrmann Hemmerde[7] at Halle, so as from there to spread the poet's fame speedily throughout the whole world. When the *Messias* (also in the large complete edition by Göschen) had appeared, the poet (who once had been a pupil at Schulpforta) on March 20, 1800, sent the beautiful volume to the rector there, Karl Wilhelm Ernest Heimbach, with the proposal that the most qualified student should place it in the library, and when opportunity came, to have placed on the grave of the co-rector, Stübel (the favorite among his former teachers), flowers, or young branches, or buds, or something such as the spring first produced. It was a high festival day in Schulpforta when the wishes of the poet were carried out. On Easter Day flowers were placed first on the grave of the teacher, amid song and the recitation of an ode. The teachers and pupils then marched into the library. Accompanied by music, two pupils carried the book, which was lying on a white silk cushion, decorated with young green foliage from the woods, and in the library they placed it on an altar that had been built for it, which was itself bedecked with white silk, garlanded with the green branches from the fir tree, and had flowers strewn in front of it. On the *Messias* an olive branch was placed. A speech by the rector concluded the celebration.[8]

Wieland, the poet of the cheerful and sensual art of living, who himself put great store by the good designing of books and who owned an exquisite library of four thousand volumes,[9] generally speaking was lucky and successful with the publishing of his books (which were gladly read). Closely connected with them are three publishers: the House of Orell, Gessner and Company in Zurich, to whom the poet Salomon Gessner also belonged and whose son, Heinrich, was later married to Wieland's daughter, Lotte; then, Weidmann and Reich in Leipzig, and finally, Georg Joachim Göschen, in Leipzig and Grimma. Wieland's chief works have been published by the heirs of Weidmann and Reich, among which was also the *Agathon* of 1773, with four full-page illustrations and four vignettes of children by Meil. In the epilogue, the poet expressed his joy over the many orders submitted prior to the work's publication: "Such a large number of the most honorable and noble names in our nation, which can be seen in the following list, cannot but be the most fortunate omen for the German Muses." Proud names are in fact in the list; besides numerous German princes, there are Herr Gottfried August Bürger, the chief magistrate of the court of Altengleichen, Herr Salomon Gessner, the senator in Zurich, the consistorial counsel, Herr Herder in Bückeburg, and Herr Dr. Goethe in Frankfurt am Main.

Weiland's *Musarion* appeared in 1769 on Dutch paper with a small vignette. There followed immediately two daring unauthorized reprints on bad paper, together with the poet's original preface, in which it is stated that the publisher had acquired a good Dutch paper for the publication. Of the nice little volumes, *Die Grazien* ("The Graces"), which contained a charming title page of Oeser, six full-page illustrations and eight decorative pieces, the Freiburg co-rector opined, with a sigh, concerning the text's small composition, "that it is as if one were to eat soup with a coffee spoon." Wieland's third publisher, Göschen, who had set for himself the goal of offering all the great German poets in splendid editions, as well as in inexpensive printings, between 1787–1802 issued Wieland's *Schriften* ("Works") in thirty-six volumes, and four supplements in four different formats: a costly quarto edition on vellum paper, with copperplate engravings by Ramberg,[10] Schnorr and Füger in 350 copies at the cost of 250 thalers, a large cotavo edition of the same design in five hundred copies for 125 thalers, a further format with only occasional pictures for 112 thalers, and a small octavo edition on ordinary paper and without the pictures for 27 thalers. When the poet came to Leipzig in July, 1794, a festive reception was waiting for him there in Göschen's garden. In a small temple stood Wieland's bust; two boys clothed in the Greek style brought forward the first volume of the deluxe edition in a Greek carriage, and a tender hand pressed the laurel wreath onto the poet's head.

The preparations of the pictures for the edition have been the source of much irritation for the poet. Thus on February 7, 1797, Wieland wrote indignantly to Göschen about his own portrait, which had been designed by Anton Graff and engraved by Johann Friedrich Bause: "About the sample of the Bauseian concoction—what should I, or can I, say about it other than that I am shocked by it. I should have thought that I was (as I am) already ugly enough, and Herr Bause would not have found it necessary to create such a caricature of me! Whoever sees it, crosses and blesses himself. What simpleton's eyes! What a nose! What satyr-like twisted mouth, everyone says, and there is general agreement about it." Wieland was quite disappointed about the small number of orders for the expensive deluxe editions. He wrote the publisher on July 15, 1799, "Only several days ago the King of Prussia has paid me a rather large compliment, to the effect that the deluxe edition of my work would redound to the great glory of the German nation; but on account of this temporal glory there is scarcely one among twenty of his rich Sileisan noblemen who has purchased a copy of this priceless edition." The Latin type has also hurt sales; men and women from all classes had explained to him that they preferred the German letters. In spite of these disappointments, the completed project was a great event in the life of the book at that time, and a German deed that could gloriously prevail even in the face of foreign scrutiny.[11]

Göschen also became the publisher of the first complete edition of Goethe's works. It was a proud announcement at the Easter Fair of 1787 when the enterprising bookdealer could introduce Klopstock, Lessing, Wieland, Goethe and Schiller in his publisher's list. The edition of Goethe (which included the first independent printings of the poet's chief works, *Egmont, Faust, Iphigenie,* and *Tasso*) Göschen brought on the market in the years 1787 to 1790 with eleven pictures, with eight title vignettes, and two decorative pieces. When Göschen refused to publish Goethe's *Metamorphose der Pflanzen* ("Metamorphosis of Plants"), the upset poet severed the relationship. Goethe's *Neue Schriften* ("New Works") were issued between 1792 and 1800 in seven volumes by Johann Friedrich Unger in Berlin and they excited the greatest delight his mother, who wrote to her son on June 15, 1794: "Herr Unger deserves praise and commendation on account of the beautiful paper and for the letters, which are unsurpassable. I am glad about all that you express, and that your publications, both old and new, have seen the light of the world not with the Latin types, which are so disagreeable to me; with the "Roman carnival" they may be all right, but for the rest, I beg you, remain German, even in the types."

Goethe's works in thirteen volumes followed, published between 1806 and 1810 by Johann Friedrich Cotta in Tübingen, with whom the poet always remained associated, despite the fact that ill humor was also not entirely lacking in this relationship.[12]

With the departing century, the exterior of the book was noticeably altered. Book design becomes simpler, the ornamentalism of the Baroque period disappears just as does the Rococo book's overladen fullness of decoration. Even the title page becomes more austere in composition and calmer in its typographical design. Schiller wrote in 1794 to his publisher, Cotta: "We want to guard against everything that is embellishment and clutter, and to me embellishment means everything in a book which is not letter or punctuation." In the same trend towards simple and clear typographic forms, there was again a tendency toward the use of the Antiqua. Even the belles-lettres were also here and there printed with Latin types; Gleim, Kleist, Bodmer, Gessner, Ramler, and the editions of classical writers, all of them published by Göschen, came out in such garb. But because the readers reacted negatively against these editions, and the German printed script found warm defenders in Breitkopf and Unger, the old relationship of the two scripts ("Scholarship in Antiqua, poetry and popular literature in Fraktur") was soon established again.

The German book trade of the Enlightenment period[13] successfully advanced with the enormous rise in German publications. At first, in the beginning of the eighteenth century, literature in the German language (which was dominated by theology) advanced farther. And already becoming prevalent were the areas of history and geography, the biographies, the Robinsonades, and also the translations (mostly from the French), and further, the lexicons and encyclopedias. The international scholarly literature in Latin visibly retreated, and with it, the Frankfurt Fair, which disappeared completely with its Easter listing of 1750.[14] The progress of the book trade advanced further through the improved means of making new publications known, and in the facilitating of literary communication.

Author and publisher attempted to represent the immeasurably increased knowledge in alphabetically arranged subject compendia. The "lexicon" quickly grew into a new form of the book that was much fostered.

Above all, the Leipzig publisher, Johann Friedrich Gleditsch, distinguished himself by publishing several great reference works. The one that had the greatest distribution was Johann Hübner's *Reales Staats-Zeitungs-und Conversations-Lexikon* (1704) which he brought out until 1728 in thirty-one editions. The largest undertaking of this kind was the one made by the publisher, Johann Heinrich Zedler, and entitled *Grosses vollständiges Universal-Lexikon aller Wissenschaften und Künste, welche bisher durch menschlichen Verstand und Witz erfunden und verbessert worden* ("Great Complete Universal Lexicon of all the Sciences and Arts, that Previously Have been Devised and Improved by Human Intellect and Wit"). Directed by the chancellor of the University of Halle, Johann Peter Ludewig, the work was published between 1732 and 1750 in sixty-four folio volumes; four supplementary volumes were issued between 1751 and 1754.[15] Even before the work came out, one could read in the *Charlatanerie der Buchhandlung* (1732): "If this lexicon should materialize, only the fewest would purchase other books, but would want to be instructed by this single lexicon." In order to obtain the funds for completing the first twelve volumes, and to continue the enormous project, the resourceful Leipzig publisher arranged for a book lottery, which was the first German one of this sort, and, despite the objections of the book dealers, he carried through with it, meanwhile issuing two thousand lots at 2.5 thalers for books 10,000 thalers; although most of the winners chiefly got less valuable goods, still some received valuable and voluminous works.

The directory to the books became ever more voluminous. The Leipzig publisher, Theophil Georgi, published in 1742 his *Allgemeines europäisches Bücherlexikon* ("General European Book Lexicon"); it was the most important list of books for the literature of its period and of the seventeenth century. This was followed in 1793 by the *Allgemeine Bücherlexicon* of Johann Wilhelm Heinsius; it attempted to list all the books of the years 1700 to 1793 with statements of their printing locale, the publisher and price. At completion, all these surveys were surpassed by the *Verzeichnis neuer Bücher* ("List of New Books"), which Johan Conrad

Hinrichs issued in 1798, with the list of the books appearing in 1797 to 1798—a work that from then on became the leader in the trade bibliography.

The century closed with an enormous rise in book production, especially in entertainment literature and in the journals. The boundaries of the scholarly and the popular literature gradually shifted as the circle of readers became broader. Publications for practical life increased in range also. The Enlightenment has not recruited in vain. The literature of the Enlightenment and the great German poets elevated the book trade immensely. Enterprising publishers were associated with the successful poets and authors in successes that up to that time had not been experienced.

This was especially the case with Philipp Erasmus Reich (1717–1787), Gellert's and Wieland's publisher, to whom Wieland once wrote: "Ducats and Louis d'or I find for my work, if need be, with others; but a heart such as yours one rarely finds in this world;"[16] Johann Gottlob Immanuel Breitkopf (1719–1794), the successful renewer of printing, of the printing of notes and of the music trade, who was influential also as the defender and the improver of the German Fraktur script which he sought to rid of needless embellishment, and which he used, changed into such a simplified form for the first time in Jean Paul's *Palingenesien* (Jean Paul type);[17] Johann Friedrich von Cotta (1764–1832) in Tübingen and Stuttgart, the prince of German bookdealers, the friend of Schiller and Goethe, the founder of the *Allgemeine Zeitung* ("General Newspaper"), and the energetic publisher who has again elevated the South German territories into a leading position in the book trade. His correspondence, which shows him as having been associated with Schiller, Goethe, Hölderlin, Lichtenberg, Wieland, Fichte, Schelling, Tieck, the brothers Schlegel, Madame de Stael, Zacharias Werner, Kleist, Jean Paul, Justinus Kerner, Rückert, Uhland, Fouqué, Schwab, Hauff and other significant contemporaries, belongs among the most important witnesses of cultural history in the classical period.[18] As if symbolically to bring all this to a conclusion, Goethe and Cotta have died in the same year.[19] To be mentioned among the leading personalities of the book trade in the classical period is finally, Georg Joachim Göschen (1752–1828), whose aforementioned significant publishing activity embraced such projects as Schiller's *Don Carlos* (1787), Goethe's *Schriften* ("Writings") in eight volumes (1787–1790), Wieland's collected works in thirty-six volumes (1794–1801), and Klopstock's works in six volumes (1798–1799); with these, Göschen has presented to the German people the first complete editions of our great poets in a worthy format.[20]

They were proud figures, these daring and successful publishers of the period around the turn of the new century; they were men who had the highest consciousness of their responsibility to their profession and who felt themselves to be the indispensable trustees of literary life, the mediators between the cultural creations and those who culturally were the receivers; they were Gutenberg's high-minded pupils and disciples who now were harvesting the ripe fruit of the great German discovery. "At no time had the art of printing been called on to communicate such a fullness of the noblest cultural treasures to the people as in the age of Lessing, Goethe, and Schiller." (Köster)

The rise of Berlin as a publishing and book trade city belongs among the most noteworthy phenomena of the book trade in this period. Here in 1723, Ambrosius Haude took over the Papen book dealership and secretly provided Crown Prince Friedrick, the later King Frederick the Great, with classic and French literature. When King Friedrich William I discovered his son's books stacked in papered-over cupboards, he took them away and had them sold. Haude again bought them, however, and gave them back to the crown prince. Karl von Holtei with amusing verses celebrated in song the secret agreement between the two.[21]

Also working in Berlin were: Christoph Friedrich Nicolai (1733–1811) (with the Frankfurt publisher, Wilhelm Fleischer, he was one of the most spirited bookdealers of the Enlightenment),[22] who with his *Allgemeine deutsche Bibliothek* ("General German Library") (1765–1806), which ultimately comprised 208 volumes, constituted one of the recognized centers of literary criticism, and as a poet then wrote the novel (which was then much read and was translated several times), *Das Leben und die Meinungen des Herrn Magister Sebaldus Nothanker* (1773–1778) ("The Life and Opinions of Magister Sebaldus Nothanker");[23] it is a good portrayal of the Enlightenment period; further, Christian Friedrich Voss, who published the several writings of Lessing and the posthumous works of Frederick the Great, who brought several pocket books on the market with copperplate engravings by Chodowiecki and the *Geschichte des Siebenjährigen Krieges* (("History of the Seven years' War") of Johann Wilhelm, Baron von Archenholz; Georg Jakob Decker (1732–1799), who published works by Iffland, Jung-Stilling, Lavater and Pestalozzi, and set up a printery in the royal castle, where between 1782 and 1789 he printed the works of Frederick the Great in German translation; and finally, Johann Friedrich Unger (1753–1804), the creator of the simplified Fraktur that was called after him, and the restorer of the art of woodcut, who with Cotta and Göschen was the main publisher of the German classic authors of Goethe's *Wilhelm Meisters Lehrjahre* ("William Meister's Apprenticeship Years") and the *Neue Schriften* ("New Writings") (1792–1800), and who likewise brought into the trade Schiller's *Jungfrau von Orleans* ("Virgin of Orleans") (1808), Schleiermacher's *Reden über die Religion* ("Discourses on Religion") (1799), August Wilhelm Schlegel's translation of Shakespeare, Ludwig Tieck's Cervantes translation, Wackenrode's *Herzensergiessungen eines kunstliebenden Klosterbruders* (1797) ("Outpourings of an art loving monk"), with its artistic and religious desire for the related artistic sensbility of the past.[24] Wackenröder's book is, according to a word of the poetess, Ricarda Huch, like one that "has lain in a church long, long years, a psalter with gold and flaming ornaments between the mystical songs that is sweet through and through from the incense that constantly has clouded around it."

We encounter a delightful personality in the Königsberg bookdealer, Johann Jakob Kanter (1738–1786). He was a friend of Hamann's; Immanuel Kant lived with him in the years 1766–1769, and he counted Herder among his frequent visitors. One can perhaps apply to him the nice portrayal that Gustav Freytag, in his *Bilder aus der deutschen Vergangenheit* ("Pictures from the German Past"), gives of the relationship of the booktrade to its customers in that period.[25]

The orphanage in Halle, and the printery associated with it, took on a special significance; it had arisen from Francke's foundation, and in connection with the

Canstein Bible Institute, it had the task of making Luther's improved Bible translation into an inexpensive popular book for Evangelical Germany. Carl Hildebrand, Baron von Canstein (1667–1719), contributed essentially to the work's success. When Canstein died, there were twenty editions of the New Testament, with 100,000 copies, and 40,000 copies of the whole Bible, in type; yet the success of the establishment had only begun; in the years 1712–1739, it disseminated 340,000 copies of the New Testament and 480,000 copies of the entire Bible.

Nuremberg maintained itself at a remarkable peak, with the art dealer, Christoph Weigel, whose chief work, the *Abbildung der Gemein-Nützlichen Haupt-Stände* ("Portrait of the Publicly Beneficial Main Professions") of 1698, which represented with 277 plates the various craftsmen at their work, is of great value for cultural history; also, with the publisher, Johann Baptist Homann (1664–1724), who with the cooperation of the geographers, Gabriel Doppelmayer in Nuremberg and Johann Hübner in Hamburg, published significant atlases, and who was able to state with pride in his *Atlas von hundert Charten* ("Atlas of a Hundred Maps"): "Before me, in my most highly prized German fatherland, no one has yet had the good fortune of bringing to light such a complete geographical work;"[26]also, with Johann Jakob Wollrab, who in 1716 brought on the market the great work of engraving by the Italian, Gregorio Lambranzi, *Nuova e curiosa de Balli Theatrali* ("New and Curious Theatrical Dance School"), which illustrates the dances of the various peoples and additionally gives the corresponding melodies, and published with Nikolaus Raspe the great pictorial works, the conchylian cabinet of Martini and Chemnitz (1769–1795), with eleven quarto volumes and 406 plates painted true to nature, and the work of Linné, with twenty-seven large octavo volumes which were rich with copperplate engravings, and Johannes Siebmacher's book of arms (1772–1788), with 1,556 plates.

In Augsburg, successful copper engraving workshops continued that city's tradition of producing great works of plates;[27] thus Johann Jakob Haid, the painter, the etcher and publisher, brought on the market Jakob Brucker's *Bilder-Saal heitiges Tages lebender und durch Gelahrtheit berühmter Schriftsteller* (1741–1755) ("Picture Gallery of Today's Living Authors Famous for Their learning"), with a hundred portraits, in which the subject represented appears more often than not with a book in his hand; and the same author's *Ehren-Tempel der Deutschen Gelehrsambeit aus dem XV, XVI, und XVII. Jahrhunderte* (1747) ("Temple of Honor of German Scholarliness form the Fifteenth, Sixteenth and Seventeenth Centuries") with fifty portraits; and then Augsburg's best known engraver, Johann Elias Riedinger (1695–1767), who has acquired great fame especially through his popular animal and hunting series,[28] and has published the *Betrachtung der wilden Tiere* ("Consideration of Wild Animals" of 1736, with verses by Barthold Heinrich Brocke, in which the cooperation of the two is announced with the strophe:

> Wir beschreiben alle beyde
> Gott zur Ehr und uns zur Freude
> Das so schöne Welt-Gebäude,
> Ich mit Tinte, Du mit Kreide

We both of us describe everything
For God's glory and our joy
The world edifice so beautiful,
I with ink, you with chalk.

Working successfully in the book trade in Vienna were Johann Thomas, Baronet von Trattner (1748–1798), the most famous and notorious reprinter of the German classic authors; Joseph Lorenz von Kurzböck (1736–1792), the Illyric-Oriental court printer and esteemed publisher of the *Weisskunig* (1775); Leopold Johann Kaliwoda (1705–1781), who published the large deluxe works of Nikolaus von Jacquin *Hortus botanicus Vindobonensis* in three folio volumes with three hundred plate engravings and the same author's *Flores Austriacae* in five folio volumes with five hundred color plates, and further, Marquard Herrgott's *Monumenta Augustae Domus Austriacae* of 1750 with 314 plates by Salomon Kleiner.

The little town of Kehl, opposite Strasbourg, has become especially noteworthy as a printing locale through the Parisian printer, Pierre Augustine Beaumarchais. In 1785 he had produced there at great expense a deluxe edition for which he could not obtain authorization in Paris; he used types purchased from John Baskerville, the English printer.[29]

Deserving of brief mention also are the excellent editions of the classical writers, which have been issued by a society of scholars since 1780 in Zweibrücken, with vignettes by Verhelst and the printer's mark, "Impressum Biponti Ex Typographia Societatis." Interrupted by the French in 1794, the activity was revived for a brief time in Strasbourg in 1798. The Greek and Latin editions of the society, which were called *Editiones Bipontinae*, enjoyed great respect in the scholarly world.[30]

As was already the case in the seventeenth century, so in this period also the work of plates was especially favored. In addition to the already mentioned works of copper engraving completed by individual publishers and printers, whole groups of comprehensive volumes of plates stood out; they belonged mainly to the natural sciences, and some among them to gardening. These illustrations of plants,[31] of birds,[32] of butterflies[33] and flower gardens[34] were primarily acquired by court libraries, and there they constituted especially popular gems in the exhibit collections. All these mostly artistically painted luxury volumes are outstandingly valuable for science, and for the history of culture. With the coloring of the copper plates, the decorative purpose did not always stand in the forefront; one also frequently desired through colors to intensify the faithfulness to nature and the clarity of the illustrations. Especially was that the case with the representations of plants. But books of costumes and works of arms also invited a colorful lay-out.[35]

The exalted professional pride of the German printers and publishers was expressed in several collections of portraits of book dealers, such as the one published in 1725 by Johann Leonhard Blanck, and between 1726–1742 by Friedrich Roth-Scholtz, both in Nuremberg.

A list memorable for the history of the German book trade was published in 1741: *Verzeichnis der meistlebenden Herren Buchhändler, welche die Leipziger und*

Frankfurter Messe insgemein zu besuchen pflegen ("List of the book dealers, most of them living, which commonly visit the Leipzig and Frankfurt Fairs"); it is the first directory of the German book trade, and at the same time it is evidence of the immense significance the German book trade had taken on. We find ninety-six German locations with 290 businesses, of which thirty-one were in Leipzig, twenty-four in Nuremberg, twenty-two in Frankfurt am Main, fourteen in Cologne, thirteen in Jena, twelve in Augsburg, and nine in Halle. Leipzig and Nuremberg are therefore the liveliest cities for the German book trade about this time.

In his *Geschichte des deuschen Buchhandels* ("History of the German Book Trade"), Goldfriedrich compares the year 1700 with the year 1900, and thus obtains the following result. The Fair catalog of 1700 lists 951 works for Germany, Austria and German Switzerland; the book listing of 1900 enumerates for the same territories 25,000 publications. The number of book trade establishments amounts in 1700 to about 450, which in the year 1900 comes to around 8,500 businesses. The German Empire counted in 1700 perhaps fourteen million inhabitants; in 1900, the number was sixty million.

The period of the increased book sales has also become, at the same time, the flourishing time for reprints. The center was above all in Vienna, with the enterprising and unscrupulous book dealer, Johann Thomas, Baronet von Trattner, who unabashedly published on May 2, 1765, an *Avertissement* ("Advertisement"), in which he advertised reprints of Gellert, Gessner, Hagedorn, Ewald von Kleist, Klopstock, Rabener, Zachariae and other authors. Further selling markets for unlimited reprints were Switzerland, Holland, Frankfurt am Main, and Karlsruhe, where Christian Gottlieb Schmieder turned out to be so unconscionable in reprinting that, following him, this whole activity was designated as *Schmiederei*, and the reprinter as *Schmieder*. Well known is the title page illustration to the second volume of Alois Blumauer's *Aeneid*, in which ugly dogs gnaw on a human head and they are identified in acid verses.

Things were in fact in a sorry plight, so far as the protection of author and publisher were concerned, as over against this proliferation of reprinting. When in 1777, the Wieland Shakespeare translation had been published by Orell, Gessner and Füssli in Zurich, it was immediately reprinted in five locales. It is understandable that the original publishers, who often had to pay rather considerable compensation to their authors and who held out for good book design (which again raised the costs of production) were utterly exasperated about this robbery by the reprinters (who had no further sacrifices to make) and above all, they tried to check them. On the other hand, the reprinter's activities did indeed contribute quite essentially to the dissemination of those publications that were in great demand. "In Trattner's reprints," Joseph Nadler pointed out,[36] "the Austria of the eighteenth century has accepted the great German literature. On Trattner's reprints depends the literary education of the new Austria. In Trattner's reprints Austria grew into its own great poetry." The struggle between the adherents and the opponents of reprinting gave vent to its fury in numerous pamphlets for and against the reprint. An initial success of the opponents was that an Electorate of Saxony mandate of December 18, 1773, forbade reprinting.[37]

Just as they did in France, printing and book design experienced a great upsurge also in England, around the middle of the century. The most significant printers were John Baskerville (1706–1775) in Birmingham, whose Vergil of 1757, Milton of 1758, Juvenal and Persius of 1761, Horace of 1762, and finally, the English Bible produced by the University of Cambridge, are to be numbered among the best English printed works; [38] William Bulmer (1754–1830), who published (1793–97) a beautiful Goldsmith edition, with woodcuts by Thomas Bewick, the restorer of the English woodcut, and from 1791 to 1802 Shakespeare's works in eleven folio volumes; and Thomas Bensley (1750–1835), who in 1789 printed a quarto edition of Lavater's *Physiogomy*, in 1796 a folio edition of Bürger's *Leonore*, in 1797 John Thomson's *Seasons* and the splendid work in five volumes, *The History of England* by David Hume. Fame came also to Samuel Richardson, (1689–1761) who, besides journals, printed his own sensitive novels and found many readers for them, also in Germany.

In Spain, Joachim Ibarra (1725–1785) in Madrid had the leadership in the growing book trade through his outstandingly beautiful printed works, such as the *Don Quixote* edition in four volumes of 1780, and the scholarly work, *Bibliotheca Hispana* of Nicolas Antonio, from the year 1783.

The reviver of the art of good printing in Italy became Giambattista Bodoni (1740–1813) in Parma, whose Homer of 1785, Tasso of 1789, Horace and Anacreon of 1791, and Vergil of 1793, are masterworks.[39]

The most famous printer-personality of America in this period was the statesman and author, Benjamin Franklin (1706–1790) in Philadelphia; among other things he had Cicero's work, *Cato Maior or Concerning Age*, produced in 1741; it was translated by James Logan and it represented the first translation in American of one of the classical writers. Franklin also issued religious publications of the Pennsylvania enthusiasts, among which were Beissel's *Göttliches Liebes-und Lobesgethöne* ("Godly Sounding of Love and Praise"); it was the first American book in the German language. Among the German printers of the new world, Christopher Sauer (1694–1758) especially distinguished himself; he was successfully active in Germantown and has produced America's first German Bible in one thousand copies[40] in 1743.

The more books that there were with the passage of time, the more it stimulated people to make this mass their own, even if only in the superficial mastery of book titles and book lists.[41] Book description practically developed into a scholarly disciple. Already at that time there were men, who, like Johann David Michaelis told about the bibliographically aware Schlüter, read auction catalogs with the same feeling with a which a poet enjoyed Haller's poetry. It was above all the rare and remarkable books that fascinated men, and the listings of these came out in impressive number. The names of Daniel Gerdes (1740), Sigmund Jakob Baumgarten (1748), Friedrich Gottlieb Freytag (1752), Jakob Wilhelm Blaufuss (1753), Johann Vogt (1753), Andreas Gottlieb Masch (1769), Johann Jakob Bauer (1770), Bernhard Friedrich Hummel (1775), are only a selection from the great number of such book enumerators. Other authors such as Michael Denis (1778), Paulin Erdt (1786), Heinrich Wilhelm Lawätz (1788) taught general bibliography or, as J.G.

Schelhorn (1788) and Albrecht Christoph Keyser (1790) spoke their minds about librarianship or, as Christian Juncker (1709), Tobias Eckhard, Petrus Jaenichius (1723), August Beyer (1731), Samuel Wenzeslaus Kroll (1735), J. Burckard (1744), Johann Christoph Mylius (1747) and Johann Friedrich Eckhardt (1775) were instructors in the history of individual libraries; others again published library catalogs: thus J.C. Dähnert issued (1775) an accurate catalog of the University Library of Greifswald.

Johann Karl Conrad Ölrichs made a typical confession in his *Entwurf einer Geschichte der Königlichen Bibliothek zu Berlin* in 1752, one of the first German library histories ever written: "I would rather have authored this publication in Latin"—he believed he had to excuse himself—"But to please the bookdealers, who today don't like to meddle with Latin things because, for the most part, as they say, they remain on the shelf, I have had to change my plan." The victory of the German language in the literature has therefore succeeded all along the line. Outstanding above all among the catalogs of manuscripts is the catalog of the Laurentiana in Florence, which was prepared by Angelo Maria Bandini (1726–1803). It was published in the years 1764–1793 in eleven folio volumes as a master work.[42]

Falling into this period also were the beginnings of incunabula research, the turning toward the earliest monuments of printing; as a result of their special design, their character as the first editions of the more valuable texts, and the fact that they were gradually becoming more and more rare, they awakened people's historical interest. Already in the seventeenth century, Johann Saubert (1643), Philipp Labbe (1653) and Cornelius von Beughem had published lists of old printed works. At first, greater significance was achieved by the *Annales typographici*, which Michael Maittaire published in the Hague in the years 1719–1741 with brief remarks concerning the printer and publishers from the beginning of early printing to the year 1664. In the last decades of the eighteenth century, several monasteries, especially in South Germany, such as SS. Ulrich and Afra in Augsburg, Rebdorf, St. Mang in Füssen, Beuerberg, and Neustift, made their incunabula known. Then there followed in 1788–1805 a list that is still useful today, the *Annalen der älteren deutschen Literatur* ("Annals of the Older German Literatur") of Georg Wolfgang Panzer and, in 1793–1803, the *Annales typographici*, by the same author, in eleven volumes. Since then the incunabula have been considered as a proud possession of libraries, and as the collector's favorites. This rising esteem was therefore already of the highest significance, because it has preserved the old printed works in the face of the threatening dissipation and destruction in the period of the dissolution of the monasteries that followed. The old printed works were now considered like the manuscripts—less as books than as valuable monuments of antiquity, which are treasures and to be carefully preserved.

For the bibliography of art history, the *Neue Nachrichten von Künstlern und Kunstsachen* ("New Reports of Artists and Art Affairs") of C.H. Heinecken (1786), meant significant progress; no less so did the list of engravings, *Peintre-graveur* of the artist and art teacher, Adam Bartsch (1803); it is still not obsolete, even today.

29

The Libraries
of the Eighteenth Century

At its beginning, the eighteenth century, like the turn of the century preceding it, has seen the foundation of a significant library, the beginnings of the British Museum in London. It was Sir John Cotton who took the initiative here. In 1700 he gave to his people for public use the valuable collection of English publications which had been set up by his grandfather, Sir Robert Cotton (1571–1631). Fortune did not initially shine on the collection, from which, incidentally, Franciscus Junius (1589–1677) (the most distinguished first publisher of the Gothic Bible translation of Bishop Ulfilas, and at the same time the leading connoisseur in that period of the Germanic languages) had already successfully used the *Beowulf* and the *Heliand* manuscripts. After the holdings had suffered harm due to several moves, a fire overtook them on October 23, 1731, and 114 manuscripts were destroyed.

Only gradually did England become conscious of its duties in respect to its national cultural properties, but then it recovered what had been neglected in the grandest way. A place was created for the collection in 1753, and for it the valuable property of the natural scientist, Sir John Sloane (1661–1734), which included 3,500 manuscripts and 40,000 printed works, was acquired for 20,000 pounds sterling, as was also the large manuscript collection of Robert and Edward Harley, Earls of Oxford, for ten thousand pounds. The project was financed by a state lottery. Montague House, which was in the same place where the British Museum is now situated, was purchased in the following year, and rebuilt for its new functions. The collection's basic stock, which was augmented in 1757 by the Royal Library's holdings, was opened on January 15, 1759, when it was already numbering over 13,200 manuscripts and 57,000 printed works; a third department of the museum comprised objects of natural science. Within the ranks of libraries, a new form of library was here taking its place, namely, one supported by the people as a whole, a collection of books that is accessible to every citizen, one that is a meaningful expression of popular will to collect the treasures of its own country, as well as to collect selectively publications from all over the world, and to make all this accessible as an inexhaustible source of scholarship and of the whole life of culture.

Countless small collections from all over England now found there way to London as if drawn by an irresistible force, and into the great national possession, until in the nineteenth century, the country felt strong enough, with its great monetary means and its world wide relations, to enlarge the acquisitions to the extent that it became one of the greatest libraries of the world.[1]

If Leibniz had still considered the chief work of public libraries to be their usefulness for the state, this conception underwent an essential transformation, when at the University Library at Göttingen after 1735 there developed, along with the newly established university, a collection of books, which, in vital relationship with the university, had but a single aim, that of promoting the most effective utilization of books in the service of the sciences. The institution initially began with rather modest means. Duplicates of the library in Hanover and students' fees were the scanty sources from which the first streams of books flowed in. But already on April 6, 1734, Gerlach Adolf, Baron von Müchhausen, who was the thoughtful patron of Göttingen University, was able proudly to announce the acquisition of Joachim Heinrich Bülow's library. The university had the good fortune of finding in the philologist, Johann Matthias Gesner (who was a friend of Johann Sebastian Bach) a scholarly attendant of its book treasures, as well as someone who was a knowledgeable administrator.

When in 1748, Gesner had to render an official judgment on "how a librarian must be constituted," he demanded, in addition to politeness, good manners, and the knowledge of languages, and above all, an acquaintance with the history of scholarship and learning. The most significant of the new goals for books was the idea that the library must own the most important works in all the scholarly disciplines of the university curriculum, and in so far as possible, they must be accessible to the users. Ample book holdings, good catalogs and full freedom of movement in the use of the book treasures – these were the fundamental presuppositions for the clearly recognized function of a scholarly library set up to be actually used – a goal which, within modest limits, the Bodleian at Oxford had already had in mind a century ago. The collecting function was therefore here no longer the main thing; it was rather the use of books in the service of the thriving sciences. It was only where books, the most important means of communicating knowledge, were actually at one's disposal that the sciences could really prosper, and it was only where the sciences were attended to that the libraries had their proper meaning, and proper respect paid them.

To have guided this advance toward an exemplary fulfillment and for all the world to see, is the lasting merit of the Göttingen institution.[2] When the professor of Old Testament, John David Michaelis, set up new administrative regulations for it in October 1761,[3] a main requirement stated: "The library must be made as useful as possible." Today this principle is quite self-evident; at that time it was so novel that in its ultimate consequences it called for a total transformation of the old form of the collection of books, where possession was the chief thing, into the modern library, the holdings of which are considered as being only a means to an end, i.e., as materials to be used in the service of scholarship. When the archeologist, Christian Gottlob Heyne (1729–1812), as Gesner's successor, assumed the administrative post at the Göttingen Library, he opined, following his initial inspection of the library's arrangement and use, that he did not know how a library could become more useful to its community.[4] And the law instructor, Johann Stephen

Pütter (1725–1807), was able proudly to report in 1765 in his *Versuch einer Gelehrten-Geschichte von der Georg-August-Universität zu Göttingen* ("Attempt at a Scholars' History of the Georg-Augusta University at Göttingen") "The great advantage of this library lies in the free and unencumbered use, an advantage that hardly any one of the libraries in Germany—or perhaps even in other regions—would dispute." The best possible utilization of books—that was the kernel of the new administrative art. Given recognition alongside the library's use was also the necessity for its uninterrupted growth through the constant acquisition of the most significant new publications. Pütter was able to boast of the library that it owned the most important principal works in all the disciplines, and that nothing essential was missing. Here, therefore, the mass of books was already part of a vital exchange in cultural properties, and the unchanging collection of books was being transformed into the versatile library. Sharing significantly in this flexible continuing development was the close connection the library enjoyed with the Society of the Sciences at Göttingen and the Göttingen *Gelehrte Anzeigen* ("Scholarly Notices"),[5] in which there was an attempt by means of reviews, continually to make known the most important new publications on the book market. Thus the library, the academy and scholarship harmoniously extended helping hands to one another.

The blossoming institution was soon exciting the attention of the entire scholarly world. When Jeremias David Reuss in 1774 submitted to the university senate of Tübingen a memorandum with the demand for more material relief in the provisions for books, he expressly reported on Göttingen's successful example. With the same approval, Johann Heinrich Landolt of Zurich, following his visit of September 23, 1782, reported on the rich holdings of Göttingen and also about the authority the professors had, which enabled them to procure the most important books in their fields, and the right of the students to be allowed, with a voucher note, to borrow as many books as they wished. On all sides, Göttingen was taken to be the model and the example. Herder saw in the library a special point of attraction for the university. When Friedrich Gottlieb Welcker (1784–1868) in 1819 was named professor and head librarian of the new university in Bonn, Wilhelm Humboldt wrote him that among all the institutions assisting scholarship, one should think mostly on the library; Göttingen, he said, owed it everything. And of Karl Goedeke, the author of the exhaustively extensive *Grundriss zur Geschichte der deutschen Dichtung* ("Foundation to the History of German Poetry"), Gustav Roethe wrote that the Göttingen library would never have prouder praises sung to it than there was in the silent eloquence of these book titles.

Among the old court libraries, which were still book museums more than useful libraries, only the collection in Vienna (which not only had built in 1727 the most splendid of all the buildings, which had been built up to that time, but which had also obtained valuable acquisitions) enjoyed increasing attention. Thus acquired were: in 1720, the valuable possession of Baron Georg Wilhelm von Hohendorf, with beautiful printed works and priceless bindings; and in 1738, the copious library of Prince Eugene of Savoy (1663–1736), with its 15,000 printed works, bound in various colors: history in red, theology in dark blue, natural history in yellow, most of them being luxury editions of the seventeenth century, in addition to 237 manuscripts, among which was the famous *Tabula Peutingeriana*, and a twelfth century manuscript of the Greek New Testament that Erasmus of Rotterdam had once used in the monastery of Corsendonck.[6] In 1756 there followed the old holdings of the Vienna University Library, with significant evidences of the humanistic movement, such as manuscripts of Enea Silvio Piccolomini, Johann Brassicanus, Johannes Cuspinianus, and Johann Fabri. Added toward the end of the century were rich accessions from the dissolved monasteries of the Jesuits and other religious orders.

The Court Library in Dresden also took a great step forward when, in 1764, the large collection of the Saxon statesman and historiographer, Heinrich, Count von Bünau (1697–1762), with 42,000 volumes, was purchased, and its industrious librarian, Johann Michael Francke, moved to Dresden with the collection.[7] The library had been located in Nöthnitz near Dresden; there, with Franck, Winckelmann had also been a librarian when he was thirty years old; and in the midst of the rich treasures, he had become an enthusiastic bibliophile, which he indeed remained all his life.[8] Dresden further obtained in 1768 the enormous book collection of Count Heinrich von Brühl (1700–1763); it contained about 62,000 volumes.

One of the last of the court libraries originated at Mannheim, where Count Palatine Karl Theodore (1724–1799) held magnificent court according to the French model. Elector since 1742, he fostered music and opera, set up a Palatine Academy of Sciences, and accommodated his book treasures in a splendid hall of his palace. He acquired valuable holdings such as, in 1769, the famous collection of letters of the scholarly family of Camerarius with priceless letters by Erasmus, Reuchlin, Luther, Zwingli, Oecolampadius, Wimpfeling, Calvin, and Beza[9]; in 1780, the exquisite library of the Italian archeologist, Pietro Vettori (1499–1584) with 250 manuscripts and 450 printed works, among which there were many first editions, with scholarly marginal notations that had been made by earlier owners. The librarian, Maillot de la Treille, reported on May 27, 1780, in a French Academy lecture, about the collection that had been acquired for 1200 florins; it is an informative historical source for getting to know the late Italian humanism.[10] The elector was an enthusiastic adherent of Voltaire, who had repeatedly been his guest and whose works he collected eagerly.[11] He owned the copy in Voltaire's handwriting of the satirical epic, *Pucelle* (Cod. gall. Monac. 226), the *Essay sur les revolutions du monde* (Cod. gall. Monac. 149, 150), and the tragedies of *Orphelin de la Chine* and *Tancrède*.

Mannheim's other priceless acquisitions included a Lower Saxon manuscript of the *Schwabenspiegel*, the single complete manuscript of the Dutch epic of *Alexanders Geesten* of Jakob von Maerland, a *sacramentarium* with ivory covers from the cathedral treasury of Verdun (Cod. lat. 10 077), an eleventh century Orosius from Toul (Cod. lat. 10 292), a Jerome manuscript of the tenth or eleventh century from Metz (Cod. lat. 10 041), an exquisite prayerbook (Cod. lat. 10 103), apparently from the possessions of the French merchant, Jacques Coeur, who was the influential counselor to King Charles VII,[12] the college book of Sebastian Münster's from the year 1515 to 1517 (Col. lat. 10 691),[13] the Parisian edition (directed by Pithou and Baluze) of Salvianus' *De Gubernatione Dei* of 1580, with manuscriptural supplements by Stephen Baluze according to manuscripts of Corvey, St. Germain des Prés and Paris (P. lat. 1740), and, finally, what was left from the library of the pugnacious parson, Johann Nikolaus Weislinger (d. 1757),[14] who was the author of the publication, *Friss Vogel oder stirb* ("Eat, bird, or die"). The library ultimately numbered 40,000 volumes and a thousand manuscripts, among which were numerous items of French origin. Following the elector's death in 1799, it was severely neglected, until Elector Maximilian I Joseph, the later first King of Bavaria, removed it in 1804 to Munich, and integrated it there with the Central Library, which is the present-day State Library.

Mannheim is a good example of how, even in the eighteenth century, venerable old book treasures could successfully be assembled if there were a passionate enthusiasm for collecting associated with corresponding financial means.

Duke Karl Eugene of Württemberg (1728–1793), who was the builder of the castles of Solitude and Hohenheim, and the founder of the Charles Academy, devoted himself with his whole soul to the enjoyment of books. The prince commissioned all his business agents in foreign courts to buy books, and he himself travelled with the same purpose in mind to Vienna, Paris, London and Oxford. In 1784, he stopped at Copenhagen and acquired the collection of the preacher, Josias Lorck, which contained five thousand printings of the Bible. Coming to him shortly thereafter was the valuable collection of Bibles owned by Panzer. The Court Library, which was removed in 1775 from Ludwigslust to Stuttgart, thus became one of the largest collections of Bibles in the world.[15]

The University Library in Erlangen acquired in 1759 the book holdings of the Margravine Wilhelmina of Bayreuth, (1709–1758), who was Frederick the Great's favorite sister; it thus obtained a characteristic book collection of the Enlightenment period.[16]

A significant event in library history occurred in 1713, in Verona, when the marchioness, Scipione Maffei (1675–1755), again rediscovered the priceless manuscripts of the library of the cathedral chapter there; at one time they had been brought to safety when threatened by an inundation of the Adige River, and then they were forgotten; with this discovery, there were found valuable literary monuments from the sixth to the ninth century; among them was an especially significant one, which later was shown by Niebuhr to be a palimpsest manuscript of Gaius. A fresh sensation was aroused when, four years later, the cathedral dean, Christoph von Hutten, rediscovered the Würzburg Cathedral Library with its valuable manuscripts; at one time, these had been hidden from the Swedes and it was then assumed that they were lost.

Learned monks were active in several monasteries with scholarly works and they thus lent their libraries a renewed significance. The Melk Benedictine, Bernhard Pez, visited fifty libraries in his researches. Among them was St. Germain des Prés, the chief site of the Maurists, and he effectively refers in his *Thesaurus anecdotorum novissimorum* (1721–1729) to the monastic treasures of books that he has used there.[17] In a similar way, Gottfried Bessel and Magnus Klein in Göttweig, Oliver Legipont of St. Martin in Cologne,[18] Froben Forster in St. Emmeran at Regensburg, Eugen Dobler in Irsee, and Eusebius Amort and Franz Töpsl in

Polling, earned enduring merit for their services both to scholarship and the monastic libraries. Franz Töpsl (1744–1796), the highly educated abbot of the Augustinian Canons in Polling near Weilheim, sent Gerhoh Steinberger, who knew books well, to Italy and France for the purpose of purchasing books, and he elevated his library so that it became one of the largest monastic collections of books in Bavaria.

From the former Paris Jesuit library, Polling acquired a series of valuable printed works and manuscripts, among which were the *Theuerdank* edition on parchment and the Koran manuscript, which was wholly inscribed with gold and is now kept in the Munich State Library; the latter manuscript had once belonged to the father-confessor of King Louis XIV, Lachaise. On all sides, the monastic libraries exerted an effort to make their book treasures known through catalogs of their holdings. SS. Ulrich and Afra in Augsburg, Rebdorf, Füssen, and Beuerberg published surveys of their incunabula. The scholarly librarian of SS. Ulrich and Afra in Augsburg, Placidus Braun, followed his list of incunabula with a detailed description of the manuscripts (1791–1799). Pius Kolb, (1712–1762), librarian of St. Gall, wrote a description of the St. Gall manuscripts, but it remained unpublished.

A second St. Gall monastery librarian, Johann Nepomuk Hauntinger, visited numerous monastery libraries in Bavaria and Swabia, laid out in 1784 a list of the books that were lacking in St. Gall, and wrote down his travel experiences. After his return home, he was not to be a librarian much longer. He had to bring his book treasures to Mehrerau to safety in 1798, in the face of the French threat. When they could get back to St. Gall, they were no longer monastery property, but became rather the impounded possession of the canton of St. Gall. But Hautinger again obtained the leadership of the handsome collection. In this or in similar ways, the fate of the last monastery libraries has repeatedly been shaped. St. Blasien has become an especially alert center of scholarly pursuit under the prince-abbot, Martin Gerbert (1720–1793); not only did he bring together a rich library and found a new large possession of books after the bad monastery fire of 1768, but he also undertook a significant scholarly project, the description of the sixty-three German dioceses in *Germania sacra*, without, however, being able to finish it.[19]

The public libraries of the eighteenth century were often simultaneously museums, in which one exhibited within the space of a splendid hall for books all that was owned in the way of rare and wonderful things, much as in the Municipal Library of Hamburg, where there were skeletons, stuffed fish, snakes in alcohol, shells, stones, instruments, or other heirloom pieces that belonged to famous personalities, weapons of foreign countries, coins, gems, and plaster castings of ancient statues.

The librarians had to show visitors especially rare or unique books. Thus candidates for positions in the Princely Library in Weimar in 1743 were supposed, besides having knowledge of the Latin, French and Italian languages, and the history of literature, to evidence skill in entertaining foreigners to the library through a scholarly discourse and giving them a sufficient report and supplementary information about the most remarkable and the rarest books.[20] The University

Library in Basel had enjoyed numerous distinguished visits, especially on account of the Amerbach cabinets that it incorporated in 1661, with their books, paintings, signs, and coins. Goethe put in an appearance there on July 8, 1775. On the following eighth of October the two Counts zu Stolberg arrived there. The book of guests further lists the bookdealer Nicolai (August, 1781), Lavater several times, Maria Sophie La Roche (August, 1784), Wilhelm von Humboldt (November 21, 1789), Heinrich von Kleist (1801), then in connection with the crossing of the Rhine by the Allies on January 14, 1814, King Frederick William of Prussia, Prince Wilhelm Ludwig of Prussia and Emperor Francis I of Austria, and on March 21, 1814, the Grand Dukes Nikolaus and Michael of Russia.[21]

The enormous increase in books was everywhere exceeding the space available in libraries and requiring extended spatial accommodations. If numerous renovations had already taken place following the end of the seventeenth century, in the eighteenth century, with the surprising rise in monasteries and church construction, an unprecedented competition was initiated in the transformation, or the production, of library buildings. There arose the beautiful Baroque and Rococo rooms, pure structures of the period's intoxicatingly sensuous culture, elegant monuments which we can still admire, especially in the South German and the Austrian monasteries.[22] Mostly encompassing two floors and including walking galleries, the wide spaces and the areas for decoration offered an endless room for play that called forth all of the arts: architecture, sculpture and painting.

Beautifully carved cases, such as those in Indersdorf, Neresheim and Hohenfurt, spiral columns, and richly detailed galleries such as those in Füssen, Metten, Scheyern, Ottobeuren, Wiblingen, Schussenried, St. Peter, Ochsenhausen, artful plaster facings, vari-colored symbols, gilding everywhere on all corners and ends, and colorful ceiling paintings — with all this splendor the books surrounded, with their gilded bindings impressively reinforcing the effect of the colors, as the jewels of the house, and only now did one see them properly as treasures to be carefully taken care of. One loved books, and the rooms for books. Beautiful libraries were also created in the Austrian monasteries: in Ranshofen, Schlierbach, Baumgartenberg, Garsten, Lambach, Waldhausen, Wilhering Zwettl, Kremsmünster, Suben, St. Florian, Göttweig, Admont,[23] Schwarzach, Klosterneuburg, Melk, Vorau, Seitenstetten and Bruck.[24]

The model for many of these halls for books became the Court Library at Vienna, where in the years 1722–26, emperor Karl VI, through Johann Bernhard and Joseph Emanuel Fischer of Erlach, had a book room built that was of unprecedented splendor.[25] Abbot Gottfried Bessel of Göttweig, in his *Chronicon Gotwicense* (which was dedicated in 1732 to the Emperor), cannot boast enough about the wonderful structure. Princely splendor and science: on these two notes all the glories of the Viennese interior decoration were designed: one saw the life-size statue of the emperor surrounded by eight other statues of princes of the house of Habsburg; one saw Minerva triumph over the two enemies of envy and ignorance, one saw frescoes with glorifications of the imperial government and with symbols of the four faculties. The Cistercian monastery of Waldsassen in the Upper Palatinate has created one of the most beautiful rooms for books in the most precise toning of color with the structures and the paintings,[26] while the gallery's twelve carved supports carry a variety of funny carvings.

Joking occasionally pursued its teasing play also in other monastic libraries. Thus in the Premonstratensian Foundation at Roggenburg near Weissenhorn one could see false book backs built for disguising the side doors, and one could read such fanciful or sarcastic titles as these: *Letzter Stich oder Sterb-Gedanken eines Spielers* ("Last Trick, or the Dying Thoughts of a Gambler"), *Vel Quasi oder Andacht der Domherren* ("Vel Quasi, or Devotions of the Canons"), *Gewissen eines Korn-händlers* ("Conscience of a Grain merchant"), *Libera me Domine oder tägliches Gebet eines Subpriors* ("Libera me Domine, or The daily prayer of a sub-prior"). The Jesuits could also point to splendid places in Trier, in Vienna, in Munich, in Bamberg, as well as elsewhere.

A proper art of library building was perfected, which understood how to create very charming rooms.[27] A special "ornament" of this sort was obtained in St. Gall, when in 1758, several artists decorated the hall for books with beautiful bookcases, stucco, and wall paintings. The splendid monastery library rooms are the last proud witness to a glorious tradition, to that deeply rooted relationship of the book with the monastic community. This concern corresponded as much to the esteem in which the book was held as it did to the growing idea that, besides a splendid house of God, nothing could contribute more effectively to the monastery's fame than an impressive library room filled with valuable books, along with a stimulating scholarly spirit as expressions of the high monastic culture.

A secular counterpart to St. Gall was the simultaneously produced Mannheim Court Library, which among the Rococo rooms was one of the most exciting, with Verschaffelt's gable frieze: Pallas Athena in the midst of the sciences and the arts, and the ceiling paintings by Lambert Krahe: Pallas Athena guides the genies of the sciences and the arts toward truth.[28] It was an impressive room in which the Mannheim Academy conducted its ceremonies surrounded by priceless book treasures.

Designers of these libraries understood in a masterful way how to use effectively the colorful bindings of the books and their rich gilding on the backs as wall decoration. Thus the books themselves helped to make the festive hall which was designed for them as handsome as possible, and book and room thus harmonized splendidly. They were truly festive rooms of the book.

If these splendid rooms were already attracting many visitors, so the treasures kept there bewitched the scholars and bibliophies even more, and moved many toward extensive travels and book investigations. Repeatedly, such travellers kept diaries for themselves, in which they report concerning the results they achieved and these are valuable evidences of the cultural life in that period. In the regulations of the University Library at Göttingen of October 28, 1761, it expressly states that if foreigners who are prominent by virture of their status or scholarship wish to see the library, they must be treated with civility.

One of the first valuable travel descriptions of a bibliographical scholar is the report of Zacharias Conrad von Uffenbach, which was published in three volumes in 1753 and 1754.[29] One hundred and six libraries were visited on the trip, which took place between 1907–1711 and took him through Holland, England, and a portion of Germany. Directors of the libraries visited do not always come off very well in these reports. Above all, it angered the critical visitor when, faced with closed doors, he had to turn around again, as in Hanover, where Leibniz refused him entry on the grounds that the holdings had not yet been brought into orderly arrangement. He was able to see the new library building in Wolfenbüttel only from the outside, because the building's interior was still not accessible. Behind such refusals he angrily perceived the jealousy of the librarian. The English librarians he credited with rather little knowledge of books. The use of manuscripts he found most sorely impeded; the rooms he found to be in an inadequate state. He was charmed most of all by the library building at Cambridge; it was the handsomest one he saw. When he came to London, the initial foundations for the future British Museum were just then being constituted: the Sloane Collection and the Bibliotheca Cottoniana, which was set up in Westminster. In the Bodleian at Oxford, he had to dispute for a long time with the librarian, until he succeeded in being admitted to the book treasures. Uffenbach's own library, which was one of the largest book collections of that time, numbered 32,000 volumes and was sold in the years 1738–1741.

The Königsberg professor, Christian Gabriel Fischer, travelled between 1727 and 1731 in over half of Europe in order to enrich his knowledge of the natural sciences, and became acquainted with about a hundred libraries in Germany, France, Italy, England, the Netherlands and Switzerland. His accounts, which in manuscript form are today with the Society of Natural Research in Danzig, give us a good view into the life of the book collections in that period that were visited.[30]

Cardinal Guiseppe Garampi (1725–1792) used an official trip in the years 1761–1763 to get an overview of the book world in the localities he visits – in Salem near Constance, Weingarten, St. Blasien, St. Gall, Rheingau, Mainz, Cologne, Utrecht, Brussels, Paris, Strasbourg, Stuttgart, Munich and Vienna. As a high clerical dignitary, he was able to gain entrance everywhere and he got a good insight into the holdings. In St. Gall the library room was just being built; therefore, the manuscripts had to be viewed in their Rorschach abode. In St. Blasien, the later abbot, Martin Gerbert, was a guide for the guests; in Munich, Andreas Felix Oefele was the guide.[31]

The prince-abbot, Martin Gerbert of St. Blasien (1720–1793), on his extended study trips visited the most important libraries of South Germany, Switzerland, France and Italy, and he reported on them in his richly informative work, *Iter Alemannicum, accedit Italicum et Gallicum* (1765).

Georg Wilhelm Zapf,[32] Philipp Wilhelm Gercken[33] and Friedrich Karl Gottlieb Hirsching[34] have also published detailed descriptions of numerous libraries that they inspected.

All these reports had no little share in enriching the knowledge of books, especially of manuscripts and of valuable printed works, of instilling in individual libraries a respect for their own possessions, and of stimulating them to increase their own book holdings. They also gave some idea for the first time in public of what rich book treasures lay extended over the entire German territories.

30

The Confiscation of Monastery Libraries as a Consequence of the Enlightenment Movement

With the Enlightenment's heightened emphasis on human reason and the state's sovereignty, the church's claims in the course of this cultural movement were drastically curtailed with respect to the shaping of thought and life. A passionate struggle against the Jesuit Order ensued primarily at the political level, until Pope Clement XIII, under pressure form the European courts, gave in for the sake of peace; and by means of his bull, *Domiue ac Redemptor noster*, issued on July 21, 1773, he abolished the Order, making reference to the accusations that had been raised against it.

The suppression of the Jesuit monasteries meant that the decisive hour of destiny had struck also for their libraries, which had enjoyed special attention; these were abolished, and their holdings destroyed, or they ended up in public libraries; individual collections were transformed into study libraries. Auctioneering at Brussels from the numerous Belgian Jesuit libraries in the years 1780 and 1781 brought in 132,084 florins; a selection for the library in Brussels had taken place prior to the auction. Book holdings of the Bohemian Jesuits mostly came to Prague. From the *Collegium* at Wiener Neustadt Emperor Maximilian's prayerbook (with an abundance of decorative miniatures) came to the Vienna Court Library, which also received substantial holdings from other Austrian Jesuit libraries. In Milan, which at that time belonged to Austria, the palace of Brera, which had been in Jesuit possession, was designated for library purposes and, as the *Bibliotheca di Brera*, it accepted the earlier Jesuit books, as well as other collections. Out of the wreckage of the dissolved Upper Italian Jesuit libraries, the Jesuit, Matteo Luigi Canonici, assembled in Venice one of the largest collections of that time, which alone numbered four thousand manuscripts and two thousand printed editions of the Bible. The manuscripts for the most part have been purchased later by the Bodleian in Oxford. The valuable possession of the famous Parisian *Collegium Clermont*, which was founded in 1561 by Guillaume Duprat, bishop of Clermont, was acquired, along with 856 priceless manuscripts, by the Dutchman and legal scholar, Gerard Meerman (1722–1771), it later came to Sir Thomas Phillips, and finally in 1886, to the Prussian State Library in Berlin.

As a second sacrificial offering to the Enlightenment movement, the numerous Austrian monasteries that were only contemplative in nature, and thus not needed for pastoral work, were dissolved in the years 1782–1786, according to the decrees of Emperor Joseph II, who was enthusiastically inspired by the Enlightenment and the idea of progress.[1] On January 12, 1782, the authorities ordered the closing of the monasteries affected by the decree and the confiscation of their holdings for the archives and libraries. On January 14, the prefect of the Vienna Court Library, Gottfried, Baron von Swieten,[2] made application to the authorities, so that, as with the dissolving of the Jesuits' libraries, the Vienna collection might also now again be considered.

On May 4 came the district authorities' command that the holdings of the libraries should be submitted to the leading authorities of the territorial office, and there they would be entered into a list for the information of the Vienna Court Library. What was not requested was supposed to be handed over to the university and lyceum libraries of the particular provinces. Duplicates might be sold, and the proceeds realized as income. Prior to the subsuming of the holdings into the libraries, a great purge had to be undertaken. According to the emperor's express decree, "The entire mass of unused prayerbooks and books of devotion, legends, and the rest of the theological nonsense" fell within the stipulation that all poor-quality works of casuists, moralists, ascetics and preachers ought to be considered as being useless, and pulped. The Enlightenment wanted to create an environment in its libraries for progress, and it therefore refused acceptance into the collection of everything that was not in accord with its spirit. "National Enlightenment" was the slogan that determined how the holdings were viewed. In an order of April 3, 1786, it says: "In a library, the value of which is based entirely on its usefulness and application, not everything can be put that has ever been printed at any time, or that exhibit mere fantasy or scholars' luxury." Books that had no other service than that they have been listed as rarities by certain bibliographers, all fifteenth century editions and the like, would be of very doubtful value for a university or for a lyceum library. Because the libraries have aimed at the direct well-being of the state, in the first place there should be physics, natural history and the medical arts. Philosophy would then follow, while legal scholarship would be less pressing, and theology could claim only the last place.

Greek and Roman literature, on the other hand, must be carefully cultivated. The sorting out of materials in keeping with such a viewpoint pronounced the death sentence over whole groups of books that had been handed down. Baron von Swieten, president of the Study and Book Censorship Court Commission, expressed the opinion in a letter that the destruction by pulping, or the sale as scrap paper, concerned only the theological rubbish, and no harm should be done even by carelessness, or at least none that would be worth the time and effort of drawing up special listings. Somewhat more carefully the librarian, Bretschneider (who had to sort out the treasures flowing into the new university library at Lemberg) wrote on January 18, 1785, "It seems to me that, among the great amount of rubbish of the preachers, the moralists, the casuists, the ascetics and other meaningless books, one can always count on half of them being items that do not absolutely merit destruction, and of these, again half of them are ones the library can use."

In Moravia and Silesia alone, there came in from the monasteries and the foundations up to 95,900 books in all, among which were 673 manuscripts, 3,117 printed works and 25,056 other books designated as useful, and the remaining 70,857 volumes were declared to be rubbish, and they fell as waste paper to the wholesale buyers. The useful portion ended up partially in Vienna, and partly in the Olmütz Provincial Library. Up to thirty-five dissolved monasteries had to contribute thereto.[3] Just as many monasteries in Bohemia fell before the dissolution; their useful books came to Prague. Numerous monasteries were also dissolved in Carinthia, and the books were transported to Klagenfurt.[4] When in the spring of 1788 the Graz duplicates were supposed to be offered for sale, the court chancellor advised not to include valueless books in the sales catalog. Such items, which the public auction would only denounce, could only be disposed of in fascicles, or as miscellanies, to book dealers, or finally, as waste paper. The dissolved Tyrolean monasteries of Bozen, Innsbruck, Josefsberg and Innichen came off no better; their books also have mostly been squandered for ridiculous prices.[5]

Deriving the greatest gain from all the confiscations was had by the Court Library of Vienna; it received 663 valuable items from Mondsee alone.

It cannot be said that these seizures of books have always had happy results. Hurrying, the poor execution of orders that had been received, an arrogant lack of knowledge on the part of unsuitable officials—all these have played havoc with the holdings, more indeed than was necessary. The men of the Enlightenment, who at best were frequently rather conceited, had no sense for the fact that books, and groups of books, as witnesses of the past, could often be of high value for the history of culture, even if they had nothing more to say to the present.

When in the summer of 1789 the French royal house collapsed and the immense state debt, together with the Enlightenment ideas, led to the confiscation of church properties, things were finished so far as the clerical book collections of the country were concerned. On November 2, 1789, the National Assembly declared the libraries of churches and monasteries, as well as the book properties of the nobility, to be the nation's property. It thus acquired an abundance of books, such indeed as could scarcely be encountered a second time anywhere in the world.

With their priceless book treasures, France's church and monastery libraries (especially St. Denis, Corbie, Fleury-sur-Loire, Rheims, Beauvais, Troyes) had been among the earliest and most active centers of cultural life in the Middle Ages. Paris alone, on the eve of the Revolution, counted about eighty clerical libraries, with over a half million books, while the whole of France could be reckoned in books as being among the richest countries on earth. For the new national library, the successor of the earlier Royal Library, the inflow of this enormous mass of books meant the glorious ascension to its present-day exemplary wealth; in the shortest time, its holdings surged upward to about 300,000 volumes. That in the confusion of the Revolution grievous losses occurred, was inevitable. Thus the library of St. Germain des Prés went up in flames, and it could only partially be saved by the director of the National Library, Johann Basilius Bernard van Praet.[6] Valuable bindings with the arms of families were threatening to fall as a sacrifice to the hatred against the Royal House and the nobility, when in the last hours of October 24, 1793, the Constitutional Convention blocked the encroachments. Books that did not end up in Parisian collections were used for the foundation for new libraries, numerous district libraries in the provinces, or for augmenting already existing institutions. The new ordering of this enormous upheaval extended far into the first decade of the following century and became the basis for the entire later development.[7]

31
France's Confiscation of Books in the Revolutionary Years 1792–1809

An enormous displacement of books such as the world had seen only in the Thirty Years' War took place when the French Army returned from its campaigns and, along with other pieces of booty, took with it numerous priceless manuscripts and rare printed works. A special authority had to direct the deliberate plundering of the occupied territories, to which the literary travel descriptions of the last decades and the published holdings lists of the individual collections offered welcome hints. In 1792 there appeared in the French capital no less than fifteen hundred manuscripts that were from Belgium alone. Not long thereafter the advance of the hostile troops was also threatening the Rhineland cities.[1] As Custine was already standing in Worms on October 4, 1792, being brought into safety at Aschaffenburg were the most valuable treasures of the ancient Mainz Cathedral Library, which had already been plundered once by the Swedes; in all there were a hundred manuscripts and fifty incunabula. What had not been removed, was ruined irretrievably on June 28, 1793, when the Germans bombarded the city and the cathedral caught fire.

The manuscript treasures of Cologne Cathedral were brought into the Electorate of Cologne's Premonstratensian monastery of Weddinghausen near Arnsberg. When the territory later came by way of the secularization to Hesse, Grand Duke Ludwig, the new owner, had the priceless booty carried off to Darmstadt. Only the peace settlement of Prussia with Hesse-Darmstadt of September 3, 1866, has awarded the two hundred manuscripts again to Cologne Cathedral.[2] The books of the old Bonn University Library were brought across the Rhine ahead of the French and fortunately succeeded to Hamburg; ultimately, however, they were sold for ridiculously low prices to benefit the compensating of the princes of Hess-Darmstadt, Nassau-Usingen, Wied-Runkel and Arenberg. Following the victory of Jourdan near Fleurus on June 26, 1794, the French immediately reached for the unprotected treasures on the left shore of the Rhine.[3] One had wanted in 1794 to bring the famous Ada manuscript into safety from Trier to Mainz; but it was seized there by the French and carried off to Paris. Again handed over following the Second Paris Peace, it came to Aachen and only in 1818 was it returned to Trier.[4] In Cologne, it was especially the libraries of the Carthusians and of the St. Pantaleon monastery that had to surrender items from among their holdings.[5]

In the Italian theatre of war, the French confiscated in 1796 the most priceless items from Ambrosiana in Milan, among which were the famous Vergil manuscript of Petrarch and documents written in their own hand by Leonardo da Vinci and Galileo. Modena lost sixty-eight manuscripts; Bologna, five hundred; Monza, 115; Mantua, fifteen; Verona, thirteen; and Venice, two hundred. The evangelary of the Milan archbishop, Eribert (d. 1045), which was also carried along, has (together with its priceless binding) remained permanently in Paris. Of a second evangelary of Eribert's (which had been presented to Milan Cathedral) only the gilded silver binding has been returned. Following the Peace Settlement of Tolentino, Pope Pius VI had on July 13, 1797 to hand over from the Vatican to Rome five hundred of the most priceless manuscripts among which were French literary monuments that at one time had come with Queen Christine's library to Rome, as well as the estate of Winckelmann's, which the Vaticana had obtained after Cardinal Albani's death in 1779.[6] There later followed five more manuscripts and 150 valuable incunabula of the Vaticana.[7] The Pope's own collection was likewise robbed of valuable items by General Daunou. The library of the House of Albani in Rome suffered the same fate; it was carried off and scattered to the four winds; several manuscripts have come into Montpellier's Municipal Library. About 1,500 manuscripts have come out of the public libraries of Italy to Paris.

After the French had brought with them over three hundred Oriental manuscripts from the campaign in Egypt, further numerous manuscripts and printed monuments were carried away from South Germany at the beginning of the new century. The French occupied Salzburg on September 15, 1800, and on February 9, 1801, General Neveu acknowledged from Munich that he had obtained about a hundred manuscripts, mostly on parchment, among which were the missal (in five volumes) of Archbishop Bernhard von Rohr, a priceless work of art by Berthold Furtmeyer, and fifty-five incunabula from Salzburg. General Lecourbe seized twelve manuscripts and printed works on his own; they have disappeared permanently. The General generously presented the Capuchin monastery in Salzburg with a manuscriptural missal on parchment, which he had carried away with him from somewhere else.

With praiseworthy courage, Professor Michael Vierthaler, who had to attend to the delivery of books in Salzburg, published a detailed report in the Salzburg literary journal in order to establish once and for all the violent acts of the French against the arts and sciences collections. The valiant example of the courageous Salzburg scholar was echoed in the *Allgemeine Literarische Anzeiger,* where on February 19, 1801, simultaneously with the printing of the Salzburg list, similar lists were requested for publication, so that all these instances of items being carried off could be entirely found in this journal. Unfortunately, the wish has only been fulfilled to a small extent, when on August 13, the librarian, Ignatius Hardt, made known in a survey about six Greek manuscripts that had been carried away from the Court Library in Munich, and on September 14, Zapf from Augsburg reported about the French in that city, where the commanders-in-chief had limited themselves to book exchange. Then in 1803, there appeared in Leipzig, issued by Rinaldo Santalone, an important list *(Recensio)* of treasures carried away from

Rome, and at the same time the people of Nuremberg published in the *Neue fortgesetzte Anzeiger* a report concerning their losses. These lists have performed a valuable service for the later return of the monuments that had been carried away.

Nuremberg was occupied in December 1800. The government commissioner, Francois Marie Neveu, demanded eighteen paintings and fifty incunabula, but he was finally satisfied with five paintings and twelve printed works. The petition of Nuremberg citizens that they might publish the items they had surrendered in the *Literarische Anzeiger* was refused.[8]

The Munich Court Library was requried at the beginning of 1801 to surrender two woodcuts, sixteen manuscripts and just as many incunabula, among which was a German calendar sheet *(Cisianus)*, that was printed in 1470 by Günther Zainer in Augsburg; this is the only known extant copy of the work.[9]

The Rhine territories were ravaged for the second time in 1802 and 1803. Six hundred forty-four incunabula and 176 manuscripts (among which were eighty-four frm Echternch)[10] were lost. In Metz, the French removed 223 printing monuments and fifteen priceless manuscripts, among which was the famous sacramentary of the Bishop of Metz, Drogo (823–855), together with its valuable ivory tablets and an evangelary of the eighth century that was bound in ivory panels and written in gold on purple parchment.

In Wolfenbüttel, the French commissioners requested the catalogs on the day before Christmas, 1806, and immediately they took seven French illuminated manuscripts with them. Later there followed 129 Latin and fifty-one Oriental manuscripts, further numerous priceless printed works, among which were twelve printed on parchment, and the rare edition of the Boner's *Fables* printed in Bamberg by Albrecht Pfister. The Potsdam castle had to surrender three books by Voltaire.

The last great confiscation occurred in Vienna, from whence the most valuable treasures had been brought to Hungary and safety at the beginning of 1809. On March 28, 1809, however, eighty-five volumes of especially priceless works were packed in eleven boxes and carried away.[11] The French occupied the city on May 13, and immediately carried off 153 Oriental manuscripts, and still later, 112 French manuscripts, 168 printing monuments, and twenty engraved works. Seventeen manuscripts were seized for Bavaria, and for Italy, 230. In all, Vienna lost 832 priceless items.[12]

The items carried away in the name of the French nation at least had the hope of finding in Paris secure accommodations. Matters turned out worse for the treasures which had been removed by generals or by troop units, and which were thus lost irretrievably. Of such plundering hardly a library was spared among the ones situated within the domain of the occupied territory. The South German monasteries, especially Rebdorf, Kaisheim and Ottobeuren, were treated particularly badly.

It was an unprecedented wealth of art works and book treasures that, little by little, was assembled in Paris from the entire world. The most select paintings of the Netherlands' masters, outstanding art works of antiquity (the Medici Venus, the

Appollo of Belvedere, the Laacoon group), and about four thousand priceless literary monuments form the venerable collections all over Europe had arrived in the French capital and had excited the wonder of the whole world. Friedrich Schlegel was in Paris already in 1802, devoting himself there with zeal to medieval art and Oriental literature; and here, Friedrich Karl von Savigny prepared, in 1805, his basic *Geschichte des römischen Rechts im Mittelalter* ("History of Roman Law in the Middle Ages"); Ludwig Uhland, in 1810, considered it a great fortune to be able to wander among these treasures and at the same time to be able to dedicate himself to scholarly works in the libraries; Jakob Grimm received here enduring stimulations for his scholarly works, and Friedrich Thiersch enthusiastically wrote on January 29, 1814: "If only, instead of three months, it would be three years in Paris! What manuscripts of Plato, of Vergil, and of Terence! The heart leaps for joy at the sight of these venerable old parchments, the pale yellow of which gleams no less pleasantly than do the old marble statues!"

When the united armies drew into Paris on March 31, 1814, the hour of freedom was to strike also for the art and book treasures. Joseph von Görres, whose angry shouts at the Rhine had been heard far and wide, had been the first to demand restitution. Of the diplomats, it was above all Prussia's representative, Wilhelm von Humboldt, who pressed for the delivery of all the bootied items that had been carried off, without any exceptions being made. He raised the matter sharply in a conversation with Talleyrand on May 27, 1814. Following long opposition, Prussia and Austria got their property handed back again.[13] Bavaria also demanded its losses back following the Paris Peace Settlement of May 30, 1814. The Munich archeologist, Friedrich Thiersch, came into the French capital on October 18, dispatched there by the duke of Montgelas; following protracted negotiations, he believed he had matters in hand, when the return of Napoleon from Elba on March 1, 1815, again threw all the arrangements overboard.

With the settlement of the Second Paris Peace the representatives of the victorious powers (even Jakob Grimm was among them as a special delegate) pressed more definitely for the handing back of all cultural properties. There now ensued an enormous wandering back of art and book treasures toward the Netherlands, toward Wolfenbüttel, toward Bavaria, and toward Italy. Not everthing got back into its original home. Bavaria, which in the Peace of Schönbrunn of October 14, 1809, had received the prince-bishopric of Salzburg, also got delivered (in addition to the Munich manuscripts) the book treasures that had been carried off from Salzburg. The thirty-eight manuscripts (among which were priceless literary monuments from Lorsch, Mainz and Freising) out of the earlier Heidelberg library that were carried from Rome to Paris went back in January 1816, not to Rome, but to Heidelberg. In return for Prussian and Austrian efforts on behalf of the return of the possessions belonging to the Vatican, (whose authorized agent was the conciliatory sculptor, Antonio Canova) the Vatican handed over to Germany (along with five hundred manuscripts) all the German manuscripts of the earlier Heidelberg library, but not the remainder of them. Joseph von Görres had already demanded their delivery before the settlement of the First Paris Peace; so had Commander Blücher. There was unbounded jubilation when on July 8, 1816, the 850 German literary monuments that had been banished so long were now again awarded to the Heidelberg library.[14]

"Think of it," Creuzer wrote Jacobs on February 10, 1816,[15] "Our entire Bibliotheca Palatina, too, has been again won for Germany. The official report came to us yesterday. It was the note, shared with the university, to our minister of Foreign Affairs von Hacke, that the pope, in order to be accommodating to the Austrian circle, had agreed to give back to the university, in addition to those thirty-eight codices, the other 847 ones that are still at the Vatican. And herewith we have it again, the old Rheinish hoard—to speak in terms of the currently much-read Nibelungs." Heidelberg, where an Arnim, a Brentano and a Görres lived, all three of them enthusiastic about the older and popular German literature, became now even more impressive as the storied center of enthusiastic Romanticism. Görres could say of the city: "Heidelberg is itself a splendid romance; there Spring envelops house and court, and everything ordinary, with flowers and vines, and the castles and forests tell a fairy-tale of yore, as if there were nothing common in the world!" And looking back on the cultural history of Heidelberg Philipp Wilken could say: "It is one of the consecrated places where mankind reflects on that which is immortal." The newly awakened study of Germany's past found in the friendly city on the Neckar (which after Vienna and Munich could now be considered as having the third most significant collection of Old German literature) an effective area of cultivation.

Many of the priceless items that were carried off, having no more found their way back, may indeed have fallen into oblivion, or they were simply not to be found in Paris. Concerning an earlier manuscripts of the Vaticana, Delisle has told us a nice story in his life memoirs. When Georg Heinrich Pertz inquired in Paris concerning the single manuscript of Nithard's history of Emperor Louis the Pious, one denied the possession there of the priceless monument, while maintaining that the manuscript had gone back to Rome. When it was not found here, Pertz got handed over a copy that was allegedly produced prior to its return to Rome. Thereafter he now issued the text in 1821, and noted therewith that the manuscript given back to Rome was, in spite of all researches, not to be found there; all the more thankful, therefore, one should be for the Parisian textual copy. In reality, however, the manuscript lay well guarded in Paris, where one indeed would not have needed to deny the treasure, since Pope Pius VII, in giving back the manuscript (which stemmed form St. Maglione in Paris) had expressly surrendered all claims to it. All this had been forgotten in Paris, and only later would it again be identified.

32
Book Collectors of the Period
of the Revolution

There has hardly ever been a better time for book collectors and buyers than the decades that followed the dissolutions of the Jesuit Order and the Austrian monasteries, and after the irruption of the French army into the Rhine territories, which in their book holdings were among the richest of all of Germany; the treasures of their defenseless foundations and monasteries now were exposed to repeated plunderings. Moving in the confusion of the totally disintegrated conditions of ownership (in addition to the serious collectors who were concerned for the preservation of the abandoned books) were intermediaries, half book collectors and half book salesmen, who expertly went for the best parts of the treasures, in order to pass them on and thereby make a profit for themselves. Even in Germany right of the Rhine disguised bibliophiles with enticing offers were skilled in inducing numerous monasteries (prior to their being dissolved) to sell valuable book monuments. Germany has been mercilessly plundered in that period.

Directly in the period of the great book upheavals falls the work of a good book connoisseur, a man who has spent most of his lifetime with manuscripts and old printed works, collecting them and carrying them off, buying them and again selling them. He is the former Benedictine, Jean Baptist Maugérard (1735–1815),[1] whose deeds are blessed in France, but cursed in Germany. In acquiring books, Maugérard especially took advantage of the connections of his Order in acquiring books. Already on January 4, 1781, he was writing to Panzer in Nuremberg that he bought and exchanged incunabula, and he asked for estimates on the duplicates in the book collections.

He was able to provide his monastery of Saint Arnold in Metz with all sorts of priceless items. Following the dissolution of his Order, in the years between 1792 and 1801 he mainly resided in Germany, where he was chiefly occupied with trading in manuscripts and in old printed works, which he sold partially to Duke Ernst II of Saxony of Gotha (1772–1804), and partially to Paris. From such provenance, Gotha owns numerous incunabula and fifty manuscripts, among which are venerable items from Murbach, Metz, Trier, Hildesheim, Erfurt, Bamberg, Würzburg, Werden, Fulda, and even the famous Echternach evangelary of Emperor Otto II, which the Echternach monks had given in trust to Erfurt in 1794. In all these monuments that were carried off, the designations of origin have carefully been removed or made unrecognizable. In this plundering, Mainz has lost three copies of the 42-line Bible, among them being the copy with the famous *Cremer* subscript and the number of the year, Metten a 36-line Bible, Donauwörth a Terence and Valerius' Maximus collective volume from the possessions of Sigismund Meisterlin. The Benedictine monasteries have especially been plundered. At the suggestion of von Praet, the director at that time of the Parisian National Library, Maugérard was in 1802 installed as the French State Commissioner for the dissolved monastery libraries for the German *Departement* and entrusted with administering in Luxembourg the mass of books from the Rhineland; this consisted of the residues of collections of the Benedictines in Münster, Echternach, St. Hubert, of the Cistercians of Orval, the Capuchins and the Recollects of Diekirch and Luxembourg, of the Dominicans and the Jesuits of Luxembourg. Although the treasures piling up in Luxembourg had already (by decrees of April 15, and July 29, 1798) been declared the property of the newly established central school, Maugérard, who with his sharp eye knew well how to discover the priceless items, had eighty-four manuscripts (among which seventy-nine were from Echternach, and five from Orval) seized and carried off to Paris. The valuable monuments, most of them manuscripts from the eighth to the twelfth century, have not been returned in 1815. A grateful Paris has dedicated a bust to the enthusiastic counselor, and a room in the National Library is named for him.

The Scottish monk, Maurus Horn, has pursued an intermediate book trade similar to Maugérard's in the German monasteries, while he wandered from monastery to monastery and mainly searched through their libraries for old printed monuments. He had belonged to the Scots' monastery in Regensburg, and he rendered services for its library, until he withdrew from the Order and then devoted himself to the book trade for England.

In the year 1799, and thus just before the dissolution of the monasteries, he was especially skilled in carrying off priceless Mainz and Bamberg incunabula from the Franconian Order houses in Bamberg and Würzburg, among them being a collective volume with printings by Albrecht Pfister, two copies of the 42-line Bible, the two Mainz psalters, and even rare broadsides, in order to sell most of them to the English collector, Earl Spencer of Althorp. Since the Scot, a good book connoisseur, had plenty of money available from England, he was successful in most instances in procuring the desired acquisitions. His German contemporary, Schaab, reports of him: "He was the true image of the crafty Maugérard, less imposing in his figure, but as flexible as a puppet."[2]

Injured the most in those times of general uncertainty were the book possessions in the Rhineland monasteries, where books and paintings had often been abandoned following the irruption of the French. Whoever wished to could easily acquire the alienated treasures of the first order. Among those who seized them without many scruples was also Joseph von Görres (1776–1848). As the brothers Boisserée in Cologne brought together that unique collection of old German paintings which today constitutes a proud possession of the Alte Pinakothek in Munich, so did Görres acquire around the turn of the century over two hundred manuscripts, which for security purposes had been brought to Ehrenbreitstein out of Rhineland monasteries, and which stemmed primarily from Himmerod in the Eifel and St. Maximim in Trier; they are outstanding monuments of the Rhineland art of writing from the Middle Ages. When the fortunate owner, who carefully protected his treasure, emigrated in 1819 to Strasbourg, he left a part of the priceless items in Coblenz, in order later to transfer them to the gymnasium there. The residue, which was conveyed to Strasbourg and later to Munich, remained forgotten for a long time, until in 1902, it was offered for sale by the Görres family heirs – to the surprise of the scholarly world. Sixty-four manuscripts, most of them literary monuments of the ninth century (among which was that collective manuscript according to which Johannes Sichardus in 1528, has published for the first time the work of Filastrius concerning the heresies), were acquired by the Prussian State Library in Berlin, as was, in 1908, an especially precious item of the collection, the evangelary from Prüm, which for a long time had been considered as a gift of Emperor Lothar to this monastery.[3] With these acquisitions, the Berlin Library has then, in 1911, also united the seventy-two manuscripts left behind at one time by Görres collection is again together in Berlin, and in public possession.[4] The famous Trier manuscript of the Benedictine Rule *(Codex regularum)* has gone to the Munich State Library (Cod. lat. 28 118).

The Rhineland book properties, once broken up, appeared to be inexhaustible. Perhaps the most valuable items thereof, Johann Wilhelm Carl Adolf Hüpsch (1730–1805) was skillful in acquiring; never particular as to his means, he occasionally even displayed false names and titles. With the excuse that he was writing a work about the Catholic liturgy, this strange man was able to acquire no less than six evangelaries and lectionaries embellished with valuable metal and ivory ornamentation. For this historical-liturgical purpose the St. Andrew Foundation in Cologne (he reports this himself) had given him its evangelaries decorated with ornaments and panels of ivory. He likewise has obtained as a present from the prince of Hohenlohe, archbishop of Breslau, similar panels and little altars from the chapel of the collegiate church of St. Gereon. There has been handed over to him from the collegiate church of St. Martin in Liège a book of the gospels with the Roman diptych of Consul Flavius Astyrius. The Cologne Foundation of St. George has let him have its best book of the gospels (the cover of which has mounted with silver plates and decorated with ivory plates) for two louis d'or. The priceless monument of art is now in the Hessian Museum at Darmstadt.

Baron von Hüpsch (it is under this name that the remarkable man continues to live in history) ultimately owned 868 manuscripts, 1,235 old monuments of printing, and over three thousand more recent works; earlier he had already sold to Landgrave Ludwig of X of Hesse 109 incunabula, to Duke Ernst of Gotha a hundred old monuments of printing, and to Duke Karl of Württemberg a gospel manuscript that he had carried off from St. James in Liège,[5] and finally, in addition to several printed Bibles, an entire Psalter manuscript written in uncials at Echternach – the so-called Merovingian psalter of the seventh century. Echternach, Werden, and St. James in Liège – those were the main monasteries form which Hüpsch has enriched himself with literary monuments. At the auction of the Liège abbey library in March 1788, he acquired eighty-one manuscripts alone for a ridiculously low price.[6] He himself once wrote that he would have had to write to abbeys and monasteries for two hundred years long before he would have assembled so much as he had purchased here for a paltry sum. Six manuscripts borrowed from the Carthusians in Xanten have been handed over to him in March 1786 in exchange for more recent works. The collection (which was ultimately estimated to be worth 36,685 franks) Hüpsch, in a generous moment before his death, bequeathed to the landgrave of Hesse; he thereby acquired merit for himself, in that the inestimably precious items went over into the public domain.[7] Today they constitute a special cause for pride in the Territorial Library in Darmstadt.

A Rhinelander yet to be mentioned as an enthusiastic collector of art works and books is Canon Ferdinand Franz Wallraf (1748–1824). His valuable book properties, with 14,500 volumes, 521 manuscripts and 1,055 incunabula have been transferred to the Municipal Library of Cologne.

In Belgium, the scholarly Charles Joseph Emmanuel Hulthem (1764–1832) zealously collected manuscripts and printed works from the dissolved monastery libraries of the country. Following his death, the Belgian government obtained the valuable estate which contained over a thousand manuscripts with the intent of building a Belgian national library in Brussels. The Belgian king authorized the new foundation on March 16, 1837. Shortly thereafter it was united with the so-called Burgundian Library, a priceless legacy of the counts of Flanders and their successors, the dukes of Burgundy, and it was elevated to, and given the name of, the Royal Library of Belgium.

33

The Dissolution of
Clerical Libraries in Germany

The wars and upheavals of the French Revolution were followed on February 9, 1801, by the Peace of Lunéville, according to which the left bank of the Rhine was transferred by the Emperor and the Empire to France, and the German princes who were thereby wronged, were supposed to be repaid by means of land in Germany. For the accomplishing of these ends, the *Deputation of the Delegates of the Empire* (Reichsdeputationshauptschluss) at Regensburg in 1803 dissolved with one fell stroke of the pen all the clerical estates, the foundations and monasteries, and their lands and other properties were confiscated. Judgment was therewith pronounced over the clerical libraries of the German territories as well.

While with the confiscation of the clerical book possessions in France, the whole country had contributed to the building up of the Bibliothèque Nationale, in Germany, with the dissolution of the monasteries only the Catholic territories were involved, and therefore primarily Bavaria, Silesia and the Rhine territories; in the Protestant territories, the Reformation had already done away with the foundations and monasteries.

That matters in Germany have not resulted in one overarching national library (as they did in France) had its basis in the German political splintering. Each sovereign territory was able to confiscate the book collections that lay within its boundaries. With the division of the enormous book treasures, frequently repeated was a distressing event like the one that had occurred several years previously in Austria, and which likewise had resulted in grievous losses and squanderings, especially of the records, but also of the books. For example, before the book stock of the Corvey monastery came into the University Library at Marburg, half the manuscripts were lost, and things have not gone much better with the printed works. The notorious auctions and sales to secondhand dealers and the pulping businesses have meant the very speedy disappearance of immense masses of paper from the former clerical possessions. The more the sources about these events are investigated, the sharper becomes the judgment about the non-sensical squandering. In the foreweord to his *Verzeichnis der deutschen Pfälzer Handschriften in Heidelberg* ("List of the German Palatine Manuscripts in Heidelberg"), Jakob Wille judges: "The carrying off of the Heidelberg Library to Rome may have meant a strike against Calvinism; but even so, it was an appreciation, yes, a veritable passion for books, which was its basis. Still, this loss represented a deliverance as compared with what at the beginning of the nineteenth century our forefathers have committed in excessive and pointless ways against the monuments of their own historical life."

Among the German book collections, it was especially the Munich Library that experienced an enormous increase in its holdings through monastical accessions; it was elevated with one stroke into a world-famous collection of selected priceless items. The Court Library of the Bavarian princes, even following its flourishing period under Duke Albrecht V and Elector Maximilian I, had not been entirely neglected by the successors; however, even under the leadership of the scholarly history researcher, Andreas Felix von Oefele (1706–1780), it had led rather a tranquil existence within its four walls. Valuable enrichments flowed into it from the dissolved monasteries of the Jesuits in Munich (1773) and the Augustinian Canons in Indersdorf (1783). With the assignment to it of the Indersdorf properties, it was expressly emphasized that the Electoral collections should be stipulated as being for general use and that they should be opened to everyone who was eager for knowledge. Thus the concept of the public nature of the courtly collection had already found an entrée also in Munich.

On March 28, 1790, the Court Library, in keeping with a decree of Elector Karl Theodore, was handed over to public use, and in connection therewith, the court librarian, Georg Stanislaus von Roccatani, has held a learned Latin discourse concerning the use of public book collections.[1] Kasimir Haeffelin, later the ambassador in Rome and ultimately a cardinal, had the superintendence of the three public court libraries in Munich, Mannheim and Düsseldorf.[2] From the reports that Haeffelin has furnished the court following the accession of Elector Max Joseph (February 1, 1799), it seems that the Düsseldorf Library (which was effectively promoted by the predecessor, Elector Karl Theodore) was already at that time no more being thought of exclusively as court property, but was already being conceived of as an object of public concern, with monetary funds coming from the diet. "It is to be wished," Haeffelin wrote on December 11, 1799, to the Count Monteglas, "that the Bavarian legislative assembly will also consider the libraries stipulated for national education and the public school institutions to be general necessities of the country and may support them with appropriate monetary contributions." The Enlightenment movement gradually came to Bavaria also. National education was the new magic word, which furnished for the libraries also the future goal of their activity. Within the range of this educational goal, Haeffelin assigned a significant place to the libraries, "the supporting pillar for the further development of knowledge and the promotion of the fatherland's enlightenment." The academy and the library were supposed to be the most important commonly useful aids for the desired national education.

Following these far-reaching ideas was the government's proposal to have a complete listing made of all the books and documents in the entire country, in order thereby to obtain an overview of all the extant literary monuments and to be able, through suitable measures, to prevent these treasures from being carried away. There seems to have been a presentiment in Munich of the secularization that was coming. All of Haeffelin's plans, however, have remained unexecuted, and they were then finally overtaken by the events of 1803, which elevated the Munich Court Library not merely to a public territorial institution in Haeffelin's sense, but also to a great collection for the fatherland of the most significant book monuments of the entire country. By this time, Haeffelin was emphasizing that in this transformation one was no longer dealing with a court library but rather with an institution of a public character which concerned the entire nation and which for the most part would be maintained by it, so that as often as not even in official documents, it would devolve into the name of "National Library." But the elector resisted the designation, because it could be objected to, on the ground that Bavaria was not really a nation, or that the designation meant a upsurpation towards the Parisian National Library, or even that the name sounded too republican. Thus the transformed institution initially came to be called Central Library, and later the Court and State Library.[3]

On March 11, 1803, the select committee of the Bavarian general territorial administration for the dissolving of the monasteries appointed three trusted men for seizing and reviewing the Bavarian monastery libraries: the Munich superintending court librarian, Johann Christoph von Aretin, for the Central Library, the former provost of the Augustinian Canons' foundation of Beuerberg, Paul Hupfauer, for the Landshut University Library, and the inspector of schools, Joachim Schubauer, for the school libraries.

It was wholly in the sense of the Enlightenment that according to an order, the reviewing of books had especially to be concerned with the "fanatical and superstitious" works. Whatever fell under these groups was supposed to be removed and auctioned off as waste paper. Fortunately for the books, appreciation for manuscripts and old printed monuments had already developed so strongly that at least these works, being monuments of antiquity, were spared the Enlightenment's fatal judgment.

The three commissioners began their difficult work on March 24, 1803; by the end of November they were finished with it. Baron von Aretin in his *Beyträge zur Geschichte und Literatur, vorzüglich aus den Schätzen der pfalzbaierischen Centralbibliothek* ("Contributions to History and Literature, chiefly out of the Treasures of the Bavarian Palatine Central Library")[4] has published descriptive letters concerning the joint activity; these give us rather good insights into the condition of the Bavarian monastery libraries prior to the dissolution, and allow us some idea of the enormous augmentation that the Munich collection was to receive. Around sixty libraries had to be visited and examined. With the treasures of all these clerical sites united, Munich's Central Library now in fact became the territorial library for the Electorate of Bavaria, in accord with what Haeffelin more or less had in mind for it; in his wildest dreams, however, he had not imagined, in addition, a collection of selected book monuments, a thoroughly priceless collection which in its unity was unique.

That which Tegernsee and Freising (or, somewhat later) Bamberg and St. Emmeram contributed were pearls out of very old cultural centers—items which only a few collections of the entire world could claim as being theirs.[5]

Of the approximately fifty thousand manuscripts of the Munich collection (the richest possession of manuscripts in Germany) attracting the attention of scholarship are, besides the wonderful manuscripts with miniature paintings, especially the numerous monuments of the older German language and literature history: the *Wessobrunner Gebet* ("Wessobrunn Prayer"), the oldest German exposition of the Lord's Prayer in the Freising *Paternoster*, the *Muspilli* poem out of St. Emmeran in Regensburg, the *Heliand* from Bamberg, Otfried von Weissenburg, the old High German harmony of the gospels from Freising, the exposition of the *Song of Songs* by the abbot of Ebersberg, Williram, the *Nibelungenlied* ("Song of the Nibelungs") in the two versions from Hohenems and from the Prunn castle, the vagabond songs *(Carmina Burana)* from Benediktbeuren, Gottfried of Strasbourg's *Tristan und Isolde*, Ulrich of Lichtenstein's *Frauendienst* ("Service of Women"), Wolfram von Eschenbach's *Parzifal* and *Titurel*, Rudolf von Ems' *Wilhelm von Orleans*, Jakob von Maerland's Dutch epic, *Alexanders Geesten*, and the so-called Colmar Songs, acquired by Jörg Wickram in 1546 for the Colmar mastersingers' school.[6]

In keeping with the Viennese and Parisian examples, one gradually in Munich sought to take in the entire country (therefore also the new Bavarian territories, which in the following years and with the elevation of Bavaria to a kingdom, came to old Bavaria) and to draw all the valuable book treasures into the capital city. Thus Bamberg had to surrender to Munich priceless pieces from the legacy of Emperor Henry II, and Augsburg had to do likewise with 219 manuscripts of the cathedral, in addition to valuable portions of the holdings of its Municipal Library (among these being the Greek *Eparchos* manuscripts). On September 18, 1807, Aretin set new requirements in a memorandum, to the effect "that all excellent literary rarities and remarkable items contained in the rest of the libraries should be handed over to the Munich Library as the central uniting point for everything which the Kingdom can show as being priceless in the treasures of literature." Aretin especially complained about the small contributions coming from the Upper Palatinate, from Nuremberg, Bamberg, and Swabia. The Municipal Library in Memmingen, a not very large but select collection, had been piled up in a granary and was being destroyed by the mice, the wind and weather. Things were faring not much better with the libraries of Augusburg. All Swabian libraries ought to be united in Augsburg and be organized by a suitable man such as the learned privy counselor, Zapf. Aretin reports frankly in the same memorandum about the many mistakes made in the takeover of the expropriated books. The library in Rottenbuch had especially been the victim of a terrible misfortune.

In all the monasteries, as a consequence of orders from the highest level, there was sorted out a class of books which, because of their superstitions and their contents were in opposition to the furtherance of popular education, and were supposed to be made into wastepaper. Due to the lack of skill on the part of the Rottenbuch commissioner, the entire monastery library now (which the exception of these rare works previously carried off) had been sold as waste paper. "In such a way," Aretin narrates, "the paper trader received a fully equipped library that contained the most prominent works in each discipline, according to the weight, one hundred pounds for fifty pfennigs. The zealous and learned monastery librarian fell into despair when he had to see this collection, for which he has used the greatest part of his life, ending up in the paper mill. It was only through prostrate pleas that the honorable man, who was then almost seventy years old, salvaged several priceless historical works, which he had to purchase himself with what was left of the monies he had saved with great difficulty.

Aretin also did not forget the monasteries of the territory of Tyrol which had fallen to Bavaria in the year 1806, and the numerous monasteries that had to be dissolved, such as St. Michael, Neustift, Gries, Wilten, Marienberg, Fiecht and Stams; in his memorandum he especially mentioned Neustift and Wilten as owners of desirable priceless pieces. The book holdings of the Tyrol did not, however, come to Munich; the greatest part of them rather went to the University Library in Innsbruck. When in 1814 the territory devolved again to Austria, and several monasteries such as Wilten, Stams, Neustift, and Marienberg were re-established, the Innsbruck library was required to return them a portion of its new accessions.

In 1809, with an appeal to Napoleon about the occupation of Bavaria in the War of Spanish Succession, Munich announced its claims to Vienna manuscripts. The seventeen items that Aretin thereby obtained from the humiliated city had to be given back again in 1816. The Munich library was more successful in 1811 when it demanded and received the valuable manuscripts of the Benedictine monastery of St. Emmeram in Regensburg, which had come into Bavaria in 1810. The year 1815, brought back again not merely the treasures the French had robbed from Munich, but also manuscripts and old printed works that had been carried off to Paris from Salzburg, which now belonged to Bavaria for a short period.

Munich further obtained manuscripts and printed works from the libraries of the Salzach district, above all from Salzburg and Ranshofen, and finally, the former episcopal library of Chiemsee, which had been accommodated in Salzburg for a long time. On June 22, 1824, there came, in addition, to Munich the valuable items from among what was left of the Mainz Cathedral Library, which had been brought for the sake of security to Aschaffenburg before the siege of the city of Mainz in 1793; among these was the priceless collection of Bonifacian letters.

Baron von Aretin has not been able to enjoy his work for very long. A difficult and inflexible personality, he had fallen into irreconcilable conflict with the Academy members, Friedrich Jacobi and Schlichtegroll, and, as vice-president of the appellate court, he had been removed in 1811 to Neuburg an der Donau. Aretin appears not always to have mastered the great difficulties of bringing a quick and functional order into the immense book treasures.[7] But it is also perhaps the most challenging assignment that a German librarian had ever been given. For the gathering of the book treasures, Aretin has undoubtedly achieved the greatest merit.

It was fortunate for the second examination of the old Bavarian book holdings that it was directed by a man who loved books and was untiring in his effort to save as much as possible for Landshut (later Munich) University.[8] Paul Hupfauer also did not allow himself in this effort to be confused by the reproach that he was transmitting nothing more than pitiful books and useless theologians. To him we are indebted for the fact that more books from the monasteries have not been destroyed. The alert natural scientist, Franz Paula von Schrank, had especially stressed this bibliothecarial activity of the earlier provost of Beuerberg with appreciative words. His calling to be librarian has been very fortunate. Scarcely had the new librarian arrived in Landshut when the book holdings were saved from being made into paperbags, and order was introduced into the chaos.

The monastery book treasures of the newly incorporated parts of the Bavarian territory remained (besides the already cited items that were carried off to Munich) in their areas and were either integrated with already existing libraries, or were utilized in new foundations. Thus did the University Library in Würzburg obtain the numerous foundation and monastery libraries of the former bishopric of Würzburg, among where were the priceless parchment manuscripts of the Cathedral Library.[9] The library of the abolished university in Bamberg was thus transformed into a handsome collection and augmented by the clerical libraries of the earlier bishopric, among which were the priceless manuscripts of the cathedral chapter and of Michelsberg. New provincial libraries were formed out of the collected book holdings in Passau, Regensburg, Amberg, Eichstätt, Dillingen, and Neuburg an der Donau.[10] Isolated monastery libraries became noblemen's possessions: so it was with Amorbach, which fell to the princes of Leiningen; the books for the most part have been sold in 1851.

The collection of the Carthusians in Buxheim initially came to the counts of Ostein, and then to the family of Waldbott-Bassenheim, and was auctioned off in 1883. The Buxheim manuscripts, to which the Carthusian, Hilprand of Brandenburg, has contributed essentially, (the same one who is known to bibliophiles as the owner of one of the oldest bookplates) have today been scattered all over the entire world. Even the princely Oettingen-Wallerstein entailed library in Maihingen, into which have come valuable holdings out of St. Marg in Füssen, from Deggingen, Donauwörth, Kirchheim and Maihingen, had for the most part been disposed of. Gradually flowing together into the Augsburg Municipal Library were the residues of Jesuit libraries and other unappropriated holdings.[11] The present-day Court Library in Aschaffenburg evidences a unique history; in its main holdings it goes back to the Court Library of the Mainz elector, Friedrich Karl Joseph von Erthal (1774–1802), and in 1792, confronted with the French threat, it was brought to Aschaffenburg for security's sake. Its director in Mainz has been the poet, Jakob Wilhelm Heinse, (author of the novel, *Ardinghello),* who was called there in 1786. He had moved, with the library, to Aschaffenburg, and his restless life has ended there on June 22, 1803. Prince Karl von Dalberg (1802–1813) had declared the book collection to be the property of the newly established principality of Aschaffenburg; following the dissolution of this small state in 1813, it was transferred as a foundation into the possession of the Bavarian state; but it has remained in Aschaffenburg.

Also in the rest of the German territories, the dissolved clerical holdings of books, so far as they were considered worth preserving, were taken in by the territorial, municipal and university libraries; all the rest were sold, auctioned off, or discarded. The main centers of this great assembling of books became Stuttgart, with the influx of books from the monastery sites of Württemberg; Freiburg im Breisgau, with the books seized from the monasteries of the Black Forest and Breisgau; Karlsruhe, with the collections out of the houses of religious Orders in Baden, among which was Reichenau alone with 267 parchment and 164 paper manuscripts;[12] Darmstadt, with additions out of Seligenstadt, Hirschhorn, Lansheim and Wimpfen; Wiesbaden with works it incorporated from the Nassau monasteries and foundations; Bonn, with portions of collections out of Marienheide, Wipperfurth and Wetzlar; Münster with enrichments from the Westphalian monasteries; Düsseldorf with items that had come in from the Bergian, Clevian and Marchian monasteries; Trier with collections from the Rhenish houses; and Marburg with what was left at Corvey.[13] The Benedictine abbey of Weingarten, together with the principality of Fulda, came to the house of Orange-Nassau. The most valuable manuscripts wandered in part toward Fulda, and partly to Stuttgart and Darmstadt.

Spurred on by Munich's example, the antiquarian, Johann Gustav Gottlieb Büsching (1783–1829) attempted in Breslau to carry out the foundation of a large "Silesian Central Library." Named by the minister, Hardenberg, in November 1810, as "Royal Prussian Commissioner for the Transfer of Libraries, Archives and Art Objects in the Dissolved Foundations and Monasteries," Büsching, who was twenty-seven years old at the time, proceeded with fiery zeal to the integrating of the rich treasures from over seventy Silesian foundations and monasteries.[14] "Too much cannot be done for a country that through its own industry in collecting has brought together such treasures as are daily disclosed to me." Inspired by this principle, the intelligent scholar had aspirations for a large facility: a central library, an art collection, an archive for the country, an antiquarian institution that would manage the duplications, an entire network of provincial, municipal, school and church libraries; he underestimated the difficulties, however, that were associated with its actual accomplishment, and he was soon clashing with the general commissioner's regulations. On September 6, 1811, he (the general commissioner) decreed that only the lists (and no more the seized books themselves) should be sent into Breslau. When Büsching was completely forced out, his far-seeing work of salvaging also remained unexecuted, and whatever immediately presented itself was pulled together, without any understanding and in the greatest hurry. There were thus gathered in Breslau only about 70,000 volumes, with around 1,700 manuscripts.

Even the libraries of individual universities were caught up in the enormous movement of books in these decades. The dissolved schools of higher learning gave their books to other universities, and insitutions that removed elsewhere took their books along with them. The library of Bützow came to Rostock, that of Duisburg fell to Bonn, that of Rinteln to Marburg, that of Frankfurt an der Oder to Breslau, the one of Wittenberg to Halle, that of Helmstedt to Marburg, Brunswick and Göttingen, and that of Altdorf to Erlangen. The towns of Dillingen, Bamberg, Herborn, Erfurt, Mainz, and Paderborn maintained their book collections, although their schools of higher learning were dissolved. Making its way with the University of Ingolstadt to Landshut in 1800 was also its library; it went to Munich in 1826.

Especially did the university in Göttingen, favored by Jérome, fare well under Westphalian government; following the dissolution of the kingdom in 1814, however, considerable holdings out of Brunswick, Gandersheim, Halberstadt, Helmstedt, Hildesheim, Magdeburg, and Quedlinburg had to be given back again. The crates from Wolfenbüttel were not even unpacked, when they had to be returned intact to their "home." Wolfenbüttel even recovered its old library from Helmstedt.[15] In the Rhineland, a furious struggle broke out among Duisburg, Düsseldorf, Neuwied, Coblenz, Cologne and Bonn concerning the allotting of the Rhenish book holdings. Pleading especially for Cologne was the Lord Lieutenant of Jülich-Cleve-Berg, Count Solms-Laubach. In all of Cologne (so he stated in his memorandum of July 23, 1816) still more complete book treasures were lying hidden, and it was especially rich in sources for the clarifying of the history of the Middle Ages, which still was so obscure, and likewise for church, legal and art history. In Bonn, on the contrary, everything that would be looked on to some extent as the foundation for a public library had disappeared. Success, however, finally went to Bonn, which from now on was to constitute the center of cultural life on the Rhine.[16]

As the storms of the French Revolution and the events following it abated, quite new libraries came into being, as well as a new conception of their significance as national property. One can without exaggeration designate the assumption of the clerical book collections so that they became public property as an event of cultural life that was of the greatest significance, as the hour of birth of the modern libraries — libraries which belong to the people as a whole and are provided for by the state. Previously there had been book collections in abundance, libraries of princes' courts, of cities and towns, of universities, of foundations and monasteries, but still missing in them all were the two chief characteristics of the new radical transformation, ownership by the entire people in an enormous and now for all practical purposes re-awakened cultural possession, and the state's duty (resulting form the seizures) to provide for regulated administration of these now public possessions, but also for increasing their holdings and making them accessible. Despite the violence of the takeover and the losses (which were condemned by all) associated with the careless overhastiness when the incorporations were going on, the "nationalization" of the clerical book properties is to be evaluated as an inestimable gain.

From the historical view one can perhaps thus best express the relationship of the "once" and "now": the monasteries and foundations, as patrons of the church that had the leading role in the Middle Ages, have been the trustees of the cultural properties, until their time had come, and with the gradual secularization of the whole of public life (itself accelerated by the Enlightenment), these properties, together with the functions associated with them, went over now to the new trustee of the community, the state. The venerable old conception of the inestimable cultural value of the book collections (which was effectively prmoted by Enlightenment ideas) now experienced a revitalization and elevated the temple of books, filled as it was with the national monumnts of the past and which even attracted the courtly possessions, into important objects of the public culture-politics. Mobilized for its victorious rise, the intellectual movement of Romanticism could with open hands draw fully on the treasures of the German past; these had at one time been scattered; but they were now united and accessible for research. The subsequent quick rise of the sciences, and the development of the historical sense, cannot be considered apart from the vital effects of libraries and the monuments of the past which are preserved within them.

Literature and the World of Books in the Modern Period After Romanticism

The stronger we see the stream of books swelling in the modern period, with its powerful political events, its proud technical achievements, and with the great upsurge of the natural sciences, the more difficult it becomes to determine the position of the book within the context of these unprecedented changes, and the harder it is to find that which is the transforming, the advancing, the essential pointing to the future, which has indeed been given to us by the world of books. A digest of all these relationships can ever be only a tentative survey.

In the history of literature, we speak of Pietism, the Enlightenment, *Sturm und Drang* ("Storm and Stress"), Classicism, Romanticism, Realism, regional art, Naturalism, and of other movements, and we thereby justifiably imagine definite forms of cultural life, eventful intellectual waves which from time to time go through the country and which change people's feeling for life and for the world. We should, however, not forget that reality never fits entirely into these artificial classifications. The developments that follow one upon another rather interpenetrate, like the generations that create and experience them.[1] Thus there has also been no entirely unified cultural structure at the beginning of the nineteenth century. One had recently designated the ascent of Germany's cultural life (which coincides approximately with Goethe's period) with the word, *Deutsche Bewegung* ("German Movement"), and thereby embraced those German reactions against the Enlightenment, such as are expressed in *Sturm und Drang*, in Pietism, in Classicism and Romanticism, and in connection with which Klopstock perhaps constitutes the beginning, and Hegel the close.[2] Each period creates the world and its values anew, believing itself to have found the best and lasting solution for life's eternal riddle, while it is only the varying demands of the period that stand ever in question.

Situated at the foreground of this feeling for life in the beginning of the century is Romanticism; with its opposing world of sensations, it is the sharpest antipol of the Enlightenment, which is sensed as being an impoverishment of life.[3] The designation Romanticism was coined by Schlegel, who was, practically speaking, the new movement's legislator. It signifies the flight of the shifting *Zeitgeist* of a period, from sovereign reason's empty world, which could not solve life's questionableness, nor give the requisite security against life's complexities, into the soul's wonderful richness, into the sensitive feeling, the imaginative faculty, into the incomprehensible, the unfathomable, the presentiment, the remoteness, the infinite, the dreamy, the impenetrable, the unreal, the unconscious, the godly, the supernatural, and in the field of poetry, into the music of fairy tales, dreams, and nature. If Classicism predominantly reflected the feeling of being alive, of a detached calm, and of perfection in a highly developed humanity, Romanticism is an infinite movement, an eternal desire, and a nostalgia for that which is distant. It is life-giving, it is the transformation of the world toward the depths of the unconscious, toward the blue flower (in accordance with Goethe's doctrine of colors), toward totality and the entirety of ceaseless, inexhaustible life, toward the final original cause of being—toward God. In Romanticism, great worlds arise inspiringly before the elated senses: nature as a symbol of the spirit, night as a magical power and protector of mysterious powers, the past as the dispenser of accumulated strengths, nationality as the myth and soul of its own nature, and fantasy as the eternal life-secret of things, the world's infinity filled with intuitions and promises.

Without wishing to present here a history of literature, we would nevertheless like in these pages to portray briefly again and again the imprint of the world of books, as in each period this was operative within a definite compact unity, and is still today vitally in evidence; we would like here to refer to its productive yield in the most important life-books and life-words, which even today have to be considered as being the pure pearls of German literature, and as the harbingers of the German soul. How does Romanticism's book world represent itself to us?

From the turn of the new century to be mentioned are Johann Peter Hebel (1760–1828) and Jean Paul Richter (1763–1824). We are familiar with the dialect poet, Hebel, through his *Schatzkästlein des Rheinischen Hausfreundes* ("Little Treasure Chest of the Rhenish House Friend"), which was distributed in many editions and was a master work of popular narrative literature. Jean Paul, the poet who was so effusive of, but who also had an infinite love for, the world of everyday, and was indeed always wrestling with these two worlds; at one time, he was influential as hardly anyone else was. Due to the formless character of his language which was so rich in imagery, he has unfortunately deprived himself of an enduring effect in his splendid works, *Leben des Quintus Fixlein* ("Life of Quintus Fixlein") (1796), *Titan*, and *Leben des vergnügten Schulmeisters Maria Wuz in Auenthal* ("Life of the happy Schoolmaster Maria Wuz in Auenthal") (1800 until 1803). In his period, he was among the most celebrated authors of the day. Gottfried Keller loved him dearly, and had his "Grüner Heinrich" doze off at the break of day, following his having read through the night, with his cheek on the beloved book.

The connection between Classicism and Romanticism is outstandingly evident in Friedrich Hölderlin (1770–1843), the great seer and singer of German peoples' desire for the everlasting kingdom, the master of linguistic form in inspired melodies and remarkable rhythmic language. His *Hyperion oder der Eremit von Griechenland* (1797–99) ("Hyperion, or the Eremite of Greece"), and his poems published in 1826 by Uhland and Schwab, are the brightest highlights of the culture of linguistic art. Concerning his musical feeling for language he himself once cheerfully uttered the jubilant word: "As Jupiter's eagle did for the song of the Muses, so do I listen to the wonderful, ceaseless harmony within myself."

What the two brothers and leaders of Romanticism, August Wilhelm von Schlegel (1767–1845), the discoverer and translator of Shakespeare, and Friedrich von Schlegel (1772–1829), the poet of *Lucinda* (1799), and both the inflluential publishers of Athenäum (1798–1800) – what they were for their time, or what even the no less effectual Ludwig Tieck (1773 until 1853), the author of the glorious *Fortunat*, signified for the advance of the cultural life at that time, even more enduringly became Friedrich Wilhelm Joseph Schelling (1775–1854), the celebrant of the idea as the world-generating spirit in nature and history, or Friedrich Schleiermacher (1768–1834). In his much noticed *Reden über die Religion an die Gebildeten unter ihren Verächtern* ("Speeches Concerning Religion to its Cultured Despisers") (1799), the latter saw the root of all religion in the feeling for the Infinite. There was also Wilhelm Heinrich Wackenröder (1773–1798), the new discoverer of medieval art, who has become familiar to us as the creator of the *Herzensergiessungen eines kunstliebenden Klosterbruders* ("Heartfelt Outpourings of an Art-loving Monk") (1797), published by Tieck. The quintessential poet of the older Romanticism is Friedrich Leopold, Baron von Hardenberg, called Novalis (1772–1801), who in his famous *Hymnen an die Nacht* ("Hymns to the Night") celebrates the veiled night as the likeness and unveiler of the true essence of the world, who seeks in his novel, *Heinrich von Ofterdingen* to transform life as a whole symbolically into poetry, and in his spiritual songs, such as "Ich sehe dich in tausend Bildern, Maria, lieblich ausgedrückt" ("I see you lovely expressed, Maria, in a thousand images"), proclaims the deepest mystical experience of feeling. Schleiermacher has celebrated him as a godly youth, for whom everything his spirit touches becomes art, and his entire world reflection a single great poem.

There is, further, Heinrich von Kleist (1777–1811), the poet whom life and the hopelessness of bad times broke, the victorious author of the dramas that are still vital today, *Der Zerbrochene Krug* ("The Broken Pitcher"), *Penthesilea* (1808), *Das Käthchen von Heilbronn* (1810) ("Kate of Heilbronn"), *Die Hermannschlacht* (1808) ("Hermann's Battle"), "Prinz Friedrich von Homburg," (1810), and creator of the masterful novella, *Michael Kohlhaas*. Ernst Theodor Amadeus Hoffmann (1776–1822), too, the unique poet and musician, with his half gay and fantastic, half weird and ghostly main works, *Elixiere des Teufels* (1815–1816) ("Elixirs of the Devil") *Nachtstücke (1817) ("Night Pieces")*, *Die Serapionsbrüder* (1821), *Lebensansichten des Kater Murr* ("Views of Life of Murr the Cat" 1822), and the novella, *Meister Martin der Küfer und seine Gesellen* ("Master Martin, the Barrel Maker and his Fellows") (1822), always has a vital strength. Friedrich de la Motte Fouqué (1777–1843), the publisher of numerous journals, is still vital for us as the author of the pretty tale, "Undine" (1811), which was set to music by Lortzing.

Ludwig Achim von Arnim(1781–1831), who has coined the words, "We want to give back to all, everything that in the many years of rolling away has kept its diamond-like firmness," and Clemens Maria Brentano (1778–1842), the discoverer of the Rhenish Romanticism, the poet of the pretty fairy tale, *Gockel, Hinkel und Gackeleia*, and the "Geschichte vom braven Kasperl und dem schönen Annerl" (1838) ("Story of the Good Kasperl and the Beautiful Annerl"). The two of them good friends, they have created the most priceless and most beautiful of all the

Romantic books, *Des Knaben Wunderhorn. Alte deutsche Lieder* ("The Boy's Magic Horn. Old German Songs") (1805–1808). Goethe wrote of it that it rightly should be in each house, where hearty people live, that it should be found on the window, under the mirror, or wherever otherwise cookbooks and songbooks are usually kept, in order that it might be opened for each mood or change of mood, where one always finds something inspiring or fitting. The folksong has since become an established part of the German literary properties. Concerning the rejuvenation that proceeded from it, Geibel has sung: "Among the flowers in the forest there trickles spring water, the folksong. There in the rejuvenating bath the Muse dips at night."

With their complete openness, the Romantics sought and found congenial dispositions in the feelings of foreign spirits, such as Shakespeare, whom August Wilhelm von Schlegel has captured for German cultural life through his masterful translations (1797–1810),[5] and likewise in respect to a similarly directed past, especially the Middle Ages, where the Romantics supposed the desire was fulfilled for an original and unified culture of all the mental powers. This increased sense for history led the Romantics to the creative Ground of all of life, to national particularity and, in connection therewith, to German antiquity. For them, mankind is an historical reality resting on customary usage and native life-forms. Herder had already been a source of profundly moving inspiration, as had Müller also. He was the first one to refer to the historical and poetic significance of the great national epic of the Nibelungs. Ludwig Tieck was thoroughly occupied with the Nibelungs, the heroic poetry, and the minne singers, and in 1803 he published *Die Minnelieder aus dem Schwäbischen Zeitalter* ("The Minnesongs from the Swabian Period"). In August 1815, August Zeune provided for an impression of the Nibelung songs as an edition issued for the army. History was again believed in as the effective life of the nation, and one enthusiastically repaired to historical research, the art of recognizing each period in its uniqueness and in its relationships.

The old folk books were treasured as valuable poetic sources; they were renewed and reedited. August Wilhelm von Schlegel declared them as being the sole real literature until now. Tieck, Friedrich von Schlegel, Arnim, Brentano, and later Görres, Büsching, von der Hagen, Schwab, and Simrock awakened them to new life. The Germanist, Friedrich Heinrich von der Hagen (1780 until 1856) published in 1808 *Der Nibelungen Lied* ("The Song of the Nibelungs"), in 1808 *Deutsche Gedichte des Mittelalters* ("German Poetry of the Middle Ages"), and in 1809, together with Docen and Büsching, the *Museum fur Altdeutsche Lieder und Kunst* ("Museum for Old German Songs and Art"), and since 1838, the *Minnesinger*. The word, *Volk*, belonged to the living language treasures of the Romantics, and the concept of *Volksgeist* ("Spirit of the People") as the compendium of all the cultural and mental powers of the entire nation, was among the greatest discoveries of this profound movement. Friedrich Ludwig Jahn (1778–1852), the founder of German gymnastics,[7] authored the book of the *Deutsche Volkstum* ("The German Nation"); and the expressions, *Volksgeist, Volksdichtung* ("Folk Poetry," "National Poetry") and *Volkslied* ("Folk Song") came into use.[8]

With their tendencies toward embracing all the cultural world, the Romantics,

under Herder's leadership, made contact with world literature and through transla-
tions, tried to make it their own. August Wilhelm von Schlegel's significant
Shakespeare translation has already been mentioned. Ludwig Tieck issued Cer-
vantes, and August Wilhelm von Schlegel also Calderon in German translation.
Reference should be made to Johann Dietrich Gies (1775–1842) with Tasso,
Ariosto, and Calderon, to Karl Friedrich Ludwig Kannegiesser (1781–1861) with
Horace, the troubadours, Dante and Byron, to Karl Streckfuss (1779–1844) with
Ariosto, Tasso, and Dante. The German book world has received a valuable enrich-
ment of its own language through these translated works.

The growing love in Romanticism for one's own people was soon to be placed
on a real-life experiment and trial in the songs and publications of the Liberation
years. Ernst Moritz Arndt (1769–1860), the brave co-contender with Baron vom
Stein in the struggle for Germany's liberation, authored in 1806 the rousing publication, *Geist der Zeit* ("Spirit of the Time"). He had to flee from the French on account
of it. In 1812, from St. Petersburg, he dispatched his *Kurzer Katechismus für
deutsche Soldaten* ("Short Catechism for the German Soldiers"), and published in
1813 his *Lieder für Teutsche* ("Songs for Germans") as well as the work, *Der Rhein,
Teutschland's Strom, aber nicht Teutschlands Gränze* ("The Rhine, German's River,
but not its Border"). The celebrant of freedom, Theodor Körner (1791 till 1813),
poeticized flaming appeals and sealed them with his own blood as a combatant in
the Lützow volunteer corps.

The pinnacle and conclusion of the younger Romanticism has been the poet
of songs and the story-teller, Joseph, Baron von Eichendorff (1788–1857). He has
enriched German poetry by his wonderful tale, *Aus dem Leben eines Taugenichts*
("Out of the Life of a Ne'er Do Well"); it has been praised by Gustav Falke, that
it "in its spring-like cheerfulness and its dreamy quality as it carries the reader and
listener with it on its varicolored butterfly wings is perhaps the fragrant flowering
of the entire Romantic art of narration." And no less do the songs of Eichendorff
make us happy; profoundly and inextricably they have sung themselves into German hearts.

Hand in hand with this independent literature of Romanticism went the
numerous journals and almanacs that disseminated the educational goal of the new
movement in wide circles almost more effectively than books, and had a great influence on the development of the feeling for life in this period. The first and most
important publication of the older Romanticism was the *Athenäum* of the brothers
Schlegel, which was published 1789–1800 by the Berlin publishers, Friedrich
Vieweg and Heinrich Frölich; excluding religion and politics, it strove for the
greatest universality possible "in what was directly aimed toward education." In the
infinite glorification of the purely spiritual, in the nature of the poetical, and in the
symbolism of art, one was seeking to gain again life's harmony which had been lost.
But this distance from the world stood in the way of the older Romanticism's effect
on everyday life; after a short but dazzling existence, the journals soon died off
again entirely. More deeply rooted in the German nationality was the *Zeitung für
Einsiedler* ("Newpaper for Solitaries"), which was published by Achim von Arnim
and Brentano, and in which the brothers Grimm, the brothers Schlegel, Ludwig

Uhland, and Justinus Kerner had collaborated. Achim von Arnim has later published it anew (1808) under the title, *Trösteinsamkeit* ("Solace of Solitude").[10]

Under the influence of Romanticism, the almanac again flourished; dedicated to the Muses,[11] it was especially cultivated by August Wilhelm Schlegel and Ludwig Tieck, with the collaboration of Chamisso, Uhland, Kerner, Eichendorff, Schwab, Schenkendorf, and Wilhelm Müller.

Close to the Romantics, and belonging already to the Biedermeier period,[12] is a considerable circle of Swabian poets, whose songs and stories are also to be considered as being among the cultural treasures of the German people: Justinus Kerner (1786–1862), with songs that have been much sung; Ludwig Uhland (1787–1862), the gallant investigator of the legend, the folksong, and of the entire Old German poetry, the master of the popular ballad, and singer of sonorous songs; Gustav Schwab, the much-read publisher of the *Fünf Bücher deutscher Lieder und Gedichte* (1835) ("Five Books of German Songs and Peoms"), of the still currently popular *Buch der schönsten Geschichten und Sagen* (1836–37) ("Book of the Most Beautiful Stories and Sagas") and the *Schönste Sagen des Klassischen Altertums* (1838–40) ("Most Beautiful Myths of the Classic Antiquity"); and finally, Wilhelm Hauff (1802–1827), the author (influenced by Walter Scott) of the romantic legend, *Lichtenstein*, of songs that have been sung again and again, or the splendid *Phantasien im Bremer Ratskeller* ("Fantasies in a Bremen Rathskeller").

Adelbert von Chamisso (1781–1838) had unusual success with his tale, which was translated into French, English, Italian and Norwegian, *Peter Schlemihls wundersame Geschichte* ("Peter Schlemihl's Wonderful Story") (1814);[13] it was one of the first books that, on account of its great demand, had been reproduced with the stereotype printing, which had been introduced shortly before. The romantic poem of the freedom fighter, Ernst Schulz, *Die bezauberte Rose* (1818) ("The Charmed Rose") was also well received and went through numerous editions, in addition to English and Czech translations. Wilhelm Müller (1794–1827), the author of the *Gedichte des reisenden Waldhornisten* ("Poems of the Travelling Horn Player") with the *Schöne Müllerin* (1821) and the *Griechenlieder* (1821) ("Greek Songs"), has become famous through Franz Schubert's musical settings. August Heinrich Hoffman von Fallersleben (1798–1874) has made a name for himself as a successful scholar of the German language and literature, in addition to being a poet of popular songs. He has been immortalized through the German's national anthem poeticized in 1814 on Helgoland: *Deutschland, Deutschland über alles.*

We will here still consider Goethe, our greatest German poet. An entire era fell with him when he died on March 22, 1832. Schelling has expressed Goethe's significance in his obituary with these words: "Germany was not deserted, not impoverished, in all of its weaknesses and inner disorders, it was great, rich and powerful in spirit, so long as Goethe was living." Novalis was of the view that Goethe had been for his life time "the true governor of the poetical spirit on earth."

We add yet Nietzsche's words: "Goethe is no German event, but a European one, a greater event than Napoleon," and finally an encomium from our own time: "No other people of recent times has had one born among them like him; his star will yet brighten the West for a long time in changing glitter with related constellations." (Hans Carossa). In Goethe, the German book has attained its cultural zenith.

Prominent also among the post-Romantics were the poets whose books still today go through the German territories as the messengers of essential things. There is Franz Grillparzer (1791–1872) who had created (besides his famous dramas, among which is the *Ahnfrau*, which has been translated into all European languages) the beautiful novella, *Der arme Spielmann* ("The Poor Musician"). Byron was of the opinion that his was certainly be a difficult name for immortality; our descendants, however, would have to learn how to pronounce him. Grillparzer was great and classic. There is Friedrich Rückert (1788–1866), whose masterful poems (1841) were produced in numerous editions with the *Liebesfrühling* ("Love Spring") (1844). There is Nikolaus Lenau (1802–1850), the poet of *Weltschmerz*, whom we treasure as the creator of the wonderfully musical *Schilflieder* ("Reed Songs") (1831). There is August, Count von Platen (1786–1835), the linguistically gifted poet of odes and sonnets, whose sonorous ballads are still now to be found in the reading books. There is Karl Immermann (1796–1840) whose satirical novel, *Münchhausen*, contains the Westphalian story, "Der Oberhof," one of the best German village stories. There is Heinrich Heine (1797–1856), who has become famous especially through his lyrical life work, the *Buch der Lieder* ("Book of Songs") and his deeply effective *Reisebilder* ("Travel Images"). Ludwig Wienberg has introduced the name for the militant group of poets, *Junges Deutschland* (1830–1840), ("Young Germany") when he in 1834 dedicated his *Aesthetische Feldzüge* ("Aesthetic Expeditions") to the *Jung Deutschland* ("Young Germany") on the proposal of the publisher, Julius Wilhelm Camp. As its main representatives, Börne, Heine, Laube, Gutzkow, Mundt, Kühne, and Weinberg have repeatedly been opposed by the German Diet of the German Confederation and so have even their publishers, Hoffman and Camp in Hamburg and C. Löwenthal in Mannheim.[14]

Ernst, Baron von Feuchtersleben (1806–1849), presented in 1938 the small publication, *Zur Dialektik der Seele* ("On the Dialectics of the Soul"), which became one of the books most read in the period. Edward Mörike (1804–1875) will remain one of the first favorite poets of the German people; he is the author of much read poems, of the *Stuttgarter Hutzelmännlein* ("Little Goblin of Stuttgart") with the tender *Historie von der schönen Lau* (1853) ("Story of the Beautiful Lau"), and finally of the fine novella, *Mozart auf der Reise nach Prag* (1854) ("Mozart on the Journey to Prague"), of which Hebbel opined that it seemed to him to solve the actual task of the novella to the extent that it had a world develop from a mustard seed, and lovingly allowed it to develop. Karl Simrock (1802–1876) has especially become known through his translation of the *Nibelungenlied* (1827), which came out in over fifty editions, and also through his poems with the Rhine song. In the turbulent year of 1848 he had appearing *Das deutsche Kinderbuch* ("The German Children's Book"), a collection of children's songs that became of incomparable effect for an entire generation. Concerning the Westphalian, Annette von Droste-Hülshoff (1797–1848), the greatest German poetess, her wonderful poems, which were related to nature (in addition to her ballads and *Die Judenbuche*), have fit into the poetical crown-jewels of the Germans. The poetess has once expressed the desire: "I may not be (and do not want to be) famous, but fifty years from now I'd like to be read."

About the middle of the century a change again took place in the German feeling of life. The world of imagination turned away from the Romanticist realms, and attached itself to practical reality. The poetry of realism set in.[15] It also has given us books of lasting value. Willibald Alexis (1798–1871) wrote his successful Brandenburg novels, and the Swiss Jeremias Gotthelf (1797–1854) his stories praising the peasantry.[16] Berthold Auerbach(1812–1882) has become one of the most read story tellers through is *Schwarzwälder Dorfgeschichten* ("Black Forest Village Stories") (1843). Adalbert Stifter (1805–1868), the sensitive listener to and messenger of, nature, the illuminator and inspirer of daily life with beauty and inwardness, formed his collection of novellas (that were fashioned in crystal clear and picturesque language), *Studien* (1854–55) and *Bunte Steine* ("Varicolored Stones") (1852), in addition to the novels, *Der Nachsommer* (1857) ("Indian Summer") and *Witiko* (1865–1867);[17] Friedrich Hebbel (1813–1863) cast his powerful tragedies, among them being the *Nibelungen,* in which the Nibelungs epic is newly awakened and dramatically fashioned, in addition to the splendid book, *Meine Kindheit* ("My Childhood"), one of the most beautiful German autobiographies; Otto Ludwig (1813–1865) presented his impressive dramas, as well as the fine novel, *Zwischen Himmel und Erde* (1856) ("Between Heaven and Earth"), and the artistic novella, *Die Heiterethei und ihr Widerspiel* (1857). Ferdinand Freiligrath (1810–1876) has become known through his excellent translations of English and French poetry, in addition to popular songs such as "Ich kann den Blick nicht von euch wenden" ("I Can't Stop Looking at You") and "Prince Eugen der edle Ritter ("Prince Eugene the Noble Knight").

Inspired by neo–Romantic feelings, Oskar, Baron von Redwitz (1823–1891), poeticized in his verse tale, *Amaranth* (1849), and had such success with it that it could appear in no fewer than thirty-six editions up to the year 1886. Otto Roquette (1824 until 1896) found the same unusual effect with his fairy tale, *Waldmeister's Brautfahrt* ("Waldmeister's Wedding Trip") (1851). Up to the year 1893, it had already gone through sixty-five editions.

Contributing to this increasing dissemination of German poetry had been not merely the author's fortunate creative power, but also the stronger resonance that there was in significantly wider circles of readers – the progressing participation of the German people in cultural life. Without such responses, the poet remains alone, and his work of no effect. To portray this external revolution concretely: how the book world – ever widening and being filled with richer content – how this world constantly gains more numerous readers, and how in that way the responsibility and the success for publisher and bookdealers increase, through which new culturally creative powers are ever and again attracted, which then strengthen anew the flow of books – all that would be the handsomest task assigned the history of the book. Friedrich Martin Bodenstedt's (1819–1982) *Lieder des Mirza Schaffy* (1851) stimulated by the publishing company, went through 160 editions before the turn of the century.[18]

Gustav Freitag (1816–1895) also had an exemplary success with his works—especially with the masterly novel, *Soll und Haben* ("Debit and Credit"), (1855 and the *Bilder aus der deutschen Vergangenheit* ("Images from the German Past") (1859–1862). Even Klaus Groth (1819–1899) and Fritz Reuter (1810–1874) were still able to achieve popular significance with their publications, although their works were strictly limited, being poems in dialect; Groth with his *Quickborn* (1852) and Reuter with the poems, *Olle Kamellen* (1959–60) and *Ut mine Stromtid* (1863–1864). Theodor Storm (1817–1888) has won German hearts no less profoundly with his impressive poems, and likewise with the wonderful novella, *Immensee* (1851) and with the *Schimmelreiter* (1888). Paul Heyse called Storm's language "colored as tenderly as young blossoms, as fragrant as the dust on the butterfly wings." Gottfried Keller (1819–1890), the poet of the great educational novel, *Der grüne Heinrich (1854–*1855), ("The Green Heinrich") has had to struggle a long time for recognition until his splendid collection of novellas, *Die Leute von Seldwyla* ("The People of Seldwyla") (1856) and the *Züricher Novellen* (1881), in addition to the unique *Sinngedicht* ("Epigram") and the *Sieben Legenden* ("Seven Legend") (1872), with the delightful *Tanzlegendchen* ("Little Dance Legends"), and finally, his poems (1889) won for him not merely the love of the people in his own region, but of Germans everywhere. Storm and Keller have helped the novella achieve its rightful place in German literature. A poet and a composer at the same time, Richard Wagner (1813–1883), created a world for himself; in the triology, *Der Ring der Nibelungen* (1853) and in the festival for the dedication of a stage, *Parsifal*, he has wanted (through dramatic means) to bring close to his people the German sagas and myths, and he sought to solve the secret of the highest art in the collaboration of all the arts. Still there was pearl on pearl to be strung up in the German book world.

Wilhelm Raabe's (1831–1910) novel, *Die Chronik der Sperlingsgasse* (1857), *Der Hungerpastor* (1862–63), and *Der Schudderump* stimulated the same success that Joseph Viktor von Scheffel (1826–1868) did in works disseminated in an immense number of editions: the epic, *Der Trompeter von Säckingen* (1854), the historical novel *Ekkehard* (1857), in addition to the much sung drinking and roving songs. Raabe expressed his poetical goal in the verses:

Im engsten Ringe
Weltweite Dinge!
Gib acht auf die Gassen
und siech nach den Sternen!

World wide matters
in the narrowest circles!
Watch out in the alleys
To look toward the stars!

Further, Conrad Ferdinand Meyers' (1825–1898) creations have achieved lasting significance: the epic-lyrical poem, "Huttens letzte Tage" ("Hutten's Final Days") (1871), the novel, *Jürg Jenatsch*, and in addition, elegantly polished poems.

Evidencing great success also have been Theodor Fontane's (1819–1890) marital tragedy *Effi Briest* (1865) and of the poetess and mistress of aphorism, Marie von Ebner-Eschenbach (1830–1916), *Dorf und Schlossgeschichten* (1883) ("Village and Castle Stores"), as well as *Das Gemeindekind* 1887) ("Public Ward of the Community"). Emanuel Geibel from Lübeck (1815–1884), who has said of himself, "In me three are one, the Greek, the Christian and the German," is present to us with his much read and much sung songs. The critic and aesthetician, Friedrich Theodor Vischer (1807–1887), surprised the world in his old age with one of the most unique and knotty novels, the witty book of life, *Auch Einer* (1879), (54th ed., 1912). Many readers further discovered new depths of life in Paul Heyse's (1830–1914) finished novellas (Selected 6th ed., 1898), the poetess Ricarda Huch's *Leben des Grafen Federigo Confalonieri*, ("Life of Count Federigo Confalonieri") and Gerhart Hauptmann's revealing social dramas, which were rooted in the Silesian homeland, *Vor Sonnenaufgang* ("Before Sun-Up") and *Die Weber* ("The Weavers") (1892).

We must yet attempt a brief look into the influence of foreign countries on the German world of books. Prepared by Comte, Spencer, Mill, Darwin, and Taine (who would see in mankind an essence and a social reality determined by heredity and environment) and founded by Balzac, Flaubert, Maupassant, Zola, Björnson, Ibsen, Jacobsen, Tolstoy, and Dostoevsky, the naturalistic movement (which rejects everything supernatural and would have reality as the only valid condition) has also won its adherents in Germany. As a needed counter-movement, the growing neo-Romanticism turned again to the ultimate grounds for everything that is; it concentrated on the longing for new symbols and, influenced by the original Romanticism, sought for its most essential vital strengths in mysticism and in the home. From foreign lands, Ruskin, Gobineau, Baudelaire, Verlaine, Mallarmé, Poe, Whitman, and Wilde made waves roll toward Germany.

Under the influence of the neo-Romantic movement, almost all the Romantics came out again in new editions: E. Th. A. Hoffmann, Novalis, Eichendorff, Kleist, Jean Paul, Annette von Droste-Hülshoff, Klemens Brentano, Achim von Arnim, the brothers Schlegel, Fichte, Hegel, Hamann, and Herder. Working in the service of this trend in literature, with a publishing goal set on nationality *(Volkstum)*, legend and myth, was especially the Jena publisher, Eugen Diederichs. Also, otherwise enterprising publishers gladly fostered literature groups that were related to each other, and they united their authors into a fellowship. For the German literature, Werner Mahrholz referred with some emphasis to this phenomenon: "In the main, one can always put a publishing house in the center of the cultural movements in Germany: what Cotta meant for the classical authors, Hoffmann and Campe did for the "Junge Deutschland," what Samuel Fischer meant for nationalism, the Insel-Verlag and Diedrich have become for the neo-Romanticism, and Kurt Wolff and Ernst Rowohlt for Expressionism. Indeed, one could write the history of German literature by writing a history of publishing."[19]

We approach now the most recent past, and, in the confusion of the present, we do well to yield consideration of the book world in this period to the judgment of what we hope is a better future.

Since Classicism and Romanticism loosed the tongue of our language and developed the word to all sorts of capabilities of presentation,[20] the artistic shaping of the word has achieved for itself ever wider areas within scholarly literature — primarily in history, in biography and in the geography of countries. German prose underwent significant development and gave us books that will always be among the cultural properties of the German people. For the first time in the history of the German book, historiography especially rose to a masterly representation of the significant temporal periods, or the important cultural developments.

Romanticism has awakened a sense of history in the widest circles and thus has prepared the way for a favorable acceptance of good historical representations. The *Deutsche Geschichte* ("German History"), published in 1816, of the senior school inspector, Friedrich Kohlrausch, came out in sixteen editions until 1865, and the *Allgemeine Geschichte* ("General History") of Karl von Rotteck (in spite of its nine volumes) was issued within the years 1813–1868, in twenty-five editions, with over ten thousand copies. Friedrich Raumer's *Geschichte der Hohenstaufen und ihrer Zeit* ("History of the Hohenstaufens and Their Times" (1823–25) has become Romanticism's most successful historical work. Barthold Georg Niebuhr's *Römische Geschichte* ("History of Rome") ((1811–32) was also read with pleasure and is still vital today.

The leader of German historiography became Leopold Ranke (1795–1866), the great master of careful research into sources and of artistic representation of history. His chief works, the *Geschichte der römischen Päpste im 16. und 17. Jahrhundert* (1834–36) ("History of the Roman Papacy in the Sixteenth and Seventeenth Centuries") and the *Deutsche Geschichte im Zeitalter der Reformation* ("German History in the Period of the Reformation") (1839–47) are among the most outstanding monuments of German literature.

Contemporaries have also been enthusiastic readers of Johann Gustav Droysen's *Leben des Grafen Yorck zu Wartenburg* ("Life of Count Yorck zu Wartenburg") (1852–53, 10th ed., 1890) or Wilhelm Griesebrecht's brilliantly written *Geschichte der deutschen Kaiserzeit* ("History of the German Imperial Period") (1855). There followed an artistic representation of the history of the other periods: Theodor Mommsen's *Römische Geschichte* ("History of Rome") (1854–57), Heinrich von Sybel's *Geschichte der Revolutionszeit 1789–1800* ("History of the Revolutionary Period 1789–1900") (1852–57), and *Begründung des Deutschen Reichs durch Kaiser Wilhelm I* ("Founding of the German Reich by Emperor Wilhelm I"), the archeologist Ernst Curtius' *Griechische Geschichte* ("History of Greece") (1857, 6th ed., 1887/88), Ludwig Hausser's *Deutsche Geschichte vom Tode Friedrichs d. Gr. bis zur Gründung des deutschen Bundes* (1854–57) ("German History from the Death of Frederick the Great to the Founding of the German Federation"), Jakob Burckhardt's *Kultur der Renaissance in Italien* ("Culture of the Renaissance in Italy") (1860, then over fifteen editions), Ferdinand Gregorovius' *Geschichte der Stadt Rom im Mittelalter* ("History of the City of Rome in the Middle Ages") (1859–1872), and Heinrich von Treitschke's *Deutsche Geschichte im 19. Jahrhundert* (1879–94) ("German History in the Nineteenth Century"). The Catholic-focused *Geschichte der Päpste* ("History of the Papacy") by Ludwig von

Pastor, in spite of its immense bulk, also went through numerous editions, as well as translations into Italian, French, English and Spanish; considered from the aspect of its historical consequences, it is one of the most successful publications in scholarly literature. One of the most read historical works is Johannes Janssen's *Geschichte des deutschen Volks seit dem Mittelalter* ("History of the German People Since the Middle Ages") (Vols. 1–8; 187–94); history is here considered from the Catholic standpoint. The work, which is replete with material, has been issued in many editions. Karl Lamprecht's *Deutsche Geschichte* ("German History") (3rd ed., 1902) in nineteen volumes has achieved for itself an established place among the most successful historical representations, as the first comprehensive history of the German people seen from the aspect of cultural history. Conspicuous in the series of the biographies that have had a rich flowering in the decades from 1870 to 1890, are Karl Justi's handsome representations of Winckelmann (1866–72) and Velasquez (1888), Wilhelm Dilthey's *Leben Schleiermachers* ("Life of Schleiermacher") (1887), Rudolf Haym's *Herder* (1880–85), and Hermann Grimm's *Michelangelo* (1860–63, 14th ed., 1909).

In the field of military science, General Karl von Clausewitz (1780–1831) has left behind the culturally and linguistically highly significant *Vom Kriege* ("Concerning War") (1832).[21] Among scientific books to be mentioned above all is Alexander von Humboldt's *Kosmos* (1848–62); translated into all the civilized languages, it is a magnificent condensation of the wealth of forms in nature within the unity of all of life, a work that on the basis of strict scholarship gives a total picture in noble language of cosmic space; it has conferred prestige of the first order on German scinece as hardly any other work has. Reckoned as being among the valuable and successful popular books might also be the much-read work of the scientist, Jakob Schleiden, *Die Pflanze und ihr Leben* ("Plants and Their Life") (6th ed., 1864), Joseph Johann Littrow's *Wunder des Himmels* (8th ed., 1895–97) ("Miracle of the Heavens"), which was a favorite book of Karl von Clausewitz, and Alfred Emanuel Brehm's *Tierleben* ("Animal Life") (1863–69, 4th ed., 1911).

In the philosophical area, three philosophers achieved significant success with their books in the widest circles: Johann Gottlieb Fichte (1762–1814), Arthur Schopenhauer (1788–1860) and Friedrich Nietzsche (1844–1900); such a breadth of effect was denied to Georg Wilhelm Friedrich Hegel (1770–1831), who was the glorifier of thought as the all-motivating cosmic power, as well as the advocate of the state as the noblest creation of the world spirit. Fichte, the inspired patriot of the period of the Liberation Wars, was the messenger of a new concept of law and the state in the sense of a new idealism, in which the state is the means for educating the nation into a pure humanity, as well as for the fulfillment of the nation's cultural destiny. Fichte has become especially dear to Germans through his *Reden an die deutschen Nation* (1808) ("Speeches to the German Nation"); directed against Napoleon's plans for world domination, at its centerpiece there stands an unshakeable faith in the future of his (German) people. Schopenhauer, Hegel's opponent and the master of a flowing and impressive language, was especially effective in his at first little, but then much-honored, chief work, *Die Welt als Wille und Vorstellung* ("The World as Will and Idea") (1819); it sees the original nature of the world not in the mind, but in the will, in the desires, which being constantly in conflict, are to be denied. Still honored more enthusiastically were Schopenhauer's essays, *Parerga und Paralipomena*. Here he devotes worthwhile considerations to the book: "Über Schriftsteller und Stil" ("Concerning Author and Style"), and "Über Lesen und Bücher" ("Concerning Reading and Books").

Nietzsche, the creator of formally unusual poetry, the passionate world affirmer, the herald of an heroic humanity, the linguistically powerful summoner to creativity and growth, presented both to his people and to the world the philosophical poetry that was fashioned in jubilating language roaring in like a stormy wind, *Also Sprach Zarathustra* ("Thus Spake Zarathustra") (1883–85). Nietzsche himself wrote of it to Erwin Rohde: "With this *Zarathustra*, I fancy myself to have brought the German language to its completion. After Luther and Goethe there was still a third step to take: Look here, old comrade of the heart, whether strength, suppleness and harmony in our language have already been so brought together . . . my style is dance; a play of the symmetries of all sorts and a leaping beyond, and a ridicule of these symmetries. That goes even as far as the choice of the vowels."

Wilhelm Heinrich Riehl (1823–1897), who with Jakob Grimm was the founder of German cultural history, has given pioneering insights into the structure of German life, and in his *Naturgeschichte des Volkes als Grundlage einer deutschen Sozialpolitik* (1851–69) ("Natural History of the People as the Basis of a German Social Politics") he has created a work of sources for our national history that is still not exhausted by a long shot. Of Victor Hehn (1813–1876), one of our most linguistically adept authors in the modern period, and one to whom the Italian experience and the cultural encounter with Goethe have become the motivating forces in his life, we possess the handsome and much-read books, *Italien*, ("Italy"), *Kulturpflanzen und Haustiere in ihrem Übergang von Asien nach Europa* ("Cultivated Plants and Domestic Animals in their Passage from Asia to Europe") and *Gedanken über Goethe* ("Thoughts about Goethe"), a work that is among the best of the literature on Goethe. That even more remote areas of knowledge, if grasped in their total depth and shaped artistically with great power, could become an established part of one's general education, the archeologist Erwin Rohde (1845–1898) had taught us with his choice book, *Psyche* (1893); it allows us to appreciate in subtle representation the religion of the Greeks, their cult of the soul and their belief in immortality. In the same discipline the philologist, Theodor Gomperz (1832–1912), has given us the handsome book, *Griechische Denker* ("Greek Thinkers"). Friedrich von der Leyen has found the following words to portray this exalted literature: "We have several books in Germany that for special discipline were of basic or pioneering significance and which at the same time, because they have grown out of a total intellectual culture, almost wonderfully promote each reader's intellectual growth. The works of Jakob Burckhardt, of Erwin Rohde and Karl Justi are justifiably called classics."[22]

Several significant philosophy-of-life type books form a group that, following the founding of the new Empire, powerfully summoned the growing German people, exhorting them again and again and warning them about reflecting on life's real values: The *Deutsche Schriften* ("German Publications") (1878–81) of the German Orientalist, Paul Anton de Lagarde (1182–1891), who, himself a passionate champion of national ideas, saw in the fostering of the German natural disposition the way to the health of his people, but saw the actual form of the life of the nation as being in the state; the deeply effective *Rembrandt als Erzieher* (1890, 49th ed., 1909) ("Rembrandt as Educator") from the pen of the "German Rembrandt," Julius Langbehn (1851–1907), who in the pattern of the most Germanic of all the German painters saw the pleasant example of a native world view and philosophy of life which rested in a Northern personality formation.

Belonging to the significant popular literature that has something to say to all Germans, are also those books that bring to view the experience and the works of our great men in the literary reports they have written of their own thoughts and deeds, letters or biographies. Here we encounter proud works that are filled with the powers of soul of the more significant men of our past: General Field Marshal Hellmuth, Count von Moltke's *Gesammelte Schriften und Denkwürdigkeiten* (8 vols. 1891–98) ("Collected Works and Memoirs"), and *Briefe an seine Braut und Frau* ("Letters to his Bride and Wife") (5th ed., 1911), Prince Otto von Bismarck's (the master of the German language) *Gedanken und Erinnerungen* ("Thoughts and Memories") (1898) which he was induced to write by the House of Cotta, or the *Briefe an seine Braut und Gattin* ("Letters to his Bride and Spouse") (1900), Ludwig van Beethoven's *Sämtliche Briefe* ("Collected Letters") (1923), Werner von Siemens' *Lebenserinnerungen* ("Life Memories") (1892), Richard Wagner's autobiography, *Mein Leben* ("My Life"), (1911), Ludwig Richter's memoirs (10th ed., 1905), Anselm von Feuerbach's *Ein Vermächtnis* ("A Testament") (7th ed., 1910), Carl Benz' *Lebensfahrt eines deutschen Erfinders* ("Life course of a German Inventor") (2nd ed., 1936),[23] Karl von Goebel's *Ein deutsches Forscherleben in Briefen* ("A German Researcher's life in Letters"), (1870–1932), published by Ernst Bergdolt, in Berlin, 1942. Letters, memoirs, and biographies have the power to take us deep into the creations of significant men and thereby to enrich our own lives infinitely. In the best sense of the word, they are books of life, which have the power to elevate the individual being into a larger humanity.

Our modern literature is filled with collections of letters, voluntary confessions, and diaries. Represented here are the best names: Hölderlin, Kleist, Novalis, Bettina von Arnim, Hoffmann, Hebbel and Jean Paul. Of the letter collections subsequently published, the letters of the musicians have especially enjoyed great popularity, such as the ones by Richard Wagner, Mozart, Beethoven, Robert Schumann, and Peter Cornelius; our great musicians are, after all, the preferred favorites of the German people.

The enormous increase in the literature from the professional and workaday life constitutes a remarkable peculiarity of the modern day world of books.

In technology and the trades, in agriculture and domestic economy, independent books and pamphlets compete with a great quantity of journals related to these disciplines, and contribute essentially to the development of the individual's professional ability, as well as to the strength of the people as a whole.

Taking on a likewise enormous compass since the middle of the nineteenth

century was the socialistic literature, which applied itself against the privileges enjoyed by the propertied classes, and in the great masses it found an entire social
class as its readers. At the pinnacle of this appeal stands the *Kommunistisches
Manifest* ("Communist Manifesto") of Karl Marx (1181–1883) and Friedrich Engels
(1820–1895), with the famous closing sentence: "Proletarians of all countries,
unite!" The basic book of the socialistic movement became: *Das Kapital. Kritik der
politischen Ökonomie.* ("Capital. Criticism of the Political Economy.") of Karl Marx,
after whom this whole societal concept received the name of Marxism. The movement created further books of social dogma with a high number of editions, in
Friedrich Engel's *Der Ursprung der Familie, des Privateigentums und des Staates*
("The Origin of the Family, of Private Property and the State") (24th edition, Berlin,
1938), August Bebel's *Die Frau und der Sozialismus* ("Women and Socialism")
(50th ed., 1910), Karl Kautsky's *Das Erfurter Programm* (21st ed., 1922), and Franz
Mehring's *Geschichte der deutschen Sozialemokratie* ("History of German Social
Democracy").[24]

It is not possible within the space of these pages to sketch, even with brief
strokes, the enormous wealth of the modern scholarly literature production. Several
views into this wide territory, however, should nevertheless attempt to circumscribe
at least approximately the extent of this world of books.

The nineteenth and twentieth centuries can reasonably be called the age of
science. The fostering of research was clearly so predominant in intellectual life,
and this was promoted by the founding of further important universities: Berlin in
1810, Breslau in 1811, and Bonn in 1818. Not merely have the individual research
monographs, and the textbooks, taken on an enormous—yes, an alarming—range;
even the great collective works and the works of sources, and no less the numerous
journals, fill the rooms of libraries with a quantity of materials that can scarcely any
more be surveyed.

Something that should not be overlooked in these successes is the fact that the
great German publishing houses (whose significant work in the service of scholarship will still be briefly evaluated in another place) have had a great share in them.
Not only have they produced countless textbooks, outlines, handbooks and
voluminous works—the encyclopedias belong among them, too—at their own risk,
but they have also come to the assistance of the extensive projects of academicians
and the learned societies with the energy and the prestige of their great traditions.
Inversely, the significance of the scholarly book for the publishing situation is
already to be deduced from the fact that numerous publishers have devoted
themselves, whether wholly or for the greater part, to the scholarly book.

Scholarship at the beginning of the nineteenth century drew a chief strength
from the loosened soil of Romanticism and its preference for the old German nationality in poetry, language, history, law and mythology. Out of the romanticist
cultural world and its feelings issued especially the gigantic work of German
historical sources of the Middle Ages *(Monumenta Germaniae historica),* which
Karl, Baron vom Stein (1757–1831), embarked upon in 1816. When after the Wars
of Liberation his dream of a free and independent *Reich* would not be fulfilled, he
withdrew into the Empire of the past, and under the influence of Johannes Müller,

he took hold of the far sighted plan of giving to the German people a comprehensive collection of medieval historical sources, so that, above all, the great period of the German imperial glory might be resurrected. Even though many priceless possessions had been ruined with the outflow of manuscripts, of old printed works, documents and monuments of art from the dissolved monasteries, the scattering of valuable monuments still awakened within wide strata of the population a sense for the antiquities of the German people. The birth hour of the new scholarly enterprises fell in this very period of the increasing inclination toward Germany's past. On January 20, 1819, Baron vom Stein founded at Frankfurt am Main the *Gesellschaft für ältere deutsche Geschichte* ("Society for Ancient German History"), which had as its task the preparation of the proposed work. In the following year, the "Archives" of the society began to appear; these were supposed to publish the most important preliminary studies and their results.[25] Baron vom Stein himself patiently looked through manuscript lists and attempted to obtain the catalog of the Vaticana in Rome for reviewing, but he did not prevail with the librarian, Angelo Mai. In 1820–21, Goethe conveyed, with the joyful consent of Grand Duke Karl August, descriptions of the Jena manuscripts, which have been published in the third volume of the "Archives."

Especially distinguishing himself among the other collaborators through the purposeful concept that he had of his task ("Representing the author in his full characteristic quality") was the very promising young scholar, Heinrich Pertz. After May 29, 1820, he searched through the important manuscripts of Austria, with great success. In 1821 he took his assignment to Italy, where he searched through the St. Mark's Library in Venice, the Laurentiana in Florence, and the Vaticana in Rome. In the *Bibliotheca Chigi* he found the *Chronicles* of Benedictus of Saint' Andrea; in the Vaticana he found the *Annales Nazariani*, and in Monte Cassino he was able to inspect the important manuscript of Gregory of Tours. Following a brief stay in Naples and in Sicily he turned back toward Germany, going by way of Rome, and here he was entrusted with the scholarly leadership of the undertaking. For publishing a text, the one or the other manuscript of the text that was, as it were, accidentally offered, did not suffice for him; the comparison of all manuscripts within reach was an established requirement of Baron vom Stein, and a basic requirement for all preliminary study. Thus for the edition of Paul the Deacon, over a hundred manuscripts were consulted.

In August 1826, there was issued the first volume of the *Monumenta*, with the annals and chronicles of the Carolingian period; in spite of some faults, it was greeted everywhere and admired. New trips led the manuscript researcher in 1826, by way of Cologne, Liège, Brussels, Louvain, Antwerp and Ghent to Paris, and, in the following year, to London. Called to the leadership position of the Royal Library in Hanover on September 14, 1827, Pertz in 1833, searched through the libraries of Fulda, Würzburg, Bamberg, and Munich. When on December 24, 1840, the head of the Royal Library in Berlin, Friedrich Wilken, had died, Pertz was called on February 26, 1842, as his successor, and with him, the great undertaking was moved to Berlin.[26]

In the meanwhile, volume had been added to volume within the five subdivisions: *Scriptores, Leges, Diplomata, Epistolae,* and *Antiquitates.* The *Moumenta Germaniae historica* and their German translations, *Geschichtschreiber der deutschen Vorzeit* ("Historiographers of the German Antiquity") have for a long time been the most used historical sources, and the volumes of the "Archives" have been among the most significant evidences of medieval bibliography and of information on manuscripts. With their exemplary critical methods they have also influenced similar publications of other peoples.

So as to touch on at Romanticism's further influence on the development of the disciplines,[27] it may be sufficient to mention several names and books, such as Friedrich Carl von Savigny and his *Geschichte des römischen Rechts im Mittelalter* ("History of Roman Law in the Middle Ages") (1815), Friedrich Schlegel's work that marked a new departure, *Über die Sprache und Weisheit der Inder* ("Concerning the Language and Wisdom of India") (1808), Friedrich Creuzer's *Symbolik und Mythologie der Alten Völker, besonders der Griechen* (1810–12) ("Symbolics and Mythology of the Ancient Peoples, especially the Greeks"), Wilhelm von Humboldt's treatment *Uber die Kawissprache* (1836) ("About the Kawis Language"), and Franz Bopp's basic *Vergleichende Grammatik des Sanskrit* (1833) ("Comparative Grammar of Sanskrit"). The most significant scholarly creations for which we are indebted to Romanticism, have been preserved in the works of Jakob Grimm (1755–1863), the great investigator of German nationality and of the German language, the informed collector of *Kinder-und Hausmärchen* (1812–22) ("Children's and House Fairy Tales") and the *Deutsche Sagen* (1816) ("German Tales"), the worthy author of the *Deutsche Grammatik* (1819–1837), of the *Deutsche Mythologie* (1834) and of the *Geschichte der deutschen Sprache* (1848) ("History of the German Language"), and the founder of the *Deutsche Wörterbuch* (since 1852) ("German Dictionary"). The prestige of Grimm's works, which are among the greatest achievements of German scholarship, already speaks for itself on the basis of the fact that they (especially the *Deutsche Grammatik* and the *Deutsche Wörterbuch)* have become examples and models for other languages.[28] The Grimm fairy tales (which have been translated into all the civilized lanugages) are *the* German children's book, and it has become a true book of the people.[29]

If we consider that total, almost unsurveyable, series of great scholarly works of modern times, we encounter at the beginning of the nineteenth century the voluminous *Allgemeine Encyklopädie der Wissenschaften und Künste* ("General Encyclopedia of the Arts and Sciences"). Founded in 1818 by the two scholars, Johann Samuel Ersch and Johann Gottfried Gruber, it sought to include the whole knowledge of the period, and until the year 1890, swelled to one-hundred sixty-seven volumes, but ultimately remained incomplete. Already expressed in these works is an essential attribute of the newer scholarly activity, the cooperation of several forces in the creating of the projects that go beyond the work limitations and the lifetime of the individual. Scholarly investigation has here been joined by scholarly organization, the division of labor, and to a large extent it is now dominant in the world of scholarly publication.

At the forefront of these common works are the great projects of the scholarly academies, which, promoted by the state, can raise larger financial sums and thus also risk larger works, and continuing publications, which could not be borne alone by the free economy.[30] Thus the Bavarian Academy of Sciences has published the comprehensive *Monumenta boica* (1763 to 1932) with its fifty volumes; the weighty *Allgemeine Deutsche Biographie* ("General German Biography") (1st vol., 1875; 56th vol., 1892), the enormous *Geschichte der Wissenschaften in Deutschland* ("History of Scholarship in German") (Vol. 1, 1864; vol. 24, 1913), the *Chroniken der deutschen Städte* ("Chronicles of German Towns") (Vol. 1, 1862; Vol. 36, 1931), and thus we owe the Prussian Academy at Berlin for enormous works, such as *Die griechischen christlichen Schriftsteller der ersten drei Jahrhunderte* (since 1897, 40 vols. until now) ("The Greek Christian Authors of the First Three Centuries"), the *Corpus inscriptionum latinarum* (since 1863, 16 vols.), the *Die deutschen Texte des Mittelalters* (since 1904, 41 vols.) ("The German texts of the Middle Ages"), The *Politische Korresondenz Friedrichs des Grossen* ("Political Correspondence of Frederick the Great") (since 1879, 41 vols.), The *Acta Borussica. Denkmäler der Prussischen Staatverwaltung im 18. Jahrhunderte (Acta Borussica.* "Monuments of the Prussian State Administration in the Eighteenth Century") (1894, 26 vols.), and finally the complete editions that were undertaken of the works of Leibniz, Kant, Wilhelm von Humboldt, and Kepler. The Vienna Academy has taken on the *Fontes rerum Austriacarum. Oesterreichische Geschichtesguellen* ("Austrian Sources of History") (since 1855, 79 vols.), the *Archiv für die Kunde österreichischer Geschichtsquellen* ("Archive for Information on Austrian Sources of History") (since 1848), the *Corpus Scriptorum ecclesiasticorum latinorum* (since 1866, 69 vols.); the scholarly society in Göttingen has taken on the editing of the Septuagint, the collection of papal documents edited by Paul Fridolin Kehr, and the works of the one-time professor at Göttingen and comprehensive master of the natural sciences, Karl Friedrich Gauss.

Where even the resources of individual academies or other learned societies were not sufficient to publish quite comprehensive works, the German academies at times closed ranks into a cartel, in order to be able, with united means and capabilities, to take on such projects. Initiated in 1906 in this way was the enormous *Thesaurus linguae latinae*, a joint project by Berlin, Göttingen, Leipzig, Munich and Vienna; in the same way, the *Mittelalterliche Bibliothekskataloge* ("Medieval Library Catalogs") has been published (since 1918), and the *Encyklopaedie der mathematischen Wissenschaften mit Einschluss ihrer Anwendungen* (since 1896) ("Encyclopedia of Mathematical Sciences with Inclusion of their Applications") is so issued. For a time it seemed as if the academies of the entire world could be included in a federation, and the international tasks of scholarship accomplished in common work.[31] These efforts, however, have not got beyond the planning and initial stages.

In addition to the German academies, there are still further scholarly societies or state agencies that publish the continuing larger works; thus there is the Society for the History of Education and Instruction that published (since 1886, 63 vols.) the *Monumenta Germaniae paedogogica*, the Luther Society, which is carrying out acomplete critical edition of Luther's works (since 1883, 4 vols.), the Prussian Archives Administration, which since 1878 had brought out over ninety *Publikationen*

aus den Preussischen Statsarchiven ("Publications from the Prussian State Archives"), the Literary Association of Stuttgart, to whom we are obliged for over two
hundred ninety valuable and rare texts of the German and Romantic literature, of
history and cultural history, and also the new printing of the *Carmina Burana*, the
Weingarten manuscripts of songs, the first German Bible, and of the works of Hans
Sachs.[32]

Among the disciplines which are most closely related to the history of the book,
and which have been greatly stimulated in recent times, are philology and
literature, both of which devote themselves mainly to investigating language and
literature – and therefore the chief basis of the world of books. To be mentioned
here as principal books are the successful works of Gervinus, Koberstein, Vilmar,
König, Scherer, Hettner, Vogt and Koch, as well as Karl Goedeke's *Grundriss zur
Geschichte der deutschen Dichtung* ("Outline of the History of German Poetry")
(1859), which lists the belletristic literature in completeness that had been unknown
until then.[33] Josef Nadler, in his *Literaturgeschichte der deutschen Stämme und
Landschaften* (1911–1928) ("Literature History of the German Tribes and
Regions") gives an original interpretation of German literature, with a somewhat
opinionated standpoint, from its growth out of region and nationality into the unity
of race, language, custom and settlement.

Several very large collections disclose numerous texts of the Middle Ages and
of the modern period, such as *Althochdeutsche Glossen* ("Old High German
Glosses") of Elia Steinmeyer and Edward Sievers (5 vols. 1879–1932), Karl
Müllenhoff's and Wilhelm Scherer's *Denkmäler deutscher Poesie und Prosa aus dem
VIII bis XII Jahrhundert* (2nd ed., 1892) ("Monuments of German Poetry and Prose
from the Eighth to the Twelfth centuries"), Josef Kürschner's *Deutsche Nationalliteratur bis zu Goethes Tode* ("German National Literature up to Goethe's
Death"), (since 1885) in two hundered twenty volumes and, since 1928, the
*Deutsche Literatur. Sammlung literarische Kunst-und Kulturdenkmäler in Ent-
wicklungsreihen* ("German Literature. Collection of Monuments of Art and Culture
in the Order of their Development"), which amounted to two hundred fifty volumes.
Valid for the investigation of German life in the past are the deeply illuminating
publications of Alwin Schultz: *Das höfische Leben zur Zeit der Minnesänger* ("The
Courtly Life at the Time of the Minnesingers") (2nd ed., 1889); of Moritz Heyne:
Fünf Bücher deutscher Hausaltertümer ("Five Books of German Domestic Antiquities") (3 vols., 1899–1933); and of Karl Müllenhoff: *Deutsche Altertumskunde*
(5 vols., 1870–1900) ("German Archeology").

Art publications[34] have in the course of the nineteeth century undergone an
unparalleled advance through photography and the art of reproduction, means of
assistance which, as an illustrative supplement, are directly of the greatest
significance for the history of art.

The creations of the older art of sculpture have been, as it were, first discovered
through the reproduced picture. The number of works of plates is almost unsurveyable. There is scarcely a painting, a plastic work of art, a building or otherwise an artistic creation of significance that has not been reproduced and included
in a book. The artists themselves find their evaluation in numerous individual

writings, or in the voluminous *Allgemeines Lexikon der bildenden Künstler* ("General Lexicon of Artists") of Ulrich Thieme and Felix Becker (since 1907). Multi-volume works illustrating their architectural and art monuments have been produced by almost all the German territories. The growing interest in art publications, in which the world and the creations of the artists (the picture-shaping symbols of human life) are reflected, expresses itself as much in the rich fullness of the published works as in the large number of editions that numerous books, such as the publications of Franz Kugler,[35] Wilhelm Lübke,[36] Anton Springer,[37] George Dehio,[38] Heinrich Wölfflin,[39] and Wilhelm Pinder, have gone through. Jakob Burckhardt's *Cicerone, Anleitung zum Genuss der Kunstwerke Italiens* ("Cicerone: Introduction to the Enjoyment of the Art Works of Italy") (1855), has been for many decades the leader in art history for German travellers in Italy, and has been translated into English, French, Swedish and Danish.

Several more recent philosophical books and books of cultural history have also evidenced very great successes (not a bad sign of the times). Especially in this the case with the works of Rudolf Hermann Lotze,[40] Eduard Zeller,[41] Kuno Fischer,[42] Wilhelm Wundt,[43] Rudolf Eucken,[44] Wilhelm Dilthey,[45] Ludwig Klages,[46] Eduard Spranger,[47] Karl Jaspers, Martin Heidegger, Oswald Spengler, Max Scheler and others.

In the unprecedented development of the sciences and of medicine[48], the observation of nature and the experiment do indeed stand in first place; but the book has still contributed essentially in these areas, in maintaining the flow of inquiry and in passing on the knowledge gained. In the book as well as in the journal, this scientific and technical literature production has assumed dimensions larger than those that could have been thought possible. Many of the leading German scientific and medical books, such as the works of the physiologist, Johan Müller (1801–1858), and Emil Du Bois-Reymond (1818–1896), of the physicists, Karl Friedrich Gauss (1777–1855), Gustav Theodor Fechner (1801–1887), and Hermann von Helmholtz (1821–1894), of the chemist, Justus von Liebig (1803–1873), of the scientist, Robert von Mayer (1814–1878), of the anthropologist, Rudolf Virchow[49] (1821–1902), of the medical doctors, Ignaz Semmelweis (1818–1865), Robert Koch (1843–1910), Friedrich Loeffler (1852–1915) Emil von Behring (1854–1917), and those of other scholars, have become world famous.

It is especially in the scientific, medical and technical areas of knowledge that the book has an exalted function to fulfill in the international traffic in intellectual properties. In these sciences, the results belong in a special sense to the whole world. What a Louis Pasteur, a Giovanni Battista Morgagni, and a Rudolf Virchow have discovered and inquired into, passes over into their books as an invaluable present to mankind as a whole. The valuable scientific books break the barriers set by peoples and states and become the cultural property of the entire world. It might be mentioned that one of the earliest aerodynamic books was the pioneering work of the engineer, Otto Lilienthal, *Der Vogelflug als Grundlage der Fliegerkunst* ("The Flight of Birds as Foundation of the Art of Flying") (1889). Since then an immense literature has arisen in this area.

Thanks to the progress of the art of reproduction, such enormous projects as the great illustrated work of Adalbert Seitz, *Die Grosschmetterlinge der Erde* ("The Large Butterflies of the Earth") could be undertaken; since 1905 about twelve hundred plates in colored hand lithography have appeared. Here the possibilities for reproduction in color have been of inestimable value, as they have been in so many other scientific works.[50] The picture, which in the period of early printing was a popular "extra" destined for wider circles, has now become a very essential "aid" in scientific books.

Geography also has great works to display, which have made their way through the entire world; mentioned here should be only the five-volume travel experiences of Baron, Ferdinand von Richthofen, *China* (1877–1912), and his *Tagebücher aus China* ("Diaries from China"), in two volumes (1907); further, Gustav Nachtigal's (1834–1885) *Sahara and Sudan* (1879–81), the best of all the African travel works. Geology has offered us the work in three volumes, *Das Antlitz der Erde* (1885–88) ("The Face of the Earth") by Eduard Suess (1831–1914). Into many hands have come Hans Kraemer's four volumes, *Weltall und Menschheit* ("Universe and Humankind") (1906); it was richly decorated with pictures.

That German scholarship, even in the period following the collapse of Germany in the World War I, could to some extent be maintained, has chiefly been due to the Emergency Society (then the Research Society) of German Science,[51] which was founded in 1920 under the chairmanship of Dr. Friedrich Schmidt-Ott, who at that time was state minister; not only has it stood ready with financial means for the printing of numerous scholarly works, but as an important auxiliary office for research, it has also, by means of central purchasing, made possible the acquisition of the most indispensable journals, in addition to the most important foreign literature.[52] It is only to be desired and hoped that the newly founded Research Society of the German Sciences, in Bad Godesberg (near Bonn) may attain the same successes. The German book urgently needs this help anew.[53]

If the significance of the scholarly book world is to be fully evaluated, its effect in foreign countries has then also to be described. That is to say that a good part of the German prestige rests on the scholarly book. For the most part, the book exports to foreign countries consisted of scholarly literature. The world trade in cultural properties has great national importance.

It is of far-reaching significance, for example, that Germany has produced such prominent books about Italy, as Jakob Burckhardt's *Cicerone* (1855) and *Die Kultur der Renaissance in Italien* ("The Culture of the Renaissance in Italy") (10th ed., 1912), and then the *Geschichte der Stadt Rom im Mittelalter* ("History of the City of Rome in the Middle Ages") by Ferdinand Gregorovius (1859 until 1878; 5th ed., 1905), Victor Hehn's *Italien* ("Italy") (1866, 9th ed., 1905) and Ludwig Pastor's *Geschichte der Päpste seit dem Ausgange des Mittelalters* ("History of the Papacy Since the Waning of the Middle Ages") (4th ed., 6 vols., 1899–1913).

The more common that the book in modern times has become, the clearer, the more elegant, and skillfully fashioned has the title of the book, or the book's entry, developed.[54] The title's beginnings in the early printing period has already been briefly considered. A thorough overview must certainly touch upon further changes in the individual centuries, the flowery, grandiloquent and embellished praises of the Baroque period, and the popular designations of certain periods, such as: little books, little tracts, *Spiegel* ("Mirror"), opinions, *Lustgarten* ("Garden for Pleasure"), *Nebenstunden* ("Incidental Hours"), the short headlines with the German classics, the accurate namings in Konrad Ferdinand Meyer's novellas, and the unexcelled challenge of Nietzsche, who was the master of short and eloquent titles; here reference may be made only to a special phenomenon.

Many titles have been established as household words, after the force of their attraction has won for them a community of readers. Belonging here are Goethe's *Dichtung und Wahrheit* ("Poetry and Truth"), Jean Paul's novel, *Die Flegeljahre* ("The Years of Indiscretion"), Friedrich Maximilian Linger's drama, *Sturm und Drang* ("Storm and Stress"), "the dearest and most wonderful that has flowed out of my heart" (Klinger to Ernst Schleiermacher), Schopenhauer's work, *Die Welt als Wille und Vorstellung* ("The World as Will and Idea"), Karl Immermann's novel, *Die Epigonen*, Nietzsche's impressive renderings, *Menschliches, Allzumenschliches* ("Human, All Too Human"), *Jenseits von Gut und Böse* ("Beyond Good and Evil"), *Der Wille zur Macht* ("The Will to Power"), *Der Wanderer und sein Schatten* "The Wanderer and His Shadow"), *Die fröhliche Wissenschaft* ("Joyful Science"), and then *Irrungen, Wirrungen* ("Errors and Confusions") of Fontane, *Das Glück im Winkel* ("Fortune in the Corner") of Herman Sudermann, *Die Welträtsel* ("The Riddles of the World") by Ernst Haeckel, Ludwig Büchner's *Kraft und Stoff* ("Force and Matter"), Friedrich Spielhagen's *Problematische Naturen* ("Problematical Natures"), Wilhelm Busch's *Max und Moritz*, Friedrich Delitzsch's *Babel und Bibel, Briefe, die ihn nicht erreichten* ("Letters that Never Reached Him") by Baroness von Heyking, and *Volk ohne Raum* ("People without Room") by Hans Grimm. Included here also might be Baron Adolf Knigge's educational work, *Über den Umgang mit Menschen* (1788) ("About Dealing with People"). From the sixteenth century comes *Die Wittenbergisch Nachitgall* ("The Wittenberg Nightingale") of Hans Sachs. Every publisher knows how significant the title can be for sales. The title often works like a magic charm. That Oswald Spengler's work, *Der Untergang des Abendlandes* ("The Decline of the West"), which was first published in 1918, and had already by 1921 achieved an edition 53,000 copies, or that Johan Huizinga's *Herbst des Mittelalters* ("Autumn of the Middle Ages") owed their unusual success partly to their gripping titles, cannot be doubted.

With this brief look into the form of the title and its significance, a further aspect of the cultural history of the book has already been touched upon, the story of its effect and the secret of its success. Reference has already been made repeatedly in the foregoing pages to the especially successful books. The subject, however, is exciting enough to call for a brief comprehensive survey.

In what consists books' irresistible power to charm? At the lowest stages of influence, perhaps in stimulating or relaxing conversation, in amusement and in passing the time, in the stilling of curiosity, in the joy of adventure or the hunger for suspense; in the higher stages, in achieving fulfillment, in extending one's own experience or in increasing or elevating it, in the participation in the beauties of the arts of word and language. In the world of books, poets and thinkers have created nothing short of a second existence, an inspired copy of the real world that omnipotently attracts to them people of thought and feeling. How is life outside one's own existence? How do other people see and experience existence? How do they handle life and its bewildering aspects? Everyone would like to know and experience that, and indeed in an answer that is most impressive on, and most in accord with, his nature. "Say something that is self-evident for the first time and you are immortal," thought Marie von Ebner-Eschenbach. There lies the book's deepest relationship to the reader, and there also the changes constantly taking place in the market's taste, in reading material, in the reading circles. These interrelations are among the most essential vital processes within the world of books; a cultural history of the book has to investigate them especially attentively.

We call "best sellers" works that, without making any claims to prestige or immortality, still are so capable of arousing the interest of the present generation and posterity that they have succeeded into thousands of hands, yes, they belong to the cultural household effects of the period, without any value judgment needing to be expressed. Their character and significance appear quite differently, in accordance wit their goal. We enumerate several such children of fortune in the world of books. That practical books for everyday life could already have a large market, such publications as Schlömilch's *Fünfstellige logarithmische und trigonometrische Tafeln* ("Fifth Place Logorithmic and Trigonometric Tabels") (The Verlag Vieweg had prepared it in around 730,000 copies), or Henriette Davidis' infinitely often requested cookbook, can perhaps teach us. Sebastian Kneipp's *Wasserkur* ("Hydropathic Treatment") (1886), a book that would serve not only for promoting of health but also the care of culture, could already announce it fiftieth edition after eight years.

Schoolbooks and calendars have also frequently gone through a considerable number of editions. Christoph von Schmid's *Biblische Geschichten* ("Biblical Stories") (1801) could already in 1911 evidence 285 editions, and the Hoffmann primer, 398 editions. Even the encyclopedia is among the successful book works, and it is a unique manifestation of clever publisher insight into the structure of cultural life and its radiations in the world. Numerous "success books" are further connected with the world of children. The best known among them are Christoph von Schmid's tales, *Genovefa* (1810), *Die Ostereier* ("Easter Eggs") (1816), *Heinrich von Eichenfels* (1818), and *Rosa von Tannenberg* (1820). *Gesamtausgabe* ("Complete Edition") (1844–46, 28th edition, 1927), the competent artist, Gustav Sues' *Hähnchen Kirkeriki* (1853) ("Cockerel Cock-a-doodle-do") in many editions, further Heinrich Hoffmann's *Struwelpeter* ("Shock-headed Peter"), perhaps the most famous and most disseminated picture book (it was translated into several languages), of which over five hundred editions were published; and finally, Wilhelm Busch's *Max and Moritz* (1865),[55] a lovely book in verse and pictures, that is even now the delight of all children.

In an unprecedented triumphal progress the novel, with its possibility of being the most comprehensive and most thrilling replication of the variations and discordances of human life and an image of the world in a particular period, has captured the book world, and indeed, it can be designated as the most successful book genre.[56] Its development is among the most remarkable sections of the history of the book's effects.

This also encompasses the cheap novel of the unbridled authors, publishers, and readers, as an expression of bad taste, as well as the chivalric romances or the robber novels,[57] as Rinaldo Rinaldini of Christian August Vulpius, and no less the "novel-factory" of Hedwig Courts-Mahler, which especially counted on exciting suspense, and whose productions have been distributed in about twenty-four million copies, also the favorite novels for youth by Karl May, which are in the hands of about fourteen million young and old,[58] further the detective stories, and finally, the great development novels and historical novels of Walter Scott, Goethe, Manzoni, Hauff, Alexis, Scheffel, and Richarda Huch. Of the specially successful novels these should be mentioned: Gustav Freytag's *Soll und Haben, Die letzte Reckenburgerin* by Louise von Francois (1871), with sixty-three editions (1925), Friedrich Theodor Vischer's *Auch einer* (1879), with 125 editions (1923), Felix Dahn's *Kampf um Rom* ("Struggle for Rome") (1886), with 615,000 copies, Ludwig Ganghofer's *Schloss Humbertus* with 677,000 copies, Gustav Frensen's *Jörn Uhl* (1901) with 512,000 copies, *Zwei Menschen* ("Two Men") by Richard Voss (1931) with 860,000 copies, *Die Heilige and ihr Narr* by Agnes Günther with 121 editions, *Die Buddenbrocks* by Thomas Mann (1901 with 234 editions (1945). Ina Seidel, *Das Wunschkind* ("The Child Planned For") and 500,000 copies, Gulbransson's, *Und ewig singen die Wälder* ("And the Forests Sing Forever") (1935) with 214 editions, Ganghofer's *Martinklause* (1895) with 172 editions, Binding's *Opfergang* ("Sacrifice of Life") (1912), with 168 editions, Rilke's *Cornet* (1912), with 168 editions, Kröger's *Das Vergessene Dorf* ("The Forgotten Village") (1934), with 140 editions. (Hans F. Schulz, *Das Schicksal der Bücher und der Buchhandel.* Berlin, 1952, p. 22.) ("The Destiny of Books and the Book Trade").

Portrayals of adventurous experiences that are full of suspense will always be uppermost among the enthusiastic youthful readers. The *Seeteufel* ("Sea Devil") of Count Felix von Luckner has been distributed in over 470,000 copies. Jules Verne has delighted countless readers with his fantastic novels.

It is a remarkable thing about the effect of a book. When the English art writer, John Ruskin, had published his brilliant colored portrayals, *Stones of Venice* (1851–53), whole bands of inspired readers departed for the celebrated city of lagoons, and when Washington Irving had presented his American readers the impressive little work, *The Alhambra,* hundreds of his charmed readers were drawn to Andalusia, in order to be able to appreciate the most beautiful Arabic building monument on European soil. Those were success books of far reaching effect, which especially depended on the thrilling portrayal of strange worlds. The American, Harriet Elizabeth Beecher Stowe, who could vitally portray the life of the North American slaves as it was experienced by the slaves themselves, got her moving work, *Uncle Tom's Cabin,* through to the entire world. The famous book of Charles Robert Darwin, *On the Origin of Species by Means of Natural Selection* (1859) has not only had countless editions and translations into almost all living languages, but has also attracted a quite large literature in agreement with it, as well as in the defense against it. Henry Ford's autobiography, *My Life and Work* has been translated into all the world's languages. Many books of the Indian poetic philosopher, Rabindranath Tagore, attained up to two hundred editions and translations. With such successes one can often no longer distinguish between the original effect of the work itself and what is fashionable.

Warm friends of the book have occasionally expressed themselves concerning their favorite books, and thus have given us insight into the effect that the world of books has had. Thomas Abbot writes in this treatment, *Vom Verdienst* (1765) ("Of Merit") about Gellert's fables, "Again and again they have slipped into houses where otherwise nothing was ever read. Ask the first best daughter of a country pastor about Gellert's fables! Those she knows; about the works of other famous poets, nothing!" Nietzsche pronounces quite a severe judgment on the German literature of his time when he says, "When one takes into account Goethe's writings and especially Goethe's conversations with Eckermann, the best German book there is — what remains actually of the German prose literature that deserves to be read again and again? Lichtenberg's *Aphorisms*, the first volume of Jung-Stillings' biography, Adalbert Stifter's *Nachsommer* ("Indian Summer") and Gottfried Keller's *Leute von Seldwyla* ("The Folk of Seldwyla"), and with those, for the time being, it is at an end." Karl Julius Weber drew his circle essentially wider and also included works of world literature in it. He thinks: "Klinger says, "If I had to dispose of my influx of books, I'd limit myself to *Nathan, Musarion, Oberon*, Goethe's *Tasso* and Iphigenia, Schiller's *Don Carlos*, Voss' *Luise* and Thümmel's travels. But I could not do that. Did Kling not think on the Bible and Homer and on other worthy old ones, such a Plutarch or Lucian? Did he not consider Ossian and Shakespeare, Ariosto and Tasso, Montaigne, Montesquieu, Rousseau, and Voltaire? Hume and Kant? Hippel and Lichtenberg? How about several excellent historians and scientists, on so many glorious travels and novels, such as those by Cervantes, Fielding and Sterne?"

The magical power that belongs to the book is also expressed in the belief that prevails here and there, to the effect that a child becomes clever if one puts a book under her little head, or that she learns well if one allows a newborn to see a book. The school child puts under her pillow the book from which she is supposed to learn something by memory, and then she hopes, upon awakening, to have conquered the material.[59] The fate of the redskins has been expressed in the fable, that the "Great Spirit" has once permitted the white man and the red man to choose one of two gifts, the bow and arrow, or a book. The red man has chosen the bow, and white man the book. In this way, the white man has become master of the earth, and the red man has become his servant.

Many works take people and the market by storm. Schiller's *Wallenstein* appeared in 1800 in 3,500 copies, and it was already sold out by the beginning of September. Gerhart Hauptmann's fairy-tale drama, *Die Versunkene Glocke* ("The Sunken Bell") had attained twenty-eight editions in scarcely a half year. At his birthday in 1932, 1,640,000 copies of his works had been disseminated, the *Weber* alone in 222,000 copies. Other works succeed only gradually. Eckermann's *Gespräche mit Goethe* (1836) ("Conversations with Goethe") took a long time before it prevailed; today it is viewed as being the most honored book in the Goethe literature. Nietzsche has maintained that it is the best German book. Only in more recent times has Emil Brachvogel's novel, *Friedemann Bach* (1858) captured the market. That access to the market and the art of selling on the part of the book trade play big roles in the success of books is shown by the triumphal progress of the trade series, *Universalbibliothek* ("Universal Library"), the *Inselbücher* ("Island Books"), the *Bücher der Rose*, and other such projects. The publisher, Friedrich Weidling, had once heard the lecture of the assistant master of the Friedrich-Werder Trade School in Berlin, Georg Büchmann, concerning *Landläufige Zitate* ("Well-known Quotes"), and persuaded the well-read scholars then to transform the lecture into a book. Thus Büchmann's *Geflügelte Worte* ("Household Words") has originated; it is today distributed in over a million copies, and it has vitally preserved the quotation treasury of the German people.

That even the books which were in the nature of a philosophy of life could win a large circle of readers has been shown in the successful authorship activity of David Friedrich Strauss, who at one time was a theologian (1808–1874). His publications, *Der alte und der neue Glaube* (1872) ("The Old and The New Faith") went through fifteen editions, *Ulrich von Hutten*, six, *Das Leben Jesu* ("Life of Jesus") (1864) thirteen, and *Voltaire*, eight. Ernst Haeckels' *Natürliche Schöpfungsgeschichte* ("Natural History of Creation") attained the ninth edition in 1898, and Ludwig Büchner's *Kraft und Stroff*, the twenty-first edition in 1904.

We thus see that the modern period has an abundance of "best sellers" to show, and that the book stands high in popular estimation. The art of poetry, historiography, philosophy, biography, natural history — yes, almost all the areas of literature — have a share in these operations. Whether the success be fleeting or enduring always depends above all on what the author, in a noble fashioning of words, has to say out of the depths of his own view of life concerning the tensions between man and the world. The more fullness there is in agreement or opposition, the more profoundly he creates from the ground of life in which mankind rests, the more urgently, picturesquely, and clearly he knows how to express the feeling for life in a period — the desire of the people according to eternal values, the more powerfully he is able to comprehend life and human will, being and the becoming, the rest and the movement of people as a whole, the more capable he is of rising out of the narrowness of the everyday into the wide kingdom of that which is essential and everlasting, the stronger his effect will therefore be on his readers, and he will inspire their spirits all the more.

"What actually constitutes the writer for people," says Georg Christoph Lichetenberg, "is faithfully to state what the greatest part of what men think or feel without being conscious of it. The average writer says only what each person would have said." Only the real life-books and the books of wisdom of the German people may enter into the halls of essential literature.[60]

Something else should yet be added to that. The German book is indebted for its triumphal progress not only to the increased intellectual and cultural life in the modern period, but especially also to the rich flowering of the language and style as the visible effects of mysticism, Classicism and Romanticism. Beauty always affects people. The ancients have always considered the sound of speech as being among the beautiful arts, and so did the humanists of the fifteenth and sixteenth centuries. The foreign word, "belletristic" *(belles lettres)*, is for us another designation for the entertainment literature and the beautiful literature, as it rests mainly on poetry. Our poets have in fact lent to the word a new effectiveness in sound and fullness, in breadth and depth, and in delicacy and weight. The style of a Walther von der Vogelweide, of a Luther, Klopstock, Goethe, Hölderlin, Nietzsche, Rilke, and George is a mysterious kingdom of wonderful beauty. Goethe and Nietzsche have increased the German language to an incomparable fullness of power that knows what to call everything that rests and lives within the inexhaustible souls of men. As Goethe uniquely says, "To do something right—in that consists the discipline of an enire life." And Nietzsche profoundly warns us: "Education is life in the sense of a great mind with the purposes of great goals." In such poetic words the wonderous work of language is revealed—its total capability of recoining each experience and the spirit of the age in nobler style. It is through the book that all of these wonders flow to us.

Alexander von Humboldt, deeply moved, describes for us in his *Kosmos,* how his artistic inspiration and his ability, at once nobly and truly to represent life's fullness and the unity of its manifoldness, positively intoxicated him and filled him with a joyful reverence for the German language. Wonderfully mysterious threads run between the recognition on the one side, and the shaping of it through words on the other. The richer and the more complete a language becomes, the more varied and full becomes also the experience of the world.

Those considerations also which have to do with the inner experience of literature, as questions closely related to the book, penetrate deeply into the cultural history of the book.[61]

The reader,[62] a further important force in the life of the book (without which the book is indeed not to be thought of at all), has already received a hearing in the most varied places in our consideration. Basically everything that there was to say about the effect of the book belongs also to him, the reader.

Something still, however, is to be added. The roll, the manuscript, and the printed work have all developed for the reader; it is for him that all the enhancements of lucid arrangement, such as title page, the number of pages, the shaping of the type, and the index have been undertaken. It is no less the case with the book's content. Already the selection of a subject for representation is determined mostly according to demand, and the execution (that is, the carrying out of the publishing process) is in accord with the circle of presupposed buyers. Our entire popular literature follows this rule. The book publisher looks around at the circle of readers before he decides on undertaking a publication. The size (that is, the number of copies) of an edition and the price of the book are likewise determined according to this view of things. One can say that it is the higher or lower claims of the reader which determine the high or the low level of a people's literature.

Novalis requires of the true reader that he must be an extension of the author— that is, he has to make what is read his own, and let it work itself upon him further. The responsibilities of the reader coincide with the art of intellectual comprehension. Goethe once expressed himself to Eckermann concerning those people who, without any preparatory studies and information, would like immediately to read each philosophical and scientific book as if it were nothing more than a novel. "The good folk," he said, "don't know what sort of effort it takes to learn to read. I've used up eighty years with it, and now I cannot yet say that I am at the goal." As in all life situations, Goethe was simply the born artist, and he knew what he owed to literature and its inclusion within his own self. Occasionally in his work he set the tone from a work by someone else. Where Werther and Lotte let a thunder-shower affect them: "We stepped to the window. It was thundering to the side and the glorious rain was rushing onto the land and the refreshing good smell in all the fullness of a warm air rushed to us. She stood propped on her elbows, her look penetrated the environ, she looked to the heavens and to me; I saw her eyes full of tears; she laid her hand on mine and said, 'Klopstock'."

It would be a beautiful task to track down similarly deep effects of the world of books on important men.[63] In many biographies we find valuable reference to such relationships. Not always does it come so easily as with the army commander, Helmut von Moltke; in his later years, he was asked by a foreign journalist what books had been the greatest influence on him, and which have been read by him as his favorites; he has given a true disclosure and mentioned Justus von Liebig, Gellert, Hebbel, Reuter, but above all, Homer and Goethe. Not seldom do we find in hidden places remarkable disclosures about the effects of a significant book. Gottfried Keller engagingly portrays the power that has flowed from Goethe's works on to this hero, the *Grüne Heinrich* ("Green Heinrich"). He had read the complete works of the poet in forty days, until they had been carried off by the bookdealer, who had made them available to him only for viewing. "It was as if a band of shining and singing spirits left the room, so that it seemed at once to be still and empty." Hans Carossa acknowledges in *Führung und Geleit* ("Guidance and Escort") early Goethe impressions: "At my fifteenth Christmas celebration I received Goethe's works. Something inexplicable arrested me after the first pages; it released me, and drew me in again. The darkest, most remote places of the second *Faust*, of the *West-östliche Divan*, of the *Wanderjahre*, of the *Metamorphose der Pflanze* I knew soon forever by heart, without suspecting what sort of enormous elements I thereby was accepting into my small life. It was at first sufficient for me to allow myself to be carried away by the blessed sound of magic words. Thus does a child play with the high and dangerous things of the spiritual world as with beautiful young animals, which one day will disclose themselves as lions."

Arnold Böcklin read and he loved the ancients very much, especially Homer; but dear to him were also Boccaccio, Ariosto, and Goethe, whom (with Homer) he valued most, and further, Peter Hebel, Jean Paul and Gottfried Keller. We know how deeply Schopenhauer's main work has influenced directly the very distraught twenty-two-year-old Nietzsche, from his moving letter concerning the read book in which he perceives the world, life, and his own soul in their frightful uniqueness." In a similar way did Friedrich Theodore Vischer's *Kritische Gänge* ("Critical Remarks") upsettingly grasp the poet, Konrad Ferdinand Meyer, and it signified to him that he had to change his life. Ina Seidel has beautifully portrayed for us how strongly rhythm and the spatial structure of verse can work on receptive readers, when in her novel, *Unser Freund Peregrin* ("Our Friend Peregrin") she has the hero say: "At that time for the first time I conceived the magic of poetry. Where I found a book whose pages had been printed only in the middle in a space-wasting way, these columns of words meanwhile were divided uniformly from each other by separated blocks; then I was enchanted, when it permeated me, even before I began to read, as with the rhythmic waves of a distant music." She goes on to say that she has in no way comprehended why otherwise word sequences and communications in her favorite books, the poems of Clemens Brentano, had been able to exercise, in this restrained and resonant form, so relaxing, yes, so redeeming an influence on the soul; but she had unreservedly been prepared to surrender to it.

Through the art of strictly developed representation, the literature that depends on scholarship has also attained far-reaching power. All of the aforementioned historical or scientific works that we might reckon as being among the "life-books" of the German people, such as the publications of Alexander von Humboldt, Leopold von Ranke, Theodore Mommsen, Jakob Burckhardt, Heinrich Treitschke, Erich Marcks or Johannes von Haller, are all of them at the same time master works of language.[64] The artistic fashioning of a significant world of vitality is always also the great secret in the success of scholarly representation, and of every other representation in prose.

The "Law Concerning the Authorship Rights to Works of Literature and Music" of June 19, 1901 (with its supplements of May 29, 1910), constituted an important event for the whole of modern literature.[65] The law has a long history. Following the discovery of printing there was still no protection for literature and for printed books. The printers only gradually applied (and on occasion, also the author or the publisher) to the Emperor for copyright reserve. In fact, the imperial chancellor granted permits for individual works or for several proposed projects, which awarded the petitioner the sole rights to trading in the works that were cited in the application.[66] Such privileges, however, were concerned only with the privileges for production and for trade, and not with the protection of the cultural performance, although there is repeated reference in the permits to the great significance of literature for scholarship and education. Even in the copyright reserves of later centuries there still is scarcely any talk of protection for the cultural work; only the publishers' protection was catered to.

It was only at the beginning of the nineteenth century that the claim of the intellectual authors came more strongly into the foreground, until finally in the Prussian law for the protection of the ownership of works of scholarship and art against reprinting and reproduction of June 11, 1837, the idea got through that the right to distribute a literary or artistic work resides in the person of the intellectual author, and that it should be protected by law. Through federal resolution, this Prussian law was carried over to all the states within the Federation, but without total uniformity being achieved. That was only achieved, following Germany's political unification, by means of the authorship law (which was gradually adopted everywhere) of June 11, 1870, at the head of which stands the sentence that the right of mechanical distribution of a book is an entitlement belonging solely to the author, and that this expires only thirty years after his death. The final unified conception followed on June 19, 1901, with the principles of May 22, 1910, and it was supplemented by the law of December 13, 1934, which extended the period of protection to fifty years.

Because an intellectual production can be distributed throughout the entire world, it was merely a continuance of the idea of the right of cultural production to legal protection, that international agreements (literature conventions) were prepared for the reciprocal supernational protection of intellectual work. The most important regulation in this direction was the Berne Convention, which was concluded on September 9, 1886, and which almost all civilized states have joined. Following it, on November 13, 1908, at Berlin, was the "Revised Berne Convention for the Protection of Works of Literature and Art." Special agreements were struck on January 15, 1892, with the United States, on the basis of the American author law (Copyright Act) promulgated on March 3, 1891. Through the Copyright Code of March 4, 1909, it was determined that all German books that wanted to share in the publisher protection of the United States, must contain the copyright-notice with a declaration of country, year, and publisher.

A consequence of the author laws, taking effect on June 19, 1901, was the law concerning the publishing right, which regulates the relationship between author and publisher.[67]

Associated in a certain, even if looser, relationship with the author and publishing right is the right of compensation (which is itself closely associated with the book as the author's intellectual production). As with the protection of intellectual work, so does its payment also have a lengthy history. Basically, it has only been entered into with the German classical authors and their also economically highly valued publications. The great masters of poetry knew what their works signified intellectually, and they knew that they would find a market and would have a claim to be evaluated as an economic good. Since then, the intellectual creation, transformed into the book, has, as a consequence of the increased demand, become a desired commodity, a power worthy of recompense. This significance of literature, which rests especially in its dissemination and in the reader, the author right and the publishing right now also come to express symbolically. Thus the achieved protection of intellectual performance has again had as its consequence a valuable upsurge in social and economic status. The intellectual work in the form of the book is now cultural value of a special kind.[68]

A brief word should yet be devoted to the book review, which has the function of making known the literature to the public with a brief evaluation of its contents.

In its beginnings the review goes back to the brief announcements, or the book-dealers' advertisements, for disseminating the book; in their further development, reviews have become the responsible guardians of printed materials generally. As a public establishment, they become, when properly conceived, an objective judge of the value, or lack of value, in the books that are being published; they undertake the judging examination for the reader; they are the book's resonance in the conscience of the world. He or she who exercises this office has two great responsibilities, one toward the author, who has the right that his effort and work should be evaluated without prejudice, but it certainly must also suffer being rejected if its performance is not good; and thus then over against the reader and the public, which may demand that they get an objective examination as to whether the book is a valuable one or not. Only he who is conscious of this double duty fulfills the presuppositions for a helpful book review, which has an important assignment to fulfill in the service of literature and, therewith, of the entire people. He is the promoting or protective guardian of the literature, the counselor and the trustee of the public in the co-administration of the book world as valuable cultural property. The book review is consummated in the journals and newspapers, where it has become an indispensable constituent of the current communications, and it finds there many readers. For the public, the book announcement is the most important source for becoming acquainted with the books being published for the first time. Already from that base is derived the review's great significance fo the book and its effect. To be sure, a review's date of publication is frequently of decisive importance. Reviews appearing too late are the cause for embarrassment and anger, especially when the book has already gone out of print in the meantime.

Especially due to the improved transportation arrangements, the journal has achieved a surpassing place for itself in modern literature. In extent and significance, it carries almost the same weight as the book, and for the entire new literature it has become of decisive significance. What lends it a certain superiority as over against the book is, for one, its flexibility in weekly, monthly or quarterly appearances, as well as the variety of contents that may claim far more readers than the individual book, and finally, the welcome apportioning of the purchase price over an entire year. It is impossible in a few lines to portray the wealth and the variety of the newer current journals, even only approximately. There stand out clearly from among the great number (as in the rest of the literature) three groups: first, the scholarly, second, the literary, entertaining and educative; and thirdly, the journals devoted to a particular discipline, and the professional journals.

The scholarly journal has followed the necessary separation of the main disciplines into numerous individual areas, and here it constitutes the corresponding supplement to the scholarly special publications. Especially the scientific, the medical and the technical journals achieved in the greatest variety of branches a fullness hardly anymore to be surpassed. Most important in the applied sciences is the quick disseminating of information about advances and discoveries, a function that only the journal, and never the book, can fulfill. References to the abundance in journals will follow the report concerning the German publishers. The literary, entertaining and instructional journal is again only the mirror-image of the corresponding belletristic and popular literature, and it presents the cultural fare in the most convenient and versatile form.

Leading family journals of this sort (which are today mostly superseded by new ones) were such ones as *Die Gartenlaube* (1853 "The Garden Arbor"), which gradually obtained 100,000 subscribers, *Westermann's Monatshefte* ("Monthly") (1856), *Über Land und See* ("Over Land and Sea") (1859), *Daheim* ("At Home") (1864), and Velhagen and Klasing's *Monatshefte*. They have gone through edition sizes the likes of which only a few books have had. Also, the unlimited recourse they had to pictorial design turned out to be very favorable for them. That goes especially for the illustrated journals, such as the Leipzig *Illustrierte Zeitung* ("The Leipzig Illustrated") (1842) or the *Fliegende Blätter* ("Flying Leaves") (1844). They enjoyed almost fabulous circulation figures. Thus the *Berliner Illustrierte Zeitung* in 1894, counted up to 14,000–and in 1927, up to 1,750,000 subscribers.[69] While the journal perhaps draws away readers from the book, through the successful extension of the class of readers, it attracts them again to the book and doubly makes up for it through the book review, which, directly promoted here with enthusiasm, contributes so much to making books known and to dissemination for the world of books. Without the journal, the modern writer's domain is indeed unthinkable.

The newspaper–"the conversation that time carries on about itself," as Robert Prutz called it–has already been briefly portrayed, at least in its initial development until its detachment from the book. It has gone its special way, and only in the nineteenth century has it experienced its brilliant triumphal march, following the Wars of Liberation, when the public's interest in political events began to grow appreciably. Fashioned along political party lines, the newspaper then everywhere became the popular leader.[70] Its general influence grew still further when it began also to foster increasingly the instructive and entertaining areas in supplements and in the feuilleton[71] enthusiastically pursued by the *Junges Deutschland* ("Young Germany").

In these additions (which have nothing to do with the news reports that were the original kernel and goal of the newspaper), the newspaper is placed within the domain of literature, and in successful competition with the book and the journal. As a reciprocal gift, it awakens and maintains, with its endless stream of knowledge and entertainment, the interest of the broadest public in the things of cultural life as a whole, and thus it also becomes a breeding ground for the actual literature.

German literature has a special function to fulfill in the service of the German community in foreign lands.[72] For Germans in other countries, the German book is the most valuable connection with their people, their language, their home and their culture. If this task has retreated strongly as a consequence of the two last world wars that have been lost, with the rise of the German people it will doubtless achieve again its great significance.

The heart and center of Europe, Germany with its fluid boundaries, stands open as no other country does to the stream of foreign culture.[73] This represents a gain if that which is foreign moves lightly and enriches what is one's own, but it is a loss and a curse if that which is foreign overruns and dilutes what is one's own. Indeed no people on earth has so many translations of foreign literature to exhibit as has the German. This is a sign of Germany's high culture, but it nevertheless often represents a threatening foreign infiltration of its own character and literature. The Saxon court counselor, Wilhelm Gottlieb Becker, says already in 1780, in the preface to the *Magazin der neueren Französischen Literatur* ("Magazine of the More Recent French Literature"): "No country concerns itself so much with the literature of foreign lands as does Germany." And Goethe once expressed the hope that Germany, through its translation work, might become in some measure the market of world literature. He surrounded himself with the "greats" of world literature and in dialogue with them created his immortal works that from their side have again become world literature. Homer, Dante and Shakespeare have found nowhere in foreign lands so firm a domicilary right as they have in Germany. If we briefly consider the modern body of publications of foreigners, in so far as this has influenced Germany, we thus encounter a considerable number of names, whose poems and ideas have penetrated from beyond our borders to us. Here there should be mentioned only those that have been disseminated the most, as valuable accessories to our own body of publications.

Of the numerous French poets who as a result of their works (or with translations) have had a strong influence on German readers, especially to be cited are: Alfred Victor, Count of Vigny, Victor Marie Hugo, Alexandre Dumas the Elder, Pierre Jean Béranger, Honore de Blazac, Georg Sand, translated by Feiligrath and Geibel, Alfred de Musset, Eugène Sue, Marie Henry Beyle, Prosper Mérimée, Théophile Gautier, Pierre Charles Baudelaire, translated by Stefan George, Anatole France, Paul Verlaine, Alexandre Dumas the Younger, Victorien Sardou, Gustave Flaubert, Claude Tillier (whose novel, *My Uncle Benjamin*, was a favorite book of Gottfried Keller's) Jules Barbey d'Aurevilly, Jules Verne, the brothers Goncourt, Émile Zola, Alphonse Daudet, Guy de Maupassant, Marcel Prévost, Frédéric Mistral, Jean Arthur Rimbaud, Francis Jammes, Romain Rolland, Paul Valéry, Stefan Marllarmé, Paul Bourget, Jules Romain (Louis Farigoule), Paul Claudel, and Henry Barbusse. Of the French historiographers, those who have become especially influential are: François Giuzot, Augustin Thierry, Philippe von Ségur, Adolphe Thiers, Jules Michelet, Hippolyte Taine, Ernest Renan, Alexis Clérel de Tocqueville, and Joseph de Maistre. Also François René de Chateaubriand, the author of the famous work about Christianity, *Génie du Christianisme* (1802), the authoress and opponent of Napoleon, Anne Louise Germaine de Stael-Holstein, who with her well-informed book, *De l'Allemagne* (1810), has been successful in making her fellow countrymen acquainted with German intellectual life, the philosophers, Henri Bergson, Comte Joseph-Arthur de Gobineau and Jacques Maritain have been much read in Germany.[74]

Penetrating from England there have been: Lord Georg Noel Gordon Byron,[75] England's most significant poet of the modern period, whom Goethe has designated as being the greatest genius of the century, Percy Bysshe Shelley, Walter Scott, Thomas Moore, Charles Dickens (who was often translated into German), Alfred Tennyson, Edward Bulwer Lytton, Dante Gabriel Rosetti, Walter Pater, John Galsworthy, John Henry Newman (Caldista, 9th German edition, 1897), the navigators, John Ross and Sir James Clarke Ross, Robert Louis Stevenson, Henry Thomas Buckle, Rudyard Kipling, Thomas Babbington Macaulay, the excellent connoisseur of, and inquirer into, German literature, Thomas Carlyle,[76] William Makepeace Thackeray, John Ruskin, Henry Morton Stanley, Charles Darwin, Herbert Spencer, John Stuart Mill, George Henry Lewes (*Life of Goethe*, 1855, German 18th ed., 1903), Katherine Mansfield, Gilbert Keith Chesterton, Herbert

George Wells, Thomas Stearns Eliot, and also the literary men, Oscar Wilde and George Bernard Shaw.[77]

Introduced into Germany from America have been: Henry Wadsworth Longfellow (translated by Freiligrath), further, James Fenimore Cooper *(The Last of the Mohicans)*, Washington Irving, Edgar Allen Poe, Walt Whitman, Harriet Elizabeth Beecher Stowe *(Uncle Tom's Cabin)*, Mark Twain (Samuel Langhorne Clemens), Ralph Waldo Emerson, Upton Sinclair, Francis Bret Harte, Lewis Wallace *(Ben Hur)*, Hervey Allen, Taylor Caldwell, Theodore Dreiser, Margaret Mitchell, John Habberton, Herman Melville, Lewis Sinclair, Thornton Wilder, John Roderigo Dos Passos, and Ernest Thompson Seton.

The classic authors, Luiz de Camões, Miguel de Cervantes, Lope Felix de Vega, and Pedro Calderon have early found admittance from the Spanish literature.[78] José Zorrila, Gustavo Adolfo Bécquer, Juan Valera, and Pedro Antonio de Alarcon have been translated several times.[79]

Among the Italian poets who have been disseminated in Germany, especially to be placed in the forefront are: Count Alessandro Manzoni and his principal work, *Die Verlobte* ("The Bethrothed") to the effectiveness of which Goethe has essentially contributed, Count Giacomo Leopardi, Silvio Pellico, Antonio Fogazzaro,[80] Giosué Carducci,[81] Giovanni Verga, and Gabriele d'Annunzio; among the historiographers, Cesare Cantù and Francesco de Sanctis, and Giovanni Papini and Benedetto Croce among the philosophers.

To be designated as the most read Danish poet in Germany is Hans Christian Andersen, the famous fairy tale poet; his fairy tales (1844) have been enthusiastically accepted in Germany,and have been illustrated by renowned artists such as Ludwig Richter, Theodore Hosemann, Franz Pocci, and Otto Speckter. Besides that there are: the creator of the Danish comedy, Ludwig von Holberg, Denmark's greatest national poet, Adam Gottlob Oehlenschläger, to whom Grillparzer has on July 12, 1844, directed the dedication, "to the great poet in two languages in a period where there were few in one (language)," Jens Peter Jacobsen, who was much treasured by Rainer Maria Rilke, Karl Adolf Gjellerup, Henrick Pontoppidan, Herman Joachim Bang,[82] and finally the influential philosopher Sören Kierkegaard, and the literary historian, George Brandes.

Sweden has achieved a special domiciliary right in Germany, and an extensive field of operation there. We mention Esias Tegnér (Frithjofsaga), Erik Gustav Geijer, Per Daniel Amadeus Atterbom, August Strindberg, Verner von Heidenstrum, Gustav Fröding,[83] Gustav af Geijerstam, Selma Lagerlöf with her successful children's book, *Die Reise des kleinen Nils Holgerson mit den Wildgänsen* ("Travels of the Small Nils Holgerson with the Wild Geese") (1906), Pär Lagerkvist and Sven Hedin.

Out of Norway there are principally Henrik Ibsen, Björnstjerne Björnson, Knut Hamsun,[84] Peter Egge, Johannes Bojer, Jonas Lie, Roald Amundsen, and Fridtjof Nansen who have won Germany. It might finally be said of the entire Scandinavian literature that it has found an unusually wide distribution in Germany; one may almost say it has found a second home.[85] From Iceland there is to be mentioned Gunnar Gunnarson.

Among the Netherlands writers, Hendrik Tollens, Jakob van Lennep, Maurice Maeterlinck, Emile Verhaeren have been much read; among the Flemish, Multatuli (Eduard Douwes Dekker), Hendrik Conscience, Charles de Coster with his popularly significant work, *Ulenspiegel*, which the Flemish people honor as the "Flemish Bible," Felix Timmermans and Stijn Streuval, have been read a great deal.

Finland is to be found in works translated into German, especially ones by Johann Ludwig Runeberg, Alexis Kivi, Juhani Aho; Hungary can be found in works by Alexander Petöfi, Maurus Jókai, Josef, Baron Eötvös, and Lorinc Szabo; modern Greece is so represented by Dimitrios Bikelas.

Russia is very richly represented in the translation literature.[86] Mainly to be mentioned here are: Alexander Sergeyevich Pushkin, Mikhail Yuryevich Lermontov,[87] Nikolay Vasilyevich Gogol, Ivan Sergeyevich Turgenev, Fedor Mikhailovich Dostoyevsky,[88] Alexey Nikolayevich Tolstoy, Nikolay Semenovich Leskov, Vsevolod Mikhaylovich Garshin, Anton Chekhov, Alexey Maximovich Gorky, Vladimir Sergeyevich Solovyev, Dimitry Sergeyevich Merezhkovsky, and the explorer, Vladimir K. Arseniev.

Gathered into the German translated works from the Polish literature have been Adam Mickiwiecz, Juliusz Slowacki, Zygmunt Kasinski, Józef Pilsudski, Michel Choromański, Jalu Kurek, Henryk Sienkiewicz, Stanislaus Przybyszewski and Wladislaw Reymont.

Chiefly contributing to the dissemination of the older— as well as the more recent—foreign literature have been the large collective works of the German publishers, such as the Brockhaus project, *Bibliothek Klassischer Romane und Novellen des Auslandes (1825*–1838), ("Library of Classic Romances and Novellas from Foreign Countries") or the *Belletristische Ausland* ("Foreign Belletristics"), which was edited by Karl Spindler, and issued by the Brothers Franck in Stuttgart (1843–1865). Considered here may also be the Tauchnitz Edition (to be mentioned in another place), which has widely distributed on German soil British and American literature in the original tongue.

To the more recent German translation art several significant masters of language, such as Freiligrath, Geibel, Heyse, Leuthold, Gildemeister, Herwegh, and Bodenstedt have successfully contributed. Many of their translations have become outstanding poetic renditions and new creations.

Foreign countries have had a deep influence on the shaping of German poetry. Arno Holz has at one time coined the sentence: "Zola, Ibsen, Leo Tolstoy—a world lies in the words." It would not perhaps be an easy thing to draw up the account, and to answer the inquiry, how much the German literature has been translated into foreign languages.[89] That here already a considerable number would emerge, several evidences from the statistics show us. These indicate that in 1929, about 2140 German works had been translated into foreign languages, and about 1235 foreign books translated into German. In 1934, 397, and in 1935, about 1964, foreign works received German translations; in 1938, up to 1772, and in 1939, up to 1936 German books were translated into foreign languages, especially into English.

Since our classical period, German literature has asserted itself in all countries.

German literature has won respect in Scandinavia, in the Netherlands, and France. Almost all the significant poetry of the flourishing period, but also creations by Heyse, Keller, Storm, Konrad Ferdinand Meyer, Raabe, and Ebner-Eschenbach, have been translated into French. In England, Thomas Carlyle, William Taylor, Samuel Coleridge, and Walter Scott have distinguished themselves as good connoisseurs of the German book.

35
The Book Trade of the Modern Period[1]

(The author is indebted for this section about the modern book trade—
something that today is especially difficult for the non-specialist to grasp—to the outstanding expertise of Dr. Wilhelm Olbrich (who is active in publishing), who here
has conveyed from quite a new perspective his observations of the subject.)

The nineteenth century in Germany began under the banner of Napoleon's dic-
tatorship. As was the case with the economic life as a whole, the book trade at that
time was also limited and restricted in its development. Censor stipulations, sale
prohibitions and threats of penalty hindered production and sales, and not least
even in France itself. In the political literature a general lethargy obtained, which
for the first time was interrupted in a pamphlet published in the summer of 1806,
Deutschland in seiner Tiefen Erniedrigung ("Germany in its Deep Humiliation"). Its
publisher was the Nuremberg book dealer, Johann Philipp Palm. The French arrested him, and when he refused to reveal the author's name, he was shot in Bran-
nau on August 26, 1806. The author of the militant publication has remained
unknown to this day. Mentioned in this connection are Johann Konrad von Yelin,
or the Altdorf rector, Johann Chr. Hrch. Adler, or (according to Hans Wecker) Dr.
Joh. Gg. Leuchs.[2]

Following the liberation struggle, better times also ensued for the German book
trade. Significant technical discoveries made the costs of production less expensive,
and they nevertheless improved the layout of books: the paper machine, stereotype
printing, which instead of the expensive new typesetting made possible essentially
cheaper, unaltered reprints with the help of poured gypsum plates (later paper
matrices); lithography, a discovery by Alois Senefelder, Friedrich König's
mechanical press, the renewal and the technical perfecting of woodcut, steel
engraving, dichromatic printing, and, finally, photography. The technical
possibilities had thus created for production an ever higher number of editions.
This factor balanced the increasing demand for books.

The struggles for freedom of the press, and for legal protection against
unauthorized reproduction and underselling, served to link the members of the
book trade more closely together. This led on April 30, 1826, to the founding of
the *Börsenverein der deutschen Buchhändler* ("Exchange Association of German
Bookdealers") in Leipzig. On January 3, 1834, there appeared the first number of
the *Börsenblatt*, which at first came out each week, and then from 1866, was issued
on a daily basis. On June 11, 1837, Prussia decreed a law against unauthorized

reproduction, in which the German Federation concurred on the following November 9. The printing festival of 1840 overwhelmingly documented the efficacy of the German book and also seemed to linked more closely together the book trading circles, so far as organization was concerned.

The year 1848 brought about the abolition of censorship. On November 1, 1867, through a decision of the German Confederation, the copyright for all authors who had been dead for more than thirty years was obliterated. With it, the so-called "everlasting copyright for editions of classical authors" ceased. The result was that 1867 became a "year of the classical authors." Again and again (and even into the next decades) there came out new inexpensive complete editions, and editions with scholarly commentary. One of the most active publishers was Gustav Hempel in Berlin; his *Nationalbibliothek sämtlicher deutscher Klassiker* ("National Library of All German Classical Authors"), begun in 1867, brought him sales in a short time of 300,000 items. In the same year, Goethe's *Faust* appeared as the first volume in Reclam's *Universalbibliothek* ("Universal Library"). On June 11, 1870, there was issued the copyright law ("Author's rights"), which then was drafted on June 19, 1901, together with the contemporary copyright law ("Publisher's rights"), which finally regulated the author and publisher relationship.

The general upswing in the Second Empire and the increasing numbers in the population also redowned to the good of the book trade. Progress in the transportation system and in technology could not remain without effect on production and on sales. Leipzig became the principal locale for the German book trade.[3] Here, at the site of the Exchange Association, there especially developed the scholarly publishing and the transactions on commission. The book trade constituted a considerable sector at the two annual fairs; on Cantate Sunday, there ensued the single reciprocal settlements, the chief assembly deliberated, and the committees of experts held their discussions. Architecturally there arose an entire book dealers' quarter, in which were interwoven large printeries and art establishments. Close by, Berlin, the capital city of the Empire, was growing, initially with a certain preference for modern belletristics, and then for specialized publishing. The next centers arose in the South, in Munich, Stuttgart and Vienna, while Cologne, Frankfurt and Hamburg were in retreat. Individual university cities achieved significance for the scholarly literature.

In the later years there developed, with the prevailing modes of the great serial and illustrated works and with the cheap colporter literature, a new kind of marketing in the pedlary and travelling book trade. Since about 1882, and in close association with it, the railroad station book trade arose; it was founded by the Berlin firm of Stilke. A closely knit network of booksellers—about five thousand of them—gradually dispersed throughout Germany, Austria and Switzerland. Two events witnessed from afar to the high status of the German book trade: On September 25, 1912, the Exchange Association concluded the founding of the "German Library *(Bücherei)*" in Leipzig as a complete archive of the German publications after 1913, and on May 6, 1914, there was opened in Leipzig the *Internationale Ausstellung für Buchgewerbe und Graphik* ("International Exhibition of the Book Trade and Graphics").

But then there came the World War, and it destroyed the hopes of that exhibition for the power of the book to bind peoples together, it ruptured the traffic in books with foreign countries, it shut down many great projects, and with the increasing shortage of paper, it rendered more difficult the production of new works, and it brought many journals and ongoing projects to a standstill. The military, political and economic breakdown of the Empire almost totally destroyed the book trade.

Such, approximately, was the course of the general development in the book trade of the modern period. Up to that time—that is, up to 1913—it has been depicted in its individual parts in the *Geschichte des deutschen Buchhandels* ("History of the German Booktrade"), in four volumes, of Friedrich Kapp and J. Goldfriedrich, which came out in the years 1886–1913. As a source work, it had been preceded since 1878, by the *Archiv für Geschichte des deutschen Buchhandels* ("Archive for the History of the German Book Trade").

History becomes vital, however, only if one recognizes behind it the bearers of the events, the men and their creations. In the book trade, the shaping element is in the first place the publishing firm. Therefore, there is also no book history that would not at the same time be a publishing history, and that would not consider the names (frequently supported by the tradition of entire generations) of those who through their own inner willingness, their own ideas, their enterprising spirit, and their financial risk-taking have worked together in originating the world of books, and who through their own personal engagement have created and distributed great works and library type series. "The dispersal of a book throughout the world is almost as difficult and weighty a work as the preparing of it," Schiller has on one occasion written to Cotta, his publisher.

Therefore, in what follows, the attempt is made to give a concise survey of the history and nature of the imperial German publishing firms; the survey is arranged first by period, and then by subject. What we are dealing with here is only an attempt, one that is undertaken in a time when everything is still in flux. Precision, therefore, in any final sense is not possible, nor is completeness, since until now no *Geschichte des deutschen Verlages* ("History of German Publishing") exists—yes, at present there is not even an address book, from which the present location of the publishing firms and the nature of their most recent production could be gathered. We shall have more than once to be content with the data prior to 1945.

The position of the "pure" publisher is relatively new. Until the middle of the eighteenth century, the person of the publisher was frequently identical with the printer—a connection that was effective until into the twentieth century. Publishing houses whose foundations reach back into these oldest periods are, therefore, mostly to be evaluated in their beginnings as printeries or booksellers. The independent publisher developed only gradually from both these trades. Up until then the financing and payment of fees for published works essentially resulted from donations and by way of subscription. There were no mass editions and scarcely a significant "publisher-personality" in the current sense.

Only in the second half of the eighteenth century was there a change: the general education grew, the position of the professional author developed through the introduction of the fee payment, and in place of the earlier exchange trade (which was conditioned by the *Sortimenterverleger*, or bookseller-publisher), stepping in now was the free "traffic in commodities" in the form of the publisher's delivery on his own; and the arrival on the scene of the journals hastened the rise of the entrepreneur-publisher.

Thus does it come about that around 1750, we see emerging in increasing density a series of publisher names that are still well-known today. The accompanying table designates a number of such firms by the year of their foundation, without wanting therewith to give more than examples.

1659	Cotta'sche Buchh. Nachf., Stuttgt.
1680	Weidmann, Leipzig-Berlin
1682	Metzler'sche Vlgsbchh., Stuttgt.
1719	Breitkopf & Härtel, Leipzig
1733	Schwetzschke & Gebauer, Halle
1735	Vandenhoeck &[R., Göttingen
1763	Beck, Nördlingen-Munich
1770	Schott's Söhne, Mainz
1780	Barth, Leipzig
1781	Hoffmann & Campe, Hamburg
1785	Perthes, J., Gotha
1785	Grote, Berlin
1786	Vieweg, Braunschweig
1789	Stalling, Oldenburg
1791	Hinrichs, Leipzig
1792	Schroedel, Halle-Hannover
1792	Steinkopf, Stuttgart
1796	Perthes, F.C., Gotha
1798	Duncker & Humblot, Berlin
1800	Peters, Leipzig
1801	Mohr, Tübingen
1801	Bagel, Düsseldorf
1805	Brockhaus, Leipzig
1810	Schrag, Nuremberg
1811	Teubner, Leipzig
1811	Engelmann, W., Leipzig
1818	Bachem, Cologne
1821	Schwann, Düsseldorf
1822	Franckh, Stuttgart
1822	Winter, Heidelberg
1826	Bibliogr. Institut, Leipzig
1826	Pustet, Regensburg
1826	Schweizerbarth, Stuttgart
1827	Baedeker, Leipzig

1828 Reclam, Leipzig
1830 Manz, Regensburg
1834 Weber, J.J., Leipzig
1835 Velhagen, Bielefeld
1837 Tauchnitz, Leipzig
1838 Westermann, Braunschweig

From these names of the pioneers of the present-day publishing trade we would now like to take several, in order to show in a somewhat more detailed representation the history of their firms, what their work and their successes consisted of, how and where they began and how the shape of their firm in the course of time has changed, so that through several generations they remained productive and significant up until the present time.

Even today these old firms have their special quality that sets them into bold relief as over against the other publishers. In those initial periods a common character bound them together much more. At that time, almost all of them were general publishers, that is, their activity comprised the most varied areas at the same time. To be sure, theology, jurisprudence, philology, or music were also at that time already playing a role; leading, however, was the fostering of literature, "belletristics" in the broadest sense, and the accompanying humanistic disciplines of history, the history of scholarship, geography and technology. One was aiming at a broad class of readers, at a general knowledge, at the education and learning of the middle classes, whether in lexical form, in the popular representation, in inexpensive editions, or in the entertaining and versatile journals for the home and family.

The lexical type of book was, in and of itself, no new idea. It was a creation of the eighteenth century, and the works of Hübner and Zedler at that time had already been significant publishing projects. These were large, multi-volumed and expensive books.[4]

They only became popular, however, when Friedrich Arnold Brockhaus (1772–1823), hit upon the idea of creating out of the Löbel's encyclopedia, (which he took over in 1808) through an entirely new kind of arrangement and wording, a practical reference work, which in a brief representation brought out what was worth knowing about all the persons and events and things of life. Brockhaus,[5] who originally had been a cloth merchant in Holland, established himself as a book dealer in Altenburg, and in 1817, he removed to Leipzig, and lived to experience the great success of the work. The first edition came out in 1809 in two thousand copies; before his death the fifth edition in 32,000 copies had already been disseminated. In 1818, a printery was acquired; and in 1836, a type foundry. The firm received an enormous impetus under his son, Friedrich (1800–65). There appeared significant scholarly journals such as Oken's *Isis*, and *Hermes*, the *Urania;* Jean Paul, Rückert, Voss, Fouqué, Körner, Steffens, Raumer and Schopenhauer were among the firm's authors. Through five generations the publishing firm in Leipzig remained as one of the largest publishing enterprises. To the *Grosse Brockhaus* ("Great Brockhaus") there was added the smaller

Handbuch and the one-volume *Volks-Brockhaus* ("People's Brockhaus"). A publishing house of valuable travel and expeditionary works was added, with publications of Stanley, Schliemann, Hansen, Nordenskjöld, Sven Hedin, Colin Ross and Filchner.

In the youngest generation, under Eberhard Brockhaus, a new publishing house was founded in 1946 in Wiesbaden, which again took up with renewed vigor the production that had diminished in Leipzig under the pressure of the political situation. Here appeared in two volumes the *Kleine Brockhaus* ("Little Brockhaus"), the *Sprach-Brockhaus* ("Language Brockhaus"), the *Gesundheits-Brockhaus* ("Health Brockhaus"), the *Brockhaus der Naturwissenschaften und Technik* ("Brockhaus of the Sciences and Technology") – all of them vital witnesses of how one firm through long years' success can itself become almost a generic term denoting quality. In that regard, however, the name of the founder should not to be forgotten; he was a German patriot, and in word and writing *(Deutsche Blätter)* (1813–1816) he pursued the aim, "to awaken the common sense – to raise the German national dignity; to instill hatred toward foreign subjugation and a trust in ourselves."

No less sonorously tied with the sound of his name is that of Friedrich Christoph Perthes (1772–1843).[6] He was a learned book dealer; he had founded a retail bookstore in Hamburg in 1796, and in 1822, he moved to Gotha, where he devoted himself entirely to publishing. He was also a friend of the Fatherland who played a big role in the liberation movement. He was in touch with Arndt, Stein, Niebuhr, Savigny and Görres, and he consciously put his publishing house in the service of the German reconstruction. He was a leading contributor in the organization of the German book trade and the co-founder of the Exchange Association. In his publication, *Der deutsche Buchhandel als Bedingung des Daseyns einer deutschen Literatur* (1816) ("The German Book Trade as the Condition for the Existence of a German Literature") he demanded a conscious promotion of the profession by the state. His son, Friedrich Andreas Perthes, is the founder (1854) of the firm of F.A. Perthes, which remained in Gotha until 1922, and which was especially devoted to history, to church history, and to literature for youth. Its largest undertaking was the *Geschichte der europäischen Staaten* ("History of European States"), by Heeren-Ukert, with one hundred eighty volumes.

Close by, there grew in Gotha the publishing establishment of Justus Perthes, which was founded in 1785, by Justus Perthes, the uncle of Friedrich Christoph. It quickly developed into one of the most significant publishers in the subject areas of cartography and geography and genealogy. Its most successful undertakings were the Gotha Court Calendar (and its various subspecies) and the great atlases of Stieler, Berghaus, Spruner, Sydow, Langhans, and especially also *Petermanns' Mitteilungen* ("Petermann's Communications") (since 1855), which for a time was the best known geographical journal in Germany.[7]

In addition to Brockhaus and Perthes, as the third of the leading publisher personalities of that early period there must be mentioned Georg Andreas Reimer (1776–1842).[8] He had participated as officer in the wars of liberation, and likewise had contributed significantly to the organizational life of the book trade. He was one of the leading publishers of the Romantics. Schleiermacher's *Monologe* were published by him, as well as the works of the brothers Schlegel, of Fichte, Tieck, Novalis, of Arndt, Kleist, Fouqué, Schenkendorf and Jean Paul, of Niebuhr, Lachmann and others. In 1819, he acquired the Berlin Council bookshop with its printery, annexed several other publishers, and in 1822, took over the Weidmann bookshop in Leipzig, which his sons moved to Berlin in 1854. The family firm, on the other hand, was transferred to Walter de Gruyter in 1897.

The Weidmann Book Dealership was one of the oldest in Germany. Founded in 1680 in Frankfurt, already in 1681 it was being removed by Moritz Gg. Weidmann to Leipzig, where in the seventeenth and eighteenth centuries, under Gleditsch, Georg M. Weidmann and Ph. E. Reich, it became the leading publisher of literature. Published with Weidmann were Wieland, Gellert, Lessing and Lavater.[9] Following its removal to Berlin, and under the leadership of the successors of Georg Reimer, the firm extended its area of work in the direction of pedagogy and philology, history, philosophy and literary scholarship, and finally, sports and the radio. Among their most famous authors in this more recent period were scholars such as Dahlmann, Mommsen, Curtius, Lamprecht, Wilamowitz-Möllendorf, Wilhelm Scherer, Haupt, Burdach and Hermann Diels.

To the support of contemporary literature and of the arts, firms of smaller compass have also devoted themselves at that time with love and success. Thus Heinrich Wilhelm Hahn in Hanover has become the first publisher of *Monumenta Germaniae Historica*, while he was later building up the business more toward the pedagogical aspect. Jakob Christian Mohr, the ancestor of the later Tübingen publisher, had published in Heidelberg *Des Knaben Wunderhorn* ("The Youth's Magic Horn"), as well as works by Arnim, Tieck, Jean Paul, Görres, and other Romanticists.[10] Schrag in Nuremberg was a center for late Romanticism. He has published first editions of Eichendorff, Fouqué, Jean Paul and Rückert, as also Chamissos' *Peter Schlemihl*.[11] Ferd. Dümmler in Bonn published *"Goethe's Briefwechsel mit einem Kinde"* ("Goethe's Letter Exchange with a Child") in 1835.

The publishing firm of Hans Friedrich Vieweg (1761–1835) in Brunswick, which today is known as a great publisher for technical works, began with literary works, already in the time of the classical authors. In his *Taschenbuch für Frauenzimmer* ("Pocketbook for Women") of 1798, there was contained the first printing of *Hermann und Dorothea*. There followed works by Herder, by the brothers Schlegel, and by Humboldt. The founder's son, Eduard, has made the tales of Andersen known in Germany, and had Klaus Groth's *Quickborn* published; he has achieved no success, however, with the initial editions of Gottfried Keller's *Grüne Heinrich* (1854–55) and the *Leute von Seldwyla* ("People of Selwyla").[12]

Even a a firm such as Breitkopf and Härtel in Leipzig, which already since its founding (1719) had been a music publisher, could not wholly ignore the swing toward the literary. The works of Luise von Francois and Felix Dahn were published by it. The popular editions of *Kampf um Rom* ("Struggle for Rome") and *Julian* have still had great success about 1930.

In the belletristic area were situated the beginnings of the firm of Bernhard Tauchnitz in Leipzig.[13] It was founded in 1837 by Christian Bernhard Tauchnitz.

His uncle, Karl Christoph Traugott Tauchnitz, was already a publisher and printer. He developed his publishing house, founded in 1798, more in line with technology, and as the first one in Germany to do so, he used stereotype. In addition to the splendid illustrated editions, he created small pretty volumes as the forerunner of the inexpensive entertainment literature. At the same time he was bringing out carefully executed editions of the ancient classical authors. His nephew, Christian Bernhard, then laid in 1841 the foundations in his own publishing house to the world famous *Collection of British and American Authors,* which grew in course of the following century to almost 5,500 volumes. Through the Tauchnitz Edition almost all the significant writers of Britain and America were distributed on the continent at inexpensive prices.

Also serving the cheap dissemination of popular literature was the *Pfennig-Magazin* ("Penny Magazine"), which was founded in 1833, by Johann Jakob Weber (1803–1880), and which attained a total subscriptions of 100,000. Adolf Menzel drew up four hundred sketches for the *Geschichte Friedrichs des Grossen* ("History of Frederick the Great"). Weber's publishing establishment achieved great merit in the revival of the woodcut. His *Leipziger Illustrierte Zeitung* (1843) achieved a world reputation. Even his manuals for artisans *Katechismen* ("Catechisms") were for a while great success.[14]

In that early period, a new idea for a book always seemed quickly to find a favorable field for operation. Thus Joseph Meyer (1796–1856), who had issued about 1823 in Gotha a *Correspondenzblatt für Kaufleute* ("Correspondence Sheet for Salespeople"), inexpensive Shakespeare translations and the novels of Sir Walter Scott, hit on the idea of publishing works that would be issued serially. In 1826, he founded his *Bibliographisches Institut,*[15] removed himself to Hildburghausen and here brought out the German classical authors in inexpensive editions. His historical-geographical educational work, *Universum,* had in the more than thirty years 80,000 subscribers and was published in twelve languages.

Between 1839–52 there appeared the *Grosse Konversationslexikon* ("Large Encyclopedia") in fifty-two volumes[16] and immediately it had 70,000 purchasers. His son, Hermann Julius Meyer (1826–1909), moved the firm to Leipzig. Under him the firm grew large with publishing, the printery, cartography, and the bookbindery. It produced the *Lexikon* in eight editions up to 1936. In 1862, Meyer's *Reisebücher* ("Travel Books") was founded, and in 1858, *Meyer's Sprachführer* ("Meyer's Language Guides"). The many editions of classical authors with commentaries, the *Grosse Duden,* the *Grosse Handatlas* were published, as were the well-known standard works: Vogt's and Koch's *Geschichte der deutschen Literatur* ("History of German Literature"), Helmolt's *Weltgeschichte* ("World History"), Steinhausen's *Kulturgeschichte* ("History of Culture"), Ranke's *Der Mensch* ("Man"), Brehm's *Tierleben* ("Animal Life"), Kerner's *Pflanzenleben* ("Life of Plants"), Ratzel's *Die Erde und das Leben* ("The Earth and Life"), and the *Grosse Weltatlas* (1933) ("The Large Atlas of the World"). Almost all of these successful books had been commissioned by the publisher.[17]

If it was through the range and the variety in the nature of its production that the "B.I." has become one of the largest German publishers, so the house of Philipp

Reclam probably became the most popular. It had resulted form the *Literarische Museum* ("Literary Musem"), which Anton Philipp Reclam (1807–96) had created in 1828. The firm, which since 1947 has maintained a branch business in Stuttgart, is today owned by the family's fourth generation. The publishing house became known world wide through the *Universalbibliothek* ("Universal Library"), which was begun in 1867 (at that time it was twenty pfennig per number). Beginning with Goeth'e *Faust*, today it comprises over eight thousand numbers and contains almost the entire literature of the world. Of the volumes with the German classical authors, about eighteen million have been printed; about eight and half million of the classical authors of antiquity have been printed. There are two and a half million copies of the *Tell* alone, of Ibsen there are four and a half million, but even philosophers such as Kant attained eight hundred thousand copies, and Schopenhauer six hundred thirty thousand. Very popular also where the affordable *Helios* classical authors. Of the large scale serial work, *Deutsche Literatur*, about a hundred volumes have appeared since 1930. The journal *Universum* (since 1884) was one of the most read ones for three decades.

The publishing house of Velhagen and Klasing in Bielefeld, which was founded in 1835, has also become known since about 1865, through the good and general entertainment journal. At that time it began with the sheet for families, *Daheim* ("At Home") and in 1886, with the essentially more sophisticated *Monatshefte* ("Monthly Issues"), which is still published today. As a book publisher, its success lay in the areas of geography (Andree's *Handatlas*), history ("Putzger's *Historischer Atlas)* and in the larger, well illustrated series, *Land und Leute* ("Land and People") and *Monographien zur Geschichte der Kunst* ("Monographs on the History of Art"). Besides these, schoolbooks were published, especially school editions of foreign language texts and publications for youth.

Thirty years before Velhagen's *Monatshefte*, those by Georg Westermann appeared in Brunswick.[18] They attained at times an edition of 30,000 copies, and they are still being published today. Founded in 1836, and supported by its own printery and bookbindery, the firm developed into a great concern, especially in the area of cartography. Westermann's *Weltatlas* ("World Atlas") and the school atlases of Diercke were enduring successes. Pedagogy, the modern languages, school books and instructional materials filled out the further areas of work. Even the belletristic production was kept faithful to the older tradition.

If with the portrayal of the publishing history up to this point the belletristic literature has stepped strongly into the foreground, one ought nevertheless not get the impression that the subject literature had not also played a big role for the development of these firms. It is much rather that, even in this early period, the majority of the firms were already (in addition to the literature) fostering scholarly publications, even if they were initially more in the direction of the human sciences. But in addition to this, there were already at that time several publishers (which today are still significant), that from the beginning had the character of specialized subject publishers.

Karl Baedeker is, for example, one such firm. It was founded in 1827, in Coblenz, and removed in 1872 to Leipzig, which only in 1951 did it exchange for

Hamburg. Here are now published the well known travel handbooks, which became so famous all over the world that the red volume accompanying them became simply characteristic for travellers. As forerunners there were published in 1829, the *Führer von Koblenz* ("Guide to Coblenz"), and in 1832, the *Rheinreise von Mainz bis Köln* ("Rhine Trip from Mainz to Cologne"), and already since 1846, also editions in foreign languages. All the volumes that followed, with their valuable maps and city plans, are known to those who travel. The first four volumes, which again were published after 1945, were city guides: Leipzig, Stuttgart, and Munich; the first territorial volume was a new edition of northern Bavaria.[19]

The firm of Duncker and Humblot (which was founded in 1809 in Berlin) appeared in its beginnings as a specialized publisher for history. In spite of many changes in locale and proprietorship it has maintained this area until now, and beyond that, has devoted its attention especially to law, and the political and social sciences. Its most famous author was Leopold von Ranke, and one of its most voluminous publications the *Allgemeine deutsche Biographie* ("General German Biography").[20]

There is one firm, however, that constitutes the worthy conclusion of this section, the name of which is even today still well known to each pupil of a gymnasium. In 1811, Benedikt Gotthelf Teubner (1784–1846) founded the firm of B.G. Teubner through the acquisition of a Leipzig printery, to which he had annexed a publishing house in 1824. It was out of this relationship of printery and publishing house that the later world firm grew, which became a leading one in the areas of school books for the higher instructional institutions, for classical philology and archeology, for pedagogy, for mathematics and for the sciences. Every pupil is acquainted with the editions of the Latin and Greek classical authors in the *Bibliotheca Teubneriana;* it extended to over five hundred volumes. No less known was the collection (since 1898) of *Aus Natur und Geisteswelt* ("Out of Nature and the World of Thought"). The *Thesaurus linguae latinae,* the *Enzyklopedie der mathematischen Wissenschaften* ("Encyclopedia of Mathematical Sciences"), and the *Kultur der Gegenwart* ("Culture of the Present") were all large, multi-volumed serial works. Numerous journals were published by the firm. In the 1890's the firm (whose sole location even now is still in Leipzig) went over into the possession of the female line (Giesecke).[21]

We would thus conclude the introductory presentation of the history of individual firms and turn to the development of German publishing within the last hundred years.

Two tendencies in increasing measure are characteristic of the structure of publishing in this last period: on the one hand, as a more technical principle, the striving for breadth, and on the other hand, as a general principle, the tendency toward limitation and apparent narrowing—or more precisely put, the mass editions and the predominance of specialized publishing.

With the growth of the general popular education and the affluence of broader classes of people, from the widest circles there came new and always more purchasers of the book. One did not read only that which was entertaining, but one read in order to learn and for the purpose of self-cultivation. On this basis, there came about new kinds of books, inexpensive and versatile book series, the most varied "libraries" of novels and great illustrated works. The entertaining journals and those that fostered the sciences for a popular audience prospered. The numbers of editions of handbooks and dictionaries increased. The layout of books becomes more sophisticated, and through the printing of a higher number of editions, the average price nevertheless came down. It increases about 1930 up to the famous 2 mark 85 books, which in spite of some questionable aspects, were wonders in German book production. The technical discoveries of this period (the composing machine, a rotation press, autotype, intaglio, and offset printing) served to make everything less expensive through speed and mass printing. This prevalence of inexpensive books also gives the newer productions substantially a quite definite direction in terms of content: "What pleases is allowed." It is a phenomenon that even today is still not finished. In the search for even larger classes of purchasers one has come upon new forms of organization, of distributing books, and of advertising. One of these phenomena is the book club which during the twenties sprang up here and there. Initially hotly contested, they have nevertheless prevailed. Undertakings such as the German book club, or the book guilds of the printers' unions, are today publishing enterprises of high production and large economical volume. The effort for greater extension was naturally expressed most strongly in belletristics. So about 1900 there was a large number of publishers that excelled through inexpenisve editions of the classic writers: Reclam and the Bibliographical Insitute, the Verlag Bong with its *Goldene Klassiker* ("Golden Classic Writers"), Max Hesse and the *Insel-Verlag* with its *Volks-Goethe* ("People's Goethe"), Cotta in Stuttgart and the *Propyläen-Verlag* in Berlin. In addition, there were innumerable select and separate editions that found their way into the bourgeois bookcase through the wholesale book trade and the commercial houses.

The market for contemporary literature was smaller and only a few novels at that time attained an edition of over fifty thousand. Youth literature had the most "hits." Of *Struwelpeter*, of *König Nußknacker* ("King Nutcracker") or the immortal *Familie Pfäffling*, new editions (with a large number of copies) could be printed again and again. The new less expensive illustration procedures worked in favor of the picture books and the fairy tale books. *Robinson Crusoe, Uncle Tom's Cabin, The Leatherstocking Tales, Münchhausen, Gulliver* and *Till Eulenspiegel*—these achieved mass editions; Karl May became, and remained, the classic author of older children. The fairy tale books of Wildermuth, Spyri, and Rhoden *(Der Trotzkopf)* were large and lasting successes. With the invention of four color printing and of color-offset, a new picture-book industry arose. The youth literature alone claimed about six percent of the entire publishing production.

The share of the so-called belletristic literature amounted in 1920 to about eighteen percent. Here lay the choice area for the large numbers of editions. Nevertheless, before 1910, there was still scarcely the concept of the American bestseller. A success such as that of Frenssen's *Jörn Uhl*, which was distributed between 1901 and 1910, in 200,000 copies, was an exception. If one understands by bestseller a work that attains a very large number of editions within a short time following its initial appearance, there is then still nothing like this in Germany today; only

Remarque's *Im Westen nichts Neues* ("All Quiet on the Western Front") alone could in the year of its publication (1929) be printed in one hundred eighty editions, which might correspond to the quantity of about one million copies. All the other most successful books, which Hans Ferdinand Schulz had put together for 1950, in his recently appeared work *(Das Schicksal der Bücher*—"The Fate of Books," Berlin, 1952) have attained their largest numbers of editions within a life span of twenty to fifty years. To them belong Thomas Mann's *Buddenbrooks*, Ganghofer's *Martinklause* ("Martin's Hermitage"), and *Schloss Humbertus* ("Humbertus' Castle"), Schleich's *Besonnte Vergangenheit* ("The Sunny Past"), Grimm's *Volk ohne Raum* ("Nation Without Room"), Kröger's *Vergessenes Dorf* ("Forgotten Village"), the *Opfergang* ("Sacrifice") by Binding and Rilke's *Cornet*. In that connection one has to observe that the last two novellas have been published in the popular and inexpensive *Inselbücherei*, and the first four novels have appeared in popular editions at 2 marks 85. *Buddenbrooks* is especially typical of how a work merely through modern means of technology can be led to an enormous distribution through mass editions and increased advertising.

By the way, with the mention of the *Inselbücherei* there emerges a characteristic type of book that has shown itself to be very functional for the further increasing of sales and of editions. They are the so-called "Book series," the "collections," "libraries" and series. Almost all of them have had great success through the low prices made possible by high editions and an established stock of subscribers. At first they dealt with belletristics, lyrics and epics, but then also with the most varied areas of the human sciences, the natural sciences and technology. Their unity is for the most part purely external: the title, which relates either to the publishing firm (Collection Göschen, Kröner's pocket editions, Collection Dietrich, Insel books, Weber's "Catechisms," Engelhorns library of novels, Schaffstein's *Blaue Bändchen, Bibliotheca Teuberiana, Ullsteinbücher,* Collection Kösel, *Reclam's Univeral Bibliothek)* or they are designated in accord with the contents, generally or symbolically ("Out of Nature and the World of the Mind," "Science and Education," "the Bluebooks," "Books of the Rose," "Silver Books," "The Knowledge of the Present"). They have all of them a standard design layout and a uniform price. There gradually came to be such series for all subject areas, where for the purposes of teaching they have often assumed the character of surveys. The best have withstood two world wars and are now once again the bookseller's daily bread.

As over against them, a third type of book (which was more sophisticated) was, thanks to the new production technology, also widely diffused. It consisted in the definitive presentation in its totality of a larger and generally interesting field of knowledge, such as history, the history of literature or of art, geography and technology, biology, botany or zoology, in the form of one or two volume standard works, that had easily understandable narratives and which were frequently illustrated. as already mentioned, the Bibliographical Institute has been a leader in this field. These were objects that brought about new trading methods: the travelling book trade, the development of a corps of sale representatives, purchase on installments, and the like.

As a fourth type of book of the greatest general effect there then must still be mentioned the lexicon (or encyclopedia). At first it was an "everything," a book of all, and a book for all. In this way, like the older examples of the "large" Brockhaus, Meyer or Herder, in the course of the years it only underwent modifications into something smaller, shorter and less expensive: in addition to the handbooks of four and two volumes, there arose the thick one-volume popular edition until we got the Knauer Popular Encyclopedia for 2 marks 85. At the same time, however, the type was encroaching on almost all special areas of knowledge and practical life. Today there are lexica for every field, lexica for literature and history, pedagogy and philosophy, for art and music, for all branches of legal science, technical lexica and scientific lexica, lexica for manual workers, salesmen and industrial, sport and model lexica, lexica for the art of cooking, and for manners and morals. The various biographical dictionaries also belong here.

All of these productions grew out of the historically conditioned and economically evaluated efforts at diffusion. They were based on the extended areas for sales, but they could only be successful in content areas that were really of interest to a large public.

In addition, developing since about 1870, in speedily increasing tempo, was a production of an apparently opposite sort. The effort here goes toward limitation and refinement. Specialization arises in science, in economics and in technology. But since books are always a mirror of the world, it was inevitable that the publisher would also follow this specialization. Ever larger became the number of books that were not meant for the general reader, but were written for the subject specialist. It was of no importance here whether he was a scholar, an artist, a technician, a salesman, or a manual worker. Specialist books appeared even in the most narrow sub-discipline. The smaller the circle of those who were interested, the smaller the edition, and therefore the higher the price. They were even higher in those areas that required difficult composition (Mathematics, Chemistry) or highly valued illustrations (medicine, art). But the price here is not decisive. Decisive are the contents and the purpose of the book, the new, the unique, and the practical value, that make it into indispensable work material, a book for studying and for using. Belonging thereto are the textbooks, the handbooks, the reference works, the commentaries and monographs of every kind. On these books rests the foundation of the new type of publisher, the specialist publisher; it became the most solid foundation of the modern publisher, and was mostly associated with the founding of corresponding specialists' journals. In this form, German publishing has withstood even the catastrophes of the two world wars, yes, thanks to the specialist books, there has been no real "catastrophe" for the book trade. The constantly growing export of the German book also depends on the specialist book.

This development initially began in the area of the human sciences, of music, theology and jurisprudence. Then there were formed the specialist publishers for children's books and books for youth, of school books and of medicine. The unusually speedy development of technology had as its result the aggregate (which had many branches) of technical and industrial publishers. The publishers for chemistry and physics went right along. In the last decade, the complicating of the economic, social and trade life has generated new specialist publishers. In addition to the old firms that accommodated themselves to the new conditions, after about 1900, new firms again and again came into existence (many of them emerged quickly and again disappeared, but others of them grew into extensive operations), which towered significantly over the earlier general publishers. On the average, these specialist publishers of the sciences are economically stronger and financially more fit than the specialist publishers for the human sciences, or the belletristic firms.

It isn't possible within a short space to give a presentation of the history of these many publishers. In the years 1910–1940, the number of German publishers of books and journals amounted to about 3,200. Around 1,500 names were registered in 1951, for West Germany and West Berlin. The general public is scarcely familiar with a hundred of them, but even the expert can only with effort get for himself some adequate conception of them. How extraordinarily numerous alone are the religious publishers, the publishers of the colporter novels, of area guides and of maps, the technical or the tax-law publishers, and very especially the pure publishers of propaganda, concerning the number and names of which no associational registry gives information.

One may nevertheless not entertain too large a conception of the publishing firms of the present day. Middle-sized and small operations are prevalent. According to a statistic of 1925, for example, of 1,700 publishers, only 52 of them had more than fifty employees, only 250 had more than ten and fully half had only five or less. Big publishers such as Springer or de Gruyter are rare.

We want now in what follows to attempt to give the reader at least an approximate picture of the current structure of the German publishing system, while from time to time we want to bring forward, in a section devoted to the most important subject areas, several of the most well known names as representatives of their subject areas.

Due to their number and popularity of the names, the publishers of belletristics still stand even today in first place. Also in the second half of the nineteenth century, there were firms appearing in this field which today are known to us only as specialist publishers in other areas. Thus, for example, did the first editions of Alexis and Gutzkow issue from Brockhaus, of Anzengruber, Dahn and Louise von Francois from Breitkopf and Härtel, and of Gustav Freitag from S. Hirzel. The publishers of Heine, Börne and Hebbel were Hoffmann and Campe in Hamburg. Gottfried Keller first appeared with Vieweg, and later with Göschen; his compatriot, C.F. Meyer, appeared with Haessel in Leipzig. Schuster and Löffler published the works of Liliencron, Dehmel and Bierbaum in Berlin, those by Storm, Paetel and Westermann; Stifter, on the other hand, was published by Heckenast in Budapest.

Berlin became the leading publishing locale for the modern belletristics after the turn of the century.

The Grote'sche publishing establishment had already moved in that direction by 1865. In its *Sammlung zeitgenössischer Schriftsteller* ("Collection of Contemporary Authors") it produced works of Raabe, Frenssen, Fontane, Federer, Jul. Wolff, Wildenbruch and Ganghofer. Its greatest success was Frenssen's *Jörn Uhl*.[22]

S. Fischer became the leading publisher of naturalism and of modernity. Founded in 1886, it was partly continued during the years 1935–45 in the emigration, and partly by Suhrkamp in Berlin, and has currently removed to Frankfurt. Appearing with this publisher were the complete works of Gerhart Hauptmann, Dehmel, Fontane, Hofmannsthal, Schnitzler, Wassermann, the great Scandinavians Ibsen, Björnson, Jacobsen, and Hamsun, the translations of Dostoevski, Tolstoy, Zola, the Goncourts, of Joseph Conrad and Shaw. It produced the first works of Hesse, Thomas Mann, Emil Strauss and Stehr, Friedrich Huch and Schaffner, of Bahr and Hartleben and of Manfred Hausmann. The inexpensive yellow volumes of *S. Fischer's Romanbibliothek* ("S. Fischer's Library of Novels") were widely disseminated.[23]

The most widely distributed *Romanbibliothek* ("Novel Library") of the purely entertainment type of literature in that period was created by Ullstein, with its little volumes bound in red linen that sold for one Mark.

Thanks to the active personality of its founder, the publishing house of Ernst Rowohlt in Berlin, since 1908, has developed as the literarily most versatile publisher, and with a great measure of success. Its initial successes were the biographies of Ludwig and the Balzac editions. The firm then had a changing destiny; it was newly founded in Stuttgart in 1946, and it finally moved to Hamburg. Rowohlt is an experimenter in the new book forms. His latest ideas were the novel in journal form and in a colportage-like make-up, both of them applied to material that was, qualitatively speaking, first class — especially the foreign novel. Besides that, he is devoted to current problems as this was perhaps expressed, for instance, in Salomon's *Fragebogen* ("Questionnaire").

The Berlin publishing house of Paul Neff (founded 1829) proves to be more inclined toward the literature of entertainment; publishing (among others) Rudolf Herzog and Bruno Brehm, it had its greatest success with the novels of Muschler; besides that, however, it also maintained considerable art publishing.

Through the 1936 removal from Frankfurt to Potsdam, there entered also into the Berlin circle the publishing firm of Rütten and Löning, which had been founded already in 1844. Its authors were Binding, Bonsels, Bengt Berg, Undset, Gjellerup, and Romain Rolland. Today it is located in Darmstadt.

In addition to Berlin, the goal of which was more directed toward the modern problematic novel or the light entertainment novel emphasizing the erotic, in the southern part of the Empire, Munich and Stuttgart developed as further center of belletristic literature.

In Munich in 1931, there arose, through the union of the old publishing houses of Georg Müller (founded 1903: Bierbaum, Wedekind, Strindberg) and Albert Langen (founded 1893: Hamsun, Lagerlöf, "Simplicissmus"), the concern of Langen Müller Publishers, as the greatest of the belletristic firms in South Germany.[24] Paul Ernst, Griese, Hans Grimm *(Volk ohne Raum)*, Hamsun, Lagerlöf, Thoma and Ernst Wiechert belonged (with others) among the authors of the firm. When the business disintegrated in 1945, its publishing rights were taken over by the most varied Munich firms, but the founding of the firm anew is now imminent.

To the publishing firm of Kurt Desch, newly established in 1945, came the works of Ernst Wiechert; it henceforth developed a considerable belletristic production.

R. Piper took over the works of Ludwig Thomas. Founded in 1904 by its senior chief, Richard Piper, the publishing firm has (as the first one to do so in Germany) produced the works of Dostoevsky in a complete edition.[25]

One is acquainted with the publishing houses of Braun & Schnieder[26] and Bassermann as the publishers of works by Wilhelm Busch. Wilhelm Langewiesche has in 1906, in nearby Ebenhausen, founded his famous brown series, the *Bücher der Rose*, which have been disseminated in more than four million copies; of them, 800,000 alone were of the anthology, *Die Ernte deutscher Lyrik* ("The Harvest of German Lyrics") of Will Vesper, the Goethe volume, *Alles um Liebe* ("Everything for Love") and Kügelgen's *Jugenderinnerungen* ("Memories of Youth").

The publishing house of Georg W. Dietrich had especially become known through it *Kleinodien der Weltliteratur* ("Jewles of World Literature") and the *Münchener Künstlerbilderbücher* ("Munich Art Picture Books"). The *Kinderheimat in Liedern* ("Children's Home in Songs") illustrated by Josef Mauder, has won many friends for itself.[27]

The most significant publisher of novels under Catholic direction is the firm of Kösel in Munich. Appearing here were works by Dörfler, of Handel-Mazetti and Weismantel. A still more successful book, however, was Sebastian Kneipp's *Meine Wasserkur* ("My Water Cure"). The activity of the newly founded firm of Franz Ehrenwirth, the publisher of the works of Gertrude von le Fort, ran in a similar direction. And, finally, we will again recall the old "General" publishers, when we can establish firms such as Beck (-Biederstein), Bruckmann or Carl Hanser as belletristic publishers.

Seen from the economic side of the printing function, the belletristic share in the publishing life of Stuttgart always played a more dominant role there than it did in Berlin or Munich. Regarding the content, predominating there was the tradition of the good (and as a whole bourgeois in orientation) entertainment novel.

Thus Cotta found similar successes with the novels of Sudermann and Heer, as it had had in its time with works by Mörike, Auerbach and W.H. von Riehl. Engelhorn, whose "novel library" was gladly read in all families about 1900, and which reached over a thousand volumes, had its greatest recent success with Kluge's *Herr Kortum*. Works of Scheffel, Karl Stieler and Ganghofer appeared with Adolf Bonz.[28] The Steinkopf firm's "Best-seller" became Agnes Günther's *Die Heilige und ihr Narr* ("The Saint and her Fool"). The *Deutsche Verlagsanstalt* ("German Publishing Establishment"), a large concern founded in 1848, with versatile productions, produced in the belletristic area poems and stories of Bierbaum, Flaischlen, Börries von Münchhausen, Bonsels, Max Eyth and Finckh. Its more recent authors are Ina Seidel, Ernst Zahn, Henry Benrath, Otto Rombach and Erhard Wittek. The *Union*, the second large operation in Stuttgart, in its time enjoyed large sales with the novels of Marlitt and Heimburg. In nearby Heilbronn, Egen Salzer[29] fostered the Swabian native literature; Hesse and Ludwig Finckh, Anna Schieber and Auguste Supper belong to its circle of authors. In Tübingen, the Reiner

Wunderlich publishing firm founded in 1926 by Hermann Leins, advanced very quickly. The collection of letters, *Das Herz ist wach* ("The Heart is Awake"), by Kennicott, was its first large success. Next to it stand the novels of Isolde Kurz, Gertrude Bäumer, Isabel Hamer and religiously oriented tales, as well as current biographies.

The city of Leipzig had its strength more in scholarly than in belletristic publishing. Today the relevant firms of Leipzig have left, or they have, at least, shifted their main production to the West.

Thus the main site of the publishing firm of Paul List, founded in Leipzig in 1894, is now in Munich. It has published Carl Hauptmann, Wilhelm von Scholz, H.E. Busse, Hermann Stehr, and Marg. zur Bentlage, has produced translations of Lawrence and Kipling, and illustrated editions of Gustav Freytag. Its further special areas are books of adventure and biographies, such as those of Hagenbeck, Henry Ford and others. Its greatest success was the *Buch von San Michele* ("Book of St. Michele") by Axel Munthe.[30]

In addition to Reclam and to Quell & Meyer, the publishing firm of Staackmann in Leipzig (now located in Bamberg) had devoted itself above all to the entertainment novel. Its specialty was the German-Austrian literature: Rosegger, Greinz, Bartsch, Müller-Guttenbrunn, Schönherr, Gagern, Ginzkey, Strobl and Wildgans have been published by it; so have the German authors, Spielhagen, Otto Ernst, Max Geissler, A. de Nora, and Paul Schreckenbach.[31]

The Insel-Verlag[32] has also shifted the site of its main production to Wiesbaden in 1945. Founded in 1902, it developed under the inspired leadership of Anton Kippenberg into a center for the fostering of Goethe and into a guardian of the German book culture. One of its greatest more recent authors was Rainer M. Rilke, whose *Stundenbuch* ("Book of Hours") appeared with the *Insel* already in 1905. In 1912, there followed Rilke's *Cornet*, which, as an *Insel* book, went through one hundred sixty-eight editions in the course of the following forty years. Carossa, Binding, Ricarda Huch, Albrecht Schäffer and Stefan Zweig have published a portion of their works with the *Inselverlag*. Financially, the greatest undertakings were the colorful reprints of the *Manessische Lieder* manuscript and the Gutenberg Bible, the multi-volumed collective editions of Goethe and Schiller that were printed on thin paper, the *Volks-Goethe* ("People's Goethe") and the *Volks-Stifter* ("People's Stifter"). Series such as the *Romane der Weltliteratur* ("Novels of World Literature"), the books of the German mystics, artists' monographs and *Deutsche Meister* ("German Masters") served to extend its field of effective operation. The name of the publishing house became the most popular through the *Inselbücherei*, which was founded in 1912, and which in the first twenty-five years brought out five hundred numbers in around twenty million copies. Rilke's poems and *Cornet*, Binding's *Opfergang* ("Sacrifice") and, earlier, Karl Stieler's *Winteridyll* achieved powerful sales in this edition (of these works). In spite of the uniformity of the series in format and price, each volume in its combination of word, type, paper and binding had a well-formed individuality, was typographically perfect, and was a singular bargain.

The belletristic publishing house did not achieve similar traditional significance in the other cities of the Empire. The present-day firms in Hamburg such as Wolf, Krüger, Govert, Marion v. Schröder, Todt or Chr. Wegner are relatively young. On the other hand, smaller cities have several of the older firms. To mention here would be Velhagen & Klasing in Bielefeld (founded in 1835), which, to be sure, has become known less through its novels than through its journal for the family, *Daheim* ("At home") (1864) and since 1886, through its *Monatshefte*. The stories of Raabe and Storm, Timm Kröger and Scharrelmann and, recently, of Hermann Claudius, Konrad Beste and H. Kutzleb, have been published by Georg Westermann in Brunswick (founded in 1838), which is the other publishing house of the *Monatshefte*. C. Bertelsmann in Gütersloh has had great success at times with the novels of Schöer. The most significant of these publishers, however, was Eugen Diederichs[33] in Jena (now in Düsseldorf), who started his publishing firm in 1904, in accord with the ideas of Neo-Romanticism. He was a promoter of the new book culture, and was open to all the modern intellectual and national currents; he was a fatherly friend of the youth movement, and a great cultural publisher. He has discovered the *Til Eulenspiegel* of Charles de Coster, has achieved great success with the *Werwolf* of Löns, and has been effective in a wide public with the women's novels of Helene Voight-D., Lulu von Strauss and Torney, and of J. Berens-Totenohl. His mutli-volume series were great publishing undertakings: The *Märchen der Weltliteratur* ("Fairy Tales of World Literature") with thirty-three volumes, the collection, *Thule* (with the "Edda") with twenty-four volumes, the *Monographien zur deutschen Kulturgeschichte* ("Monographs on German Cultural History"), and the *Deutsche Volksbücher* ("German Popular Books").

Related to the belletristic (and frequently united with it in the same firm) is the publishing of works for youth. The main location for it is in South Germany, and in the first place, Stuttgart. The *Union* has for decades possessed good advertising organs for its books for youth in its leading journals, *Der gute Kamerad* ("The Good Comrade") and *Das Kränzchen* ("The Little Club"). The Franckh'sche publishing company, the publisher of the *Kosmos*, fostered the scientific book for youth. K. Thienemann is known for his well-illustrated fairy tales and stories; J.F. Steinkopf emphasized more the historical and regional aspects, and the publishing firm of Loewe and Herold the simpler and less expensive children's book. Balzer in Heilbronn, and Enssling & Laiblin in Reutlingen are representatives with the broader environment. A certain basic Catholic attitude in Freiburg emerged with Herder; in Cologne, it was Bachem, and in Paderborn, Schöningh. Schaffstein in Cologne devoted himself to artistic picture books, and, in addition, created in 1907, the blue *Volksbücher*, which were disseminated in the millions. The art institute of Josef Scholz in Mainz-Wiesbaden (founded 1793) is well known through its picture and coloring books. Rütten and Löning in Frankfurt had a world-wide success with Hoffmann's *Struwelpeter* and the *Kñig Nußknacker*. The Sebaldus publishing firm in Nuremberg maintains the old tradition of the field, while the series of the earlier Nuremberg picture books came to Oldenburg, and was continued by Stalling in valuable illustrated stories for youth. The firm of E. Wunderlich in Worms and Leipzig, with its well-thought-through children's books, pursues pedagogical intentions. Westermann, with its versatile graphics department, is also active in this area.

Mentioned also are E. Keyser in Heildelberg, Hegel & Schade in Bonn, and Bertelsmann in Gütersloh. In Berlin there is a "Children's Book" publisher, and in Augsburg there is the specialist publisher, Franz Schneider, from Leipzig.

Schoolbook publishing had since 1870 experienced a quick increase; today, however, it is endangered in several countries through foundations by the state. In the Eastern Zone, school book publishing is socialized through the collectively owned enterprise, *Volk und Wissen* ("Nation and Knowledge"). The Bavarian school book publishing house in Munich is a state establishment. Otherwise the publishing of popular school books is decentralized by locale, while the publishing of the books for middle schools is less spatially defined. New foundations of school book publishing firms are rare; the old school book publishers are mostly connected with their own printeries. It is logical that some of these publishers deal at the same time with pedagogical, linguistic and scholarly-literary productions.

Beginning in the South, the most well-known school book publishers are the following: in Munich, the firms of Oldenbourg, Kösel and Ehrenwirth; in Bamberg, Buchner; in Stuttgart, E. Klett; in Heidelberg, Quelle & Meyer; in Frankfurt, M. Diesterweg. Düsseldorf is the site of the 150 year-old firm of A. Bagel,[34] and also of the Schwann publishers. Aschendorff in Münster and the middle school publisher, Schrödel (founded 1792), which moved from Halle to Hanover, are old well-known firms. Also to be mentioned here are Schöningh in Paderborn, Westermann in Brunswick, and Velhagen. Leipzig firms, such as Dürr and Klinkhardt, have moved to Bonn and Bad Heilbrunn. A new foundation is the publisher of instructional materials in Offenburg. The old firms of Vandenhoeck & Ruprecht in Göttingen, Winter in Heidelberg, and Weidmann in Berlin attend to certain subject fields of the books for the unviersities. B. G. Teubner is the only classic school book publisher who has remained in Leipzig.

Notable in Heidelberg is a special preference for the fostering of linguistic scholarship. Important instructional books in the modern languages were published by Kerle and Groos. Elwert in Marburg has also occupied itself with modern philology. The classic publisher for philology is Max Niemeyer in Halle and Tübingen. Publications of the Germanists, Paul and Braune, the *Neudrucke deutscher Literaturwerke des 17. und 18. Jahrhunderts* ("Reprints of German Literary Works of the 17th and 18th Centuries") (287 volumes), the *Altdeutsche Textbibliothek* ("Library of Old German Texts"), the *Romanische Bibliothek* ("Romance Library"), and important specialized journals.[35] De Gruyter in Berlin produced Paul's important *Grundriss der Germanischen Philologie* ("Outline of Germanic Philology"). It is also the publishing firm of Kürschner's *Deutscher Gelehrten Kalender* and the *Literaturkalender*.[36] The multi-volume famous Grimm dictionary was published by G. Hirzel in Leipzig. Metzler in Stuttgart produced Pauly-Wissowa's *Realencyklopädie der Klassischen Altertumswissenschaft* ("Encyclopedia of Classical Archeology"); Kolhammer produced several foundational works for classical philology at that very place. In Munich, C.H. Beck has been active in Germanistics as well as in the classical philological areas also. The best known larger histories of scholarship have been published by Beck, by Kröner in Stuttgart, by the Bibliographical Institute in Leipzig, and in the Propyläen-Verlag in Berlin.

As a publisher of foreign language dictionaries, the Langenscheidt'sche publishing firm in Berlin (founded 1856) has acquired a world wide reputation through its special methods. Its correspondence courses and pocket dictionaries have been disseminated in the many thousands.[37]

The publishers of historical literature are essentially more numerous than those of historical scholarship: historical biographies, for example, are sometimes in vogue, and are then popular with all publishers and for their sale they do not require any of the special experience of the specialist publishers; neither do the many locally oriented historical treatments. The publishers Beck, Bruckmann, Callwey, Kösel, and Oldenbourg in Munich, K.F. Koehler, Kohlhammer and the German Publishing Institution in Stuttgart, Kerle in Heidelberg, Diedrichs and the Droste-Verlag in Düsseldorf, Duncker & Humblot, Weidmann and de Gruyter in Berlin — by the nature and the range of their production these all manifest themselves as historical publishers; and so do the four publishers of the *Monumenta Germaniae historica:* Hahn in Hanover, Weidmann in Berlin, Boehlav in Weimar, and Hiersemann in Leipzig-Stuttgart.

With the geographical publishers, one has also to differentiate between those firms which are concerned with general presentations of geography and ethnology, with portrayals of travels and expeditions, and with pictorial works, and those firms that attend to the expressly specialist scholarly literature, and finally, such firms as are occupied first of all with producing maps and area guides.

To the first group belong the publishers such as Brockhaus, with its already earlier mentioned authors; the Zurich-Freiburg Atlantis-Verlag, with its journal of the same name, and its large series of pictorial works, *Orbis terrarum*, belongs here, as does also D. Reimer in Berlin, who published the events of the Altai-Pamir expedition in 1928. The Bibliographical Institute, Velhagen and Westermann, Ravenstein in Frankfurt, Lax in Hildesheim and Flemming in Hamburg are cartographic institutions and publishers of atlases. Here once again, Baedeker has to be mentioned, the travel books of which obtained their world wide reputation not least because of their first-rate maps. De Gruyter in Berlin has been active as a scholarly publisher. The most significant specialist publisher in the geographical field was, and remains, the already earlier mentioned firm of Justus Perthes in Gotha.

The center of the German art publishers is situated in Berlin and Munich. In Berlin, there was Bruno Cassirer, there was the German Art Publishing Firm (Deutscher Kunstverlag) with its large pictorial archives, with which only the Scholarly Art Seminar in Marburg could compare, in Berlin the Propyläen-Verlag produced its grand illustrated history of art in several volumes, Woldermar Klein his *Silberne Reihe* ("Silver Series"), and Wasmuth his large pictorial works for the history of arts and crafts. Equally sophisticated in terms of their illustrations were the monumental works that the publishing firm of Karl W. Hiersemann in Leipzig published for the history of tapestry, of porcelains, of lace, of goldsmith works and of medieval miniature paintings.

In that very place, in Leipzig, E.A. Seemann was developing after 1861 into one of the most important publishers for art scholarship. It published the

Zeitschrift für bildende Kunst ("Journal for Fine Art"), the art histories of Woermann, Springer and Pinder, Burckhardt's *The Culture of the Renaissance*, but above all it did the art encyclopedia (in thirty-eight volumes) of Thieme-Becker.

The art publishers in Munich are represented through firms such as Bruckmann, Callwey and R. Piper. Bruckmann has published large works with plates illustrating archeology and the Italian Renaissance architecture, many monographs in the history of art, alpine pictorial works, and two widely distributed art journals. Callwey, the publisher of the *Kunstwart* ("Art Outlook"), attended to art and architecture. With its "Piperdrucke," ("Piper Printings"), R. Piper produced outstanding facsimiles of the most outstanding paintings. It founded the series of printings of the Marees-Society and advanced modern graphics though works by and about Barlach, Beckmann and Kubin. The Prestel-Verlag, which had moved from Frankfurt to Munich, also devoted itself to the reproduction of graphics.

In Stuttgart, art publishing emphasized architecture and the arts and crafts. The firms of Alexander Koch and Julius Hofmann have exercised decisive in fluence through their publications. The publishing firm of E. Spemann[38] produced art lexica and annually it produced its popular art calendar. The *Reallexikon der deutschen Kunstgeschichte* ("Encyclopedia of German Art History") of Otto Schmitt was published at Metzler's.

For disseminating knowledge of German art, the publishing house of Robert Langewiesche in Königstein has also achieved great merit through the inexpensive series of its *Blaue Bücher* ("Blue Books").

As the final group of these specialist publishers for the human sciences, there must be still mentioned within the space of this book those firms that have primarily devoted themselves to bibliography in its narrow sense, the scholarship on the book itself.

The leading German firm here is the publishing house of Karl W. Hiersemann, which was founded in 1884, in Leipzig, and since 1949, has been in Stuttgart. It is the publisher of the *Gesamtkatalog der Wiegendruck* (GKW) ("Whole Catalog of Incunabula"), of Schramm's *Bilderschmuck der Frühdrucke* ("Pictorial Decoration of the Early Printing Period"), of the multi-volumed Austrian catalog of illuminated manuscripts, of the three-volume *Lexikon des gesamten Buchwesen* ("Lexicon of the Book in its Totality"), of Schottenloher's *Bibliographie zur deutschen Geschichte im Zeitalter der Glaubensspaltung* ("Bibliography of German History in the Age of the Religious Division"). Here appeared the bibliographical "Introductions," numerous bibliographies, reproductions of manuscripts and basic works for the history of the journal and of the newspaper. The young publishing house in Stuttgart has maintained the proven tradition: Nissen's *Botanische Buchillustration* ("Botanical Book Illustration") contains the history and bibliography of all illustrated botanical books, the *Romanführer* ("Guide to Novels") makes more extensive the group of bibliographies of novels, and George Schneider's *Schlüsselliteratur* ("Roman à Clef") is the first monograph about this specialized area of world literature.[39]

The similarly disposed firm of Otto Harrassowitz in Leipzig-Wiesbaden is the publisher of the *Zentralblatt für Bibliothekswesen*. It published the first edition of Milkau's *Handbuch der Bibliothekswissenschaft* ("Handbook of Library Science").[40]

The publishing house of J.C. Hinrich in Leipzig (founded in 1791) historically gets the credit for having published until 1915 the *Wöchentliches Verzeichnis des deutschen Buchhandels* ("Weekly List of the German Book Trade'), which the publishing establishment of the Exchange Association then took over, and which became the basis for the present-day book trade bibliographies of the Exchange Associations in Leipzig and Frankfurt.[41] It is supplemented through the bibliography of the international journals of the publishing firm of Felix Dietrich in Osnabrück. In Stuttgart, the scholarly trade publishing firm of C.E. Poeschel[42] has produced various important works for the history and technology of printing the book trade, among which is the famous book by Stanley Unwin, *Das wahre Gesicht des Verlagsbuchhandels* ("The True Face of the Publishing House").

Theological publishing constitutes one of the largest groups of the specialized publishing establishments. The number of these publishers is almost uncontrollable if one would understand as being among them all of those firms that are mainly concerned with the production of religious literature. Anyway, a number of publishers here also have attained a leading position on account of their age and the range, in connection with which the difference between Catholic and Evangelical firms is already recognizable from the locales of the publishers. They are less frequently situated in the large cities than they are in the central points of religious life.

The largest theological publisher of Germany is the firm of Herder, which was founded in 1801, and since 1808, has been in Freiburg. Here are published most of the liturgical and religious scholarly works, multi-volume series, journals and lexica *(Kirchenlexikon, Lexikon für Theologie und Kirche, Staatslexikon,* i.e. "Church Lexicon," Lexicon for Theology and Church," "State Lexicon"). Even their other projects, such as the *Grosse Herder*, the historical works and the works of literary scholarship (Janssen, Pastor, Kraus), the belletristics and the publications for young people are built upon a Catholic foundation. A network of booksellers scattered into the entire world provides for distribution.[43] A second center of Catholic publishing is situated in the Rhineland-Westphalia: Bachem in Cologne,[44] Schwann in Düsseldorf, the Paulus publishing house in Recklinghausen, Butzon and Bercker in Kevelaer, the Paulinus-Verlag in Trier, in Münster, Aschendorff *(Corpus Catholicorum* 1–22,; *Reformationsgeschichtliche Studien und Texte 1–75),*[45] and Regensberg, Schöningh in Paderborn, the Mathias-Grünewald Verlag in Mainz, and the Lahn-Verlag in Limburg. The third center is Bavaria: The Verlag Kösel in Munich belongs to the most significant Catholic publishers, also in scholarly and philosophical respects; the publisher, *Ars sacra* is a Catholic art publishing establishment, the Regensburg firms of Manz, Habbel and Pustet,[46] and Auer in Donauwörth prefer the liturgical printings, and in the most recent period the Echter-Verlag has developed in Würzburg.

Evangelical publishing has its center in Württemberg. One of the oldest firms is J.C.B. Mohr (Paul Siebeck) in Tübingen, which has an emphatic scholarly character. In Stuttgart there are the Evangelische Verlagswerk ("Evangelical Publishing Works"), the Evangelische Missionsverlag, the Quell-Verlag and W.

Kohlhammer. The Württemberg Bible Institution annually sends many thousands of its Bibles out into all the world. Further examples in South Germany are Salzer in Heilbronn and Kaiser in Munich. Vanderhoeck & Ruprecht[47] in Göttingen, Bertelsmann in Gütersloh and the publishers that have remained in the Eastern zone, such as Böhlau in Weimar (the great editions of Luther)[48] and Hinrichs in Leipzig (theological literature journal), maintain their Evangelical tradition. The Evangelische Verlagsanstalt ("Evangelical Publishing Institution"), Toepelmann and the Furche-Verlag, are situated in Berlin.

The leading philosophical publishing establishment is that of Felix Meiner in Leipzig-Hamburg. It produced the complete editions of Hegel's works, of the mystic, Eckart, and the series, *Philosophische Bibliothek* ("Philosophical Library"). Spengler's *Untergang des Abendlandes* ("Decline of the West") was published by Beck in Munich, as were the publications of Albert Schweizer. The Nietzsche editions from the Kröner Verlag in Stuttgart have been widely disseminated.

The speeches of the Buddha have been published by Piper in Munich, and recently also the works of Karl Jaspers. The Munich publishing firm of Ernst Reinhardt has also concentrated mainly in the religious and philosophical areas (Forel, Kafka, Heiler, Schnitzer, Verweyen). Kösel in Munich and Lambert Schneider in Heidelberg emphasize philosophy in their production. Diederichs in Jena published the works of Maeterlinck, of Kierkegaard and of the German mystics.

The most significant legal specialist publisher currently is the C.H. Becksche publishing house in Munich.[49] Founded in 1763, in Nördlingen, it was originally related more to the human sciences (archeology, literary scholarship, history, pedagogy and philosophy) and it had its greatest success with Spengler's *Untergang des Abendlandes*. But since the takeover of the legal publishing rights from Berlin firms, it has strengthened this area so much that, with its quickly appearing red law editions and commentaries, it today holds almost a monopoly position as the publishing firm for law. Further older publishing houses for legal science are Mohr in Tübingen, Kohlhammer in Stuttgart, Böhlau in Weimar, de Gruyter in Berlin, and Elwert in Marburg.[50] Besides these, the publishing firms of Aschendorff in Münster and Schwann in Düsseldorf are rather active as publishers of the texts of laws.

Incidentally, precisely this area has branched out especially strongly into individual specialized areas, such as economic and social law, state and administrative law, work, trade, tax and criminal law, and it has thus also correspondingly been relatively departmentalized to a great degree. There is a large number of newer and smaller firms that are successfully engaged with these quite specialized disciplines, or even with only the publishing of an individual specialized journal. Thus, for example, such well-known firms as Duncker & Humblot in Berlin, Hanser in Munich, G. Fischer in Jena,[51] the Piscator publishing house in Stuttgart, or Vandenhoeck & Ruprecht in Göttingen, give their attention above all to the economic and the social sciences.

A necessary consequence of the speedy development and specialization of technology in the last eighty years was the complete reconstruction of technical publishing. The emphasis in production here lies almost more with the journals than it does with the books, the number of which is as large as that of the publishers. They were naturally situated in the large cities and in the industrial centers, above all in the Ruhr district. Their significance and their range is hard for lay people to recognize.

In Berlin, the firm of Julius Springer (founded 1842) increasingly concentrated on technology. Part of the over one hundred journals published by Springer are devoted to a variety of technological subjects. The publisher has almost a monopoly in some areas because of great collective works and the most diversified specialized monographs.[52] The most successful book of technical publishing firm of Wilhelm Ernest & Sohn was the well-known pocketbook for engineers, *Die Hütte* ("Iron and Steelworks"). The publishing house of de Gruyter also devoted one of its series, as well as some of the volumes of its *Sammlung Göschen* ("Collection Göchen") to technological problems. The newly founded publishing concern, "Technik," is expressly devoted to specialist works.

Into the Rhineland industrial center of Düsseldorf there recently moved the publishing house of the Association of German Engineers, the specialist journal of which belongs among the most widely disseminated organs. The publishing establishment of Stahleisen, in the very same place, is a newly arisen large undertaking. The firms of Girardet and the mining publishing agency, Glückauf, have settled down in Essen. In Middle Germany, the old publishing firm of Vieweg in Brunswick transformed itself ever more exclusively into a specialized firm for technology. Teubner in Leipzig also opened a technical sector and Wilhelm Knapp in Halle devoted itself to the literature concerning coal and ores, photography and filming techniques. Wittwer in Stuttgart, G. Braun in Karlsruhe, and Oldenbourg and Carl Hanser in Munich are to be mentioned as examples for South Germany.

The artisan specialist publishers are sharply divided according to their specialities. Here there are less the old, well-known, large enterprises (such as perhaps Westermann in Brunswick) than much more the smaller publishing firms quite attuned to their special function. Pflaum in Munich, Herrose & Ziemsen in Wiesbaden, Matthaes in Stuttgart, Pfanneberg in Giessen, the Sebaldus-Verlag in Nuremberg, and Colemann in Lübeck are several of the most active firms today.

The leading agricultural publishing house is also currently still the Firm of Paul Parrey in Berlin,[53] which was founded in 1848. It publishes several specialist journals encompasses all areas (forest economy, horticulture and so forth). Ulmer in Stuttgart has developed as a second comprehensive publisher. There recently arose in Munich the Bavarian Agricultural Publishing House. The firms of Carl in Nuremberg and Schaper in Hanover work in this area.

There is no special publisher for mathematics, but the firms of Teubner and Herzel in Leipzig, Niemeyer in Halle-Tübingen and Aschendorff in Münster, have already devoted their special attention to this sector within the context of their other activity. The firm of R. Oldenbourg in Munich has several specialist journals that encompass the fields of mathematics and applied technology; but it also evidences general works, such as the *Geschichte der Wissenschaften in Deutschland* ("The History of Scholarship in Germany").[54]

Thus there remains, as the last ones, the important group of specialist publishers, the advance of which falls temporarily in the last period—the scientific publisher.

Here there are several firms whose emphasis lies with medicine, and others whose emphasis is in physics and chemistry. Reference should be made here to the important role of the journal as the communicator of the most recent research results.

Until 1945, Leipzig was the main site of medical publishing. here there was already founded in 1780, the publishing house of Joh. Ambros Barth,[55] with its many specialist journals; here since 1886, there was developing the firm of Georg Thieme,[56] the publishing firm of the *Deutsche medizinische Wochenschrift* (today with its main place of business in Stuttgart) ("German Medical Weekly Journal); here S. Hirzel and the Academic Publishing Society (today Geest & Portig) published their large basic research works and textbooks. In nearby Jena, Gustav Fischer produced therapeutic specialist literature. Theodore Steinkopf in Dresden applied itself to pharmacy. Both of the large Berlin houses, Springer and de Gruyter, have significant medical departments. Also the leading Viennese firm of Urban & Schwarzenberg supported a branch business in Berlin.[57] In Stuttgart, besides Thieme and Hirzel, Ferdinand Enke[58] was active for the longest time as a medical publishing house. The Munich medical publishers are Bergmann, Hanser (Dentistry) and the publishing firm of J.F. Lehmann, which has become active again with the revival of the *Münchener medizinische Wochenschrift* ("Munich Medical Weekly").[59]

Most of these medical firms are at the same time significant scientific publishers, and they publish large and basic publications, especially in physics and chemistry, as well as the standard specialist journals. This holds for Springer and de Gruyter in Berlin, for Geest & Portig, Barth, Thieme and Hirzel in Leipzig, for Gustav Fischer in Jena, in Stuttgart for Enke and the new foundations, Thieme, Hirzel and the Piscator-Verlag. Especially emphasized is the scientific production outside medicine itself, with the Naturwiss Verlag ("Scientific Publishing House"), formerly Bornträger[60] in Berlin, with Teubner and Wilhelm Engelmann in Leipzig, Vieweg in Brunswick, and Vandenhoeck & Ruprecht in Göttingen. The Leipzig firm of Quelle & Meyer[61] has established itself in Heidelberg, which has had a worldwide success with its zoological and botanical textbooks by Schmeil. Of the Stuttgart firms of Schweizerbarth[62] and Franckh, the latter (as the publisher of the journal *Kosmos*) has more the tendency of popularizing. The publishing firm of Chemie in Berlin and Weinheim is the most significant specialist publisher in this quite specialized area. In Munich, the publishing firm of Oldenbourg also always fostered this special area.

So approximately does German publishing present itself in the present moment as the result of its development in the last century. The foundation period, in which the personalities and the names of the founders have entered into the history of the book trade, is concluded at the beginning of this period. The old names of the firms have become established concepts that now are less connected with the person of the owner than with the character of the production. The old firms have maintained their definitive character which tradition has shaped for them. Many new firms have arrived on the scene during this time. The most recently arrived still require, in spite of strong initial results, the confirmation that duration brings. The older ones, founded in the years prior to 1900, generally have maintained the way taken at the beginning. Publishing is to that extent a conservative trade. The sudden acceptance of production areas which are contrary to the direction taken up until now has seldom held true. As a whole, there was an immense increase up until 1914, and then there was an interruption due to the First World War, and apparent flowering in the inflationary period, again an increase, then threatening years from 1929 to 1932, and then an enormous production into the Second World War. The year 1945 was the greatest catastrophe that the German book trade has experienced. For the private book publishing of the East, it practically meant the end. Firms with century old traditions have disappeared or migrated from their old ancestral sites; still, their new location, their new production, and their continuation can scarcely be evaluated yet. The German publishing in the West also had initially the difficult period of licensing and production control to overcome, and only since the introduction of free trade in the three occupation zones did there once again arise a free and stimulating publishing life.

Fallen on destruction and into confusion is likewise the once so well-ordered structure of the organization of the German book trade with its headquarters in Leipzig. In addition to the Exchange Association there, today there is a second one in Frankfurt; besides the German Library in Leipzig there is a German Library in Frankfurt, and each of these institutions publishes its own bibliography. The central offices for settlement of accounts and ordering exist no more, and the Commission's book trade and the wholesale bookstores have to struggle. The "Iron Curtain" hinders the exchange of books and the intellectual intercourse of the Germans from this side to the other.

Even in the free territory of the West, serious dangers have arisen for the book due to the enduring increase in production costs and the loss of the East as buyers. Experience, efficiency, tenacity and enterprise will help to overcome these problems.

In periods of threatened sales, the advertisement plays an even more important role. From the side of the publisher it has unquestionably become more modern, original, versatile and amusing. The most important and the broadest foundation for the marketing of all the works that are published has remained the retail book-trade, just as it was before. In spite of all the modern varieties as these have taken shape in the travel, shipping, railway or export book trade, the book trade of the shop even still today is unassailably the standard mediator between the publishing houses and the bookbuyers. The "shop book trade is the art of bringing books among the people," Friedrich Perthes wrote. The best book is useless if it is not sold and read. The book shop is the heart of the book trade. The network of bookstores stretches over the whole of the old Empire, and in no country of Europe is it so strong, so traditionally proven, so versatile and so well organized.

Book production has increased enormously since 1800. At that time about 2,600 books were appearing (in a year). In 1830, there were over 7,000, in 1860, over 9,000, in 1890, over 18,000, and in 1913 even 35,000. In 1920, the number fell to 28,000, in 1925 it grew to 31,500, in 1933 amounted to around 21,500, in 1938, to approximately 25,500, and in the last years of the war, 1943–44, only 15,500 and 11,200. The year 1950 will register 18,000 books and twelve hundred journals, and there is no doubt that, in spite of paper shortages and all the other problems, it is moving increasingly forward. One can well accept it that in these numbers there is expressed a certain over-production and that, in the belletristic area, there are many books that could be dispensed with. The numbers are nevertheless an evidence that the German book trade is beginning again to recover from the effects of the war, that the book plays—as it did previously—a role in economic life, which in spite of all the financial difficulties, and in spite of the film, radio and sports, books are begin bought and read, as before.

36
Book Design in the Modern Period

The book changes imperceptibly almost daily. New ideas enliven it, new ways of production transform it, and new feelings for form give it another face. In the everlasting stream of culture, the book is always on the move. The aforementioned technical advances of the machine age were thus already operating mightily on the forms of the book; they made possible the less expensive mass production, and they also found receptive readers for the book. Added to that were the revolutionary new techniques in the pictorial reproduction, where woodcut and copper-engraving were more and more displaced by the various applications of photochemical processes, through ectypography, autotype, steel engraving,[1] heliography, lithography and phototype. This infinitely extended and rendered less expensive, pictorial reproduction again worked in favor of increased book sales. The book and the illustration arrived at a new successful relationship. That Germany had a significant share in all these transformations is almost to be considered as being self-evident. Standing out clearly visible with these transformations were above all two leading forces: Aloys Senefelder (1771 until 1854), the discoverer of lithography,[2] and Friedrich König (1774–1833),[3] the first builder of the mechanical press driven by steam. Senefelder has set forth his discovery and its results in his own work, the *Vollständiges Lehrbuch der Steindruckerey* ("Complete Textbook of Lithography") (1818). The work has to be classed with the most valuable German books. As a consequence of the discovery, Franz Hafstängl created the large publication of the Dresden Gallery, which is a master work of lithographic art, and Franz Wishaupt in 1928 brought about in Munich the first attempt with the impression of differently colored stones in color plates for the travel work by Spix and Martius on Brazil. Friederich König's mechanical press was put into operation for the first time on November 28, 1814, for the printing of the *Times* in London, and for the first time on the continent on January 25, 1823, for the production of the Haude and Spener newspaper in Berlin. Here, on April 10, King Frederick William examined the new printing machine, and in that connection, he expressed his misgivings concerning what indeed would become of printers if the machine took work away from them.

If the machine age has offered books infinite possibilities for increased production and distribution, it has certainly not conferred any high book culture – much in contrast with the early printing period, which has bestowed on mankind not merely the great discovery of printing, but also an exquisitely beautiful cultivation of books as material objects. Perhaps this has been much easier for the fifteenth

century, because the fashioning power of handwork was still connected with
the great tradition of the manuscriptural period, and printing also had to overcome
the competitive trade in the manuscriptural production of books. This struggle
has given wings to the forces that were at work. Both of them were lacking in
the new advance in book technology. It is not that the twentieth century has given
us no beautiful books.[4] Artists can indeed embellish and decorate a book; but
that still does not create a uniform form of the book—something that has its own
laws.

Associated with the effects of Romanticism is a series of able artists, who have
devoted themselves to books with warm love and have scattered in them delightful
decorations and small illustrations about fairy tales, stories, fables and rhymes.[5]
These books and the illustrated broadsheets are pleasant testimonies to the art of
popular illustration and remaining symbols of German character, created out of
legends and sagas, fairy tales and popular song. In addition to Eugen Neureuther,
whose *Randzeichnungen zu Goethe's Balladen und Romanzen* ("Marginal Illustrations to Goethe's Ballads and Romances") (1829) (which had charmed the prince
of poetry to the highest degree), there is above all Ludwig Richter, the sensitive artist of the German landscape and of the German heritage, who, encouraged by the
publisher, Otto Wiegand, knew how to vivify impressively, besides the popular
books, the fairy tale books of Karl Musäus (1842) and Ludwig Bechstein (1853).
Franz, Count Pocci, cooperated in Friedrich Wilhelm Güll's delightful
Kinderheimat in Bildern und Liedern ("Children's Home in Pictures and Songs")
(1837), created numerous splendid books for children, and published a serious-
minded *Totentanz mit Bildern und Sprüchen* (1862) ("Dance of Death with Pictures
and Texts").[6]

Moritz von Schwind, the born teller of fairy tales, contributed eloquent pictures
to several books of his period, such as to Scherer's *Alte und Neue Kinderlieder* ("Old
and New Songs for Children"). Otto Speckter decorated the *Fünfzig Fabeln für
Kinder* ("Fifty Fables for Children") of Wilhelm Hay (1833); it was issued by the
Verlag Perthes, with outstanding drawings that elevated the little work into one of
the most beautiful German books for children. Speckter's *Gestiefelter Kater* (1843)
has become no less famous. Alfred Rethel (1816–1859) has created in 1848, a
weighty work of popular force in his *Totentanz* ("Dance of Death"); it was cut by
Hugo Bürkner and accompanied by verses of Robert Reinick. "The old ways of the
leveller, Death, have been executed in these eight masterful sheets with new, unique poesie and it has charged the pamphlet style of the sixteenth century with new
life" (von Lützxow). The artist, Theodore Horsemann, who was chiefly active with
the energetic Berlin Verlag Winckelmann, contributed handsome drawings to
Zacharia's *Renommisten* (1845) ("Boastings"), to *Des Freiherrn von Münchhausen
wunderbaren Reisen und Abenteuern* ("Baron von Munchhausen's Wonderful
Travels and Adventures") (1849), and to Immermann's *Tulifäntchen* ("Little
Tulip"). The painter and poet, Robert Reinich (1805–1852), gave to children and
to the nation his *Deutscher Jugendkalender* ("German Youth Calendar")
(1847–1851), as well as the especially successful *Märchen-, Lieder- und
Geschichtenbuch*)"Book of Fairy Tales, Songs and Stories") (16th ed., 1922).

Georg Scherer's *Illustriertes deutsches Kinderbuch* (1849) ("Illustrated German Children's Book"), which was rich with illustrations by Peter von Cornelius, Wilhelm von Kaulbach, August von Kreling, Oscar Pietsch, Franz Pocci, Ludwig Richter, Moritz Schwind, and Paul Thumann, found a large circulation.

In 1880, Max Klinger created an outstandingly beautiful book-edition in his fairy tale poem, *Amor und Psyche*, by Apuleius. Dedicated to the musician, Johann Brahms, it had numerous fine etchings and decorations, and was published by Max Stroeter in Munich.

With his exciting picture books, *Schlafende Bäume* ("Sleeping Trees"), *Wiesenzwerge* (1902) ("Meadow Dwarfs") (in which the secret life between flowers and the grass is masterfully represented), *Gartentraum* (1912) ("Garden Dream"), *Bei Gnomen und Elfen* ("With Gnomes and Elves") (1928), and *Grashupfer* (1931) ("Grasshopper"), the artist, Ernst Konrad Theophil Kreidolf, has gained many friends for himself among both young and old. He has also successfully supplied the illustrations for foreign works.

Taking first place by a wide margin among the illustrated books of the nineteenth century is the *Geschichte Friedrichs des Gorssen* ("History of Frederick the Great") of Franz Kugler (1840), which was decorated with four hundred pictures by Adolf Menzel (1815–1905). It is a work that has become a pure German folkbook.[7] The same artist has also supplied the pictures for the princely editions of the works of Frederick the Great, which were published in thirty volumes on commission from King Friederich Wilhelm IV in the year 1846–1857, as well as Franz Dingelstedt's edition of the Heinrich von Kleist comedy, *Der zerbrochene Krug* ("The Broken Jug"). In 1851, he published a booklet, *Versuche auf Stein mit Pinsel und Schabeisen* ("Attempts in Stone with Pencil and Scrapers"), which produced outstanding lithographs.

The renewal of the artistic woodcut and of the woodcut book (for which, above all, the cutters, Johann Georg Unger and Friedrich Wilhelm Gubitz are to be thanked) had an essential share in the successful increase of the decorated books; the renewal has brought about a second flourishing period for the German woodcut. Gubitz has himself designed (and has chiefly become famous for) his *Deutscher Volkskalender* (1835). The German woodcut has demonstrated its greatest efficacy in the *Fliegende Blätter* ("Broadsheet"), the *Münchener Bilderbogen* ("Munich Picture Sheet"), and the *Leipziger Illustrierte Zeitung*, in which the illustrations were by Busch, Meggendorfer, and Oberländer. Here it has become a pure folk art.

So far as foreign countries are concerned, it was primarily the French book art that was influential in Germany.[8] Here it was Eugène Delacroix (1798–1883) who had the greatest influence; he was able to illustrate Goethe's *Faust* so impressively that the poet let it be known concerning the illustrations that his own imagination had been excelled by the artist; and there was further, Gustave Doré from Strasbourg (1832–1883), who drew illustrations to Rabelais, Balzac, Cervantes, Dante, Chateaubriand, and Ariosto. Through editions of the Bible, his grand designs for Biblical literature have gone throughout the entire world.[9] Of the English book artists, it was especially John Flaxman (1755–1826), with his fine line drawings to the Iliad and the Odyssey (1803), to Dante (1802), and to Hesiod (1817), who found numerous German admirers.

Even though, since the time when the publishing houses advanced, the independent significance of the printeries for book promotion has more and more retreated, individual printeries did obtain for themselves so surpassing a place that they may not be overlooked as successful sites for fostering the book. Thus the Vienna printer, Joseph Vinzenz Degen (1761–1827), produced select luxury editions, such as those of Ovid (1803) and Uz (1804). When in 1814 the Royal Court and State Printer was established in Vienna, Degen became its director.[10] The printing establishment of Rudolf Ludwig Decker took a similar development in Berlin (1804–1877). He had printed the already mentioned princely editions of the works of Frederick the Great and, for the London Industry Exhibition of 1851, Luther's New Testament with illustrations by Peter Cornelius and Wilhelm von Kaulbach: he was elevated to the nobility in 1863. Following his death on January 12, 1877, the printery went over into the possession of the Empire and from April 1, 1879, was continued as the imperial printer, with the aim of doing exemplary printing work.[11]

The uniform shaping of the design of the book took a visible upswing in the decades following 1874, when several printeries, such as those of Max Huttler and Georg Hirth in Munich, Heinrich Wallau in Mainz, W. Drugulin in Leipzig, and Otto von Holten in Berlin, followed the example of the Gothic and Renaissance book in producing handsome printing layouts; and in this they were successfully supported by artists such as Otto Hupp, Rudolf Seitz, Peter Halm and Ernst Doepler. Otto Hupp has especially become well known through his *Münchener Kalender* ("Munich Calendar"), which was issued after 1885 with the splendid illustrations of heraldic arms.[12] The Central Association for the Book Trade, which was later called the German Book Trade Association, and which was founded in 1884 by Oscar von Hase, has also gradually worked in the interest of better book design.

A genuinely new enlivening, however, of the highly valued art of the book came only from England. There William Morris, with the most extreme care in the selection of the paper, of typecuts, of printing color, and by the artistic fashioning of the entire preparation for printing, and supported by Walter Crane (the printer and illustrator), created a pure art of the book which depended on the uniform shaping of the entire book. His chief work, issued in 1896, was adorned with beautiful borders and with eighty-seven pictures by the artist Edward Burne-Jones, and it contained writings of the poet Geoffrey Chaucer; it has rightly become famous as one of the most beautiful books of modern times. The printed works of the Kelmscott Press (so did Morris call the workshop after his favorite residence of Kelmscott) had significant influence on book design in the entire world, and in all circles it set the stage for greater care in the production of books.[13]

As the beginning in Germany of an increased concern for books one can designate the art journal, "Pan," which was directed by Otto Julius Bierbaum[14] from 1895 to 1900, printed by Drugulin, and decorated by significant artists such as Klinger, Greiner, Thoma,[15] Sattler and Fidus (Höppener), in addition to the

Munich journal, *Jugend* ("Youth") (since 1896), and *Insel*,[16] which was founded in 1899, by Heymel, Schröder and Bierbaum. Soon there was an impressive series of artists for decorating books. Joseph Sattler, the successful designer of two large sets of pictures, *Die Wiedertäufer* ("The Anabaptsits") and *Totentanz* ("Dance of Death"), contributed such an effective decoration to the *Geschichte der rheinischen Städtekultur* ("History of the Rhineland Cities' Culture"), by Heinrich Boos (1897–1901), that the work has become one of the best German book creations decorated with pictures. Sattler contributed with similar success to the artistic design of the *Nibelung* editions, which were produced by the imperial printer for the world exhibition in Paris in 1900, with six hundred extremely fine initials. Appearing for the same exhibition (it was published by the German Book Trade Association at Leipzig), was the *Katalog der Deutschen Buchgewerbe-Austellung* ("Catalog of the Book Trade Exhibition") in a worthy design that Johann Vinzenz Cissarz[17] had artistically directed. Belonging also to the most beautiful books are two of Melchior Lechter's excitingly designed works: Maurice Maeterlinck's *Schatz der Armen* ("Treasure of the Poor") (1898) and Stefan George's *Teppich des Lebens* (1899) ("Tapestry of Life"). Johann Vincenz Cissarz, Heinrich Vogeler, Peter Behrens, Marcus Michael Douglas Behmer and other artists have likewise been in the service of outfitting the book.

No less effective were the various attempts, setting book ornamentation aside, to bring about a distinguished typography solely through the artistic design of the types. Here above all the Paris World Exhibition has proven to be an effective challenge. Attention was enthusiastically given to the art of shaping type, just as there had been in the period of early printing. Significant type designers such as Rudolf von Larisch, Georg Schiller, Otto Hupp, Heinz König, Otto Eckmann, Anna Simmons, Otto Reichert, Peter Behrens, Fritz Helmut Ehmcke, Rudolf Koch,[18] Walter Tiemann, Emil Rudolf Weiss, Ernst Schneider, Friedrich Wilhelm Klenkens, Herbert Post,[19] Paul Renner, Ernst Engel, and others, created a plethora of excellent types.[20]

The German type foundries cooperated in this matter in an exemplary way.[21] Interested printing workshops such as Otto von Holten, W. Drugulin, Poeschel[22] and Trepte likewise began to look for uniformity of script in the compact composition and for a calm elegance in the total arrangement of type. Carl Ernst Poeschel and Walter Tiemann joined together in purposefully artistic printing work in the Janus Press, and produced typographically outstanding works, such as Goethe's *Römische Elegien* (1907) and Goethe's *Tasso* (1910). With the same aims, Friedrich Wilhelm Kleukens founded the Ernst Ludwig Press in Darmstadt on commission from the Grand Duke of Baden. Other manual printeries worked in the same direction and produced an impressive number of handsomely printed books.[23]

The plethora of beautiful books would seemingly not come to an end. Included among them might also be the luxury printings, projects that were more graphic art works than they were books decorated with pictures; on account of their costliness, only a small circle of buyers came here into consideration; Max Slevogt, Lovis Corinth, Karl Walser, Hans Meid, Walo von May, and Emil Preetorius furnished the lithographs or the etchings for them; from the very first, they were not concerned to be in accord with the techniques of printed works and were designed quite independently.

The most important factor for an enduring forward movement of book design was that the enterprising publishers—above all, Eugen Diederichs and Anton Kippenberg (the director of the Insel Verlag)—wanted to produce not only individual beautiful books, but in counsel with a circle of sympathetic artists, such as Cissarz, Fidus, Vogeler, Behrens, Weiss, and Ehmcke, attempted in matters relating to type and illustration, to permeate artistically their entire publishing work, and thus by success and example they effectively guided the uniform book design into new heights.

It ought to be noted that the provision of the Insel Verlag for its books extended to the inexpensive cardboard covers which it had decorated with brightly colored papers. Through such assiduous care for its artistic fashioning, the book of the modern period, whether it be simply attired or made up in a festive manner, has maintained a distinctive design throughout. Even into the most recent period numerous artists have contributed to book design,[24] and the book trade has striven for choice handicraft work.

The bound book has yet found a further supplement in the decorative and promotional book jacket. In and of itself, the jacket is there only to protect the book externally, and thus it is also called a protective cover. What an idea it was when this cover was realized as an advance sheet and one gave it a pleasing and enticing look! Whoever now looked into the book dealer's show window, or let the bright display of books in a bookshop affect him, was surprised by the rich fullness of the most varied kinds of design for the book jacket, which had earlier been so sober. Sometimes it was an effective front with the title of the book, sometimes an illustration from the contents, sometimes a small graphic art work in bright colors; always it was something that led one toward the book, that wanted to awaken the onlooker's participation. Assisted by the possibility of the most varied sorts of production, the protective cover has become an effective means of advertising and a part of the art of the book.[25] To be seen in the decorative cover is an entirely effective advertisement for the book, and to be recognized at the same time is its higher value as a means for disseminating the book. This success in the advertising also means cooperation in the fulfillment of the book's purpose.

Karl Woerman[26] once says concerning art: "It lies grounded in the organic laws of the development of art history, that a situation of pure balance in the artisitc creation of the people tends to hold no longer than a generation. It remains left to a new generation to seek out new goals, or to stay with a now rigid tradition." Without further ado we may also apply this law to book design, and hope that it will again find new and rejuvenating strengths.

37
Libraries Since the Early 1800s

One may perhaps call the nineteenth, and the beginning of the twentieth, century the most fortunate age in library history.[1] If within the boundaries of the nineteenth century, there had been assembled in numerous preferred centers an unprecedented plethora of books, developing from public administration and growth of these treasures were aims and functions that had to organize the entire life of this book world from the ground up. With the confiscation of the monastery libraries, the state had assumed the enormous responsibility of deliberately increasing the intellectual wealth (which was now defined as community property), and of making it accessible to scholarship. A whole host of forces was necessary for examining, arranging and increasing the abundance of books which had been accumulated. A new spirit was introduced everywhere – even where no such access was forthcoming. Although the state economized more than was necessary, the most needed expenditures soared to new levels by leaps and bounds.

For the Berlin Library, the monetary resources grew in the year 1827, from 4,000 thalers to 8,626, of which 4,050 thalers were for acquisitions. In 1845, ten thousand thalers stood at their disposal for acquiring books; at Vienna, the figure was 19,000 florins, in Munich 17,300 florins, and in Göttingen, 5,000 thalers. Indeed these were still entirely insufficient amounts, but taken together the sums dispensed in the whole of Germany amounted to a far higher figure than that which the courts, churches and monasteries had previously allotted, and the newly acquired book treasures, being now more comprehensive and more accessible to the entire nation, were far more beneficial, and especially so to scholarship. And no less significant for the effect of the world of books was the growing number of librarians who were dedicated to it. With the increased functions, there were concerns sufficient so that soon there was a need for a public advisory office for all questions relating to book maintenance. In January 1840, as preparations were going on for the fourth centenary celebration of the invention of printing, the Leipzig municipal librarian, Robert Naumann, inaugurated *Serapeum. Zeitschrift für Bibliothekswissenschaft, Handschriftenkunde und ältere Literatur* ("Journal for Library Science Inquiry into Manuscripts and the Older Literature").

Articles were supposed to be published there about the manuscripts and printed works of the libraries and concerning the history of individual institutions, or about specialties in the book world. In 1841, the librarian, Julius Petzholdt, founded the *Anzeiger für Literatur der Bibliothekswissenschaft* ("Reporter for the

Literature of Library Science"); it was supposed to make known the current publications on bibliology and librarianship. Issuing from the literary reports of the *Anzeiger* in 1866 has been Petzholdt's *Bibliotheca bibliographica*, a quite valuable total survey of the bibliography of that period. With the fragmentation of their strength, the two journals then, however, came to an end: the *Serapeum* ceased publication in 1870, and the *Anzeiger* in 1884. It was in this year, under more fortunate conditions, that the *Zentralblatt für Bibliothekswesen* (which was founded by Otto Hartwig[2] and then edited for a long time by Paul Schwenke) took its beginning; here, in its continuing reports and researches, bibliography and librarianship in their totality found a valuable center.

All the fruitful buds of fresh life in the library came to the strongest development when, in 1871, the German people came together in a political and economic unity.[3] Libraries are rooted, as are all public institutions, in the entire nation, and they participate in the total life of the period, in the political ascendancy, as well as in the people's welfare, or in the development of education and science. The idea became even more strongly established that the fostering of scholarship and the means of assisting it are among the concerns of the state, which issued in a development the full significance of which we can scarcely anymore measure. The enormous advances in scholarship, with the innumerable sources, editions, individual publications, journals, series of continuations—these all went hand in hand with the richest development of the book trade, which obtained its strongest and securest backing in the publicly accessible libraries. Whoever is only slightly familiar with the history of scholarship knows that here indeed rests that which is essential for the results of research activity, but that also among the important preconditions for all prosperous development are the external conditions of life. The invention of printing, the development of the book trade, technical progress in the book industry, the working up of the market, the possibilities for richer book uses in larger or smaller libraries—these are the factors that play the greatest role of all in the life of scholarship. The acquisition, preservation and making accessible of cultural treasures were seen more and more as being sufficiently important and responsible for increasing recognition to be accorded these functions in public life. If the book collections in an older time were primarily collections for the preservation of book treasures, so now there are likewise scholarly places for research and education, in which the books, in constant circulation, serve to stimulate and to assist.

One has only to walk through one of the spacious reading rooms of a large library and survey the works placed there from all the disciplines or fetched there from the stacks—the great reference books, the lexica, encyclopedias, sourceworks, and journals, the almost unsurveyable bibliographical aids, the multi-volumed printed catalogs of London, Paris or the German *Gesamtkatalog* ("Whole Catalog"), and consider what daily and hourly emanates from this mass of books to the challenge of education, of knowledge and research. Or one should step into one of the reading rooms for research into manuscripts—say in Berlin, Munich, Vienna, Paris or Rome—and observe the handbooks provided there, with their valuable reproductions of manuscripts from all over the world, with their numerous specimens of scripts and illustrations from the past, with the catalogs of manuscripts from the entire globe, with the infinite series of texts of all sorts; the power of this world of books, which encompasses many centuries and has been prepared for scholarship, is simply overwhelming. If one then would add, finally, the hundreds and thousands of books that can assist and be of use to scholars, the students and to all those thirsty for knowledge who are in the rooms of libraries, or who by day and night are in quiet hours at home, one would then be able to some extent to measure the enormous effective powers of this immense cultural equipment of humankind. This side of the growing effectiveness of the book world in the libraries is also part of the cultural history of the book.

In addition to the effects of the individual collections of books was the successful amalgamation of all the German scholarly libraries in the exchange of manuscripts and printed works along the routes of the German interlibrary loan, in the inquiries of the Information Bureau of the German Libraries for books that were sought after,[4] and finally in the common publications, such as especially the *Gesamtkatalog der Wiegendrucke* (GKD) ("Whole Catalog of Incunabula") and in the large German *Gesamtkatalog* ("Whole German Catalog"). If now, following the war, these valuable arrangements have partially been broken off, it is to hoped that they can somehow be again revitalized in the forseeable future.

Among the German book collections of modern times, it was above all the Prussian State Library in Berlin (now: Public Research Library) that through a remarkable rise came into such prominence. At the beginning of the nineteenth century, it was warmly promoted by Wilhelm von Humboldt, and it was placed on a broader foundation in 1810 through the establishment of the University in Berlin, and the collection was able to increase its holdings in manuscripts and printed works considerably, such as, since 1850, by the purchase of the collections of Diez,[5] of Nagler,[6] and Meusebach. Gradually it won a leading place in the German book world. That in Germany it did not (as in France, England, or America) become a towering national library, lay (as already mentioned) in the development and the organization of the German Empire. The fostering of art and science remained left, as before, to the individual territories. Prussia, however, the largest of the federal states, by a generous cultural policy, also frequently undertook duties that belonged to the entire Empire.

Controlled by Heinrich von Treitschke and Friedrich Althoff, the library at Berlin on November 16, 1855, received the commission to collect in the future the German literature in as much completeness as possible, and the foreign literature in a suitable selection, and to assume therewith (with certain limits) the function of a German Reich Library – something which had been tried several times, but had not been attained. This high goal, and ever richer financial means, lent to the institution rejuvenated strengths that in their development have redowned to the good of the whole of the native German librarianship. Evidences for that are three catalogs, published since 1886, of the university publications, the printed titles for the printed works acquired annually in Berlin and Prussia, the *GKW* ("Whole Catalog of Incunabula"), the production of a union catalog of German libraries,[7] the creation of an information department of the German book collections, and the new home in Berlin, which is among the greatest library buildings in the world.[8]

He, however, who would discern the full consequences for the book that issued from the German book collections must proceed from the totality of the numerous libraries. The high standing of German librarianship rests especially on the unsurpassed wealth of books which are scattered throughout the entire country.[9] One needs only to think of the forty large German state and municipal libraries – besides the Berlin one – the Munich State Library, the Vienna National Library, the Dresden Territorial Library, and the Stuttgart Territorial Library, or the twenty-three university libraries, in order to be able to form an approximate notion of the almost unsurveyable wealth of books and book circulation for the whole of the intellectual centers of Germany. A few numbers may focus this image still more clearly. As a whole, Germany shows approximately a thousand scholarly libraries with about one hundred million volumes. In 1942, the State Library in Berlin owned: 3,030,418 volumes and 71,602 manuscripts; Munich had 2,173,147 volumes and 48,645 manuscripts; Vienna owned 1,406,000 volumes and 34,646 manuscripts.

The huge book production in modern times has necessarily led (if the libraries should carry out their functions) to weighty increases in monies for acquisitions. Prior to 1870, for the purchasing of German publications (with about 11,305 items), about 37,000 Marks were needed; in 1880, about 65,000 Marks were needed for 14,941 items, in 1890, for 18,875 items 87,000 Marks, and in 1900, 105,000 Marks for 24,792 items. Worth noting with this increase is the fact that one and the same work (whether an independent book or a journal) increased considerably in size and price in the later editions, or in its continuation. Thus Georg Voigt's *Wiederbelebung des klassischen Altertums* ("The Revival of Classical Antiquity") cost only 6.75 Marks in 1859; in the 3rd edition in 1893, it cost 20 Marks; the *Zeitung für wissenschaftliche Theologie* ("Journal for Scholarly Theology") cost only 31 Marks in 1870, but in the year 1910, it was already costing 143 Marks.[10] Book purchases in 1940 totaled 203,143 Marks at the Berlin State Library; at the Munich State Library the figure was 135,979 marks, and at the Vienna National Library it was 128,703 Marks. In the same year the Berlin Library supplied its visitors with 266,226 volumes; in Munich this figure was 89,892, and in Vienna 20,417 volumes were supplied to visitors.

Almost every one of the numerous German libraries has a specialized function to fulfill in the preservation and the preparation work of the book world. The territorial libraries primarily care for the assembling of the domestic literature of the various territories and groups. Where there is no effective territorial library, the university libraries assume these responsibilities. Thus Königsberg collects[11] East Prussian literature, Breslau the Silesian, Göttingen that of Lower Saxony, and Greifswald that of lower Germany. There are also special places for collecting foreign literature; thus Göttingen provides for Anglo-Saxon literature, Bonn for Dutch, Breslau and Posen for Slavic, and Freiburg im Breisgau for Swiss and Spanish literatures.

A few German libraries can invite additional special appreciation. When in 1870, the German armies laid siege to the city of Strasbourg, the choir of the new Dominican church (in which the unviersity and city library had been accommodated) was hit by one of the first projectiles on the evening of August 24. The whole building was soon engulfed in flames, and the next morning one saw only the outer walls and the charred remains of the masses of books – among which there were valuable manuscripts. One of the most aggravating losses was the destruction of the *Hortus deliciarum* (which was rich in illustrations) of the learned Abbess of St. Odilien, Herrad von Landsberg, who had compiled in her collective book all that was worth knowing in her time (the twelfth century) for instruction in the monastery. Since several copies were happily extant as well as the tracings of Count Bastard, the Society for the Preservation of Historical Monuments in Alsace was still able in 1902 to publish 263 facsimiles of the 336 miniature paintings. In November 1871, at the instigation of Karl August Barack, there was formed an association for the reestablishment of the library, and on May 1, 1872, when the German University of Strabourg was opened, the new collection (devoted to the school of higher learning, as well as to the whole of the territory of Alsace) was already counting 200,000 volumes. It stood in third position among the German libraries before the First World War. Since the World War, it again shares in the changeful destiny of the Alsatian border country.

A second great library with a similar fate originated on the eastern border: the Kaiser Wilhelm Library at Posen.[12] In its main contents a scholarly collection, the new institution was at the same time supposed to serve the general education of the city and its surrounding area and thereby introduce into Germany for the first time the special form of educational library for all classes of people – the kind that had spread so vigorously in Britain and America. A special peculiarity of the new foundation lay in the affiliation with it of a mobile library, which was supposed to carry to the scattered district libraries of the province fresh reading matter throughout the whole year. Like the Strasbourg Library, the flourishing Posen institution has also been lost in the collapse of the German Empire.

A third significant collection of books was initiated on September 25, 1912, by the Association of German Bookdealers in the book city of Leipzig. Under the name of Deutsche Bücherei ("German Library"), it was intended to collect and preserve the entire German literature published in Germany and in foreign countries from January 1, 1913, forward.[13] The cornerstone was laid on July 21, 1914, and on May 27, 1916, the German Library could already begin its move into the enormous building, which was capable of holding ten million volumes. On September 2, on Sedan Day (the day marking the decisive defeat of the French at Sedan in 1870), the dedicatory celebration took place in the presence of the King of Saxony. Its specialized functions consist, on the one hand, in the collecting of German literature, by which the German book trade, according to a voluntary obligation, places at its disposal on a cost-free basis the whole of the literature being published; and on the other hand, in the issuance of the *Deutsche Nationalbibliographie*, as well as the *Literarisches Zentralblatt*. A vital activity (which up to then was unusual in the German library situation) in making the German world of books accessible through title entries is therefore the further specialty of this new, consciously and successfully unusual German sister institution.

Among the non–German libraries of the nineteenth century, the library of the

British Museum in London above all took an unprecedented upswing which speedily placed it in the first rank of the great collections of books in the world, and insured for it an enormous influence on the nature of collecting in the other nations.
This unique development is the more remarkable, as the library constituted only
a part of the enormous British Museum, which, together with the remaining departments in natural monuments of antiquity, represented the most comprehensive collection in the world. The library first obtained a valuable enrichment in 1823, when
the collection of King George III (numbering over 65,250 volumes) fell to it; this
collection had been assembled primarily from the dissolved continental Jesuit
libraries, and it contained valuable atlases. A second priceless accession consisted
of the numerous parchment printings, Shakespeare editions and Italian and
Spanish romances that Sir Thomas Grenville (1755–1846) had assembled. The
most important event for the aspiring collection was that it obtained a leader in 1837
in the person of the Italian political refugee, Antonio Panizzi (1797–1879), who was
later a close friend of the French professional author, Prosper Mérimée, and who
prescribed for the library large goals for the future: the collecting of literature in
English, together with the most important literature of the world and the best possible use of its book holdings. The famous memorial of the year 1845, the *Ninety-One
Rules*, the Magna Charta of librarianship, has become the foundation of the British
Museum's quick ascent into the ranks of a world library.[14] The grateful British
Museum had decorated the entrance to the reading room (containing space for
three hundred visitors) with the bust of its bibliothecarial master; it was executed
by Marocchetti.

Antonio Panizzi in London and Léopold Delisle in Paris are brilliant examples
of how much great goals and strong will power may be able to do in responsible
positions. That was "the new" in this collection, which was becoming ever more
richly equipped – namely, that the British people saw in it a proud national monument and, as such, they bestowed on it all their love and sacrifice. Whoever gives
something here, (that was the general idea) gives it to the entire nation. The journal
Serapeum could already boast in 1843 that the British Museum was providing, as
was no other institution, for the accessibility of its treasures, so that the collection
was surpassing all the libraries of the world in its exemplary order, the purposeful
making of its books accessible, and the broad-minded administration, when Panizzi
carried through a new building with the famous reading room (1857).[15] Visible
testimonies of the progressive spirit are also the numerous publications from the
treasures of the collection, the valuable listings of the manuscripts, the highly significant catalog of its own holdings of incunabula,[16] the subject catalog to the new acquisitions of the library (it is one of the most comprehensive catalogs of books in
the world),[17] but quite especially, in the catalog of the entire holdings of printed
works, which has been issued since 1882, and which finally numbered 115
volumes; it was published in a second edition in 1932.[18] Paleography and
manuscript research have nowhere been so effectively fostered as they have in the
rich London manuscript collection.[19] The total holdings of the British Museum today number about 4.5 million books, 55,000 manuscripts and 84,000 documents.

Also reckoned as being among the most significant foundations of the modern period is the John Rylands Library at Manchester in the North of England, which is pleased to be called "the British Museum of the North." Enriqueta Augustina Rylands, the widow of the great English industrialist, John Rylands (d. 1888), has, as a memorial to her husband, transferred to the public her handsome properties in manuscripts and books on October 6, 1899. Famous collections, such as the priceless items of Lord George John Spencer *(Bibliotheca Althorpiana)*, that once was administered by the librarian, Thomas Frognall Dibdin, with its valuable editions of the classical authors; the Mainz Gutenberg Bible, the *Psalterium* of 1457, rare English incunabula by William Caxton and Wynkyn de Worde, 108 works printed on parchment, to which were added significant portions of the *Bibliotheca Lindesiana* of Alexander William, Earl of Crawford, with thirty luxury volumes and two thousand Oriental manuscripts—these were among the holdings, and in 1906, the magnanimous donor still gave it the rich Dante collection of the Florentine scholar, Passerini, with around five thousand volumes.[20] Exhibitions, lectures and publications provided for the priceless treasures being as useful as possible.

The Vaticana in Rome, which time and again accepted large individual collections, essentially pursues the aim of serving the acquisition of, and inquiry into, manuscripts, and in connection therewith, of maintaining a large and up-to-date scholarly reference library after the example of the Paris National Library. For the enlargement of the holdings, it has acquired in the more recent period the Borghese Library with about seven hundred manuscripts, the Barberini collection (1902) with about ten thousand (among them being 593 Greek and 164 Oriental manuscripts), to which were added four thousand works (among them being books from the property of Torquato Tasso and the Gutenberg Bible on parchment), the *Bibliotheca Chigi* (1923) from the properties of the Chigi family with its three thousand manuscripts and thirty thousand printed volumes, and finally,the *Bibliotheca Rossiana* (1923), which was founded by Gian Francesco de Rossi, with 1,195 manuscripts, 2,247 incunabula, and around nine thousand printed works.

When a university on the German model was founded in Athens in 1837, and a library was connected with it, Austria and Germany contributed rich presents of books. The emperor of Austria had the collective duplicates of the Vienna Court Library sent over to Athens. The German publishers likewise turned up with valuable books.

In the Eastern world, one of the largest modern libraries has developed at Leningrad. Constituting the basic stock thereof is the rich collection of the Duke and Great Assessor of the Crown of Poland, Joseph Andreas Zaluski (1702 until 1774), who has gifted his entire book properties with 230,000 volumes and 11,000 manuscripts to the Polish nation as a public property in 1748. The collection of the Jesuits has been transferred to it in 1761, when it had been declared state property following the dissolution of the Order. Transferred at the command of Empress Katherina in 1795 to Petersburg, it was quickly increased with other collections— among which were many Oriental manuscripts. Further, the Russian embassy attache, Dubrowksy, brought valuable collections along with him from Paris, among which were priceless items from the library of St. Germain, such as the famous

Tetra-Evangelium Anglosaxonicum; it was acquired in 1805. The forward movement of the Petersburg library suffered an involuntary interruption through the political events of 1812 when Napoleon appeared in Russia. One hundred fifty thousand volumes were brought to safety on the waterways to the north and only at the end of 1812, were they again returned by ship. The library was transferred to the public on January 2, 1814. It is unique in its rich possession of Old Slavic and Oriental manuscripts, and with its almost five million volumes and over 300,000 manuscripts, it is reckoned as being among the largest libraries of the world.[21] Here Victor Hehn has also discharged his office as librarian for a long time and has had the opportunity, not only to come to know the rich treasures of the collection, but also the mysterious world of the East.

Leading all the libraries of the United States of America is the Library of Congress in Washington, which has experienced its enormous upsurge in the nineteenth century and which, with its five million volumes, its enormous building, and its exemplary administrative arrangements, is now among the most significant collections of books on earth. So, even in the new world, the book has created a temple scarcely surpassed in size and splendor, a national library in the grand style; it is one of the main things worth seeing in Washington. Very closely connected with the Library is the Smithsonian Institute (which was founded by the Englishman, James Smithson, for the dissemination of knowledge); it is a quite important place for research, richly equipped as it is with appropriate research tools; free of charge, it simultaneously arranges for the exchange of its own, and of foreign, publications, as well as the officially printed government documents and Congressional reports of the United States with all the outstanding libraries and scholarly offices of the world.[22]

All civilized countries now have their large national library, in which the whole of their literature (to which is added at least a portion of the foregin literature) is acquired and preserved.[23] Thus Egypt possesses the library in Cairo, Argentina the National Library in Buenos Aires, Belgium the Royal Library in Brussels, Brazil the National Library in Rio de Janeiro, Bulgaria the National Library in Sofia, Chile the National Library in Santiago, China the National Library in Peking, Denmark the Royal Library in Copenhagen, France the Bibliothèque Nationale in Paris, Greece the National Library in Athens, Great Britain the Library of the British Museum in London, Holland the Royal Library in 's Gravenhage,[24] Japan the Imperial Library in Tokyo, Italy the National Libraries in Rome and Florence, Mexico the National Library in Mexico City, Norway the Royal University Library in Oslo, the Soviet Union the Public Library in Leningrad (to which is added the Lenin Library in Moscow), Sweden the Royal Library in Stockholm, Switzerland the Territorial Library in Bern, Spain the National Library in Madrid, and the United States of America, the aforementioned Library of Congress in Washington. The book has thus been recognized in all countries has a highly valued national and cultural property and it everywhere enjoys public protection.

If the general scholarly book collections bascially attempt to give an accurate picture of the total literature, the increasing fragmentation of the public and scholarly life has also pressed toward libraries which provide for only certain knowledge areas and thus seek here to attain a certain completeness. Especially do the essential resources have to be available for state officials and other authorities in the execution of their daily assignments. So have the large governmental libraries arisen, such as those owned by the German *Reichstag*, the German Reich Court, the Reich Patent Office, the Reich Justice Ministry, the Ministry of Health, the General Staff, and the Foreign Ministry. Most of these specialized libraries have issued printed lists of their holdings and so have created valuable resources for bibliography that go far beyond the purpose of the catalog.

Nor has this changeover to specialized libraries ceased with the fulfilling of governmental assignments. As knowledge more and more was divided into completely separated individual areas with an unsurveyable plethora of publications, so inquiries began to demand independent specialized libraries for the specialized scholarly literature. The book collections of the specialized schools, of the technical schools of higher learning,[25] and of the large museums, were shaping themselves more and more into comprehensive special libraries with significant results for the book. Still to be mentioned here are the book collections of the German Academy of Scientific Research in Halle, the German Museum in Munich, and the Senckenberg Library for National Science in Frankfurt am Main.

As technology and the natural sciences have in many relationships worked together for the transformation of the nature of research and instruction, also to be attributed to them primarily is the triumphal progress of the scholarly seminars and institutes in the German schools of higher learning, which were built on the basis of common research areas and practices. Occurring there is not only a vital exchange of both knowledge and research between teacher and student, but also a close connection of the scholarly recruits with the literature of the individual specialized areas. The seminar, or the institute, library has the task of making the young disciple of scholarship familiar with the specialized books of the field in which he is working, and of producing a connection with the books of the more comprehensive university library.[26] While earlier the lectures, with submission to oral instruction, have signified the "one and only" of the instructional program in the school of higher learning, now exercise and the book have been added as forces which have equal entitlement. The seminar library thus represents a very significant victory for the book within the instructional operations of the school of higher learning. How practical this arrangement has proven itself to be can be seen in the fact that it has found heedful cultivation even in America and it has acquired numerous individual libraries of Europe. Entire scholars' libraries — such as the ones of Franz Bopp (1868), Robert von Mohl (1875), Leopold von Ranke (1886), Wilhem Scherer (1886), Friederich Zarncke (1891), Matthias Lezer (1892), Paul de Lagarde (1893), Heinrich von Brunn (1894), Emil Dubois-Reymond (1896), Ernst Curtius (1896), and Konrad von Maurer (1904) have journeyed across the sea and effectively and honorably assisted with the building up of the university and institute libraries of the United States of America.

Associated with the earlier printing privileges and censorship stipulations today in almost all civilized states is the legally adopted so-called depository copy, which must be surrendered to the state by the publisher for each work issued by him as a gift in return for the protection afforded to the book, and in connection with which the stipulated library of the territory is able to collect in the greatest completeness possible the native literature (and above all the ephemeral literature that is so easily exposed to ruin) and to preserve it as a national property of the people for all times.[27] In earlier periods, the German printers or publishers who requested a protective letter for a projected published work against its being pirated have been responsible for surrendering several copies of the publication to the imperial chancellor as evidence, or as a means for censorship. Out of these evidential copies deposited at the chancellory there has come since the seventeenth century the national despository copy (the word is a nineteenth century designation) for incorporation into the intellectual collective properties of the German people. While already in France, Konrad Néobar, with his appointment as the royal printer on January 17, 1538, has been required to surrender copies of his Greek first editions to the King's library, so that if the edition encountered harm, it would remain preserved for posterity. In the Reich we hear of such a transition into public possession only in an order of Emperor Ferdinand II of August 26, 1624, to the collective book dealers and booksellers of Frankfurt am Main, according to which the surrendered works had to be given to the Imperial Library in Vienna. Today the individual depository copy goes into the closer territorial library, while the whole German publishing industry still surrenders a further copy of its publications to the German Library at Leipzig, which has taken on the function of an archive for the German book trade and for German literature.

In the fullness of the times, the incessant stream of books gradually had to break asunder the large splendid hall of the earlier centuries and imperatively demand suitable buildings with flexible rooms.[28] Considered as forerunners of that in Germany can already be the building occupied in 1723, in Wolfenbüttel, which was designed after Palladios' so-called Villa rotunda near Vicenza, and the library that was opened in Berlin in 1748, on order from Frederick the Great and called in the vernacular on account of its curved form, "The bow-front chest of drawers." The actual period of the great library buildings—in which, again, as with other forms already in the seventeenth and eighteenth centuries, great tasks have been given to architecture by the book world—began only in the nineteenth century, when the great upheavals of the Napoleonic period and the mighty growth of the book market allowed enormous masses of manuscripts, printed works, journals, newspapers, and new books to flow together into the possession of the public.

There arose in the decade of 1832–1843 at Munich the huge palace of King Ludwig I, with its massive street side and its stone statues of Greek philosophers on the outside staircase; it was simultaneously a symbol of the new set of vital relationships of libraries, of their development into independent scholarly insitutions, which depended on their valuable holdings (it was built by Friedrich Gärtner); the halls for books in London and Paris were immeasureably extended; Württemberg erected its handsome territorial library in Stuttgart (1878); then Wolfenbüttel saw arise its gorgeous temple in the Italian Renaissance style, with its exquisite middle room (1882–1886); there then followed the National Library at Athens, which was built of the noblest marble by Ernst Ziller (1887–1901), the beautiful library building in Strasbourg (1889–1894) as a stimulating monument of German culture in Alsace (which at that time had been won again) and the simply infinite number of new buildings in Amsterdam, Basel, Christiana, Erlangen, Freiburg im Breisgau, Giessen Göttingen, Graz, Greifswald, Halle, Heidelberg, Karlsruhe, Kassel, Kiel, Königsberg, Leyden, Leipzig, Mainz, Marburg, Münster, Rostock, Stockholm, Tübingen, Wiesbaden and Zurich. Exceeding all of these in mass and size was the Prussian State Library at Berlin, a huge building of fabulous size, such as the world does not possess a second time. The cost for the lot came to 11.5 million marks, and for the construction and furnishing, 14.5 million. The magnificent dedication took place on March 22, 1914, in the presence of Kaiser William II; it was the last great courtly celebration of the second German Empire. Shells fired during the revolt impacted the walls of the same building in November, 1918. The last of the great German places for books arose finally in Leipzig in the German Library which was opened on September 2, 1916; it was a luxuriously equipped creation, which the German bookdealers and Saxony have, with many sacrifices, dedicated to German literature.[29] The two enormous buildings in Berlin and Leipzig may be considered as the end for the time being of the rich modern building activity in the service of the book.

In the new world, the American nation in its unbounded advance, built one "palace" after another for the widest dissemination of the book.[30] Especially prominent among all the many buildings is the Library of Congress in Washington (1897), an architectural wonder in size and arrangement. Joining it with outstanding significance are the public libraries in Boston (1910) and New York (1911), the latter built entirely of white marble in Italian Renaissance style for nine million dollars, and equipped with appropriate reading rooms for Orientalia, Judaica, Slavic items, engravings, maps, art, genealogy, technology, national economics and sociology. Andrew Carnegie, the king of gifts for the dissemination of books, has created a suitable form of functional and dignified library buildings.

What differentiates all the new buildings from the earlier ones is the separation of the rooms for the books themselves and the administration of the collection; the greatest possible use is made of the available space through the utmost compression of the books arranged in the stacks area with mezzanines and false ceilings. Only in the reading room has a small section remained from the earlier hall-library; here the book stands directly at the disposal of the reader. The growing flow of books and of enthusiastic readers will, however, expand even here beyond this tight compression of books. Then instead of the one reading room for the whole library, there will be several rooms having formal specialized libraries, individual reading rooms; for the user this is the best solution, but for the total house it is again an undesired expansion, and a subverting of the space-saving goal that formerly was aimed at. Fortunate attempts to do justice to the insatiable pressure of expansion of the book world are made in the dome rooms of London and Berlin.

Although the public libraries are the best-secured protective rooms for the book treasures that are here stored up in definitive public possession, there are still dangers lurking even here, which can threaten and destroy the holdings. The main enemies are fire and war. Both (frequently in union with one another) have destroyed or injured innumerable collections, from the destruction of the library in Alexandria up until the current wars being waged. Several examples will relate the story of such fates. Fire broke out in the Escorial in 1671, and it consumed a large portion of the priceless book treasures amassed there. The Heidelberg Castle suffered a similar fate and valuable holdings from the possessions of the Palatine counts (who so enjoyed books) were thereby lost. The fire in Stockholm Castle in 1697, destroyed eleven hundred manuscripts and over 17,300 printed works. In 1768, the fire in the monastery of St. Blasien in the Black Forest reduced the priceless book treasures to ashes; among them were also three St. Gall manuscripts from the ninth century, which had been borrowed. The University Library at Valencia was destroyed by the attack of Marshal Suchet on the city. At the fire of the city of Abo, the University Library there was also burnt completely to the ground. The Cathedral Library at Strengnaes (which grew in the Thirty Year's War with many manuscripts carried off from Bohemia and Moravia) suffered a severe injury from fire. The destruction of the Strasbourg Municipal Library in 1870, has already been mentioned.

From the 23rd to the 24th of May, 1871, the rioting commune in Paris set the library of the Louvre[31] on fire at the same time as the Tuilleries, and they thereby destroyed a large collection of revolutionary writings, as well as numerous splendidly executed works. The books and the collections of the historiographer, Theodore Mommsen, burned in Charlottenburg on July 12, 1880; among the items destroyed were valuable manuscripts from Berlin, Breslau, Heidelberg and Vienna. Especially painful is the loss of the Heidelberg *Jordanis* manuscript, which is the oldest and the best transmission of the text. The fire at Turin on January 25–26, 1904, brought with it one of the severest losses of modern times; it destroyed irreplaceable holdings of the Biblioteca Nazionale there, with 3,400 manuscripts, among which were the famous *Livre d'heures* of the dukes of Berry from the year 1403, with miniatures by Van Eyck, the *Historia Augusta*, with miniature paintings of Pisanello and Pasti; added to these were 24,700 printed works.

Destroyed in the First World War was the valuable University Library at Louvain, which was accommodated in the old Gothic hall for books; it had about 250,000 volumes and 250 manuscripts. "That is no more merely a Belgian loss; the entire world has thereby become poorer."[32] Reestablished by Germany, it suffered the same fate at the entry of the German troops in the summer of 1940. The Public Library at St. Paul in Minnesota was sacrificed to fire in 1915. The Lippian Territorial Library in Detmold caught fire on November 22, 1921, and had valuable losses to bemoan. Also in the future one will have to fear for our large collections and all provisions must be made for their protection, especially following the experiences of the last war. Never have the German book properties suffered so badly as they did in the last universal conflagration. Entire libraries lie in rubble and ashes; others have severe individual losses. Added thereto are the enormous destructions of books in the countless bookstores, the antiquarian booksellers, the bookbinderies, and in individual possession. Germany will have to expend the greatest effort in order to be able to make relatively good again its public losses in books. Many priceless items have been forever lost.[33]

38
Oriental Book Holdings in the West

If in the fifteenth and sixteenth centuries, the most vital among the European nations had turned to Roman and Greek literature, the nineteenth century likewise began enthusiastically to search out Oriental languages and literature, especially since it had been recognized that all the Indo-Germanic languages can be traced back to a common root. Relations to the mysterious countries of the rising Sun, and to the homeland of the great books of religion, the Bible, the Koran, of the Egyptian Book of the Dead, of the *Zendavesta,* and of the Vedas, had already existed. Above all, the Holy Land had been from time immemorial the passionate goal of pious pilgrims, of Knights strong in the faith, and of adventurers eager for new experiences. There, following the break-up of the Western Roman Empire, the Arabs had pushed the culture of Islam forward to Spain, to Sicily and to northern Africa. The vital trade connections there had exported not merely wares, but also the knowledge of languages and literary monuments, from the East to the West. On Epiphany 1212 there arrived in the monastery of Drasark (the seat at that time of the archbishop and imperial chancellor of the small Armenian Kingdom) the bishop of Hildesheim, Wilbrand of Oldenburg, in order to bring to the king of the country a message from the German emperor. The monks in the community proudly displayed for their guests the gospel books written on parchment and decorated with colorful miniature paintings.

Apparently among these treasures was that priceless Armenian gospel manuscript, which is provided with pictures, with ornamental letters and borders from the year 1113, and which now belongs to the University Library in Tübingen, and is exhibited as the most significant evidence for a miniature painting school influenced by Persia. Then with the Renaissance there had come the period of the great renewal of learning, which took such pleasure in books, and it had been a tremendous support especially for comparative philology and for the acquisition of Oriental books. Johann Albrecht Widmanstetter proudly exhibited the numerous manuscripts he owned in the most varied languages of the East;[1] they were gazed at in wonder, as a marvel.

In the course of the sixteenth century, impressive manuscript holdings from the Orient came together in Rome, Paris, Vienna and in the Escorial. The early printing primarily embraced the Hebrew literature, but also other Eastern language monuments. King Ferdinand received from Moses of Marden a Syrian manuscript of the gospels in thanksgiving for the fact that in 1555, he had the New Testament printed in Vienna in the Syrian language and script. Venice became a main center for the distribution of books from foreign countries. Knowledge of Oriental languages received a significant boost when Pope Urban VIII founded the *Collegium pro fide propaganda* in Rome in 1627, in order to give missionaries the opportunity to learn foreign languages. Mission activity, and the stimulating comparative philology connected with it, brought valuable property into the Vaticana; today it preserves around 1,260 Oriental manuscripts. Generally speaking, however, interest in the Oriental languages and literatures was awakened only in particular places, without becoming of greater significance.

A fresh advance in the exploration into Oriental literature ensued when, after the end of the eighteenth century, several societies originated for inquiry into the Oriental languages—in 1779, the Bataviaasch-Genootschap van Kunsten en Wetenschappen, in 1784, the Asiatic Society of Bengal at Calcutta, in 1821, the Société Asiatique in Paris, in 1823, the Royal Asiatic Society of Great Britain and Ireland in London, and in 1845, the German Oriental Society in Halle. Since then, there was eager traversing of the Eastern countries in order to search for foreign literary monuments. Charles Schefer, who for a time was the French ambassador in Constantinople (1849–1857), collected 276 Arabic, 276 Persian, and 239 Turkish manuscripts; in December 1899, the priceless legacy was acquired for the National Library in Paris. Constantinople has always been an important trading place, both for the buying and selling for Greek literature, but for Oriental literature also. As at one time the Greek manuscripts did, so now hundreds, and even thousands, of Arabic, Armenian, Turkish, Persian, Syrian, Japanese and Chinese manuscripts found their way to Europe, in order ultimately to "land" in the book collections of London, Oxford, Paris, Madrid, Rome, Berlin, Munich, Dresden, Leipzig, Tübingen, and Vienna, and here to provide the indispensable foundation for the comparative philology that was being pursued more and more zealously.[2]

In the meanwhile, unfortunately, whole libraries in the East, such as those in Baghdad, Tripoli, and Cairo, had been ruined by war and fire. England now owns the richest collections of Oriental literature: London, with its rich holdings of the India Office and the British Museum, and Oxford with its valuable treasures in the Bodleian. The National Library in Paris especially has a significant wealth of Chinese publications, and Madrid is outstanding for its large Arabic holdings, with valuable portions of the Arabic literature. In Germany, the Prussian State Library in Berlin has mainly taken a successful interest in acquiring Oriental manuscripts. If the year 1817 was already bringing valuable Oriental items from the property of the Orientalist and friend of Goethe, Heinrich Friedrich von Diez (1751–1817), so over 840 Indian manuscripts (including a complete series of Vedas in good copy) were acquired in 1842, by von Bunsen, the Legation counsel, from the estate of the Englishman, Sir Robert Chambers. Wilhelm von Humboldt called attention to the estate following the owner's death (May 9, 1803). Following these, there were valuable collections of Wetzstein (1852), Petermann (1857), Sprenger (1857), Minutoli (1864), Schoemann (1979), Laudberg (1884), Sachau (1884), Glaser (1887) and Pander (1889), to which was added in 1906, the Dutch-Indian library acquired from the city of Delft, with its valuable holdings in the Malayan and Japanese languages. In their totality, these were rather extensive and valuable holdings, which were sufficiently significant and important to generate the establishment on April 1, 1919, of an Oriental department.[3]

In 1858, the Munich State Library added to its priceless collections of Johann Albrecht Widmanstetter from the sixteenth century the significant library of the French Orientalist, Etienne Marc Quatremère (1792–1857), with more than 1,200 Oriental manuscripts;[4] it later acquired valuable Sanskrit and Zend (the Old Persians) manuscripts, as well as Chinese books.[5] The choice collection of the historiographer of the Turkish (Osmanian) Kingdom, Joseph, Baron von Hammer-Purgstall (1744–1856), passed into the possession of the Viennese Court Library. So Berlin, Munich and Vienna made considerable sacrifice in order to advance the investigations into Oriental languages and literatures. The Royal Library in Stockholm acquired a rich collection of Japanese materials, which Adolf Erik, Baron von Nordenskjöld, has brought home with him from the Vega-Expedition of 1878/1879. The United States of America has also been concerned to acquire Oriental manuscripts and books. The Newberry Library in Chicago in 1907 had acquired over twelve hundred works in 21,400 volumes in China and Japan.

Of the larger collections, most of the institutions have issued printed lists of their holdings. In their totality, these surveys are valuable guides through the literature of the East.[6] The monuments themselves signify not merely important materials of the foreign languages and of cultural groups, but they also afford us a valuable view into an entirely new world of forms (and one that is strange to us) in the structure of Eastern literature and bibliography.[7] The kingdom of the book has extended itself for us into the realm of the infinite and the wonderful.

39
The Book in the Popular Libraries

If the scholarly library is considered primarily as being for the collecting, preservation and preparation of the most important literary properties in the service of the nation, of research and scholarship, taking a place beside it in modern times has been the popular library, the educational library, and the reading rooms which have the goal of serving the general education, instruction, and the cultural recreation of the entire citizenry.[1] If the scholarly collection has devoted itself to the past, the present and the future regardless of period, the popular library is adapted to the present day and hour, so as to be able to make accessible to contemporaries the sources of knowledge, of professional improvement, and of poetry. Those are the external differences of the two institutions for books; there are, however, the most manifold approaches, supplementations and overlappings. The scholarly library closes its doors to no one, when the concern is with a serious effort toward professional improvement and knowledge; and, as a matter of fact, many scholarly libraries have annexed a popular department so as to be able to work on a broader basis. Conversely, the reading rooms provided with large financial means could develop far beyond their narrow tasks if they kept and encompassed the literature of the period in the widest range, or if they carried through a special collection task, such as one that would serve knowledge of, and research into, the geography and folklore of the locale in which they were situated.

The popular library is also linked inseparably to the development of cultural life. Only hesitatingly did the oldest printers venture into the issuance of books in German, so strongly did the Latin literature (the scholarly literature of the waning Middle Ages and of the early printing period) hold sway. Even Luther had the scholarly libraries mainly in mind for the use of preachers and of secular officials, when he recommended the building and cultivation of libraries. Only on occasion were isolated voices raised which, like Caspar Hedio, emphasized the heightened significance of German works and translations into German for the cultural (and even more for the religious) elevation of the people. Several centuries had to go by first, before the power of thought and of knowledge in the Enlightenment period began to instruct with alluring words and, in connection therewith, a literature grew up that had something to say in understandable German—and something not merely for the scholars, but for the entire people.

The Anglo-Saxon countries, Britain and America, have become the home of the new book movement, which belongs to the greatest cultural movements of the nineteenth century. Knowledge is power—this magic formula that was carried throughout the country primarily by Edward Edwards (1812–1881), one of the most significant English librarians and author of the outstanding work, *Memoirs of Libraries* (1859), created in England on July 30, 1850, a law (The Public Libraries Act), which empowered communities to support public libraries and museums with the aid of an additional tax. The first popular libraries were opened in Manchester and Liverpool in the year 1852; Birmingham followed in 1861, and quickly built a library system on a grand style.[2] The establishments were soon considered in England as being necessary constituent parts of public life, as important supplements to the popular compulsory education, and as significant enhancements of useful participation in public life. In the libraries, where the world of books was available for all the people until far into the night, as well as on Sundays, each person was supposed to be given the possibility of caring for his continuing education according to his own will and judgment, and to participate in the cultural properties of his nation and of the entire world.

The popular library associated itself even more closely with the public life of the United States of America. Here the educational library, defined as being for the public, purposely joined the rest of the popular educational efforts in lectures, exhibits and annual celebrations. In the course of half a century the American people have created an entire network of large and small libraries with the aim of making the cultural treasures accessible to each person for the freest and most convenient usage during the entire day. Hemmed in by no historical traditions and establishments, borne by an economic upsurge which was unparalleled, and furthered by means of rich gifts, the public library, as a continuing school for all that is enthusiastically provided for and used, has become a vital expression of the America spirit.[3] The unequalled legacies which Andrew Carnegie (1855–1919) and numerous other patrons have given to their nation, are visible evidences of how securely anchored this educational establishment is in American life. Since 1869, Carnegie, in grateful consideration of impressions he had received as a youth in a lending library, gradually spent more than one hundred million dollars for the founding of libraries, which he normally set up in such a way that the city, community, or corporation being considered was supposed to apply each year at least ten of each hundred dollars offered to the support of the institution thus erected. In such a way more than 2,800 library buildings have been established by him.[4] He has set down his goal in the famous book, *The Gospel of Wealth.*[5]

Among all the numerous libraries of America (which always are provided with handsome buildings) primarily outstanding are the New York Public Library with its two million volumes (among which are valuable manuscripts), the Boston Public Library, and the Public Library of Chicago, which for the human sciences is supplemented by the Newberry Library, and for the natural and social sciences, by the John Crear Library. It is a special distinction of the American library situation that the rich monetary funds which are here applied come for the most part out of voluntary contributions. What lends the American public library its successful powers of enlistment and efficacy is the far-reaching accessibility of its holdings for the entire population in rooms that are comfortable, which are opened the whole day long, and which, with catalogs and information, guide the visitor to the books in the quickest way possible. Thus America, with the passage of time, has become the land of reading rooms, in which everyone has the possiblity of educating himself, of being instructed or entertained, by means of the book. Here the book, fostered by a strong faith in its educative and formative powers, and in association with the whole movement for popular education, becomes a cultural guide for the people. Not the book as applied to the Muse, or to deep questions concerning the meaning and purpose of life itself, but the world-affirming, joyful book, the book that shows the way to forward-looking thought, to the iron will, and to brilliant economic success — it is this book, as the expression of the dominant vitality, which is the favorite of the American people.

In Germany, it took a long time before the popular library could be effected. The initial beginnings go back to the after-effects of the Enlightenment period. In 1797, the journalist, Heinrich Stephani, in his *Grundriss der Staatserziehungs-wissenschaft* ("Foundations of the Science of National Education") outlined a great plan for popular reading institutions, with the village and town libraries being subject to the comprehensive national library, which would include the individual institutions, and this proposal found a vital agreement with the later Prussian minister, Julius von Massow. Still, these advances initially only remained on paper. Greater successes were allotted to the Saxon revenue official, Karl Preusker, who founded a citizen's library in Grossenhain in Saxony in 1828, and in addition, in his publication of 1839/40, *Über öffentliche Vereins- und Privatbibliotheken sowie andere Sammlungen, Lesezirkel und verwandte Gegenstände mit Rücksicht auf den Bürgerstand* ("Concerning Public Associational and Private Libraries, as well as other Collections, Reading Circles and Related Objects, with Respect to the Middle Classes"), he effusively espoused the cause of the general educational library. When the historiographer, Friedrich von Raumer, returned in 1841 from a trip to North America, he urgently propagandized in Berlin for the institution that he knew to be full of significance, and in 1850, he pushed through the founding of four popular libraries. As a result, several educational associations embraced the concern, and in a series of towns this led to the setting up of libraries. The first municipal reading rooms were opened in Berlin and Düsseldorf in 1896. Three years later the Comenius Society called on the magistrates of all German towns and cities to build free public libraries, and on July 18, 1899, the Prussian culture minister, Bosse, issued an order according to which the state authorities were directed to support the movement vigorously.

The Prussian territorial assembly granted an annual subsidy of 50,000 marks; later it was 100,000. Essen had considerable success with the library that was established by Friedrich Alfred Krupp; Jena did likewise with its famous Zeiss foundation, and so did Charlottenburg and Elberfeld with their large municipal popular reading rooms. The experiences of these book halls and reading rooms have taught us that no miracles can be demanded of them. But they can serve to promote and to assist, and they can communicate knowledge and information in all areas. The book, however, has to come to the people, just as the people have come to the book. That requires a functional division of popular librarianship, both in its conception and in its operation, by the setting up of branches in the most varied quarters of the large cities, as well as the establishing of good reference departments. Above all, the book will become more accessible as a means of education, even to country people. The village library, suggested already in 1885 by Heinrich Sohnrey, has to become the communicator of the educational assets which are contained within the book.

Belonging to the earliest manifestations of effective communication through books is the educational goal of the Catholic Borromeo Association, which was founded in 1844, and which made it its concern to disseminate doctrinally conforming publications to be personally owned or also to be borrowed, and which has spread a dense network of libraries all over Germany. Its own journal, *Die Bücherwelt* ("The World of Books") represents the hub and the exchange of ideas for this book movement. The considerable range of this solicitation in the service of the book is shown by the distribution of 305,500 volumes in 1931, and further by the total holdings of its libraries which came to 4,300,000 volumes in the same year, as well as by the lending of 10,156,000 volumes of the association, or the budget of 1,860,000 marks.

The worker's libraries of the great industrial plants are devoted to practical productions. The book can also give much of value to workers. Workers' libraries provide them with the opportunity of deepening their specialized knowledge, of extending their general knowledge, of becoming acquainted with the treasures of German poetry, and of enabling them to participate in the nation's cultural assets. Among the most significant industrial libraries of this sort are the libraries of the Allgemeine Elektrizitäts-Gesellschaft ("General Electricity Company"), the Siemens-Schukkert Werke, the German Potassium Syndicate (all three of these are in Berlin), the Friedrich Krupp Aktiengesellschaft in Essen, and the Interessengemeinschaft Farbenindustrie in Höchst am Main and in Leverkusen.

Modern forms of circulating the book further include the book clubs and the lending libraries. The book clubs are retail trades, whose director publishes his own works, or those of other houses, in a large number of issues at lower prices to the members, who are bound by the payment of annual fee to accept a certain number of volumes. The largest German enterprises of this sort were the Deutsche Buchgemeinschaft ("German Book Club") and the Volksverband der Bücherfreunde ("Popular Association of Bibliophiles"), both of them in Berlin. Lending libraries[6] primarily stock works of entertainment and lend their holdings for the payment of a borrowing fee. The reading circle, the lending exchange of journals which is operated like a trade, brings a selection of weekly and monthly publications to the participant in his home; they are exchanged on a regular basis.

The Librarian in the Service
of the World of Books

As demanding as the book is, for its production and distribution it requires not merely printer, publisher and bookdealer, but also those who in the book rooms attend to its maintenance and communication, which are so decisive for the book's lasting effect. We have already made reference repeatedly in these pages to the work of the librarian in the service of the world of books; but it is perhaps worthwhile to bring together the individual aspects of the phenomena in a small total picture, so as to illustrate the great significance that this profession has in the operation of the world of books.

The flourishing period of the ancient librarianship in Alexandria shows us the scholar, who did indeed also have to maintain the external order of his domain, but who still considered his chief task as being the scholarly mastery of his treasures through the examination, sorting and classification of the texts. Then in the Middle Ages we encounter especially the work of the monastery librarian, who watched over the busy hands of the monks in the scriptorium, administered the collection of books, but who in most instances still had other responsibilities to fulfill, such as the division of the daily work or directing the singing in church. As a consequence of the reawakening of the Roman and Greek antiquities, which heightened the esteem in which public collections of books were held, and the inviting image of the scholarly Alexandrian librarian, the scholar was once more looked on as the proper leader of the new libraries. The famous mural in which Pope Sixtus IV calls the historiographer, Platina, who took pleasure in books, to be head of the Vaticana, expresses this relationship in a picturesque way. In Germany, the earliest forerunners are Conrad Celtes and Georg Spalatin, and in Vienna, the most effective representative of the development is Hugo Blotius. This image of the librarian, as it then represents itself most impressively in Peter Lambeck in Vienna, had been the dominant one for centuries. Constituting the high point have been the seventeenth and eighteenth centuries, the age of great learning and scholarship, when Leibniz and Muratori performed their duties in the book rooms.

Rather unique assignments have often fallen to the keepers of libraries. When the subsequently great philosopher, Immanuel Kant, was installed in 1766 as the second librarian at the Castle Library in his hometown of Königsberg, he was required to attend to it that in the library everything would remain in good order, "especially with the mob of young rough people who have ventured in here at times to withdraw books according to their pleasure, and have dared to use the library room as a public promenade." Kant has soon removed himself again from the library.[1]

The activities of one of the most famous librarians of the eighteenth century, Gotthold Ephraim Lessing, have to be judged from the standpoint of a closely confined courtly activity.[2] The poet was freed of an intolerable external situation when he was called in May 1770 from Hamburg to Wolfenbüttel, in order to administer the court library there for eleven long years. Initially he occupied spacious quarters in the castle, in the "fortress of Wolfenbüttel" which he later frequently cursed; later when Eva König became his wife, he lived in a house, with garden, which was fixed up for him. What his function was, he described in a letter to his father from July 27, 1770, with the following words: "Actual official business I have only to the extent that I myself create it. I might mention that the hereditary prince has seen to it that I should use the library rather than the library using me. Meanwhile I shall try to connect the two: or to speak actually, have one follow upon the other."

Abbot Jerusalem reported on March 12, 1770, to Karl Friedrich Bahrdt in the same vein concerning the ultimate purpose of Lessing's appointment. What Lessing considered his function to be is shown in his publications of 1777 and 1774, *Zur Geschichte der Literatur aus den Schätzen der herzoglichen Bibliothek zu Wolfenbüttel* ("A History of Literature from the Treasures of the Ducal Library at Wolfenbüttel"), in which he reported about his discoveries and conclusions. In the lectures he expresses himself in detail concerning the need for a new history of the Wolfenbüttel library. He thinks that Burckhard, the first historiographer of the collection, seems simply not to have considered what the history of a library chiefly consists of; it is not one that, with an anxious conscientiousness, reports the indifferent facts of its origin and the collection's growth in general (that would at best be the genealogy of the library), but is one that shows "whereto now also it has been used by scholarship and the scholars, that so many books have been brought together here at so much cost; these above are the deeds of the library; and without deeds there is no history." Despite all the freedom he was afforded there, the eleven years Lessing spent in lonely Wolfenbüttel were not to his liking. Thus he once wrote that it would never have been his inclination for the rest of his life to tend to books, removed from the company he needed, and in a place like Wolfenbüttel. Those talents for the work of organizing and the making materials accessible, which managing a library demanded, he felt, were lacking in him. Even the scholarly work on Wolfenbüttel's treasures didn't interest him very much. When he announced to his brother the first volume of the publications from the treasures of the library, he wrote in addition: "Such dry library work allows for rather pretty writing, but all without participation, without the slightest mental strain. Still I can always rest with the confidence that I am sufficiently performing my office, and I can learn much thereby, even though not one-hundredth of these things is valuable enough to be learned." Added to this discontent there was still the unpleasantness that issued from the copying of an alleged Wolfenbüttel manuscript, which in reality was a posthumous treatment by the philosopher, Hermann Samuel Reimarus, the

Fragmente eines Unbekannten ("Fragments of an Unknown"). In a heated quarrel with the Hamburg pastor, Johann Melchior Goeze, Lessing voiced the idea that he would not like to be the dog that kept watch over the house, or the groom who carried to each hungry horse the hay in the hay rack; whereupon his sharp-witted opponent replied that he would have to call a library administered according to such a concept, a churchyard (i.e., cemetary), and the librarian therein an undertaker.

Guidance and advice were the main functions that Lessing officially had to administer. For example, on June 5, 1771, Duke Karl wrote him from Brunswick: "My dear Mr. Lessing: The princes of Sweden will come to Wolfenbüttel on the sixth toward midday, in order to view the library there. Keep yourself therefore in readiness so that they can be shown the items that are the most outstanding and the most remarkable. The eldest is very curious about old things." On another occasion he had to comment on the claim of the University of Helmstedt to the Wolfenbüttel duplicates. He expressed himself as being against the surrendering of them, and he proposed making a profit from these superfluous books in order to increase the stock of his own library. Among the German people, Lessing is remembered not as the librarian of Wolfenbüttel, but rather as the great cultural leader and the gifted master of the German tongue.

The effective emphasis of these scholarly librarians of the eighteenth century lay more in the service of scholarship than in the art of administration. Thus even Lodovico Antonio Muratori (1672–1750), who initially was at the Ambrosiana in Milan and then, after 1700, at the library of the princes in Modena for a half-century long, was considered a marvel of scholarship. There are evidences for that even now in his famous editions of the Italian historiographers, *Rerum Italicarum scriptores* with its twenty-five volumes, and the *Annales* with twelve. The chief aim of his library work was making the book collections entrusted to him accessible to scholarship. A list of the New Testament writings from the end of the second century, which was discovered by him in an Ambrosiana manuscript of the ninth century, bears permanently the name of the fortunate finder *(Muratori Fragment)*.

Adreas Felix Oefele (1706–1780), the director of the Munich Court Library, spent most of his time with scholarly activities. Although he also accepted organizational tasks and built a catalog in twenty-four volumes of the classics in his collection, his library work primarily revolved around the tireless compiling of individual scholarly details in such fullness, that he had no energy left to do anything with them. Only the collection of the Bavarian historical sources, created from the libraries in Munich, Ingolstadt, Augsburg and Tergernsee, saw publication. Oefele was in stimulating conversation with the scholars of his period; with Töpsl, Quirini, Muratori, and Bianconi, he industriously exchanged letters; Montfaucon sent him his *Bibliotheca bibliothecarum*, with a handwritten dedication. His son, Klemens, increased his own book collection with the Sulzbach church library, in order than to sell the greatest part of it to the Augustinian Canons' foundation in Rottenbuch. From there most of the books came again in 1803, to Munich and here, a century later, they found themselves together again with Oefele's scholarly legacy, which had been handed over by his heirs.[3]

When in the first decades of the nineteenth century, calm again entered into the libraries' holdings, which had been thrown into such confusion, it then became necessary to bring order and life into the hastily assembled books. It was a rare mixture of people, this generation of librarians who were called to transform the great accumulations of books into beneficial assistance to scholarship. Not always was there suitable personnel available who were qualified to cope with this enormous work. Where large tasks wait on a solution, it is easiest to distinguish the able ones from the rest. The most suitable still seemed to be the former monks, who in their quiet cells have taken a fancy to the world of books, or who had already earlier administered their monastic collections. Paul Hupfauer, Martin Schrettinger, and Heinrich Joachim Jäck (all three of whom were at one time unworldly inhabitants of the monastery, and later became able librarians) may be mentioned as examples of such assistants. Jäck, the wise organizer of the proud treasures of Bamberg, was engaged by such love for the collection entrusted to him that he offered his own financial means so as, with assistants, to bring it into serviceable order. For the most part, it was lacking in suitable places for arranging the books, in heated rooms for working, in assistance in the discharge of the most pressing activities, and in money for increasing the book treasures. Individual niggardly foundations (and added thereto, the notorious auctions and sales) frequently constituted the sole, quickly exhausted sources for the scanty money. In order to be able to sell as many duplicates as possible, one sometimes broke up the old collective volumes and therewith destroyed valuable marks of their origin or important connections between the works thus united with one another.

In the books themselves there is so strong an attraction that, even under the most unfavorable existential conditions they knew, as it were, how to develop their life. When through the union of valuable book treasures unprecedently rich centers of literature had been formed, it was then a joy for the professional attendants of these treasures, hand-in-hand with their work of organizing, to create out of the fullness of their riches, and to suprise the scholarly world with discoveries of all sorts. There thus now ensued (just as once it did in the time of Humanism) a period of numerous discoveries, a time that has brought to book collections an increase in the value ascribed to them by public opinion, especially in the scholarly world. Working successfully in this sense was the already mentioned director of the Central Library, Johann Christoph, Baron von Aretin, who, as the deserving publisher of *Beyträge zur Geschichte und Literatur, vorzüglich aus den Schätzen der pfalzbaierischen Centralbiblioteck zu München* ("Contributions to History and Literature, Selected from the Treasures of the Palatine-Bavarian Central Library at Munich"), not merely sought deliberately with his own treatises to make the rich treasures in the Munich collection accessible, but also engaged zealous collaborators. Among these were Ignaz Hardt, the later describer of the Munich Greek manuscripts, Johann Baptist Bernhart (1759–1821), the outstanding connoisseur of early printing and book rarities,[4] who was called to make known the rich treasures of the Munich incunabula in a fruitful way, as Ludwig Hain has done a decade later in his *Repertorium bibliographicum* which has become famous; Bernard Joseph Docen (1782–1828), the fortunate discoverer of valuable German language monuments, who issued several not yet published (or only defectively published) Old High German monuments: a section from the Bamberg *Heliand* manuscript, proofs of the Windberg Psalter, and the inestimable Tegernsee glosses, and then several Middle High German texts, among which are the significant fragments of Wolfram's *Titurel*, which he dedicated to August Wilhelm Schlegel and to Martin Schrettinger, the author of the oft-cited *Handbuch der Bibliothekswissenschaft* (Handbook of Library Science), and founder of the currently still useful old Munich subject catalog.

How fundamentally had the assessment of the literary monuments of the German past changed since the times of the scoffer of *Sanssouci!* When Christoph Heinrich Müller sent Frederick the Great his *Sammlung Deutscher Gedichte aus dem XII, XIII and XIV. Jahrhundert* ("Collection of German poetry from the XII, XIII and XIV Centuries"), with the first complete edition of the *Nibelungenlied,* he has been mockingly and negatively answered from Potsdam on February 22, 1784: "You judge much too favorably your poems from the twelfth, thirteenth and fourteenth centuries, the printing of which you have promoted and which you hold to be so useful to the German language. In my view such things are not worth a shot of gunpowder, and they don't deserve to be drawn from the dust of the past. At least I should not put up with such stuff in my book collections; I would rather throw it out. The copy of it sent to me may therefore await its fate in the large library there. Not many people will ask for it there either." Now all professional persons rejoice over such discoveries from the treasures of libraries. When Max Joseph of Bavaria visited the University Library in Jena in 1823, the Grand Duke presented him with an artistic reproduction fromt he Jena *Minnesänger* manuscript; the remarkable specimen is kept together with an accompanying letter to the Grand Duke signed by Goethe on May 18, 1823, in the Munich State Library. Goethe had at that time superintendence over the libraries of Jena and Weimar, and he was always filled with the greatest reverence for the holdings, with which he felt himself in the presence of a great capital stock that would silently bear incalculable interest.[5]

John Andreas Schmeller (1785-1852) became the most significant Munich librarian. Born in the same year as Jakob Grimm, and tossed hither and yon for a long time by fate, he entered the Munich library in 1829, and with an outburst of enthusiasm initiated that successful work on the manuscript treasures which has brought fame alike to him and to the institution.[6] One of his first activities was that he again brought together according to their provenance the Latin manuscripts which had been broken up into individual collections by Docen, so as to preserve the historical connection with their country of origin. The next was that, like Docen, he made priceless antiquities accessible: the old Saxon *Heliand* poetry of the gospels (1830), which was discovered by Docen, the *Muspilli* poem (as it was called by Schmeller), the Old High German translation of the harmony of the gospels of Ammonius (1841), the priceless vagabond songs of Benediktbeuern *(Carmina Burana,* 1847), and the *Jagdlied* ("Hunting Song") of Hadamar von Laber (1850). His chief scholarly work has become the *Bayerische Wörterbuch* ("Bavarian Dictionary"), which drew on the abundant resources of a comprehensive knowledge.

Besides Docen and Schmeller, two further significant devotees of German archeological research worked in the bibliotecarial office: Jakob and Wilhelm Grimm.[7] The older brother, Jakob, (1785–1863) came into relation to the world of books already early when in 1806 (he was then only 21 years old), through the intercession of the historiographer, Johannes von Müller, he became for a brief period the librarian of King Jérome of Westphalia in Wilhelmshöhe. In 1815, he spent a while in Paris in the company of the Prussian statesman, Johann Albrecht Friedrich Eichhorn, in order to take back the Rhenish manuscripts which had been carried off to France. In the meantime, his brother, Wilhelm (1786 until 1859), had on February 4, 1814, obtained employment in the library at Kassel, and a special circumstance willed that from May 1, 1816 on, both brothers had to work thirteen years long with the same niggardly household economy in the same library at Kassel. It was not the happiest period in their lives. In order to furnish visible proof of their work there, they had to write a catalog of eighty folio volumes. "This business," Jakob Grimm groaned at the time, "I must say has become for me the hardest in my life."

In 1830, the inseparable brothers moved to Göttingen as professors and librarians; but here also they felt so strongly pressured by the library and other official work until, dismissed among the "Göttingen Seven," they found greater freedom of movement for their scholarly researches in Berlin. On June 5, 1885, on the birthday of Jakob Grimm, a later generation has honored the Kassel activities of both the deserving scholars by placing their busts in the library at Kassel. By calling and inclination they have, like Lessing, been no exemplary librarians; like him, however, they have enriched the libraries with immortal works.

As the last librarian from the "camp" of the archeological research of this period, August Heinrich Hoffman von Fallersleben, should be mentioned; he was the poet of *Deutschland, Deutschland über alles*.[8] The unquiet course of his life has brought him into connection with libraries several times. When in 1818 he visited the brothers Grimm in the library at Kassel, he was steered toward German antiquity. After he had applied in vain for a position in the library at Göttingen, he entered in 1819 into the newly founded University Library at Bonn, and he threw himself enthusiastically into the collecting of material for research into the German language, German customs and character. The initial results were the *Bonner Bruchstücke von Otfried* ("Bonn Fragments of Otfried"), which he had discovered in the covers of the Duisburg manuscripts. When his director, Friedrich Gottlieb Welcker, submitted the printed edition to the Ministry, he believed that he had to note therein that the fragments had been discovered and published by an assistant who, as such, did not do much work, but who zealously rummaged through the library for his literary purposes.

Hoffmann spent Christmas Eve 1822 with the Baron von Meusebach in Berlin, and he formed a lasting friendship with the zealous collector of German language monuments. Application for an office in the Berlin library failed. He was named curator of the Central Library in Breslau on March 4, 1823. His application to be the successor to Ebert in Wolfenbüttel was not successful. In 1830, he obtained a position as Professor Extraordinary for the German Lanugage and Literature in Breslau, but he kept his library work. The handsome results of further scholarly library travels he made known in his *Fundgruben für Geschichte deutscher Sprache und Literatur (1830–1837)* ("Treasure Troves for the History of German Language and Literature"). In 1841, he published a *Verzeichnis der altdeutschen Handschriften der K.K. Hofbibliothek zu Wien* ("Catalog of the Old German Manuscripts of the Royal Court Library in Vienna"). He was let go in 1842, on account of his *Politische Lieder* ("Political Songs"), and for a long time he led an unquiet life of wandering until, in March 1860, Duke Victor von Ratisbon, at the recommendation of Princess Maria von Wittgenstein-Sayn (a daughter of the female friend of Franz Liszt), named him as his librarian at the Corvey castle near Höxter an der Weser. Here the poet lived and worked until his death, and he found his final resting place beside the old monastery church, a symbolic grave for a poet: close by there at one time stood the famous monastery library, which had handed over to the Renaissance Pope, Leo X, the Tacitus manuscript for its first printed edition.

Other poets of this period also tried their luck as librarians[9]: Hermann Kurz in Tübingen, Friedrich von Matthisson, (whose song, "Adelaide," Beethoven has set to music), Franz Dingelstedt and Friedrich Haug in Stuttgart, Friedrich Hölderlin in Hamburg, August Count von Platen, Otto Roquette in Darmstadt, Franz Grillparzer in Vienna, and Joseph Victor von Scheffel in Donaueschingen. Grillparzer entered in 1813 as the unsalaried candidate into the Vienna Court Library; but he left it in the same year with the humorous poem, "Abschied von der Hofbibliothek" ("Farewell to the Court Library"). Later applications on two occasions by Grillparzer for the directorship of the Vienna Court Library have remained without success. Joseph Victor von Scheffel, the poet of the *Trompeter von Säckingen* ("Trumpeter of Säckingen") and of the historical romance, *Ekkhard,* which was prepared in the Abbey Library at St. Gall, has been busy with the organizing of the library of the Baron von Lassberg until he has, with this collection, moved to Donaueschingen. He remained there only two years (1857–1859), just long enough to publish his listing, *Die Handschriften altdeutscher Dichtunger der Fürstlich Fürstenbergischen Hofbibliothek* (1859) ("The Manuscripts of Old German Poems of the Princely Furstenberg Court Library"). He then offered his resignation in order to be able to give himself wholly in the service of the Grand Duke at Weimar.[10]

The more the production of books grew into enormous proportions, and the flow of them into libraries increased, the more the scholarly disciplines developed, with all of them demanding access to the collections of books, the more vigorously did the new aim of the public research libraries carry through, that of making the old and new library holdings as fruitful as possible in the service of scholarship (a goal that initially had to establish itself firmly on administrative principles and strategies that depended on experience) and all the more successfully was the idea instilled that bibliotecarial activity would be a match for its increased functions, only if it claimed the full strength of its devotees and was itself based on a planned professional development. One of the first men who, by a sharp insight recognized the distress of the library profession in its office as a secondary occupation, and who tried to overcome it, was Friedrich Adolf Ebert (1791–1834), one of the bibliographically best informed librarians of the previous century.

Already as a young man he was filled with the highest esteem for the new libraries, and he saw in them the most important centers for modern education and for the historical literary monuments. When only twenty years old, he wrote a small work, *Über öffentliche Bibliotheken, besonders deutsche Universitätsbibliotheken und Vorschläge zu einer zwekcmäßigen Einrichtung derselben* ("Concerning Public Libraries, especially German University Libraries and Proposals for a Functional Organization of the Same"), and he complained therein primarily about conditions in the libraries of the schools of higher learning. One sentence from it has become famous: "What are the majority of our academic libraries? Dusty, desolate and unvisited rooms in which the librarian must stay on account of his office, so that he is quite alone at this time. Nothing interrupts the deep stillness other than the sad gnawing of the bookworm here and there." The far-seeing author demanded primarily two things for a thriving development of the book collections: the disengagement first of all of the librarian from the other employments and a better professional development for this profession. Two years from that time, Ebert applied himself to the library profession and he remained faithful to it as long as he lived. With a fiery youthful enthusiasm he threw himself into his new assignments in the handsome library at Dresden, and, delighted by the plethora of the priceless book treasures stored there, he asserted that he would now become a more complete librarian, "because in this company to maintain an average and ordinary stance would be a mortal sin."

The Dresden Library became a school of higher learning for him, to which he owed his comprehensive knowledge. For that he gave it back his best labor, the development of its history (1822); it is one of the earliest representations of library history, and it had an enormous effect on the later works by Wilken (1828), Irmischer (1829), Jäck (1831), and Mosel (1835). In the small publication of 1820, *Die Bildung des Bibliothekars* ("The Education of the Librarian") he espoused yet again the cause of the independence of the librarian's profession and methodical preparation for it. His Wolfenbüttel listing of manuscripts signified remarkable progress in the important task of bibliography — to recognize the manuscripts as being historical monuments in all their relationships to the environment of the past. With good sense he saw in the art of administration a second indispensable condition for the fulfillment of the bibliotecarial task. For him, however, it did not become a purpose in itself, but in his innermost being, the question was always there: How do I best unlock the world of books entrusted to me so that they are effective with the public? To attend to the book as something of intellectually productive value: that was his highest aim.[11]

This sought-for development of the bibliotecarial office into an independent profession was inseparably involved with economic conditions, and it only came to maturity with the progress in the general welfare following the establishment of the German Empire. Certain of general agreement, the Jena librarian, Anton Klette, could vigorously raise these demands anew in the publication that appeared without his name in 1871, *Die Selbständigkeit des bibliothekarischen Berufes* ("The Independence of the Bibliotecarial Profession").[12] It was not long before the desire was fulfilled in numerous schools of higher learning, such as Jena, Freiburg im

Breisgau, Breslau, Munich, Heidelberg, Kiel, Halle and Strasbourg. Of significance for these successes was the fact that outstanding instructors in schools of higher learning (who were librarians at the same time), such as Wilhelm Brambach and Friedrich Ritschl, effectively supported the demand. The quick results thoroughly vindicated their views. When Karl Dziatzko (1842–1903) took over the Breslau Library as a full-time position, the number of borrowed books amounted to 3,922 volumes, while in the next year they climbed to 16,937 and in 1886, swelled to 41,869 volumes. The justification for the new office could not have been more forcefully evidenced. What Dziatzko has meant for the Breslau library, Fritz Milkau[13] (whom we may reckon as being among our best German librarians) has described with extolling words.[14] Dziatzko was also closely connected in other ways with the forward movement of Prussian and German librarianship. As one of the first ones to do so at a German school of higher learning, he held lectures and gave seminars in the knowledge area of the book, from which several profound works have emerged. He was also among those who saw in the librarian's detachment (so that he could be exclusively engaged in administrative work) a danger for the bibliotecarial profession, which with its service to books has always to be primarily devoted to the advancement of knowledge.[15]

Perhaps the most significant devotee of the profession in the modern period, the Bibliothèque Nationale at Paris, has had in Léopold Delisle (1826–1910), the outstanding master of the administration of books and the unexcelled researcher of the rich manuscript treasures of Paris.[16] His immortal works in the service of the world of books and of scholarship are the printing of the printed holdings of the Paris Library and the *Cabinet des manuscrits de la Bibliothèque Nationale,*[17] which is a significant history of the library that almost amounts to a medieval cultural history of France. "With a clarity not previously attained, from widely visible position he has shown through action what high significance is due to libraries in the cultural life of humankind." (Milkau).

The great merits that Antonio Panizzi (one of the most capable librarians of the modern period) has achieved in the growth of the British Museum in London have already been touched on. They consist, first of all, in the fact that he had not merely placed before the institution the high aim of becoming a great national library, but that he made acceptable a new conception of the necessity of the greatest usefulness possible for a library in the service of culture.

In the period of its impressive growth, American librarianship has found its master in William Frederick Poole (1821–1894). He was the advocate of the united author and subject catalog (dictionary catalog), the founder of the enormous subject index to the British and American periodicals for the years 1802–1906, the advocate of a combined room for books as well as for study for each of the scholarly disciplines, with a general reading room being added thereto, and finally he was the creator of two large, brand new libraries: the Public Library of Chicago and the Newberry Library in the same city.[18]

Schrettinger, Ebert, Jäck, Förstemann, Zoller, and Klette had already forcefully referred to the necessity for librarians' professional education. There were already attempts being made in the spring of 1863, to connect with the Germanic

National Museum in Nuremberg a scholarly teaching institution for archivists, librarians and the curators of the national collections. In 1878, Prussia introduced lectures in the University of Göttingen on the book and librarianship. Through a decree of December 15, 1893, Prussia instituted professional training for the next generation of librarians. Bavaria followed with introductory library courses at the Munich State Library and with corresponding stipulations relating to preparatory instruction.

In the course of these endeavors there has come into vogue the designation "library science" for the discipline concerned with the book and with libraries. One has earlier called both areas simply *Buch- und Bibliothekskunde* ("Bibliography and Information on the Library") ("Bibliothecy"),[19] and therewith hit upon perhaps more properly the kernel of the matter, because the book, the foundation of the entire structure, has therewith better come into its own. The matter might be more suitably designated as "Book and Library Science." Adjacent to bibliothecarial activity will always be the book and the scholarly spirit that surrounds it. Printed catalogs of manuscripts, the *GKW* ("Whole Catalog of Incunabula"), the German Union Catalog *(der deutsche Gesamtkatalog)*, stimulated participation in bibliology in the widest range, whether research into manuscripts or bibliography[20] — these are in fact evidences of such successful activity in the service of the book. Several names have already been mentioned: Schmeller, Ebert, Dziatzko, Delisle, Milkau, Leidinger, and Haebler: they could be shining examples. Delisle tells us in his youthful memoirs that, out of love for old parchments and papers, he has become a passionate bibliophile and a researcher into books, and that from here he had advanced into the essence and operation of the individual libraries. Such enthusiasm has not been given to everyone. But a little bit of the ardor of love for the book and for scholarship should not be lacking in one who devotes his entire life to the service of these forces.

The founding of the general libraries that were stipulated as being educational libraries for the entire nation has created a new type of librarian — the popular public librarian. He also has to deal with the providing and making accessible of the world of books. But while the scholarly libraries left the visitors to make use of the books offered them through means of catalogs, information, and exhibits, the popular librarian enters independently into the service of the book; he selects and offers it, and he tries to make it as useful as possible. He thereby takes on an educational task, while he places the book in the service of the extension of knowledge and of culture. The book for him is no object for research as it is for the scholars and students, but it is primarily a means for the extending and deepening of cultural and professional improvement — a means for the education of the entire people. The presupposition for this work in the service of popular culture is also knowledge and indeed, a saturation in the world of books, in the concept of cultural history, empathy with the German nature, in the tasks of his own nation, and in the cultural-political goal of the state leadership. Of special interest here is the valuable and the helping book, the book that extends the horizon, that enriches vitality, that deepens one's sense for beauty, that nourishes one's love for one's own people, and that fortifies the national consciousness.

41
Modern Bibliography

The enormous world of books would gradually have become like a large and thick forest that would be impenetrable, if individual paths and guideposts did not lead us through it. Paths through the world of books include bibliology, which traces for us the development of the book, and bibliography, which lists the literature according to certain subject areas. But even bibliography is already again become almost inextricable, and indeed requires a plan, like the paths through the forest, which gives a total overview.[1] There are already thousands of works that contain only lists of books. They fill entire rooms in the large libraries, and in every collection of books they are the ones most used. Whosoever occupies himself with any area of knowledge has to consult them.

Following the uniting of countless masses of books in the large libraries of the nineteenth century, there emerged an incomparably better possibility for investigating the development of the book and of literature than was the case in earlier times. Thus especially did the knowledge of manuscripts and of incunabula experience significant growth. A legion of reproductions of individual descriptions, and catalogs from numerous libraries are evidences of the rich flowering of the research into manuscripts since the beginning of the nineteenth century.[2] By means of all these publications the acquaintance with the medieval book and literature has grown extraordinarily. The first fruit of the improved possibilities for comparison in the area of incunabula research is the *Repertorium bibliographicum* by Ludwig Hain (1826–38); it is based on the extensive holdings of the State Library of Bavaria. With its hitherto unattained number of careful descriptions, it represented an outstanding advance in our knowledge of old monuments of printing.[3]

The further development of information concerning incunabula devoted itself chiefly to research into the stock of types in the individual workshops, in order on this basis to determine the provenance of the numerous works that were published without declaration of locale and printer, and thus to bring order into the entire history of printing. This research method is based on the necessary correspondence of items printed from types cast from the same set of types and illustrations that were printed from the same wood block. Numerous works with plates, with models of types, and woodcuts support this research. Such works of reproduction Holtrop (1857–1868) published for the Netherlands, Thierry-Poux (1890) for France, Konrad Burger for Germany (1892–1313), and for the Gesellschaft für Typenkunde ("Society of Information about Types"), and Konrad Haebler did for Spain. The bookdealer, Anatole Claudin (1833–1906) had devoted a deluxe work to the early French printing; it is richly illustrated with models.[4] Henry Bradshaw, Robert Proctor and Konrad Haebler[5] share the credit for having successfully carried out, through exact research into types, the new working methods, and for having put our research into incunabula on a more secure foundation. Constituting the conclusion of all these efforts is the *Gesamtkatalog der Wiegendrucke* (GKW) ("Whole Catalog of Incunabula") which has been published since 1925, and which lists in alphabetical order all the printed works that have appeared in Europe up to the year 1500, and seeks to determine precisely the locale and the time of their publication. The work that has now grown to the heading, "Federicis," will some day be one of the most significant monuments of German scholarship and it will fulfill a glorious duty that the German people owe to the nation's great son, Gutenberg.[6]

Progress in our information on incunabula has also successfully redowned to the favor of Gutenberg research. Constituting a landmark here was the magnificent Gutenberg festival at Mainz in 1900, which was simultaneously the foundation year of the Gutenberg Museum at Mainz, which set itself the task "to gather, to sort out, to work through, to exhibit, and to make known in the widest circles through scholarly publications everything that bears witness to Gutenberg's discovery, but also everything that concerns the history of the whole art of printing in all the civilized countries on earth."[7] Backing up the Gutenberg Museum was the Gutenberg Society, which has the double task of fostering the Gutenberg Museum and at the same time of being a center for research into the history of printing.[8] The Gutenberg Museum in Bern has also been founded in the same year of 1900; it would likewise represent in its collections the development of printing, with special regard being paid to the art of printing in Switzerland.[9] Thus two important centers of the history of the book have been created here. Falling in line with it, and having similar goals, was the "German Museum for Book and Script" (Deutsches Buchmuseum) in Leipzig, which, supported by the "German Association for the Book and Script" and enriched out of the holdings of the "International Exhibit for the Book Trade and Graphics in Leipzig, 1914," would advance the entire book trade and the history of which it would explore in publications; it was heavily hit, however, in the last war. The book also found here effective attention.[10] The book trade side of the world of books was elucidated with full devotion, and according to the most varied aspects, in the Archiv für Buchgewerbe und Gebrauchsgraphik ("Archive for the Book Trade and the Graphic Art"), which was issued by the German Association of the Book Trade.

While scholarly bibliography has pursued the aim of making accessible the literature concerning a certain subject area, about a personality, or concerning historical developments, the book trade had striven to make known the new publications of the day. In their chief purpose matters of business advertisement, these listings are at the same time valuable—yes, indispensable—sources for acquaintance with current literature, and therefore they are important literature lists. The large older surveys of Heinsius, Kayser, Hinrichs (to which should be added the subject catalog of Karl Georg and Leopold Ost) have succeeded so effectively that they belong among the most important bibliographical reference works of modern times. Still more significant became the transformation of these projects (which to an extent stood in sharp competition with one another) into the *Deutsche Nationalbibliographie* ("German National Bibliography"), which was taken over by the Association of German Bookdealers and published in Leipzig by the German Library. Its value rests primarily in the reliable completeness of the German literature included, which according to the statutory stipulations of the Association is deposited by the publishers immediately at the German Library in Leipzig and is there directly recorded by subject in daily and weekly listings.

The strong demand for books will again and again also call the comprehensive surveys that are concerned with especially valuable publications. For the belles-lettres, the histories of literature[11] and the literary journals fulfill this function. For the rest of the popular literature, there are reviews in journals and newspapers, or the surveys of the best publications of the year, to draw on. The divisions of the book world are too extensive, and the desires of the readers too varied, for us to be able to set up lists of the most significant books as unconditionally reliable guides (as this tends to happen, especially in Britain and America). All such attempts will always be time-bound and therefore already insufficient.[12]

42

The Book and the Art of Reproduction

It can certainly not be sufficiently emphasized how valuable is the illustration, as an assisting, exhibiting medium, to the effectiveness of the book. If one cannot well imagine the manuscript without miniature paintings, one can especially not think of the old printed work without woodcut and copper engraving. The photograph and the art of reproduction that depends on it have altogether made possible an enrichment of the book which has evoked a total revolution in the history of literature. The illustration has become the book's indispensable accompaniment. Especially there, where the illustrative representation of an object surpasses in clarity the best verbal description—there, primarily in aethetics and archeology, in the geography of countries and regions, in anthropology, zoology, botany, mineralogy, and medicine, there has been an inseparable connection between the book and the illustration, and by sensory perception it supplements the word in the most fortunate manner. As with printing, technology has thus once again come to the effective assistance of the book. But photography and the art of reproduction still have a further great significance for the world of books.

The attempt has already early been made to render whole manuscripts (or individual parts of them) into multiple copies so as to obtain the significant literary monuments independent of the priceless original, and to make them accessible to scholarship. Among the first attempts were the reproducing of individual pages from the prayerbook of Charles the Bold (which was printed in 1583)[1] and the Echternach *Martyrologium Hieronymianum*, which Heribert Rosweyda (one of the first collaborators in the *Acta Sanctorum)* has published at Antwerp in 1626. Signifying the most important landmark in these endeavors were the large undertakings of the Frenchman, Count Auguste Bastard d'Estang (d. 1883), who set himself the life-long task of reproducing in colorful copies the scripts, illustrations, and decorations of the most significant literary monuments. The expensive work,[2] which was begun in 1833, has—with its twenty parts and two hundred twenty plates according to the Paris and Strasbourg manuscripts—remained uncompleted, and it is now a rarity of the first order.[3] Since the Strasbourg manuscripts were destroyed by fire in 1870, the reproduction of numerous illustrated pages from them have at least been preserved.

Then in 1840, Friedrich Ritschl considered publishing textually important Greek and Roman manuscripts in facsimile reproduction; but the ambitious plans came to naught. Among the first complete reproductions of manuscripts is the famous St. Gall Antiphony of S. Gregorius, which was published in 1851, by Neumann[4] and was written under Pope Hadrian for the Emperor Charlemagne, and which is one of the oldest monuments of Latin Church song; and further, the Utrecht Psalter of the British Museum; published in 1875, it comes from the second quarter of the ninth century; it was written in the monastery of Hautvillers in Northern France and was decorated with valuable pen drawings from the Rheims school.[5] Meanwhile, Edward Auguste Bond, the distinguished head of the manuscript department of the British Museum in London, founded the Paleological Society (1873–1894), with the aim of providing facsimile copies from the most varied manuscripts. Until 1894, four hundred fifty-five specimens of script have appeared.[6] In other ways, Leyden took up the competition in 1896 with London; the Leyden librarian, Du Rieu, got together with the publishing house of Sijthoff, in order gradually to offer to scholarship under the title, *Codices Graeci et Latini* the most important old manuscripts of the entire world in reliable facsimile. When Du Rieu died a short time thereafter, his successor, De Vries, took over the project. The initial volume brought the famous Leyden Greek Bible manuscript of the fifth century (from Sarrau), with individual illustrations from Paris and St. Petersburg fragments. There followed the Iro-Scottish Berne collective volume, Codex 363, with its valuable Horace and Ovid texts.

Now there lined up, as it were, gift on gift, into a unique succession of priceless texts and literary monuments, as in such fullness they have hardly ever been united into one single collection: the famous Oxford Plato manuscript from the library of Arethas of Caeserea; the Heidelberg Plautus Codex, which at one time was carried off to Rome, and given back by way of Paris; the standard Tacitus-copy of the Laurentiana in Florence; the illustrated Terence manuscript of the Ambrosiana in Milan, with numerous specimen illustrations from other manuscripts, and at the same time, valuable source works for the history of ancient and medieval book decoration;[7] the *Iliad* manuscript from Venice; the textually significant copy of Aristophanes from Ravenna; the unique Vienna Dioscurides manuscript, which was dedicated about 512 to the Byzantine emperor's daughter, Juliana Anicia; the transmission of Livy of the fifth century, which came from the Lorsch monastery, and which was used in 1531 by Grynäus and which is likewise kept in Vienna; the Leyden Latin *Aesop*, which is rich in illustrations, and which was from the possesions of the archeologist, Isaac Vortius, and which had been united with other parts in the eleventh century by the presbyter, Ademar, in the monastery of St. Martial near Limoges, to make an important collective manuscript; the Heidelberg manuscript of the Greek anthology, which with its first volumes, like the incomplete Plautus, has returned to Paris; the fateful Propertius manuscripts, which was acquired in 1710, for Wolfenbüttel, with the library of Marquard Gude, on commission from the philosopher, Leibniz; along with it were valuable bearers of the tradition for Lucretius, Isodorus, Tibullus and Cicero. The Leyden collection thus represents the entire library of valuable literary monuments.[8]

That was the great advance in the new art of reproduction, that by means of photography, reproductions faithful to the original could be produced directly. Numerous further reproductions of manuscripts of individual collections followed the Leyden project. Thus in 1899 the Vaticana inaugurated a lengthy series of reproductions, in which (among others) the two famous Vergil manuscripts, and then the *Pontificale Ottobonianum*, the Joshua Roll, the Canzoniere manuscript of Petrarch, the Fronto pamlipsest, and *Menologium* of Basilius, have been published.[9] And thus the Bibliothèque Nationale in Paris, which has already published its valuable Demosthenes manuscript in 1892,[10] made accessible after 1901 a large number of its miniature manuscripts,[11] the Vienna National Library made accessible its wonderful Greek *Genesis*[12] and the *Seelengärtlein* ("Little Garden of the Soul"),[13] the Laurentiana in Florence did the same with its inestimable *Pandects* manuscript,[14] the Escorial Library the chess board book of King Alphonse from the year 1283,[15] the Ambrosiana at Milan made accessible its *Iliad* fragment decorated with illustrations,[16] as well as the oversized volume of Leonardo da Vinci,[17] the Bodleian at Oxford made accessible its precious uncial manuscript of the Eusebian Chronicle of St. Jerome,[18] the Munich State Library its most valuable illuminated manuscripts, among which were the famous *Codex aureus* from St. Emmeram in Regensburg, the French Boccaccio, and the Babylonian Talmud[19]; the Heidelberg University Library made accessible its unique *Manesse* songs manuscript,[20] the Stuttgart Territorial Library the songs manuscript from Weingarten[21], the Public Library in Dresden the Greek manuscripts of the thirteen letters of Paul, written in the ninth century in St. Gall[22]; and the University of Uppsala the luxury manuscript of the Gothic Bible.[23] A special society was formed in Paris in 1911, for the publication of reproductions of valuable illuminated manuscripts (Société française de reproductions de manuscrits à peintures).

The first publication was the Bible Moralisée from the thirteenth century; it was designed with many small round illustrations, and is now kept in Paris, Oxford and London.[24] The chief value of these expensive projects lies in the guarantee that their texts, all unique monuments of irreplaceable value, are saved forever from destruction through reproduction, and they are useful for research throughout the entire world, without the works themselves being endangered. For that is indeed a special concern of these libraries—that their treasures be not merely made accessible, but that they also are protected from destruction or decomposition. It is to the merit of the scholarly director of the Vaticana and outstanding librarian, Franz Ehrle,[25] that in 1898, there came about in St. Gall an international assembly of experts for consultation concerning the best ways of preserving and restoring the endangered manuscripts. It was then established[26] that all manuscripts from the first six centuries, and thus especially the *Codex Alexandrinus* (the oldest Bible manuscript of the British Museum),[27] the Plautus manuscript of the Ambrosiana, the *Codex Marchallianus* (the second oldest manuscript of the Vaticana), the transmission of the *Pandects* of the Laurentiana, are as a result of their fine parchment and the special quality of the ink, exposed to certain deterioration and require the most careful handling.

Not any less endangered, after the experiences gained, are all the palimpsests in Verona, Milan, Rome, and Paris, which their first discoverers in every case have treated with sharp acids in order to freshen the original text. Here photography everywhere performs inestimable service. More and more, the dark room becomes indispensable in all large book collections,[28] and the provision of as many photographs as possible out of one's own holdings and out of foreign holdings becomes an imperative requirement for researching manuscripts as well as for bibliography.

The perfecting of color photography printing today permits an almost totally corresponding copy of the text.[29] The art of color reproduction has offered handsome evidence of its productive power in the splendid reproduction of the magnificent *Breviariaum Grimani* (1904), with its 1,568 pages decorated with pictures and ornaments; it was based in the priceless original owned by the Marciana in Venice.[30] That the Viennese *Seelegärtlein* ("Little Garden of the Soul"), a Dutch artistic creation[31] dedicated to the Archduchess Margareta of Austria (the sister of Emperor Maximilian I), and the famous Munich prayerbook of Kaiser Maximilian I, with its fine pen drawings by Albrecht Dürer, are now available, is an inestimable gain for our knowledge of the final flowering of the artistic miniature painting and sixteenth century book design. All these reproductions of entire manuscripts, or of parts of them, and added thereto, the numerous reproductions of scriptural specimens,[32] ornaments and illustrations, already comprise an enormous library[33] with large volumes, which even by itself would be capable of effectively affording an approximate picture of the nature of the medieval book, and of the research into manuscripts with illustrations, recollections, connections and comparisons. That such unique and expensive works (the reproduction of the Vienna *Genesis* cost 1100 marks, and the *Manesse* songs manuscript cost 3000) could come about, is due not only to the highly developed book trade, but also to the enterprising inclinations of the large publishers, and the sales possible to the large libraries.

It was to be expected that the art of reproduction would also take on rare and memorable printed works which, due to their scholarly meaning, or their significance in the history of art, are in sufficient demand that a further dissemination in faithful reproduction appears to be desirable.[34] Baron von Aretin was already in 1808 having the *Mahnung der Christenheit wider den Tüken* ("Urging of Christendom against the Turks") (which was preserved in only one copy in the Bavarian State Library) reproduced with the help of lithography, which had been discovered shortly before then. Many further valuable reproductions of printed works have appeared since then, such as Boner's *Edelstein*, Ulrich von Richental's *Concilium* book, the 42-line Bible, Hartmann Schedel's *World Chronicle*, Lirer's *Swabian Chronicle*, Johann von Ketham's *Fasciculus medicinae*, Hieronymus Brunswig's *Chirurgia* ("Surgery"), several of Caxton's printed works, the Columbus letter, Luther's Bible translation of 1534, a folio edition of Shakespeare, and numerous other monuments of printing from later centuries. In time, all the rarities that are in some way significant will exist in reproductions.

Through the art of reproduction, the original shape of a valuable cultural work is promised immortality as well as the widest possible dissemination. The book's will to recognition has here again achieved a handsome success.

43

Book Exhibitions

The book is like the human being, its creator, in that it has no individual being for itself; rather does each belong much more to a certain circle; each one has its forerunners, relatives, successors, and each operates in community. Goethe's *Faust* belongs to the poet's creation as a whole; it belongs to Classicism and Romanticism, and belongs to the production series of the *Faust* material. And so does the individual work live for the most part within the larger world of books — a phenomenon that, from the aspect of the history of culture, lends to the consideration of literature its quite special charm. Nowhere does this come to the surface more evidently than in book exhibitions, in which books that in some way belong together is visibly presented, and affords insights (as some large picture book might) which, by itself, are for the most part not accessible to pure thought.

Bibliophiles have always recognized and exploited the attractive power of the show pieces among their possessions. The ability to exhibit special priceless items has always been the pride of monasteries, of courts, and of cities. Luxurious rooms of the seventeenth and eighteenth centuries have mostly served simultaneously as exhibition rooms in which "book gems" (to which other things worth seeing were added) were shown to the visitor. From the economic perspective, the store or the show-window of the bookseller (and also the antiquarian bookseller) early sought to show the book to good advantage. To be seen in these offerings of specially handsome, priceless, rare pieces or advertising of modern publications are the beginnings of the public book exhibitions.

There is now a considerably wider circle that seeks through exhibitions to make the world of books visibly accessible. In the foremost ranks stand the public research libraries[1] which, with their large holdings, are book museums — that is to say, they are collecting the stations of the shaping of literature by the book trade and can additionally claim as theirs unique book gems, priceless manuscripts, rare early printed works, woodcut books, and book monuments from famous property holdings or that possess remarkable entries. Robert Naumann in Leipzig was the first librarian who recognized in such activity an important task for libraries and collections and called this to the public's attention.[2] From the double aspect of the history of culture and of the book trade, it is a fine task and obligation of libraries to show their treasures to the outside world and thereby announce that they have to operate and assemble materials not merely for the scholarly world, but that they are a proud national cultural possession, in which the entire people ought to participate. In exhibiting their possessions the libraries meanwhile have the best possibility of bringing their own significance to bear. Here the book—one backed up to the other—receives an enormously increased efficacy, and becomes a public and popular concern in the best sense of the word.

It is well justified if a library primarily sets before the public—either permanently, or from time to time—its most valuable holdings, or its unique possessions. When in 1905, at the hundredth anniversary of Friedrich Schiller's death, the Munich State Library instituted a memorial exhibition, it joined with it a large exhibit concerning its rich holdings in linguistic and literary monuments from the *Muspilli* manuscript and the *Wessobrunner Gebet* ("Wessobrunn Prayer") on up into the most recent period. A composition (in his own hand) of Schiller's with verses from the poet's *Zerstörung von Troja* ("Destruction of Troy") was followed by pictures, works, translations and musical settings. Valuable mementos out of a gift by Schiller's daughter, the Baroness Emilie von Gleichen-Russwurm, with letters of Schiller that he had written with his own hand (among them being significant writings to Körner from September 12, 1788, about the initial encounter with Goethe) lent the exhibit—with its meaningful uniting of letter and book—an enticingly personal tone.[3] The Territorial Library at Weimar (the hall of fame of the great Weimar period) has an especially high mission to fulfill; the library is richly decorated with sculptures and busts from the period of German Classicism. That the library in Wolfenbüttel has its own Lessing Room with a permanent exhibit of illustrations, letters, manuscripts, and first editions of the great poet, is thoroughly in order as a distinguished form of ancestor glorification. In the same sense the Biblioteca Nazionale Braidense at Milan has devoted to the poet, Allessandro Manzoni, a room decorated with a bust of the poet presented by King Humbert. One could only wish that many such memorial places would spring up—just as there are, in a similar way, special collections: possibly the Luther Hall in Wittenberg or the Melanchthon House in Bretten, which are dedicated to the memory of the two reformers.

Belonging among the most popular and the most effective exhibitions of book collections will always be the book shows that are devoted to book design. The consequences that have come, for example, from the exhibitions of the miniature manuscripts in Vienna (1901),[4] Bamberg (1907),[5] London (1908)[6] and Munich (1909 and 1950)[7] have endured far beyond their day, and they have become valuable stimulations of discussion about art. The investigations into printing in the exhibitions of 1840, 1900 and 1940, have likewise given valuable insights into the development of printing. Exhibitions of handsome bindings have, on account of their stress on the artistic aspects, enjoyed a special power to attract. The Gutenberg Museum at Mainz, the German Museum for Book and Script at Leipzig, and the Gutenberg Museum at Bern devote to the book permanent demonstrations of its external development. The city of Antwerp possesses in its Plantin-Moretus Museum a quite unique collection of typographical monuments and documents, which in rich mementos demonstrates the work during three centures of the famous printing house.[9]

That the libraries participated in scholarly conferences[10] and in memorial celebrations of great men by displaying their treasures from the knowledge areas appertaining, has generally introduced a further opportunity for these institutions to bring their holdings publicly to bear, and this deserves to be considered a permanent responsibility. Walther von der Vogelweide, Columbus, Luther, Zwingli, Hans Sachs, Orlando di Lasso, Galileo, Racine, Leibniz, Klopstock, Lessing, Goethe, Schiller, Beethoven, Karl Maria von Weber, and Richard Wagner—all of them, and numerous other cultural leaders, have already had their days of honor in the libraries, and they have had thereby an effect on the widest circles. In a similarly significant manner, Königsberg has, in 1894, celebrated the 350th year festival of the university there with the showing of the silver library of Duke Albrecht of Prussia. Lübeck has displayed a Lübeck-Nordic exhibition for Nordic Week in September 1921, Breslau has in February 1929, for the Silesian Cultural Week, shown "Seven Hundred Years of Silesian Literature," and Augsburg has displayed a Reformation exhibit in 1930, at the Four Hundredth Annual Memorial to the Augsburg Imperial Diet of 1530.

For demonstrating political or cultural connections, the book world of the large public collections is inexhaustible. The variety of such insights may be characterized through a selective survey of the hitherto most important exhbitions in the two great libraries in Berlin and Munich. Berlin has shown: in 1916, bookbindings; in 1917, Luther; in 1921 Beethoven, Romanticism; in 1922, E.T.A. Hoffmann, the history of musical literature and printing; in 1923, Oriental manuscripts and printing; Evangelical hymnbooks in 1924, as well as Hoffman von Fallersleben, Kant, the nature of the books and libraries of the Mark Brandenburg, and Lower German literature; in 1925, Hans Christian Andersen; in 1827, Johann Sebastian Bach, German script; in 1928, Beethoven, Heinrich von Kleist; in 1929, Berlin printing, Schubert, Lessing, F.K. von Savigny; in 1930, Walter von der Vogelweide; in 1931, Napoleon's library; in 1932, Goethe and Music; in 1933, Heinrich Schütz, Luther; beautiful manuscripts in 1934; 1935, two hundred years of German music, Victor Hugo, Bach-Händel-Schütz; in 1936, German physical training in book and picture; in 1937, sports in the Middle Ages, Karl Maria von Weber, the German folk song, Brahms, Sweden—its land and people in books; in 1938, five hundred years of German gardens, Schumann and Wagner; in 1939, the "Farmers of the Empire," Portugal; and finally, German printing and German history in 1940.

To be listed for Munich are: in 1894, Orlando di Lasso with Hans Mülich's illumination of the penitential psalms in its center, and Hans Sachs; in 1899, medical manuscripts and autographs; Gutenberg in 1900, Schiller in 1903, a history of miniature painting in 1909, manuscripts from the Islamic cultural circle in 1910; in 1911, the Wittelsbachs; in 1924, Oriental manuscripts, and manuscripts of astronomy and astrology; Franz Pocci in 1927; the history of German script in 1928; in 1929, manuscripts for the history of bibliography; 1930, the art of the book in the Bavarian manuscripts of the Middle Ages; in 1931, the Munich book from the Middle Ages to the present, and the self-promotion of the journal; in 1933, the Germans in Russia, Papyrus, and Joseph Ponten; in 1936, German woman-German book, and physical training and sports in literature; in 1937, Max Reger, chess, and books on plants; in 1938, German book illumination, and the Italian press; in 1939, German book illumination of the Middle Ages, Spain in books and pictures, handsome bookbindings, the insect in pictorial representation, and the French press past and present; in 1940, monuments from the first century of the art of printing; and in 1941, the German Alsace. Besides Berlin and Munich, numerous other libraries have also prepared exhibitions in connection with most varied occasions.

Even the book trade agency and the German trade association have in recent times taken up the book exhibition in stronger measure. Thus the foreign department of the association has repeatedly arranged book shows: in Florence,[11] in Barcelona, and Stockholm. The book received an especially effective inauguration in 1914 at the International Exhibition for the Book Trade and Graphics at Leipzig, which was supposed to give an account of what the book world has meant as the bearer of culture and as a cultural force binding the peoples together. It was by a terrible fate that shortly after the brilliant opening of the exhibition, the World War nullified all the expectations from the strenuously organized undertaking.[12] "Goethe in the Book Art of the World" was the object of an impressive show that the Association of German Book Artists demonstrated to the public in Leipzig in the Goethe year of 1932.

44
Bibliography and Book Collecting

There is scarcely anyone who does not own books and keep them as faithful friends. Still, this relationship to the book that we daily encounter does not belong to those activities of bibliophily and of book collecting which, due to their influence on cultural life, have such significance for the history of culture.[1] There can indeed be a limited individual possession of great consequence, if it be in the care of a significant personality that, in its development, is furthered by it now and then. It is thus certainly not an indifferent matter which books a Lessing, a Goethe, a Schiller, Herder or Wieland have owned and read; proven to have formerly been their properties, these works then have to assume a value for us.[2] The actual bibliophiles who collect within a larger compass comply for the most part with two essential presuppositions: an enduring, inspired, and self-sacrificing love for the book which extends beyond the concerns of the day, and thus a deliberate methodicalness in the collecting of certain books, or groups of books.

Persons who embrace their treasures in this way acquire books because they see their charges as being indispensable assistants in elevating life, or they have a special liking for the external appearance of books, and possibly for certain specialties in the world of books. A scholar, for example, acquires the publications of his discipline within the widest range, and in such a way assembles a valuable specialized library. Books are thus examined and collected as notable cultural creations, possibly the works and the editions of Dante, Cervantes, Luther, Shakespeare, and Goethe, as well as all the works about them. Or the varied representations of certain objects serve as stimuli to collect entire groups of books, such as costume books, works on plants, architectural books, the classics, songbooks, books on the *Totentanz* ("Dance of Death"), robinsonades, or cookbooks. No less enticing is the book's external form.

The book productions of the Gothic period, the Renaissance, the Baroque, and of Romanticism—all of these have their special friends; and in no less degree the famous workshops do also, as for example those of Aldus, Giunta, Estienne, Elzevir, Baskerville, Didot, Bodoni, or those that come from the hand presses of modern times. Added to that are the rare and remarkable books, the incunabula, parchment printings,[4] woodcut books, engraved works, censured works, productions from monastery and castle printeries, and works that have come from well-known properties or estates, and that contain remarkable entries or that possess priceless bindings. Even rarities such as books on silk, or those of the smallest size, can arouse an interest in collecting.[5] At the Paris World Exhibition of 1900, there was exhibited a "Liliput Library," with 1500 books (mostly Dutch) in a case that was 50 cm. high and 30 cm. wide.[6]

Mention has already been made repeatedly in these pages of the valuable individual possessions of the earlier period. Several names may now be advanced also for the more recent period. As we have already mentioned, the decades following the French Revolution and the great monastery confiscations have been particularly favorable for the activity of collecting. The books could literally be picked up on the street and acquired by enthusiastic collectors, so as ultimately to find their way into public libraries, or to disappear in the book market. Love for the monuments of the past, intensified by Romanticism, has contributed much to the saving of these treasures.

It is entirely from this mind set, i.e. from the love and passion for the German past, that the enthusiastic collector and prominent connoisseur of Fischart's works, Karl Harting Gregor, Baron von Meusebach, has come (1781–1847). Through the wise limiting of himself to the German literature of the sixteenth, seventeenth and eighteenth centuries, and chiefly to the spiritual and secular songs, collections of proverbs, newspapers, astrologies, controversial writings, joke books, the pamphlets, and all the small printings "which may be called the stuffing of literature," Meusebach has gained immortal merit for himself for saving valuable German literary works. When the baron died, the collection was threatened with dispersal, although maintaining it found warm advocates. On September 5, 1847, Bettina von Arnim, the sister of the poet, Clemens Brentano, warmly interceded in a letter to the King of Prussia for the maintenance of the collection. And Ludwig Uhland wrote to Moritz Haupt on February 10, 1850: "May a favorable star still rule over the Meusebach legacy, so that a collection may not thus become the victim of a calamity or deplorably be destroyed, one that so properly belongs to the most characteristic life of the German people and which, once thrown away, would not be retrievable any more." Finally, on November 5, 1850, the collection (which numbered about 25,000 items, among where were 3,500 issues of Luther's publications) was acquired by King Friedrich Wilhelm IV for 40,700 thalers and incorporated into the Berlin State Library.[7]

As Meusebach did in northern Germany, so did Joseph, Baron von Lassberg (1770–1855), constitute an effective focal point of the Romantic love for German antiquities in the South. The two brothers Grimm, Lachmann, Schmeller, Uhland, and Franz Pfeiffer exchanged letters with him, or they visited him, in order to sustain their enthusiasm for the German past through him and his collection. On February 21, 1838, he acquired the legendary castle of Meersburg on Lake Constance and here in an atmospheric environment he lived with his old paintings, documents and priceless monuments of German poetry. The baron's sister-in-law, our great German poetess, Annette von Droste-Hülshoff, frequently despaired when the old men sat at the table for long hours and spoke of nothing else but their old books, concerning which the poetess thought that it was sometimes as if she were wandering between dry bean husks and was hearing nothing around her other than a dry rattling and crackling. At the end of his days, the baron knew the joy of being able to put into caring hands the handsome collection, with its 12,000 printed volumes and 273 manuscripts, among which were the famous *Nibelungen* manuscript C, which was acquired in 1815 in Vienna and which had been used at one time by Bodmer at the Hohenems Castle, a parchment manuscript of the twelfth century, and the two oldest manuscripts of the *Schwabenspiegel*, as Prince Karl Egon II of Fürstenberg (1796–1854) acquired them for 27,000 florins. So long as the collector was still living, the treasures remained at Meersburg; after his death (March 15, 1855), they were moved to Donaueschingen and here found in Joseph Victor Scheffel their appreciative organizer.[8]

The individual book collection is considerably increased in value, if in such ways it serves higher goals. The publisher-bookseller, Franz, Baron von Lipperheide, brought together the most important literature on the historical study of costumes; bewteen 1896–1905, he published a valuable catalog about it and he bequeathed the entire contents of his collection to the Prussian state. The possession was incorporated within the State Art Library in Berlin. The Hungarian, Alexander, Count Apponyi (1843–1925), aimed at acquiring all literature concerning Hungary that was published in foreign countries; he published an introductory catalog of the holdings and finally presented the collection to the Hungarian National museum in Budapest.[9] The collection of manuscripts has especially remarkable results to exhibit. Sir Thomas Coke, Earl of Leicester (d. 1759), obtained in his travels priceless manuscripts, among them being the Greek manuscripts collection of Giustiani in Venice, which he acquired in 1721. Richly increased by Thomas William Coke, the library set up in Holkham has become one of the largest collections of books in private possession that is for public use.[10]

America is particularly rich in collections of benefit to the public; several great libraries there that are open to the public go back to large gifts. Thus Henry Edward Huntington (1850–1927) assembled 5,400 incunabula, 20,000 first English editions and 55,000 Americana, and he bequeathed the entire valuable collection to the State of California and therewith founded the library in San Marino which is named for him.[11]

The book as an object for collecting lives by quite other laws than does the book intended to be used. Above all, the economic value changes according to demand and supply. Added to that are the factors of fashion and accidents in the classification of the collector. The best sources for acquaintance with the values and with the market are the antiquarian booksellers' catalogs, to which are added the auction lists and the advertisement lists, which, if they be carefully prepared, represent at the same time valuable aids to bibliography and have already brought to light many a priceless item.[12]

Book collecting, which in its development is an exciting phenomenon in the history of culture, always has countless curiosities to exhibit, ones which faithfully reflect the book world's mighty power to attract, and at the same time contribute to the general intelligibility of mankind's irresistible love for collecting. When at the auction of the book collection of John Ker, Duke of Roxburghe, in May and June of 1812, Christopher Valdarfer's rare edition of Boccaccio's *Decameron* from 1471, passed to the Marquis of Blandford following a stubborn struggle with Lord

Spencer for the unprecedented price of around 45,000 Marks, the chief participants were so inspired by the course of this auction that on June 17, 1812, they founded the Roxburghe Club, which set itself the task of publishing reproductions of manuscripts and/or rare printed works. It was the first bibliophilic association. England has also henceforward remained the leading country of the large book auctions.

Thus coming under the hammer in December 1884 were the valuable holdings of Sir John Hayford, among which were the Gutenberg Bible for about 78,000 Marks, the Mainz Psalter of 1459, for 99,000 Marks, and the Mainz Bible of 1462 on parchment and having on its cover the arms of Prince Eugene of Savoy, for 20,000 Marks. There followed in 1889 the rest of the famous Alexander Hamilton collection, out of which the most important item, the Gospels manuscript presented by King Herny VIII to Pope Leo X, had previously in a roundabout way already come to the generous collector of books, John Pierpont Morgan, so as to increase his rich collection of books by one further piece. One of the most significant German auctions was the sale of the Leipzig collection of Theodore Oswald Weigel in May of 1872; the richly illustrated work, *Die Anfänge der Druckerkunst* ("The Beginnings of the Art of Printing") by T.O. Weigen and A. Zestermann (1866) is based on it. From this collection, the British Museum acquired several woodcut works, such as *Ars moriendi* for 7150 thalers, an *Apocalypse* for 3110 thalers, a *Salve Regina* for 1605 thalers, and two *Biblia pauperum* for 2360 and 2001 thalers, respectively.

Seldom has an individual possession caused so much comment as did the voluminous library of the Englishman, Sir Thomas Phillipps (1792–1872) in Cheltenham – perhaps the largest manuscript collection that a mortal has ever possessed. Like many libraries of that period the handsome possession went for the most part back to the unclaimed properties in books on the Continent in the Napoleonic period, and especially back to accquisitions from the collections of the former Dominican and later Marburg professor, Leander van Ess (1863), with its three hundred valuable manuscripts from Rhenish monasteries such as Camp, Coesfeld, Marienmünster, Jakobsberg near Mainz, and the Carthusian house of St. Barbara in Cologne. The most precious item that Philipps, a wealthy eccentric, acquired in that period so rich in books, were the eleven hundred manuscripts of the Paris Jesuit monastery; these were bought in 1824 from the estate of the Dutchman, Johann Meermann, for 131,000 Dutch gulden, the monastery having been dissolved in 1764. What was hospitably displayed to visitors (among whom were Pertz and Ranke) in Middlehill (Worcestershire) and later in Cheltenham, was a collection the likes of which in size and significance could scarcely be found anywhere else in the entire world. When in 1886 the heirs began to auction off the handsome possession, the entire world participated in the event. Decades passed over the individual auctioning off of over seven thousand manuscripts and bibliophiles were kept permanently in suspense. The patrons of scholarship made possible in 1887 the acquisition by the Prussian State of 620 manuscripts (for 285,359 Marks) for the Berlin State Library. The pricelss items (individual items of which extended back into the Merovingian times) stemmed almost all of them out of the Paris monasteries and have for the most part earlier belonged to French and Lorrainese monasteries. Thirty-three monuments alone have come from St. Vincent's in Metz. The Berlin Library was able to acquire another eighty-four manuscripts in 1912.[13]

A further great event for books was the London auction of the collection of A.L. Huth in November 1911. The highest prices in connection therewith were 116,000 Marks for the Gutenberg Bible, 61,000 for the Mainz Bible of 1462, 10,400 Marks for the Strasbourg Eggestein Bible, 24,000 for the woodcut printing of the Apocalypse, and 30,000 Marks for an *Ars moriendi*.

The history of the book also has something to tell us about the opposite side of bibliography, about the passion for the book which is associated with avarice, and which does not shrink from grabbing property even when it involves misdemeanor and crime. The sale of the valuable English book collection of Lord Bertram of Ashburnham (1797–1878) brought out into the open an unprecedentedly enormous robbery; the collection consisted of three large parts, which were the Stowe collection that came from the Buckingham auction, the Libri collection (with its 1923 manuscripts) that was acquired in 1847, and the Barrois holdings purchased in 1848.[14] It was no less a personage than Leopold Delisle who, following ceaseless and laborious manuscript researches, could prove that the greatest part of the manuscripts carried off by Guglielmo Libri Caruccii (among which were priceless items from the Merovingian and Carolingian periods) stemmed from ancient centers of culture in France and had been stolen from the public libraries of Orléans, Lyons, Tours, Troyes, Grenoble, and Montpellier. Libri had had access to them as the secretary of the commission for the production of a union catalog of the manuscripts in the public libraries of France. With the return of twenty-three manuscripts from Tours in 1888 (as has already been mentioned), the German imperial goverment was able to acquire, by way of exchange, the *Mannesse* Songs manuscript. Delisle then also demonstrated about the collection of the French deputy, Joseph Barrois, that a large number of manuscripts, most of them medieval French poetry, had been stolen from the Bibliothèque Nationale in Paris. The two collectors had therefore stolen two hundred manuscripts from the libraries and archives of France.

With our brief sketches already several of the most expensive books (apart from the priceless manuscripts that seldom come on the market) have been mentioned: the Gutenberg Bible, which ultimately cost around one and a half million marks in a parchment copy from St. Paul in Carinthia as yet the costliest book in the world and then the *Psalterium* of 1457, at 200,000 Marks, and the Mainz *Catholicon* of 1460, at 45,000 Marks. Among the later printed works of the fifteenth century, the handsome woodcut books are the highest (in cost). We read for the Veronese Valturius editoin of 1472, 7000 Marks, and for the Ulm Boccaccio of 1473, with its eighty woodcuts, 6000 Marks. Paid for very highly are the quite rare printed works of Caxton, the oldest English printer: his *Royal Book* was auctioned in 1902 by Sotheby in London for about 45,000 Marks. Among the printed works of the sixteenth century, the *Theuerdank* (as one of the books most sought after) brought about four thousand marks; if printed on parchment and artistically illustrated, the price was raised. Everything that is connected with the discovery of America or with the oldest ship travels on the seas is sought after, and is expensive. England pays the highest prices for Shakespeare, as it does also for Caxton. Shakespeare's folio edition of 1623 has been sold in 1899, for 11,700 Marks, and the work *Passionate Pilgrime* of 1612, for 43,000 Marks in 1901. Very honored and paid for dearly are the French illustrated books of the eighteenth century—especially if they exhibit good copper plates, or are furnished with handsome bindings. The *Fables* of La Fontaine, from 1755–59, were valued at five thousand Marks, the Ovid edition 1667–70, at three thousand Marks, and Montesquieu's publication, *Le temple de Gnide* of 1772, at 4500 Marks. Beautiful bindings are very much sought after and are paid for dearly. The chief questions for determining the economic value relate to the book as a product of its culture, as a monument of antiquity, as a work of beautiful printing or art, as a memorial of a famous author or of a previous owner, or as in some other way being a curiosity. Precisely the rarity, or certainly the uniqueness, of a book exercises on many bibliophiles an irresistible attraction.

Bibliophiles have sometimes joined together in union so as in community to dedicate themselves to the care of books, to exchange books, to publish rarities, or to publish journals devoted to the inquiry into the book.[15] Besides, to be sure, much chaff, valuable publications have also issued from these endeavors.

Among the bibliophilic journals, the *Zeitschrift für Bücherfreunde* ("Journal for Bibliophiles"), which was founded in 1897 by Fedor von Zobeltitz, obtained the first place. It has ceased publication, with its fortieth successive year, in 1936.

Bibliophily is of the greatest significance for the book trade. It has a favorable effect on book design through the preference it has for the beautiful book; it is a vital presupposition for the antique booktrade and for the book auction.

Bibliophily has attained its significance fo the history of culture chiefly through the countless valuable collections which it has assembled in the various centuries and has made useful to scholarship. By a fortunate providence, they frequently have gone over into public possession. There are numerous examples of that fact in the previous pages; they could be increased into infinity. Each large public library contains valuable holdings out of such lovingly cared-for possessions and gratefully it remembers its collector.

Postscript

We bid farewell now to this biography of the book world. The story itself has naturally not come to an end with our presentation: it rather proceeds further, as does life as a whole. How will its future be shaped? We don't know. The last terrible decades which lie behind us now and which have not yet been overcome, have severely affected the kingdom of books also. It is up to us, by our increased concern, to contribute to its rebuilding. Its main vitality certainly depends on free flow in the world of ideas, and it cannot be awakened through external means. Thinking and writing, researching and fashioning—these are the business of the spirit, in the enlightened heights of grace, and they are linked by mysterious forces of Fate. They thrive better, however, when they can make their way through the world accompanied by benevolence and love. In our survey we have seen that the flourishing periods of books (which are the chief bearers of intellectual life) have been mostly conditioned somehow by, or effectively furthered through, the patronage of understanding princes, the encouraging assent of public opinion, and through self-sacrificing and enterprising publishing firms and booksellers. External aids can indeed prepare the ground for the thriving growth of cultural life. For these connections, we need only recall the peak periods of the Renaissance, of Classicism and Romanticism. A chief goal of our examination was to underscore the great significance that the world of books has for culture as a whole, and to reinforce the high regard the book enjoys in public opinion. That which is recognized as valuable has a significant effect, and at the same time, it calls for responsibility. The states' *Kulturpolitik* has large assignments here in the sevice of cultural life: we need but mention the support of the scholarly academies, of the learned societies, of the libraries and of the research associations of German science. Today they all require—as they always have—encouragement and support.

In our currently difficult situation of crisis, we require quite extraordinarily high aims, and the success of promising forces, for the healing and the recuperation of our essential nature, threatened as this is. As so often in our history, this especially has to do with the recalling of our unity and our concord. May our book world, which is an incomparable cultural possession, prove itself (as it has over the centuries) to be a binding pledge of our belonging together, and of our intellectual prowess.

We stand at an important turning point of world history and therefore also of our national life. How will our book world present itself as over against the coming new tasks? Perhaps in the future a report will contain in one of its sections the heading: The book in the service of the Western concept of the world, and of the reconciliation of the peoples of Europe.

Notes

Translators' Preface

1. Geldner, Ferdinand. *Festgabe der Bayerischen Staatsbibliothek für Karl Schottenloher*. *Mit either Bibliographie der Veröffentlichungen Karl Schottenlohers von Otto Schottenloher*. Munich, Karl Zink Verlag, 1953.
2. *Ibid.*, p. 5.

Introduction. Outline of a Cultural History

1. Adolf von Harnack, "Über Anmerkungen in Büchern," in his *Aus Wissenschaft und Leben*, vol. 1, Giessen, 1911, p. 148. Compare also his *Reden und Aufsätze*, N.F.4, Giessen, 1923, p. 218. — On the meaning of a cultural history of the book, see also Friedrich Oldenbourg's *Buch und Bildung*, Munich 1928, p. 31.
2. From the general literature on the book these should be mentioned: W. Koehler's *Das Buch im Strom des Verkehrs*, Heidelberg, 1905. — W. Koehler, *Geschichte des literarischen Lebens vom Altertum bis auf die Gegenwart*, 2 vols., Gera, 1906. — *Das Buchgewerbe und die Kultur. Sechs Vorträge*. Leipzig, 1907. — Oskar Weise, *Schrift- und Buchwesen in alter und neuer Zeit*, 3rd ed., Leipzig, 1910. — Richard Pietschmann, "Das Buch" in *Die Kultur der Gegenwart*, I, 1. 2nd ed. Leipzig, 1912, p. 556. — Albert Schramm, *Schreib- und Buchwesen einst und jetzt*. Leipzig, 1922. — Svend Dahl, *Bogens Historie*. Copenhagen, 1927; Authorisierte Übersetzung aus dem Dänischen von Lina Johnsson. Leipzig, 1928; 2d improved ed., Leipzig, 1941. — Hanns Bohatta, *Einführung in die Buchkunde*. Vienna, 1927. — Hugo von Hofmannsthal, *Das Schrifttum als geistiger Raum der Nation*. Munich, 1927. — Frdr. Oldenbourg, *Buch und Bildung*. Munich, 1928. — Josef Nadler, *Buchhandel, Literatur und Nation in Geschichte und Gegenwart*. Berlin, 1932. — Hans Heinrich Bockwitz, *Buchform und Buchfunktion im Wandel der Zeit*. Leipzig, 1933. — *Lexikon des gesamten Buchwesens*. Hrsg. von Karl Löffler und Joachim Kirchner. Unter Mitwirkung von Wilh. Olbrich. Vols. 1–3. Leipzig, 1935–1937. — *Die Welt des Buches; eine Kunde vom Buch*. Hrsg. von Hellmuth Langenbucher. Ebenhausen, 1938; 3rd ed., 1942. — Hans Köster, *Buch und Leben*. Potsdam, 1938. — Wilhelm H. Lange, *Das Buch im Wandel der Zeiten*. Hamburg, 1941; 2d ed., 1942. — H. Hesse, *Magie des Buches*, Olten, 1942. — Ernst Robert Curtius, "Schrift- und Buchmetaphorik in der Weltliteratur," *Deutsche Vierteljahrsschrift für Literaturwissenschaft und Geistesgeschichte*, 20(1942), p. 359. — M. Hausmann, *Von der dreifachen Natur des Buches*. Bielefeld, 1942. — Ermin Stein, *Von der Sendung des Buches*. Frankfurt am Main, 1950. — Richard Mummendey, *Von Büchern und Bibliotheken*. Bonn, 1950. — R. Hoecker and J. Vorstius list the rich literature appearingannually: *Internationale Bibliographie des Buch- und Bibliothekswesens Jahrgang 1- , 1926- . On illustrative presentations of the connection between humankind and the book, see Otto Glauning's "Der Buchbeutel in der bildenden Kunst," Archiv für Buchgewerbe und Buchgraphik, 63(1926), p. 121. — Adolf Heckel, Über ein Buch gebeugt*. Leipzig, 1937. — Kurt Gerstenberg, "Das Bücherstilleben in der Plastik," in *Deutschland-Italien: Festschrift für Wilhelm Waetzoldt*. Berlin, 1941, p. 135. — Compare also the background report by J. Schmidt, "In angello cum libello," *Zeitschrift für Bücherfreunde*, N.F. 15(1923), p. 4.

3. Ernst Schultze, *Die Schundliteratur; ihr Vordringen, ihre Folgen, ihre Bekämpfung.* Halle, 1909. (Is now dated.)

Chapter 1. Books in Antiquity

1. Konrad Bämminger, *Kleine Philosophie des Schrifttums.* Bern, 1940.

2. Theodor Birt, *Das antike Buchwesen in seinem Verhältnis zur Literatur.* Berlin, 1882.—C. Castellani, *Le biblioteche nell'antichità.* Bologna, 1884.—Hugo Landwehr, "Studien über das antike Buchwesen," *Archiv für lateinische Lexikographie und Grammatik,* 6(1889), pp. 219, 419.—C. Haeberlin, "Beiträge zur Kenntnis des antiken Bibliotheks- und Buchwesens," *Zentralblatt für Bibliothekswesen,* 6(1889), p. 480.—Friedrich Blass, "Palaeographie, Buchwesen und Handschriftenkunde," *Handbuch der Klass. Altertumswissenschaft.* vol. 1, 2nd ed. Munich, 1892, p. 297.—K. Dziatzko, "Bibliotheken" in Paulys *Real-Encyclopädie der classischen Altertumswissenschaft,* vol. 3, (1899), col. 405.—Theod. Birt, "Zur Geschichte des antiken Buchwesens," *Zentralblatt für Bibliothekswesen, 17(1900), p. 545.—K. Dziatzko, Untersuchungen über ausgewählte Kapital des antiken Buchwesens.* Leipzig, 1900.—Theod. Birt, *Die Buchrolle in der Kunst; archäologisch-antiquarische Untersuchungen zum antiken Buchwesen.* Leipzig, 1904; 2d ed., 1907.—Ernst Pfuhl, "Zur Darstellung von Buchrollen und Grabreliefs," *Jahrbuch des Deutschen Archäologischen Instituts,* 22(1907), p. 113.—Theod. Birt, "Nachträgliches zur Buchrolle in der Kunst," *Jahrbuch des Deutschen Archäologischen Instituts,* 23(1908), P. 112.—Victor Gardthausen, *Das Buchwesen im Altertum und im byzantinischen Mittelalter,* 2d ed. Leipzig, 1911.—Frederic K. Kenyon, *Books and Readers in ancient Greece and Rome.* Oxford, 1932.—Fritz Milkau, *Geschichte der Bibliotheken im alten Orient.* Leipzig, 1935.—Carl Wendel, "Neues aus alten Bibliotheken," *Zentralblatt für Bibliothekswesen,* 34(1937), p. 585; 35(1938), p. 641.—Heinz Gernoll, "Bibliographie des griechisch-römischen Bibliothekswesens, 1899–1938," *Buch und Schrift,* N.F. 1(1938), p. 96.—Carl Wendel, "Das griechisch-römische Altertum," pp. 1–63 in *Handbuch der Bibliothekswissenschaft,* vol. 3: *Geschichte der Bibliotheken.* Leipzig, 1940.

3. Bruno Meissner, "Wie hat Assurbanipal seine Bibliothek zusammengebracht?," *Aufsätze Fritz Milkau gewidmet.* Leipzig, 1921, p. 244.

4. H.V. Hilprecht, *Die Ausgrabungen der Universität von Pennsylvania im Bel-Tempel zu Nippur.* Leipzig, 1903.

5. Franz Poland, "Öffentliche Bibliotheken in Griechenland und Kleinasien," *Historische Untersuchungen; Ernst Föstemann gewidmet.* Leipzig, 1894, p. 7.

6. Moise Schwab, *Bibliographie d'Aristote.* Paris, 1896.

7. C. Wachsmuth, "Die pinakographische Tätigkeit des Kallimachos," *Philologus,* 16(1860), p. 653.—Augusto Rostagni, "I bilbiotecarii alessandrini nella cronologia della letteratura ellenistica," *Atti della R. Accademia delle Science di Torino,* 50(1914/15), p. 241.—F. Sitzler, "Die alexandrinischen Bibliothekare," *Wochenschrift für klassische Philologie,* 34(1917), col. 1087.—Frdr. Schmidt, *Die Pinakes des Kallimachos.* Berlin, 1922.

8. G. Parthey, *Das alexandrinische Museum.* Berlin, 1838.—Fr. Ritschl, *Die alexandrinischen Bibliotheken.* Opuscula I. Breslau, 1838, p. 1.—V. Gardthausen, "Die alexandrinische Bibliothek," *Zeitschrift des Deutschen Vereins für Buchwesen und Schrifttum,* 5(1922), p. 73.

9. Fred J. Teggart, "Caesar and the Alexandrian Library," *Zentralblatt für Bibliothekswesen,* 16(1899), p. 470.

10. A. Langie, *Les Bibliothèques publiques dans l'ancienne Rome et dans l'empire romaine.* (Thesis) Fribourg, 1908.—M. Ihm, "Die Bibliotheken im alten Rom," *Zentralblatt für Bibliothekswesen,* 10(1893), p. 513.—G. Garbelli, *Le biblioteche in Italia all'epoca romana.* Milan, 1894.

11. Ch. Jensen, "Die Bibliothek von Herculaneum," *Bonner Jahrbücher,* 135(1930), p. 49.

12. Ernst Kornemann, *Die neue Livius-Epitome aus Oxyrhynchus.* Leipzig, 1904.—*Guide to a Speical Exhibition of Greek and Latin papyri, presented to the British Museum by the Egypt Exploration Fund, 1900–1914.* London, 1914.

13. Adolf Erman and Fritz Krebs, *Aus den Papyrus der Königlichen Museen zu Berlin.* Berlin, 1899.

14. Alfred Körte, "Was verdankt die klassische Philologie den literarischen Papyrusfunden?," *Neue Jahrbücher für das klassische Altertum, Geschichte und deutsche Literatur,* 20(1917), p. 281.— Compare also Adolf Deissmann's *Licht vom Osten; das neue Testament und die neuentdeckten Texte der hellenistisch-römischen Welt.* Tübingen, 1909.

15. Ludwig Mitteis and Ulrich Wilcken, *Grundzüge und Chrestomathie der Papyruskunde*. I. II. Leipzig, 1912. — Wilh. Schubart, "Papyrusfunde und griechische Kultur," *Internationale Monatsschrift für Wissenschaft, Kultur und Technik*, 8(1914), cols. 1181, 1269. — Wilh. Schubart, *Einführung in die Papyruskunde*. Berlin, 1918. — Wilh. Schubart, *Das Buch bei den Griechen und Römern*, 2d ed. Berlin, 1921. — Frederic G. Kenyon, *Ancient Books and Modern Discoveries*. Chicago, 1927. — Karl Preisendanz, "Zur Papyruskunde" in *Handbuch der Bibliothekswissenschaft*, vol. 1. Berlin, 1931, p. 300. — Karl Preisendanz, *Papyrusfunde und Papyrusforschung*. Leipzig, 1933. — Frederic G. Kenyon, *Papyrus; alte Bücher und moderne Entdeckungen*. Übertragen von Gertrud Lehmann-Viereck. Brünn, 1939. — Emil Kiessling, "Papyruskunde," *Zentralblatt für Bibliothekswesen*, 57(1940), p. 101.

16. Compare A. Conze's "Die pergamenische Bibliothek," *Sitzungsberichte der Preussischen Akademie der Wissenschaften 1884*, II, p. 1259 ff. — K. Dziatzko, "Die Bibliotheksanlage von Pergamon," *Sammlung bibliothekswissenschaftliche Arbeiten*, 10(1896), p. 38. — Emil Jacobs, "Neue Forschungen über antike Bibliotheksgebäude," *Zentralblatt für Bibliothekswesen*, 24(1907), p. 118. — Wilh. Wilberg, "Die Fassade der Bibliothek in Ephesus," *Jahreshefte des österreichischen Archäologischen Insitutes in Wien*, 11(1908), p. 118.

Chapter 2. *The Ancient Literary Tradition*

1. Georg Wissowa, *Bestehen und Vergehen in der römischen Literatur*. Halle, 1908.

2. Ludwig Feuerbach, "Der Schriftsteller und der Mensch," in his *Sämtliche Werke*, vol. 1, Stuttgart, 1903, p. 269.

3. Remigio Sabbadini, *Storia e Critica di Testi Latini: Cicero, Donato, Tacito, Celso, Plato, Quintiliano, Livio e Sallustio, Commedia ignota*. Catania, 1914.

4. Georg Voigt, "Die handsriftliche Überlieferung von Ciceros Briefen" in *Berichte über die Verhandlungen der sächsischen Gesellschaft der Wissenschaften zu Leipzig. Philosophische- historische Classe*, 31(1879), p. 41. — Th. Zielinski, *Cicero im Wandel der Jahrhunderte*. Leipzig, 1908.

5. Domenico Comparetti, *Vergilio nel medio evo*. Livorno, 1872; 2nd ed., 1895. — Charles Knapp, *Bimillennium Vergilianum; a Vergilian Exhibition Held at the New York Public Library; List of Books and Manuscripts with an Introductory Essay*. New York, 1930. — Joachim Kirchner, *P. Vergilius Maro im Spiegel der literarischen Überlieferung*. Frankfurt am Main, 1930. For the early period of printing, see W.A. Copinger's "Incunabula Virgiliana," *Transactions of the Bibliographical Society* 2(1893/4), p. 123.

6. Konrad Burdach, "Die humanistichen Wirkungen der Trostschrift des Boëthius im Mittelalter und in der Renaissance," *Deutsche Vierteljahrsschrift für Literaturwissenschaft und Geistesgeschichte* 11(1933), p. 530. — A. van de Vyrer, "Les traductions du De Consolatione philosophiae de Boèce en littérature comparée,' *Humanisme et Renaissance* 6(1939), p. 247.

7. Victor Burr, "Byzantiner und Araber" in *Handbuch der Bibliothekswissenschaft, vol. 3: Geschichte der Bibliotheken*. Leipzig, 1940, pp. 64–89.

Chapter 3. *The Early Christian Period*

1. Rudolf Eucken, *Die geistesgeschichtliche Bedeutung der Bibel*. Leipzig, 1917. — Konrad Burdach, *Die nationale Aneignung der Bibel und die Anfänge der germanischen Philologie*. Halle, 1924. — Hans Vollmer, *Die Bibel im deutschen Kulturleben*. Leipzig, 1938. — Hans Rost, *Die Bibel im Mittelalter*. Augsburg, 1939.

2. Adolf von Harnack, "Julius Afrikanus, der Bibliothekar des Kaiser Alexander Severus," *Aufsätze Fritz Milkau gewidmet*. Leipzig, 1921, p. 42.

3. Karl Wendel, "Der Bibel-Auftrag Kaiser Konstantins," *Zentralblatt für Bibliothekswesen*, 56(1939), p. 165.

4. Compare Richard Stettner's *Die illustrierten Prudentiushandschriften*. Berlin, 1895–1905.

5. Adolf von Harnack, "Die älteste Inschrift über einer öffentlichen Kirchen-Bibliothek," *Beiträge zum Bibliotheks- und Buchwesen: Paul Schwenke gewidmet*. Berlin, 1913, p. 111.

6. Adolf von Harnack, "Tertullians Bibliothek Christlicher Schriften," *Sitzungsberichte der Preussischen Akademie der Wissenschaften*, 1914, I, p. 303.

7. Alexander, Comte de Laborde, *Les Manuscrits à Peintures de la Cité de Dieu de Saint Augustin*. I. II. Paris, 1909.

8. G. Misch, *Geschichte der Autobiographie*, vol. 1: *Das Altertum*. Leipzig, 1907.—Werner Mahrholz, *Deutsche Selbstbekenntnisse. Ein Beitrag zur Geschichte der Selbstbiographie von der Mystik bis zum Pietismus*. Berlin, 1914.

Chapter 4. Papyrus Rolls and Parchment

1. Compare Emil Jacobs in *Zentralblatt für Bibliothekswesen*, 26(1909), p. 31.
2. Ulrich Wilcken, "Zur Geschichte des Codex," *Hermes*, 44(1909), p. 150.
3. Victor Schultze, "Rolle und Kodex. Ein archäologischer Beitrag zur Geschichte des Neuen Testaments," in *Greifswalder Studien: Theologische Abhandlungen Hermann Cremer dargebracht*. Gütersloh, 1895, p. 147.
4. "Die Wiener Genesis." Edited by Wilhelm, Ritter von Hartel, and Granz Wickhoff. Supplement to vols. 15, 16 of *Jahrbuches der Kunsthistorischen Sammlungen des Kaiserhauses*. Vienna, 1895.—Hans Gerstinger, *Die Wiener Bilder-Genesis, Farbenlichtdruckfaksimile der griechischen Bilderbibel aus dem 6. Jahrhundert*.Vienna, 1931.
5. Anton von Premerstein, "Anicia Juliana im Wiener Dioskorides," *Jahrbuch der Kunsthistorischen Sammlungen des Kaiserhauses* 24(1903), p. 105.
6. J.H. White, "The Codex Amiatinus and Its Birthplace," *Studia biblica et ecclesiastica*, 2(1898), p. 273.—Joseph Schmid, "Zur Geschichte des Codex Amiatinus," *Theologische Quartalschrit*, 89(1907), p. 577.—Angelo Mercati, "Per la storia del codice Amiatino," *Biblia*, 3 (1922), p. 324.
7. Enrico Rostagno, *Il Codice Medice di Virgilio*. (With a reproduction of the manuscript). Rome, 1931.
8. Ernst Meyer, "Zur Geschichte des Codex argenteus Upsaliensis," *Zentralblatt für Bibliothekswesen*, 28(1911), p. 544.—Otto von Friesen and Andres Grape, *Codex Argenteus Upsaliensis iussu Senatus Universitatis phototypice editus*. Uppsala, 1927. Compare Helmut de Boor's "Der Codex Argenteus und seine neueste Ausgabe," *Buch und Schrift*, 2 (1928), p. 39.
9. C.L. Bethmann, "Die Evangelienhandschrift zu Cividale," *Neues Archiv der Gesellschaft für ältere deutsche Geschichtskunde*, 2(1876), p. 113.
10. On the development of medieval script, see Erich Petzet's and Otto Glauning's *Deutsche Schrifttafeln des IX bis XVI Jahrhunderts aus den Handschriften der Staatsbibliothek in München*. Munich, 1910–1912.—E.A. Lowe, "A Handlist of Half-uncial Manuscripts," *Miscellanea Francesco Ehrle*, 4(1924), p. 34.—Hermann Delitsch, *Geschichte der abendländischen Schriftformen*. Leipzig, 1928.—Hermann Degering, *Die Schrift: Atlas der Schriftformen des Abendlandes vom Altertum bis zum Ausgang des 18. Jahrhunderts*. Berlin, 1929.
11. Otto Jahn, "Die Subscriptionen in den Handschriften der römischen Classiker," *Berichte der Königliche Sächischen Gesellschaft der Wissenschaften zu Leipzig. Philologische-Historische Classe*, 3(1851), p. 327.
12. Ad. Goldschmidt, *Die Elfenbeinskulpturen aus der Zeit der karolingischen und sächsischen Kaiser*, 2 vols. Berlin, 1914–18.—Hans Loubier, *Der Bucheinband von seinen Anfängen bis zum Ende des 18. Jahrhunderts*. 2d ed. Leipzig, 1926.—M. Husung, "Geschichte des Bucheinbandes," in *Handbuch der Bibliothekswissenschaft*, vol. 1. Leipzig, 1931, p. 666.

Chapter 5. To the Early Middle Ages

1. Otto Bardenhewer, *Patrologie*. 3rd ed. Freiburg im Breisgau, 1910, p. 546. Compare also L. Spengel's "Die subscriptio der institutiones des Cassiodorus im Bamberger Codex," *Philologus*, 17(1861), p. 555.—A. Franz, *M. Aurelius Cassiodorus Senator*. Breslau, 1872.—P. Corssen, "Die Bibeln des Cassiodorus und der Codex Amiatinus," *Jahrbücher für protestantichen Theologie*, 9(1883), p. 619.—Wilhelm Weinberger, "Handschriften von Vivarium," in *Miscellanea Francesco Ehrle*, 4. Rome, 1924, p. 75.—Ernst Heinrich Zimmermann, *Vorkarolingische Miniaturen*, Berlin, 1916, where the portrait that apparently comes from the *Codex grandior* of the sixth century is reproduced. The *Institutiones* of Cassiodorus have been handed down to us in an especially valuable manuscript of the State Library in Bamberg *(Patr. 61)* with a signature of the eighth century, which appears to go back directly to the original script.—Fritz Milkau, "Zu Cassiodor," in *Festschrift für Ernst Kuhnert*. Berlin, 1928, p. 23.—H. Thiele, "Cassiodor," *Studien und Mitteilungen des Benediktiner-Ordens*, 50(1932), p. 378.

2. A.E. Anspach, "Das Fortleben Isidors im 7.–9. Jahrhundert" in *Miscellanea Isidoriana*. Rome, 1936, p. 323.

3. Charles H. Beeson, *Isidor-Studien*. Munich, 1913, p. 133.

Chapter 6. The Book in the Middle Ages

1. From the rich literature concerned with the medieval books, the following works should be mentioned: Friedrich Adolf Ebert, *Zur Handschriftenkunde*. Leipzig, 1825.—L. Delisle, "Documents sur les Livres et les Bibliothèques au Moyen Age," in *Bibliothèque de l'école des Chartes*, III, 1, 1849, p. 216.— Karl Bartsche, *Albrecht von Halberstadt und Ovid im Mittelalter*. Quedlinberg, 1861.—Lëopold Delisle, *Le Cabinet des Manuscrits de la Bibliothèque imperiale*, 3 vols. Paris, 1868–1881.—Franz Rühl, *Die Verbreitung des Justinus im Mittelalter*. Leipzig, 1871.—Franz Anton Specht, *Geschichte des Unterrichtswesens in Deutschland von den ältesten Zeiten bis zur Mitte des dreizehnten Jahrunderts*. Stuttgart, 1885.—Adolf Ebert, *Allgemeine Geschichte der Literatur des Mittelalters im Abendlande*, 3 vols. Leipzig, 1874–1889.—M. Manitius, "Beiträge zur Geschichte römischer Prosaiker (und Dichter) im Mittelalter," *Philologus*, 47(1887), pp. 562, 710; 49(1890), p. 554; 50(1891), p. 354; 51(1892), p. 156; 56(1897), p. 535.—M. Manitius, *Analekten zur Geschichte des Horaz im Mittelalter (bis 1300)*. Göttingen, 1893.—I. Haury, "Über Prokophandschriften," in *Sitzungsberichte der philosophische und der historische Classe der bayerische Akademie zu München*, 1895, p. 125.—Wilh. Wattenbach, *Das Schriftwesen des Mittelalters*, 3d ed. Leipzig, 1896.—Geo. H. Putnam, *Books and their Makers during the Middle Ages*, 2 vols. New York, 1897.—K.O. Meinsma, *Middeleeuwsche Bibliotheken*. Zütphen, 1903.—Hilarius Felder, *Geschichte der wissenschaftlichen Studien im Franziskanerorden bis um die Mitte des 13. Jahrhunderts*. Freiburg im Breisgau, 1904.—M. Manitius, "Zur überlieferungsgeschichte mittelalterlicher Schulautoren," *Mitteilungen der Gesellschaft für deutsche Erziehungs- und Schulgeschichte*, 16(1906), p. 232.—J.W. Clark, *The Care of Books*, 2d ed. Cambridge, 1909.—Karl Holl, *Die handscriftliche Überlieferung des Epiphanius*. Leipzig, 1910.—Sigm. Tafel, *Die Überlieferungsgeschichte von Ovids "Carmina amatoria." Verfolgt bis zum 11. Jahrhundert*. Dissertation. Munich, 1910.—Ernest A. Savage, *Old English Libraries; the Making, Collection and Use of Books during the Middle Ages*. London, 1911.—M. Manitius, *Geschichte der Lateinischen Literatur des Mittelalters*, 3 vols. Munich, 1911–31.—Paul Lehmann, *Aufgaben und Anregungen der lateinischen Philologie des Mittelalters*. Munich, 1918.—Paul Lehmann, "Quellen zur Feststellung und Geschichte mittelalterlicher Bibliotheken, Handschriften und Schriftsteller," *Historisches Jahrbuch*, 40(1920), p. 44.—Karl Löffler, *Deutsche Klosterbibliotheken*, 2nd ed. Bonn, 1922.—Karl Löffler, *Einführung in die Handschriftenkunde*. Leipzig, 1929.—Karl Löffler, "Allgemeine Handschriftenkunde," in *Handbuch der Bibliothekswissenschaft*, vol. 1. Berlin, 1931, p. 254.—Paul Lehmann, *Erforschung des Mittelalters*. Leipzig, 1941.

2. G. Bötticher, "Die dichterischen Stoffe des deutschen Alterthums in ihrer nationalen Bedeutung," *Preussische Jahrbücher*, 53(1884), p. 145.

3. Paul lehmann, "Deutschland und die mittelalterliche Überlieferung der Antike," *Zeitschrift für deutsche Geistesgeschichte*, 1(1935), p. 136.

4. Ludwig Traube, *Autographa des Johannes Scotus*. Munich, 1912.

5. Ludwig Schmidt, "Zur Geschichte der Dresdner Thietmarhandschrit," *Neues Archiv für Sächische Geschichte und Altertumskunde*, 16(1895), p. 129.—Ludwig Schmidt, *Die Dresdner Handschrift der Chronik des Bischofs Thietmar von Merseburg in Faksimile hrsg.* Dresden, 1905.

6. Martin Grabmann, "Das Albertusautograph in der Hofbibliothek zu Wien," *Historisches Jarhbuch*, 35(1914), p. 352.—Paul Lehmann, "Autographe und Originale namhafter Schriftsteller des Mittelalters," *Zeitschrift des Deutschen Vereins für Buchwesen und Schrifttum*, 3(1920), p. 6.—Martin Grabmann, "Die Autographe von Werken des hl. Thomas von Aquin," in *Historisches Jahrbuch*, 60(1940), p. 514.

7. C. Becker, *Catalogi bibliothecarum antiqui*. Bonn, 1885.—*Mittelalterliche Bibliothekskataloge Österreichs*, I, II. Munchen, 1915–29. *Mittelalterliche Bibliothekskataloge Deutschlands und der Schweiz*, I: *Bistum Konstanz und Chur, 1928*; II: *Erfut, 1928*: III: *Augsburg, Eichstädt, Bamberg*, 1933–39.

8. Compare Theodor Gottlieb's *Über mittelalterliche Bibliotheken*. Leipzig, 1890.—J.W. Thompson, *The Medieval Library*. Chicago, 1939.—Karl Christ, "Das Mittelalter," p. 90 ff. in *Handbuch der Bibliothekswissenschaft*, vol. 3: *Geschichte der Bibliotheken*. Leipzig, 1940.—Konrad Jos. Heilig, "Mittelalterliche Bibliotheksgeschichte als Geistesgeschichte," *Zeitschrift für Geistesgeschichte*, 1(1935), p. 12.

9. Karl Konrad, "Angekettete Bücher," *Zeitschrift für Bücherfreunde*, N.F. 4(1912), 1, p. 21.

10. W. Schürmeyer, "Die Pultbibliothek des Mittelalters," *Zeitschrift für Bücherfreunde*, N.F. 22(1930), p. 9.

11. Ernst Kuhnert, *Die Königliche- und Universitäts-Bibliothek zu Königsberg i. Pr.* Königberg, 1901.

12. J.A. Schmeller, "Über Büchercataloge des 15. und früherer Jahrhunderte," *Serapeum*, 2(1841), p. 241.

13. Engelbert Mühlbacher, *Die literarischen Leistungen des Stiftes St. Florian.* Innsbruck, 1905, p. 33.

14. G.A. Schneider, *Der Hl. Theodor von Studion, Sein Leben und Wirken: ein Beitrag zur byzantinischen Mönchsgeschichte.* Münster in Westfalen, 1900, p. 56 f. It is indeed a significant consequence of Theodore's work if an illustrated manuscript important for the history of the Greek Church, containing the text of the Greek Psalter and today in the British Museum *(Addit. 19 352)* in London, has originated in the Studion Monastery in 1066.

15. W. Wattenbach, *Das Schriftwesen im Mittelalter*, 3rd ed. Leipzig, 1896, p. 244.

16. Concerning the maintenance of books in the later nunneries, see A. Hauber's "Deutsche Handschriften in Frauenklöstern des späteren Mittelalters," *Zentralblatt für Bibliothekswesen*, 31(1914), p. 341.

Chapter 7. Important Places in the Cultural Tradition

1. Andrea Caravita, *I codici e le arti a Monte Cassino.* 3 vols. Monte Cassino, 1869—Oderisco Piscicelli Taeggi, *Le miniature nei codici Cassinesi.* Monte Cassino, 1887.

2. Edward Sullivan, *The Book of Kells*, 3rd ed. London, 1927.

3. I.O. Westwood, *Facsimilies of the Miniatures and Ornaments of Anglo-Saxon and Irish Manuscripts.* London, 1868.—H. Zimmer, "Über die Bedeutung des irischen Elements fü die mittelalterliche Cultur," in *Preussische Jahrbücher*, 59(1887), p. 27.—Walter Schultze, "Die Bedeutung der iroschottischen Mönche für die Erhaltung und Fortpflanzung der mittelalterlichen Wissenschaft," *Zentralblatt für Bibliothekswesen*, 6(1889), pp. 185, 233, 281.

4. The Celtic inhabitants of Ireland were called Scots, *Scoti* in the Middle Ages; only at the waning of the Middle Ages is the migrated population of Britain's northern parts so called.

5. *Kultur der Gegenwart*, I. 11.I., p. 81.

6. C. Scherer, *Die Codices Bonifatiani in der Landesbibliothek zu Fulda.* Fulda, 1905.

7. O. Seebass, "Handschriften von Bobbio in der Vatikanischen und Ambrosianischen Bibliothek," *Zentralblatt für Bibliothekswesen*, 13(1896), p. 1.—Franz Steffens, "Über die Abkürzungsmethoden der Schreibschule von Bobbio" in *Mélanges offerts à M. Emile Chatelain.* Paris, 1910, p. 244.—Heinz Gomoli, "Zu Cassiodors Bibliothek und ihrem Verhältnis zu Bobbio," *Zentralblatt für Bibliothekswesen*, 53(1936), p. 185.

8. Emile Chatelain, "Les Palimpsestes latins," in *École pratique des hautes études. Annuaire*, (1904), p. 5.—Émile Chatelain, "Notes sur quelques palimpsestes de Turin," *Revue de Philologie*, 27(1903), p. 37.

9. *Königsbrief Karls d. Gr. an Papst Hadrian über Abt-Bischof Waldo von Reichenau-Pavia; Palimpsest-Urkunde aus Cod. lat. Monac. 6333.* Hrsg. von Emmanuel Munding. Beuron, 1928.

10. *Gai Codex Rescriptus in Bibliotheca Capitulari Ecclesiae Cathedralis Veronensis. Cura et studio eiusdam bibliothecae custodi phototypice expressus, mit einleit. lateinischen Text von Don Antonio Spagnola.* Leipzig, 1909.

11. A.W. von Schröter, "Übersicht der vorzüglichsten seit dem Jahre 1813 besonders durch Codices rescripti neuendeckten Stücke der griechischen und römischen Literatur," *Hermes*, 24(1824), p. 318; 25(1826), p. 271.—Alban Dold, "Palmipsest-Handschriften," in *Gutenberg-Jahrbuch*, (1950), p. 16 ff.

12. Raphael Kögel, *Die Palimpsestphotographie in ihren wissenschaftlichen Grundlagen und praktischen Anwendungen.* Halle, 1920.—*Texte und Arbeiten.* Herausgegeben durch die Erzabtei Beuron. Beuron, 1917-.

Chapter 8. The Carolingian Period

1. Carmina barbara et antiquissima, quibus veterum regum actus et bella canebantur, scripsit memoriaeque mandavit (Einhard: *Vita Karoli*).

2. Paul Lehmann, "Büchersammlung und Bücherschenkungen Karls des Grossen," *Historische Vierteljahrschrift*, 19(1920), p. 237.

3. Elias Avery Lowe, *Codices Lugdunenses antiquissimi; Le scriptorium de Lyon, la plus ancienne école calligraphique de France*. Lyons. 1924.

4. E. Lesne, *Les Livres, "Scriptoria" et bibliothèques du commencement du VIIIe à la fin du XIe siecle*. Lille, 1938.

5. Franz Friedr. Leitschuh, *Geschichte der Karolingischen Malerei*. Berlin, 1894. — A.C.L. Boinet, *La Miniature Carolingienne*. Paris, 1913.

6. From the extensive literature on illumination, see Hugo Janitschek, *Geschichte der Deutschen Malerei*. Berlin, 1890. — J. A. Herbert, *Illuminated Manuscripts*. London, 1911. — Georg Leidinger, *Meisterwerke der Buchmalerei: Aus Handschriten der Bayerische Staatsbibliothek Muchen ausgewählt und beschrieben*. Munich, 1921. — Adolph Goldschmidt, *Die deutsche Buchmalerei*, 2 vols. Munich, 1928. — Albert Boeckler, *Abendländische Miniaturen bis zum Ausgang der römanischen Zeit*. Berlin, 1930. — Albert Boeckler, "Die Buchmalerei," in *Handbuch der bibliothekswissenschaft*, I. Berlin, 1931, p. 150. — Albert Boeckler, *Schöne Handschriften aus dem Besitz der Preussische Staatsbibliothek*. Berlin, 1931. — Albert Boeckler, *Ars sacra: Kunst des frühen Mittelalters; Ausstellung*. Munich, 1950.

7. *Beschreibendes Verzeichnis der illuminierten Handschriften und Inkunabeln der Nationalbibliothek in Wien*. Hrsg. v. Herm. Jul. Hermann. Teil 1–7. Leipzig, 1923–38.

8. L. Delisle, "Mémoire sur l'École calligraphique de Tours au IXe siècle," *Mémoires de l'Académie des inscriptions et belles-lettres*, 32(1886), I, p. 29. — E.K. Rand, *A Survey of the Manuscripts of Tours*. Cambridge, Mass., 1929. — Wilhelm Köhler, *Die Schule von Tours*, 2 vols. Berlin, 1930–33.

9. Louis Weber, *Einbanddecken, Elfenbeintafeln, Miniaturen, Schriftproben aus Metzer liturgischen Handschriften*. Metz, 1913.

10. F.M. Carey, "The Scriptorium of Reims during the Archbishopric of Hincmar," in *Studies in Honor of E.K. Rand*. New York, 1928, p. 41.

11. Léopold Delisle, "Recherches sur l'ancienne Bibliothèque de Corbie," *Bibliothèque de l'école des Chartes*. Fifth series, I(1860), pp. 393, 498.

12. Joachim Prachno, "Das Bild des Hrabanus Maurus, ein Beitrag zur Geschichte des Porträts," in *Kultur- und Universalgeschichte. Walter Goetz dargebracht*. Leipzig, 1927, p. 15.

13. Franz Falk, *Beiträge zur Rekonstruktion der alten Bibliotheca fuldensis und Bibliotheca laureshamensis*. Leipzig, 1902, and in *Zentralblatt für Bibliothekswesen* 25(1908), p. 556. — Karl Löffler, "Die Fuldaer Klosterbibliothek," Zeitschrift für Bücherfreunde, N.F. 10(1918/19), II, p. 194. — Paul Lehmann, *Fuldaer Studien*. Munich, 1925, 1927. — Paul Lehmann, "Fulda und die antike Literatur" in *Aus Fuldas Geistesleben* (Fulda, 1928), p. 9 — Karl Christ, *Die Bibliothek des Klosters Fulda in 16. Jahrhundert*. Leipzig, 1933.

14. Paul Clemen, "Die Schreibschule von Fulda," *Repertorium für Kunstwissenschaft*, 13(1890), p. 123. — Julius von Schlosser, "Eine Fuldaer Miniaturhandschrift der K.K. Hofbibliothek," in *Jahrbuch der Kunsthistorischen Sammlungen des Kaiserhauses*, 13(1892), p. 1. — E.H. Zimmermann, "Die Fuldaer Buchmalerei in karolingischer und ottonischer Zeit," in *Kunstgeschichtliches Jahrbuch der K.K. Zentralkommission für Kunst und historische Denkmale*, 4(1910), p. 1. — Gregor Richter and Albert Schönfelder, *Sacramentarium Fuldense saeculi X. Cod. Theol. 231 der Universitätsbibliothek zu Göttingen*. Fulda, 1912. — Albert Boeckler, *Der Codex Wittekindeus*. Leipzig, 1938.

15. Cf. J. Schnetz, *Ein Kritiker des Valerius Maximus im 9. Jahrh*. Neuburg a. D., 1901.

16. M. Manitius, "Lupus von Ferrières, ein Humanist des 9. Jahrhunderts," *Rheinisches Museum für Philologie*, N.F. 48(1893), p. 313 ff. — Charles Henry Beeson, *Lupus of Ferrières as Scribe and Text Critic*. Cambridge Mass., 1930. — Emmanuel von Severus, *Lupus von Ferrières. Gestalt und Werk eines Vermittlers antiken Geistesgutes an das Mittelalter im 9. Jahrhundert*. Münster, 1940.

17. *Bibliothek und Schreibstube der mittelalterlichen Reichenau*. Beiträge von Albet Boeckler, Theodor Längin, Paul Lehmann, Karl Preisendanz. (Sonderdruck aus; *Die Kultur der Abtei Reichenau*). Munich, 1925.

18. Franz Weidmann, *Geschichte der Bibliothek von St. Gallen seit ihrer Gründung um das Jahr 830 bis auf 1841*. St. Gallen, 1841. — I.B. Näf, "Die Bibliothek des ehemaligen Benediktinerstiftes Sankt Gallen," *Studien und Mitteilungen zur Geschichte des Benediktinerordens*, N.F. 1(1911), pp. 205, 385. — Adolf Merton, *Die Buchmalerei in St. Gallen vom 9. bis zum 11. Jahrhundert*. 2nd ed. Leipzig, 1923. — Heinrich Brauer, *Die Bücherei von St. Gallen und das althochdeutsche Schrifttum*. Halle, 1926. — Adolf Fäh, *Die Stiftsbibliothek in St. Gallen: Der Bau und seine Schätze*. St. Gallen, 1929.

19. Franz Landsberger, *Der St. Galler Folchart-Psalter: eine Initialstudie*. St. Gallen, 1912.
20. Phil. Jaffé and Wilh. Wattenbach, *Ecclesiae metropolitanae Coloniensis codices manuscripti*. Berin, 1874.—Anton Decker, "Die Hildebald'sche Manuskriptensammlung des Kölner Domes," in *Festschrift der 43. Versammlung deutscher Philologen und Schulmänner*. Bonn, 1895, p. 215.—Paul Lehmann, 'Erzbischof Hildebald und die Dombibliothek von Köln," *Zentralblatt für Bibliothekswesen*, 25(1908), p. 153.—L.W. Jones, *The Script of Cologne from Hildebald to Hermann*. Cambridge, Mass., 1932.
21. Aug. Wilmanns, "Der Katalog der Lorscher Klosterbibliothek aus dem 10. Jahrhundert," *Rheinisches Museum für Philologie*, N.F. 23(1868), p. 385.—The entry in the Lorsch books designating ownership reads: "Iste liber est monasterii b. Nazarii in Laurissa."
22. Edm. W. Braun, *Beiträge zur Geschichte der Trierer Buchmalerei im früheren Mittelalter*. Trier, 1896.—Keuffer, "Bücherei und Bücherwesen von St. Maximin im Mittelalter," in *Jahresbericht der Gesellschaft für nützliche Forschungen zu Trier 1894-1899*, p. 48.—*Die Trierer Ada-Handschfrift*. Bearbeitet und herausgegeben von K. Menzel, P. Corssen, H. Janitschek, A. Schnügen, F. Heltner, K. Lamprecht. Leipzig, 1889.
23. *Die Handschrift des Wessobrunner Gebets. Faksimile-Ausgabe von A. von Eckardt*. Munich, 1922.
24. Ludwig Traube, *Textgeschichte der Regula S. Benedicti*, 2nd ed., Munich, 1911.
25. Georg Leidinger, *Der Codex aureus der Bayer. Staatsbibliothek*. Munich, 1921-25.—Bernh. Bischoff, "Literarisches und künstlerisches Leben in St. Emmeram," *Studien und Mitteilungen aus der Geschichte des Benediktinerordens*, 51(1933), p. 102.

Chapter 9. The Saxon and Frankish Emporers (919–1125)

1. W. Vöge, *Eine deutsche Malerschule um die Wende des ersten Jahrtausends*. Freiburg, 1891.—F.X. Kraus, *Die Miniaturen des Codex Egberti*. Freiburg, 1884.—H.V. Sauerland and A. Haseloff, *Der Psalter Egberts von Trier*. Trier, 1901.—*Die Kunst des Klosters Reichenau im 9. und 10. Jahrhundert*. Freiburg, 1906.—Hans Jantzen, "Das Wort als Bild in der frühmittelalterlichen Buchmalerei," *Historisches Jahrbuch*, 60(1940), p. 507.
2. Adolf Schmidt, *Die Miniaturen des Gerokodex. Ein Reichenauer Evangelistar des 10. Jahrhunderts. Handschrift 1948 der Landesbibliothek zu Darmstadt*. Leipzig, 1924.
3. A. Boeckler, in *Die Kultur der Abtei Reichenau*, vol. 2. Munich, 1925, p. 977.
4. H.V. Sauerland and A. Haseloff, *Der Psalter des Erzbischofs von Trier*. Trier, 1901.
5. Stephan Beissel, *Des hl. Bernward Evangelienbuch im Dome zu Hildesheim*. Mit Handschriften des 10. und 11. Jahrhunderts verglichen. Hildesheim, 1891.
6. August Potthast, "Tacitus und Corvey," *Anzeiger für Kunde der deutschen Vorzeit*, N.F. 10(1863), col. 358.—Georg Hüffer, *Korveyer Studien. Quellenkritische Untersuchungen zur Karolinger-Geschichte*. Münster i. W., 1898.—Karl Löffler, "Die Bibliothek von Korvei," *Zeitschrift für Bücherfreunde*, N.F. 10(1918/19), I, p. 136.—Paul Lehmann, *Corveyer Studien*. Munich, 1919.
7. Paul Clemen, *Der Echternacher Evangeliencodex in Gotha*. Bonn, 1930.
8. Paul Th. Hoffmann, *Der mittelalterliche Mensch, gesehen aus Welt und Umwelt Notkers des Deutschen*, 2nd ed. Leipzig, 1937.
9. Jos. Becker, *Textgeschichte Liudprands von Cremona*. Munich, 1908.
10. *Plautus-codex Heidelbergensis 1613 Palatinus C. phototypice editus*. Praefatus est Carolus Zangemeister. Leyden, 1900.
11. G.F. Warner and H.A. Wilson, eds., *The Benedictional of Saint Aethelwold*. Oxford, 1910.
12. H.A. Wilson, *The Missal of Robert of Jumièges*. London, 1896.
13. Rud. Beer, *Die Handschriften des Klosters Santa Maria de Ripoll* (Sitzungsberichte der Akademie der Wissenschaften in Wien. Philos. -Histor. Klasse 155, 3 and 158, 2). Vienna, 1907/08.
14. Robert Fawtier, "la bibliothèque et le trésor de l'abbaye de Saint-Évre-les-Toul. Nancy, 1911.
15. Heinrich Wölfflin, *Die Bamberger Apokalypse. Eine Reichenauer Bilderhandschrift vom Jahre 1000*, 2nd ed. Munich, 1921.
16. Max Huattmann, "Das Bamberger Elfenbeinrelief Cim. 57 aus der Hof- und Staatsbibliothek zu München," *Die christliche Kunst*, 5(1909), p. 123.—Georg Leidinger, *Das Perikopenbuch Kaiser Heinrichs II*. Munich, 1914.
17. Georg Leidinger, *Evangeliarium aus dem Domschatze zu Bamberg (Cod. lat. 4454)*. Munich, 1921.

18. Ludwig Traube, *Bamberger Fragmente der vierten Dekade des Livius*. Munich, 1904.—Hans Fischer and Ludwig Traube, *Neue und alte Fragmente des Livius*. Munich, 1907.—Hans Fischer, "Die kgl. Bibliothek in Bamberg und ihre Handscriften," *Zentralblatt für Bibliothekswesen*, 24(1907), p. 364.—About Emperor Heinrich's presentation of books, see *Mittelalterliche Bibliothekskataloge Deutschlands und der Schweiz*, vol. III, part 3, Munich, 1939, p. 321: "Bistum Bamberg," Edited by Paul Ruf.

19. Georg Leidinger, *Das sogenannte Evangeliarium Ottos III*. Munich, 1912.

20. A. Boeckler, *Das goldene Evangelienbuch Heinrichs III*. Berlin, 1933.

21. Stephan Beissel, *Das Evangelienbuch Heinrich III aus dem Dome zu Goslar in der Bibliothek zu Upsala in seiner Bedeutung für Kunst und Liturgie*. Düsseldorf, 1900.

Chapter 10. The High Middle Ages (12th–14th Centuries)

1. J.A. Endres, *Honorius Augustodunensis. Beitrag zur Geschichte des geistigen Lebens im 12. Jahrhundert*. Kempten, 1906.

2. Eduard Thoma, *Die Tegernseer Buchmalerei*. Dissertation. Munich, 1910.—E.F. Bange, *Eine bayerische Marlerschule des 11. und 12. Jahrhunderts*. Munich, 1923.

3. A. Boeckler, *Die Regensburg-Prüfeninger Buchmalerei des 12. und 13. Jahrhunderts*. Munich, 1924.

4. Franz Jansen, *Die Helmarshausener Buchmalerei zur Zeit Heinrichs des Löwen*. Hildesheim, 1933.

5. Herm. Krabbo, "Der Reinhardsbrunner Briefsteller aus dem zwölften Jahrhundert," *Neues Archiv der Gesellschaft für ältere deutsche Geschichtskunde*, 32(1907), p. 51.—For Reinhardbrunn, still see Karl Wenck, "Ein Handschriftenkatalog des Klosters Reinhardsbrunn vom Jahre 1514," *Zeitschrift des Vereins für Thüringische Geschichte und Altertumskunde*, 12(1885), p. 279.—R. Ehwald, "Reste der Reinhardsbrunner Bibliothek," *Mitteilungen der Vereinigung für Gothaische Geschichts- und Altertumsforschung*, 1907, p. 63.

6. Jean Loubier, "Die Herstellung der mittelalterlichen Bücher nach einer Miniatur des 12. Jahrhunderts," *Zeitschrift für Bücherfreunde*, 12(1908–09), II, p. 409.

7. A. Straub and G. Keller, *Herrade de Landsberg. Hortus deliciarum*. Strasbourg, 1899.

8. E. Winkler, *Das Rolandslied*. Heidelberg, 1919.

9. Friedrich Wilhelm, *Zur Geschichte des Schrifttums in Deutschland bis zum Ausgang des 13. Jahrhunderts*. Munich, 1920–21, p. 60.

10. Karl Löffler, *Der Landgrafenpsalter. Eine Bilderhandschrift aus dem Anfang des 13. Jahrhunderts in der Württembergischen Landesbibliothek*. Leipzig, 1925.

11. Martin Lintzel, "Die Mäzene der deutschen Literatur im 12. und 13. Jahrhundert," *Sächsische Zeitschrift für Geschichte und Kunst*, 22(1933), p. 47.—Werner Fechter, *Das Publikum der mittelhochdeutschen Dichtung*. Frankfurt am Main, 1935.

12. Theod. Abelin, *Das Nibelungenlied und seine Literatur*. Leipzig, 1907–09.—H.A. Korff, "Deutschlands Anteil an der Weltdichtung," *Zeitschrift für Deutschkunde*, 1931, p. 433.

13. K.J. Benziger, *Parzival in der deutschen Handschriftenillustration des Mittelalters*. Strasbourg, 1914.

14. Herm. Schneider, *Heldendichtung, Geistliche Dichtung, Ritterdichtung*. Heidelberg, 1943.

15. Walter Goetz, "Die Enzykopädien des 13. Jahrhunderts. Ein Beitrag zur Entstehung der Laienbildung," *Zeitschrift für deutsche Geistesgeschichte*, 2(1936), p. 227.—Bernhard Wendt, *Idee und Entwicklungsgeschichte der enzyklopädischen Literatur*. Würzburg, 1941.

16. Rochus, Baron von Liliencron, *Über den Inhalt der allgemeinen Bildung in der Zeit der Scholastik; Festrede*. Munich, 1876.

17. Fritz Hoyer, *Einführung in die Papierkunde*. Leipzig. 1914—A. Renker, *Das Buch vom Papier*, 2nd ed. Leipzig, 1936.—Bockwitz. *Zur Kulturgeschichte des Papiers*. Stettin, 1935.

18. *Miniatures du Psautier de S. Louis*. Leyden, 1902.

19. Georg Graf Vitzthum, *Die Pariser Miniaturmalerei von der Zeit des hl. Ludwig bis zu Philipp von Valois und ihr Verhältnis zur Malerei in Nordwesteuropa*. Leipzig, 1907.

20. Albin Czerny, *Die Bibliothek des Chorherrnstiftes St. Florian*. Linz, 1874.

21. Ulrich Schmid, *Otto von Lonsdorf, Bischof zu Passau 1254–1265*. Würzburg, 1902.

22. J. Damrich, *Ein Künstlerdreiblatt des 13. Jahrhunderts aus Kloster Scheyern*. Strasbourg, 1904.

23. J.A. Schmeller, *Carmina Burana, 4th ed. Breslau, 1904.* — Alf. Hilka and Otto Schumann, *Carmina Burana*, 2 vols. Heidelberg, 1930.

24. Karl von Amira, *Die Dresdener Bilderhandschrift des Sachsenspiegels.* Leipzig, 1902.

25. G. Homeyer, *Die deutschen Rechtsbücher des Mittelalters und ihre Handschriften.*Revised by Conrad Borchling, Karl August Ekkardt and Julius von Gierke. Section 1. Weimar, 1934.

26. Rudolf Sillib. *Zur Geschichte der grossen Heidelberger (Manesseschen) Liederhandschrift und anderer Pfälzer Handschriften.* Heidelberg, 1921.

27. Karl J. Trübner, "Die Wiedergewinnung der sog. Manesseschen Liederhandschrift," *Zentralblatt für Bibliothekswesen,* 5(1888), p. 225.

28. Karl Zangemeister, "Zur Geschichte der grossen Heidelberger, sog. Mannesischen Liederhandschrift," *Westdeutsche Zeitschrift für Geschichte und Kunst,* 7(1888), p. 325. — E. Stange. *Die Miniaturen der Manessischen Liederhandschrift und ihr Kunstkreis.* Dissertatio. Königsberg, 1909. — Rudolf Sillib, *Zur Geschichte der grossen Heildeberg (Manesseschen) Liederhandschrift und andere pfälzer Handschriften.* Heidelberg, 1921. — *Die Manessesche Handschrift.* Facsimile edition. Leipzig, 1929. — Karl Preisendanz, "Zum Aufbewahrungsort des Grossen Liederbuchs," *Neue Heidelberger Jahrbücher,* N.F. 1939, p. 97. — Fr. Panzer, "Zur Bibliotheksgeschichte der Manessischen Handschrift," *Neue Heidelberger Jahrbücher,* N.F. 40(1941), p. 92. — Karl Preisendanz, "Die Rückkehr der Manesseschen Liederhandschrift aus Paris 1887/88," *Sitzungsberichte der philolog. -histor. Klasse der Heidelberger Akademie,* 1942.

29. Albert Boeckler, *Heinrich von Veldeke, Eneide. Die Bilder der Berliner Handschrift (Ms. germ. fol. 282).* Leipzig, 1939.

30. Adolf von Oechelhäuser, *Der Bilderkreis zum Wälschen Gaste des Thomasin von Zerclaere nach den vorhandenen Handschriften untersucht und beschrieben.* Heidelberg, 1890.

31. Edward Schröder, "Echte, rechte, schlechte Titel in der altdeutschen Literaturgeschichte," *Imprimatur,* 8(1938), p. 153. — E. Schröder. *Anfänge des deutschen Buchtitels.* Nachrichten von der Gesellschaft der Wissenschaft zu Göttingen. Phil. -hist. Klasse. Fachgruppe 4. N.F. I, 1. Göttingen, 1937.

32. Ludwig Volkmann, *Iconografia Dantesca; Die bildlichen Darstellungen zur Göttlichen Komödie.* Leipzig, 1897. — Ernst Robert Curtius, "Das Buch als Symbol in der Divina Commedia," in *Festschrift zum 60. Geburtstag von Paul Clemen.* Bonn, 1926, p. 44. — G. Mambelli, *Annali dell'Edizioni Dantesche.* Bologna. 1931.

33. Remarkable things can happen to books: The Berlin State Library in 1868 received from the legacy of the Germanist, Franz Pfeiffer, a manuscript of the mystic, Suso (Cod. germ. qu. 840). Dr. Karl Bihlmeyer was able to authenticate that this, the best manuscript of this mystic, was the same one that had belonged to the Knights of Malta Library in Strasbourg, and then to the University of Strasbourg. The (book) monument had escaped the 1870 fate, and with the permission of the Prussian government was returned to Strasbourg in 1907.

34. Tauler's "Sermon weisende auf den nahesten waren wegk in geiste wandern," ("Sermon Pointing to the Nearest Path of the Spiritual Journey") was printed for the first time in 1489 at Konrad Kachelofen's in Leipzig.

35. Maurice Faucon, *La librairie des papes d'Avignon, sa formation, sa composition, ses catalogues (1316–1420),* 2 vols. Paris, 1886. — Franz Ehrle, *Historia bibliothecae Romanorum pontificum tum Bonifatianae tum Avenionensis,* vol. 1. Rome, 1890.

36. Cod. lat. Monac. 1312 of the Munich State library.

37. Gabriel Maier, *Heinrich von Ligerz, Bibliothekar von Einsiedeln im 14. Jahrhundert.* Leipzig, 1886. — Karl J. Benziger, *Geschichte des Buchgewerbes im fürstlichen Benediktinerstifte U.L.F. von Einsiedeln.* Einsiedeln, 1912.

38. G. Kaufmann, "Zu dem Philobiblon des Richard de Bury," *Zentralblatt für Bibliothekswesen,* 6(1889), p. 337. Final edition by M.J. Husung, Weimar, 1931.

Chapter 11. The Early Renaissance

1. Jakob Burckhardt, *Die Kultur der Renaissance in Italien,* 16th edition, edited by W. Goetz. Leipzig, 1927. Also compare Georg Voigt's *Die Wiederbelebung des klassischen Altertums oder das erste Jahrhundert des Humanismus, I–II,* 3rd edition, edited by M. Lehnerdt. Berlin, 1893.

2. P. de Nolhac, "Manuscrits à miniature de la Bibliothèque, de Pétrarque" *Gazette*

Archéologique, 14(1899), p. 25ff.—L. Delisle, "Notice sur un manuscrit des poésies de Pétrarque rapporté d'Italie en 1494 par Charles VIII," *Bibliothèque de l'École des Chartes*, 41(1900), p. 450.—P. de Nolhac, *Pétrarque et l'humanisme*, New edition, I–II. Paris. 1907.—Karl Schneider, "Die Bibliothek Petrarcas und ihre Schicksale," *Zeitschrift für Bücherfreunde*, N.F. 1(1909), I, p. 157.

3. According to Ludwig Geiger's *Renaissance und Humanismus in Italien und Deutschland*. Berlin, 1882, p. 24.

4. O. Hecker, *Boccaccio-Funde*. Braunschweig, 1902. Cf. *Zentralblatt für Bibliothekswesen*, 19(1902), p. 479.

5. Alfred von Martin, *Coluccio Salutati und das humanistische Lebensideal*. Berlin, 1916.

6. Remigio Sabbadini, "Niccolò da Cusa e i conciliari di Basilea alla scoperta dei codici," *Rendiconti della R. Accademia dei Lincei. Classe di scienze morali, storiche e filol.*, 20(1911), p. 9.—Paul Lehmann, "Konstanz und Basel als Büchermärkte während der grossen Kirchenversammlungen," *Zeitschrift des Deutschen Vereins für Buchwesen*, 4(1921), p. 6, 17.

7. A.C. Clark, "The Literary Discoveries of Poggio," *Classical Review*, 13(1899), p. 119.—Ernst Walser, *Poggius Florentinus. Leben und Werke*. Leipzig, 1914.

8. Hermann Blass, "Über die von Poggio zu den Zeiten des Konstanzer Conzils gefundenen Handschriften des Quintilian und von Statius Silven," *Museum für Philologie*, 30(1875), p. 458ff.

9. Cf. also Rudolf Till's *Handschriftliche Untersuchungen zu Tacitus Agricola und Germania. Mit einer Photokpoie des Codex Aesinas*. Berlin, 1943.

10. R. Sabbadini, *Le scoperte dei codici latini e graeci ne' secoli XIV e XV*, 2 vols. Florence, 1905–14.

11. Emil Jacobs, "Eine Instruktion niccolò Niccolis für die Durchsuchung deutscher Klöster nach Handschriften," *Wochenschrift für Klassische Philologie*, 30(1913), cols. 701, 929.

12. B. Podesta, "Documenti inediti per la Storia della Libreria Laurenziana," *Rivista delle Biblioteche*, I(1888), pp. 18, 59, 95, 186.—Eugène Müntz, *Les collections des Medicis au XVe siècle*. Paris, 1888.

13. Wilhelm Hoffmann, "Florentiner Buchkunst der Medici-Zeit. Die Bücherschau der Medici-Ausstellung in Florenz," *Philobiblon*, 11(1939), p. 306.

14. Enea Piccolomini, "Delle condizioni e delle vicende della libreria medicea privata dal 1494 al 1508" *Archivio storico Italiano III*, 19(1874), p. 101; 20(1875), p. 51; 21(1876), p. 102.

15. Gg. Gronau, "Dokumente zur Entstehungsgeschichte der neuen Sakristei und der Bibliothek von S. Lorenzo in Florenz," *Jahrbuch der Preussischen Kunstsammlungen*. Beiheft, 32(1911), p. 62.

16. *Vite di uomini illustri, riveduti da L. Frati*, 3 vols. Bologna, 1892/93. German: selected by Paul Schubring. Jena, 1914; English: London, 1926. Cf. Paul Schubring's "Vespasiano da Bisticci," *Mitteilungen des Kunsthistorischen Institutes in Florenz*, 3(1919–1932), p. 64, and *Zeitschrift für Bücherfreunde*, N.F. 11(1919/20), II, p. 183.—Arnim Lucchesi, "Der Buchhändler des Cosimo de' Medici. Aus den Erinnerungen des Vespasiano da Bisticci," *Philobiblon*, 11(1939), p. 292.

17. Raimondo Zazzeri, *Sui codici e libri a stampa della Bibliteca Malatestiana di Cesena ricerche ed osservazioni*. Cesena, 1887.

18. *Si cupis his positi quonam sint ordine libri Discere, qui transis, carmina pauca lege: Dextra sacrorum iurisque volumina servat, Philosophos, physicos, nec geometer abest. Quicquid cosmographi, quicquid scripsere poetae Historicique omnes, dat tibi laeva manus.* Cf. Cesare Guasti's "Inventario della Libreria Urbinata, compilato da Federigo Veterano, bibliotecario di Federigo I. da Montefeltro," *Giornale storico degli Archivi toscani*, 6(1862), p. 127; 7(1863), p. 130.—Karl Voll, "Josse von Ghent und die Idealporträts von Urbino," *Repertorium für Kunstwissenschaft*, 24(1901), p. 54.

19. Cosimo Stornajolo, *Codices Urbinates Graeci bibliothecae Vaticanae*. Rome 1895.

20. Ramon D'Alos, "Documenti per la storia della biblioteca d'Alfonso il Magnanimo," in *Miscellanea Francesco Ehrle*, 5(1924), p. 390.

21. Giuseppe Mazzatinti, *La Biblioteca dei Re d'Aragona in Napoli*, Rocca di Cascia, 1897.—H. Omont, "Inventaire de la bibliothèque de Ferdinand I. d'Aragon, roi de Naples à 1481," *Bibliothèque de l'École des Chartes, 70(1909), p. 456*.

22. *Laura Pittoni, La Libreria di S. Marco. Cenni storici*. Pistoia, 1903.—Giulio Coggiola, "Della 'Libreria' del Sansovino al Palazzo Ducale. Un episodio della vita della Marciana 1797–1812," *Rivista delle Biblioteche e degli Archivi, 16(1905), p. 34*.

23. Cf. E.G. Vogel's "Bessarions Stiftung oder die Anfänge der S. Marcusbibliothek in Venedig," *Serapeum*, 2(1841), p. 90 ff; p. 138f.—H. Omont, "Inventaire des manuscrits grecs et latins donnés à Saint Marc de Venise par le Cardinal Bessarion en 1468," *Revue des bibliothèques*, 4(1894), p. 129

ff.—R. Rocholl, *Bessarion. Studie zur Geschichte der Renaissance.* Leipzig, 1904.—Ludwig Mohler, *Kardinal Bessarion als Theologe, Humanist und Staatsmann.* Paderborn, 1923.

24. Eugène Müntz, *La Bibliothèque du Vatican au 16. siècle.* Paris, 1886.—Joseph Hilgers, "Zur Bibliothek Nikolaus V," *Zentralblatt für Bibliothekswesen,* 19(1902), p. 1.

25. August Schmarsow, *Melozzo da Forli.* Berlin, 1886, p. 25.—Paul Fabre, "La Vaticane de Sixte IV," *Mélanges d'archéologie et d'histoire,* 15(1895), p. 455.

26. A friend of Conrad Celtis. Cf. Rupprich's *Der Briefwechsel des Konrad Celtis* (Munich, 1934), p. 69, and Reicke's *Willibald Pirckheimers Briefwechsel.* Vol. 1(Munich, 1940), p. 199.

27. Julian Klaczko, "Dans la Camera della Segnatura," *Revue des deux mondes,* 124(1894), p. 241.—Franz Wickhoff, "Die Bibliothek Julius II," *Jahrbuch der Preussischen Kunstsammlungen,* 14(1893), p. 49 ff.—León Dorez, "La bibliothèque privée du pape Jules II," *Revue des Bibliothèques,* 6(1896), p. 97 ff.—I Schlosser, "Giustos Fresken in Padua und die Vorläufer der Stanza della Segnatura," *Jahrbuch der Kunstsammlungen des Kaiserhauses,* 17(1896), p. 83.—Georg Leyh, "Die Camera della Segnatura ein Bibliothekraum?," in *Festschrift für Georg Leidinger.* Munich, 1930, p. 171.

28. Otto Eduard Schmidt, "Die Visconti und ihre Bibliothek zu Pavia," *Zeitschrift für Geschichte u. Politik,* 5(1888), p. 444.

29. Hermann Julius Hermann, "Zur Geschichte der Miniaturmalerei am Hofe der Este in Ferrara," *Jahrbuch der kunsthistorischen Sammlungen des Kaiserhauses,* 21(Vienna, 1901), p. 117 ff.— Giulio Bertoni, *La Biblioteca Estense e la coltura ferrarese ai tempi del duca Ercole I (1471*–1505). Turin, 1903; G. Fumagalli, *L'Arte della legatura alle corte degli Estensi à Ferrara o à Modena dal sec. XV. al XIX.* 1913.—Domenico Fava, *La Biblioteca Estense nel suo sviluppo storico.* Modena, 1925.

30. H.J. Hermann, "Miniaturhandschriften aus der Bibliothek des Herzogs Andrea Mateo III. Acquaviva," in *Jahrbuch der kunsthistorischen Sammlungen des Kaiserhauses,* 19(Vienna, 1898), p. 190.

31. Piero Misciattelli, *La Libreria Piccolomini nel Duomo di Siena.* Siena, 1922.—Georg Leyh, "Renaissance Bibliotheken," *Lexikon des gesamten Buchwesens,* 3(1937), p. 114.

32. Giulio Coggiola, *Das Breviarium Grimani in der St. Marcus-Bibliothek in Venedig.* (Authorized German translation by Kurt Preise). Leyden, Leipzig, 1908–10.

33. C. Castellani, "Pietro Bembo, bibliotecario della libreria di S. Marco 1530–1543," *Atti del R. Istituto veneto di scienze,* 54(1896), p. 862.

34. Concerning the earlier carrying off of an especially valuable manuscript from Bobbio, see Sabbadini, Remigio, "Zur Überlieferungsgeschichte des Codex Mediceus (M) des Vergilius," *Rheinisches Museum für Philologie,* N.F. 65(1910), p. 475.

35. Von Gebhardt, "Ein Bücherfund in Bobbio," *Zentralblatt für Bibliothekswesen* 5(1888): 343.

36. Carol Thulin, *Die Handschriften des Corpus agrimensorum Romanorum.* Abhandlungen der Preussischen Akademie der Wissenschaften. Philos.-histor. Klasse. 1911. Anhang. Abh. II. Berlin, 1911.

37. Léopold Delisle, *Facsimilé de livres copiés et enluminés pour le roi Charles V.* Paris 1903.— Léopold Delisle, *Recherches sur la librairie de Charles V.* Paris, 1907.

38. Paul Durrieu, *Les très belles heures de Notre-Dame du Duc Jean de Berry.* Paris, 1922.—Paul Durrieu, *Les trois riches heures du Jean de France, duc de Berry.* Paris, 1904.—Hippolyte Fierens-Gevaert, *Les très belles heures de Jean de France, duc de Berry.* Paris, 1924.

39. August Schestag, "Die Chronik von Jerusalem. Eine für Philipp den Guten verfertigte Miniaturhandschrift der Wiener Hofbibliothek," *Jahrbuch der kunsthistorischen Sammlungen des Kaiserhauses,* 26(1899), p. 195.

40. A. Boinet, "Un bibliophile du XVe siècle, le grand bâtard de Bourgogne," *Bibliothèque de l'école des Chartes,* 67(1906), p. 255.

41. Antoine Le Roux de Lincy, "La Bibliothèque de Charles d'Orléans à son château de Blois en 1427," *Bibliothèque de l'école des Chartes,* 5(1844), p. 59—Pierre Champion, *La Librairie de Charles d'Orléans.* Paris, 1910.

42. Henry Omont, *Heures d'Anne de Bretagne.* Paris, 1906.

43. Cf. Max Dvorak, "Die Illuminatoren des Johann von Neumarkt," *Jahrbuch der Kunsthistorischen Sammlungen des Kaiserhauses,* 22(Vienna, 1901), p. 33 ff.

44. Julius von Schlosser, "Die Bilderhandschriften König Wenzels I," *Jahrbuch der kunsthistorischen Sammlungen des Kaiserhauses,* 14(Vienna, 1893), p. 214.—H.J. Hermann, "Eine unbeachtete Wenzelhandschrift in der Wiener Hofbibliothek," *Mitteilungen für österreichische Geschichtsforschung,* 21(1900), p. 162.

45. Joseph Neuwirth, "Die Herstellungsphasen spätmittelalterlicher Bilderhandschriften," *Repertorium für Kunstwissenschaft,* 16(1893), p. 76.

46. Phil. Strauch, *Pfalzgräfin Mechthild in ihren literarischen Beziehungen*. Tübingen, 1883.—Fr. Behrend and Rudolf Wolkan, *Der Ehrenbrief des Püterich von Reichertshausen*. Weimar, 1920.

47. Karl Bartsch, *Die altdeutschen Handschriften der Universitäts-Bibliothek in Heidelberg*. Heildeberg, 1887.—Konrad Burdach, "Die pfälzischen Wittelsbacher und die altdeutschen Handschriften der Palatina," *Zentralblatt für Bibliothekswesen*, 5(1888), p. 111.—Karl Christ, *Die alfranzösischen Handschriften der Palatina*. Leipzig, 1916.

48. Ludwig Fischer, *König Matthias Corvinus u seine Bibliothek*. Vienna, 1878.—Joh. Csontosi, *Bildnisse des Königs Matthias Corvinus und der Königin Beatrix in den Corvin-Codexen*. Sonder-Abdruck aus der Ungar. Revue. Budapest, 1890.—Lodovico Frati, "Della Biblioteca Corvina," *Rivista delle Biblioteche*, 4(1893), p. 7.—Victor Rácsey, "Über den jetzigen Stand der Frage der Corvina-Bibliothek," *Mitteilungen des österreichischen Vereins für Bibliothekswesen*, 5(1901), p. 114.—Wilhelm Weinberger, "Beiträge zur Handschriftenkunde. I. Die Biblioteca Corvina," *Sitzungsberichte der philos. -hist. Klasse der Wiener Akademie der Wissenschaften*, 159(1908), Abh. 6.—André de Hevesy, *La bibliothèque du roi Mathias Corvin*. Paris, 1923.—V. Fraknói, J. Fógel, P. Gulyás, and Edith Hoffmann, *Bibliotheca Corvina*. Budapest, 1927.—Wilhelm Weinberger, "Erhaltene Handschriften des Königs Mathias Corvinus u. des Graner Erzbischofs Johann Vitéz," *Zentralblatt für Bibliothekswesen*, 46(1929), p. 6.

49. Wilhelm Fraknói, "Die Bibliothek des Johann Vitéz," *Literarische Berichte aus Ungarn*, 2(1878), p. 113.

50. Cf. Johann Csontosi, "Corvinische Handschriften von Attavantes," *Zentralblatt für Bibliothekswesen*, 3(1886), p. 209.—P. d'Ancona, "Attavante," in *thieme-Becker Lexikon der bildenden Künstler*, vol. 2, p. 214.

51. Josef Fitz, "König Matthias Corvinus und der Buchdruck," in *Gutenberg-Jahrbuch*, 1939, p. 128.

52. A. von Reumont, "Die Bibliothek König Matthias Corvinus," in supplement to *Allgemeine Zeitung*, June 16, 1877, no. 167.

53. Eugen Abel, "Die Bibliothek des Königs Matthias Corvinus," *Literarische Berichte aus Ungarn*, 2(1878), p. 556.

54. M. Maitius, *Bildung, Wissenschaft und Literatur im Abendlande von 800 bis 1100*. Crimitschau, 1925.

55. Julius von Schlosser, *Die Darstellungen der Encyclopädie insbesondere der sieben freien Künste*. Sitzungsberichte der phil. -hist. Klasse der Akademie der Wissenschaften, 123. Vienna, 1891, p. 128.—Julius von Schlosser, "Giusto's Fresken in Padua und die Vorläufer der Stanza della Segnatura," *Jahrbuch der kunsthistorischen Sammlungen des Kaiserhauses*, 17(1896), p. 13.

56. Hans Schmölzer, "Der Bibliothekssaal im Castell zu Trient," *Mitteilungen der K.K. Centralkommission für Erforschung u. Erhaltung der Kunst- u. historischen Denkmale*, N.F. 27(1901), p. 37.

Chapter 12. The Perfecting of Printing

1. For the history of early printing see Georg Wolfg. Panzer's *Annalen der älteren deutschen Literatur. I.: Von Erfindung der Buchdruckerkunst bis 1520. II: 1521–1526*. Nuremberg, 1788–1805.—Georg W. Panzer, *Annales typographici. I–V: 1450–1500. VI–XI: 1501–1536*. Nuremberg, 1793–1803.—Ludwig Hain, *Repertorium bibliographicum, in quo omnes libri ab arte typographica inventa usque ad annum 1500 typis expressi recensentur*. Stuttgart, 1826–38.—M.F.A.G. Campbell, *Annales de la Typographie néérlandaise au XVe siècle*. La Haye, 1874–90.—Anton von der Linde, *Geschichte der Erfindung der Buchdruckerkunst*. Berlin, 1886.—G.E. Klemming, *Sveriges bibliografi 1481–1600*. Uppsala, 1889.—*Festschrift zum 500jährigen Geburtstage von Johann Gutenberg*. Mainz, 1900.—Robert Proctor, *An Index to the Early Printed Books in the British Museum*. London, 1898–1903.—Heinrich Meisner and Joh. Luther, *Die Erfindung der Buchdruckerkunst*. Bielefeld, 1900.—A. Claudin, *Histoire de l'imprimerie en France au XVe et au XVIe siècle*, 4 vols. Paris, 1900.—Konrad Burger, *The Printers and Publisher of the XVth Century*. London, 1902.—*Catalogue of Books Printed in the XVth Century now in the British Museum*. London, 1908 ff.—Ernest Voulliéme, *Dei deutschen Drucker des 15. Jahrhunderts*, 2d ed. Berlin, 1922.—Konrad Haebler, *Geschichte des spanischen Frühdrucks in Stammbäumen*. Leipzig, 1923.—Konrad Haebler, *Handbuch der Inkunabelkunde*. Leipzig, 1925.—*Gesamtkatalog der Wiegendrucke*, vol. 1 ff. Leipzig, 1925 ff.—R. Teichl, "Der Wiegendruck im Kartenbild," in *Festschrift der Nationalbibliothek Wien*. (Supplement). Vienna, 1929.—*Der Buchdruck des 15. Jahrhunderts. Eine bibliographische Übersicht*. Hrsg. von der

Wiegendruck-Gesellschaft, 5 parts. Berlin, 1929–36. – Erich von Rath, "Buchdruck und Buchillustration bis zum Jahre 1600," in *Handubch der Bibliothekswissenschaft*, vol. I. Berlin, 1931, p. 332. – Carl Wehmer. *Deutscher Buchdruck im Jahrhundert Gutenbergs. Zur 500 Jahrfeier der Erfindung des Buchdrucks.* Hrsg. v. der Preuss. Staatsbibliothek und von der Gesellschaft für Typenkunde des 15. Jahrhunderts. Leipzig, 1940. – *Denkmale aus dem ersten Jahrhundert des Buchdrucks. Ausstellung der Bayerischen Staatsbibliothek im Gutenbergjahr.* Munich, 1940. – Concerning the history of printing as a whole, cf. C. Falkenstein's *Geschichte der Buchdruckerkunst in ihrer Entstehung und Ausbildung*, 2d ed. Leipzig, 1856. – Carol B. Lorck, *Handbuch der Geschichte der Buchdruckerkunst*, 2 parts. Leipzig, 1882. – *Das alte Buch und seine Ausstattung vom XV. bix zum XIX Jahrhundert.* Mit einem Vorwort von Heinr. Röttinger. Vienna, 1915. – Karl Schottenloher, *Das alte Buch*, 2d ed. Berlin, 1921. – William Dana Orcutt, *The Kingdom of Books.* London, 1927. – Walther G. Oschilewski, *Der buchdrucker Brauch und Gewohnheit in alter und neuer Zeit.* Jena, 1935. – Laurence C. Wroth, *A History of the Printed Book.* New York, 1938. – Gustav Adolf Ernst Bogeng, *Geschichte der Buchdruckerkunst.* Hellerau, 1939. – Herm. Barge, *Geschichte der Buchdruckerkunst von ihren Anfängen bis zur Gegenwart.* Leipzig, 1940. – Konrad F. Bauer, *Aventur und Kunst. Eine Chronik des Buchdruckgewerbes.* Frankfurt am Main, 1940. – Julius Rodenberg, *Die Druckkunst als Spiegel der Kultur in fünf Jahrhunderten.* Berlin, 1942.

2. Cf. Aloys Ruppel's *Johannes Gutenberg: Sein Leben und sein Werk.* Berlin, 1939.

3. Ernst Kyriss, "Schriftdruck vor Gutenberg," *Gutenberg Jahrbuch.* 1942–43, p. 40.

4. Carl Wehmer in *Einleitung zu dem Tafelwerk: Deutscher Buchdruck im Jahrhundert Gutenbergs.* Leipzig, 1940.

5. *Hic liber non calami, stili aut penne suffragio sed mira patronarum formarumque concordia, proporcione et modulo impressus atque confectus est.*

6. Carl Wehmer, *Mainzer Probedrucke in der Type des sogenannten Astronomischen Kalenders für 1448. Ein Beitrag zur Gutenbergforschung.* Munich, 1948. Cf. Walter Menn's "Ein neues Dogma um Gutenberg?" in *Aus der Welt des Buches Festgabe zum 70. Geburtstag von Georg Leyh.* Leipzig, 1950, p. 65 ff.

7. Edward Schröder, "Philologische Beobachtungen zu den ältesten Mainzer und Bamberger Drucken in deutscher Sprache," *Zentralblatt für Bibliothekswesen*, 19(1902), p. 432.

8. Gottfried Zedler, *Die älteste Gutenbergtype.* Mainz, 1902.

9. Arthus Wyss, "Der Türkenkalender für 1455. Ein Werk Gutenbergs," in *Festschrift zum 500jährigen Geburtstage von Johann Gutenberg.* Mainz, 1900, p. 305.

10. Edward Schröder, "Das Mainzer Fragment vom Weltgericht, ein Ausschnitt aus dem Deutschen Sybillenbuche," *Veröffentlichungen der Gutenberg-Gesellschaft*, 5, 6, 7(1908), p. 1.

11. *Calixtus III. die Türkenbulle. Ein deutscher Druck von 1456 in der ersten Gutenbergtype.* In Nachbildung hrsg. von Paul Schwenke. Mit einer geschichtlich-sprachlichen Abhandlung von H. Degering. Berlin, 1911.

12. Facsimile edition by Paul Schwenke. Leipzig, 1913–1923. – Gottfried Zedler, *Die sogenannte Gutenbergbibel sowie die mit der 42zeiligen Bibeltype ausgeführten kleineren Drucke.* Mainz, 1929.

13. M.E. Kronenberg, "De Rubricator en zijn werk," *Het Boek*, 6(1917), p. 19.

14. Léopold Delisle, *A la mémoire de Jean Gutenberg.* Paris, 1900, p. 21. – Ernst Freys, "Zum Rubrikenverzeichnis der 36zeiligen Bibel," *Zentralblatt für Bibliothekswesen*, 35(1918), p. 167.

15. Wilhelm Meyer, *Die Buchstaben-Verbindungen der sogenannten gothischen Schrift.* Abhandlungen der Gesellschaft der Wissenschaften zu Göttingen. Philol.-histor. Klasse. N.F. 1, 6. Berlin, 1897. – Paul Schwenke, *Untersuchungen zur Geschichte des ersten Buchdrucks.* Berlin, 1900. – Stanely Morison, *Meisterwerke gotischer Schrift. Deutsche Inkunabeln im Britischen Museum.* Berlin, 1928.

16. Rudolf Stöwesand, *Der heutige Bestand der Welt an Gutenbergbibeln.* Wolfenbüttel, 1929. – E. Lazare, *Die Gutenberg-Bibel. Ein Census.* In deutscher Sprache bearbeitet und erganzt von M.O. Krieg. Vienna, 1951.

17. The origin of the 36-line Bible is still more unclear than that of its 42-line precusor. Ferdinand Geldner has recently pointed to Heinrich Kefer (who was Gutenberg's journeyman and an assistant to Johann Sensenschmidt) as its possible printer. ("Hat Heinrich Kefer aus Mainz die 36 zelige Bible gedruckt?," in *Gutenberg-Jahrbuch*, 1950, p. 100). This supposition, which chiefly depends on an already known mark of Kefer's ownership in a collective volume with pamphlets printed by Sensenschmidt and which was brought by chance to Bamberg, is just as little proven as the rest of the guessing games about the Bible, which indeed remains an everlasting mystery. Cf. V. Scholderer in the *Gutenberg-Jahrbuch*, 1951, p. 56.

18. In 1843 the antiquarian bookseller, J. Hess of Ellmagen has obtained a parchment copy from the Cathedral Library of Eichstadt and has passed it on, along with the volumes of *Acta Sanctorum,* to the Territorial Library in Stuttgart for about 120 florins. In 1857 the King of Württemberg gave about 7000 florins to the King of Prussia for the rarity. it is preserved today in the State Library in Berlin. So changefully is the destiny of books fulfilled.

19. Cf. Gottfried Zedler's *Das Mainzer Catholicon.* Mainz, 1905. Concerning early printing in Mainz, further see A. Tronnier's *Die Missaldrucke Peter Schöffers und seines Sohnes Johann.* Mainz, 1908.—I. de Ricci, *Catalogue raisonné des premières impressions de Mayence (1445–1467).* Mainz 1911.—Aloys Ruppel, *Peter Schöffer aus Gernsheim.* Mainz, 1937.—Carol Wehmer, *Mainzer Probedrucke in der Type des sogenannten astronomischen Kalenders für 1448. Ein Beitrag zur Gutenbergforschung.* Munich, 1948.

20. Ernst Crous, "Die Abkürzungszeichen in den Wiegendrucken," in *Gutenberg-Festschrift zur Feier des 25jährigen Bestehens des Gutenbergmuseums in Mainz,* 1925, p. 288.

21. Karl Schottenloher, "Der Frabenschmuck der Wiegendrucke" in *Buch und Schrift,* 4(1930), p. 81.

22. Erich von Rath, "Randleisten," in *Lexikon des gesamten Buchwesens,* 3(1937), p. 80.

23. Cf. Gottfried Zedler's *Die Bamberger Pfisterdrucke und die 36zeilige Bibel.* Mainz, 1911.

24. Cf. E. Voulliéme, *Der Buchdruck Cölns bis zum Ende des 15. Jahrhunderts.* Bonn, 1903.

25. E.W.E. Roth, "Zur Geschichte der Eltviller Buchdruckerei bis 1476," *Zentralblatt für Bibliothekswesen,* 18(1901), p. 117.—Aloys Ruppel, *Eltville als Frühdruckstadt.* Mainz, 1938.

26. Kurt Ohly, "Die Anfänge des Buchdrucks in Basel," *Zentralblatt für Bibliothekswesen,* 47(1940), p. 247.

27. Franz Stock, *Die ersten deutschen Buchdrucker in Paris um 1500.* Freiburg, 1940.—Concerning Paris printing see further George Lepreux's *Gallia typographica ou répertoire biographique et chronologique de tous les imprimeurs de France depuis les origines de l'imprimerie jusqu'à la révolution.* Paris, 1904–14.—A. Claudin, *Documents sur la typographie et la gravure en France au XVe et XVIe siècles.* Paris, 1916.

28. Gyula von Sebastyen in *Gutenberg Festschrift,* 1925, p. 29 ff.

29. Konrad Haebler, *The Early Printers of Spain and Portugal.* London, 1897.

30. W. Blades, *The Life and Typography of William Caxton,* 2 vols. London, 1861—Rudolf Hittmair, *William Caxton.* Innsburck, 1931.

31. Cf. Konrad Haebler's *Die deutschen Buchdrucker des 15. Jahrhunderts im Auslande.* Munich, 1924.—J. Rodenberg, G. Menz and F. Bergemann, "Buch und Büchereiwesen," *Handwörterbuch des Grenz-und Auslandsdeutschtums,* vol. 1. Breslau, 1933, p. 567.

32. Leo Baer, "Bernhard, Maler von Augsburg und die Bücherornamentik der italienischen Frührenaissance," *Monatshefte für Kunstwissenschaft,* 2(1909), p. 46.

33. P. Riccardi, *Saggio di una bibliografia euclidea.* Bologna, 1887–93.—Charles Thomas Stanford, *Early Editions of Euclid's Elements.* London, 1926.

34. Cf. Gilbert R. Redrave's *Erhard Ratdolt and his Work at Venice.* London, 1894.—Karl Schottenloher, *Die liturgischen Druckwerke Erhard Ratdolts aus Augsburg, 1485 bis 1523.* Mainz, 1922.—Robert Diehl, *Erhard Ratdolt.* Vienna, 1933.

35. Axel L. Romdahl, "Die Illustrationen in Stephen Arndes Bibel 1494 und andere Lübecker Holzschnitte," *Zeitschrift für Bücherfreunde,* 9(1905–06), II, p. 591.—Hans Wahl, *Die 92 Holzschnitte der Lübecker Bibel.* Weimar, 1917.

36. A. Claudin, *Origines de l'Imprimerie à Albi en Languedoc (1480–1484). Les pérégrinations de J. Neumeister, compagnon de Gutenberg en Allemagne, en Italie et en France (1463–1484). Son éstablissement-définitif à Lyon (1485–1507).* Paris, 1880.—Henry Joly, "Le missel Lyonnais et le psautier de Jean Neumeister," *Gutenberg-Jahrbuch,* (1932), p. 147.

37. King Manuel, *Early Portugese Books, 1489–1600.* Cambridge, 1929.

38. *L'Histoire de la belle Mélusine de Jean d'Arras. Reproduction en facsimile de l'édition de Genéve, imprimée par A. Steinschaber en 1478.* Avec une preface par W.J. Meyer, Bern, 1924.

39. *Quae doctos latuit Graecos Italosque peritos, ars nova Germano venit ab ingenio.* Cf. Alfred Börkel's *Gutenberg.* Giessen, 1897, p. 88 ff.

40. Friederich Kapp and Johann Goldfriedrich, *Geschichte des deutschen Buchhandels,* 5 vols. Leipzig, 1886–1903.

Chapter 13. The Incunabula Period

1. In the autobiography of the Basel schoolman and printer, Thomas Platter (1495–1582), is found the following interesting report on how he came to be a printer: "Da ich gsach, wie Harvagius und andere Truckerherren ein gute sach hatten, mit wenig arbeit gross gut gewunnen, dacht ich, möcht ich auch ein Truckerherr werden" ("Since I saw how Hervagius and other printers had a good thing, achieving great profit with little work, I thought that I'd like to become a printer also"). Cf. Karl Schottenloher's *Der Buchdrucker als neuer Berufsstand des 15. und 16. Jahrhunderts*. Mainz, 1935.—H. Kruse, "Die wirtschaftliche und soziale Lage im deutschen Buchgewerbe des 16. Jahrhunders," *Archiv für Buchgewerbe*, 13(1936), p. 396.—Wilhelm Port, "Buchdruckerschicksale am Oberrhein," *Gutenberg-Jahrbuch*, 1942/43, p. 126.

2. Robert Steele, "What Fifteenth Century Books are About," *The Library*, N.S. 4(1903), p. 337; 5(1904), p. 337; 6(1905), p. 137; 8(1907), p. 225.—Bonaventura Kruitwagen, "Wat men in de Nederlanden las in de 15e eeuw," *Bibliotheekleven*, 10(1925), pp. 41, 51, 87, 102.

3. W.L. Schreiber, "Heiligenlegenden," *Lexikon des gesamten Buchwesens*, 2(1936), p. 75.

4. W.L. Schreiber and E. v. Rath, "Heiligtumsbücher," *Lexikon des gesamten Buchwesens*, 2 (1936), p. 77.

5. Franz Falk, *Die Druckkunst im Dienste der Kirche zunächst in Deutschland bis zum Jahre 1520*. Cologne, 1879.

6. Paul Pietsch, *Ewangely und Epistel Teutsch, Die gedruckten hochdeutschen Perikopenbücher (Plenarien) 1473 bis 1523*. Göttingen, 1927.

7. Roderich Stintzing, *Geschichte der populären Literatur des römisch-kanonischen Rechts in Deutschland am Ende des 15. und im Anfang des 16. Jahrhunderts*. Leipzig, 1867.—Gustav Homeyer, *Die deutschen Rechtsbücher des 15. Jahrhunderts*, 1903, p. 58.

8. Giuseppe Manacorda, "Libri scolastici del Medio Evo e del Rinascimento," *La Bibliofilia*, 17(1916), p. 397; 18(1917), p. 240.

9. Dietrich Riechling, *Das Doctrinale des Alexander de Villa-Dei*. Berlin, 1893.

10. M.B. Stillwell, "The Fasciculus Temporum," in *Bibliographical Essays: A Tribute to Wilberforce Eames*. Cambridge, Mass., 1924, p. 409.—L. Baer, *Die illustrierten Historienbücher des 15. Jahrhunderts*. Strasbourg, 1903, p. 58.

11. Otto Schottenloher, ed., *Drei Frühdrucke zur Reichsgeschichte*. Veröffentlichungen der Gesellschaft für Typenkunde des XV Jahrhunderts. Seltene Frühdrucke in Nachbildungen, 2. Leipzig, 1938.

12. Karl Welzhofer, *EinBeitrag zur Handschriftenkunde der Naturalis Historia des Plinius*. Progr. Munich, 1878.

13. E. von Rath, "Hortus sanitatis," *Lexikon des gesamten Buchwesens*, 2(1936), p. 120.

14. Karl Sudhoff, *Der Fasciculus medicinae des Johannes de Ketham*. Facsimile edition. Milan, 1923.

15. Chr. Fr. Harless, *Die Literatur der ersten hundert Jahre seit der Erfindung der Typographie*. Leipzig, 1840.—R. Landau, "Die ältesten medizinischen Drucke," *Mitteilungen zur Geschichte der Medizin und der Naturwissenschaften*, 3(1904), p. 246.—Ludwig Choulant, *Graphische Incunabeln für Naturgeschichte*. Leipzig, 1924.—Karl Sudhoff, *Deutsche medizinische Inkunabeln*. Leipzig, 1908.—W.L. Schreiber, *Die Kräuterbücher des XV. und XVI Jahrhunderts* (offprint of the epilogue to the facsimile edition of *Hortus sanitatis*, German; Peter Schöffer, Mainz, 1485), Munich, 1924.

16. Justin Winsor, *A Bibliography of Ptolemy's Geography*. Cambridge, 1884.—J. Fischer, *Der Deutsche Ptolemeus (um 1490) in Faksimiledruck*. 1910.

17. Erwin Holzer, "Die frühesten und wichtigsten Drucke über die Entdeckung und Erforschung Amerikas," *Philobiblon*, 10(1938), p. 469.

18. Oscar Hase, *Die Koberger, 2nd ed.* Leipzig, 1885; reprint, 1886.

19. Gustav Klein, *Das Frauenbüchlein des Ortolff von Bayerland, gedr. vor 1500*. Munich, 1910.—K. Löffler, "Arzneibücher," *Lexikon des gesamten Buchwesens*, 1(1935), p. 88.

20. Alfred Hartmann, *Die Amerbachkorrespondenz. 1. Bd. Die Briefe aus der Zeit Johann Amerbachs 1481–1513*. Basel, 1942.

21. On Heilsbronn see Bruno Griesser's *Schreibstube und Bibliothek des Klosters Heilsbronn unter Abt Deinnke von Hirschlach 1282–1317*. Festgabe um Priesterjubiläum von Gregor Müller. Bregenz, 1926, p. 37.

22. O. Hartlich, "Giovanni Andrea dei Bussi, der erste Bibliothekar der Vaticana," *Philologische Wochenschrift*, 59(1939), cols. 327, 364, 395.

23. Cf. Joseph Schlecht's *Sixtus IV. and die deutschen Drucker in Rom.* Festschrift zum 1100 jährigen Jubiläum des deutschen Campo Santo in Rom. Freiburg im Breisgau, 1897, p. 270 ff.

24. The Vaticana in Rome owns a Strabo ms. *(Cod. Vat. lat. 2049)* with Bussis' own notation to the effect that he has gone through the manuscript on May 2, 1462, in the hosue of his master, Cardinal Nicholas of Cusa, Cf. R. Sabbadini in: *Il libro e la stampa*, 3(1909), p. 7.

25. Ernst Zinner, "Die wissenschaftlichen Bestrebungen Regiomontans," *Beiträge zur Inkunabelkunde*, N.F. 2(1938), p. 89.

26. Karl Schottenloher, "Tagebuchaufzeichnungen in immerwährenden Buchkalendern der Frühdruckzeit," in *Otto Glauning zum 60. Geburtstag*, vol. 2. Leipzig, 1938, p. 88ff.

27. Concerning early printing in Italy, see Lippmann, "Der italienische Holzschnitt im 15. Jahrhundert," *Jahrbuch der Preuss. Kunstsammlungen*, 3 and 5(1882 and 1884).—P. Kristeller, *Italienische Buchdrucker- und Verlegerzeichen bis 1525*. Strasbourg, 1893.—A. W. Pollard, *Italian Book Illustrations, Chiefly of the Fifteenth Century*. London, 1894.— L'arte della Stampa nel rinascimento italiano. Venice, 1894–95.—D. Marzi, "I tipografi tedeschi in Italia durante il secolo XV," *Festschrift zum 500jährigen Geburtstage von Johann Gutenberg*. Mainz, 1900, p. 505.—G. Fumagalli, *Lexikon typographicum Italiae*. Florence, 1905.—K. Haebler, *Der italienische Wiegendruck in Original-Typenbeispielen*. Munich, 1927.—William Dana Orcutt, *The Book in Italy during the 15th and 16th Centuries*. London, 1928.—V. Scholderer, "Der Buchdruck Italiens im 15.Jh.," in *Beiträge zur Inkunabelkunde*, N.F. 2(1938), p. 17.—Max Sander, *Le Livre à figures italien depuis 1467 jusqu'à 1530*, 1–6. Milan, 1942.

28. Concerning Greek printing see Robert Proctor's *The Printing of Greek in the Fifteenth century*. London, 1900.—Victor Scholderer, *Greek Printing Types 1465–1927*. Facsimiles. London, 1927.— Busso Loewe, "Die Ausbreitung der griechischen Typographie in Deutschland," in *Gutenberg-Jahrbuch*, 1940, p. 297.—W.P. Greswell, *A View of the Early Parisian Greek Press*. Oxford, 1833.

29. George C. Keidel, *A Manual of Aesopic Fable Literature*. Baltimore, 1896.

30. On Aldus Manutius, see A.A. Renouard's *Annales de l'imprimerie des Aldes*, 3d ed. Paris, 1834.—Julius Schück, *Aldus Manutius und seine Zeitgenossen in Italien und Deutschland*. Berlin, 1862.—Ambroise Firmin-Didot, *Alde Manuce et l'hellénisme à Venise*. Paris, 1878,—Pierre de Nolhac, *Les correspondants d'Alde Manuce (1483–1514)*. Rome, 1888.—Marco Ferrigni, *Aldo Manuzio*. Milan, 1925.

31. Henri Omont, *Catalogues de livres Grecs et Latins imprimés par Alde Manuce à Venise (1448, 1503, 1513) reproduits en phototypie*. Paris 1892.

32. W. Schümeyer, "Die Hypneromachia Polifili des Francesco Colonna," *Zeitschrift für Bücherfreunde*, N.F. 10)1912), I. p. 44.—Graziano Paolo Clerich, "Tiziano e la Hypnerotomachia Poliphili," *La bibliofilia*, 20(1919), pp. 183, 240.—Georg Leidinger, *Albrecht Dürer und die 'Hypnerotomachia Poliphili.'* Munich, 1929. The treatment rests on the handwritten entry in the Bavarian State Library's copy, according to which the book has been purchased by one D. Erasmus Flock (not Hock) on August 13, 1555, from the library of Albrecht Dürer. The entry refers to the not unknown Nuremberg mathematician and physician, Dr. Erasmus Flock (1520–1568), whom Philipp Melanchthon has recommended to Nuremberg on March 27, 1538, for a medical stipend *(Zeitschrift für Kirchengeschichte*, 35, (1914), p. 277). Flock has been active in Nuremberg after 1545; he has also died there (Bruhns in *Allg. Deutsche Biographie*, 8(1877), p. 280). He can thus indeed have acquired the volume from Dürer's legacy, even if care is advised concerning the undoubted later origin in the Mannheim Court Library, where many doubtful items have been hastily acquired. On Flock see also Otto Clemen's "Erasmus Flock, ein Nürnberger Arzt und Mathematiker," *Zeitschrift f. Bayer. Kirchengeschichte*, 2(1939), p. 195.—With the handsome Aldus edition, see also the pretty bibliophilic novel by Emanuel Stickelberger, *Der Liebestraum des Polyphilos*. Gütersloh, 1943.

33. Victor, Prince d'Essling, *Les Livres à figures Venetiens de la Fin du XVe siècle et due commencement du XVIe*. Florence, 1907–1914.

34. Cf. Rudolf Kautzsch's *Einleitende Erörterungen zu einer Geschichte der deutschen Handschriftenillustration im späteren Mittelatler*. Strasbourg, 1894.—Hans Wegener, "Die deutschen Volkshandschriften des späten Mittelalters," in *Mittelalterliche Handschriften*. Festgabe für Hermann Degering. Leipzig, 1926, p. 316 ff.—Helmut Lehmann-Haupt, *Schwäbische Federzeichnungen. Studien zur Buchillustration Augsburgs im 15. Jahrhundert*. Berlin, 1929.

35. P. Poppe, *Über das Speculum humanae salvationis*. Dissertation. Strasbourg, 1887.

36. Cf. Rudolf Kautzsch's "Diebold Lauber und seine Werkstatt in Hagenau," *Zentralblatt für Bibliothekswesen*, 12(1895), p. 57 ff and *Archiv für Buchgewerbe und Gebrauchsgraphik*, 63(1926),

p. 42. – W. Fechter, "Der Kundenkreis des Diebold Lauber," *Zentralblatt für Bibliothekswesen*, 55(1938), p. 121.

37. Cf. W.L. Schreiber, "Darf der Holzschnitt als Vorläufer der Buchdruckerkunst betrachtet werden?," *Zentralblatt für Bibliothekswesen*, 12(1895), p. 200.

38. R. Hochegger, *Die Entstehung und Bedeutung der Blockbücher*. Leipzig, 1891. – W.L. Schreiber, *Livres xylographiques et xylo-chirographiques* (vols. 4, 7, 8 of his *Manuel*). Leipzig, 1895–1902.

39. Th. Musper, "Die Urausgabe der Biblia pauperum und der Apokalypse," *Gutenberg Jahrbuch*, 1938, p. 53.

40. W.L. Schreiber, "Ars moriendi," *Lexikon des gesamten Buchswesens*, I(1935), p. 86.

41. Konrad Burdach, *Der Dichter des Ackermanns aus Böhmen und seine Zeit*. Berlin, 1926–1932.

42. Emil Weller, "Einige unbekannte Ausgaben der alten Volksbücher," *Serapeum. Intelligenzblatt*, 30(1869), p. 43; 31(1807), p. 168. – Paul Heitz and Franz Ritter, *Versuche einer Zusammenstellung der deutschen Volksbücher des 15. und 16. Jahrhunderts*. Strasbourg, 1924. – Heinz Kindermann, *Volksbücher vom sterbenden Rittertum*. Weimar, 1925. – Lutz Mackensen, *Die deutschen Volksbücher*. Leipzig, 1927. – W. Liepe, "Volksbuch," *Reallexikon der deutschen Literaturgeschichte*, 3(1928–1929), p. 481.

43. Edward Schroder, *Das goldene Spiel vom Meister Ingold*. Strasbourg, 1882.

44. W. Schmidt, *Die 24 Alten Ottos von Passau*. Dissertation, University of Berlin. Berlin, 1936.

45. Karl Schorbach, "Die Historie von der schönen Melusine," *Zeitschrift für Bücherfreunde*, 1(1897–98), I, p. 132.

46. Karl Schorbach, *Studien über das deutsche Volksbuch Lucidarius und seine Bearbeitungen in fremden Sprachen*. Strasbourg, 1894.

47. *Nec stili barbaries terreat verum sententiarum veritas alliciat.*

48. Friedrich Teudeloff, *Beiträge zur Übersetzungstechnik der ersten gedruckten deutschen Bibel auf Grund der Psalmen*. Berlin, 1922. – Ernst Gössel, *Der Wortschatz der Ersten Deutschen Bibel.*Giessen, 1933. – Erich Zimmermann, "Die deutsche Bibel im religiösen Leben des Spätmittelalters," *Bibel und deutsche Kultur*, 8(1938), p. 1, and *Buch und Schrift*, N.F. 1(1938), p. 77. – Hans Rost, *Die Bibel im Mittelalter*. Augsburg, 1939.

49. Richard Benz, "Geist, Schrift und Bild im Buch des 15. Jahrhunderts," *Imprimatur. Jahrbuch für Bücherfreunde*, 5(1934), p. 9.

50. Concerning various editions of this, perhaps the most handsome of the popular books of the 15th century, cf. Hans Naumann's *Die Holzschnitte des Meisters vom Amsterdamer Kabinett im Spiegel menschlicher Behaltnis* (gedr. zu Speyer bei Peter Drach). Strasbourg, 1910.

51. Paul Hankamer, *Die Sprache, ihr Begriff und ihre Deutung im 16. und 17. Jahrhundert*. Bonn, 1927, p. 4. – Max Böhme, *Die grossen Reisesammlungen des 16. Jahrhunderts und ihre Bedeutung*. Strasbourg, 1904. – G.A.E. Bogeng, "Reisewerke," *Lexikon des gesamten Buchswesens*, 3(1937), p. 106.

52. *Buch und Leben des hochberühmten Fabeldichters Aesopi. Mit einer Einführung von W. Worringer und sprachlicher Erneuerung von R. Benz*. Munich, 1925.

53. H. Wegener, *Bidpai, das Buch der Beispiele alter Weisen*. 1926.

54. Hermann Wunderlich, "Der erste deutsche Terenz," in *Studien zur Literaturgeschichte, Michael Bernays gewidmet*. Hamburg, 1893, p. 201

55. Rudolf Kautzsch, *Die Holzschnitte der Kölner Bibel von 1479*. Strasbourg, 1896. – Georg Gerlach, "Der Drucker und die Ausgaben der Kölner Bilderbibel," *Sammlung bibliothekswissenschaftlicher Arbeiten*, 13(1900). Otto Zaretzky, "Die Kölner Buchillustration im 15. und 16. Jahrhundert," *Zeitschrift für Büchertreunde* 3(1899/1900) I, p. 129. – Wilhelm Worringer, *Die Kölner Bibel*. Munich, 1923. – Erich von Rath, "Buchdruck und Buchillustration des 15. und 16. Jahrhunderts in Köln," *Zentralblatt für Bibliothekswesen*, 54(1937), p. 421.

56. Hugh William Davies, *Bernhard von Breydenbach and his Journey to the Holy Land 1483/4. A Bibliography*. London, 1911.

57. Franz Stadler, *Michael Wolgemut und der Nürnberger Holzschnitt im letzten Drittel des 15. Jahrhunderts*. Strasbourg, 1914.

58. M. Thausing, "Michael Wolgemut als Meister W und der Ausgleich über den Verlag der Hartmann Schedel'schen Weltchronik," *Mitteilungen des Instituts für Österreichische Geschichtsforschung*, 5(1884), p. 121. – V. von Loga, "Die Städteansichten in Hartmann Schedels Weltchronik," *Jahrbuch der Preussischen Kunstsammlungen*, 9(1888), p. 93.

59. W. Weisbach, *Der Meister der Bergmannschen Officin und Albrecht Dürers Beziehungen zur*

Basler Buchillustration. Strasbourg, 1896.—Rudolf Kautzsch, *Die Holzschnitte zum Ritter vom Turn.* Strasbourg, 1903.

60. Paul Heitz, *Flugblätter des Sebastian Brant.* Strasbourg, 1915.

61. Richard Muther, *Die deutsche Bücherillustration der Gotik und Frührenaissance (1460 bis 1530),* 2 vols. Munich, 1884.—Carl von Lützow, *Geschichte des deutschen Kupferstiches und Holzschnittes.* Berlin, 1891.—C. Dodgson, *Catalogue of Early German and Flemish Woodcuts Preserved in the Department of Prints and Drawings in the British Museum,* I, II. London, 1903–1911.—Hans Koegler, *Über Buchillustrationen in den ersten Jahrzehnten des deutschen Buchdrucks.* Mainz, 1911.— Wilhelm Worringer, *Die altdeutsche Buchillustration.* Munich, 1912.—Alfred W. Pollard, *Fine Books.* London, 1912.—W.L. Schreiber, *Manuel de l'amateur de la gravure sur bois et sur métal au 15. siècle. T.5. Catalogue des incunables à figures imprimés en Allemagne en Suisse, Autriche-Hongrie et en Scandinavie.* Berlin, 1911/12.—Paul Kristeller, *Kupferstich und Holzschnitt in vier Jahrhunderten,* 4th ed. Berlin, 1922.—A.W. Pollard, *Early Illustrated Books.* London, 1917.—W.L. Schreiber, *Der Buchholzschnitt im 15. Jahrhundert.* Munich, 1929.—Albert Schram, *Der Bilderschmuck der Frühdrucke,* 23 vols. Leipzig, 1920–42.—Max Geisberg, *Die Deutsche Buchillustration in der ersten Hälfte des 16. Jahrhunderts.* Munich, 1930.

62. Erich von Rath, "Totentanz," *Lexikon für gesamte Buchwesen,* 3(1937), p. 414.

63. Hans Wahl, *Die 92 Holzschnitte der Lübecker Bibel.* Weimar, 1917.—Max J. Friedländer, *Die Lübecker Bibel.* Munich, 1923.

64. Martin Rade, "Zur Apokalypse Dürers und Cranach," in *Gesammelte Studien zur Kunstgeschichte. Eine Festgabe für Anton Springer.* Leipzig, 1885, p. 120.

65. W.L. Schreiber und P. Heitz, *Die Deutschen Accipies-und Magister-cum-discipulis Holzschnitte.* Strasbourg, 1908.—Hans Koegler, "Zwei unbeschriebene deutsche Accipies- oder Magister-Holzschnitte vom Ende des XV. oder Anfang des XVI. Jahrhunderts," *Zeitschrift für Bücherfreunde,* N.F. 2(1910–11), I. p. 491.—F. Schubert in *Reallexikon zur deutschen Kunstgeschichte,* I(1933), p. 110.

66. The Strasbourg printer, Heinrich Knoblochtzer, also belongs among the chief promoters of the German book. Cf. Karl Schorbach and Max Spirgatis's *Heinrich Knoblochtzer in Strassburg (1477–1488).* Strasbourg, 1888.

67. P. Kristeller, *Early Florentine Woodcuts.* London, 1897.—Erich von Rath, "Florentiner Buchillustration," *Lexikon des gesamten Buchwesens,* I; (1935), p. 551.

68. Franz Lippmann, *Le chevalier délibéré.* London, 1898.

69. Karl Schottenloher, "Die Druckersippen der Frühdruckzeit," *Zentralblatt für Bibliothekswesen,* 57(1940), p. 232.

70. Thus did the Salzburg Archbishop, Bernhard von Rohr (1466–1482) have bindings of manuscripts and printed works decorated with engravings of his arms and a crowned "M" as a sign of respect for the B.V.M. and the motto, "Unica spes mea" About the leather bindings, see H. Schreiber in: *Lexikon des gesamten Buchwesens,* 2(1936), p. 304, and P. Ruf in: *Festschrift Eugen Strollreither.* Erlangen, 1950, p. 229.

71. Karl Schottenloher, "Die Buchbinderwerkstätte des Klosters Tegernsee 1488–1518," *Allgmeiner Anzeiger für Buchbindereien,* 61(1948), p. 91.

72. Concerning book binding, see H. Loubier's *Der Bucheinband von seinen Anfängen bis zum Ende des 18. Jahrhunderts,* 2nd ed. Leipzig, 1926.—M.J. Husung, in *Handbuch der Bibliothekswissenschaft,* I(1931), p. 666.—W. Meyer, *Bibliographie der Buchbinder-Literatur.* Leipzig. 1925; supplements, 1934.

Chapter 14. The Waning Middle Ages

1. In the Munich ms. *Cod. lat. 18442* they are called by the abbot: *Libri, quos comparavit, constant 1100 fl. Bibliotecam construxit, quae anno 1525 solotenus deiecta reedificata est a domino Mauro, ut cernitur.*—Cf. G. Virgil Redlich's *Teggernsee und die deutsche Geistesgeschichte im 15. Jahnhundert.* Munich, 1921.

2. J.J. Bühler, *Die Schriftsteller und Schreiber des Benediktinerstifts St. Ulrich und Afra in Augsburg während des Mittelalters.* Dissertation. Munich, 1916.

3. Carl Wehmer, "Leonard Wagner und seine Proba centum scripturarum," *Beiträge zur Inkunabelkunde,* N.F.1. (1935):78.—Die Munich ms. *Cod. lat. 4340* has the following colophon by the 65 year-old: *Explicit commune sanctorum per fratrem Leonhardum Wirstlin alias Wagner de*

Schwabmenchingen presbyterum et conventualem monasterii Sanctorum Udalrici et Afrae in Augusta Vindelicorum in die sancti Pauli primi heremitae anno domini 1519, aetatis suae sexagesimo quinto.

4. Karl Schottenloher, "Ein handschriftlicher Inkunabel-Katalog aus dem Jahre 1500," *Zeitschrift für Bücherfreunde* 23(1931): supplement, col. 92.

5. Hugo, Graf von Waldersdorff, "Hrotsuit von Gandersheim," *Verhandlungen des histor. Vereins von Oberpfalz und Regensburg* 29(1874): 89.

6. Magnus Bernhard, "Die Buchdruckerei des Kolsters Ottobeuren," *Studien und Mitteilungen aus dem Benediktinerorden* 2(1881), p. 313, Cf. the supplements thereto by Ed. Gebele, *ibid.* 43(1925): 205.

7. Paul Lehmann, "Nachrichten von der Sponheimer Bibliothek des Abtes Johannes Trithemius," *Festgabe für Hermann Grauert.* (Freiburg im Breisgau, 1910), p. 205.

8. Fritz Schillmann, *Wolfgang Trefler und die Bibliothek des Jakobsklosters zu Mainz.* Leipzig, 1913.

9. Berthold Cernik, "Das Schrift- und Buchwesen im Stift Klosterneuburg während des 15. Jahrhunderts, *Jahrbuch des Stiftes Klosterneuburg,* 5(1913), p. 97.

10. Paul Lehmann, *Bücherliebe und Bücherpflege bei den Karthäusern.* Miscellanea Francesco Ehrle, vol. 5. Rome, 1924, p. 364.

11. Ludwig Sieber, *Informatorium bibliothecarii Cartusiensis domus Vallis beatae Margarethae in Basilea Minori ex autographo fratris Georgii Carpentarii.* Basel, 1888.

12. Bernhard Walde, *Christliche Hebraisten Deutschlands am Ausgange des Mittelalters.* Münster, 1916, p. 74.

13. *Tractatus contra perfidos Judeos.* Esslingen, Konrad Fyner, 1475.

14. Franz Falk, *Die Presse zu Marienthal im Rheingau und ihre Erzeugnisse.* Mainz, 1882.

15. Karl Löffler, "Das Schrift- und Buchwesen der Brüder vom gemeinsamen Leben," *Zeitschrift für Bücherfreunde,* 11(1907–08), II, p. 286.—On the Augustinians of this period, see Hedwig Vonscholt's *Geistiges Leben im Augustinerorden am Ende des Mittelalters und zu Beginn der Neuzeit.* Berlin, 1915.

16. E. Fromm, *Die Ausgaben der Imitatio Christi in der Kölner Stadtbibliothek.* Cologne, 1886.—A. de Baker, *Essai bibliographique sur le Livre De imitatione Christi.* 1864.

17. Jos. A. Hanslik, *Geschichte und Beschreibung der Prager Universitätsbibliothek.* Prague, 1851.—Joh. Loserth, "Der älteste Katalog der Prager Universitätsbibliothek," *Mitteilungen des Instituts für österreichische Geschichtsforschung,* 11(1890), p. 301.

18. J.C. Herm. Weissenborn, *Amplonius Ratinck de Berka u seine Stiftung.* Erfurt, 1878.—W. Schum, *Beschreibendes Verzeichnis der Amplonianischen Handscriftensammlung zu Erfurt.* Berlin, 1887.

19. Th. Pyl, *Die Rubenow-Bibliothek.* Greifswald, 1865.

20. Axel Nelson, "Richard de Burys Philobiblon und die Festrede Matthaeus Hummels, des ersten Rektors der Albert-Ludwigs-Universität zu Freiburg," *Zentralblatt für Bibliothekswesen,* 40(1923), p. 269.

21. Jos. Rest, "Die älteste Geschichte der Freiburger Universitätsbibliothek," *Zentralblatt für Bibliothekswesen,* 39(1922), p. 7.

22. P. Lehmann, "Dr. Johannes Tröster, ein humanistisch gesinnter Wohltäter bayerischer Büchersammlungen," *Historisches Jahrbuch,* 60(1940), p. 646.

23. Cf. Wilhelm John's "Das Bücherverzeichnis der Ingolstädter Artistenfakultät von 1508," *Zentralblatt für Bibliothekswesen,* 59(1942), p. 381 ff., with illustrations of the attested bookplates.

24. Herm. Keussen, "Die älteren Bibliotheken der Kölner Universität insbesondere die Artistenbibliothek," *Westdeutsche Zeitschrift für Geschichte und Kunst,* 18(1899), p. 315.

25. Goerg Leidinger, *Kleine Studien zu Andreas von Regensburg. 1. Ein Handschriftenvermächtnis an die Stadt Regensburg vom Jahre 1430. Hermann Grauert-Festgabe.* Freiburg im Breisgau, 1910, p. 111.

26. Petz, "Urkundliche Beiträge zur Geschichte der Bücherei des Nürnberger Rates 1429 bis 1538," *Mitteilungen des Vereins für Geschichte der Stadt Nürnberg,* 6(1886), p. 123.—Paul Ruf in *Mittelalterliche Bibliothekskataloge Deutschlands und der Schweiz,* vol. 3, pt. 3. Munich, 1939, p. 774.

Chapter 15. The World of Dürer's Time

1. G. Agnelli and G. Ravegnani, *Annali delle edizioni Ariostee,* 2 vols. Bologna, 1933.

2. Pierre- Paul Plan, *Bibliographie Rabelaisienne. Les Éditions de Rabelais de 1532 à 1711.* Paris, 1904.

3. On Murner's relationship to the book, see M. Sondheim's "Thomas Murner als Illustrator," *Frankfurter Bücherfreund,* 9(1911), p. 78 and 10(1912), p. 307.

4. Karl Schottenloher, "Der Holzschnitt-Titel im Buch der Frühdruckzeit," *Buch und Schrift,* 2(1928), p. 17.

5. Johann Luther, *Die Titeleinfassungen der Reformationszeit.* Leipzig, 1900–13.–J. von Pflug-Harttung, *Rahmen deutscher Buchtitel im 16. Jahrhundert.* Stuttgart, 1909.–Alfred Forbes Johnson, *German Renaissance Title-borders.* Oxford, 1929.

6. Gustav Könnecke, *Bilderatlas zur Geschichte der deutschen Nationalliteratur,* 2d ed. Marburg, 1895.–A.F. Johnson, *One hundred Title Pages, 1500–1800.* London, 1928.–Julius Mäser and Otto Westram, *Der Titelsatz und seine Entwicklung bis zur Neuzeit,* 2d ed. Leipzig, 1920.–Gerh. Kiessling, "Die Anfänge des Titelblattes in der Blütezeit des deutschen Holzschnitts 1470–1530," *Buch und Schrift,* 3(1929), p. 9. (Issued as book, 1930).–Karl Schottenloher, "Titelsatz, Schrift und Satzspiegel im alten und neuen Buch," *Archiv für Buchgewerbe und Gebrauchsgraphik,* 76(1939), p. 167.

7. Stanley Morison, *Handbuch der Druckkunst. 250 Beispiele mustergültiger Antiquadrucke aus den Jahren 1500–1900.* Berlin, 1925.

8 .*Druckschriften des 15. bis 18. Jahrhunderts in getreuen Nachbildungen herausgegeben von der Direktion der Reichsdruckerei.* Berlin, 1884/87.–Karl Burger, *Monumenta Germaniae et Italiae typographica. Deutsche und italienische Inkunabeln in Getreuen Nachbildungen.* Herausgegeben von der Direktion der Reichsdruckerei. Berlin, 1892–1903.–*Veröffentlichungen der Gesellschaft für Typenkunde des 15. Jahrhunderts.* 1 ff. Leipzig, 1907 ff.–Karl Brandi, *Unsere Schrift.* Göttingen, 1911.–Rud. Kautzsch, *Die Entstehung der Frakturschrift.* Mainz, 1922.–A. Hessel, "Von der Schrift zum Druck," *Zeitschrift des deutschen Vereins für Buchwesen und Schrifttum,* 6(1923), p. 89.–Stanley Morison, *Meisterwerke aus vier Jahrhunderten. Die Entwicklung des Buchdrucks in lateinischer Schrift.* Berlin, 1924.–Gust. Milchsack, *Was ist die Fraktur?,* 2d ed. Braunschweig, 1925.–Hans Degering, *Die Schrift. Atlas der Schriftformen des Abendlandes vom Altertum bis zum Ausgang des 18. Jahrunderts.* Berlin, 1929.–W.H. Lange, *Schriftfibel,* 3rd ed. Wiesbaden, 1951.

9 .Hinr. Alfr. Schmid, "Holbeins Tätigkeit für die Baseler Verleger," *Jahrbuch der Preuss. Kunstsammlungen* 20(1899), p. 233.–Hans Holbein. *Initialen.* Herausgegeben von Gustav Schneeli und Paul Heitz. Strasbourg, 1900.–W.L. Schreiber, "Der Initialschmuck in den Druckwerken des 15. bis 18. Jahrhunderts," *Zeitschrift für Bücherfreunde,* 5(1901/02), I., p. 209; II., p. 302.–Oskar Jennings, *Early Woodcut Initials.* London, 1908.–A.F. Butsch, *Bücherornamentik der Renaissance und Hochrenaissance.* Leipzig, 1878–81.–A.F. Johnson, *Decorative Initial Letters.* London, 1937.

10. G. Sello, "Die Glücksgöttin auf Buchdruckerzeichen des XVI. Jahrhunderts," *Zeitschrift für Bildende Kunst* 12 (1877) p. 115.–Paul Heitz, *Die Büchermarken oder Buchdrucker und Verlegerzeichen,* 7 vols. Strasbourg, 1892–1908.–Paul Heitz, *Die Zürcher Buchermarken.* Zürich, 1895.–Hans Koegler, "Basler Büchermarken bis zum Jahre 1550," *Zeitschrift für Bücherfreunde,* 12(1908/09), I., p. 253; II., p. 283.–Annemarie Meiner, *Das deutsche Signet.* Leipzig, 1922.–Marie Louis Polain, *Marques des Imprimeurs et Libraires en France au XVe Siècle.* Paris, 1926.–*Die deutschen Drucker und Buchhändler-marken.* 1 ff. Munich, 1924 ff.–Hugo Alker, "Die älteste Druckermarke im Psalterium Moguntinum von 1457," *Gutenberg-Jahrbuch,* (1950), p. 134 ff.

11. Albrecht Kirchhoff, *Beiträge zur Geschichte des deutschen Buchhandels.* Leipzig, 1851/53.

12. Max von Boehn, *Albrecht Dürer als Buch- und Kunsthändler.* Munich, 1905.–Friedrich Bock, "Albrecht Dürer und das Buch," *Ostdeutsche Monatshefte,* 9(1928–29), p. 147.

13. Hans Vollmer, "Die Illlustratoren des 'Beschlossen gart des rosenkranz mariae.' Ein Beitrag zur Kenntnis des Holzschnittes der Dürerschule," *Repertorium für Kunstwissenschaft,* 31(1908), p. 18.

14. Franz, Frhr. von Soden, *Beiträge zur Geschichte der Reformation.* Nuremberg, 1855, p. 292.

15. O. Clemen, *Der Gilgengart.* Zwickauer Faksimiledrucke, 16. Zwickau, 1913.

16. Karl Schottenloher, "Der Augsburger Verleger Sigmund Grimm und sein Geschäftszusammen-bruch im Oktober 1527." *Der Sammler,* 11(Berlin, 1921) p. 344.

17 .Wilhelm Fraenger, *Altdeutsches Bilderbuch. Hans Weiditz u. Sebastian Brant.* Leipzig, 1930.

18. Heinr. Alfr. Schmid, "Holbeins Tätigkeit für die Baseler Verleger," *Jahrbuch der Preussischen Kunstsammlungen,* 20(1899), p. 233.

19. "Historiarum veteris instrumenti icones" and "Les Simulachres et historiees faces de la mort." Cf. A. Goette's *Holbeins Totentanz und seine Vorbilder.* Strasbourg, 1897.

20. Urs. Graf, *Die Holzschnitte zur Passion. Mit einer Einführung von Wilhelm Worringer.* Munich, 1923.

21. Konrad Varrentrap, "Sebastian Brants Beschreibung von Deutschland und ihre Veröffentlichung durch Caspar Hedio," *Zeitschrift für die Geschichte des Oberrheins,* 50(1896), p. 288.

22. Fr. Ritter von Wieser, *Die Cosmographiae introductio des Martin Waldseemüller (Ilacomilus) in Facsimiledruck.* Strasbourg, 1907.

23. Concerning America's oldest literature, see Henry Harrisee's *Bibliotheca Americana Vetustissima. A Description of Works Relating to America Publsiehd Between 1492 and 1551,* 2 vols. Paris, 1866–72; new printing, Leipzig, 1926.—J. Fischer and Fr., Ritter von Wieser, *Die älteste Karte mit dem Namen Amerika aus d. J. 1507 und die Carta marina aus d. J. 1516 des Martin Waldseemüller.* Innsbruck and London, 1903.

24. J. Ferguson, "The Margarita philosophica of Gregor Reisch," *Transactions of the Bibliographical Society,* II, 10(1930), p. 194.

25. Hildegard Zimmermann, *Lukas Cranach d. Ae., Folgen der Wittenberger Heiligtümer und die Illustration des Rhau'schen Hortulus animae.* Halle, 1929.—Ernst Schulte-Strathaus, "Die Wittenberger Heiligtumsbücher vom Jahre 1509." *Gutenberg-Jahrbuch,* (1930), p. 175.

26. Eduard Flechsig, *Adam von Fulda. Ein sehr andechtig cristenlich Buchlein. Mit 8 Holzschnitten von Lukas Cranach.* Photocopy. Berlin, 1914.

27. Gabr. von Terey, *Cardinal Albrecht von Brandenburg und das Halle'sche Heiligtumsbuch von 1520.* Strasbourg, 1892. On the unknown printer, see Joseph Benzing's "Die Anfänge des Buchdrucks zu Halle an der Saale," *Gutenberg Jahrbuch.* 1939, p. 202. The decorative illustrations are reproduced in Georg Hirth's *Liebhaberbibliothek alter Illustratoren,* vol. 13. Leipzig, 1889.

28. F. Weinkauff, "Zwei Briefe Sebatstian Francks,"*Alemannia,* 4(1877), p. 24.—Ad. Fluri, "Ein Brief des Chronisten Sebastian Franck an Eberhard von Rümlang," *Anzeiger für Schweizerische Geschichte,* N.F. 7(1894–97), p. 539, and 8(1898–1901), p. 48.—Alfred Hegler, *Beiträge zur Geschichte der Mystik in der Reformationszeit.* Berlin, 1906, pp. 196, 208.

29. *Novus orbis regionum ac insularum veteribus incognitarum.*

30. *Die New Welt der Lanschaften und Insulen.* Cf. V. Hantzsch's *Deutsche Reisende des 16. Jahrhunderts.* Leipzig, 1895.

31. Elsbeth Bonnemann, *Die Presse des Hieronymus Rodler in Simmern. Eine fürstliche Hofbuchdruckerei des 16. Jahrhunderts.* Leipzig, 1939.

32. Martin von Hase, "Die in Erfurt von Mathes Maler und Melchior Sachse gedruckten Ausgaben der Rechenbücher von Adam Riese," *Gutenberg Jahrbuch* (1937), p. 121.

33. Cf. p. 120.

34. Ernst Zinner, *Geschichte und Bibliographie der astronomischen Literatur in Deutschland zur Zeit der Renaissance.* Leipzig, 1941.

35. Gustav Hellmann, *Aus der Blütezeit der Astrometeorologie. J. Stöfflers Prognose für das Jahr 1524."* Veröffentlichungen des Preussischen Meteorologischen Instituts, no. 273. Berlin, 1914, p. 5.

36. Otto Hupp, *Ein Missale speciale. Vorläufer des Psalteriums von 1457.* Munich 1898.—Konrad Häbler, "Das 'Missale speciale Constantiense'," *Gutenberg-Jahrbuch.* (1930), p. 67.

37. Victor, Prince d'Essling, *Les Missels imprimés a Venise de 1481 à 1600.* Paris, 1894.—Adolf Tronnier, *Die Missaldrucke Peter Schöffers und seines Sohnes Johann.* Mainz, 1908.—Hanns Bohatta, *Katalog der Liturgischen Drucke des XV. und XVI. Jahrhunderts in der Herzogl. Parma'schen Bibliothek in Schwarzau am Steinfeld.* Vienna, 1909.—Wilhelm L. Schreiber, *Christus am Kreuz. Kanonbilder der in Deutschland gedruckten Messbücher des 15. Jahrhunderts.* Strasbourg, 1910. K. Schottenloher, *Die liturgischen Druckdenkmäler in ihrer Blütezeit.* Mainz, 1910.—H. Bohatta, *Liturgische Bibliographie des XV. Jahrhunderts mit Ausnahme der Missale und Livres d'heures,* 2d ed. Vienna, 1924.—H. Bohatta, *Liturgische Drucke und liturgische Drucker.* Festschrift. Regensburg, 1926.—W.H. James Weale, *Bibliographia liturgica. Catalogus missalium ritus latini ab anno 1474 impressorum. Iterum edidit H. Bohatta.* London, 1926.—Hanns Bohatta, *Bibliographie der Breviere 1501–1850.* Leipzig, 1937. Ernst Schulze gives a thorough discussion of the book in: *Beiträge zur Inkunabelkunde, N.F. 2(1938), p. 179.*

38. *Wilhelm Loose, Anton Tuchers Haushaltsbuch.* Stuttgart, 1877, p. 155.

39. John Macfarlane, *Antoine Verard.* London, 1908.—Aug. Bernard, "Antoine Vérard et ses livres à miniatrues au XVe siècle," *Bulletin du bibliophile et du bibliothécaire,* 14(1860), p. 1589.

40. Felix Soleil, *Les heures gothiques et la Littérature pieuse au XV. et XVI. siècle.* Rouen, 1882.—W. von Seidlitz, "Die gedruckten illustrierten Gebetbücher des 15. und 16. Jahrhunderts," *Jahrbuch der Preuss. Kunstsammlungen,* 5(1884), p. 128; 6(1885), p. 22.—Georg Domel, *Die Entstehung des*

Gebetbuches und seine Ausstattung bis Anfang des 16. Jahrhunderts. Cologne, 1921.—Hanns Bohatta, *Bibliographie der Livres d'heures, officia, Hortuli animi, Coronae B.M.V., Rosaria und Cursus B.M.V. des XV. und XVI. Jahrhunderts,* 2d ed. Vienna, 1924.

41. Franz Friedr. Leitschuh, "Die Bamberger Halsgerichtsordnung," *Repertorium für Kunstwissenschaft,* 9(1886), p. 59.—Cf. Karl Schottenloher's "Der Frühdruck, im Dienste der öffentlichen Verwaltung," *Gutenberg-Jahrbuch.* 1944/49, p. 138 ff.

42. K. Schottenloher, *Der Münchener Buchdrucker Hans Schobser.* Munich, 1925.

43. Carl F. Becker, *Die Tonwerke des 16. und 17. Jahrhunderts,* 2d ed. Leipzig, 1855.—Rob. Eitner, *Bibliographie der Musiksammelwerke des 16. und 17. Jahrhunderts.* Berlin, 1877.—Hugo Riemann, *Notenschrift und Notendruck. Bibliographisch-typographische Studie.* Leipzig, 1896.—Adolf Thürling, "Der Musikdruck mit beweglichem Metallsystem im 16. Jahrhundert und die Musikdrucke des Mathias Apiarius in Strassburg und Bern," *Vierteljahrschrift für Musikwissenschaft,* 8(1892), p. 389.—Rob. Eitner, "Der Musiknotendruck und seine Entwicklung," *Zeitschrift für Bücherfreunde,* 1(1898), II., p. 630.—Carl Wendel, "Aus der Wiegenzeit der Notendrucke," *Zentralblatt für Bibliothekswesen,* 19(1902), p. 569.—Herm. Springer, "Die Musiktypographie in der Inkunabelzeit," in *Beiträge zur Bücherkunde und Philologie. August Wilmanns gewidmet.* Leipzig, 1930, p. 173.—Jos. Mantuani, *Über den Beginn des Notendrucks.* Vienna, 1901.—Raph. Molitor, *Deutsche Choral-Wiegendrucke.* Regensburg, 1904.—Ludwig Volkmann, "Musikalische Bibliophilie," *Zeitschrift für Bücherfreunde,* N.F. 1(1909), I., p. 121.—Max Seiffert, "Bildzeugnisse des 16. Jahrhunderts für die instrumentale Begleitung des Gesanges und den Ursprung des Musikkupferstiches," *Archiv für Musikwissenschaft,* 1(1919), p. 49.—G. Kinsky, "Musikbücher," *Lexikon des gesamten Buchwesens,* 2(1936), p. 502.—Walter zur Westen, *Musiktitel aus vier Jahrhunderten.* Leipzig, 1921.—Kathi Meyer, "Die Illustrationen in den Musikbüchern des 15.–17. Jahrhunderts," *Philobiblon,* 10(1938), pp. 205, 278.

44. Ph. Renouard, *Bibliographie des impressions et des oeuvres de Josse Badius Ascensius (1462–1535),* 3 vols. Paris, 1909.—J. Lieure, *La gravure en France au XVIe siècle.* Paris, 1927.—A.F. Johnson, *French Sixteenth Century Printing.* London, 1928.

45. P. Renouard, *Bibliographie des éditions de Simon de Colines (1520–1546).* Paris, 1894. Cf. also R. Brun's *Le Livre illustre en France au XVIe siècle.* Paris, 1930.

46. Franz Dülberg, "Lucas van Leyden als Illustrator," *Repertorium für Kunstwissenschaft,* 31(1898), p. 36.—D. Campbell, "Beschreibendes Verzeichnis der Buchillustrationen Lucas van Leydens," *Repertorium für Kunsturissenschaft,* 53(1908), p. 43.—N. Beets, *De houtsneden in Vorstermann's bijbel van 1528.* Amsterdam, 1915.—E. von Rath in *Lexikon des gesamten Buchwesens,* 2(1936), p. 334.

47. Franz Delitzsch, *Studien zur Entstehungsgeschichte der Polyglottenbibel des Kardinals Ximenes.* Leipzig, 1871 and 1886.

48. The Cardinal's care also extended to worthy books for worship. In the missal for Toledo, printed in 1512 at Burgos it is promulgated: *Faciant alii templorum fundamenta, construant parietes, erigant turres, testitudines suspendant, dum nobis relinquant dicare bibliothecas, comportare libros atque sacris codicibus sacerdotes, ministros atque aedituos instruere.* He would have all worship books printed on parchment.

49. L.C. Treviranus. *Die Anwendung des holzschnittes zur bildlichen Darstellung von Pflanzen.* Leipzig, 1855.—Claus Nissen, *Die botanische Buchillustration,* 2 vols. Stuttgart, 1951.

50. Kunstbuch des Peter Flötner, Zürich, Rudolf Wyssenbach, 1549; reproduction: Berlin, 1882.

51. Alfred Lichtwark, *Das Modelbuch des Peter Quentel. Gesammelte Studien zur Kunstgeschichte. Eine Festgabe für Anton Springer.* Leipzig, 1885, p. 143.—Alfred Lichtwark, *Der Ornamentstich der deutschen Frührenaissance.* Berlin, 1888, p. 115.—E. von Ubisch, "Über Spitzenbücher und Spitzen," *Repertorium für Kunstwissenschaft,* 16(1893), p. 89.—Arthur Lotz, "Die Eutstehung der Modelbücher," *Zeitschrift für Bücherfreunde,* N.F. 18(1926), p. 45.—Arthur Lotz, *Bibliographie der Modelbücher. Beschreibendes Verzeichnis der Stick- und Spitzenmusterbücher des 16. und 17. Jahrhunderts.* Leipzig, 1933.

52. J.H. Slater, *Illustrated Sporting Books.* London, 1899.

53. Hans Wegener, *Küchenmeisterei.* Faksimile. Mit einem Glossar und einer Bibliographie. Leipzig, 1939.

54. J. Stockbauer, "Die Bücher der Schreibmeister des 16. bis 18. Jahrhunderts im Germanischen Museum," *Mitteilungen aus dem germanischen Nationalmuseum,* 1(1884–86), p. 77.—Arthur Lotz, "Schreibmeisterbücher," *Lexikon des gesamten Buchwesens,* vol. 3. Leipzig, 1937, p. 234.—Arthur Lotz, "Die deutschen Schreibmeisterbücher," *Philobiblon,* 10(1938), pp. 379, 434.

55. W. Schürmeyer, "Technische Bücher," *Lexikon des gesamten Buchwesens*, 3(1937), p. 375.
56. Georges Duplessis, *Essai bibliographique sur les différentes éditions des oeuvres d'Ovide ornées de planches publiées aux 15. et 16. siècles*. Paris, 1889. — M.D. Henkel, "Illustrierte Ausgaben von Ovids Metamorphosen im XV., XVI. und XVII. Jahrhundert," *Vorträge der Bibliothek Warburg*. 1930, p. 58.
57. Jaro Springer, "Der Farbenholzschnitt," *Die Graphischen Künste*, 16(1893), p. 11. — Walter Gräff, "Älteste deutsche Farbenholzschnitte," *Zeitschrift für Bücherfreunde*, N.F. 1(1909/10), II, p. 336.
58. Friedrick Warnecke, *Die deutschen Bücherzeichen (Ex libris) von ihrem Ursprunge bis zur Gegenwart*. Berlin, 1890. — G. Seyler, *Illustriertes Handbuch der Exlibris-Kunde*. Berlin, 1895. — Walter zur Westen, *Exlibris, (Bucheignerzeichen)*. Bielefeld, 1901. — K.E., Graf zu Leiningen-Westerburg, *Deutsche und öesterreichische Bibliothekszeichen*. Stuttgart, 1901. — *Exlibris. Zeitschrift für Bücherzeichen seit 1892.* — *Jahrbuch der österreichischen Exlibris-Gesellschaft seit 1906.*

Chapter 16. The German Humanists

1. *Clarorum virorum epistolae latinae, graecae et hebraicae variis temporibus missae ad Johannem Reuchlin*. Tübingen, Thomas Anshelm, 1514; 2d ed., with a second book 1519.
2. *Epistolae obscurorum virorum ad venerabilem virum Magistrum Ortuinum Gratium Daventriensem*. Hagenau, Heinrich Gran, 1515; new edition by Aloys Bömer. Heidelberg, 1924.
3. *Porro felices vos putate, qui in hoc seculum incidistis, in quo non solum linguae Latina, Graeca et Hebraica revixerunt, sed et disciplinae bonae omnes atque adeo Theologia ipsa ac Philosophia renascunter.*
4. *Tua officina laudatissimos autores suppeditat Latinis, Graecis et Hebraeis formulis excusos et his quidem longe elegantissimis.* Borrowing from Aldus Manutius, Anshelm proudly called his operation "Academia Anshelmiana."
5. Cf. my treatment that will appear shortly, "Die Widmungsvorrede im Buche des 16. Jahrhunderts," *Reformationsgeschichtliche Studien und Texte*, 75.
6. Clemens I, *Recognitionum libri X*. Basel, 1526.
7. Erasmus, *Paraphrases in Evangelia et Epistolas*. Basel, Johann Froben, 1522.
8. Carl Meyer, "Der griechische Mythus in den Kunstwerken des fünfzehnten Jahrhunderts," *Repertorium für Kunstwissenschaft*, 16(1893), p. 261. — Otto Clemen, "Die Titelbordüre mit dem Parisurteil," *Zeitschrift für Bücherfreunde*, N.F. 11(1919/20), II, p. 162.
9. Annemarie Meiner, "Signete des Humanismus," *Imprimatur*, 7(1937), p. 51.
10. Paul Joachimsohn, "Aus der Bibliothek Sigismund Gossembrots," *Zentralblatt für Bibliothekswesen*, 11(1894), p. 249 and 297.
11. Heinrich Karmm, *Deutsche Bibliotheken unter dem Einfluss von Humanismus und Reformation. Ein Beitrag zur deutschen Bildungsgeschichte*. Leipzig, 1938.
12. K. Morneweg, *Johann von Dalberg, ein deutscher Humanist und Bischof*. Heidelberg, 1887.
13. Rich. Stauber, *Die Schedelsche Bibliothek*. Freiburg im Breisgau, 1908. — K. Schottenloher, "Hartmann Schedel 1440–1514," *Philobiblon*, 12(1940), p. 279.
14. Erich König, *Peutinger-Studien*. Freiburg im Breisgau, 1914.
15. Erich König, *Konrad Peutingers Briefwechsel*. Munich, 1923, p. 340.
16. Theod. Herberger, "Conrad Peutinger in seinem Verhältnisse zu Kaiser Maximilian I," in *Jahresbericht des histor. Vereins von Schwaben und Neuburg*, 15 and 16(1851), p. 29.
17. Karl Schottenloher, "Johann Reuchlin und das humanistische Buchwesen," *Zeitschrift für die Geschichte des Oberrheins*, 37(1922), p. 295. — Karl Christ, *Die Bibliothek Reuchlins in Pforzheim*. Leipzig, 1924.
18. Fritz Husner, "Die Bibliothek des Erasmus," *Gedenkschrift zum 400. Todestage des Erasmus von Rotterdam*. Basel, 1936, p. 228.
19. Erwin Rosenthal, "Dürers Buchmalereien für Pirckheimers Bibliothek," *Jahrbuch der preuss. Kunstsammlungen*, 49(1928), p. 1. — Emile Offenbacher, "La bibliothèque de Willibald Pirckheimer," *La bibliofilia*, 40(1938), p. 241.
20. Alfons Semler, "Die Bibliothek des Humanisten Jakob Spiegel," *Zeitschrift für die Geschichte des Oberrheins*, 71(1917), p. 85.
21. Karl Krause, "Bibliologisches aus Mutians Briefen," *Zentralblatt für Bibliothekswesen*, 10(1893), p. 1.
22. Beriah Botfield, *Prefaces to the First Editions of the Greek and Roman Classics and of the Sacred*

Scriptures. London, 1861.—Karl Schottenloher, "Handschriftenforschung und Buchdruck im XV. und XVI. Jahrhundert," *Gutenberg-Jahrbuch*, 1931, p. 73.

23. They practically have the effect of a book exhibition and give us a pretty picture of the appearance of the bindings at that time. Cf. Hans Loubier's *Der Bucheinband*, 2d ed. Leipzig, 1936, p. 198.

24. Ludwig Enthoven, "Über Druck und Vertrieb Erasmischer Werke," *Neue Jahrbücher für Pädagogik*, 14(1911), p. 33.—P.S. Allen, "Erasmus Relations with his Printers," *Transactions of the Bibliographical Society*, 13(1916), p. 297.—B. Kruitwagen, *Erasmus en zijn drukkers-Uitgevers. Een Fragment uit hun Briefwisseling.* Amsterdam, 1923.

25. August Bludau, *Die beiden ersten Erasmus-Ausgaben des Neuen Testaments und ihre Gegner.* Freiburg im Breisgau, 1902.

26. *Erasmi Roterdami Encomium moriae, i.e. Stultitiae laus, Lob der Torheit.* Basel edition of 1519 with the border designs by Hans Holbein the Younger. In facsimile, with an introduction edited by Heinrich Alfred Schmid. Basel, H. Oppermann, 1931. Cf. Fritz Homeyer's "Wie Holbein das 'Lob der Narrheit' illustrierte," *Zeitschrift für Bücherfreunde*, N.F. 23(1931), p. 117.

27. Rud. von Raumer, *Geschichte der Germanischen Philologie vorzugsweise in Deutschland.* Munich, 1870, p. 4.—Hans Tiedemann, *Tacitus und das Nationalbewusstsein der deutschen Humanisten Ende des 15. und Anfang des 16. Jahrhunderts.* Berlin, 1913.—Cf. also Jos. Knepper's *Nationaler Gedanke und Kaiseridee bei den elsässischen Humanisten.* Freiburg im Breisgau, 1898.

28. Anton Ruland, "Der Original-Codex der Roswitha und die Herausgabe desselben durch Conrad Celtis," *Serapeum*, 18(1875), p. 17.

29. A. Fechter, *Die Amerbachische Abschrift des Vellegjus Paterculus und ihr Verhältnis zum Murbacher Codex und zur Editio princeps.* Basel, 1844.

30. Cf. K. Schottenloher, "Der Druckfehlerteufel der Reformationszeit," *Zeitschrift für Bücherfreunde*, N.F. 23(1931), p. 111.

31. Adalbert Horawitz, "Des Beatus Rhenanus literarische Tätigkeit," *Sitzungsberichte der philos. -histor. Classe der Akademie der Wissenschaften.* vol. 71. Vienna, (1872), p. 634; vol. 72. Vienna, (1872), pp. 323–376.—Adalbert Horawitz, "Die Bibliothek und Correspondenz des Beatus Rhenanus zu Schlettstadt," *Sitzungsberichte der philos. -histor. Classe der Akademie der Wissenschaften*, vol. 78. Vienna, 1874, pp. 313–340.—Gustav Carl Knod, "Aus der Bibliothek des Beatus Rhenanus," in *Die Stadtbibliothek zu Schlettstadt.* Strasbourg, 1889, Book II, p. 1.

32. Franz Falk, "Der Livius-Herausgeber und Übersetzer Nicolaus Carbach zu Mainz," *Zentralblatt für Bibliothekswesen*, 4(1887), p. 218.

33. Paul Lehmann, *Johannes Sichardus und die von ihm benutzten Bibliotheken und Handscriften.* Munich, 1911.

34. Karl Schottenloher, "Widmungsvorreden deutscher Drucker und Verleger des 16. Jahrhunderts," *Gutenberg-Jahrbuch.* 1942, p. 248.

35. Paul Lehmann, *Franciscus Modius als Hanschriftenforscher.* Munich, 1908.

36. Anton Ruland, "Franciscus Modius und dessen Enchiridion," *Serapeum*, 14(1853), p. 81.

37. Concerning a similar papal stipulation, see J.A.F. Orban's "Eu panselijk verbod tegen hed opgbruiken van handschriften anno 1566," *Tijdschrift voor boek- en bibliotheekwezen*, 5(1907), p. 62.

38. List in *Pal. lat.* 1925 of the Vaticana in Rome.

39. *Pal. lat.*, 1951.

40. *Pal. graec. 431* of the Vaticana.—*Il rotulo die Giosuè. Codice Vaticano Palatino greco 431 riprodotto.* Milan, 1905.

41. *Pal. lat., 1921.*

42. Karl Christ, "Zur Geschichte der griechischen Handschriften der Palatina," *Zentralblatt für Bibliothekswesen*, 63(1919), p. 3.

43. Hans Lietzmann, "Zur Datierung der Josuasrolle," in *Mittelalterliche Handschriften. Festgabe zum 60. Geburtstage von Hermann Degering.* Leipzig, 1926, p. 181.

44. Wilh. Port, *Hieronymus Commelinus, 1550–1597.* Leipzig, 1938.—Karl Preisendanz, "Friedrich Sylburg als Verlagsberater," *Gutenberg-Jahrbuch.* 1937, p. 193.—Karl Preisendanz, "Aus Friedrich Sylburgs Heidelberger Zeit," *Neue Heidelberger Jahrbücher.* 1937, p. 35.

45. Gottfr. Smend, *Jan Gruter. Sein Leben und Wirken.* Bonn, 1939.

46. Anton Ruland, "Erasmus Neustetter, der Maecenas des Franciscus Modius, nach des letzteren Tagebuch" *Archiv des historischen Vereins von Unterfranken und Aschaffenburg*, 12(1853), nos. 2 and 3, p. 1.

47. Karl Löffler, "Die 'Bibliotheca Eckiana'," *Zentralblatt für Bibliothekswesen*, 36(1919), p. 195.

Chapter 17. The Reformation

1. Otto Clemen, *Luthers Lob der Buchdruckerkunst*. Zwickau, 1939.

2. The famous Nuremberg booksellers' establishment.

3. Concerning these frequently printed (and in several instances, richly illustrated) postils, see W.L. Schreiber, "Guillermus-Postille," *Lexikon des gesamten Buchwesens*, 2(1936), p. 32.

4. Gustav Wustmann, "Luthers erster Bibeldrucker," in his *Aus Leipzigs Vergangenheit. Gesammelte Aufsätze*, N.F. Leipzig, 1898, p. 116. – Paul Pietsch, "Bibliographie der deutschen Bibel Luthers" in *D. Martin Luthers deutsche Blbel (D. Martin Luthers Werke*. Kritische gesamtausgabe, Abt. 3), v. 2. Weimar, 1909, p. 201. – Wilhelm Walter, *Luthers deutsche Bibel. Festschrift zur Jahrhundertfeier der Reformation*. Berlin, 1917. – Albert Schramm, *Die Illustration der Lutherbibel*. Leipzig, Hiersemann, 1923.

5. Martin Luther, *Tischreden oder Colloquia, so er in vielen Jahren gegen gelarten Leuten, fremden Gästen und seinen Tischgesellen geführet*. Nach den Hauptstücken unserer christlichen Lehre zusammengetragen (von Johannes Aurifaber). Eisleben, Urban Gaubisch, 1566. – Cf. *D. Martin Luthers Tischreden 1531–46* (Edited by E. Kroker), in *Martin Luthers Werke*. Kritische Gesamtausgabe. Weimar, 1912–21.

6. E. Thiele, "Die Original-Handschriften Luthers," in *Lutherstudien zur 4. Jahrhundertfeier der Reformation*. Weimar, 1917, p. 233. – G. Kattermann, "Luther's Handexemplare des antijüdischen Porchetus in der Landesbibliothek Karlsruhe," *Zentralblatt für Bibliothekswesen*, 55(1938), p. 45.

7. *Die Schmalkaldischen Artikel vom Jahr 1537. Nach D. Martin Luthers Autograph in der Universitätsbibliothek zu Heidelberg*. Hrsg. von Karl Zangenmeister. Heidelberg, 1883.

8. K. Schottenloher, "Schicksale von Büchern und Bibliotheken im Bauernkrieg," *Zeitschrift für Bücherfreunde*, 12(1908–09), II., p. 396.

9. K. Schottenloher, "Beschlagnahmte Druckschriften aus der Frühzeit der Reformation," *Zeitschrift für Bücherfreunde*, N.F. 8(1916/17), p. 305 ff. – K. Schottenloher, "Buchdrucker und Buchführer im Kampf der Schwärmer und Wiedertäufer," in *Buch und Papier. Buchkundliche u. papiergeschichtliche Arbeiten*. Hans H. Bockwitz dargebracht. Leipzig, 1949, p. 90 ff.

10. Wilhelm Meyer, "Über das Gebetbuch Karls des Kahlen," *Sitzungsberichte der philos., philolog. und histor. Classe der bayer. Akademie der Wissenschaften*, 1883, 3, p. 424.

11. Gustav Abb, "Von der Verschollenen Bibliothek des Klosters Lehnin," in *Mittelalterliche Handschriften*. Festgabe zum 60. Geburtstage von Hermann Degering. Leipzig, 1926, p. 1.

12. O. Radlach, "Die Bibliotheken der evangelischen Kirche und ihre rechtsgeschichtliche Entwicklung," *Zentralblatt für Bibliothekswesen*, 12(1895), p. 153.

13. Ludwig Schmidt, "Beiträge zur Geschichte der wissenschaftlichen Studien in sächsischen Klöstern," *Neues Archiv für Sächsische Geschichte und Altertumskunde*, 20(1899), p. 1.

14. James Montague Rhodes, *The Ancient Libraries of Cambridge and Dover*. Cambridge, 1903. – James Montague Rhodes, *A Descriptive catalogue of the Manuscripts in the Library of Corpus Christi College, Cambridge*, 2 vols. Cambridge, 1909–13.

15. *Sapiens atque eloquens pietas*, as this educational goal was described by Johann Sturm.

16. Wilhelm Preger, *Matthias Flacius Illyricus und seine Zeit*, 2 vols. in 1. Erlangen, 1861, p. 413. – J. Wilhelm Schulte, "Beiträge zur Entstehungsgeschichte der Magdeburger Centurien," *19. Bericht der Philomathie in Neisse*. (1874/77), p. 50. – A. Nürnberger, "Die Bonifatiusliteratur der Magdeburger Centuriatoren," *Neues Archiv der Gesellschaft für ältere deutsche Geschichte*, 11(1886), p. 9. – Ernst Schaumkell, *Beitrag zur Entstehungsgeschichte der Magdeburger Centurien*. Ludwigslust, 1898.

17. Viktor Bibl, "Der Briefwechsel zwischen Flacius ünd Nidbruck," *Jahrbuch der Gesellschaft für die Geschichte des Protestantismus in Österreich*, 17(1896), p. 1; 18(1897), p. 201; 19(1898), p. 96; 20(1899), p. 83.

18. K. Schottenloher, "Handschriftenschätze zu Regensburg im Dienste der Zenturiatoren 1554–1562," *Zentralblatt für Bibliothekswesen*, 34(1917), p. 65.

19. H. Schneider, "Die Bibliotheksreisen des Marcus Wagner," *Zentralblatt für Bibliothekswesen*, 50(1933), p. 678.

20. R. von Stintzing, *Georg Tanners Briefe an Bonifacius und Basilius Amerbach 1554 bis 1567. Ein Beitrag zur Geschichte der Novellen-Editionen.* Bonn, 1879. —Viktor Bibl, "Nidbruck und Tanner. Ein Beitrag zur Entstehungsgeschichte der Magdeburger Centurien und zur Charakteristik König Maximilians II," *Archiv für österreichische Geschichte,* 85(1898), p. 379.

21. *Etiam non sunt istiusmodi res toti regno ac ecclesiae necessariae privati iuris aut professionis propriae sed publici.* Cf. E. G. Vogel's "Ein Löblicher Vorschlag von Matth. Flacius," *Serapeum,* 8(1847), p. 270.

22. K. Schottenloher, "Reichenbacher Handschriften der Münchener Staatsbibliothek," *Zentralblatt für Bibliothekswesen,* 48(1931), p. 245.

23. Konrad Ziegler, "Zur Überlieferungsgeschichte des Firmicus Maternus De errore profanarum religionum," *Rheinisches Museum für Philologie,* N.F. 60(1905), p. 417. —*Julii Firmici Materni De errore profanarum religionum edidit Konrad Ziegler.* Leipzig, 1907. —Alfons Müller, *Zur Überlieferung der Apologie des Firmicus Maternus.* Dissertation, University of Tübingen. Tübingen, 1908.

24. Konrad Burdach, *Die nationale Aneignung der Bibel und die Anfänge der germanischen Philologie.* Halle (Saale), 1924,pp. 11, 62. —On Werden Abbey, see Adolf Schmidt's "Handschriften der Reichsabtei Werden," *Zentralblatt für Bibliothekswesen,* 22(1905), p. 241.

25. *De statu religionis et reipublicae Carolo Quinto Caesare Commentarii.* Strasbourg, 1555. C.f. Walter Friedensburg's *Johann Sleidanus.* Leipzig, 1935. —Otto Winckelmann, "Zur Geschichte Sleidans und seiner Kommentare," *Zeitschrift für die Geschichte des Oberrheins,* 53(1899), p. 565. —K. Schottenloher, "Johann Sleidanus und Markgraf Alcibiades," *Archiv für Reformationsgeschichte,* 35(1939), p. 193.

26. Ch. F. Schnurrer, *Slavischer Bücherdruck in Württemberg im 16. Jahrhundert.* Tübingen, 1799. —Franjo Bučar in *Carniola,* N.F. 7(1916), pp. 104, 178. —Karl Löffler, "Slawischer Buchdruck in Württemberg im Jahrhundert der Reformationszeit," *Zeitschrift für Bücherfreunde,* N.F. 21(1929), p. 93.

27. Cf. *Archiv für Buchbinderei,* 39(1939), p. 41.

28. Heinrich Reusch, *Der Index der verbotenen Bücher.* Bonn, 1883. —Heinrich Reusch, *Die Indices librorum prohibitorum des 16. Jahrhunderts.* Tübingen, 1886. —Jos. Hilgers. *Der Index der verbotenen Bücher.* Freiburg im Breisgau, 1904. —Bernhard Duhr, *Geschichte der Jesuiten in den Ländern deutscher Zunge,* v. 1. Freiburg im Breisgau, 1907, p. 635.

29. Cf. also Joh. Cardona's *De expurgendis haereticorum propriis nominibus etiam de Libris, qui de religione ex professo non tractant.* Rome, 1576.

30. Munich State Library: 4° Polem. 1738.

31. Johannes Aventinus, *Annalium Boiorum libri septem.* Ingolstadt, Alexandrum & Sam. Weissenhorn, 1554; Munich State Library: Rar. 790.

32. Karl Schottenloher, "Zensur-Eingriffe in der Münchener Jesuitenbibliothek im Jahre 1578," *Buch und Schrift,* N.F. 2(1939), p. 59. One of the two censors was not, as I have here assumed Dietrich Canisius, but the famous Petrus Canisius. Cf. the valuable supplement by J.M. Metzler in *Archivum Historicum,* 1940, p. 137.

33. Adolf Ulm, "Ein bayrischer Index erlaubter Bücher vom Jahre 1566," *Archiv für Geschichte des Deutschen Buchhandels,* 1(1878), p. 176. —Karl Theodor Heigel, "Die Censur in Altbaiern," *Archiv für Geschichte des Deutschen Buchhandels,* 2(1879), p. 5.

34. J. Zahn, "Zum Bücherwesen der Vorzeit," *Zeitschrift für deutsche Kulturgeschichte,* N.F. 4(1875), p. 189.

35. Otto Braunsberger, "Ein Freund der Bibliotheken und ihrer Handschriften," in *Miscellanea Francesco Ehrle,* 5(1924), p. 455. But even just as enthusiastically does Canisius express himself for ecclesiastical censorship. Cf. *Zeitschrift für deutsche Kulturgeschichte,* N.F. 4(1875), p. 213 ff.

36. Moritz Grolig, *Die Buchdruckerei des Jesuitenkollegiums in Wien, 1559–65.* Vienna, 1909.

37. Bernhardt Duhr, *Geschichte der Jesuiten in der ersten Hälfte des 17. Jahrhunderts* (Freiburg i.B., 1913). Part 2: 376, 642; Part 3: 295; Part 4, 1: 425. Cf. also H.O. Lange, "De forste europaeiste Bogtrykt i Macao 1588," *Nordisk Tidskrift for bok- och biblioteksväsen,* 10(1923), p. 137. —A. Huonder, *Die Verdienste der katholischen Heidenmission um die Buchdruckerkunst in überseeischen Ländern.* Aachen, 1923. —A. Väth, "Missionsdruckereien der Jesuiten," *Jesuiten- Lexikon* (L. Koch, ed.). Paderborn, 1934, col. 1213.

38. Otto Braunsberger, *Entstehung und erste Entwicklung des Katechismus des seligen Petrus Canisius.* Freiburg im Breisgau, 1893. —Friedrich Streicher, *S. Petri Canisii Catechismi Latini et Germanici.* Rome-Munich, 1933.

39. Alfred Goetze, *Die hochdeutschen Drucker der Reformationszeit*. Strasbourg, 1905.—Otto Clemen, *Die lutherische Reformation und der Buchdruck*. Leipzig, 1939.

Chapter 18. The Princely Courts of the Sixteenth Century

1. Karl Schottenloher, "Buchwidmungsbilder in Handschriften und Frühdrucken," *Zeitschrift für Bücherfreunde*, N.F. 12(1920/21), p. 149.
2. *Kaiser Maximilians I. Gebetbuch mit Zeichnungen von Albrecht Dürer und anderen Künstlern*. Faksimiledruck hrsg. von Karl Giehlow. Vienna, 1907.—*Aus den Gebetbuch Kaiser Maximilians*. Insel-Bücherei, 550.--Georg Leidinger, *Albrecht Dürers und Lukas Cranachs Randzeichnungen zum Gebetbuch Kaiser Maximilians I. in der Bayerischen Staatsbibliothek zu München*. Munich, 1922.
3. *Teuerdank. Ein literarischer, künstelerischer und historischer Ausschnitt. Nach dem illuminierten Pergamentexemplar im Besitz der Preussischen Staatsbibliothek herausgegeben von Hermann Degering*. Bielefeld, 1927.
4. Th. Gottlieb, *Büchersammlung Kaiser Maximilians I. Mit einer Einleitung über älteren Bücherbesitz im Hause Habsburg*. Leipzig, 1900.
5. G. Buchwald, "Archivalische Mitteilungen über Bücherbezüge der Kurfürstlichen Bibliothek und Georg Spalatins in Wittenberg," *Archiv für Geschichte des Deutschen Buchhandels*, 18(1896), p. 7.—C.G. Brandis, "Luther und Melanchthon als Benützer der Wittenberger Bibliothek," *Theologische Studien und Kritiken*, 90(1917), p. 206.—E. Hildebrandt, "Die kurfürsHiche Schloss- und Universitätsbibliothek zu Wittenberg," *Zeitschrift für Buchkunde*, 2(1925), p. 34.—G. Buchwald, "Zu Spalatins Reisen insbes. nach Wittenberg in Angelegenheiten der Kurfürstlichen Bibliothek," *Archiv für Bibliographie, Buch- und Bibliothekswesen*, 2(1928/29), p. 92.—Walter Friedensburg, *Urkundenbuch der Universität Wittenberg*, Part 1. Magdeburg, 1926, pp. 154, 158, 186, 225, 234, 297.
6. Bernh. Willkomm, "Die Bedeutung der Jenaer Universitätsbibliothek für reformationsgeschichtliche Forschung," *Zentralblatt für Bibliothekswesen*, 30(1915), p. 245.—Carl Georg Brandis, *Beiträge aus der Universitätsbibliothek zu Jena zur Geschichte des Refomationsjahrhunderts*. Jena, 1917.
7. J. Förstemann, "Felix König (Rex), erster Bibliothekar des Herzogs Albrecht von Preussen," *Zentralblatt für Bibliothekswesen*, 16(1899), p. 306.
8. Paul Schwenke and Konrad Lange, *Die Silberbiliothek Herzog Albrechts von Preussen*. Leipzig, 1894.—E. Kuhnert, "Die Nova Bibliotheca des Herzogs Albrecht," in *Aufsätze Fritz Milkau gewidmet*. Leipzig, 1921, p. 209.—A. Rohde, *Die Silberbibliothek des Herzogs Albrecht in Königsberg*. Königsberg, 1928
9. Konrad Haebler, *Deutsche Bibliophilen des 16. Jahrhunderts. Die Fürsten von Anhalt, ihre Bücher und ihre Bucheinbäude*. Leipzig, 1923.—Paul Wahl, "Fürst Georgs Bibliothek," *Zentralblatt für Bibliothekswesen*, 44(1927), p. 359.
10. August Wilmanns, "Der Katalog der Lorscher Klosterbibliothek aus dem zehnten Jahrhundert," *Museum für Philologie*, N.F. 23(1868), p. 385.
11. Jakob Wille, *Die Deutschen Pfälzer Handschriften des 16. u. 17. Jahrhunderts der Universitätsbibliothek in Heidelberg*. Heidelberg, 1903.—Karl Schottenloher, *Pfalzgraf Ottheinrich und das Buch*. Münster in Westfalen, 1927.—K. Preisendanz, "Neue Ottheinrich-Bände," *Forschungen u. Fortschritte*, 15(1939), p. 21.—K. Schottenloher, "Kurfürst Ottheinrich von der Pfalz und Herzog Albrecht V. von Bayern," *Archiv für Buchgewerbe u. Gebrauchsgraphik*, 1940, p. 73.
12. Max Georg Zimmermann, *Die bildenden Künste am Hof Herzog Albrechts V. von Bayern*. Strasbourg, 1895. p. 47.
13. Paul Durrieu, *Les Antiquités Judaiques et le peintre Jean Fouquet*. Paris, 1908.—Paul Durrieu, *Le Boccace de Munich*. Munich, 1909.
14. Otto Hartig, *Die Gründung der Münchener Hofbibliothek durch Albrecht V. und Johann Jakob Fugger*. Munich, 1917.
15. Ilse Schunke, "Die Pariser Büchersendungen des Hubert Languet an Kurfürst August von Sachsen 1566," in *Festschrift Martin Bollert*. Dresden, 1936, p. 49.
16. K. Berling, *Der kursächsische Hofbuchbinder Jakob Krause*. Dresden, 1897.—Christel Schmidt, *Jakob Krause*. Leipzig, 1923.—Ilse Schunke, "Methodische Fragen zur Krause-Forschung," *Archiv für Buchbinderei*, 28(1928), p. 73.—Ilse Schunke, *Krause-Studien*. Leipzig, 1932.
17. Albert Duncker, *Landgraf Wilhelm IV. von Hessen, genannt der Weise, und die Bergründung der Bibliothek zu Kassel im Jahre 1580*. Kassel, 1881.

18. O. Smital, "Miszellen zur Geschichte der Wiener Palatina. Hugo Blotius," in *Festschrift der Nationalbibliothek in Wien.* Vienna, 1926, p. 771.

19. Franz Babinger, "Hans Dernschwam, ein Kleinasienforscher des 16. Jahrhunderts," *Deutsche Rundschau für Geographie*, 35(1913), p. 535; 36(1914), p. 133; 37: 37.—Franz Babinger, *Hans Dernschwams Tagebuch einer Reise nach Konstantinopel und Kleinasien* (1553/55). Munich, 1923.

20. Hans Gerstinger, "Johannes Sambucus als Handschriftensammler," in *Festschrift der Nationalbibliothek in Wien.* Vienna, 1926, p. 251.

21. H. Michelant, *Catalogue de la Bibliothèque de Francois Ier à Blois en 1518.* Paris, 1863.—P. Arnauldet, "Inventaire de la librairie du chateau de Blois en 1518," *Le bibliographe moderne*, 6(1902), p. 145.

22. *Das spanische Schachzabelbuch des Königs Alfons des Weisen vom Jahre 1283. Vollständige Nachbildung der Handschrift in 194 Lichtdrucktafeln*, (Herausgeber John G. White). Leipzig, 1913.

23. Rud. Beer, "Niederländische Büchererwerbungen des Benito Arias Montano für den Escorial im Auftrage König Philipps II. von Spanien," *Jahrbuch der kunsthistorischen Sammlungen des Kaiserhauses*, 25(1905), II, p. 1.

24. J. Zarco Cuevas, "La Biblioteca y los bibliotecarios de San Lorenzo el Real de El Escorial," *Ciudad de Dios*, 144(1926), p. 192; 145(1926), p. 332.

25. Rud. Beer, "Die Handschriftenschenkung Philipps II. an den Escorial vom Jahr 1576," *Jahrbuch der kunsthistorischen Sammlungen des Kaiserhauses*, 23(1903), no. 6.

26. E.G. Vogel, "Erinnerung an Ant. Agustins Bibliothek," *Serapeum*, 8(1847), p. 161.

Chapter 19. *Greek Manuscripts in the Renaissance Period*

1. Concerning the transmitting of the Greek literature, see Henri Bardier's *Description des peintures et autres ornements contenus dans les manuscrits Grecs de la Bibliothèque Nationale.* Paris, 1883.—Emile Legrand, *Bibliographie Hellénique ou description raisonnée des ouvrages publiés en Grec par des Grecs au XVe et XVIe Siècles*, 4 vols. Paris, 1885–1906.—Albert Ehrhard, "Der alte Bestand der griechischen Patriarchalbibliothek von Jerusalem," *Zentralblatt für Bibliothekswesen*, 9(1892), p. 441, and *Archäologische Ehrengabe der Römischen Quartalschrift zu De Rossi's 70. Geburtstage*, Rome, 1892, p. 354.—Wilhelm Wattenbach, *Anleitung zur griechischen Palaeographie*, 3d ed. Leipzig, 1895.—Carl Haeberlin, "Griechishe Papyri," *Zentralblatt für Bibliothekswesen*, 14(1897), p. 1.—Karl Krumbacher, *Geschichte der byzantinischen Literatur von Justinian bis zum Ende des oströmischen Reiches (527 bis 1453)*, 2d ed. Munich, 1897.—Viktor Gardthausen, *Sammlungen und Cataloge griechischer Handschriften.* Leipzig, 1903.—Thod. Schermann, "Griechische Handschriftenbestände in den Bibliotheken der christlichen Kulturzentren des 5. bis 7. Jahrhunderts," *Oriens christianus*, 4(1904), p. 151.—Viktor Gardthausen, *Griechische Paläographie*, 2d ed. 2 vols. Leipzig, 1911–1913.—Sir Edward Maunde Thompson, *An Introduction to Greek and Latin Paleography.* Oxford, 1912.—Wilhelm Schubart, "Papyrusfunde und griechische Literatur," *Internationale Monatsschrift für Wissenschaft, Kunst und Technik*, 8(1914), pp. 1182–1218.—Otmar Schissel, *Kataloge griechischer Handschriften.* Graz, 1924.

2. Adolph Harnack, "Die Überlieferung der griechischen Apologeten des zweiten Jahrhunderts in der alten Kirche und im Mittelalter," *Texte und Untersuchungen zur Geschichte der altchristlichen Literatur*, 1, I and II(1889), p. 36.

3. W. Gass, *Zur Geschichte der Athosklöster.* Giessen, 1865—Spyridion Lambros, *Ein Besuch auf dem Berge Athos.* Würzburg, 1881.—Spyridion Lambros, *Die Bibliotheken der Klöster des Athos.* Bonn, 1881.—Spyridion Lambros, *Catalogue of the Greek Manuscripts on Mount Athos.* Cambridge, 1895–1900.—Heinrich Brockhaus, *Die Kunst in den Athos-Klöstern*, 2d ed. Leipzig, 1921. Cf. also A. Berendts' *Über die Bibliotheken der Meteorischen und Ossa-Olympischen Klöster. Texte und Untersuchungen zur Geschichte der altchristlichen Literatur*, 26. Leipzig, 1904, II, p. 67.

4. Constantin von Tischendorf, *Die Sinaibibel. Ihre Entdeckung, Herausgabe und ERwerbung.*Leipzig, 1871.—Viktor Gardthausen, *Catalogus codicum Graecorum Sinaiticorum.* Oxford, 1886.—Johann Georg von Sachsen, *Das Katharinenkloster am Sinai.* Leipzig, 1912.

5. W. Studemund, "Das Inventar der Bibliothek des Klosters St. Johannis auf der Insel Patmos im 16. Jahrhundert," *Philologus*, 26(1867), p. 167.—Ch. Diehl, "Le Trésor et la bibliothèque de Patmos au commencement du 13e Siècle," *Byzantinische Zeitschrift*, 1(1892), p. 498.

6. Pierre Batiffol, "Vier Bibliotheken von alten basilianischen Klöstern in Unteritalien," *Römische Quartalschrift*, 3(1889), p. 39.—Pierre Batiffol, *L'abbaye de Rossano. Contribution à l'histoire de la Vaticana.* Paris, 1891.—A. Rocchi, *De coenobio Cryptoferrantensi eiusque bibliotheca et codicibus.*

Tusculum, 1893.—Sofronio Gassisi, "I Manoscritti Autografi di S. Nilo Juniore fondatore del Monastero di S.M. Grottaferrata," *Oriens christianus*, 4(1904), p. 308.

7. Oskar von Gebhardt and Adolf Harnack, *Evangeliorum codex Graecus purpureus Rossanensis.* Leipzig, 1880.—Arthur Haseloff, *Codex purpureus Rossanensis.* Berlin, 1898.—Antonio Muñoz, *Il Codice purpureo di Rossano e il frammento Sinopense.* Rome, 1907.

8. A. Calderini, "Ricerche intorno alla biblioteca e alla curtura greca di Francesco Filelfo," *Studi italiani della filologia classica*, 20(1913), pp. 204–424.

9. Henricus Stevenson, *Codices manuscripti Palatini Graeci Bibliothecae Vaticanae.* Rome, 1885.—Pierrre Batiffol, *La Vaticana de Paul III à Paul V.* Paris, 1890.

10. Léon Dorez, "Recherches et documents sur la bibliothèque du cardinal Sirleto," *Mélanges d'archéologie et d'histoire*, 11(1891), p. 457.—H. Omont, "La Bibliothèque Vaticane sous le cardinal Sirleto. Archats et reliures de Livres 1578–1580," *Revue des Bibliothèques*, 23(1913), p. 369.

11. Fernand Benoit, "La Bibliothèque grecque du cardinal Farnèse suivie d'un choix de lettres d'Antoine Eparque, Mathieu Devaris et Fulvio Orsini," *Mélanges d'archéologie et d'histoire*, 39(1922), p. 167.

12. Rich. Förster, "Cyriacus von Ancona zu Strabon," *Rheinisches Museum*, N.F. 51(1896), p. 481.—Hans Graeven, "Cyriacus von Ancona auf dem Athos," *Zentralblatt für Bibliothekswesen*, 16(1899), pp. 209, 498.

13. Wilhelm Dindorf, "Über die venezianische Handschrift des Athenaeus und deren Abschriften," *Philologus*, 30(1870), p. 73.

14. I.L. Heiberg, "Die Archimedeshandschrift Georg Vallas," *Philologus*, 42(1884), p. 421.

15. Léon Dorez, "Latino Latini et la Bibliothèques capitulaire de Viterbe," *Revue des Bibliothèques*, 5(1895), p. 237.

16. Konrad Escher, "Das Testament des Kardinals Johannes de Ragusio," *Basler Zeitschrift für Geschichte u. Altertumskunde, 16(1917), p. 208.—Phil. Schmidt, "Die Bibliothek des ehemaligen Dominikanerklosters zu Basel," Basler Zeitschrift für Geschichte u. Altertumskunde*, 18(1919), p. 160.

17. Rich. Foerster, *De antiquitatibus et libris manuscriptis Constantinopolitanis commentatio.* Rostock, 1877.—F. Blass, "Die griechischen und lateinischen Handschriften im alten Serail zu Konstantinopel," *Hermes*, 23(1888), pp. 219, 622.—Stephen Gaselee, *The Greek Manuscripts in the Old Seraglio at Constantinople.* Cambridge, 1916.—Emil Jakobs, *Untersuchungen zur Geschichte der Bibliothek im Serail zu Konstantinopel.* Heidelberg, 1919.

18. A.F. Villemain, "Laskaris ou les Grecs du XVe Siècle." Paris, 1825.—E.G. Vogel, "Literarische Ausbeute von Janus Lascaris Reisen im Peloponnes ums Jahr 1490," *Serapeum*, 15(1854), p. 154.—E. Piccolomini, "Due documenti relativi ad acquisti di codici greci, fatti da Giovanni Lascaris per conto di Lorenzo de' Medici," *Rivista di filologia*, 2(1874), p. 401; 3(1875), p. 150.—K.K. Müller, "Neue Mitteilungen über Janos Laskaris und die Mediceische Bibliothek," *Zentralblatt für Bibliothekswesen*, 1(1884), p. 333.—Pierre de Nolhac, "Inventaire des manuscrits Grecs de Jean Lascaris," *École francaise de Rome. Mélanges d'archéologie et d'histoire*, 6(1886), p. 250.—G. Mercati, "Cenni di A. del Monte e G. Lascaris sulle perdite della Biblioteca Vaticana nel sacco del 1527," *Miscellanea Ceriani*, Milan, 1910, p. 605.

19. E.G. Vogel, "Constantin Lascaris und seine Handschriften-Sammlung," *Serapeum*, 6(1845), p. 40.—Hugo Rabe, "Konstantin Laskaris," *Zentralblatt für Bibliothekswesen*, 45(1928), p. 1.

20. H. Omont, "Liste de manuscrits grecs de la Bibliothèque Vaticane. Par Constantin Palaeocappa," *Revue des Bibliothèques*, 19(1909), p. 432.

21. Rich. Förster, "Handschriften des Antonios Eparchos," *Rheinisches Museum für Philologie*, N.F. 37(1882), p. 491.—H. Omont, "Catalogue des manuscrits grecs d'Antoine Eparque 1538," *Bibliothèque de l'école des chartes*, 53(1892), p. 95.—Léon Dorez, "Antoine Eparque," *Mélanges d'archéologie et d'histoire*, 13(1893), p. 281.—Wilh. Weinberger, "Griechische Handschriften des Antonios Eparchos," in *Festschrift Theodor Gomperz.* Vienna, 1902, p. 303.

22. Ludw. Schmidt, "Andreas Darmarius," *Zentralblatt für Bibliothekswesen*, 3(1886), p. 129.

23. About the Greek copyists, cf. E.G. Vogel, "Verzeichnis griechischer Abschreiber aus dem 11.-16. Jahrhundert," *Serapeum*, 5(1844), pp. 257, 273, 295, 312, 324, 246.—C.R. Gregory, "Die Schreiber der griechischen Handschriften," *Theologisches Literaturblatt*, 8(1887), col. 393 ff.—Joseph Sturm, "Franciscus Graecus, ein unbekannter Handschriftenschreiber des. 16. Jahrhunderts," *Byzantinische Zeitschrift*, 5(1896), p. 560 ff.—Marie Vogel and Viktor Gardthausen, *Die griechischen Schreiber des Mittelalters und der Renaissance.* Leipzig, 1909.—Josef Bick, *Die Schreiber der Wiener griechischen Handschriften.* Vienna. 1920.

24. J. Fesenmair, *Diego Hurtado de Mendoza, ein spanischer Humanist des 16. Jahrhunderts.* Progr. Munich. 1882–1884.

25. Martin Schanz, "Über Arnold Arlenius Peraxylus," *Zeitschrift für das österreichische Gymnasium,* 35(1884), p. 161.

26. Emil Jacobs, "Francesco Patricio und seine Sammlung griechischer Handschriften in der Bibliothek des Escorial," *Zentralblatt für Bibliothekswesen,* 25(1908), p. 19.

27. E. Miller, *Catalogue des manuscrits grecs de la bibliothèque de l'Escurial.* Paris, 1848.—Ch. Graux, *Essai sur les origines due Fonds grec de l'Escurial.* Paris, 1880.

28. Rich. Förster, "Die griechischen Handschriften von Guillaume Pellicier," *Rheinisches Museum für Philologie,* N.F. 40(1885), p. 453.—H. Omont, "Catalogue des manuscrits grecs de Guillaume Pellicier," *Bibliothèque de l'école des chartes* 46(1885):45, 594.—H. Omont, "Inventaire de la Bibliothèque de Guillaume Pellicier," *Revue des Bibliothèques,* 1(1891), p. 161.

29. Ernest Quentin-Bauchart, *La bibliothèque de Fontainebleau et les livres des derniers Valois à la Bibliothèque nationale* (1575–1589). Paris, 1891.

30. Leroux de Lincy, "Notice sur la Bibliothèque de Catharine de Medici," *Bulletin du Bibliophile el du Bibliothècaire,* 13(1858), p. 915.—H. Omont, "Un premier catalogue des manuscrits grecs du cardinal Ridolfi," *Bibliothèque de l'école des chartes,* 49(1888), p. 309.

31. H. Omont, *Fac-similés de manuscrits grecs des XVe et XVIe siècles reproduits d'après les originaux de la Bibliothèque Nationale.* Paris, 1887.—H. Omont, *Catalogues des manuscrits grecs de Fontainebleau sous François I. et Henri II.* Paris, 1889.—H. Omont, *Inventaire sommaire des manuscrits Grecs de la Bibliothèque Nationale et des autres bibliothèques de Paris et des Départements.* Paris, 1898.

32. H. Omont, "Inventaire des manuscrits Grecs et Latins données a Saint Marc de Venise par le Cardinal Bessarion 1468," *Revue des Bibliothèques,* 4(1894), p. 129.—H. Omont, "Deux registres de prêts de manuscrits de la bibliothèque de Saint-Marc à Venise 1545–1559," *Bibliothèque de l'école des chartes,* 48(1887), p. 651.—Giulio Coggiola, "Il presitto di manoscritti della Marciana dal 1474 al 1527," *Zentralblatt für Bibliothekswesen,* 25(1908), p. 47.—Carlo Volpati, "Per la storia e il prestito di codici della Marciana nel sec. XVI," *Zentralblatt für Bibliothekswesen,* 27(1910), p. 35.

33. Fr. Roth in *Archiv für Refomationsgeschichte,* 1(1904), p. 111.

34. Cf. the Imperial Court Council's protocol in *Jahrbuch der Kunsthistor. Sammlungen des Kaiserhauses,* 19(1898). II. S. II. No. 16062.

35. Rud. Sillib, "David Hoeschels Beziehungen zur Heidelberger Palatina," *Zentralblatt für Bibliothekswesen,* 37(1920), p. 174.—Wilhelm Port, "David Hoeschel u. Hieronymus Commelinus 1595–1597," *Neue Heidelberger Jahrbücher,* N.F. 1936, p. 93.

36. See the extensive literature on Busbeck in my *Bibliographie zur deutschen Geschichte im Zeitalter der Glaubensspaltung,* vol. 1. Leipzig, 1933, col. 89; 5(1939), col. 36.

37. Stephan Gerlach, *Tage-Buch.* Frankfurt am Main, 1674. Cf. also Martin Crusius' *Turcograeciae libri octo.* Basel, 1584, pp. 419, 427, 467.

38. Emilie Legrand, "Notice biographique sur Jean et Thèodose Zygomalas," *Publications de l'école des langues orientales vivantes* III, 6(Paris, 1889), p. 67.

39. Basileos A. Mystakidés, "Martin Crusius und Andrea Darmarios aus Epidauros in Tübingen 1584," in *Forschungen und Versuche zur Geschichte des Mittelalters und der Neuzeit. Festschrift Dietrich Schäfer.* Jena, 1915, p. 499.

40. Henri Omont, "Martin Crusius, Georges Dousa et Theodose Zygomalas," *Revue des Études grecques,* 10(1897), p. 66.—Basileos A. Mystakidés, *Notes sur Martin Crusius, ses livres, ses ouvrages et ses manuscrits.* Paris, 1898.—Basileos A. Mystakidès, *Notes sur Martin Crusius, ses livres, ses ouvrages et ses manuscrits.* Paris, 1898.—Basileos A. Mystakidès, *Germano-Graeca. Konstantinopolis-Tubingae.* Constantinople, 1922.

41. So it is in the Munich manuscripts, Cod. gr. 39, 9 and 141.

42. Emil Jacobs, "Johann Hartung zum Gedächtnis," in *Aus der Werkstatt,* Freiburg im Breisgau, 1925, p. 89.

43. *Catalogus librorum, quos Georgius Douza Constantinopoli secum advexit.* The Hague, 1598. Several of the manuscripts have come into the possession of the befriended Bonaventura Vulcanius.

Chapter 20. The Second Flowering in the Later Sixteenth Century

1. H. Grotefend, *Christian Egenolff, der erste ständige Buchdrucker zu Frankfurt am Main und seine Vorläufer.* Frankfurt am Main, 1881.

2. Heinrich Pallmann, *Sigmund Feyerabend, sein Leben und seine geschäftlichen Verbindungen.* Frankfurt am Main, 1881.

3. E. von Ubisch, *Virgil Solis und seine biblischen Illustrationen für den Holzschnitt.* Leipzig, 1889.

4. W.L. Schreiber, "Jost Ammans Bibelbilder von 1573," *Zeitschrift für Bücherfreunde,* 10(1906/07), II, p. 267.—Cf. Albrecht Kirchhof, "Zu Sigismund Feyerabends Streit mit Christoph Walther in Wittenberg," *Archiv für Geschichte des Deutschen Buchhandels,* 6(1881), p. 261.

5. Hoder, "Turnierbücher," *Lexikon des gesamten Buchwesens,* 3(1937), p. 44.

6. *Das älteste Faustbuch. Historia vom D. Johann Fausten. Nachbildung mit einer Einleitung von Wilh. Scherer.* Berlin, 1884.

7. A. von der Linde, "Drei- Baseler Verleger- und Lagerkataloge aus den Jahren 1553 und 1554," *Neuer Anzeiger für Bibliographie und Bibliothekswissenschaft,* 46(1885), p. 65.

8. Leonhardt Fuchs, *New Kreütterbuch.* Faksimileabdruck der ersten deutschen Augsabe (1543) vermehrt durch einen wissenschaftlichen Anhang von Heinrich Marzell. Leipzig, 1938.

9. Andreas Vesalius, *Andreae Vesalii Bruxellensis icones academicae.* Ediderunt Academia medicinae Nova-Eboracensis et Bibliotheca universitatis Monacensis. Munich, 1935.

10. Viktor Hantzsch, *Sebastian Münster.* Leipzig, 1898.

11. Friedrich Bachmann, *Die alten Städtebilder.* Leipzig, 1939.—Friedrich Bachmann, *Die alte deutsche Stadt.* Leipzig, 1941.

12. Münster's letter to Johann Albrecht, Duke of Mecklenburg, Dec. 9, 1550 in: Frdr. Wilh. Schirrmacher, *Johann Albrecht, Herzog von Mecklenburg,* Part 2. Wismar, 1885, p. 375.

13. Count Palatine Ottheinrich to Christoph Arnold, Weinheim, Nov. 19, 1547 (Rott, Hans. *Ott Heinrich und die Kunst.* Heidelberg, 1905, p. 59.)

14. T. Schiess, "Sebastian Münster und die Engadiner," *Sonntagsbeilage der Allg. Schweiz. Zeitung,* 1901, 5 and 6.

15. *De ortu et causis subterraneorum libri V. De natura eorum, quae effluunt ex terra libri IV. De natura fossilium libri X. De veteribus et novis metallis libri II. Bermannus sive de re metallica dialogus.*

16. E. Müntz, "Le Musée de Portraits de Paul Jove," *Mémoires de l'Institut National de France. Académie des inscriptions et belles-lettres,* Notes—36(1901), p. 249.

17. E. von Rath, "Porträtwerke," *Lexikon des gesamten Buchwesens,* 3(1937), p. 38.

18. Ernst Zinner, *Geschichte und Bibliographie der astronomischen Literatur in Deutschland zur Zeit der Renaissance.* Leipzig, 1941.

19. Ad Ioannem Schonerum de libris revolutionum Doctoris Nicolai Copernici per quendam iuvenem, Mathematicae studiosum narratio prima. Danzig, Franciscus Rhodus, 1540.—Cf. *Des Georg Joachim Rhetikus Erster Bericht über die Bücher des Kopernikus von den Kreisbewegungen der Himmelsbahnen.* Translated and introduced by Karl Zeller. Munich, 1943.

20. Heinrich Röttinger, *Die Holzschnitte zur Architektur und zum Vitruvius des Walther Rivius.* Strasbourg, 1914.—B. Ebhardt, *Die zehn Bücher der Architektur des Vitruv und ihre Herausgeber seit 1487.* Berlin, 1919.—Erich von Rath, "Architekturbücher," *Lexikon des gesamten Buchwesens,* 1(1935), p. 80.

21. Hans Doege, "Die Trachtenbücher des 16. Jahrhunderts," *Beiträge zur Bücherkunde und Philologie.* Aug. Wilmanns gewidmet. Leipzig, 1903, p. 429.—Karl Spiess, "Trachtenkunde," *Deutsche Geschichtsblätter,* 8(1907), p. 145.—Walter Schürmeyer, "Trachtenbücher," *Lexikon des gesamten Buchwesens,* vol. 3. Leipzig, 1937, p. 419.

22. Paul Leemann-van Elck, *Die Offizin Froschauer. Zürichs berühmte Druckerei im 16. Jahrhundert.* Zürich, 1940.

23. *Gemeiner loblicher Eydgnosschaft Stetten, Landen und Völkeren Chronik wirdiger thaaten beschreybung.* Cf. Paul Leemann-van Elck's *Der Buchschmuck der Stumpfschen Chronik.* Bern, 1935.—Ruthardt Oehme, "Die kartographische Bedeutung der Landtafeln des Johannes Stumpf," in *Otto Glauning zum 60. Geburtstag,* vol. 2. Leipzig, 1938, p. 53.

24. The artist, Heinrich Vogtherr.

25. *Zwingliana,* 1(1904), p. 146.

26. Paul Leeman-van Elck, *Der Buchschmuck in Conrad Gessner's naturgeschichtlichen Werken.* Bern, 1935.—On the printing of illustrations in scientific works, see Claus Nissen's "Naturwissenschaftliche Illustration," *Lexikon des gesamten Buchwesens,* 2(1936), p. 99.

27. Johannes Hanhart, *Conrad Gessner.* Winterthur, 1824.—Hans Lutz, "Konrad Gessners

Beziehungen zu den Verlegern seiner Zeit nach seinen Pandekten von 1548," *Mélanges offerts à Marcel Godet*. Neuchâtel, 1932, p. 109.

28. Claus Nissen, "Fischbücher," *Lexikon des gesamten Buchwesens*, 1(1935), p. 541.

29. W. Becher, "Zacharias Ursins Briefe an Crato von Crafftheim," *Theologische Arbeiten aus dem rhein. wissenschaftl. Prediger-Verein*, 12(1892), p. 85.

30. Konrad Gesner, *De lacte et operibus lactariis libellus*. Zürich, 1541.

31. Alfred Nehring, *Über Herberstain und Hirsvogel*. Berlin, 1895.—Anton Schlossar, "Sigmund von Herberstein und seine 'Moscovia'," *Zeitschrift für Bücherfreunde*, 8(1904/05), I.

32. K. Schottenloher, "Ehemalige Klosterdruckereien in Bayern," *Das Bayerland*, 24(1912), p. 136.—A. Mitterwieser, "Die Anfänge des Buchdrucks in der Abtei Tegernsee," in *Gutenberg-Jahrbuch*, 7(1932), p. 178.—A. Mitterwieser, "Der Druck des Chronicon Gottwicense in der Abtei Tegernsee," *Gutenberg-Jahrbuch*, 10(1935), p. 275.

33. Julius, Ritter von Schlosser, *Die Kunstliteratur*. Vienna, 1924, pp. 243, 369.

34. H. Averdunk and J. Müller-Reinhard, *Gerhard Mercator und die Geographen unter seinen Nachkommen*. Gotha, 1914.—F. van Ortroy, "Bibliographie sommaire de l'oeuvre mercatorienne," *Revue des Bibliothèques*. 24(1914), p. 113; 25 and 26(1916), pp. 9, 119.

35. Erich von Rath, "Emblematik," *Lexikon des gesamten Buchwesens*, 1. Leipzig, 1935, p. 478.

36. *Emblemata nobilitatis. Stamm- und Wappenbuch von Isaak und Theodor de Bry*. Mit einem Vorwort über die geschichtliche Entwicklung der Stammbucher, herausgegeben von Friedr. Warnecke. Berlin, 1884.

37. Robert and Richard Keil, *Die deutschen Stammbücher des 16. bis 19. Jahrhunderts*. Berlin, 1893.—Willibald Franke, "Deutsche Stammbücher des 16. bis 18. Jahrhunderts," *Zeitschrift für Bücherfreunde*, 3(1899/1900), II, p. 329.—Max Rosenheim, "The Album Amicorum," *Archaeologia*, 62(1910), p. 251.—A. Hildebrandt, *Stamm-Bücher-Sammlung Friedrich Warnecke*. Leipzig, C.G. Boerner, 1911.—M. Lankorońska, "Die Studenten-Stammbücher des 18. Jahrhunderts," Imprimatur, 5(1934), p. 97.

38. *Mess-Memorial des Frankfurter Buchhändlers Michael Harder, Fastenmesse 1569*. Herausgegeben von Ernst Kelchner und Richard Wülcker. Frankfurt am Main, 1893.—Philipp Rath, *Das Mess-Memorial des Frankfurter Buchhändlers M. Harder 1569 und der Frankfurter Volksbücherverlag des H. Gülfferich*. 1926.

39. Gabr. Putherbi, *Traktat von Verbot und Aufhebung der Bücher und Schriften, so nicht mögen gelesen werden, in das hochdeutsche transferirt* (von Joh. Bapt. Fickler). Munich, Adam Berg., 1581. Fickler's dedicatory prologue to Urban, Bishop of Passau.

40. Max Rooses, *Christoph Plantin imprimeur Anversois*, 2 vols. Antwerp, 1882.—Maurits Sabbe, *Plantin, les Moretus et leur oeuvre*. Brussels, 1926.

41. S. Bongi, *Annali di Gabriele Giolito de'Ferrari da Trino*, 2 vols. Rome, 1890–95.—A.J. Butler, "The Gioliti and their Press at Venice," *Transactions of the Bibliographical Society*, 10(1910), p. 83.

42. G. Zaccaria, *Catalogo ragionato di opere stampate per Francesco Marcolini da Forli*. 1850–53.—Sc. Casali, *Annali della tipografia veneziana di Francesco Marcolini*. 1861.

43. D. Moreni, *Annali della tipografia fiorentina di Lorenzo Torrentino*. 1819.—G.J. Hoogewerff in: *Het Boek*, 15(1926), pp. 273, 369.

44. G. Fumagalli and G. Belli, *Catalogo delle edizioni romane di A. Blado ed eredi* (1516 to 1593). 1891.—G. Fumagalli, *A. Blado*, 1893.

45. Claus Nissen, "Vogelbücher," *Lexikon des gesamten Buchwesens*, 3(1937), p. 527.

46. A.A. Renouard, *Annales de l'imprimerie des Estienne*, 2d ed. Paris, 1843.

47. Wilh. Meyer, *Henricus Stephanus über die Regii Typi Graeci*. Göttingen, 1902.

48. Henr. Stephanus. *Artis typographicae querimonia de illiteratis quibusdam typographis, propter quos in contemptum venit. Epitaphia Graeca et Latina doctorum quorundam typographorum*. Paris, 1569.

49. Henr. Stephanus, *Francofurtiense emporium*. Frankfurt, 1574.—*Der Frankfurter Markt oder die Frankfurter Messe von Henricus Stephanus*, hrsg. von J. Ziehen. Frankfurt am Main, 1919.

50. L. Williams, "Ameet Tavernier en de invoering der civilité-Letter in Zuid-Nederland," *Tijdschrift vor boek- en bibliothekwezen*, 5(1907), p. 241. Maurits Sabbe and Maurius Audin, *Les caractères de civilité de Robert Granjon et les imprimeurs flamands*. 1921. Translated into German by Herbert Reichner. Vienna, 1929.

51. C.H. Rother, "Nikolaus Laurentii und seine Dante-Ausgabe vom Jahre 1481," *Zeitschrift für Bücherfreunde*, N.F. 13(1921), p. 78.

52. Erich von Rath, "Die Entwicklung der Kupferstichillustration im sechzehnten Jahrhundert," *Archiv für Buchgewerbe und Gebrauchsgraphik*, 64(1927), p. 1.—Erich von Rath, "Die Kupferstichillustration im Wiegendruckzeitalter," *Die Bibliothek und ihre Kleinodien. Festschrift zum 250jähr. Jubiläum der Leipziger Stadtbibliothek.* Leipzig, 1927, p. 59.—Erich von Rath, "Zur Entwicklung des Kupferstichtitels," *Buch und Schrift*, 3(1929), p. 51.

53. *Ibid.* 4: 221.

54. H. Lempertz, "Das 'Städte-Buch' von G. Braun u. Hogenberg," *Annalen des hist. Vereins für den Niederrhein*, 36(1881), p. 179.—Reproduction of 24 sheets in color, edited by Wolfgang Bruhn. Leipzig, 1938.

55.*Lexikon des gesamten Buchwesens*, 2(1936), p. 23.

56. From the rich literature concerning these volumes, see Johannes Rudbeck's "Nagra italienska bokband fran 1500-talet," in *Bok-och Bibliothekshistoriska Studier tillägnade Isak Collyn*. Uppsala, 1925, p. 411.—E. von Frisch, "Ein Buch aus der Bibliothek Ulrich Fuggers," *Gutenberg-Jahrbuch*. 1950, p. 376.

Chapter 21. Promotion and Bibliology in the Incunabula Period

1. Cf. in that connection the following: Karl Burger, *Buchhändleranzeigen des 15. Jahrhunderts. In getreuen Nachbildungen herausgegeben.* Leipzig, 1907.—Supplements by Ernst Voulliéme in : *Wiegendrucke und Handschriften. Festgabe Konrad Haebler.* Leipzig, 1919, p. 1.—Jacques Rosenthal, *Eine unbekannte Bücher-Anzeige des XV. Jahrhunderts.* Munich, 1927.

2. *Ibid.* p. 133 ff.

3. *Ibid.* p. 125 ff.

4. Karl Schorbach, "Eine Buchanzeige des Antwerpener Druckers Geraert Leeu in niederländischer Sprache 1491," *Zeitschrift für Bücherfreunde*, 9(1906/07), I. p. 139.

5 .O. Clemen, "Bücher-und Vorlesungsankündigungen," *Neues Archiv für Sächsische Geschichte*, 19(1898), p. 108.—Wilh. Riedner, "Liepziger Buch- und Vorlesungsanzeigen," *Zeitschrift für Bücherfreunde*, N.F. 3(1912), II, p. 277.—Ludw. Bertalot, "Humanistische Vorlesungsankündigungen in Deutschland im 15. Jahrhundert," *Zeitschrift für Geschichte der Erziehung u. des Unterrichts*, 5(1915), p. 1.

6. K. Schottenloher, "Titelreime mit Buchanpreisungen aus der Frühdruckzeit," *Börsenblatt für den deutsche Buchhandel*, 94(1927), no. 33.

7. Libri, quos variis in scientiis et artibus conscriptos nuper edidit et ad nundinas Francfordianas misit Academia Veneta. 1559.

8. Wilh. Fuchs, "Die Anfänge juristischer Fachbibiliographie im 16. Jahrhundert," *Archiv für Bibliographie, Buch- und Bibliothekswesen*, 2(1929), p. 44.—K. Schottenloher, "Die Anfänge der neueren Bibliographie," *Festschrift für Georg Leidinger.* Munich, 1930, p. 233.—Werner Kienitz, *Formen literarischer Ankündigung im 15. u. 16. Jahrhundert.* Dissertation. Cologne, 1930.

9. *Verzeichnis der Bücher, welche in Sigismund Feyerabends Buchladen diese Herbstmess anno 1579 gefunden werden.* Munich, State Library: Broadsheet VIII. 7b.

10. Gustav Schwetschke, *Codex nundinarius Germaniae literatae bisecularis. Messjahrbücher des deutschen Buchhandels 1564 bis 1846.* Halle, 1850–1877.—Max Spirgatis, "Die litterarische Produktion Deutschlands im 17. Jahrhundert und die Leipziger Messkataloge," *Sammlung bibliothekswissenschaftlicher Arbeiten*, 14(1901), p. 24.—Kurt Fleischhack, *Vom Messkatalog zum Deutschen Bücherverzeichnis 1931–1935.* Leipzig, 1937.

11. Johannes Trithemius, *Liber de scriptoribus ecclesiasticis.* Basel, 1494.

12. Herm. Escher, "Die Bibliotheca universalis Konrad Gessners," *Vierteljahrsschrift der Naturforschenden Gesellschaft in Zürich*, 79(1934), p. 174.—Herm. Escher, "Konrad Gessner über Aufstellung und Katalogisierung von Bibliotheken," in his *Ausgewählte bibliothekswissenschaftliche Aufsätze.* Zürich, 1937, p. 153.—Hans Lutz, Konrad Gessners Beziehungen zu den Verlegern seiner Zeit nach seinen Pandekten von 1548," *Mélanges offerts à Marcel Godet.* Neuchâtel, 1937, p. 109.

13. *Necessarium est extare publicas bibliothecas veterum librorum manuscriptorum et antiquissimarum etiam impressionum.*

Chapter 22. The Seventeenth Century

1. G. Jenny, *Miltons verlorenes Paradies in der deutschen Literatur des 18. Jahrhunderts*. St. Gallen, 1890.

2. Charlotte von Dach, *Racine in der deutschen Literatur des 17. jahrhunderts*. Bern, 1941.

3. Manuel Henrich, *Iconografia de las Ediciones del Quijote de Miguel de Cervantes Saavedra*, 3 vols. Barcelona, 1905. — Adam Schneider, *Spaniens Anteil an der Deutschen Literatur des 16. und 17. Jahrhunderts*. Strasbourg, 1898.

4. Herm. Tiemann, *Lope de Vega in Deutschland*, Hamburg, 1939, and *Romanische Jahrbücher*, 1(1948), p. 233.

5. Jacob Ter Meulen, *Concise Bibliographie of Hugo Grotius*. Leyden, 1925.

6. Willi Flemming, *Deutsche Kultur im Zeitalter des Barock*. Potsdam, 1937.

7. *Aristarchus sive de contemptu Linguae Teutonicae*. 1617.

8. Artur Bechtold, "H. M. Moscherosch und der Kupferstecher Aubry," *Zeitschrift für Bücherfreunde*, N.F. 8(1916/17), II, p. 250. — A. Bechtold, *Kritisches Verzeichnis der Schriften Johann Michael Moscheroschs*. Munich, 1922.

9. Manfred Koschling, *Grimmelshausen und seine Verleger*. Leipzig, 1935.

10. Alois Jesinger, *Die Buchgewerbe in den Traktaten Etwas für alle des P. Abraham a Santa Clara*. Mit den Kupfern von Christoph Weigel. Vienna, 1936.

11. *Methodus novus*. 1615.

12. August Schmarsow, *Leibniz und Schottelius. Die unvorgreiflichen Gedanken untersucht und herausgegeben*. Strasbourg, 1877.

13. Christian Franz Paullini, *Kurzer Bericht vom Anfang und bisherigen Fortgang des vorhabenden historischen Reichs-Collegii*. Frankfurt am Main, 1694.

14. Johann Giefel, "Ulrich Pregitzers Reise nach Oberschwaben im Jahre 1688," *Württembergische Vierteljahrshefte für Landesgeschichte*, 11(1888/89), p. 36.

15. Ernst von Moeller, *Hermann Conring, der Vorkämpfer des deutschen Rechts 1606 bis 1681*. Hanover, 1915.

16. Gabriel Eckhard, *Das deutsche Buch im Zeitalter des Barock*. Berlin, 1930. — Julius Rodenberg, "Der Buchdruck von 1600 bis zur Gegenwart," *Handbuch der Bibliothekswissenschaft*, 1(1931), p. 461. — Arthur Lotz, "Ornamentaler Buchschmuck im deutschen Barock und Rokoko," *Philobiblon*, 11(1939), p. 233.

17. H. Eckhardt, *Matthäus Merian, Skizze seines Lebens und ausführliche Beschreibung seiner Topographia Germaniae*, Basel, 1887. 2d ed., 1892. — C. Schuckhard, "Die Zeiler-Merianschen Topographien. Bibliographisch beschrieben," *Zentralblatt für Bibliothekswesen*, 13(1896), p. 193. — Mathhäus Merian, *Topographia Bavariae*. Edited by Otto C. Clemen. Zwickau, 1914. (First published, 1644). — Facsimile reporductions of the individual volumes in the publishing firm of the Frankfurt Art Association, 1924–26. — Fr. Bachmann, *Die alten Städtebilder*. Leipzig, 1939. -F. Bachmann, *Die alte deutsche Stadt*, vol. 1. ff. Leipzig, 1941, ff.

18. K.K. Eberlein, "Ein Empfehlungsschreiben für Matthäus Merian," *Zeitschrift für die Geschichte des Oberrheins*, 75(1925), p. 226.

19. Olga Pöhlmann, *Maria Sibylla Merian*. Berlin, 1935.

20. *Metamorphosis Insectorum Surinamensium*. Amsterdam, 1705. Cf. excerpt in Insel book: *Das Kleine Buch der Tropenwunder*. Kolorierte Stiche. Geleitwort von Frdr. Schnack. Leipzig, 1935.

21. Herm. Bingel, *Das Theatrum Europaeum, ein Beitrag zur Publizistik des 17. u. 18. Jahrhunderts*. Dissertation, University of Munich. Munich, 1909.

22. F. Ferchl, "Die Augsburger kupferstecherfamilie Kilian im Dienst der pharmazeutischen Buchillustration," *Philobiblon*. 1934, p. 385.

23. Paul Kutter, *Joachim von Sandrart als Künstler*. Strasbourg, 1907.

24. Theodor Hampe, "Paulus Fürst und sein Kunstverlag," *Mitteilungen des Germanischen Nationalmuseums*, 1914/15, p. 55; 1920/21, p. 1.

25. Frdr. Oldenbourg, *Die Endter. Eine Nürnberger Buchhändlerfamilie (1590–1740)*. Munich, 1911.

26. Fr. Schulze, "Das deutsche Antiquariat in geschichtlicher Entwicklung," *Wissenschaft und Antiquariat. Festschrift für Gustav Fock*. Leipzig, 1929, p. 57.

27. H.O. Lange, "De hollandske Bogauktioner i derer første halve Aarhundrede," *Nordisk Tidskrift för Bok- och Biblioteksväsen*, 1(1914), p. 133.

28. Bernh. Wendt, *Der Versteigerungs- und Antiquariats-Katalog im Wandel dreier Jahrunderte.* Leipzig, 1937.

29. Schwetschke, *Codex nundinarius Germaniae literatae bisecularis.* 1850–77.

30. *Bibliotheca classica.* Frankfurt am Main, 1610. 2d ed., 1625.

31. Joh. Goldriedrich, *Geschichte des deutschen Buchhandels,* 2 vols. Leipzig, 1908, p. 502.

32. Charles Pieters, *Annales de l'Imprimerie Elseviriennne,* 2d ed. Ghent, 1858.—A. Willems, *Les Elzevier.* Brussels, 1880; supplements by J. Bergmann. Stockholm, 1885–97.—G. Frick, "Die Elsevirschen Republiken," *Zeitschrift für Bücherfreunde,* 1(1897/98), II, p. 609.—H.B. Copinger, *The Elzevier Press.* London, 1927.

33. Emil Weller, *Lexicon pseudonymorum 1856–67,* 2d ed. Regensburg, 1886.

34. Max Rooses, *Titels en Portretten gesneden naar P.P. Rubens voor de Plantijnsche Druckerij.* Antwerp, 1877.—Max Rooses, *Petrus Paulus Rubens en Balthasar Moretus.* Antwerp, 1894.

35. Lauritz Nielsen, *Dansk Typografisk Atlas 1482–1600.* Copenhagen, 1934.

36. Edward Luther Stevensen, *Willem Janszoon Blaeu 1571–1638.* New York, 1914.—W. Nijhoff, "De verschillende uitgaven van de stedenboeken van J. van Blaeu," *Het Boek,* N.R. 2(1933/34), p. 33.

37. F.A. Duprat, *Histoire de l'Imprimerie impériale de France.* Paris, 1861.—August J. Bernard, *Histoire de l'Imprimerie royale du Louvre.* Paris, 1867.

38. H.B. Plomer, "The Printers of Shakespeare's Plays and Poems," *The Library,* N.S. 8(1906).—K. Schneider, "Die Drucker Shakespeares," *Zeitschrift für Bücherfreunde,* 11(1907/08), II, p. 345.—Alfred W. Pollard, *Shakespeare's Folios and Quartos.* London, 1909.—W. Jaggard, *Shakespeare Bibliography.* Stratford-on-Avon, 1911.—Max Förster, "Zum Jubiläum der Shakespeare-Folio," *Zeitschrift für Bücherfreunde,* N.F. 16(1924) p. 49.

39. Stphan Kekulé von Stradonitz, "Über Superexlibris," *Zeitschrift für Bücherfreunde,* 8(1904/05), II, p. 33 ff.

40. H. Lehmann-Haupt, *Das amerikanische Buchwesen.* Leipzig, 1937.

Chapter 23. Seizure in the Thirty Years' War

1. Friedr. Wilken, *Geschichte der Bildung, Beraubung und Vernichtung der alten Heidelbergischen Büchersammlungen.* Heidelberg, 1817.—Augustin Theiner, *Die Schenkung der Heidelberger Bibliothek durch Maximilian I. an Papst Gregor XV. und ihre Versendung nach Rom.* Munich, 1844.—Gessert, "Theiner über die Schenkung der Heidelberger Bibliothek durch Kurfürst Maximilian I. von Bayern an Papst Gregor XV," *Serapeum,* 6(1845), p. 1.—Christian Bähr, "Die Entführung der Heidelberger Bibliothek nach Rom im Jahre 1623,'" *Serapeum,* 6(1845), p. 113.—Chrn. Bähr, "Zur Geschichte der Wegführung der Heidelberger Bibliothek nach Rom in Jahre 1623," *Heidelberger Jahrbücher der Literatur,* 65(1872), p. 481.—Giovanni Beltrani, *Relazione sul trasporto della Biblioteca Palatina da Heidelberg a Roma scritta da Leone Allacci.* Florence, 1882 (From *Rivista Europea,* 28, 1882, p. 5).—F. Roediger, "Instruzione a V.S. Dottor Leone Allacio scrittore Greco della Biblioteca Vaticana per andare in Germania," *Il Bibliofilo,* 6(1885), p. 165.—H. Omont, "Lettre de Leone Allacio relative au transport à Rome de la bibliothèque de Heidelberg," *Zentralblatt für Bibliothekswesen,* 8(1891), p. 123.—E. Erdmannsdörfer, "Zur Geschichte der Heidelberger Bibliotheca Palatina," *Neue Heidelberger Jahrbücher,* 1(1891), p. 349.—Curzio Mazzi, *Leone Allacci e la Palatina di Heidelberg.* Bologna, 1893.—Jakob Wille, *Aus alter und neuer Zeit der Heidelberger Bibliothek.* Heidelberg, 1906.—Ludwig Pastor, *Geschichte der Päpste,* 13, I. Freiburg, 1928, p. 184.

2. The most important source for the carrying off of the library is *Cod. Vat. lat.* 7762.

3. O. Walde, *Storhetstidens litterära krigsbyten En kulturhistorisk-bibliografisk studie.* I. II. Uppsala, 1916/20. Cf. J. Collijn in: *Nordisk Tidskrift för Bok- och Biblioteksväsen,* 3(1916), p. 294.

4. Otto Handwerker, *Die Hofbibliothek des Würzburger Fürstbischofs Julius Echter von Mespelbrunn.* Uppsala, 1925.

5. O. Walde, "Die herzogliche Bibliothek in Gotha und die literarische Kriegsbeute aus Würzburg," *Nordisk Tidskrift for Bok- och Biblioteksväsen,* 17(1930), p. 14.

6. Friedr. Leitschuh, "Zur Geschichte des Bücherraubes der Schweden in Würzburg," *Zentralblatt für Bibliothekswesen,* 13(1886), p. 104.

7. Franz Falk, *Die ehemalige Dombibliothek zu Mainz, ihre Entstehung, Verschleppung und Vernichtung.* Leipzig, 1897.—Gustav Binz, "Literarische Kriegsbeute aus Mainz in schwedischen Bibliotheken," *Mainzer Zeitschrift,* 12/13(1917/18), p. 157.

8. P. Jürges, "Die Ausplünderung der Eberbacher Klosterbibliothek, im Dreissigjährigen Kriege," *Nassauische Heimatblätter*, 20(1916), p. 63.

9. Jos. Kolberg, "Bücher aus ermländischen Bibliotheken in Schweden," *Zeitschrift für die Geschichte und Altertumskunde Ermlands*, 9(1916), p. 496.

10. Isak Collijn, *Die in der Universitätsbibliothek zu Uppsala anfbewahrten Bücher aus dem Besitze des Leipziger Professors und Ermländer Domhernn Thomas Werner*. Uppsala, 1909.

11. Fr. Jacobs and F.A. Ukert, *Beiträge zur älteren Litteratur oder Merkwürdigkeiten der Herzogl. öffentlichen Bibliothek zu Gotha*. 3 vols. Leipzig, 1835–43.

12. Rud. Roth, *Die fürstliche Liberei auf Hohentübingen und ihre Entführung im Jahr 1635*. Tübingen, 1888.—E. Nestle, "Zur Entführung der Tübinger Bibliothek," *Blätter für württembergische Kirchengeschichte*, 3(1888), p. 87.

Chapter 24. Seventeenth Century Libraries

1. Johannes Kemke, *Patricius Junius (Patrick Young), Bibliothekar der Könige Jakob I. und Carl I. von England*. Leipzig, 1898.

2. William Dunn Macray, *Annals of the Bodleian Library*, 2d ed. Oxford, 1890.—H.A.L. Degener, "Die Bodleian Library in Oxford," *Zeitschrift für Bücherfreunde*, 8(1904/05), I, p. 89.—Falconer Madan, *The Bodleian Library at Oxford*. Oxford, 1919.—Sir Thomas Bodley, *Letters to Thomas James, First Keeper of the Bodleian Library*. Edited by G.W. Wheeler. Oxford, 1926.

3. A. Rivolta, *Un gran bibliofilo del secolo XVI. Contributo a uno studio sulla biblioteca di Vincenzo Pinelli*. Monza, 1914.—A. Rivolta, *Catalogo dei codici Pinelliani dell' Ambrosiana*. Milan, 1933.

4. L. Beltrami, *Il Libro d'Oro Borromeo alla Bibliotheca Ambrosiana*. Miniato da Cristoforo Preda. Milan, 1896.—L. Beltrami, *La Biblioteca Ambrosiana*. Milan, 1896.—A. Saba, "La Biblioteca Ambrosiana 1609–1632," *Aevum*, 6(1932), p. 531.

5. Ignaz Franz, Edler von Mosel, *Geschichte der Kaiserl. Königl. Hofbibliothek zu Wien*. Vienna, 1935.

6. M.A.H. Fitzler, *Die Entstehung der sogenannten Fuggerzeitungen in der Wiener Nationalbibliothek*. Vienna, 1937.

7. Heinrich Modern, "Die Zimmernschen Handschriften der k. k. Hofbibliothek. Ein Beitrag zur Geschichte der Ambraser Sammlung und der k. k. Hofbilbiothek," *Jahrbuch der kunsthistor. Sammlungen des Kaiserhauses*, 20(1899), p. 113. Cf. *Zeitschrift für Bücherfreunde*, 3(1899/1900), p. 401.

8. *Commentarii de Augustissima Bibliotheca Caesarea Vindobonensi*. 8 vols. Vienna, 1665–79.

9. Karl Oberleitner, "Beiträge zur Biographie des k. Historiographen u. Bibliothekars Peter von Lambeck," *Notizenblatt Beilage zum Archiv für Kunde österreichischer Geschichtsquellen*, 8(1858), p. 382.—Frdr. Lorenz Hoffmann, *Peter Lambeck (Lambecius) als bibliotgraphisch-literarhistorischer Schriftsteller und Bibliothekar*. Soest, 1864.—Th. G. von Karaian, *Kaiser Leopold I. und Peter Lambeck. Votrag*. Vienna, 1868.

10. K. Tautz, *Die Bibliothekare der Churfürstlichen Bibliothek zu Cölln an der Spree*. Leipzig, 1925.

11. Kurt Tautz, *Die Räume der Churfürstlichen Bibliothek zu Cölln an der Spree*. Burg, 1924.

12. L.C. Bethmann, *Herzog August der Jüngere, der Gründer der Wolfenbüttler Bibliothek*. Wolfenbüttel, 1863.—Paul Zimmermann, "Herzog August der Jüngere zu Braunschweig und Lüneburg als Bibliothekar," *Zentralblatt für Bibliothekswesen*, 45(1928), p. 665.

13. Karl Löffler, *Die Handschriften des Klosters Weingarten*. Leipzig, 1912.

14. Cf.A. Wetzel in *Zentralblatt für Bibliothekswesen*, 6(1889), p. 211.

15. P. de Nolhac, *La Bibliothèque de Fulvio Orsini*. Paris, 1887.

16. A 1660 catalog of the library from the hand of Holstes can be found in the Vaticana *(Cod. Vat. 7764)*.

17. W.H. Grauert, *Christine, Königin von Schweden und ihr Hof*. 2 vols. Bonn, 1837–42.—Léon Dorez, "Documents sur la Bibliothèque de la reine Christine de Suède," *Revue des bibliothèques*, 2(1892), p. 129.—O. Walde, "Till Kristinabibliotekets Historia," *Nordisk Tidskrift för Bok- och biblioteksväsen*, 2(1915), p. 122.

18. A. Franklin, *Histoire de la Bibliothèque Mazarine et du Palais de l'Institut*. 2d éd. Paris, 1901.

19. J.V. Rice, *Gabriel Naudé 1600–1653*. London, 1939.—C. Moreau, *Bibliographie des Mazarinades*. 3 vols. 1850–51.

20. L. Auvray, "La collection Baluze Notes—a la Bibliothèque nationale," *Bibliothèque des chartes,* 81(1920), p. 93.

21. Andr. Bigelmair and Fr. Zoepfel, *Nikolaus Ellenbogs Briefwechsel.* Nuremberg, 1938.

22. Ap. Brequet, "Notes sur la Bibliothèque et les armoires de J. Aug. de Thou," *Bulletin du Bibliophile et du bibliothècaire,* 14(1860), p. 896.

23. H. Omont, "Les manusrits de Pacius chez Peiresc et Holstenius 1629–1631," *Annales du Midi,* 3(1891), p. 1.—Wachsmuth, "Der codex Peirescianus," *Berichte über die Verhandlungen der sächsischen Gesellschaft der Wissenschaften zu Leipzig. Phil. histor. Classe,* 45(1893), p. 261.—Joh. Kemke, "Die Geschichte einer Handschriften-Versendung," *Beiträge zur Bücherkunde und Philologie. Aug. Wilmanns gewidmet.* leipzig, 1903, p. 489.—Gamille Pitollet, *Sur la destinée de quelques manuscrits anciens. Contribution a l'histoire de Fabri de Peiresc.* Paris, 1910.

24. M. Castelbarco Albani della Somoglia, "La Biblioteca Angelica e il suo fondatore," *La Bibliofilia,* 28(1926/27), p. 382.

25. A. Rocca, *Bibliothea Apostolica Vaticana a Sixto V. in splendiorem locum trasnlata.* Rome, 1541.

26. Léon G. Pélissier, "Les amis d'Holstenius," *École française de Rome. Mélanges d'archéologie et d'histoire,* 6(1886), p. 554; 7(1887), p. 62; 8(1888), pp. 323, 521.—Hugo Rabe, "Aus Lucas Holstenius' Nachlass,' *Zentralblatt für Bibliothekswesen,* 12(1895), p. 441.

27. Rich. Beck, "Die Beziehungen des Florentiners Antonio Magliabecchi zu Christian Daum, Rektor zu Zwickau," *Zentralblatt für Bibliothekswesen,* 15(1898), p. 97.—Domenico Fava, *La Biblioteca Nazionale Centrale di Firenze e le sue insigni raccolte.* Milan, 1939.

28. Richard Kukula, *Die Mauriner-Ausgabe des Augustinus. Ein Beitrag zur Geschichte der Literatur und der Kirche im Zeitalter Ludwigs XIV.* Sitzungsberichte der philos.-histor. Classe der Akademie der Wissenschaften, 121–128. Vienna, 1890–98.—A. Goldmann, "Beiträge zum Mauriner-Briefwechsel," *Studien u. Mitteilungen aus dem Benedictiner- und dem Cistercienser-Orden, 11(1890),* p. 597.—Jos. Anton Endres, *Korrespondenz der Mauriner mit den Emmeramern und Beziehungen zu den wissenschaftlichen bewegungen des 18. Jahrhunderts.* Stuttgart, 1899.—I.E. Kathrein, "Aus dem Briefverkehr deutscher Gelehrter mit den Benediktinern der Congregation von St. Maur," *Studien u. Mitteilungen aus dem Benedictiner- und dem Cistercienser-Orden,* 23(1902), p. 111.

29. H. Omont, "Mabillon et la Bibliothèque du Roi," in *Mélanges et Documents publiés a l'occasion du 2e centenaire de la mort de Mabillon.* Paris, 1908, p. 105.

30. Emanuel de Broglie, *Mabillon et la societé de l'abbaye de Saint Germain des Prés à fin du dix-septième siècle 1664–1707.* 2 vols. Paris, 1888.—Suitbert Bäumer, *Johannes Mabillon. Ein Lebens u. Literaturbild aus dem XVII. und XVIII Jahrhundert.* Augsburg, 1892.—Alfred Hessel, "Mabillons Musterbibliothek," in *Mittelalterliche Handschriften. Festgabe zum 60. Geburtstage von Hermann Degering.* Leipzig, 1926, p. 119.

31. H. Omont, "Voyage littéraire de Paris à Rome en 1698. Notes de D. Paul Briois, compagnon de Montfaucon," *Revue des Bibliothèques,* 14(1904), p. 1.

32. Bernardus de Montfaucon, *Diarium italicum, sive monumentorum veterum, bibliothecarum, musaeorum, etc. notitiae singulares in itinerario italico collectae.* Paris, 1702.—H. Omont, "Note sur les manuscrits du Diarium italicum de Montfaucon," *Mélanges d'archéologie et d'histoire,* 11(1891), p. 437.

33. Bernard de Montfaucon, *Bibliotheca Coisliniana, olim Segueriana, sive manuscriptorum omnium Graecorum, quae in ea continentur, accurata descriptio.* Paris, 1715.

34. *Bibliotheca bibliothecarum manuscriptorum nova.* Paris, 1739. Concerning Montfaucon, cf. Emanuel de Broglie's *Bernard de Montfaucon et les Bernardins 1715–1750.* 2 vols. Paris, 1891.

35. Jos. Greven, "Die Bollandisten," *Der Belfried,* 2(1918), p. 163.—Hippolyte Delehaye, *A travers trois siècles. L'oeuvre des Bollandistes 1615–1915.* Brussels, 1920.

Chapter 25. The Journal and Newspaper

1. Emil Weller, *Die ersten deutschen Zeitungen.* Mit einer Bibiographie (1505–1599). Stuttgart, 1872.—Concerning one of the oldest (1505) and most famous "Neuen Zeitungen" see H.H. Bockwitz' "Die 'Copia der Neuen Zeitung aus Presilg Lang,' *Zeitschrift des Deutschen Vereins für Buchwesen und Schrift,* 3(1920), p. 27.—Cf. also Karl Schottenloher's *Flugblatt und Zeitung.* Berlin, 1922.

2. Felix Stieve, *Über die ältesten halbjährigen Zeitungen oder Messrelationen und insbesondere über deren Begründer Frhn. Michael von Aitzing.* Munich, 1881.
3. *Die Relation des Jahres 1609.* In Faks.-Druck hrsg. von Walter Schöne. Leipzig, 1940.
4. *Der Aviso des Jahres 1609.* In Fas.-Druck hrsg von Walter Schöne. Leipzig, 1939.
5. Henriette Schöne-Rieck, *Die Zeitungen des Jahres 1609.* Leipzig, 1943.
6. Walter Schöne, *Die deutsche Zeitung des 17. Jahrhunderts in Abbildungen. 400 Faksimiledrucke.* Leipzig, 1940.
7. The chief works about the newspaper are: Salomon, Ludwig. *Geschichte des deutschen Zeitungswesens.* 3 vols. Oldenburg, Leipzig, 1900–06. —Otto Groth, *Die Zeitung.* 4 vols. 1928–30.— Karl Börner, *Bibliographisches Handbuch der Zeitungswissenschaft.* Leipzig, 1929.—Karl Börner. *Internationale Bibliographie des Zeitungswesens.* Leipzig, 1932.—*Handbuch der Zeitungswissenschaft.* Hrsg. von Walther Heide. Bearbeitet von Ernst Lehmann. Leipzig, 1940. ff.
8. Concerning the mistaken attempt of Fritz Muths to prove the "Monatsgespräche" of Johann Rist as the oldest of the journals see Hellmut Rosenfeld's "Um die älteste Zeitschrift!," *Zentralblatt für Bibliothekswesen,* 58(1941), p. 133.
9. Joachim Kirchner, "Zur Entstehungs- und Redaktionsgeschichte der Acta Eruditorum," *Archiv für Buchgewerbe,* 65(1928), p. 75.
10. On the journal, see especially Joachim Kirchner's *Die Grundlagen des deutschen Zeitschriftenwesens. Mit einer Gesamtbibliographie der deutschen Zeitschriften bis zum Jahre 1790.* 2 parts. Leipzig, 1928–31.—E.H. Lehmann, *Einführung in die Zeitschriftenkunde.* Leipzig, 1936.—J. Kirchner, "Zeitschrift," *Lexikon des gesamten Buchwesens,* 3(1937), p. 611.—Joachim Kirchner, *Das deutsche Zeischriftenwesen. Seine Geschichte u. seine Probleme. Teil I: Von den Anfängen des Zeitschriftenwesens bis zum Ausbruch der Französichen Revolution.* Leipzig, 1942.

Chapter 26. Leibniz and the World of His Time

1. Wilhelm Wundt, *Leibniz,* Leipzig, 1917.
2. On Leibniz as a librarian, see G.E. Guhrauer's "Bibliothekarisches aus Leibnizens Leben und Schriften," *Serapeum,* 12(1851), pp. 1, 16, 33.—Eduard Bodemann, "Leibnizens Briefwechsel mit dem Herzog Anton Ulrich von Brauschweig-Wolfenbüttel," *Zeitschrift des Historischen Vereins von Niedersachsen.* 1888, p. 73.—Archibald L. Clarke, "Leibniz as a Librarian," *The Library,* 3.S.5.(1914), p. 140.—Karl Löffler, "Leibniz als Bibliothekar," *Zeitschrift für Bücherfreunde,* 9(1917), I, p. 95.
3. Fr. Bertram, "G.W. von Leibnizens Beziehungen zu Z.K. von Uffenbach," *Zeitschrift für Bücherfreunde,* 10(1907), I, p. 195.
4. Oskar, Frhr. von Mitis, "Leibniz in der Wiener Hofbibliothek," *Mitteilungen des österreichischen Vereins für Bibliothekswesen,* 7(1903), p. 145.
5. G.E. Guhrauer, *Gottfried Wilhelm Freiherr von Leibniz.* 2 parts. Breslau, 1842, p. 198.— Ludwig Grote, *Leibniz und seine Zeit.* Hanover, 1869, p. 5.
6. Joh. Goldfriedrich, *Geschichte des Deutschen Buchhandels.* 2 vols. Leipzig, 1908, p. 33.
7. Edmund Pfleiderer. *Gottfried Wilhelm Leibniz als Patriot, Staatsmann und Bildungsträger.* Leipzig, 1870.—F.W. Dafert, *Gottfried Wilhelm Leibniz als Deutscher.* Vienna, 1883.—Dietr. Mahnke, *Leibniz als Gegner der Gelehrtenäusserlichkeit.* Stade, 1912.—Alfr. Brunswig, *Leibniz.* Vienna, 1925.

Chapter 27. The Enlightenment

1. H.A. Korff, *Voltaire im literarischen Deutschland des XVIII. Jahrunderts.* 2 vols. Heidelberg, 1918.
2. Julian Schmidt, *Geschichte des geistigen Lebens in Deutschland von Leibniz bis auf Lessings Tod 1681–1781.* 2 vols. Leipzig, 1862–64.—Christian Frdr. Weiser, *Shaftesbury und das deutsche Geistesleben.* Berlin, 1916.—H.A. Korff, *Voltaire im literarischen Deutschland des XVIII. Jahrhunderts. Ein Beitrag zur Geschichte des deutschen Geistes von Gottsched bis Goethe.* 2 vols. Heidelberg, 1917.— Emil Ermatinger, *Barock und Rokoko in der deutschen Dichtung.* Berlin, 1926.—*Deutsche Literatur. Reihe Aufklärung.* Hrsg. von Fritz Brüggemann. v. 1-ff. Leipzig, 1928 ff.—Emil Ermatinger, *Deutsche Kultur im Zeitalter der Aufklärung.* Potsdam, 1934.—Franz Koch, *Deutsche Kultur des Idealismus.* Potsdam, 1935.—Richard Benz, *Klassik und Romantik.* Berlin, 1938.

3. Ferdinand Avenarius, ed., *Balladenbuch*. 3d ed. Munich, 1910.—Börries, Frhr. von Münchhausen, *Meisterballaden*. 1923.—Wolfgang Kayser, *Geschichte der deutschen Ballade*. Berlin, 1936.

4. On the group of fairy tale books, see Linck, "Märchenbücher," *Lexikon des gesamten Buchwesens*, 2(1936), p. 390.

5. Heinz Kindermann, *Klopstocks Entdeckung der Nation*. Danzig, 1935.

6. Adolph Kohut, *Autor und Verleger. Kritische Essays und Randglossen aus Schriftsteller- und Verleger-Werkstätten*. Heidelberg, 1908.—H.H. Borchert, *Das Schriftstellertum von der Mitte des 18. Jahrhunderts bis zur Gründung des Deutschen Reiches*. 1923.

7. A. Kippenberg, *Robinsonaden in Deutschland bis zur Insel Felsenburg*, (1731–1743). Hanover, 1892.—Edgar Breitenbach, "Robinsonaden," *Lexikon des gesamten Buchwesens*, 3(1937), p. 130 ff.

8. Wilhelm Vollrath, *Goethe und Grossbritannien*. Erlangen, 1920.—Jean-Marie Carré, *Goethe en Angleterre*. Paris, 1920.

9. Karl Berger, *Schiller*. 13th ed. Munich, 1921, p. 92.

10. L.M. Price, *English and German Literary Influences*. Berkeley, Calif., 1910.—Gerda Mielke, "Englische Literatur," *Reallexikon der deutschen Literaturgeschichte*, 1(1926), p. 779.

11. Walter Fränzel, *Geschichte des Übersetzens im 18. Jahrhundert*. Leipzig, 1914.

12. J. Barnstorff, *Youngs 'Nachtgedanken' und ihr Einfluss auf die deutsche Literatur*. Bamberg, 1895.

13. R. Wood, *Der Einfluss Fieldings auf die deutche Literatur*. Dissertation. Heidelberg, 1895.

14. Rudolf Unger, *Hamann und die Aufklärung. Studien zur Vorgeschichte des romantischen Geistes im 18. Jahrhundert*. Jena, 1911.

15. Karl Mollenhauer, *Justus Mösers Anteil an der Wiederbelebung des deutschen Geistes*. Brunswick, 1896.

16. Eduard von der Hellen, *Goethe's Anteil an Lavaters physiognomischen Fragmenten*. Frankfurt am Main, 1888.—Charlotte Steinbrucker, *Lavaters phsyiognomische Fragmente im Verhältnis zur bildenden Kunst*. Berlin, 1915.

17. Hans Glogau, *Die Moderne Selbstbiographie als historische Quelle*. Marburg, 1903.

18. Karl Hobrecker, *Alte vergessene Kinderbücher*. Berlin, 1924.—Irene Graebsch, *Geschichte des deutschen Jugendbuches*. Leipzig, 1942, p. 29.

19. J. Goldfriedrich, *Geschichte des deutschen Buchhandels*. vol. 2. Leipzig, 1908, p. 394.

20. Christian August Vulpius (the later brother-in-law of Goethe) in 1797 authored his *Rinaldo Rinaldini*, the model for numerous robber novels.

21. Gustav Roethe, *Vom literarischen Publikum in Deutschland. Festrede*. Göttingen, 1902. Cf. also Georg Steinhausen's "Was man vor Zeiten gern las," in his *Kulturstudien*. Berlin, 1893, p. 44.—Walter Rumpf, *Das literarische Publikum und sein Geschmack in den Jahren 1760–1770*. Dissertation. Frankfurt am Main, 1926.

22. Kohlfeld, "Lesegesellschaften," in supplement to the *Allgememe Zeitung*, Feb. 22, 1899.—Alois Jesinger, *Weiner Lekturkabinette*, Vienna, 1928.

23. Ernst Milberg, *Die moralischen Wochenschriften des 18. Jahrhunderts*. Meissen, 1881.—Oskar Lehmann, *Die deutschen moralischen Wochenschriften des 18. Jahrhunderts als pädagogische Reformschriften*. Leipzig, 1893.—M. Stecher, *Die Erziehungsbestrebungen der moralischen Wochenschriften*. Langensalza, 1914.—J. Wiegand, "Moralische Wochenschrift," *Reallexikon der deutschen Literatur*. vol. 2. 1926/28, p. 404.

24. Theod. Vetter, *Der Spectator als Quelle der 'Discourse der Maler'*. Frauenfeld, 1887.

25. Ernst Herbert Lehmann, *Die Anfänge der Kunstzeitschrift in Deutschland*. Leipzig, 1932.—Lisl Grüssen, *Die deutsche Zeitschrift als Ausdrucksmittel der Literaturströmungen. Deutung des Werdens der deutschen Literaturzeitschrift vom Humanismus bis zum deutschen Idealismus*. Munich, 1937.

26. Frdr. Meyer, *Schillers Horen als Verlagswerk betrachtet*. Leipzig, 1941.

27. Hans Köhring, *Bibliographie der Almanache, Kalender und Taschenbücher für die Zeit von ca. 1730–1860*. Hamburg, 1929.

28. Arthur Rümann, "Historisch-genealogische Kalender," *Philobiblon*, 11(1939), p. 7.

29. Arthur Rümann, "Historische Almanache und Taschenbücher," *Philobiblon*, 11(1939), p.185.

30. Maria and Leo Lanckoronska, "Deutsche Musenalmanache des 18. Jahrhunderts," *Philobiblon*, 11(1939), p. 97.—J. Wiegand, "Musenalmanache," *Reallexikon der deutschen Literatur*, 2(1928), p. 21.

31. Hans Grantzow, *Geschichte des Göttinger und des Vossischen Musen-Almanachs*. Berlin, 1909.

32. Wolfg. Seyffert, *Schillers Musenalmanache*. Berlin, 1913.

33. Johann Goldfriedrich, in his *Gechichte des Deutschen Buchhandels*, 3 vols. Leipzig, p. 343, gives a good survey concerning the censorship relations of the period. — Cf. also H.H. Houben's *Verbotene Literatur von der Klassischen Zeit bis zur Gegenwart*. 2 vols Berlin, 1924–28.

Chapter 28. Design and Marketing in the Classic Period

1. Loys Delteil, *Manuel de l'amateur d'éstampes du XVIIIe siècle*. Paris, 1910. — Henry Cohen, *Guide de l'amateur de liveres à gravures du 18e siècle*. 6. èdition par Seymour de Ricci, Paris, 1912. — W. Hausenstein, *Rokoko. Französische und deutsche Illustrationen des 18. Jahrhunderts*. Munich, 1912; 4th ed. 1924. — Hans Wolfg. Singer, *Französische Buchillustrationen des achtzehnten Jahrhunderts*. Munich, 1923. — Lothar Brieger, *Das goldene Zeitalter der französischen Illustration*. Munich, 1924. — Karl Madsen, *Franske Illustratorer fra det XVIII Aarhundrede*. Copenhagen, 1929. — H. Fürstenberg, *Das französische Buch im 18. Jahrhundert*. Weimar, 1929.

2. Ernst Schulte-Strathaus, *Bibliographie der Originalausgaben deutscher Dichtungen im Zeitalter Goethes*. Munich, 1913. — Lothar Brieger, *Ein jahrhundert deutscher Erstausgaben (1750–1880)*. Stuttgart, 1925. — Arthur Rümann, *Die illustrierten deutschen Bücher des 18. Jahrhunderts*. Stuttgart, 1927. — Hans Wegener, "Die Buchillustration im 17. und 18. Jahrhundert," in *Handbuch der Bibliothekswissenschaft*, v. 1. Berlin, 1931, p. 569. — Maria Lanckoronska und Richard Oehler, *Die Buchillustration des XVIII Jahrhunderts in Deutschland, Österreich und der Schweiz*. 3 parts. Frankfurt am Main, 1932–34.

3. Rich. Oehler, "Adam Friedrich Oeser, Goethe's Lehrer als Buchillustrator," in *Gutenberg-Festschrift*. Mainz, 1925, p. 214. — Arthur Rümann, *Adam Friedrich Oeser. Bibliographie*. 1931.

4. Wilhelm Dorn, *Meil-Bibliographie*. Berlin, 1928.

5. Wilhelm Engelmann, *Chodowieckis sämtliche Kupferstiche*. Leipzig, 1857. — Wolfgang von Oettingen, *Daniel Chodowiecki*. Berlin, 1895. — Ulrich Thieme and F. Becker, eds., *Lexikon der bildenden Künstler von der Antike bis zur Gegenwart* (1907–1950), v. 6, p. 519. — Olga Amberger, *Zeitgenossen Chodowieckis. Lose Blätter schweizerischer Buchkunst*. Basel, 1920.

6. For this chief piratical printer the one who so reproduced materials was called "Schmieder."

7. Franz Muncker, "Briefwechsel Klopstocks und seiner Eltern mit Karl Hermann Hemmerde und Georg Friedrich Meier," *Archiv für Literaturgeschichte*, 12(1883), p. 225.

8. Friedrich G. Klopstock an den Rektor M. Karl Wilh. Ernst Heimbach in Schul-Pforta: *Allg. Literatur-Anzeiger*, 5(1800), col. 969.

9 .W. Deetjen, "Wielands Bibliothek" in *Funde und Forschungen. Eine Festgabe für Julius Wahle*. Leipzig, 1921. Heinrich Meyer, Goethe's friend, in the 1815 *Züricherischen Beyträgen zur wissenschaftlichen und geselligen Unterhaltung* has reported things worth reading about the library's auction, June–July, 1815.

10. F. Stuttmann, *Johann Heinrich Ramberg*. Munich, 1929.

11. Max Ziegert, "Wieland und seine Verleger," *Berichte des Freien Deutschen Hochstiftes zu Frankfurt am Main*, N.F. 3(1886), II, p. 11.

12. Otto Friedrich Vaternahm, *Goethe und seine Verleger*. Dissertation. Frankfurt am Main, 1916.

13. Rud. Jentzsch, *Der deutsch-lateinische Büchermarkt nach den Leipziger Ostermess-Katalogen von 1740, 1770 und 1800 in seiner Gliederung Wandlung*. Leipzig, 1912. — Otto Bettmann, *Die Entstehung buchhändlerischer Berufsideale im Deutschland des XVIII. Jahrhunderts*. Leipzig, 1927. — Walter G. Oschilewsky, "Der Berufsstand der deutschen Buchdrucker im achtzehnten Jahrhundert," *Imprimatur*, 8(1938), p. 48.

14. Felix von Schroeder, *Die Verlegung der Büchermesse von Frankfurt am Main nach Leipzig*. Leipzig, 1904.

15. Alfred Rüffler, "Die Pressezensur und Zedlers Universal-Lexikon im vorpreussischen Berslau," *Schlesische Geschichtsblätter*, 1927, p. 63.

16. Karl Buchner, *Wieland und die Weidmannsche Buchhandlung*. Berlin, 1871. — Karl Buchner, *Aus den Papieren der Weidmannschen Buchhandlung*. Berlin, 1871. — Ernst Vollert, *Die Weidmannsche Buchhandlung in Berlin 1680 bis 1930*. Berlin, 1930.

17. Oskar von Hase, *Breitkopf u. Härtel, Buch- und Notendrucker, Buch- und Musikalienhändler in Leipzig*. 2 vols. Leipzig, 1917–19. — Ludw. Volkmann, *Johann Gottlob Breitkopf als Vorkämpfer der deutschen Schrift*. Leipzig, 1932.

18. Wilh. Vollmer, ed., *Briefwechsel zwischen Schiller und Cotta*. Stuttgart, Cotta, 1876–J.G. Cotta (firm). *Briefe an Cotta*. 3 vols. Stuttgart, 1925–27.

19. Albert Schäffle, *Johann Friedrich Cotta*. Berlin, 1895.

20. George Joachim Goschen, Viscount. *Das Leben Georg Joachim Göschens*. Deutsche Ausgabe Übersetzt von Th. A. Fischer. 2 vols. Leipzig, 1903.

21. Konr. Weidling, *Die Haude & Spenersche Buchhandlung in Berlin in den Jahren 1614 bis 1890*. Berlin, 1902, p. 25.–*Stolze Vergangenheit–lebendige Gegenwart. 325 Jahre Haude & Spenersche Buchhandlung zu Berlin*. Berlin, 1939.

22. Karl Aner, *Der Aufklärer Friedrich Nicolai*. Giessen, 1912.

23. New edition by Fritz Brüggemann, *(Deutsche Literatur. Reihe Aufklärung*, Vol. 15, Leipzig, 1938).

24. Flodoard, Frh. von Biedermann, *Johann Friedrich Unger im Verkehr mit Goethe und Schiller*. Berlin, 1927.

25. Gustav Freytag, *Bilder aus der deutschen Vergangenheit*. 4 vols. Leipzig, 1911, p. 129.

26. Wilhelm Heinrich Riehl, "Der Homannische Atlas" in his *Kulturstudien aus 3 Jahrhunderten*. 7th ed. Stuttgart and Berlin, 1910, p. 3.–Chrn. Sandler, *Johann Baptista Homann*. Berlin, 1886.

27. Olgerd Grosswald, *Der Kupferstich des XVIII. Jahrhunderts in Augsburg und Nürnberg*. Munich, 1912.

28. Concerning the hunting books which were especially popular in the eighteenth century see R. Souhart's *Bibliographie des ouvrages de la chasse*. Paris, 1886.–J. Thiébaud, *Bibliographie des Ouvrages francais sur la chasse*. Paris, 1934.–Karl Löffler and Erich von Rath, "Jagdbücher," *Lexikon des gesamten Buchwesens*, 2(1936), p. 133.

29. Robert Diehl, *Beaumarchais als Nachfolger Baskervilles. Entstehungsgeschichte der Kehler Voltaire-Ausgabe in Baskerville-Typen*. Frankfurt am Main, 1925.

30. Frdr. Butters, *Über die Bipontiner und die Editiones Bipontinae*. Programm. Zweibrücken, 1897.–H.H. Bockwitz, "Die Editiones Bipontinae," *Archiv für Buchgewerbe*, 79(1942), p. 325.

31. Claus Nissen, "Botanische Prachtwerke 1740–1840," *Philobiblon*, 5(1933), p. 243.–Claus Nissen, "Pflanzenbücher," *Lexikon des gesamten Buchwesens*, 3(1937), p. 6.–Claus Nissen, *Die botanische Buchillustration. Ihre Geschichte und Bibliographie*. 2 vols. Stuttgart, 1951–52.

32. Claus Nissen, "Die ornithologische Illustration," *Philobiblon*, 8(1935), p. 23.–Claus Nissen, *Schöne Vogelbücher. Ein Überlick der ornithologischen Illustration*. Vienna, 1936.–Jean Anker, *Bird books and Bird Art. An Outline of the Literary History and Iconography of Descriptive Ornithology*. Copenhagen, 1938.

33. H.A. Hagen, *Bibliotheca Entomologica. Die Literatur über das ganze Gebiet der Entomologie bis zum Jahre 1862*. 2 vols. Leipzig, 1863.–M.A. Pfeiffer, "Schmetterlings- und andere Insektenwerke," *Philobiblon*, 9(1936), p. 51.

34. Walter Schürmeyer, "Die Gartenwerke des 18. Jhs.," *Imprimatur*, 7(1936/37), p. 125.

35. Claus Nissen, "Handkolorierung," *Lexikon des gesamten Buchwesens*, 2(1936), p. 52.

36. *Buchhandel, Literatur und Nation in Geschichte und Gegenwart*. Berlin, 1932, p. 23.

37. Cf. also Rud. Krauss' "Zur Geschichte des Nachdrucks und Schutzes der Schillerschen Werke," *Württembergische Vierteljahreshefte für Landesgeschichte*, N.F. 13(1904), p. 187.

38. R. Straus and R.K. Kent, *John Baskerville*. Cambridge, 1907.

39. Herm. Falk, *Giambattista Bodonis Typenkunst*. Mainz, 1905.–H.C. Brooks, *Compendiosa bibliografia di edizione Boboniane*. Florence, 1927.–H. Bohatta, "Zur Bodoni-Bibliographie," *Gutenberg-Jahrbuch*, 1935, p. 280.–Fritz Schröder, *Giambatista Bodoni*. Berlin, 1938.

40. Gustav Mori, "Der Buchdrucker Cristoph Sauer in Germantown," *Gutenberg-Jahrbuch*. 1934, p. 224.–H. Lahmann-Haupt, *Das amerikanische Buchwesen*. Leipzig, 1937.

41. Always to be consulted for the history of surveys of books is Georg Schneider's *Handbuch der Bibliographie*, 4th ed. Leipzig, 1930.

42. *Catalogus codicum latinorum Bibliothecae Mediceae Laurentianae*. Florence, 1764–93. Cf. Adolf Schmidt's "Una lettera di Angelo Maria Bandini sul suo Catalogo dei manoscritti della Laurenziana," *La Bibliofilia*, 22(1921), p. 283, with Bandini's letter to Baron Hüpsch from May 8, 1779.

Chapter 29. The Eighteenth Century

1. Edward Edwards, *Lives of the Founders of the British Museum*. 2 vols. London, 1870.–H.A.L.

Degener, "Die Bibliothek des British Museum," *Zeitschrift für Bücherfreunde*, 6(1902/03), I, p. 1.–H.C. Shelley, *The British Museum*. London, 1911.–A. Esdaile, *National Libraries of the World*. London, 1934, p. 3.

2. K.J. Hartmann and H. Füchsel, *Geschichte der Göttinger Universitätsbibliothek*. Göttingen, 1937.

3. Georg Leyh, "Die Gesetze der Universitätsbibliothek zu Göttingen vom 26. October 1761," *Zentralblatt für Bibliothekswesen*, 37(1920), p. 1.

4. Georg Leyh, "Chr. G. Heynes Eintritt in die Göttinger Bibliothek," in *Aufsätze, Fritz Milkau gewidmet*. Leipzig, 1921, p. 220.–Rich. Fick, *Ein Bericht Heynes aus der westfälischen Zeit und seine programmatische Bedeutung*. Göttingen, 1924.

5. Gustav Roethe, "Göttingische Zeitungen von gelehrten Sachen," in *Festschrift zur Feier des 150jährigen Bestehens der Gesellschaft der Wissenschaften zu Göttingen*. Berlin, 1901, p. 567.

6. Wilhelm Weinberger, "Die griechischen Handschriften des Prinzen Eugen von Savoyen," *Wiener Eranos zur 50. Versammlung deutscher philologen und Schulmänner in Graz*. Vienna, 1909, p. 137.

7. Heydenreich, "Die Bibliothek des Grafen von Bünau in Nöthnitz," *Neuer Anzeiger für Bibliographie und Bibliothekswissenschaft*, 1878, p. 90.–Werner Schultze, "Die Bibliothek Heinrich von Bünaus," *Zentralblatt für Bibliothekswesen*, 52(1935), p. 337.

8. Martin Bollert, "J.J. Winckelmann als Bibliothekar des Grafen Bünau," in *Festschrift für Georg Leidinger*. Munich, 1930, p. 19.–M. Bollert, "Johann Joachim Winckelmann als Bibliothekar," *Zentralblatt für Bibliothekswesen*, 53(1936), p. 482.

9. Karl Felix von Halm, "Über die handschriftliche Sammlung der Camerarii und ihre Schicksale," *Sitzungsberichte der bayer. Akademie der Wissenschaften. Philos. -philol. -hisotr. Classe*, v. 3 (1873), p. 241.

10. Maillot de la Treille, Über Peter Vettoris Leben und Büchersammlung," *Rheinische Beiträge zur Gelehrsamkeit*, 2(1780), p. 37.

11. Karl Theod. Heigel, "Karl Theodor von Pfalz-Bayern und Voltaire," in his *Essays aus neuerer Geschichte*. Munich, 1892, p. 145.–Leo Jordan, "Voltaire und Karl Theodor von Pfalz-Bayern," *Archiv für das Studium der neueren Sprachen und Literaturen*, 127(1911), p. 12; 128(1912), p. 371; 129(1912), p. 388; 131(1913), p. 347.

12. Franz Boll, "Jacques Coeurs Gebetbuch in der Münchener Hof und Staatsbibliothek," *Zeitschrift für Bücherfreunde*, 6(1903), I, p. 49.–Hans Prutz, "Jacques Coeur als Bauherr und Kunstfreund," in *Sitzungsberichte der Bayer. Akademie der Wissenschaften, Philos. -philolog. u histor. Klasse*. Munich, 1911, p. 1.

13. Aug. Wolkenhauser, *Sebastian Münsters Kollegienbuch aus den Jahren 1515–18 und seine Karten*. Berlin, 1909.

14. J. Alzog, "Über Johann Nicolaus Weislinger," *Freiburger Diöcesan-Archiv*, 1(1865), p. 405.–Wolfgang Pfeiffer-Belli, "Johann Nicolaus Weislingers deutsche Schriften," *Euphorion*, 29(1928), p. 82. The State Library in Munich preserves the library's catalog (acquired in 1750) under Cod. Bav. Cat. 581.

15. Laurentius Hanser, "Karl Eugen von Württemberg in Scheyern," *Altbayerische Monatschrift*, 15(1920), p. 34.–Karl Löffler, *Gechichte der Württembergischen Landesbibliothek*. Leipzig, 1923.

16. Rich. Fester, "Die Bibliothek der Markgräfin Wilhelmine," in *Festschrift dem Prinzregent Luitpold von Bayern dargebracht von der Universität Erlangen*. Erlangen, 1901, p. 137.

17. Eduard E. Katschthaler, *Über Bernhard Pez und dessen Briefnachlass*. Jahresbericht des Obergymnasiums zu Melk, 39. Melk, 1889.

18. Paulus Volk, "Ein Briefwechsel aus der deutschen Wissenschaftsgeschichte des 18. Jahrhunderts," *Zeitschrift für deutsche Geistesgeschichte*, 1935, pp. 23, 92.

19. Georg Pfeilschifter, *Die St. Blasianische Germania Sacra. Ein Beitrag zur Historiographie des 18. Jahrhunderts*. Kempten, 1921.–Georg Pfeilschifter, *Korrespondenz des Fürstabtes Martin II. Gerbert von St. Blasien*. 2 vols. Karlsruhe, 1931–34.–A. Bömer, "Der Wiederaufbau der durch Brand zerstörten Bibliothek St. Blasien unter Fürstabt Martin II Gerbert," *Zentralblatt für Bibliothekswesen*, 55(1938), p. 307.

20. W. Deetjen, "Eine Bibliothekarprüfung des achtzehnten Jahrhunderts," *Zentralblatt für Bibliothekswesen*, 45(1928), p. 302.

21. Andr. Heusler, *Geschichte der öffentl. Bibliothek der Universität Basel*. Progr. Basel, 1896. On the libraries of the eighteenth century also see Johann von Nepomuk Hauntinger's *Süddeutsche Klöster*

vor hundert Jahren. Reisetagebuch. Hrsg. von Gabriel Meier. Cologne, 1889.—Karl Meyer, "Bibliotheksnachrichten in Tagebüchern deutscher Schriftsteller des 18. Jahrhunderts," *Zentralblatt für Bibliothekswesen,* 55(1938), p. 211.

22. Walter Schürmeyer, *Bibliothekräume aus fünf Jahrhunderten.* Frankfurt am Main, 1929.—Cf. Georg Leyh in: *Zentralblatt für Bibliothekswesen,* 46(1929), p. 506.—Gert Adriani, *Die Klosterbibliotheken des Spätbarock in Österreich und Süddeutschland.* Graz, 1935.

23. Anton Mayr, "Beziehungen des Augsburger Malers und Kupferstechers Gottfried Bernhard Götz zum Stifte Admont," in *20. Jahresbericht des Carl Ludwig-Gymnasiums im XII. Bezirke von Wien,* 1903, p. 1.

24. Gollinger, "Die Fresken am Plafond der ehemaligen Bibliothek der Prämonstratenser-Abtey Bruck an der Thaja," *österreichisches Archiv für Geschichte, Erdbeschreibung, Staatenkunde, Kunst u. Literatur,* 2(1832), pp. 368, 373.

25. Camillo List. *Die Hofbibliothek in Wien. Zwanzig Tafeln in Lichtdruck.* Vienna, 1897.

26. Felix Mader, *Die Kunstdenkmäler Bayerns. Oberpfalz und Regensburg. Heft 14: Bezirksamt Tirschenreuth.* Munich, 1908, p. 127.—Cf. Also Leonia Lorenz' *Das Geheimnis des Bibliotheksaales zu Waldsassen.* Regensburg, 1927.

27. Gustav Münzle, "Die Bibliotheksfiguren Christian Wenzingers im Kloster St. Peter," *Schau ins Land* 47–50. 1923: 70, with an illustration depicting the library hall.

28. Max Oeser, *Städtische Schlossbücherei Mannheim. Kurzer Führer durch ihre Sammlungen.* Mannheim, 1926.

29. Zach. Konr. von Uffenbach, *Merwürdige Reisen durch Niedersachsen, Holland und Engelland. 3 Theile.* Frankfurt 1753/54. Cf. also G.A. Bogeng, "Über Zacharias Conrad von Uffenbachs Erfahrungen und Erlebnisse bei der Benutzung deutscher, englischer, holländischer öffentlicher Büchersammlungen 1709–1711," in *Beiträge zum Bibliotheks- und Buchwesen. Paul Schwenke gewidmet.* Berlin, 1913, p. 30.—J. Becker, "Die Bibliothek des Zacharias Konrad von Uffenbach," in *Festschrift Georg Leyh.* Leipzig, 1937, p. 129.

30. Albert Predeek, "Bibliotheksbesuche eines gelehrten Reisenden des 18. Jahrhunderts: Christian Gabriel Fischer," *Zentralblatt für Bibliothekswesen,* 45(1928), pp. 221, 342, 393.

31. Grg. Palmieri: *Giuseppe Garampi, Viaggio in Germania, Baviera, Suizzera, Olanda e Francia compiuto negli anni 1761–1763. Diario.* Rome, 1889. Cf. Gabr. Meier's "Cardinal Garampis litterarische Reise durch Deutschland 1761–1763," *Zentralblatt für Bibliothekswesen,* 7(1890) p. 481.

32. *Litterarische Reisen durch einen Theil von Baiern, Franken, Schwaben, und der Schweiz.* Augsburg, 1786—*Reisen in einige Klöster Schwabens, durch den Schwarzwald und in die Schweiz.* Augsburg, 1786.

33. *Reisen durch Schwaben, Baiern, angränzende Schweiz, Franken und die rheinischen Provinzen in den Jahren 1779–82.* Parts 1–4. 1783–88.

34. *Verusuch einer Beschreibung sehenswürdiger Bibliotheken Teutschlands.* Vols. 1–4. Erlangen, 1786–91.

Chapter 30. The Confiscation of Monastery Libraries

1. Simon Laschitzer, "Die Verordnungen über die Bibliotheken und Archive der aufgehobenen Klöster in Österreich," *Mitteilungen des Instituts für österreichische Geschichtsforschung,* 2(1881), p. 401.—Rudolf Hittmair, *Der Josefinische Klostersturm im Lande ob der Enns.* Freiburg im Breisgau, 1907.

2. F. Mencik, "H.G. Bretschneider und G. van Swieten," *Mitteilungen des österreichischen Vereins für Bibliothekswesen,* 10(1906), p. 11.

3. Anton Schubert, "Die ehemaligen Bibliotheken der von Kaiser Josef II. aufgehobenen Mönchsklöster in Mähren und Schlesien, sowie der Exjesuiten zu Teschen und Troppau," *Zentralblatt für Bibliothekswesen,* 17(1900), p. 321.

4. Simon Laschitzer, "Geschichte der Klosterbibliotheken und Archive Kärntens zur Zeit ihrer Aufhebung unter Kaiser Josef II," *Carinthia,* 73(1883), pp. 129, 161, 193.

5. Pirmin Lindner, "Die Aufhebung der Klöster in Deutschtirol 1782–1787," *Zeitschrift des Ferdinandeums für Tirol u. Vorarlberg.* 3, F. 29(1885), p. 157; 29(1885), p. 145; 30(1886), p. 9.

6. Baron von Reiffenberg, "Biographische Notiz über John. Bas. Bern. van Praet," *Serapeum,* 1(1840), p. 310.

7. V. Mortreuil, *La Bibliothèque Nationale.* Paris, 1878.—Léon Vallée, *La Bibliothèque Nationale.* Paris, 1894.—H. Marcel, H. Bouchot and E. Babelon, *La Bibliothèque Nationale.* Paris,

1907. — Otto Löhmann, "Der Kampf um die politischen Ideololgien der französischen Revolution in der Verfassungsgeschichte der Pariser Nationalbibliothek," *Zentralblatt für Bibliothekswesen*, 56(1939), p. 348.

Chapter 31. France's Confiscation of Books 1792–1809

1. Herm. Degering, "Französischer Kunstraub in Deutschland 1794–1807," *Internationale Monatsschrift für Wissenschaft, Kunst und Technik*, 11(1916/17), p. 1.
2. Frenken, *Das Schicksal der im Jahre 1794 über den Rhein geflüchteten Wertgegenstände des Cölner Domes, insbesondere die Zurückführung der Manuskriptenbibliothek*. Cologne, 1868.
3. W. Classen, "Beiträge zur Geschichte der Klosterbibliotheken und -archive am linken Rheinufer zur Zeit der französischen Herrschaft 1794 ff," *Düsseldorfer Jahrbuch*, 39(1937), p. 279.
4. G. Kentenich and E. Jacobs, "Zum Schicksal der Bibliothek der Benediktinerabtei St. Maximin bei Trier," *Zentralblatt für Bibliothekswesen*, 24(1907), p. 108. — Max Keuffer, "Das Schicksal der Trierer Stadtbibliothek in französischer Zeit," *Trierische Chronik*, 6(1910), p. 73.
5. H. Degering, "Geraubte Schätze. Kölnische Handschriften in Paris und Brüssel," *Beiträge zur Kölnischen Geschichte*, 2(1917), p. 38. — Cf. also M. Domarus' "Die Eberbacher Klosterbibliothek und die Nationalbibliothek in Paris im Jahre 1797," *Mitteilungen des Vereins für Nassauische Altertumskunde und Geschichtsforschung*, 1906/07, p. 21.
6. André Tibal, *Inventaire des manuscrits de Winckelmann déposés à la Bibliothèque Nationale*. Paris, 1911. — Eugène Müntz, "La Bibliothèque du Vatican pendant la Révolution française," in *Mélanges Julien Havet*. Paris, 1865, p. 579.
7. E. Steinmann, "Die Plünderung Roms durch Bonaparte," *Internationale Monatsschrift*, 11(1916/17), cols. 641, 819.
8. Otto Glauning, "Neveu und der Raub Nürnberger Kunst- und Bücherschätze im Jahre 1801," *Mitteilungen des Vereins für Geschichte der Stadt Nürnberg*, 22(1918), p. 174.
9. Karl Schottenloher, "Bayern und der französische Bücherraub im Jahre 1800," *Das Bayerland*, 29(1918), p. 207. — Heinr. Huber, "Die Wiedergewinnung der von den Franzosen im Jahre 1800 aus München entführten Kunstschätze," *Gelbe Hefte*, 5(1929), p. 349.
10. Herm. Degering, "Handschriften aus Echternach und Orval in Paris," *Aufsätze Fritz Milkau gewidmet*. Leipzig, 1921, p. 48.
11. O. Doublier, "Die Wiener Hofbibliothek in Kriegsgefahr," *Zentralblatt für Bibliothekswesen*, 53(1936), p. 33.
12. F. Mencik, "Die Wegführung der Handschriften aus der Hofbibliothek durch die Franzosen," *Jahrbuch der Kunsthistorischen Sammlungen des Kaiserhauses*, 28(1909/10), II, p. IV.
13. H. Schlitter, "Die Zurückstellung der von den Franzosen entführten Archive, Bibliotheken und Kunstsammlungen," *Mitteilungen des Instituts für österreichische Geschichtsforschung*, 22(1901), p. 108.
14. Hubert Bastgen, "Vatikanische Dokumente zur Herausgabe der Codices an die Heidelberger Universität im Jahre 1816," *Neue Heidelberger Jahrbücher*, N.F., 1929, p. 50. — Wilhelm Port, "Deutsche Akten über die Rückgabe der Bibliotheca Palatina an den Vatikan im Jahre 1815/16," *Ibid.* p. 100.
15. *Zentralblatt für Bibliothekswesen*, 30(1913), p. 22.

Chapter 32. Book Collectors in the Revolution

1. Ludwig Traube and R. Ewald, "Jean Baptiste Maugérard," *Abhandlungen der histor. Klasse der Akademie der Wissenschaften Munchen*, 29, 2. Munich, 1904, p. 301. — Emil Jacobs, "Zur Kenntnis Maugérards," *Zentralblatt für Bibliothekswesen*, 27(1910), p. 158, and in *Wiegendrucke u. Handschriften. Festgabe Konrad Haebler dargebracht*. Leipzig, 1919, p. 64. — B. Vollmer, "Die Entführung niederrheinischen Archiv-, Bibliotheks- und Kunstguts durch den französischen Kommisar Maugérard," *Annalen des Histor. Vereins für den Niederrhein*, 131(1937), p. 120.
2. K. Schottenloher in *Zentralblatt für Bibliothekswesen*, 29(1912), p. 68.
3. Herm. Degering, "Das Prümer Evangeliar in Berlin," in *Fünfzehn Jahre Königliche und Staatsbibliothek*, Berlin, 1921, p. 132.

4. Emil Jacobs, "Die Handschriftensammlung Joseph Görres'," *Zentralblatt für Bibliothekswesen*, 23(1906), p. 189.—Fritz Schillmann, *Die Görreshandschriften*. Berlin, 1919.

5. Adolf Schmidt, "Ein Evangeliar aus St. Jakob in Lüttich," *Zentralblatt für Bibliothekswesen*, 42(1925), p. 265.

6. Paulus Volk, "Baron Hüpsch und der Verkauf der Lütticher S.t Jakobsbibliothek 1788," *Zentralblatt für Bibliothekswesen*, 42(1925), p. 201.

7. Adolf Schmidt, *Baron Hüpsch und sein Kabinett. Ein Beitrag zur Geschichte der Hofbibliothek und des Museums zu Darmstadt*. Darmstadt, 1906.—Adolf Schmidt, "Baron Hüpsch in Köln als Inkunabelsammler und Händler," in *Wiegendrucke und Handschriften. Festgabe Konrad Haebler zum 60. Geburtstage*. Leipzig, 1919, p. 45.

Chapter 33. Dissolution of Clerical Libraries

1. *Oratio, Quum bibliotheca ad usum commodum aperta est*. Munich, 1790.

2. Karl Schottenloher, "Der bayerische Gesandte Kasimir Haeffelin in Malta, Rom und Neapel 1796–1827," *Zeitschrift für bayerische Landesgeschichte*, 5(1932), p. 380.

3. August Rosenlehner, "Ein alter Reorganisationsplan der kurpfalzbayrischen Hofbibliotheken 1799," *Zentralblatt für Bibliothekswesen*, 25(1908), p. 433.

4. Vols. 1–9. Munich, 1803–1812.

5. Karl Schottenloher, "Die Münchener Staatsbibliothek als Buchmuseum," *Börsenblatt für den Deutschen Buchhandel*, 97(1930), August 30, no. 201.

6. E. Petzet, "Die deutschen Handschriften der Münchener Hof und Staatsbibliothek," *Germanisch-romanische Monatsschrift*, 3(1911), p. 15.—E. Petzet, *Die deutschen Pergamenthandschriften Nr. 1–200 der Staatsbibliothek in München*. Munich, 1920.

7. E. Petzet, "Friedrich Jacobi über die Münchener Staatsbibliothek vor 100 Jahren," Supplement to *Allgemeinen Zeitung*, 1907, no. 225, p. 421.

8. Chr. Ruepprecht, "Vermehrung der Universtätsbibliothek zu Landshut bzw. München aus den altbayerischen klosterbibliotheken 1803," *Monatsschrift des Historischen Vereins von Oberbayern*. 1893, pp. 93, 111.—A. Hilsenbeck, "Die Universitätsbibliothek Landshut-München und die Säkularisation," in *Festschrift Georg Leyh*. Leipzig, 1937, p. 180.

9. Otto Handwerker, "Zur Geschichte der Handshriftensammlung der Würzburger Universitätsbibliothek," *Zentralblatt für Bibliothekswesen*, 26(1909), p. 485.

10. Adolf Hilsenbeck, "Eine Denkschrift Aretins über die bayerischen Provinzialbibliotheken," in *Aufsätze Fritz Milkau gewidmet*. Leipzig, 1921, p. 153.

11. Joseph Rottenkolber, "Die Schicksale Allgäuer Klosterbibliotheken in der Zeit der Säkularisation," *Zentralblatt für Bibliothekswesen*, 49(1932), p. 431.

12. Alfred Hoder and Karl Preisendanz, *Die Reichenauer Handschriften*. 3 vols. Leipzig, 1906.

13. Fritz Behrend, "Corveys elfhundertjährige Geschichte im Spiegel seiner Büchersammlungen," *Zeitschrift für Bücherfreunde*, N.F. 15(1923), p. 11.

14. Joh. Gust. Büsching, *Bruchstücke meiner Geschäftsreise durch Schlesien, unternommen in den Jahren 1810, 11, 12*. Vol. 1. Breslau, 1813.

15. Otto von Heinemann, *Die Handschriften der Herzoglichen Bibliothek zu Wolfenbüttel*. Abt. I–IV. Wolfenbüttel, 1884–1913.

16. Wilh. Ermann, *Geschichte der Bonner Universitätsbibliothek 1818–1901*. Halle, 1919.

Chapter 34. Literature After Romanticism

1. Wilhelm Pinder, *Das Problem der Generation in der Kunstgeschichte Europas*. 2d ed. Berlin, 1928.

2. Heinz Kindermann, *Durchbruch der Seele. Literaturhistorische Studie über die Anfänge der 'Deutschen Bewegung' vom Pietismus zur Romantik*. Danzig, 1928.

3. Cited from the rich literature about Romanticism should be: Oskar Walze's *Deutsche Romantik*. 5th ed. Leipzig, 1923/25.—Cajetan Osswald, *Die blaue Blume. Ein Büchlein von romantischer Kunst und Dichtung*. Munich, 1924.—Sigmond von Lempicki, "Bücherwelt und wirkliche Welt. Ein Beitrag zur Wesenserfassung der Romantik," *Deutsche Vierteljahrsschrift für Literaturwissenschaft und*

Geistesgeschichte, 3(1925), p. 339.—Rud. Haym, Die romantische Schule. 5th ed. Edited by O. Walzel. Berlin, 1928.—Fritz Strich, *Deutsche Klassik und Romantik oder Vollendung und Unendlichkeit. Ein Vergleich.* Munich, 1928.—*Deutsche Literatur. Reihe Romantik.* Hrsg. von Paul Kluckhohn. Leipzig, 1930 ff.—Paul Kluckhohn. *Das Ideengut der deutschen Romantik.* 2d ed. Halle, 1942.

4. Otto Mallon, *Arnim-Bibliographie.* Berlin, 1925.

5. Friedr. Gundolf, *Shakespeare und der deutsche Geist.* 7th ed. Berlin, 1933.—*Shakespeare in Deutschland.* Hrsg. von Gustav Würtenberg. Bielefeld, 1942.

6. Fridr. Pfaff, *Romantik und Germanische Philologie.* Heidelberg, 1886.

7. Alfred Baeumler, "Jahns Stellung in der deutschen Geistesgeschichte," in his *Politik und Erziehung.* Berlin, 1937, p. 139.

8. Paul Kluckhohn, *Die Idee des Volkes im Schrifttum der deutschen Bewegung von Möser bis Grimm.* Berlin, 1934.

9. Heinrich Hubert Houben and Oskar F. Walzel, *Zeitschriften der Romantik.* Berlin, 1904 ff.

10. Frdr. Pfaff, *Arnims Tröst Einsamkeit.* Freiburg im Breisgau, 1883.—*Neudrucke romantischer Seltenheiten.* 1. Athenäum. Eine Zeitschrift von August Wilhelm Schlegel u. Friedrich Schlegel. 1798–1800.—2. Phoebus. Ein Journal für die Kunst. Hrsg. von Heinr. von Kleist und Adam H. Müller. 1808.—3. Troest Einsamkeit. Hrsg. von Ludwig Achim von Arnim. 1808. Munich, 1924.

11. Anton Schlossar, "Taschenbücher und Almanache zu Anfang unseres Jahrhunderts," *Zeitschrift für Bücherfreunde*, 3(1899/1900) I, p. 49; II, p. 298.—R. Pissin, *Almanache der Romantik.* Berlin, 1910.

12. Paul Kluckhohn, "Die Biedermeierzeit als literarische Epochenbezeichnung," *Deutsche Vierteljahresschrift für Literaturwissenschaft und Geistesgeschichte*, 13(1935), p. 1.

13. Phil. Rath, *Bibliotheca Schlemihliana. Ein Verzeichnis der Ausgaben u. Übersetzungen des Peter Schlemihl.* Berlin, 1919.

14. Cf. Joh. Proelss, *Das Junge Deutschland.* Stuttgart, 1892.—F. Kainz, "Junges Deutschland," *Reallexikon der deutschen Literaturgeschichte*, 2(1926/28), p. 40.—Cf. also H.H. Houben's *Die Zeitschriften des Jungen Deutschlands.* 1906–1909.

15. Ernst Volkmann, *Wege zu realistischem Lebenserfassen. Junges Deutschland und Frührealismus 1830–1848.* Deutsche Literatur. Reihe Deutsche Selbstzeugnisse, 12. Leipzig, 1943.

16. W.A. Aeberhardt, "Die Illustratoren der Schriften Jeremias Gotthelfs," *Schweizerisches Gutenbergmuseum*, 18(1932), p. 193.

17. Cf. Ina Seidel, "Mein Erlebnis mit Adalbert Stifter," in her *Dichter, Volkstum und Sprache.* Stuttgart, 1934, p. 202.

18. Friedrich von Bodenstedt, *Ein Dichterleben in Briefen an das Verlagshaus R. v. Dekker 1850–1892.* Hrsg. von Gustav Schenk. Berlin, 1893.

19. Werner Mahrholz, *Deutsche Literatur der Gegenwart.* Durchgesehen und erweitert von Max Wieser. Berlin, 1930, p. 309.

20. Konrad Krause, *Werkstatt der Wortkunst. Eine Poetik in Selbstzeugnissen deutscher Dichter.* Munich, 1942.

21. Walter Malmsten Schering and Carl von Clausewitz, *Geist und Tat. Das Vermächtnis des Soldaten und Denkers.* Stuttgart, 1941. The fifth edition of the work, *Vom Kriege* (1905) has been introduced by Alfred, Graf von Schlieffen.

22. Friedrich von Der Leyen, *Das Studium der deutschen Philologie.* Munich, 1913.

23. Cf. Paul Siebertz' *Karl Benz, Ein Pionier der Motorisierung.* 2d ed. Stuttgart, 1950.

24. Cf. Jos. Stammhammer's *Bibliographie des Socialismus und Communismus.* 3 vols. 1893–1909.—P. Lensch, *Sozialistische Literatur.* Leipzig, 1907.—Joh. Sassenbach, *Verzeichnis der in deutscher Sprache vorhandenen gewerkschaftlichen Literatur.* 4th ed. Berlin, 1910.—Ernst Drahn, *Zur Entwicklung und Geschichte des sozialistischen Buchhandels und der Arbeiterpresse.* Leipzig, 1913.—E. Drahn, *Führer durch das Schrifttum der deutschen Sozialdemokratie.* 2d ed. Berlin, 1920.—E. Drahn, *Systematische Bibliographie der wissenschaftlichen Literatur Deutschlands der Jahre 1914–1923.* Berlin, 1924.—Leop. Winarsky, "Etwas über sozialistische Bibliophilie," *Deutscher Bibliophilen-Kalender für 1916*, col. 62.—*Geschichte des Sozialismus in Erst- und Original-Ausgaben.* Ausstellung. Vienna, 1926.

25. Harry Bresslau, *Geschichte der Monumenta Germaniae historica.* Hanover, 1921.—Heinrich Schreiber, "Friedrich Adolf Ebert und die Monumenta Germaniae," in *Festschrift Martin Bollert.* Dresden, 1936, p. 82.

26. Georg Waitz, "George Heinrich Pertz und die Monumenta Germaniae historica," *Neues Archiv der Gesellschaft für ältere deutsche Geschichtskunde*, 2(1877), p. 451.—Adalbert Hortzschansky,

"Heinrich Pertz' Berufung zum Oberbibliothekar der Königlichen Bibliothek in Berlin," in *Beiträge zum Bibliotheks- und Buchwesen. Paul Schwenke zum 20. März 1913 gewidmet.* Berlin, 1913, p. 115.

27. *Deutsche Literatur. Reihe Romantik. Band 13: Romantische Wissenschaft.* Bearbeitet von Wilhelm Bietak. Leipzig, 1940.

28. Wilhelm Schoof, "Kritik um das Grimmsche Wörterbuch," *Archiv für das Studium der neueren Sprachen,* 174(1938), p. 145.

29. E. Probst, *Die deutschen Illustrationen der Grimmschen Märchen im 19. Jahrhundert.* Disseration. Würzburg, 1935.

30. Axel von Harnack, "Die Akademien der Wissenschaften," *Handbuch der Bibliothekswissenschaft,* 1(1931), p. 850.

31. K. Th. von Heigel, *Die Anfänge des Weltbundes der Akademien.* Munich, 1907.

32. Wilh. Olbrich, "Der Literarische Verein Stuttgart," *Philobiblon,* 12(1940), p. 229.

33. Carl Diesch, *Der Goedecke. Werdegang eines wissenschaftlichen Unternehmens.* Dresden, 1941. — Cf. also Josefl Körners' extensive *Bibliographisches Handbuch des deutschen Schrifttums.* 3rd ed. Bern, 1949.

34. Julius Schlosser, *Die Kunstliteratur. Ein Handbuch zur Quellenkunde der neueren Kunstgeschichte.* Vienna, 1924.

35. *Handbuch der Kunstgeschichte.* 5th ed. 1871/2.

36. *Geschichte der Architektur.* 6th ed. 1884. — *Grundriss der Kunstgeschichte.* 14th ed. 1907/10. — *Geschichte der Plastik.* 3rd ed. 1880.

37. *Handbuch der Kunstgeschichte.* 12th ed. Leipzig, 1923.

38. *Handbuch der deutschen Kunstdenkmäler.* 1905–12. 5th–7th eds. 1926–37.

39. *Renaissance und Barock.* 4th ed. 1926. — *Die klassische Kunst.* 7th ed. 1924. — *Die Kunst Albrecht Dürers.* 5th ed. 1926. — *Kunstgeschichtliche Grundbegriffe.* 7th ed. 1929.

40. Hermann Lotze, *Mikrokosmus. Ideen zur Naturgeschichte und Geschichte der Menschheit.* Leipzig, 1865; 5th ed. Leipzig, 1896.

41. *Die Philosophie der Griechen* ——— dargestellt von Dr. Eduard Zeller. 6th ed. 3 vols. Leipzig, 1920.

42. Kuno Fischer, *Geschichte der neueren Philosophie.* 6 various editions. Heidelberg, 1867–1923.

43. Wilh. M. Wundt, *Grundriss der Psychologie.* 15 various editions. Leipzig, 1896–1922. — WIlh. M. Wundt, *Grundzüge der physiologischen Psychologie.* 6 editions. Leipzig, 1874–1911. — Wilh. Max Wundt, *Völkerpsychologie; eine Untersuchung der Entwicklungsgesetze von Sprache, Mythus und Sitte.* 4 vols. in 4 editions. Leipzig, 1904–1922.

44. Rudolf Christof Eucken, *Die Lebensanschauungen der grossen Denker.* Leipzig, 1890; 15th and 16th eds. Berlin, 1921. — Rudolf Christof Eucken, *Der Sinn und Wert des Lebens.* 6th ed. Leipzig, 1918.

45. *Erlebnis und Dichtung. Lessing, Goethe, Novalis, Hölderlin.* 1906; 4th ed., 1916. Cf. Gerh. Masur's "Wilhelm Dilthey und die europäische Geistesgeschichte," *Deutsche Vierteljahrsschrift für Literaturwissenschaft und Geistesgeschichte,* 12(1934), p. 479.

46. *Die Geist als Widersacher der Seele.* 3 vols. Leipzig, 1929; 2d ed., 1937/9.

47. Eduard Spranger, *Lebensformen.* 6th ed. Halle, 1927.

48. Gottfried Kricker, *Die Schrifttumsnachweise der Medizin. Übersicht über Handbücher, Bibliographien, Referatenblätter und sonstige Literaturquellen.* 2d ed. Leipzig, 1941.

49. Ludwig Aschoff, *Rudolf Virchow, Wissenschaft und Weltgeltung.* Hamburg, 1940.

50. About these groups of scientific works, see Claus Nissen's "Insekten," *Lexikon des gesamten Buchwesens,* 2(1936), p. 163.

51. *Aus fünfzig Jahren deutscher Wissenschaft. Die Entwicklung ihrer Fortschritte in Einzeldarstellungen.* Hrsg. von Gustav Abb. Berlin, 1930. (Friedrich Schmidt-Ott-Festschrift). *Deutsche Forschung. Aus der Arbeit der Notgemeinschaft.* Heft 1–27. Berlin, 1928–34. — Friedrich Schmidt-Ott, *Aus vergangenen Tagen deutscher Wissenschaftspflege.* Berlin, 1935. — A. Jürgens, "Weltgeltung der deutschen Wissenschaft und des Buches," *Börsenblatt des deutschen Buchhandels,* 108(1941), p. 109.

52. Adolf Jürgens, "Auslandsliteratur auf deutschen Bibliotheken," *Literarisches Zentralblatt für Deutschland,* 75(1924), col. 629. Cf. Karl Kerkhof's "Die internationalen naturwissenschaftlichen Organisationen vor und nach dem Weltkrieg und die deutsche Wissenschaft," *Kunst und Technik,* 15(1921), p. 237.

53. Heinrich von Sbrik, "Das deutsche wissenschaftliche Buch und seine Bedeutung für das Ausland," in *Adalbert Stifter Almanach.* 1941/1942, p. 22.

54. Rud. Fürst, "Die Mode im Buchtitel," *Das liter. Echo* 3(1901), col. 1088. — K. Bader, "Vom

Büchertitel einst und jetzt," *Zeitschrift für Bücherfreunde,* 6(1902/1903) I, p. 69.—Egon von Komorzynski, "Zur Geschichte der Blume im deutschen Buchtitel," *Zeitschrift für Bücherfreunde,* 7(1903/1904) II, p. 284.—Heinrich Meisner, "Büchertitelmoden," *Zeitschrift für Bücherfreunde,* 8(1904/05) I, p. 38.—Karl Bücher, "Welche Rücksichten sind bei der Wahl eines Buchtitels zu beobachten?," in his *Hochschulfragen.* Leipzig, 1912, p. 173.—M. Grolig, "Der Buchtitel. Eine Literaturübersicht," *Deutscher Bibliophilen-Kalender für 1916.* Vienna, 1916, p. 107.—Max Sondheim, *Das Titelblatt.* Mainz, 1937.—Hedwig Gollob, "Wiener Titelblätter und Signete der Renaissancezeit," *Gutenberg Jahrbuch,* 1942/43, p. 198.

55. Albert Vanselow, *Die Erstdrucke und Erstausgaben der Werke von Wilhelm Busch.* Leipzig, 1913.

56. I refer only to Grellmann, "Roman" in P. Merker and W. Stammler, *Reallexikon der deutschen Literaturgeschichte,* 3(1928/29), p. 63; and W. Olbrich's *Der Romanführer. Die deutschen Romane und Novellen vom Barock bis zum Naturalismus.* 2 vols Stuttgart, 1950/51.

57. Joh. Wilh. Appell, *Die Ritter-, Räuber- und Schauerromantik. Zur Geschichte der deutschen Unterhaltungs-Literatur.* Leipzig, 1859.

58. Karl May Verlag. *25 Jahre Schaffen am Werke Karl May's.* Radebeul bei Dresden, 1938.

59. *Handwörterbuch des deutschen Aberglaubens.* vol. 1. 1927, col. 1688.

60. Ina Seidel, *Dichter, Volkstum und Sprache.* Stuttgart, 1934, p. 7 ff.

61. Cf. also p. 332.

62. Concerning the relationship of the reader to books see C. Tumlirz's *Die Schwankugen des literarischen Geschmacks und ihre Ursachen.* 1900.—Gustav Roethe, *Vom literarischen Publicum in Deutschland.* Göttingen, 1902.—Wilh. Bube, "Lesebedürfnis und Bildungstrieb der Landbevölkerung," *Das Volks- u. Jugendschrifttum,* 1(1913), p. 3.—Leon L. Schücking, "Literaturgeschichte und Geschmacksgeschichte," *Germanisch-Romanische Monatsschrift,* 5(1913), p. 561.—Bruno Markwardt, "Literarischer Geschmack," *Reallexikon der deutschen Literaturgeschichte.* Hrsg. von Paul Merker u. W. Stammler. 2 vols. 1926–29, p. 241.—L.L. Schücking, *Dis Soziologie der literarischen Geschmacksbildung.* 2d ed. Leipzig, 1931.—Walter Hofmann, *Die Lektüre der Frau. Ein Beitrag zur Leserkunde und zur Leserführung.* Leipzig, 1931.—Rich. Müller-Freienfels, "Bücher und ihr Publikum," *Die Literatur,* 34(1931–32), p. 665.—Otto Görner, "Der Volkslesestoff" in Adolf Spamer's *Die Deutsche Volkskunde,* vol. 1. Leipzig, 1935, p. 388.—Horst Kunze, "Buchkunde und Literaturgeschichte. Buchkundliche Voraussetzungen zu einer Literaturgeschichte des Publikumsgeschmacks," *Buch und Schrift,* N.F. 1(1938), p. 106.—Horst Kunze, *Lieblings-Bücher von dazumal. Eine Blütenlese aus den erfolgreichsten Büchern von 1750–1860. Zugleich ein erster Versuch zu einer Geschichte des Lesergeschmacks.* Munich, 1938.—Wilhelm Schuster, "Zur Geschichte des lesenden Volkes und seiner Büchereien," *Die Bücherei,* 5(1938), p. 703.—Erich Thier, *Gestaltwandel des Arbeiters im Spiegel seiner Lektüre. Ein Beitrag zur Volkskunde und Leseführung.* Leipzig, 1939.—Herbert Barth and Walther Vontin, *Das kleine Lese-Brevier. Weisung und Zuspruch deutscher Dichter und Denker.* Ebenhausen, 1939.—Bruno Brehm, *Der Lieber Leser.* Berlin, 1940.—Karl d' Ester, *Zeitung und Leser.* Mainz, 1941.

63. Cf. Bernhard Rang's "Gottfried Keller als Leser," *Die Bücherei,* 11(1944), p. 248.—Nora Imendörffer, "Johann Georg Hamann als Bücherleser und -sammler," *Philobiblon,* 12(1914), p. 243.

64. Ewald A. Boucke, "Der Prosastil," in W. Hofstaetter and F. Panzer's *Grundzüge der Deutschkunde,* vol. 1. Leipzig, 1925, p. 71.

65. Phil. Allfeld, *Das Urheberrecht an Werken der Literatur und der Tonkunst.* 2d ed. Munich, 1928.

66. Karl Schottenloher, "Die Druckprivilegien des 16. Jahrhunderts," *Gutenberg-Jahrbuch.* 1933, p. 89.—Friedrich Lehne, "Zur Rechtsgeschichte der kaiserlichen Druckprivilegien. Ihre Bedeutung für die Geschichte des Urheberrechtes," *Mitteilungen des Österreichischen Instituts für Geschichtsforschung,* 53(1939), p. 323.

67. Phil. Allfeld, *Das Verlagsrecht.* 2d ed. Munich, 1929.—Robert Voigtländer-Elster, ed., *Gesetze über das Verlagsrecht.* 3rd ed. Berlin, 1939.—Wilhelm Olbrich, *Einführung in die Verlagskunde,* 2d ed. Leipzig, 1943.

68. Gerh. Menz, *Kulturwirtschaft.* Leipzig, 1933.—Cf. also H.H. Borchardt's "Honorar," *Reallexikon der deutschen Literaturgeschichte,* 1(1926), p. 523.—Walter Krieg, "Materialien zu einer Geschichte des Buchhonorars vom 15. bis 20. Jahrhundert," *Das Antiquariat,* 7(1951), nos. 13/16.

69. *Der Verlag Ullstein zum Weltreklame-Kongress in Berlin.* Berlin, 1929.

70. Otto Groth, *Die Zeitung,* 4 vols. Mannheim, 1930.—*Standortskatalog wichtiger Zeitungsbestände in deutschen Bibliotheken.* Leipzig, 1933.—Karl Bömer and E. Dovifat, *Handbuch*

der Weltpresse. Eine Darstellung des Zeitungswesens aller Länder, 3rd ed. Leipzig, 1937.—*Handbuch der Zeitungswissenschaft*. Hrsg. von W. Heide, bearb. von E.H. Lehmann. Leipzig, 1940 ff.

71. Ernst Meunier and Hans Jessen, *Das deutsche Feuilleton*. Berlin, 1931.—Emil Dovifat, "Feuilleton," *Handbuch der Zeitungswissenschaft*, 1(1940), p. 976.—Wilmont Haacke, *Feuilletonkunde. Das Feuilleton als literarische und journalistische Gattung*. Leipzig, 1943.

72. Georg Eltzschig, *Des deutschen Buches Wert und Wirkung für das Ausland-Deutschtum. Eine Denkschrift*. Hrsg. für die G.A. von Halem Export-und Verlagsbuchhandlung. Bremen, 1928.—Heinz Kinderman, *Rufe über Grenzen. Antlitz und Lebensraum der Grenz und Auslandsdeutschen in ihrer Dichtung*. Berlin, 1938.—*Deutschtum in Übersee und in den Kolonien. Ein Schrifttumsverzeichnis*. Berlin, 1939.

73. Helmut Hatzfeld makes a small contribution to the subject in his *Wechselbeziehungen zwischen der deutschen Literatur und den übrigen europäischen Literaturen*. Bielefeld, 1927.—Cf. also Cäsar Fleischlen's *Graphische Literatur-Tafel. Die deutsche Literatur und der Einfluss fremder Literaturen auf ihren Verlauf in graphischer Darstellung, 1890.*—R. Leppla, "Übersetzungsliteratur," in P. Merker and W. Stammler's *Reallexikon der deutschen Literaturgeschichte*, 3(1928/29), p. 394.

74. V. Rossel, *Histoire des relations littèraires entre la France et l'Allemagne*. Paris, 1897.—Ludwig Griebert, *Paul Verlaine und seine deutschen Übersetzer*. Giessen, 1928.—Hans Fromm, *Bibliographie deutscher Übersetzungen aus dem Französischen 1700–1948*. Im Auftrage des Hohen Kommissariats der Französischen Republik in Deutschland. vols. 1–4. Baden-Baden, 1950–51.

75. Richard Ackermann, *Lord Byron Sein Leben, seine Werke, sein Einfluss auf die deutsche Literatur*. Heidelberg, 1901.

76. Walther Fischer, "Varnhagen von Enses Carlyle-Bibliothek," *Die neueren Sprachen*, 24(1916), p. 449.

77. Max Koch, *Über die Beziehungen der englischen Literatur zur deutschen im 18. Jahrhundert*. Leipzig, 1883.—Anselm Schlösser, *Die englische Literatur in Deutschland von 1895 bis 1934 mit einer vollständigen Bibliographie der deutschen Übersetzungen und der im deutschen Sprachgebiet erschienenen englischen Ausgaben*. Jena, 1937. Cf. also p. 337 ff.

78. *Spanische Dramen*. Übersetzt von Karl August Dohrn. 4 vols. Berlin, 1841.—Moritz Rapp, *Spanisches Theater*. 7 vols. Leipzig, 1868–70.—Adam Schneider, *Spaniens Anteil an der deutschen Literatur des 16. und 17. Jahrhunderts*. Strasbourg, 1898.—*Meisterlustspiele der Spanier*. In freier Nachdichtung von Ludwig Fulda. 2 vols. Berlin, 1925.—Hermann Tiemann, *Das spanische Schrifttum in Deutschland von der Renaissance bis zur Romantik*. Hamburg, 1936.—H. Tiemann, *Lope de Vega in Deutschland*. Hamburg, 1939.

79. Julius Schwering, *Literarische Beziehungen zwischen Spanien und Deutschland*. Münster, i.W., 1902.

80. E. Fay, "Das Deutschland Fogazzaros," *Archiv für das Studium der neueren Sprachen*, 167(1935), p. 74.

81. Erwin Hunziker, *Carducci und Deutschland*. Aarau, 1927.

82. For the eighteenth century, cf. Leopold Magon's *Ein Jahrhundert geistiger und literarischer Beziehungen zwischen Deutschland und Skandinavien 1750–1850*. 1.Bd.: *Die Klopstockzeit in Dänemark*. Dortmund, 1926.

83. Günter Krumm, *Gustav Frödings Verbindungen mit der deutschen Literatur. Ein Beitrag zur Geschichte der geistigen Wechselbeziehungen zwischen Deutschland und Skandinavien*. Greifswald, 1934.

84. Walter A. Berendsohn, "Knut Hamsuns Aufnahme in Deutschland," *Deutschnordisches Jahrbuch*. 1929. p. 85.

85. Irmgard Gunther, *Die Einwirkung des skandinavischen Romans auf den deutschen Naturalismus*. Greifswald, 1934.—Erika Wiehe, *Gottlieb Mohnike als Vermittler und Übersetzer nordischer Literatur*. Greifswald, 1934.

86. A. Luther, "Russische Literatur," in P. Merker and W. Stammler's *Reallexikon der deutschen Literaturgeschichte*, 3(1928/29), p. 130.—Erich Boehme and Arthur Luther, "Frühdeutsche Übersetzungen aus dem Russischen," *Philobiblon*, 6(1933), pp. 277, 349.

87. Frdr. Dukmeyer, *Die Einführung Lermontows in Deutschland und des Dichters Persönlichkeit*. Berlin, 1925.

88. Theoderich Kampann, *Dostojewski in Deutschland*. Münster, 1931.

89. On this question cf. Bayard Quincy Morgan's *A Bibliography of German Literature in English Translation*. Madison, 1922; 2d ed., 1938.—*Der Auslandsdeutsche*. Sonderheft, 1930. 2 Oktoberheft:

"Die Kulturmission des deutschen Buches im Ausland." Charlotte Bauschinger, "Das deutsche Buch in fremden Sprachen. Statistik der Übersetzungen für 1935–1939," *Mitteilungen der Akademie zur wissenschaftlichen Erforschung des Deutschtums*, 1936: 473; 1937: 481; 1938: 565; 1939: 370; 1941: 221.—In vol. 13(1938) of the same journal of the German Academy, there are the following surveys: Julius Wilhelm, "Deutsche Geistes- und Literatureinflüsse auf Frankreich im 19. Jahrhundert" (p. 10).—G. Haack, "Das zeitgenössische spanische Schrifttum und Deutschland" (p. 189).—Hans Galinsky, "Das deutsche Schrifttum in England" (p. 531).—F.R. Schäfer, "Das deutsche Schrifttum in Japan" (p. 536).—Cf. further Hans Frese's *Das deutsche Buch in Amerika*. Dissertation. Marburg, 1937.—Hans Galinsky, *Deutsches Schrifttum der Gegenwart in der englischen Kritik der Nachkriegszeit (1919–1935). Ein Versuch über die Lebensbedingungen und das kulturpolitische Wirken des deutschen Buches im Ausland.* Munich, 1938.—Fritz Meyer, *Die norwegischen Übersetzungen deutscher Schönliteratur 1814–1941.* Oslo, 1942.

Chapter 35. The Modern Book Trade

1. Heinrich Lempertz, *Bilderhefte zur Geschichte des Bücherhandels.* Bonn, 1853/65.—Karl Bücher, *Der deutsche Buchhandel und die Wissenschaft.* 3rd ed. Leipzig, 1904.—Theod. Petermann, *Der deutsche Buchhandel und seine Abnehmer.* Dresden, 1906.—Gerhard Menz, *Deutsche Buchhändler. Vierundzwanzig Lebensbilder.* Leipzig, 1924.—Gerhard Menz, *Der deutsche Buchhandel.* Gotha, 1925.—Friedrich Schulze, *Der deutsche Buchhandel und die geistigen Strömungen der letzten hundert Jahre.* Leipzig, 1925.—H. Kliemann, *Die Werbung für das Buch.* 2d ed., Stuttgart, 1951.—Erich Scherer, *Das Unternehmertum des deutschen Verlagsbuchhandels.* Dissertation. Göttingen, 1926.—D. Bottmann, "Verlagsbuchhandel," in P. Merker und W. Stammler's *Reallexikon der deutschen Literaturgeschichte*, 3(1928/29), p. 442.—Max Paschke and Philipp Rath, *Lehrbuch des deutschen Buchhandels.* 7th ed. Editions 1, 2. Leipzig, 1932–35.—Wilhelm Olbrich, *Einführung in die Verlagskunde.* Leipzig, 1932; 2d ed., 1943.—A. Speemann, *Berufsgeheimnisse und Binsenwahrheiten.* Stuttgart, 1941.—Oskar Siebeck, *Die Aufgabe des wissenschaftlichen Verlags im Deutschland des 20. Jahrhunderts.* Tübingen, 1934.—Alf. Druckenmüller, *Der Buchhandel der Welt. Aufbau, Verkehrswesen, Anschriften des Buchhandels in Europa und USA.* Stuttgart, 1935.—Ernst Johann, *Die deutschen Buchverlage des Naturalismus und der Neuromantik.* Dissertation. Heidelberg, 1935.—Gerhard Menz, *Der europäische Buchhandel seit dem Wiener Kongress.* Würzburg, 1941.—Stanley Unwin, *Das wahre Gesicht des Verlagsbuchhandels.* 2d ed. Stuttgart, 1950.—Hans Ferd. Schulz, *Das Schicksal der Bücher.* Berlin, 1952.

2. Martin Riegel, *Der Buchhändler Johann Philipp Palm. Mit einem vollständigen Abdruck der Schrift 'Deutschland in seiner tiefen Erniedrigung'.* Hamburg, 1938.

3. Hans H. Bockwitz, *Stätten des Buches in Leipzig 1933.*

4. E.H. Lehmann, *Geschichte des Konversationslexikon.* Leipzig, 1934.

5. Herm. Ed. Brockhaus, *Friedrich Arnold Brockhaus.* 3 vols. Leipzig, 1872–81.—*Die Firma Friedrich Arnold Brockhaus 1805–1905.* Leipzig, 1905.—*F.A. Brockhaus in Leipzig. Vollständiges Verzeichnis der seit dem Jahre 1873 verlegten Werke.* Leipzig, 1905.—*Aus dem Archiv Friedrich Arnold Brockhaus.* Leipzig, 1926.—*Sven Hedin und Albert Brockhaus. Eine Freundschaft in Briefen.* Herausgegeben von Suse Brockhaus. Leipzig, 1942.

6. Clemens Theodor Perthes, *Friedrich Perthes' Leben.* 3 vols. 8th ed. Gotha, 1896.

7. Justus Perthes, *Justus Perthes von Gotha 1785–1883.* Munich, 1887.—*Justus Perthes' Haupt-Katalog.* Gotha, 1935.

8. Hermann Reimer, *Georg Andreas Reimer,* Berlin, 1904.—Theodor Roller, *Georg Andreas Reimer und sein Kreis.* Berlin, 1924.

9. *Verlags Katalog der W.B. in Berlin.* Berlin, 1926.—Ernst Vollert, *Die W.B. in Berlin 1680–1930.* Berlin, 1930.—Konrad Burdach, *Wissenschaftsgeschichtliche Eindrücke eines alten Germanisten. Festgabe zum 250jährigen Jubiläum der W.B.* Berlin, 1930.

10. Heinrich W.B. Zimmer, *Johann Georg Zimmer und die Romantiker.* Frankfurt am Main, 1888.—Otto Reichel, *Der Verlag von Mohr und Zimmer in Heidelberg und die Heidelberger Romantik.* Dissertation. Munich, 1913.—Jos. Körner, "A.W. Schlegel und sein Heidelberger Verleger," *Zeitschrift für die österreichischen Gymnasien*, 65(1914), p. 674.—*August Wilhelm Schlegels Briefwechsel mit seinen Heidelberger Verlegern.* Hrsg. von Erich Jenisch. Festschrift zur Jahrhundert-Feier des Verlags Carl Winter. Heidelberg, 1922.—Werner Siebeck, *Der Heidelberger Verlag von Jacob Christian Benjamin*

Mohr. Tübingen, 1926.—Oskar Rühle, *Der theologische Verlag von J.C.B. Mohr (Paul Siebeck).* Tübingen, 1926.

11. *Die Veröffentlichungen des Verlags von J.L. Schrag in Nürnberg 1810–1910.* Nuremberg, 1910.—Paul Ruf, "Ein Verlagsarchiv aus der Zeit der Spätromantik in der Staatsbilbiothek zu München," *Zentralblatt für Bibliothekswesen,* 48(1926), p. 616, and *Forschungen und Fortschritte,* 3(1927), p. 191.

12. Ernst Adolf Dreyer, *Friedrich Vieweg & Sohn in 150 Jahren deutscher Geistesgeschichte 1786–1936.* Brunswick, 1936.—Jonas Fränkel, *Gottfried Kellers Briefe an Vieweg.* Zürich, 1938.

13. Frhr. von Tauchnitz, *Fünfzig Jahre der Verlagsbuchhandlung Bernhard Tauchnitz, Leipzig 1837–1887.* Leipzig, 1887.—*Der Verlag Bernhard Tauchnitz 1837–1912.* Leipzig, 1912.—*Tauchnitz Edition. Kleiner Führer durch die gute englische und amerikanische Literatur der neuesten Zeit.* Leipzig, 1933.

14. Wolfgang Weber, *Johann Jacob Weber.* Leipzig, 1928.—Wolfgang Weber, *Dr. Felix Weber, der Neuschöpfer der Firma J.J. Weber 1845–1906.* Leipzig, 1939.

15. Joh. Hohlfeld, *Das Bibliographische Institut.* Festschrift. Leipzig, 1926.—Werner Schultze, *Aus der Chronik des B.I.* Leipzig, 1936.

16. Gerh. Menz, *Hundert Jahre Meyers Lexikon.* Leipzig, 1939.

17. *Widmungsblätter an Hans Heinrich Reclam. Beim Erscheinen der Nr. 500 von Reclams Universalbibliothek.* Leipzig, 1910.—*Ausführlicher Schlag- und Stichwortskatalog zu Reclams Universal-Bibliothek (bis Ende des Jahres 1925).* Mit Geleitwort von Heinrich Uhlendahl. Leipzig, 1926.—Th. Mann, *100 Jahre Reclam.* Leipzig, 1929.—Herm. Hesse, *Eine Bibliothek der Weltliteratur.* 2d ed. Leipzig, 1930.—Annemarie Meiner, *Reclam. Eine Geschichte der Universal-Bibliothek.* Leipzig, 1942.—Josef Nadler intended the *Reclams Universalbibliothek* to be the greatest publishing idea of modern times.

18. *Hundert Jahre Georg Westermann, Braunschweig 1838–1938.* Brunswick, 1938.—Gerhard Schönfelder, "Hundert Jahre im Dienste des deutschen Schrifttums und der deutschen Schule," *Bücherkunde,* 5(1938), p. 259.

19. *Karl Baedeker 1827–1927.* Leipzig, 1927.

20. *Verlagsverzeichnis von Duncker & Humblot in Leipzig 1866–1914.* Leipzig, 1914.

21. Friedrich Schulze, *B.G. Teubner 1811–1911. Geschichte der Firma.* Leipzig, 1911.—*Forschung und Unterricht. Einblicke in ihre Arbeit. Aus Verlagswerken von B.G. Teubner in Leipzig und Berlin.* Leipzig, 1911.

22. Hans Martin Elster, *Verlagskatalog 1849–1924.* G. Grotesche Verlagsbuchhandlung. Berlin, 1924.

23. Samuel Fischer, *Das 40. Jahr 1886–1929.* Berlin, 1929.

24. *Fünfzehn Jahre Georg Müller Verlag München 1903–1918.* Munich, 1919.

25. Reinhard Piper, *Vormittag. Erinnerungen eines Verlegers.* Munich, 1947. 2. Teil: *Nachmittag.* Munich, 1950.

26. Braun & Schneider, Munich. *Verlags-Katalog.* Munich, 1928.

27. *Zehn Jahre Verleger. Eine kleine Gedenk- und Werbeschrift mit Bildbeilagen aus Werken des Verlages Georg W. Dietrich in München 1906–1917.* Munich, 1917.

28. Adolf Bonz & Co., Stuttgart. *Ein Bücherverzeichnis zur Feier des 50jährigen Bestehens.* Stuttgart, 1926.—Adolf Bonz & Co. *Zeitgebürtige Dichtung aus dem Verlag Adolf Bonz & Comp. Ein Almanach.* Stuttgart, 1927.

29. Hans H. Gaede, *Vom Stufenreich des Lebens. 40 Jahre Eugen Salzer Verlag.* 1931.

30. *Almanach des Paul List-Verlages auf das Jahr 1931.* 1931.

31. *L. Staackmann Leipzig 1869–1919.* Leipzig, 1919.—L. Staackmann, *Verzeichnis sämtlicher erschienenen Bücher.* Leipzig, 1919.

32. *Verzeichnis aller Veröffentlichungen des Insel-Verlags 1899–1924.* Leipzig, 1924.—*Die Insel-Bücherei 1912–1937.* Leipzig, 1937.—Frdr. Michael, "Die Insel-Bücherei," *Imprimatur,* 7(1937), p. 205.

33. Gerhard Menz, *Der deutsche Buchhandel der Gegenwart in Selbstdarstellungen.* Vol. 2, no. 1: E.D. Leipzig, 1927.—F.H. Ehmcke, "Erinnerung an Eugen Diederichs," *Gutenberg-Jahrbuch.* 1931, p. 328.—*Eugen Diederichs Leben und Werk. Ausgewählte Briefe und Aufzeichnungen,* Hrsg. von Lulu von Strauss u. Torney-Diederichs. Jena, 1936.—Walter G. Oschilewski, *Eugen Diederichs und sein Werk.* Jena, 1936.—Klaus Dietze, *Eugen Diederichs und seine Zeitschriften.* Würzburg, 1940.

34. *Von der schwarzen und von der weissen Kunst. A. Bagel 1801–1951.* Text von Ilse Bartleben. Düsseldorf, 1951.

35. Max Niemeyer (Firm), Halle. *Verlags-Katalog, 1870–1930.* Halle, 1930; (annual) supplements, Halle, 1930 ff.

36. Gerh. Lüdtke, *Der Verlag Walter de Gruyter & Co. Skizzen aus der Geschichte der seinen Aufbau bildenden ehemaligen Firmen, nebst einem Lebensabriss Dr. Walter de Gruyters.* Berlin, 1921.—Gerh. Lüdtke, *Walter de Gruyter. Ein Lebensbild.* Berlin, 1929.—*Katalog von Walter de Gruyter & Co. 1749–1832.* Berlin, 1932.

37. *Geschichte und Werke der Langenscheidtschen Verlagsbuchhandlung.* Berlin, 1932.

38. Adolf Spemann, *Wilhelm Spemann. Ein Baumeister unter den Verlegern,* Stuttgart, 1943. Cf. also Adolf Spemann's *Berufsgeheimnisse und Binsenwahrheiten. Aus den Erfahrungen eines Verlegers.* 2d ed., Stuttgart, 1941.

39. *Werden und Wirken. Festschrift f. K.W. Hiersemann.* Leipzig, 1924.—*Jub. -Verlagskatalog.* 1924.—*Börsenblatt,* September 3, 1924, and December 10, 1928.—W. Goldfriedrich in the *Intern. Adressbuch d. Antiquare.* Weimar, 1930.—W. Olbrich, *Geschichte und Arbeitsgebiete der Firma Karl W. Hiersemann.* Leipzig, 1941.

40. Hans Harrassowitz, *Otto Harrassowitz und seine Firma.* Leipzig, 1922.—Heinrich Becker, "75 Jahre Otto Harrassowitz," *Zentralblatt für Bibliothekswesen,* 61(1947), p. 12.

41. J.C. Hinrichs (Firm), Leipzig. *Verlagskatalog 1845–1904.* Leipzig, 1905.

42. C.E. Poeschel (Firm), Stuttgart. *Fünfzig Jahre C.E. Poeschel Verlag, 1902–1952.* Stuttgart, 1952.

43. A.M. Weiss, *Benj. Herder,* 1890.—Franz Meister, *Barth Herder,* 1915/17.—Ph. Dorneich, *Vor 50 Jahren.* 1929.—*Der Verlag Herder im Ausland—Pionierarbeit für das deutsche Buch.* 1937.

44. Georg Hölscher, *Hundert Jahre J.P. Bachem.* Cologne, 1918.

45. S.P. Widmann, *Die Aschendorffsche Presse 1762–1912.* Münster, 1912.—Aschendorff (Firm). *Aus unserer wissenschaftlichen Verlagtätigkeit.* Münster, 1933.—*Westphälisches Schrifttum. Veröffentlichungen der Aschendorffschen Verlagsbuchhandlung.* Münster, 1937.—*130 Jahre Aschendorff 1720–1950.* Münster, 1950.

46. Otto Denk, *Friedrich Pustet. Vater u. Sohn,* 1904.—Josef Kösel und Friedrich Pustet (firm), München. *Jubiläums Almanach.* Munich, 1926.

47. Wilhelm Ruprecht, *Väter und Söhne. Zwei Jahrhunderte Buchhändler in einer deutschen Universitätsstadt.* Göttingen, 1935.

48. *Verzeichnis des Verlags von Hermann Böhlaus Nachfolgern in Weimar. Die Jahre 1853 bis 1912 umfassend.* Weimar, 1913.

49. C.H. Beck (Firm), München. *Verlagskatalog der C.H. Beckschen Verlagsbuchhandlung 1763–1913.* Munich, 1913.—C.H. Beck (Firm), München. *Fachkatalog Verlag C.H. Beck.* Munich, 1951.

50. *150 Jahre N.G. Elwert,* 1933.

51. Gustav Fischer (Firm), Jena. *Ein Verzeichnis der seit dem 1. Januar 1878 erschienenen Werke und Zeitschriften.* Jena, 1928.

52. Julius Springer (Firm), Berlin. *Verlagskatalog von Julius Springer in Berlin. . .1842–1911.* Leipzig, 1912.

53. Paul Parey (Firm), Berlin. *Verlagskatalog.* Berlin, 1911.

54. Johannes Hohlfeld, *Die Firma R. Oldenbourg, München. Ein geschichtlicher Überblick 1858 bis 1940.* Munich, 1940.

55. Johann Ambrosius Barth (Firm), Leipzig. *Verlagskatalog 1881/83.* Leipzig, 1883.—Johann Ambrosius Barth, Leipzig. *25 Jahre Verlagstätigkeit 1881–1905.* Leipzig, 1905.—Johann Ambrosius Barth (Firm), Leipzig, *Johann Ambrosius Barth, Leipzig, 1780–1930.* Leipzig, 1930.

56. *Georg Thieme Verlag, Leipzig, 1886–1936.* Leipzig, 1936.

57. Urban & Schwarzenberg, *Verzeichnis aller bis Ende 1916 erschienenen Werke, Zeitschriften und Sammelwerke.* Vienna and Berlin, 1916.

58. Enke (Firm), Stuttgart. *Hundert Jahre Ferdinand Enke Verlagsbuchhandlung,* Stuttgart. *Jubiläumskatalog, 1837–1937.* Stuttgart, 1937.

59. Julius Friedrich Lehmann, *Verleger J.F. Lehmann; ein Leben im Kampf für Deutschland; Lebenslauf und Briefe.* Hrsg. von Melanie Lehmann. Munich, 1935.

60. Bornträger Gebrüder (Firm), Berlin. *Gebrüder Bornträger Berlin und Leipzig, 1790–1930. Verzeichnis der seit 1750 erschienenen Werke und Zeitschriften.* Berlin, 1930.

61. Quelle und Meyer, Leipzig. *Verzeichnis der Veröffentlichungen des Verlages, 1906–1931.* Leipzig, 1931.

62. Schweizerbarth (Firm), Stuttgart. *Jubiläumskatalog 1826–1926.* Stuttgart, 1926.

Chapter 36. Modern Book Design

1. Kurt Volkmann, "Der Stahlstich als Buchillustration," *Zeitschrift für Bücherfreunde*, 37(1933), p. 211.

2. Luitpold Dussler, *Die Incunabeln der deutschen Lithographie 1796–1821.* Berlin, 1925.

3. Th. Goebel, *Friedrich König und die Erfindung der Schnellpresse.* 2d ed. Stuttgart, 1908.

4. On modern book design, see Ottot Grautoff's *Die Entwicklung der modernen Buchkunst in Deutschland.* Leipzig, 1901.—Rud. Kautzsch, *Die neue Buchkunst. Studien im In- und Ausland.* Weimar, 1902.—Felix Poppenberg, *Buchkunst.* Munich, 1908.—Hans Loubier, *Die neue deutsche Buchkunst.* Stuttgart, 1921.—Arthur Rümann, *Die illustrierten deutschen Bücher des 19. Jahrhunderts.* Stuttgart, 1926.—Arthur Rümann, *Das illustrierte Buch des XIX. Jahrhunderts in England, Frankreich und Deutschland 1790–1860.* Leipzig, 1930.—Julius Rodenberg, "Geschichte der Illustration von 1800 bis heute," *Handbuch der Bibliothekswissenschaft*, 1(1931), p. 625.—Karl Scheffler, *Die impressionistische Buchillustration in Deutschland.* Berlin, 1931.—Anita Fischer, *Die Buchillustration der deutschen Romantik.* Berlin, 1933.—*Das Buchgewerbe. Eine Gesamtdarstellung des graphischen Gewerbes in seinen wissenschaftlichen, technischen und künstlerischen Grundzügen.* Leipzig, 1940.—Hans Leitmeier, "Einige Zukunftswünsche aus den Erfahrungen Buchkunst unseres Jahrhunders," *Gutenberg-Jahrbuch.* 1942/3, p. 355.—Walter Tiemann, "Der Jugendstil im deutschen Buch," *Gutenberg-Jahrbuch.* 1951, p. 182.

5. Richard Benz and Arthur v. Schneider, *Die Kunst der Romantik.* Munich, 1939.—Oskar Lang, *Deutsche Romantik in der Buchillustration.* 2d ed. Munich, 1940.

6. Franz Graf von Pocci, *Das Werk des Künstler Franz Pocci.* Munich, 1926.

7. Elfriede Bock, "Die Geschichte eines Volksbuches," *Kunst und Künstler*, 13(1915), p. 450.

8. Lothar Brieger, *Das goldene Zeitalter der französischen Illustration.* Berlin, 1925.—E. Bock and Adolph Menzel, *Verzeichnis seines graphischen Werkes.* Berlin, 1923.

9. Albert Kolb, "Gustave Doré als Buchillustrator," *Guttenberg-Jahrbuch*, 3(1928), p. 142.

10. *Zur Feier des 100jährigen Bestandes der k.k. Hof- und Staatsdruckerei.* Vienna, 1904.

11. *Fünfzig Jahre Reichsdruckerei 1879–1929.* Verfasst und herausgegeben von der Direktion der Reichsdruckerei unter Mitwirkung von Ernst Crous.* Berlin, 1929.

12. Wilh. H. Lange, *Otto Hupp. Das Werk eines deutschen Meisters.* Berlin, 1939.—Annemarie Meiner, "Otto Hupp 1859–1949," *Guttenberg-Jahrbuch.* 1950, p. 318.

13. H. Halliday Sparling, *The Kelmscott Press and William Morris, Master Craftsman.* London, 1924.

14. Heinrich E.S. Bachmair, *Otto Julius Bierbaum. Ein Kapitel neuer deutscher Buchkunst.* Munich, 1927.

15. J.A. Beringer, "Hans Thomas Graphik," *Kunst für alle*, 32(1917), p. 241.

16. Georg Ramsegger, *Literarische Zeitschriften um die Jahrhundertwende unter besonderer Berücksichtigung der "Insel."* Berlin, 1941.

17. J.T. Häuselmann, "Der Maler und Graphiker Cissarz," *Die Rheinlande.* 1916, p. 329.

18. Georg Haupt, *Rudolf Koch, der Schreiber.* Jena, 1936.—Klingspor Gebrüder (Firm), Offenbach a.M. *Eine deutsche Schrift von Rudolf Koch, geschnitten und herausgegeben von Gebr. Klingspor*, Offenbach am Main, 1910.

19. Jos. Theele, "Die Drucke der Werkstätten der Stadt Halle (Burg Giebichenstein) und das Werk Herbert Posts," *Gutenberg-Jahrbuch.* 1941, p. 269.

20. F.H. Ehmcke, *Schrift. Ihre Gestaltung und Entwicklung in neuerer Zeit.* Hanover, 1925.—Karl Klingspor, *Über Schönheit von Schrift und Druck. Erfahrungen aus fünfzugjähriger Arbeit.* Frankfurt am Main, 1949.

21. Julius Rodenberg, *Die deutsche Schriftgiesserei.* Mainz, 1927.

22. Carl Ernst Poeschel, *Deutsche Buchdruck. Gestern-Heute-Morgen.* Munich, 1927.

23. Horst Stobbe, "Bibliographie der deutschen Pressen," *Die Bücherstube*, 2(1923), p. 175.—Julius Rodenberg, *Deutsche Pressen. Eine Bibliographie 1925–1931.* Berlin, 1930/3.

24. Wolfgang Bruhn, "Deutsche Buchillustration und Buchschmuck der Gegenwart," in *Das Buchgewerbe.* Leipzig, 1940, p. 529.

25. Curt Tillmann, "Über das Sammeln von Buchumschlägen," *Zeitschrift für Bücherfreunde*, 37(1933), p. 1.—Walter Hofmann, "Der Buchumschlag und seine Geschichte," in *Das Buchgewerbe.* Leipzig, 1940, p. 585.

26. Karl Woermann, *Die Kunst zur Zeit der Hochrenaissance. Leipzig, 1921, p. 81.*

Chapter 37. Libraries Since the Early 1800s

1. On the general history of libraries, see Gustav Klemm's *Zur Geschichte der Sammlungen für Wissenschaft und Kunst in Deutschland*. Zerbst, 1837. — Edward Edwards, *Memoirs of Libraries*. 2 vols. London, 1859. — Arnim Graesel, *Handbuch der Bibliothekslehre*. 2d ed. Leipzig, 1902. — Fritz Milkau, "Die Bibliotheken," in *Die Kultur der Gegenwart* I, 1, 2d ed. Leipzig, 1912, p. 580. — Victor Gardthausen, *Handbuch der wissenschaftlichen Bibliothekskunde*. 2 vols. Leipzig, 1920. — Adolf Hessel, *Geschichte der Bibliotheken*. Göttingen, 1925. — Waldemar Sensburg, *Die bayerischen Bibliotheken*. Munich, 1926. — *Geschichte der Bibliotheken*. Bearbeitet von Aloys Bomer, Viktor Burr, Karl Christ, Georg Leyh, Albert Predeek, Joris Vorstius, Carl Wendel *(Handbuch der Bibliothekswissenschaft*, hrsg. von Fritz Milkau u. Georg Leyh, v. 3). Leipzig, 1940. — Joris Vorstius, *Grundzüge der Bibliotheksgeschichte*. 4th ed. Leipzig, 1948. — Ernst Mehl, "Deutsche Bibliotheksgeschichte," in *Deutsche Philologie im Aufriss*. Berlin, 1951, p. 314 ff.

2. Otto Hartwig, *Aus dem Leben eines deutschen Bibliothekars. Erinnerungen und biographische Aufsätze*. Marburg, 1906.

3. Karl Dziatzko, *Entwicklung und gegenwärtige Stand der wissenschaftlichen Bibliotheken Deutschlands mit besonderer Berücksichtigung Preussens*. Leipzig, 1893.

4. R. Fick, "Das Auskunftsbureau der deutschen Bibliotheken," in *Fünfzehn Jahre Königl. und Staatsbibliothek. Festschrift für A. von Harnack*. Berlin, 1921, p. 172.

5. C. Balcke, "Heinrich Friedrich von Diez und sein Vermächtnis in der Preuss. Staatsbibliothek," in *Von Büchern u. Bibliotheken. Festschrift für Ernst Kuhnert*. Berlin, 1928, p. 187.

6. R. Juchhoff, "Die Büchersammlung des Generalpostmeisters von Nagler in der Preuss. Staatsbibliothek," in *Von Büchern u. Bibliotheken. Festschrift für Ernst Kuhnert*. Berlin, 1928, p. 201.

7. Fritz Milkau, *Centralkataloge und Titeldrucke*. Leipzig, 1898. — E. Kuhnert, "Zur Entstehung und Gestaltung des Gesamtkatalogs," *Zentralblatt für Bibliothekswesen*, 49(1932), p. 117. — H. Fuchs, "Der Deutsche Gesamtkatalog als Organisation und Leitung," *Zentralblatt für Bibliothekswesen*, 55(1938), p. 443.

8. Frdr. Wilken, *Geschichte der Königlichen Bibliothek zu Berlin*. Berlin, 1828. — Heinrich von Treitschke, "Die Königliche Bibliothek in Berlin," *Deutsche Kämpfe*, N.F., Leipzig, 1896, p. 303. — Albert Hortzschansky, *Die Königliche Bibliothek zu Berlin*. Berlin, 1908. — Adolf von Harnack, *Die Benutzung der Königlichen Bibliothek und die deutsche Nationalbibliothek*. Berlin, 1912. — *Fünfzehn Jahre Königliche und Preussische Staatsbibliothek*. Adolf von Harnack überreicht. Berlin, 1921. — Curt Balcke, *Bibliographie zur Geschichte der Preussischen Staatsbibliothek*. Leipzig, 1925.

9. For the literature about individual German libraries see the *Minerva-Handbücher. 1. Abt. Die Bibliotheken. Bd. 1. Deutsches Reich*. Hrsg. von Hans Praesent. Berlin, 1929. — 2. Bd. Österreich. Bearbeitet von Robert Teichl. 1932. — 3. Bd. Schweiz. Bearb. von Felix Burckhardt. 1934.

10. Adalb. Roquette, *Die Finanzlage der Deutschen Bibliotheken*. Leipzig, 1902.

11. Ernst Kuhnert, *Geschichte der Staats- und Universitätsbibliothek zu Königsberg*. Leipzig, 1926.

12. Rudolf Focke, "Die Kaiser-Wilhelm-Bibliothek," *Zentralblatt für Bibliothekswesen*, 22(1905), p. 401.

13. Heinr. Uhlendahl, *25 Jahre Deutsche Bücherei*. Leipzig, 1938.

14. *Lettere ad Antonio Panizzi di uomini illustri e di amici italiani (1823–1870) publicate da Luigi Fagan*. Florence, 1880. — Louis Fagan, *The Life of Sir Anthony Panizzi*. 2 vols. London, 1880. — Prosper Mérimée, *Lettres à M. Panizzi 1850–1870*. Publiées par L. Fagan. 2 vols. Paris, 1881. — Karl Hillebrand, "Antonio Panizzi," *Deutsche Rundschau*, 29(1881), p. 235. — A. Predeek, "Antonio Panizzi und der alphabetische Katalog des Britischen Museums," in *Festschrift Georg Leyh*. Leipzig, 1937, p. 257.

15. Karl Dziatzko, "Die Bibliothek und der Lesesaal des Britischen Museums," *Preussische Jahrbücher*, 48(1881), p. 346. — Edith Rothe, "Die Bibliothek des Britischen Museums," *Zentralblatt für Bibliothekswesen*, 53(1936), p. 681.

16. British Museum. Dept. of Printed Books. *Catalogue of Books Printed in the XVth century now in the British Museum*. 1 ff. London, 1908 ff.

17. British Museum. Dept. of Printed Books. *Subject Index of Modern Works added to the Library of the British Museum in the year 1901–1905*. Edited by G.K. Fortescue. London, 1906 (and supplements).

18. A. Grüwell, "Der Katalog des British Museum," *Mitteilungen des österreichischen Vereines für Bibliothekswesen*, 5(1901), p. 16.

19. A. Hulshof, "Das Studium der Palaeographie in England seit 1873," *Zentralblatt für Bibliothekswesen*, 33(1916), p. 281.

20. John Rylands Library, Manchester. *Catalog of an Exhibition of Medieval and other Manuscripts and Jewelled Book-Covers*. Manchester, 1924.

21. Werner von Grimm, "Studien zur älternen Geschichte der K. öffentlichen Bibliothek in St. Petersburg 1794–1861," *Zentralblatt für Bibliothekswesen*, 50(1933), pp. 301, 353, 601.—Ernst von Horstkamp-Sydow, "Seltenheiten und Kuriositäten der Kaiserlichen öffentlichen Bibliothek zu St. Petersburg," *Zeitschrift für Bücherfreunde*, 12(1908/09), I, p. 26.

22. H. Small, *Handbook of the New Library of Congress in Washington*. Boston, 1901.—G.B. Goode, *The Smithsonian Institution 1846–96*. Washington, D.C., 1879.—C. Diesch, "Smithsonian Institution," *Lexikon des gesamten Buchwesens*, 3(1937), p. 202.

23. Arundell Esdaile, *National Libraries of the World. Their History, Administration and Public Services*. London, 1934.

24. S.D.C. van Dokkum, *Nederlandsche Bibliotheekgids-Adresboek van Nederlandsche openbare bibliotheken*. Utrecht, 1924.

25. Paul Trommsdorff, *Die Bibliotheken der deutschen technischen Hochschulen*. Berlin, 1928, and *Handbuch der Bibliothekswissenschaft*, Bd. 2(1933), p. 511.

26. Karl Bücher, "Universitätsbibliothek und Institutsbibliotheken," in his *Hochschulfragen*. Leipzig, 1912, p. 145.—Gotthold Naetebus, "Instituts-Bibliotheken und andere Bibliotheken," in *Handbuch der Bibliothekswissenschaft*, Bd. 2(1933), p. 323.

27. Johannes Franke, *Die Abgabe der Pflichtexemplare von Druckerzeugnissen mit besonderer Berücksichtigung Preussens und des deutschen Reiches*. Berlin, 1889.—Alfred Flemming, *Das Recht der Pflichtexemplare*. Munich, 1940.

28. G. Fumagalli, "Edifici di biblioteche italiane," *Riviste delle Biblioteche*, 1(1888), p. 161.—Ferdinand Eichler, "Moderne Bibliotheksbauten," *Mitteilungen des österreichischen Vereins für Bibliothekswesen*, 10(1906), p. 1.—Molitor, "Über Universitätsbibliotheksbauten," *Zentralblatt für Bibliothekswesen*, 26(1909), p. 386.—Paul Pescheck, "Die Entwicklung des neueren Bibliotheksbaues," in *Aufsätze Fritz Milkau gewidmet*. Leipzig, 1921, p. 264.—Georg Leyh, "Probleme des Bibliotheksbaues," *Zentralblatt für Bibliothekswesen*, 45(1928), p. 471.

29. Gustav Wahl, "Der Bau der Deutschen Bücherei in Leipzig," *Zentralblatt für Bibliothekswesen*, 33(1916), p. 327.

30. Ernesto Nelson, *Las Bibliotecas en los Estados Unidos*. New York, 1927.

31. G.A. Erich Bogeng, "Die Bibliothèque du Louvre," *Zeitschrift für Bücherfreunde*, N.F. 4(1912), I, p. 159.

32. Fritz Milkau in *Zentralblatt für Bibliothekswesen*, 33(1916), p. 24.

33. Georg Leyh, *Die deutschen wissenschaftlichen Bibliotheken nach dem Krieg*. Tübingen, 1947.

Chapter 38. Oriental Holdings in the West

1. Now in the State Library in Munich, among which are valuable Helraic, Arabic and Armenian manuscripts. Cf. Karl Römer's *Der Codex Arabicus Monacensis Aumer 238*. Dissertation. Leipzig, 1905.—Emil Gratzl, *Drei armenische Miniaturen-Handschriften. Cod. armen. 1, 6 und 8*. Munich, 1910.—Hans Striedl, "Die Bücherei des Orientalisten Johann Albrecht Widmanstetter," in *Serta Monacensia, Franz Babinger dargebracht*. Leyden, 1952, p. 200 ff.

2. H. Hülle, "Die Erschliessung der chinesischen Bücherschätze der deutschen Bibliotheken," *Ostasiatische Zeitschrift*, 8(1920), p. 199.—Frdr. M. Trautz, "Japanbücher und japanische Bücher in Deutschland," in *Aus Wissenschaft u. Antiquariat. Festschrift zum 50jährigen Bestehen der Buchhandlung Gustav Fock*. Leipzig, 1929, p. 345.—Adolf Jürgens, "Vom Aufbau chinesischer Sammlungen in Deutschland," *Hochschule und Ausland*, 14(1936), p. 254.

3. Preussische Staatsbibliothek. *Katalog der Handbibliothek der orientalischen Abteilung*. Leipzig, 1929.

4. Emil Schlagintweit, "Die tibetischen Handschriften der kgl. Hof- und Staatsbibliothek zu München," in *Academie der Wissenschaften zu München. Philolog. und histor. Classe. Sitzungsberichte*, 1875, II. Munich, 1875, p. 67.—E. Rödiger. "Über die orientalischen Handschriften aus Etienne Quartremères Nachlass in München," *Zeitschrift der Deutschen morgenländischen Gesellschaft*, 13(1859), p. 219.—Emil Gratzl, *Katalog der Ausstellung von Handschriften aus dem islamischen Kulturkreis im*

Fürstensaal der k. Hof- u. Staatsbibliothek. Munich, 1910. — Emil Gratzl, "Die arabischen Handschriften der Sammlung Glaser in der königl. Hof- und Staatsbibliothek zu München," *Mitteilungen der Vorderasiatischen Gesellschaft*, 1916, p. 196.
    5. Georg Reismüller, "Zur Geschichte der chinesischen Büchersammlung der Bayer. Staatsbibliothek," *Ostasiatische Zeitschrift*, 8(1919/20). — Georg Reismüller, "Karl Friedrich Neumann. Seine Lern- und Wanderjahre, seine chinesische Büchersammlung," in *Aufsätze zur Kultur- und Sprachgeschichte, vornehmlich des Orients. Ernst Kuhn gewidmet.* Breslau, 1916, p. 437.
    6. Hermann Hülle, "Geschichte und Inhalt der Wissenschaft von Ostasien," *Zentralblatt für Bibliothekswesen*, 42(1925), p. 545.
    7. Friedrich Sarre, *Islamische Bucheinbände.* Berlin, 1923. — Emil Gratzl, *Islamische Buchein-bände der Bayer. Staatsbibliothek.* Leipzig, 1924. — Adolf Grohmann, "Bibliotheken und Bibliophilen im islamischen Orient," in *Festschrift der Nationalbibliothek im Wien.* Vienna, 1926, p. 431. — Kurt Tautz, *Buch und Bibliothek in Japan. Reiseeindrücke.* Leipzig, 1941.

Chapter 39. The Popular Libraries

    1. From the rich literature about the popular libraries, see Ed. Reyer's *Entwicklung u. Organisation der Volksbibliotheken.* Leipzig, 1893. — Constantin Nörrenberg, *Die Volksbibliothek, ihre Aufgabe und ihre Reform.* Kiel, 1896. — Ernst Schultze, *Freie öffentliche Bibliotheken, Volksbibliotheken und Lesehallen.* Stettin, 1900. — Emil Jaeschke, *Volksbibliotheken.* Leipzig, 1907. — Gottlieb Fritz, *Das moderne Volksbildungswesen. Bücher- und Lesehallen, Volkshochschulen und verwandte Bildungseinrichtungen.* Leipzig, 1909. — *Die öffentlilche Bücherei. Sechs Abhandlungen.* Vorwort von Paul Ladewig. Berlin, 1917. — Erwin Ackerknecht, *Büchereifragen.* 2d ed. Berlin, 1926. — Walter Hofmann, *Der Weg zum Schrifttum. Gedanke, Gestalt, Verwirklichung der deutschen volkstümlichen Bücherei.* Berlin, 1922. — C. Nörrenberg, *Die Volksbibliothek, ihre Aufgabe und Reform.* 1928. — Erwin Ackerknecht, *Skandinavisches Büchereiwesen. Ein Überblick über die heutige Volksbüchereiarbeit in Dänemark, Finnland, Norwegen und Schweden.* Stettin, 1932. — Paul Ladewig, *Politik der Bücherei.* 3rd ed. Leipzig, 1934. — Franz Schriewer, *Die staatlichen Volksbüchereistellen im Aufbau des deutschen Volksbüchereiwesens.* Leipzig, 1938. — Walter Hofmann, *Buch und Volk. Gesammelte Aufsätze und Reden zur Buchpolitik und Volksbüchereifrage.* Hrsg. von Rudolf Reuter. Cologne, 1951.
    2. Paul Trommsdorf, *Die Birmingham Free Libraries.* Leipzig, 1900.
    3. H. Bonfort, *Das Bilbliothekswesen der Vereinigten Staaten.* Hamburg, 1896. — A.B. Meyer, *Amerikanische Bibliotheken und ihre Bestrebungen.* Berlin, 1906. — Hellmut Lehmann-Haupt, *Das amerikanische Buchwesen.* Leipzig, 1937. — Louis R. Wilson, *The Geography of Reading. A Study of the Distribution and Status of Libraries in the United States.* Chicago, 1937.
    4. Theodor Wesley Koch, *A Book of Carnegie Libraries.* New York, 1917.
    5. Adolf von Harnack, "Carnegies Schrift über die Pflicht der Reichen," in his *Aus Wissenschaft und Leben. 1. Bd.* Giessen, 1911, p. 167.
    6. Menz in *Lexikon des gesamten Buchwesens*, 2(1936), p. 310. — M. Wellnhofer, "Die Anfänge der Leihbibliotheken und Lesegesellschaften in Bayern," *Heimat und Volkstum*, 17(1939), p. 289.

Chapter 40. The Librarian

    1. Ernst Kuhnert, *Die Königliche und Universitäts-Bibliothek zu Königsberg i. Pr.* Königsberg, 1901, p. 14.
    2. Otto von Heinemann, *Zur Erinnerung an G.E. Lessing.* Leipzig, 1870. — Paul Zimmermann, "Zu Lessings Wolfenbüttler Bibliothekariat," *Akademische Blätter*, 1(1884), p. 605. — Otto von Heinemann, "Lessingiana," *Euphorion*, 2(1895), p. 632. — Otto Deneke, *Lessing als Büchersammler.* Göttingen, 1907. — Paul Zimmermann, "Ein neuer Beitrag zu Lessings Wolfenbüttler Bibliothekariat," *Zentralblatt für Bibliothekswesen*, 40(1923), p. 181. — H. Schneider, "Neue Beiträge zur Geschichte der Bibliotheca Augusta zu Wolfenbüttel," *Zentralblatt für Bibliothekswesen*, 40(1923), p. 185.
    3. Georg Leidinger, "Oefeleana," *Forschungen zur Geschichte Bayerns*, 13(1905), p. 230; 14(1906), p. 226.
    4. Ernst Freys, "Johann Baptist Bernharts 'Gesammelte Schriften'. Ein Vorläufer von Haeblers

Typenrepertorim," in *Wiegendrucke und Handschriften. Festgabe Konrad Haebler zum 60. Geburtstage.* Leipzig, 1919, p. 145.

5. Heinrich Düntzer, "Goethe und die Bibliotheken zu Weimar und Jena," *Zentralblatt für Bibliothekswesen,* 1(1884), p. 89.—Wilhelm Paszkowski, "Goethes Verhältnis zum Bibliothekswesen," *Beiträge zur Bücherkunde u. Philologie. August Wilmanns gewidment.* Leipzig, 1903. p. 159.—Werner Deetjen, "Ungedruckte Briefe und Aktenstücke zu Goethes Wirksamkeit für die wissenschaftlichen Anstalten der Universität Jena," *Zeitschrift für Bücherfreunde,* 9(1917/8), II, p. 299.

6. Konrad Hofmann, *Johann Andreas Schmeller, Eine Denkrede.* Munich, 1885.—Konrad Hofmann, "Über Schmellers amtliche Thätigkeit auf der Königl. Hof- und Staatsbibliothek in München," *Serapeum. Intelligenz-Blatt,* 1855, p. 161.

7. Alb. Duncker, *Die Brüder Grimm.* Kassel, 1884.—Reinh. Steig, "Die Brüder Grimm und die Weimarische Bibliothek," *Zeitschrift für Bücherfreunde,* N.F., 4(1912), I, p. 25.—Wilh. Hopf, "Die amtliche Tätigkeit der Brüder Grimm an der Landesbibliothek Cassel," *Zentralblatt für Bibliothekswesen,* 39(1922), p. 294.—Ludw. Zoepf, "Die Brüder Grimm als Bibliothekare," *Zentralblatt für Bibliothekswesen,* 45(1928), p. 123.—Wilh. Hopf and Gust. Struck, *Die Landesbibliothek Kassel 1580-1930.* Marburg, 1930.

8. August Heinrich Hoffmann von Fallersleben, *Mein Leben.* 3 vols. Hanover, 1868.—Fritz Behrend. "Germanistenbriefe von und an Hoffmann von Fallersleben," *Mitteilungen aus dem Literaturarchiv in Berlin,* N.F., 14. Berlin, 1917.

9. R. Dedo, "Dichter unter deutschen Bibliothekaren," in *Aufsätze. Fritz Milkau gewidmet.* Leipzig, 1921, p. 37.—Hubert Schiel, "Dichterbibliothekare," *Lexikon des gesamten Buchwesens,* 1(1935), p. 421.

10. Wilh. Zentner, "Scheffel in Donaueschingen," *Badische Heimat,* 25(1938), p. 305.

11. Richard Bürger, *Friedrich Adolf Ebert. Ein biographischer Versuch.* Leipzig, 1910.—George Leyh, "Friedrich Adolf Ebert zum 100jährigen Todestag," *Zentralblatt für Bibliothekswesen,* 51(1934), p. 599.—Heinr. Schreiber, *Nachklänge zu Friedrich A. Eberts Lehrbuch der Bibliographie.* Leipzig, 1936.

12. *Jubiläums-Ausgabe.* Marburg, 1897.

13. *Aufsätze Fritz Milkau gewidmet.* Leipzig, 1921.—*Fritz Milkau zum Gedächtnis. Ansprachen, Vorträge und Verzeichnis seiner Schriften.* 1934.

14. Fritz Milkau, *Die Königliche und Universitäts-Bibliothek zu Breslau.* Breslau, 1911.

15. Cf. Dziatzko's essays: "Die internationalen gegenseitigen Beziehungen der Bibliotheken," *Zentralblatt für Bibliothekswesen,* 10(1893), p. 457.—"Eine Reise durch die grösseren Bibliotheken Italiens," *Sammlung bibliothekswissenschaftlicher Arbeiten,* 6(1894), p. 96.—"Die Beziehungen des Bibliothekswesens zum Schulwesen und zur Philologie," *Neue Jahrbücher für das klassische Altertum,* 6(1900), p. 94.

16. G.A. Crüwell, "Der neue Katalog der Bibliothèque Nationale in Paris," *Mitteilungen des österreichischen Vereins für Bibliothekswesen,* 6(1902), p. 59.—Paul Lacombe, *Bibliographie des travaus de M. Léopold Delisle.* Paris, 1902-1911.—Henri Lemaître, "Léopold Delisle," *Zeitschrift des österreichischen Vereins für Bibliothekswesen,* 1(1910), p. 113.—Fritz Milkau, "Léopold Delisle," *Zentralblatt für Bibliothekswesen,* 27(1910), p. 385.—Georges Perrot, "Notice sur la Vie et les Travaux de Léopold Delisle," *Bibliothèque de l'école des chartes,* 73(1912), p. 5.—L. Klaiber, "Léopold Delisle und die Reform der Bibliothèque Nationale," in *Aus der Welt des Buches. Festgabe zum 70. Geburtstag von Georg Leyh.* Leipzig, 1950, p. 156.

17. P. 1-3. Paris, 1868-81.

18. C. Nörrenberg, "W.F. Poole," *Zentralblatt für Bibliothekswesen,* 11: p. 526.

19. Cf. Georg Leidinger's "Was ist Bibliothekswissenschaft?," *Zentralblatt für Bibliothekswesen,* 45(1928), p. 440.—Fritz Milkau, *Handbuch der Bibliothekswissenschaft. Bd. 1.* Leipzig, 1931.—C. Diesch, in *Lexikon des gesamten Buchwesens,* 1(1935), p. 212.—F. Vorstius, "Bibliothek, Bibliothekar, Bibliothekswissenschaft," *Zentralblatt für Bibliothekswesen,* 63(1949), p. 172.—A. Predeek, "Die Bibliothekswissenschaft als Disziplin und Universitäts-Lehrfach," in *Aus der Welt des Buches. Festgabe zum 70. Geburtstag von Georg Leyh.* Leipzig, 1950, p. 169.—Joachim Kirchner, *Bibliothekswissenschaft (Buch- und Bibliothekswesen).* Heidelberg, 1951.

20. C. Wendeler, "Wissenschaftliche Bibliographie—eine Aufgabe unserer Bibliotheksbeamten," *Neue Preussische Zeitung,* 1885, no. 97/9.

Chapter 41. Modern Bibliography

1. Julius Petzholdt, *Bibliotheca bibliographica. Kritisches Verzeichnis der das Gesamtgebiet der Bibliographie betreffenden Literatur des In- und Auslandes in systematischer Ordnung.* Leipzig, 1866. – Georg Schneider, *Handbuch der Bibliographie.* 4th ed. Leipzig, 1930. – Georg Schneider, *Einführung in die Bibliographie.* Leipzig, 1936.

2. Karl Löffler, *Einführung in die Handschriftenkunde.* Leipzig, 1929. – Karl Löffler, in *Handbuch der Bibliothekswissenschaft,* 1(1931), p. 254. – *Catalogue alphabétique des livres imprimés mis à la disposition des lecteurs dans la salle de travail de la Bibliothèque nationale à Paris.* 4th ed. Paris, 1933.

3. Erich von Rath, "Zur Biographie Ludwig Hains," in *Bok-och Bibliothekshistoriska Studier tillagnade I. Collijn.* Uppsala, 1925.

4. *Histoire de l'imprimerie en France au XVe et au XVIe Siècle.* T. 1–4. Paris, 1900–1914; the 4th fol. by Paul Lacombe.

5. K. Haebler, *Typenrepertorium der Wiegendrucke.* Halle a. S., 1905–10. – K. Haebler, "Wie ich Inkunabelforscher wurde," *Philobiblon,* 5(1932), supplement.

6. W.L. Schreiber, "Holzschnitt und Inkunabelforschung," *Zentralblatt für Bibliothekswesen,* 23(1906), p. 237. – R. Galle, "Inkunabelverzeichnisse und literarische Wissenschaft," *Zentralblatt für Bibliothekswesen,* 25(1908), p. 241. – Ernst Schulz, *Aufgaben und Ziele der Inkunabelforschung.* Munich, 1924. – Konrad Haebler, *Handbuch der Inkunabelkunde.* Leipzig, 1925. – Erich von Rath, *Aufgaben der Wiegendruckforschung.* Mainz, 1925. – Erich von Rath, "Inkunabelkatalogisierung," *Lexikon des gesamten Buchwesens,* 2(1936), p. 160. – Carl Wehmer, "Inkunabelkunde," *Zentralblatt für Bibliothekswesen,* 57(1940), p. 214.

7. A. Ruppel, *Das werdende Weltmuseum der Druckkunst.* Mainz, 1934. – A. Ruppel and A. Tronnier, *Kleiner Führer durch das Gutenberg-Museum in Mainz.* Mainz, 1934.

8. The extensive *Gutenberg-Jahrbuch,* which has been published since 1926, serves especially inquiry concerning the book.

9. With the journal, *Schweizerisches Gutenbergmuseum,* since 1919.

10. With the annual, *Buch und Schrift* (since 1937) as a continuation of *Zeitschrift des Deutschen Vereins für Buch und Schrift* (since 1918). cf. H. Bockwitz' *Das deutsche Museum für Buch und Schrift.* Leipzig, 1930. – H. Bockwitz, *Deutsches Buchmuseum zu Leipzig. Rundgang durch die Sammlungen.* Leipzig, 1940.

11. Hanns W. Eppelsheimer, *Handbuch der Weltliteratur von den Anfängen bis zum Weltkrieg.* Frankfurt am Main, 1937, 2d ed., 1947.

12. On the German attempts, see perhaps Gustav Schwab and Karl Klüpfl's *Wegweiser durch die Literatur der Deutschen.* Leipzig, 1846–1864. – Max Schneidewind, *Die besten Bücher aller Zeiten und Literaturen.* Berlin, 1889. – A.E. Schönbach, *Über Lesen und Bildung.* 5th ed. Graz, 1897. – *Bücher und Wege zu Büchern.* Unter Mitwirkung von Elisabeth Foerster-Nietzsche, Peter Jessen u. Philipp Rath. Hrsg. von Arthur Berthold. Berlin, 1900. – Eduard Grisebach, *Weltliteratur-Katalog.* 2d ed. Berlin, 1905. – Hanns von Walther, *Die Bücherei eines Deutschen.* Berlin, 1923. – Josef Hofmiller, *Über den Umgang mit Büchern.* Munich, 1927. – Ferdinand Baron von Neufforge, *Über den Versuch einer deutschen Bibliothek als Spiegel deutscher Kulturentwicklung.* Berlin, 1941. (This is only the listing of the extensive, but nevertheless rather accidental, collection of authors.)

Chapter 42. The Art of Reproduction

1. *Liber precationum, quas Carolus litteris scribi aureis mandavit.* Ingolstadt, David Sartorius, 1583. Cf. p. 206.

2. *Peintures et ornements des manuscrits.* Paris, 1832–69.

3. Léopold Delisle, *Les collections de Bastard d'Estang à la Bibliothèque Nationale.* Nogent-Le-Rotrou, 1885.

4. *Antiphonaire de Saint Grégoir. Fac-Simile du manuscrit de Saint-Gall par L. Lambilotte.* Brussels, 1851.

5. E.T. De Wald, *The Illustrations of the Utrecht Psalter,* 1932.

6. A. Hulshof, "Das Studium der Palaeographie in England seit 1873," *Zentralblatt für Bibliothekswesen,* 33(1916), p. 281.

7. Cf. also Karl E. Weston's "The Illustrated Terence Manuscripts," in *Harvard Studies in*

Classical Philology, 14(1903), p. 37.—Otto Engelhardt, *Die Illustrationen der Terenzhandschriften. Ein Beitrag zur Geschichte des Buchschmucks*. Dissertation. Jena, 1905.—L.W. Jones and C.R. Morey, *The Miniatures of the Manuscripts of Terence*. 2 vols. Princeton, N.J., 1930–31.

8. W.N. du Rieu, "Phototypographische Herausgabe von Handschriften," *Zentralblatt für Bibliothekswesen*, 11(1894), p. 225.—*Codices Graeci et Latini photographice depicti duce Giulelmo Nicolao Du Rieu (et Scatone de Vries)*. Leyden, A.W. Sijthoff, 1897–1906.—A.W. Sijthoff, *Unternehmen der Codices Graeci et Latini photographice depicti*. Leyden, 1908.

9. *Codices e Vaticanis selecti phototypice expressi. Bd. 1–25*. Rome, 1899–1914. *Codices ex ecclesiasticis Italiae bibliothecis delecti phototypice expessi*. Rome, 1924 ff.

10. Henri Omont, *Demosthenis orationum codex Σ; Oeuvres complètes de Demosthène. Fac-Simile du manuscrit grec. 2394 de la Bibliothèque Nationale*. T. 1. 2. Paris, 1892/93.

11. Henri Omont, *Reproduction de manuscrits et miniatures de la Bibliothèque nationale*. Paris, 1901–1911.

12. Hans Gerstinger, *Die Wiener Bilder-Genesis. Farbenlichtdruckfaksimile der griechischen Bilderbibel aus dem 6. Jahrhundert*. Vienna, 1931.

13. *Seelengärtlein. Hortus animae. Cod. Bibl. Pal. Vindob. 2706 der k.k. Hofbibliothek in Wien*. Photomechanische Nachbildung der k.k. Hof- und Staatsdruckerei in Wien. Hrsg. unter Leitung von Fr. Dörnhöffer. Frankfurt am Main, 1907.

14. *Corpus iuris civilis. Iustiniani Augusti Digestorum seu Pandectarum Codex Florentinus, olim Pisanus*. Rome, 1912. Cf. Guido Biagi's *Riproduzioni di manoscritti miniati. Cinquanta tavole in fototipia de codici della R. Biblioteca Medicea Laurenziana*. Florence, 1914.

15. *Das spanische Schachzabelbuch des Königs Alfons des Weisen vom Jahre 1283. El Tratado de Ajedrez del Rey Alonso el Sabio del año 1283. Illustrierte Handschrift im Besitze der Kgl. Bibliothek des Escorial*. Vollständige Nachbildung hrsg. mit Einleitung von J.G. White. Leipzig, 1913.

16. Anton M. Ceriani and Ach. Ratti, *Homeri Iliadis pictae fragmenta Ambrosiana*. Milan, 1905.

17. *Il Codice Atlantico di Leonardo da Vinci nella Biblioteca di Milano*. Milan, 1894–1904.

18. John Knight Fotheringham, *The Bodleian Manuscript of Jerome's Version of the Chronicle of Eusebius*. Oxford, 1905.

19. Georg Leidinger, *Miniaturen aus Handschriften der Bayer. Staatsbibliothek*. 1 ff, Munich, 1921–1925.—Paul Durrieu, *Der Münchener Boccaccio. Reproduction der 91 Miniaturen*. Munich, 1909.—Hermann L. Strack, *Der babylonische Talmud nach der Münchener Handschrift Cod. hebr. 95 mittels Faksimile-Lichtdruck herausgegeben*. Leyden, 1912.

20. *Die Manessesche Handschrift*. Facsimile ed. Leipzig, 1925–29.

21. Karl Löffler, *Die Weingartner Liederhandschrift in Nachbildung*. Stuttgart, 1927.

22. *Codex Boernerianus der Briefe des Apostels Paulus (Msc. Dresden A 145b). Eine griechische Handschrift der 13 Briefe Pauli aus dem 9. Jahrhundert, entstanden im Kloster St. Gallen*. In Lichtdruck nachgebildet mit Vorwort von A. Reichardt. Leipzig, 1910.

23. Otto von Friesen and Anders Grape, *Codex Argenteus Upsaliensis iussu Senatus Universitatis phototypice editus*. Uppsala, 1927.

24. *La Bible moralisée, conservée à Oxford, Paris et Londres*. Reproduction intégrale du manuscrit du 13e siècle, accompagnée d'une notic par A. de Laborde. Paris, 1911 ff.

25. *Miscellanea Francesco Ehrle*. 6 vols. Rome, 1924.—Cf. M. Grabmann in *Stimmen der Zeit*, 64(1933/34), p. 217.

26. Franz Ehrle, "Über die Erhaltung und Ausbesserung alter Handschriften," *Zentralblatt für Bibliothekswesen*, 15(1898), p. 17.—Franz Ehrle, "Die international Konferenz in St. Gallen am 30. September und 1 Oktober 1898 zur Beratung über die Erhaltung and Ausbesserung alter Handschriften," *Zentralblatt für Bibliothekswesen*, 16(1899), p. 27 and 26(1909), p. 245.—Otto Posse, *Handschriften-Konservierung. Nach den Verhandlungen der St. Gallener Internationalen Konferenz zur Erhaltung und Ausbesserung alter Handschriftn von 1898 sowie der Dresdener Konferenz Deutscher Archivare von 1899*. Dresden, 1899.—Cf. also *Actes du congrès international pour la reproduction des manuscrits, tenu à Liège les 21, 22 et 23 Août, 1905*. Brussels, 1905.

27. Cf. also Frederic G. Kenyon's *Facsimiles of Biblical Manuscripts in the British Museum*. London, 1900.

28. Emile Chatelain, "La photographie dans les bibliothèques," *Revue des Bibliothèques*, 1(1891), p. 225.—Gabr. Meier, "Die Fortschritte der Palaeographie mit Hilfe der Photographie. Ein bibliographischer Versuch," *Zentralblatt für Bibliothekswesen*, 17(1900), p. 1.—W. Molsdorf, "Einige Ratschläge bei der Beschaffung photographischer Einrichtungen für Bibliothekszwecke," *Zentralblatt*

für Bibliothekswesen, 18(1901), p. 23.—Karl Krumbacher, *Die Photographie im Dienste der Geisteswissenschaften.* Leipzig, 1906.—Otto Fiebiger, "Internationale photographische Ausstellung, Dresden, 1909. Die Photographie im Dienste des Bibliothekswesens," *Zentralblatt für Bibliothekswesen,* 26(1909), p. 451.

29. Otto Pelka, "Die mittelalterliche Miniaturmalerei und die Reproduktionstechniken der Gegenwart," *Archiv für Buchgewerbe und Gebrauchsgraphik,* 63(1926), p. 213.

30. *Das Breviarium Grimani in der Bibliothek von San Marco in Venedig.* Leyden and Leipzig, 1904–1910.

31. Frdr. Dörnhöffer, *Seelengärtlein. Hortulus animae.* Frankfurt am Main, 1907–10.

32. E. Chatelain, *Paléographie des Classiques latins.* Paris, 1884–92; 1894–1900.

33. Heinr. Schreiber, "Faksimilierte Handschriften antiker Klassiker." Sonderabzug des *Börsenblatts für den deutschen Buchhandel,* 99(1932), nos. 270, 276, 282, 290, 294, 303.—Henri Omont, *Listes des recueils de fac-similés et des reproductions de manuscrits conservés a la Bibliothèque Nationale.* 3rd ed. by Philippe Lauer. Paris, 1935.

34. E. Crous, "Faksimilia von Wiegendrucken," *Zeitschrift für Buchkunde,* 1(1924), p. 148.

Chapter 43. Book Exhibitions

1. Gustav Wahl, "Statistisches über Bibliotheksausstellungen," in *Festschrift Martin Bollert.* Dresden, 1936, p. 141.—Paul Sattler, "Ausstellungen als bibliothekarische Aufgabe," *Zentralblatt für Bibliothekswesen,* 54(1937), p. 498.—J. Hofmann, "Leipzig im deutschen Buchausstellungswesen und der Anteil der Leipziger Bibliotheken seit 100 Jahren," *Buch und Schrift,* N.F. 3(1940), p. 120.

2. *Serapeum,* 8(1847), p. 193.

3. Erich Petzet, *Schiller-Ausstellung der Kgl. Hof- und Staatsbibliothek. Zum 100. Todestage des Dichters.* 2. Ausgabe. Munich, 1905.—E. Petzet, "Die Schiller-Autographen der Münchener Hof- und Staatsbibliothek," *Studien zur Vergleichenden Literaturgeschichte,* 5(1905), supplementary no., p. 334.

4. *Katalog der Miniaturausstellung.* 2d ed. Vienna, 1901.—Cf. *Kunst u. Handwerk,* 5(1902), pp. 233, 285, 451.

5. Hans Fischer, *Verzeichnis der bei der Versammlung der deutschen Bibliothekare am 23. Mai 1907 in der Kgl. Bibliothek zu Bamberg ausgestellten Handschriften.* Bamberg, 1907.

6. Burlinton Fine Arts Club. *Exhibition of Illuminated Manuscripts.* London, 1908.

7. Georg Leidinger, *Verzeichnis der wichtigsten Miniaturen-Handschriften der Kgl. Hof- und Staatsbibliothek, München.* Munich, 1912.—A. Boeckler, *Ars sacra. Kunst des frühen Mittelalters.* Munich, 1950.

8. Hans Loubier, "Eine Ausstellung von Bucheinbänden in der Königlichen Bibliothek in Berlin," *Zentralblatt für Bibliothekswesen,* 34(1917), p. 12.—W. Krag and P. Ruf, *Schöne Bucheinbände. Ausstellung der Bayerischen Staatsbibliothek.* Munich, 1939.

9. Max Rooses, *Le musée Plantin-Moretus.* Antwerp, 1914.

10. W. Brambach, "Ausstellung der Grossherzogl. Hof- und Landesbibliothek zum VII. Deutschen Geographentag in Karlsruhe," *Zentralblatt für Bibliothekswesen,* 4(1887), p. 425.

11. *Das deutsche Buch auf der zweiten internationalen Büchermesse in Florenz.* Leipzig, 1925.

12. Ludw. Volkmann, *Von der Weltkultur zum Weltkrieg.* Leipzig, 1914.

Chapter 44. Bibliography and Book Collecting

1. Jacques Charles Brunet, *Manuel du libraire et de l'amateur de livres.* 3 vols. Paris, 1810; 5th ed. 6 vols., 1860–86.—Frdr. Adolf Ebert, *Allgemeine Bibliograph, Lexikon.* 2 vols. Leipzig, 1821–30.—Jean George Theodore Graesse, *Trésor de livres rares et précieux.* 7 vols. Dresden, 1859–1869; new impression, Berlin, 1922.—Ernst Quentin-Bauchart, *Les femmes bibliophies de France XVI, XVII et XVIII Siècles.* 2 vols. Paris, 1885.—C.J. and M.A. Elton, *The Great Book Collectors.* London, 1893.—Otto Mühlbrecht, *Die Bücherliebhaberei und ihre Entwicklung bis zum Ende des 19. Jahrhunderts.* 2d ed. Bielefeld, 1898.—Edouard Rouveyre, *Connaissances nécessaires à un bibliophile.* 10 vols. 5th ed. Paris, 1899.—William Younger Fletcher, *English Book Collectors.* London, 1902.—P. Dauze, *Manuel de l'amateur d'éditions originales, 1800–1911.* 1911.—Gustav Adolf Erich Bogeng, "Klassiker und Romantiker-Bibliotheken," *Vierteljahrsschrift f. angewandte Bücherkunde,* 1(1918), p. 182.—Seymour de Ricci, *The Book Collector's Guide.* Philadelphia, 1921.—G.A.E. Bogeng, *Die grossen*

Bibliophilen. 3 vols. Leipzig, 1922.—G.A.E. Bogeng, *Einführung in die Bibliophilie.* Leipzig, 1922.— Edouard Rahir, *La Bibliothèque de l'Amateur.* 2d ed. Paris, 1924.—L. Carteret, *Le trésor du Bibliophile romantique et moderne.* Paris, 1801–1875; 1924–1927.—F.C. Lonchamp, *Manuel du Bibliophile Français.* 4 vols. Paris, 1927.—C.G. von Maassen. "Über die Seltenheit vom Romantiker-Erstausgaben," *Imprimatur,* 6(1935), p. 84.—Eberhard Hölscher, *Handwörterbuch für Büchersammler.* Hamburg, 1947 (of minor significance).—Among the bibliophilic journals to be mentioned are: *Zeitschrift für Bücherfreunde,* 1897–1936.—*La Bibliofilia,* 1899- .—*Vierteljahrsschrift für angewandte Bücherkunde,* 1918- .—*Philobiblon,* 1928- .—*Imprimatur,* 1930- .—*Sankt Wiborada,* 1933- .—*Das Antiquariat* 1, Vienna, 1945- with its insert, "Der Bibliophile."

2. Cf. Otto Deneke's *Lessing als Büchersammler.* Göttingen, 1908.—Wolfgang von Wurzbach, "Aus Schillers Bibliothek," *Zeitschrift für Bücherfreunde,* 4(1900/01), I, p. 71.—Albert Köster, "Schillers Handbibliothek," *Zeitschrift für Bücherfreunde,* 9(1905/06), I, p. 62.—Paul Ortlepp, "Schillers Bibliothek und Lektüre," *Neue Jahrbücher für das klassische Altertum, Geschichte und deutsche Literatur,* 35(1915), I. p. 375.

3. Heinr. Meisner, "Seltene Bücher," *Zeitschrift für Bücherfreunde,* 3(1899/1900), p. 147.

4. Jos. Basile Bernard van Praet, Catalogue des livres imprimés sur vélin dans les bibliothèques tant publiques que particulières. 4 vols. Paris, 1824–28. Supplement (by L. Delisle). Paris, 1887.

5. A. Kuczynski, *Verzeichnis einer Sammlung mikroskopischer Drucke und Formate im Besitz von Albert Brockhaus.* Leipzig, 1888.—Gustav Milchsack, "Die Buchformate, historisch und ästhetisch entwickelt," in *Versammlung der Philologen und Schulmänner.* Dresden, 1937.—R.L. Prager, "Kleine Bücher" und mikroskopische Drucke," *Jahrbuch deutscher Bibliophilen,* 5(1917).—Karl Jakob Lüthi, *Bücher kleinsten Formates.* Bern, 1924.

6. The incunabula period was already acquainted with printed works of the smallest design, such as the *Officium beatae Mariae Virginis* (Munich State Library. Rar. 15), which was printed in Venice by Joh. Emericus de Spira in 1489 for Lucantonio de Giunta.

7. Frdr. Zarnke, "Die Meusebach'sche Bibliothek," *Serapeum,* 11(1850), pp. 89, 109.—C. Wendeler, "Zur Geschichte des Ankaufs der Meusebach'schen Bibliothek," *Zentralblatt für Bibliothekswesen,* 1(1884), p. 213.

8. Ed. Heyck, "Eine fürstliche Hausbibliothek im Dienste der Öffentlichkeit," *Zeitschrift für Bücherfreunde,* 1(1897/8), p. 65.

9. Alexander Graf Apponyi, *Hungarica. Ungarn betreffende, im Ausland gedruckte Bücher und Flugschriften.* Munich, 1903–1925.

10. Rich. Förster, "Handschriften in Holkham," *Philologus,* 72(1884), p. 158.—Léon Dorez, *Les manuscrits à peintures de la bibliothèque de Lord Leicester à Holkham Hall, Norfolk. Choix de miniatures et de reliures.* Paris, 1908.

11. Robert Oliver Schad, *H.E. Huntington.* San Marino, Calif., 1935.

12. *American Book Prices Current.* New York, 1895- .—*Book Prices Current.* London, 1895- .—W. Robert, *Rare Books and Their Prices.* London, 1895.—C.A. Grampelt, "Bücherliebhaberei und Bücherauktionswesen," *Zeitschrift für Bücherfreunde,* 7(1903/04), II, p. 443.—Jul. Luther, "Die Preise der Lutherdrucke im deutschen Antiquariatsbuchhandel," *Zentralblatt für bibliothekswesen,* 22(1905), p. 349.—Alfr. W. Pollard, "Zur Theorie der Bücherpreise," *Zeitschrift für Bücherfreunde,* 10(1906/07), I, p. 207.—*Jahrbuch der Bücherpreise,* 1- , 1907- .—M. Sander, *Handbuch der Inkunabelpreise.* Milan, 1930.—Guenther Koch, *Kunstwerke und Bücher am Markte.* Esslingen, 1915.—Emil Starkenstein, "Der Arzt und sein Buch," *Philobiblon,* 10(1938), p. 305.—*Das Antiquariat. Halbmonatsschrift für alle Fachgebiete des Buch- und Kunstantiquariats.* 1 ff. Vienna, 1945 ff.—W. Junk, *50 Jahre Antiquar. Ein nachgelassenes Manuskript* herausgegeben von A.C. Klooster und W. Weisbach. 's-Gravenhage, 1949.

13. *Die Handschriften-Verzeichnisse der Königlichen Bibliothek zu Berlin.* Berlin, 1890.—Valentin Rose, *Die Meermann-Handschriften des Sir Thomas Philipps.* Berlin, 1893.—Emil Jacobs, "Die von der Königlichen Bibliothek zu Berlin aus der Sammlung Philipps erworbenen Handschriften," *Zentralblatt für Bibliothekswesen,* 28(1911), p. 23.

14. Paul de Lagarde, "Die Handschriftensammlung des Grafen von Ashburnham," in *Nachrichten von der Gesellschaft der Wissenschaften in Göttingen,* (1884), p. 14.—Th. Stange, "Die Bibliothek Ashburnham," *Philologus,* 45(1886), p. 201.

15. Julius Rodenberg, comp., *Deutsche Bibliophilie in drei Jahrzehnten. Verzeichnis der Veröffentlichungen der deutschen bibliophilen Gesellschaften und der ihnen gewidmeten Gaben, 1898–1930.* Herausgegeben von der Deutschen Bücherei. Leipzig, 1931.

Name Index

A

Aa, Pieter van der 257
Abbt, Thomas 330
Abraham, Bishop of Freising
42
Abraham a Santa Clara 210
Acacius (cleric) 16
Accursius, Bonus 92
Acominatos 175
Acquaviva, Andrea Matteo
III 65, 169
Adalbert, Prior of Corvey 46
Adalgaud (cleric) 37
Adalhart of Tours 35
Adalram, Archbishop of
Salzburg 39
Adam of Fulda 122
Adamantius 66
Addison, Josef 257
Adelphi, Johann 158
Adelung, Friedrich 222
Adelung, Johann Christoph
255
Ademar (presbyter) 408
Adler, Johann Chr. Heinr.
342
Adolf of Nassau 79
Aelianus 71, 143
Aemilius Paulus, Lucius 5
Aeschines 4, 93, 257
Aeschylus 4, 9, 24, 175,
177
Aesop 50, 81, 92, 99, 189,
264, 408
Aethelwold, Bishop of Win-
chester 42
Agricola, Georg 192
Agricola, Johann 203
Agricola, Michael 157
Agricola, Rudolf 133
Agrippa, Camillo 198
Agustin, Antonio 172, 180,

Aho, Juhani 340
Airnschmalz, Konrad 106
Aitzing, Michael 240
Alantsee, Leonhard 117
Alantsee, Lukas 117, 118
Alarçon, Pedro Antonio de
339
Alba, Ferdinand Alvarez,
Duke of 157, 171
Albani, Alessandro 289
Albech, called Cremer,
Heinrich 77, 294
Albertini, Francesco 63
Albertus Magnus 25, 48,
72, 87, 197
Albrecht (mathematician)
197
Albrecht, Duke of Prussia
163, 413
Albrecht, Elector of Mainz
64, 118, 122
Albrecht IV, Duke of Bavaria
109, 231
Albrecht V, Duke of Bavaria
134, 143, 158, 159, 166,
167, 171, 224, 298
Albrecht of Halberstadt 48
Alcaeus 7
Alciato, Andrea 189, 196
Alcuin 30, 33, 35, 38, 39,
106, 108
Aldrovandi, Ulisse 198
Aldus Manutius 61, 92, 93,
105, 117, 127, 136, 163,
179, 182, 202, 205, 232,
415
Alembert, Jean le Rond d'
248
Alexander, Bishop of Jeru-
salem 13
Alexander de Villa Dei 88,
202
Alexander Gallus 90

Alexander of Aphrodisias
167
Alexander Severus 13
Alexander the Great 4, 10
Alexander VII, Pope 60
Alexander VIII, Pope 233
Alexander von Hales 48, 89
Alexis, Willibald 329, 355
Allacci, Leone 220, 221
Allen, Hervey 339
Alphonse I, King of Naples
60
Alphonse X, King of Leon
171, 409
Alphonsus de Spira 90
Altdorfer, Albrecht 128
Altensteig, Johann 103
Althoff, Friedrich 377
Alto, Abbot of Weihenstep-
han 47
Alveldt, Augustin 149
Amboise, George d' 60
Ambrosius 14, 33, 47, 56,
60, 63, 72, 87, 89, 117,
121, 137, 166
Amerbach, Johann 87, 90,
139, 204
Amman, Jost 117, 189, 196
Ammianus Marcellinus 11,
24, 37
Ammonius 181, 398
Amort, Eusebius 279
Amundsen, Roald 339
Anacreon 262
Anastasius 40
Anaxagoras 4
Andersen, Hans Christian
339, 348
Andreae, Hieronymus 116
Andreae, Jakob 185
Andreae, Thorirus 57
Andronicus of Rhodes 3,
184

J

Jacobi, Friedrich 301
Jacobs, Christian Friedrich Wilhelm 292
Jacobsen, Jens Peter 315, 339, 356
Jacobssoen van der Meer, Jacob 83
Jacobus Philippines de Bergamo 70
Jäck, Heinrich Joachim 401, 402
Jacquin, Nikolaus von 271
Jaenichius, Petrus 274
Jaggard, William and Isaac 217
Jahn, Friedrich Ludwig 309
James, Thomas 226
Jammes, Francis 338
Jamnitzer, Wenzel 193
Janssen, Johann 317, 363
Jaspers, Karl 325, 364
Jenson, Nikolaus 116
Jeremias II, Patriarch 185
Jerome, Saint 13, 14, 15, 16, 31, 44, 50, 60, 63, 72, 89, 91, 117, 201
Jérôme (Bonaparte) of Westphalia 304
Jerusalem, Johann Friedrich Wilhelm 395
Joachim, Georg 192, 193
Joachim III of Brandenburg 195
Jobin, Bernhard 192
Jobst von Mähren 57
Jöcher, Christian Gottlieb 255
Johann Friedrich of Hanover 243
Johann Friedrich of Saxony 129
Johann von Neumarkt 69
Johannes de Gamundia 96
Johannes de Spira 80, 88
Johannes de Westphalia 81
Johannes Gritsch 90
Johannes Philagathos 45
Johannes von Troppau 69
John Chrysostomus 14, 18, 72, 87, 121, 137, 175, 185
John Damascene 185
John Fredrick of Saxony 150
John of Burgundy 68
John of Ragusa 153, 178
John Scotus *see* Erigena

John II of Palatine-Simmern 125, 191
Jókai, Maurus 340
Jordanes (Jornandes) 22, 39, 42, 135, 285
Josephus, Flavius 31, 38, 42, 43, 47, 180
Jourdan, Jean Baptiste 288
Judex, Matthäus 154
Jüger, Andreas 105
Juliana Anicia 17, 185, 408
Julius Africanus 13
Julius of Brunswick 168
Julius II, Pope 63
Juncker, Christian 274
Jung-Stilling, Johann H. 250, 269, 330
Junius, Franciscus 275
Justi, Karl 317, 318
Justin 47, 120
Justinian, Emperor 11, 21, 37, 72, 87, 119, 141, 144
Juvenal 5, 24, 40, 43, 47, 93, 106, 219, 273
Juvencus 13, 21, 105

K

Kachelofen, Konrad 125, 202
Kaden, Michael von 168
Kafka, Gustav 364
Kaliwoda, Leopold Johann 271
Kallierges, Zacharias *see* Callierges
Kandel, David 192
Kannegiesser, Karl Frierdrich Ludwig 310
Kant, Immanuel 248, 253, 254, 260, 269, 323, 330, 350, 395, 413
Kanter, Johann Jakob 269
Kapp, Friedrich 344
Karl August of Saxony-Weimar 321
Karl Egon II of Fürstenberg 417
Karl Eugen of Württemberg 279, 295
Karl Ludwig, Count Palatine 222
Karl Theodor, Elector 222, 251, 278, 298
Karlstadt, Andreas 141, 149, 163

Karoch, Samuel 133
Katzbeck, Michael 155
Kaulbach, Wilhelm von 371, 374
Kautsky, Karl 320
Kayser, Albrecht Christoph 274, 405
Kefer, Heinrich 80
Kehr, Paul Fridolin 323
Keller, Ambr. 105
Keller, Gottfried 253, 307, 314, 330, 333, 338, 341, 348, 355
Kepler, Johann 208, 323
Kerle (publishing firm) 360, 361
Kerner, Anton 349
Kerner, Justinus 268, 311
Kerold, Monk 41
Kessler, Johann 137
Ketham, Johann von 88, 410
Keyser, E. (publishing firm) 360
Kiekegaard, Sören 339, 364
Kilian, Balthasar 213
Kilian, Hans 153, 165
Kilian, Lukas 213
Kilian, Wolfgang 213
Kipling, Rudyard 338, 358
Kippenberg, Anton 358, 374
Kirchhoff, Hans Wilhelm 197
Kirchner, Christian 215
Kirsten, Petrus 221
Kivi (Kiwi), Alexis 340
Klages, Ludwig 325
Klein, Magnus 195, 279
Klein, Woldemar 361
Kleiner, Salomon 271
Kleist, Ewald Christian von 250, 268
Kleist, Heinrich von 263, 266, 272, 281, 315, 319, 348, 371, 413
Klett, E. (publishing firm) 360
Klette, Anton 402
Kleukens, Friedrich Wilhelm 373
Kling, Melchior 203
Klinger, Friedrich Maximilian 327, 330
Klinger, Max 371, 372

Subject Index

All undeclined initial articles are disregarded for purposes of alphabetization.

A

Aachen 33, 88; Palace School 33
Aalst 81
Aberrations in early printing 79, 115
Abbéville 234
Abo 125; library 386
Academia della Crusca 208
Academia Veneta 203
Academic libraries *see* Libraries, academic
Academic Publishing Society, Leipzig 366
Académie Française 208
Academies 256, 321, 322
Accipies woodcuts 102
Acquisition 378
Acta Borussica 323
Acta eruditorum 241
Acta sanctorum ordinis Benedicti 237
Ada – manuscript 35, 288
Aderlass calendar 76
Ad Insigne pinus – printery 184
Admont library 53, 281
Adrianople 177
Advertising 374
Aesop's *Fables* (15th-c.) 92
Africa – maps 93
Against Celsus manuscript 62
Agnetenberg 109
Agricultural publishers 365
Agrimensor 66
Aire 141
Akhmin 6
Alban Hills 176

Albani library (Rome) 289
Albelda council 171
Albi 83
Albums 196
Alcala de Henares 127
Alcuin Bible 10
Aldersbach 51
Alemannian law book 38
Alexander, comedies of 7
Alexandria xx, 13; library 4, 5, 11, 93, 140, 386, 394
Alexandrian school 4, 5
Alhambra 329
Allegories 208, 329
Allgemeiner Literarischer Anzeiger 290
Almanac of the Muses 259
Almanacs 255, 259, 311
Alpinism 194
Alsace 414
Also Sprach Zarathustra 318
Altaich yearbook 43
Altai-Pamir expedition 361
Altdorf: University library 303
Altenburg 346
Althorp 294
Altzelle 108; library 108, 153
Amadis di Gaula – romance 197
Amberg 302
Ambras 213; library 69, 229
Amelungsborn library 168
Amerbach cabinet 281
America 75, 89, 122, 382,

385, 389, 417; discovery of 420; early printing in 218; institute libraries in 218; popular education libraries in 391, 402
American publications in Germany 339
Americana 418
Amiatina Biblia 17
Amor 132
Amsterdam 216, 219; library 385
Anabaptists 152
Ancient classical writers 45, 67, 80, 90, 137; translations 67
Andalusia 329
Andechs 108
Anegray 30
Angelica library (Rome) 235
Anglo-Saxon: culture 30; popular education libraries 391
Anhalt 164
Animal hides and parchment 16
Annaburg 167
Annales Nazariani 321
Annals (Tacitus) 25
Anrede (as title) 148
Ansbach 72
Antioch 4
Antioch as center for literary transmission 5
Antiphonary of St. Gregorius 408
Antiqua 131, 132
Antiquarian books 215
Antiquarian catalogs 417